Dimensions of Sheckley

The Selected Novels of Robert Sheckley

Edited by Sharon L. Sbarsky

The NESFA Press
Post Office Box 809
Framingham, MA 01701
2002

Acknowledgements

"Introduction" by Mike Resnick appears here for the first time.
"Afterword" by Tom Gerencer appears here for the first time.
Immortality, Inc. - Avalon, 1958; Bantam 1959.
Journey Beyond Tomorrow - Signet, 1963.
Mindswap - Delecorte, 1966; Dell, 1967.
Dimension of Miracles - Dell, 1968.
Minotaur Maze - Pulphouse Press, 1990.

CONTENTS

Dimensions of Sheckley

INTRODUCTION

The late John Campbell once remarked that E. E. "Doc" Smith had given us the stars and we were still waiting for the next breakthrough.

The late John Campbell was dead wrong.

Robert Sheckley, laboring for Campbell's competitors, gave us a truly major breakthrough, and it's sitting right in the middle of this book.

But I'm getting ahead of myself.

Let's begin at the beginning, and in Sheckley's case that would be 1952, when he first broke into print. From that first story onward, he was the smoothest, most facile writer in the field, accessible to all, even easier to read than the great Alfred Bester or the masterful Henry Kuttner.

More to the point, he was funny. Hell, he was more than funny—he was hilarious.

Science fiction was a short story medium them, and Sheckley supplied them, one brilliant piece after another, with no visible effort. "Watchbird," "The Accountant," "The Lifeboat Mutiny," "The Prize of Peril," "Citizen in Space," "Native Problem," "Shall We Have a Little Talk?," and dozens more appeared on an almost monthly basis. Here and there was a straight science fiction story, as well-done as Heinlein or Asimov, tales such as "Dawn Invader," or post-*Weird Tales* horror pieces like "The Altar." The only thing you could be sure of with a Sheckley story was that finishing it would be effortless. Even his second-raters, and he had a few, were easier to finish than cast aside; he just had that touch, that accessibility that so many writers strive for and so few master.

And because he was a humorist first, he began pulling science fiction in new directions. While Heinlein all but created the competent engineer, Sheckley—especially with his AAA Ace stories—created the Stupid Hero. Not retarded, just stupid. And there are a lot more stupid people reading science fiction, its advocates' claims to the contrary, than competent engineers.

Eventually it dawned on Sheckley, as it did on just about everybody else in the field, that you can't make a living just writing short stories, no matter how prolific you are, so he turned to novels (and as you've already figured out, this book was produced to preserve some of the long out-of-print ones, plus a novella, in permanent form).

His first, in 1958, was *Immortality Delivered,* with a title change to *Immortality, Inc.* when the mass market edition came out in 1959. It is the story of Thomas Blaine and his attempt to cope in a future where you buy your way into Heaven, where immortality is a commodity, and where—and this is a theme that would become more important in future novels—humanity's surroundings may have changed and grown more sophisticated, but humanity itself remains the same stumbling, bumbling, well-meaning but not very bright creatures we are today, never quite able to cope with their problems.

(A third of a century after the book's appearance Hollywood proved that it hadn't learned any faster or better than Sheckley's characters, buying *Immortality, Inc.* and producing a painfully un-Sheckley movie called *Freejack.*)

The next novel was *The Status Civilization,* in which Will Barrent is sent to a prison planet which has created its own rules and its own society. It's pure science fiction, grim, though with a healthy dose of satire.

It was a nice enough beginning as a novelist. Two well-thought-out science fiction novels that played fair with the reader, didn't unduly strain his credulity, snuck in some satire and social commentary. In other words, they were typical of the better novels being produced at the time.

So of course they must have felt like a straitjacket to Sheckley, who would never write another "typical" or "traditional" science fiction novel.

His next one has appeared as both *The Journey of Joenes* and *Journey Beyond Tomorrow,* and it shows Sheckley starting to push the envelope, to see what he could accomplish (and what he could get away with) in a science fiction novel.

Oh, he'd always been funny before, but some of his stories, like "The Language of Love" and "Pilgrimage to Earth," were more than just funny conceits masterfully handled. They seriously examined the flaws in our society, and they did it with a maturity that was beyond every other satirist in the field except perhaps Bester and Leiber, neither of whom could turn a funny phrase with Sheckley's sure hand.

Journey Beyond Tomorrow did at length what some of his more mature satires had set the stage for. It was traditionally structured—the Noble Savage (Joenes) visiting Civilization and being appalled—but it was in the details that it departed from everything that science fiction had done before. First, it showed Sheckley's facility for taking a mildly silly situation—security in the Pentagon, in this case—and drawing it out to the proper length to show just how ridiculous it truly was. His creation of the Octagon—a military complex still under construction, so secret that no one, not even the architect, can find his way around it—is a work of sheer comic genius.

While the book is told in the third person, Sheckley had no problem inserting a couple of first-person chapters written by Joenes's hippie/beatnik friend Lum, when he feels like using that character to make his point. And along with the more meaningful satire, there's Sheckley's opinion of the typical pulp romance, as shown by Joenes's tender feelings toward the totally selfish and off-putting Tondelayo (and I'm sure Hedy Lamarr didn't mind loaning her the name).

Can you make a living when you're pulling the field in new directions, making fun of its most sacred traditions?

Probably not, so while he was coming up with his three masterworks of the 1960s, Sheckley also produced a series of five adventure novels—*Calibre .50, Live Gold, White Death, Dead Run* and *Time Limit*—starring Stephen Dain; and he also wrote the brilliant thriller *The Man in the Water,* and the very popular spy novel *The Game of X.*

I don't mean to denigrate those books—I enjoyed every last one of them—but as well-conceived and well-written as they were, Sheckley was doing his important work in the field of science fiction.

Playboy discovered him, and became a second home to him and his sophisticated wit, and subsequently brought him to the attention of a much wider readership. And some of those readers lived in Hollywood.

It wasn't long before Tinseltown bought the rights to "The Seventh Victim," turned it into *The Tenth Victim* (anyone who was alive and over 10 years old at the time will remember Ursula Andress firing a gun through her bra), and hired Sheckley himself to do the novelization.

The next major novel to appear was *Mindswap.* It used a premise that was not totally unfamiliar—in this future the technology exists to permit people to swap minds, and it becomes a popular way of taking a vacation—only in Sheckley's hands you just know things are going to get fouled up.

What you can't know is how brilliantly inventive and satirical the foul-ups get. Poor Marvin Flynn, who spends most of the book walking around with a bomb in his nose (no, don't ask), learns the Theory of Searches, which, like the Octagon, almost makes sense. (In fact, a *lot* of Sheckley almost makes sense, until you turn to stare at it head-on, and then you realize that it's just a funhouse mirror he's holding up to those aspects of society that amuse him the most. There's a lot of wit and satire here, but, oddly, very little anger.)

Then, just to show you how easy it is for him to write the kind of scene everyone else is trying to write—and to do it far better, with a tenth the effort—he sticks in Chapter 22. He also has a scene in the bar that carries the notion of a haunting melody conjuring up a mood to an absolutely crazed extent. Then, just for the hell of it, he gives you a nice medieval intrigue and battle.

And when you're sure you've seen it all, out comes the greatest invention of them all, the one that's been referred to and hinted at throughout the book, but which you never seriously expected to see: the Twisted World, where effect precedes cause, black is white, day is night, and nothing is as it seems. At a time when science fiction's New Wave writers were experimenting with colored sentences, and circular sentences, and sentences that formed patterns in the margins, Sheckley created the strangest effect of all using nothing but simple sentences and paragraphs. And, of course, a towering talent.

And then, a year later, came THE masterwork, the most brilliant work of humor ever to appear in this field, the book that all the increasingly sophisticated and mature stories and novels were leading up to: *Dimension of Miracles*. For a third of a century fanzines and interviewers have been asking me to name the greatest novels in the history of science fiction, and for just as long I have always listed this book in the top half-dozen.

It's not only brilliant, it's not only hilarious, but it's Campbell's missing breakthrough: a humor that can only work as science fiction.

From the moment Carmody is whisked to the Galactic Center, the book never lets up, and this time the themes aren't lovers and military complexes and Twisted Worlds. They're gods, such as Melichrone, and the creator of our own world (Maudsley) and the bearded old man who had ordered it. They're intelligent dinosaurs who have no idea they'll become extinct; and Bellwether, a sentient city that gives new meaning to the word *yenta*. They're a world gone mad with advertising slogans (Sheckley at his nastiest), a dream world peopled only by Hollywood actors (or, rather, their personas). And finally, when all seems lost, there is a complete and mature understanding of his life by Carmody, who then makes the only decision he *can* make— and we come to the realization that Sheckley is all through with the Stupid Hero, that Carmody's adventures have made him every bit as much of a clear-eyed realist as Sheckley himself.

Sheckley never equaled *Dimension of Miracles*. The only thing to be said on his behalf is that no one else ever equaled it either—and at least he did it once.

It was seven years before Sheckley would write another novel, and in *Options* he went off in a new direction. It's easy to see why. With *Dimension of Miracles* he'd gone as far as he could with the forms he had been playing with in the 1960s, and rather than repeat himself he began experimenting with something new: absurdist science fiction.

Did it work? Not always. It's hard to do 77 chapters, each a separate absurdist adventure, and have the whole hold together, but there's more than enough wit and invention to keep most people satisfied, and it's probably a stranger book than anyone else had attempted up to that time.

Still, he took his best shot at an absurdist novel, and then, being Sheckley, he went off in an entirely new direction. We're proud to be able to present, as the final entry in this omnibus volume, *Minotaur Maze,* a novella that saw publication only in a very limited edition from Pulphouse in 1990.

Why add it?

To show you what Sheckley's doing these days. This one's got a plot three times as complex as any of the other novels included here, yet it's barely a third of their length. It's got its absurd moments, but it's not absurdist fiction. It's got a lot of wit, but it's not exactly a funny novella. As a matter of fact, the best way to find out what it really is is to walk up to Sheckley and ask him. His answer will differ depending on his mood, and the time of day, and the weather, but what the hell—that's the essence of Robert Sheckley.

When I was a kid, just into my teens, devouring all the science fiction I could read, I knew I wanted to be a science fiction writer someday. I didn't know what kind of stories I wanted to tell, or what length, but I knew one thing: I wanted to be as accessible, as readable, as Robert Sheckley, who was, and remains, one of my very few literary heroes.

When you're through with this book, you'll know why.

—Mike Resnick

Immortality, Inc.

PART ONE

Chapter 1

Afterwards, Thomas Blaine thought about the manner of his dying and wished it had been more interesting. Why couldn't his death have come while he was battling a typhoon, meeting a tiger's charge, or climbing a windswept mountain? Why had his death been so tame, so commonplace, so ordinary?

But an enterprising death, he realized, would have been out of character for him. Undoubtedly he was meant to die in just the quick, common, messy, painless way he did. And all his life must have gone into the forming and shaping of that death—a vague indication in childhood, a fair promise in his college years, an implacable certainty at the age of thirty-two.

Still, no matter how commonplace, one's death is the most interesting event of one's life. Blaine thought about his with intense curiosity. He had to know about those minutes, those last precious seconds when his own particular death lay waiting for him on a dark New Jersey highway. Had there been some warning sign, some portent? What had he done, or not done? What had he been thinking?

Those final seconds were crucial to him. How, exactly, had he died?

He had been driving over a straight, empty white highway, his headlights probing ahead, the darkness receding endlessly before him. His speedometer read seventy-five. It felt like forty. Far down the road he saw headlights coming toward him, the first in hours.

Blaine was returning to New York after a week's vacation at his cabin on Chesapeake Bay. He had fished and swum and dozed in the sun on the rough planks of his dock. One day he sailed his sloop to Oxford and attended a dance at the yacht club that night. He met a silly, pert-nosed girl in a blue dress who told him he looked like a South Seas adventurer, so tanned and tall in his khakis. He sailed back to his cabin the next day, to doze in the sun and dream of giving up everything, loading his sailboat with canned goods and heading for Tahiti. *Ah Raïatea, the mountains of Mooréa, the fresh trade wind...*

But a continent and an ocean lay between him and Tahiti, and other obstacles besides. The thought was only for an hour's dreaming, and definitely not to be acted upon. Now he was returning to New York, to his job as a junior yacht designer for the famous old firm of Mattison & Peters.

The other car's headlights were drawing near. Blaine slowed to sixty.

In spite of his title, there were few yachts for Blaine to design. Old Tom Mattison took care of the conventional cruising boats. His brother Rolf, known as the Wizard of Mystic, had an international reputation for his ocean-racing sailboats and fast one-designs. So what was there for a junior yacht designer to do?

Blaine drew layouts and deck plans, and handled promotion, advertising and publicity. It was responsible work, and not without its satisfactions. But it was not yacht designing.

He knew he should strike out on his own. But there were so many yacht designers, so few customers. As he had told Laura, it was rather like designing arbalests, scorpions and catapults. Interesting creative work, but who would buy your products?

"You could find a market for your sailboats," she had told him, distressingly direct. "Why not make the plunge?"

He had grinned boyishly, charmingly. "Action isn't my forte. I'm an expert on contemplation and mild regret."

"You mean you're lazy."

"Not at all. That's like saying that a hawk doesn't gallop well, or a horse has poor soaring ability. You can't compare different species. I'm just not the go-getter type of human. For me, dreams, reveries, visions, and plans are meant only for contemplation, never for execution."

"I hate to hear you talk like that," she said with a sigh.

He *had* been laying it on a bit thick, of course. But there was a lot of truth in it. He had a pleasant job, an adequate salary, a secure position. He had an apartment in Greenwich Village, a hi-fi, a car, a small cabin on Chesapeake Bay, a fine sloop, and the affection of Laura and several other girls. Perhaps, as Laura somewhat tritely expressed it, he was caught in an eddy on the current of life... But so what? You could observe the scenery better from a gently revolving eddy.

The other car's headlights were very near. Blaine noticed, with a sense of shock, that he had increased speed to eighty miles an hour.

He let up on the accelerator. His car swerved freakishly, violently, toward the oncoming headlights.

Blowout? Steering failure? He twisted hard on the steering wheel. It wouldn't turn. His car struck the low concrete separation between north and south lanes, and bounded high into the air. The steering wheel came free and spun in his hands, and the engine wailed like a lost soul.

The other car was trying to swerve, too late. They were going to meet nearly head-on.

And Blaine thought, yes, I'm one of them. I'm one of those silly bastards you read about whose cars go out of control and kill innocent people. Christ! Modern cars and modern roads and higher speeds and the same old sloppy reflexes...

Suddenly, unaccountably, the steering wheel was working again, a razor's edge reprieve. Blaine ignored it. As the other car's headlights glared across his windshield, his mood suddenly changed from regret to exultance. For a moment he welcomed the smash, lusted for it, and for pain, destruction, cruelty and death.

Then the cars came together. The feeling of exultance faded as quickly as it had come. Blaine felt a profound regret for all he had left undone, the waters unsailed, movies unseen, books unread, girls untouched. He was thrown forward. The steering wheel broke off in his hands. The steering column speared him through the chest and broke his spine as his head drove through the thick safety glass.

At that instant he knew he was dying.

An instant later he was quickly, commonly, messily, painlessly dead.

Chapter 2

He awoke in a white bed in a white room.

"He's alive now," someone said.

Blaine opened his eyes. Two men in white were standing over him. They seemed to be doctors. One was a small, bearded old man. The other was an ugly red-faced man in his fifties.

"What's your name?" the old man snapped.

"Thomas Blaine."

"Age?"

"Thirty-two. But—"

"Marital status?"

"Single. What—"

"Do you see?" the old man said, turning to his red-faced colleague. "Sane, perfectly sane."

"I would never have believed it," said the red-faced man.

"But of course. The death trauma has been overrated. Grossly overrated, as my forthcoming hook will prove."

"Hmm. But rebirth depression—"

"Nonsense," the old man said decisively. "Blaine, do you feel all right?"

"Yes. But I'd like to know—"

"Do you see?" the old doctor said triumphantly. "Alive again and sane. *Now* will you co-sign the report?"

"I suppose I have no choice," the red-faced man said. Both doctors left.

Blaine watched them go, wondering what they had been talking about. A fat and motherly nurse came to his bedside. "How do you feel?" she asked.

"Fine," Blaine said. "But I'd like to know—"

"Sorry," the nurse said. "No questions yet, doctor's orders. Drink this, it'll pep you up. That's a good boy. Don't worry, everything's going to be all right."

She left. Her reassuring words frightened him. What did she mean, *everything's going to be all right?* That meant something was wrong! What was it, what was wrong? What was he doing here, what had happened?

The bearded doctor returned, accompanied by a young woman.

"Is he all right, doctor?" the young woman asked.

"Perfectly sane," the old doctor said. "I'd call it a good splice."

"Then I can begin the interview?"

"Certainly. Though I cannot guarantee his behavior. The death trauma, though grossly overrated, is still capable of—"

"Yes, fine." The girl walked over to Blaine and bent over him. She was a very pretty girl, Blaine noticed. Her features were clean-cut, her skin fresh and glowing. She had long, gleaming brown hair pulled too tightly back over her small ears, and there was a faint hint of perfume about her. She should have been beautiful; but she was marred by the immobility of her features, the controlled tenseness of her slender body. It was hard to imagine her laughing or crying. It was impossible to imagine her in bed. There was something of the fanatic about her, of the dedicated revolutionary; but he suspected that her cause was herself.

"Hello, Mr. Blaine," she said. "I'm Marie Thorne."

"Hello," Blaine said cheerfully.

"Mr. Blaine," she said, "where do you suppose you are?"

"Looks like a hospital. I suppose—" He stopped. He had just noticed a small microphone in her hand.

"Yes, what do you suppose?"

She made a small gesture. Men came forward and wheeled heavy equipment around his bed.

"Go right ahead," Marie Thorne said. "Tell us what you suppose."

"To hell with that," Blaine said moodily, watching the men set up their machines around him. "What is this? What is going on?"

"We're trying to help you," Marie Thorne said. "Won't you cooperate?"

Blaine nodded, wishing she would smile. He suddenly felt very unsure of himself. Had something happened to him?

"Do you remember the accident?" she asked.

"What accident?"

"Do you remember being hurt?"

Blaine shuddered as his memory returned in a rush of spinning lights, wailing engine, impact and breakage.

"Yes. The steering wheel broke. I got it through the chest. Then my head hit."

"Look at your chest," she said softly.

Blaine looked. His chest, beneath white pajamas, was unmarked.

"Impossible!" he cried. His own voice sounded hollow, distant, unreal. He was aware of the men around his bed talking as they bent over their machines, but they seemed like shadows, flat and without substance. Their thin, unimportant voices were like flies buzzing against a window.

"Nice first reaction."

"Very nice indeed."

Marie Thorne said to him, "You are unhurt."

Blaine looked at his undamaged body and remembered the accident. "I can't believe it!" he cried.

"He's coming on perfectly."

"Fine mixture of belief and incredulity."

Marie Thorne said, "Quiet, please. Go ahead, Mr. Blaine."

"I remember the accident," Blaine said. "I remember the smashing, I remember—dying."

"Get that?"

"Hell, yes. It really plays!"

"Perfectly spontaneous scene."

"Marvellous! They'll go wild over it!"

She said, "A little less noise, please. Mr. Blaine, do you remember dying?"

"Yes, yes, I died!"

"His face!"

"That ludicrous expression heightens the reality."

"I just hope Reilly thinks so."

She said, "Look carefully at your body, Mr. Blaine. Here's a mirror. Look at your face."

Blaine looked, and shivered like a man in fever. He touched the mirror, then ran shaking fingers over his face.

"It isn't my face! Where's my face? Where did you put my body and face?"

He was in a nightmare from which he could never awaken. The flat shadow men surrounded him, their voices buzzing like flies against a window, tending their cardboard machines, filled with vague menace, yet strangely indifferent, almost unaware of him. Marie Thorne bent low over him with her pretty, blank face, and from her small red mouth came gentle nightmare words.

"Your body is dead, Mr. Blaine, killed in an automobile accident. You can remember its dying. But we managed to save that part of you that really counts. We saved your mind, Mr. Blaine, and have given you a new body for it."

Blaine opened his mouth to scream, and closed it again. "It's unbelievable," he said quietly.

And the flies buzzed.

"Understatement."

"Well, of course. One can't be frenetic forever."

"I expected a little more scenery-chewing."

"Wrongly. Understatement rather accentuates his dilemma."

"Perhaps, in pure stage terms. But consider the thing realistically. This poor bastard has just discovered that he died in an automobile accident and is now reborn in a new body. So what does he say about it? He says, 'It's unbelievable.' Damn it, he's not really reacting to the shock!"

"He is! You're projecting!"

"Please!" Marie Thorne said. "Go on, Mr. Blaine."

Blaine, deep in his nightmare, was hardly aware of the soft, buzzing voices. He asked, "Did I really die?"

She nodded.

"And I am really born again in a different body?"

She nodded again, waiting.

Blaine looked at her, and at the shadow men tending their cardboard machines. Why were they bothering him? Why couldn't they go pick on some other dead man? Corpses shouldn't be forced to answer questions. Death was man's ancient privilege, his immemorial pact with life, granted to the slave as well as the noble. Death was man's solace, and his right. But perhaps they had revoked that right; and now you couldn't evade your responsibilities simply by being dead.

They were waiting for him to speak. And Blaine wondered if insanity still retained its hereditary privileges. With ease he could slip over and find out.

But insanity is not granted to everyone. Blaine's self-control returned. He looked up at Marie Thorne.

"My feelings, " he said slowly, "are difficult to describe. I've died, and now I'm contemplating the fact. I don't suppose any man fully believes in his own death. Deep down he feels immortal. Death seems to await others, but never oneself. It's almost as though—"

"Let's cut it right here. He's getting analytical."

"I think you're right," Marie Thorne said. "Thank you very much, Mr. Blaine."

The men, solid and mundane now, their vague menace disappeared, began rolling their equipment.

"Wait—" Blaine said.

"Don't worry," she told him. "We'll get the rest of your reactions later. We just wanted to record the spontaneous part now."

"Damn good while it lasted."

"A collector's item."

"Wait!" Blaine cried. "I don't understand. Where am I? What happened? How—"

"I'll explain everything tomorrow," Marie Thorne said. "I'm terribly sorry, I must hurry now and edit this for Mr. Reilly."

The men and equipment were gone. Marie Thorne smiled reassuringly, and hurried away.

Blaine felt ridiculously close to tears. He blinked rapidly when the fat and motherly nurse came back.

"Drink this," said the nurse. "It'll make you sleep. That's it, take it all down like a good boy. Just relax, you had a big day, what with dying and being reborn and all."

Two big tears rolled down Blaine's cheeks.

"Dear me," said the nurse, "the cameras should be here now. Those are genuine spontaneous tears if I ever saw any. Many a tragic and spontaneous scene I've witnessed in this infirmary, believe me, and I could tell those snooty recording boys something about genuine emotion if I wanted to, and they thinking they know all the secrets of the human heart."

"Where am I?" Blaine asked drowsily. "Where is this?"

"You'd call it being in the future," the nurse said.

"Oh," said Blaine.

Then he was asleep.

Chapter 3

After many hours he awoke, calm and rested. He looked at the white bed and white room, and remembered.

He had been killed in an accident and reborn in the future. There had been a doctor who considered the death trauma overrated, and men who recorded his spontaneous reactions and declared them a collector's item, and a pretty girl whose features showed a lamentable lack of emotion.

Blaine yawned and stretched. Dead. Dead at thirty-two. A pity, he thought, that this young life was snuffed in its prime. Blaine was a good sort, really, and quite promising...

He was annoyed at his flippant attitude. It was no way to react. He tried to recapture the shock he felt he should feel.

Yesterday, he told himself firmly, I was a yacht designer driving back from Maryland. Today I am a man reborn into the future. The future! Reborn!

No use, the words lacked impact. He had already grown used to the idea. One grows used to anything, he thought, even to one's death. *Especially* to one's death. You could probably chop off a man's head three times a day for twenty years and he'd grow used to it, and cry like a baby if you stopped...

He didn't care to pursue that train of thought any further.

He thought about Laura. Would she weep for him? Would she get drunk? Or would she just feel depressed at the news, and take a tranquilizer for it? What about Jane and Miriam? Would they even hear about his death? Probably not. Months later they might wonder why he never called any more.

Enough of that. All that was past. Now he was in the *future*.

But all he had seen of the future was a white bed and a white room, doctors and a nurse, recording men and a pretty girl. So far, it didn't offer much contrast with his own age. But doubtless there were differences.

He remembered magazine articles and stories he had read. Today there might be free atomic power, undersea farming, world peace, international birth control, interplanetary travel, free love, complete desegregation, a cure for all disease, and a planned society in which men breathed deep the air of freedom.

That's what there should be, Blaine thought. But there were less pleasant possibilities. Perhaps a grim-faced Oligarch had Earth in his iron grasp, while a small, dedicated underground struggled toward freedom. Or small, gelatinous alien creatures with outlandish names might have enslaved the human race. Perhaps a new and horrible disease marched unchecked across the land, or possibly the Earth, swept of all culture by hydrogen warfare, struggled painfully back to technological civilization while human wolfpacks roamed the badlands; or a million other equally dismal things could have happened.

And yet, Blaine thought, mankind showed an historic ability to avoid the extremes of doom as well as the extremes of bliss. Chaos was forever prophesized and utopia was continually predicted, and neither came to pass.

Accordingly, Blaine expected that this future would show certain definite improvements over the past, but he expected some deteriorations as well; some old problems would be gone, but certain others would have taken their places.

"In short," Blaine said to himself, "I expect that this future will be like all other futures in comparison with their pasts. That's not very specific; but then, I'm not in the predicting *or* the prophesying business."

His thoughts were interrupted by Marie Thorne walking briskly into his room.

"Good morning," she said. "How do you feel?"

"Like a new man," Blaine said, with a perfectly straight face.

"Good. Would you sign this, please?" She held out a pen and a typed paper.

"You're very damned efficient," Blaine said. "'What am I signing?"

"Read it," she said. "It's a release absolving us from any legal responsibility in saving your life."

"Did you save it?"

"Of course. How did you think you got here?"

"I didn't really think about it," Blaine admitted.

"We saved you. But it's against the law to save lives without the potential victim's written consent. There wasn't opportunity for the Rex Corporation lawyers to obtain your consent beforehand. So we'd like to protect ourselves now."

"What's the Rex Corporation?"

She looked annoyed. "Hasn't anyone briefed you yet? You're inside Rex headquarters now. Our company is as well known today as Flyier-Thiess was in your time."

"Who's Flyier-Thiess?"

"No? Ford, then?"

"Yeah, Ford. So the Rex Corporation is as well known as Ford. What does it do?"

"It manufactures Rex Power Systems," she told him, "which are used to power spaceships, reincarnation machines, hereafter drivers, and the like. It was an application of the Rex Power Systems that snatched you from your car at the moment after death and brought you into the future."

"Time travel," Blaine said. "But how?"

"That'll be hard to explain," she said. "You don't have the scientific background. But I'll try. You know that space and time are the same thing, aspects of each other."

"They are?"

"Yes. Like mass and energy. In your age, scientists knew that mass and energy were interchangeable. They were able to deduce the fission-fusion processes of the stars. But they couldn't immediately duplicate those processes, which called for vast amounts of power. It wasn't until they had the knowledge *and* the available power that they could break down atoms by fission and build up new ones by fusion."

"I know this," Blaine said. "What about time travel?"

"It followed the same pattern," she said. "For a long time we've known that space and time are aspects of the same thing. We knew that either space or time could be reduced to fundamental units and transformed into the other by a power process. We could deduce the warping of space-time in the vicinity of supernovae, and we were able to observe the disappearance of a Wolf-Rayet star when its time-conversion rate accelerated. But we had to learn a lot more. And we had to have a power source exponentially higher than you needed to set off the fusion process. When we had all this, we could interchange time units for space units—which is to say, time distances for space distances. We could then travel the distance of, say, a hundred years instead of the interchangeable distance of a hundred parsecs."

"I see, after a fashion," Blaine said. "Would you mind running through it again, slowly?"

"Later, later," she said. "Will you please sign the release?"

The paper stated that he, Thomas Blaine, agreed not to bring suit against the Rex Corporation for their unauthorized saving of his life in the year 1958 and the subsequent transporting of that life to a Receptacle in the year 2110.

Blaine signed. "Now," he said, "I'd like to know—"

He stopped. A teen-age boy had come into the room holding a large poster. "Pardon me, Miss Thorne," he said, "the Art Department wants to know will this do?"

The boy held up the poster. It showed an automobile at the moment of smashup. A gigantic stylized hand was reaching down from the sky and plucking the driver from the burning wreck. The caption read: REX DID IT!

"Not bad," Marie Thorne said, frowning judiciously. "Tell them to brighten the reds."

More people were coming into the room. And Blaine was growing angry.

"What's going on?" he asked.

"Later, later," Marie Thorne said. "Oh, Mrs. Vaness! What do you think of this poster for a teaser?"

There were a dozen people in his room now, and more coming. They clustered around Marie Thorne and the poster, ignoring Blaine completely. One man, talking earnestly to a grey-haired woman, sat down on the edge of his bed. And Blaine's temper snapped.

"Stop it!" Blaine shouted. "I'm sick of this damned rush act. What's the matter with you people, can't you behave like human beings? Now get the hell out of here!"

"Oh lord," Marie Thorne sighed, closing her eyes. "He *would* have to be temperamental. Ed, talk to him."

A portly, perspiring middle-aged man came to Blaine's bedside. "Mr. Blaine," he said earnestly, "didn't we save your life?"

"I suppose so," Blaine said sullenly.

"We didn't have to, you know. It took a lot of time, money and trouble to save your life. But we did it. All we want in return is the publicity value."

"Publicity value?"

"Certainly. You were saved by a Rex Power System."

Blaine nodded, understanding now why his rebirth in the future had been accepted so casually by those around him. They had taken a lot of time, money and trouble to bring it about, had undoubtedly discussed it from every possible viewpoint, and now were conscientiously exploiting it.

"I see," Blaine said. "You saved me simply in order to use me as a gimmick in an advertising campaign. Is that it?"

Ed looked unhappy. "Why put it that way? You had a life that needed saving. We had a sales campaign that needed sparking. We took care of both needs, to the mutual benefit of you and the Rex Corporation. Perhaps our motives weren't completely altruistic; would you prefer being dead?"

Blaine shook his head.

"Of course not," Ed agreed. "Your life is of value to you. Better alive today than dead yesterday, eh? Fine. Then why not show us a little gratitude? Why not give us a little cooperation?"

"I'd like to," Blaine said, "but you're moving too fast for me."

"I know," Ed said, "and I sympathize. But you know the advertising game, Mr. Blaine. Timing is crucial. Today you're news, tomorrow nobody's interested. We have to exploit your rescue right now, while it's hot. Otherwise it's valueless to us. "

"I appreciate your saving my life," Blaine said, "even if it wasn't completely altruistic. I'll be glad to cooperate."

"Thank you, Mr. Blaine," Ed said. "And please, no questions for a while. You'll get the picture as we go along. Miss Thorne, it's all yours."

"Thanks, Ed," Marie Thorne said. "Now, everybody, we have received a provisional go-ahead from Mr. Reilly, so we'll continue as planned. Billy, you figure out a release for the morning papers. 'Man from Past' sort of thing."

"It's been done."

"Well? It's always news, isn't it?"

"I guess once more won't hurt. So. Man from 1988 snatched—"

"Pardon me," Blaine said. "1958."

"So from 1958 snatched from his smashed car at the moment after death and set into a host body. Brief paragraph about the host body. Then we say that Rex Power Systems performed this snatch over one hundred and fifty-two years of time. We tell 'em how many ergs of energy we burned, or whatever it is we burn. I'll check with an engineer for the right terms. OK?"

"Mention that no other power system could have done it," Joe said. "Mention the new calibration system that made it possible."

"They won't use all that."

"They might," Marie Thorne said. "Now, Mrs. Vaness. We want an article on Blaine's feelings when Rex Power Systems snatched him from death. Make it emotional. Give his first sensations in the amazing world of the future. About five thousand words. We'll handle the placement."

The grey-haired Mrs. Vaness nodded. "Can I interview him now?"

"No time," Miss Thorne said. "Make it up. Thrilled, frightened, astonished, surprised at all the changes that have taken place since his time. Scientific advances. Wants to see Mars. Doesn't like the new fashions. Thinks people were happier in his own day with less gadgets and more leisure. Blaine will OK it. Won't you, Blaine?"

Blaine nodded dumbly.

"Fine. Last night we recorded his spontaneous reactions. Mike, you and the boys make that into a fifteen-minute spin which the public can buy at their local Sensory Shop. Make it a real connoisseur's item for the prestige trade. But open with a short, dignified technical explanation of how Rex made the snatch."

"Gotcha," said Mike.

"Right. Mr. Brice, you'll line up some solido shows for Blaine to appear on. He'll give his reactions to our age, how it feels, how it compares to his own age. See that Rex gets a mention."

"But I don't know anything about this age!" Blaine said.

"You will," Marie Thorne told him. "All right, I think that's enough for a start. Let's get rolling. I'm going to show Mr. Reilly what we've planned so far."

She turned to Blaine as the others were leaving.

"Perhaps this seems like shabby treatment. But business is business, no matter what age you're in. Tomorrow you're going to be a well-known man, and probably a wealthy one. Under the circumstances, I don't think you have any cause for complaint."

She left. Blaine watched her go, slim and self-confident. He wondered what the penalty was, in this day and age, for striking a woman.

Chapter 4

The nurse brought him lunch on a tray. The bearded doctor came in, examined him and declared him perfectly fit. There was not the slightest trace of rebirth depression, he declared, and the death trauma was obviously overrated. No reason why Blaine shouldn't be up and about.

The nurse came back with clothing, a blue shirt, brown slacks, and soft, bulbous grey shoes. The outfit, she assured him, was quite conservative.

Blaine ate with good appetite. But before dressing, he examined his new body in the full-length bathroom mirror. It was the first chance he'd had for a careful appraisal.

His former body had been tall and lean, with straight black hair and a good-humored boyish face. In thirty-two years he had grown used to that quick, deft, easy-moving body. With good grace he had accepted its constitutional flaws, its occasional illnesses, and had glorified them into virtues, into unique properties of the personality that resided within them. For his body's limitations, far more than its capabilities, seemed to express his own particular essence.

He had been fond of that body. His new body was a shock.

It was shorter than average, heavily muscled, barrel chested, broad shouldered. It felt top-heavy, for the legs were a little short in proportion to the herculean torso. His hands were large and callused. Blaine made a fist and gazed at it respectfully. He could probably fell an ox with a single blow, if an ox were procurable.

His face was square and bold, with a prominent jaw, wide cheekbones and a Roman nose. His hair was blonde and curly. His eyes were a steely blue. It was a somewhat handsome, slightly brutal face.

"I don't like it," Blaine said emphatically. "And I hate curly blonde hair."

His new body had considerable physical strength; but he had always disliked sheer physical strength. The body looked clumsy, graceless, difficult to manage. It was the kind of body that bumped into chairs and stepped on people's toes, shook hands too vigorously, talked too loudly, and sweated profusely. Clothes would always bulge and constrict this body. It would need continual hard exercise. Perhaps he would even have to diet; the body looked as though it had a slight tendency toward fat.

"Physical strength is all very well," Blaine told himself, "if one has a purpose for it. Otherwise it's just a nuisance and a distraction, like wings on a dodo."

The body was bad enough. But the face was worse. Blaine had never liked strong, harsh, rough-hewn faces. They were fine for sandhogs, army sergeants, jungle explorers and the like. But not for a man who enjoyed cultured society. Such a face was obviously incapable of subtlety of expression. All nuance, the delicate interplay of line and plane, would be lost. With this face you could grin or frown; only gross emotions would show.

Experimentally he smiled boyishly at the mirror. The result was a satyr's leer.

"I've been gypped," Blaine said bitterly.

It was apparent to him that the qualities of his present mind and his new body were opposed. Cooperation between them seemed impossible. Of course, his personality might reshape his body; on the other hand, his body might have some demands to make on his personality.

"We'll see," Blaine told his formidable body, "we'll see who's boss."

On his left shoulder was a long, jagged scar. He wondered how the body had received so grievous a wound. Then he began wondering where the body's real owner was. Could he still be lodged in the brain, lying doggo, waiting for a chance to take over?

Speculation was useless. Later, perhaps, he would find out. He took a final look at himself in the mirror.

He didn't like what he saw. He was afraid he never would.

"Well," he said at last, "you takes what you gets. Dead men can't be choosers."

That was all he could say, for the moment. Blaine turned from the mirror and began dressing.

Marie Thorne came into his room late in the afternoon. She said, without preamble, "It's off."

"Off?"

"Finished, over, through!" She glared bitterly at him, and began pacing up and down the white room. "The whole publicity campaign around you is off."

Blaine stared at her. The news was interesting; but much more interesting were the signs of emotion on Miss Thorne's face. She had been so damnably controlled, so perfectly and grotesquely businesslike. Now there was color in her face, and her small lips were twisted bitterly.

"I've worked on this idea for two solid years," she told him. "The company's spent I don't know how many millions to bring you here. Everything's set to roll, and that damned old man says drop the whole thing."

She's beautiful, Blaine thought, but her beauty gives her no pleasure. It's a business asset, like grooming, or a good head for liquor, to be used when necessary, and even abused. Too many hands reached to Marie Thorne, he imagined, and she never took any. And when the greedy hands kept reaching she learned contempt, then coldness, and finally self-hatred.

It's a little fanciful, Blaine thought, but I'll keep it until a better diagnosis comes along.

"That damned stupid old man," Marie Thorne was muttering.

"What old man?"

"Reilly, our brilliant president."

"He decided against the publicity campaign?"

"He wants it hushed up completely. Oh God, it's just too much! Two years!"

"But why?" Blaine asked.

Marie Thorne shook her head wearily. "Two reasons, both of them stupid. First, the legal problem. I told him you'd signed the release, and the lawyers had the rest of the problem in hand, but he's scared. It's almost time for his reincarnation and he doesn't want any possible legal trouble with the government. Can you imagine it? A frightened old man running Rex! Second, he had a talk with that silly, senile old grandfather of his, and his grandfather doesn't like the idea. And that clinched it. After two years!"

"Just a minute," Blaine said. "Did you say his *reincarnation?*"

"Yes. Reilly's going to try it. Personally I think he'd be smarter to die and get it over with."

It was a bitter statement. But Marie Thorne didn't sound bitter making it. She sounded as though she were making a simple statement of fact.

Blaine said. "You think he should die instead of trying for reincarnation?"

"*I* would. But I forgot, you haven't been briefed. I just wish he'd made up his mind earlier. That senile old grandfather butting in now—"

"Why didn't Reilly ask his grandfather earlier?" Blaine asked.

"He did. But his grandfather wouldn't talk earlier."

"I see. How old is he?"

"Reilly's grandfather? He was eighty-one when he died."

"*What?*"

"Yes, he died about sixty years ago. Reilly's father is dead, too, but he won't talk at all, which is a pity be cause he had good business sense. Why are you staring at me, Blaine? Oh, I forgot you don't know the setup. It's very simple, really."

She stood for a moment, brooding. Then she nodded emphatically, whirled and walked to the door.

"Where are you going?" Blaine asked.

"To tell Reilly what I think of him! He can't do this to me! He promised!" Abruptly her control returned.

"As for you, Blaine, I suppose there's no further need of you here. You have your life, and an adequate body in which to live it. I suppose you can leave at any time you desire."

"Thanks," Blaine said, as she left the room.

Dressed in his brown slacks and blue shirt, Blaine left the infirmary and walked down a long corridor until he reached a door. A uniformed guard was standing beside it.

"Excuse me," Blaine said, "does this door lead outside?"

"Huh?"

"Does this door lead outside the Rex Building?'"

"Yeah, of course. Outside and onto the street."

"Thank you." Blaine hesitated. He wanted the briefing he had been promised but never given. He wanted to ask the guard what New York was like, and what the local customs and regulations were, and what he should. see, and what he should avoid. But the guard apparently hadn't heard about the Man from the Past. He was staring pop-eyed at Blaine.

Blaine hated the idea of plunging into the New York of 2110 like this, without money or knowledge or friends, without a job or a place to stay, and wearing an uncomfortable new body. But it couldn't be helped. Pride meant something, after all. He would rather take his chances alone than ask assistance from the porcelain-hard Miss Thorne, or any of the others at Rex.

"Do I need a pass to get out?" he asked hopefully.

"Nope. Just to get back in." The guard frowned suspiciously. "Say, what's the matter with you?"

"Nothing," Blaine said. He opened the door, still not believing that they would let him leave so casually. But then, why not? He was in a world where men talked to their dead grandfathers, where there were spaceships and hereafter drivers, where they snatched a man from the past as a publicity stunt, then lightly discarded him.

The door closed. Behind him was the great grey mass of the Rex Building. Before him lay New York.

Chapter 5

At first glance, the city looked like a surrealistic Bagdad. He saw squat palaces of white and blue tile, and slender red minarets, and irregularly shaped buildings with flaring Chinese roofs and spired onion domes. It looked as though an oriental fad in architecture had swept the city. Blaine could hardly believe he was in New York. Bombay perhaps, Moscow, or even Los Angeles, but not New York. With relief he saw skyscrapers, simple and direct against the curved Asiatic structures. They seemed like lonely sentinels of the New York he had known.

The streets were filled with miniature traffic. Blaine saw motorcycles and scooters, cars no bigger than Porsches, trucks the size of Buicks, and nothing larger. He wondered if this was New York's answer to congestion and air pollution. If so, it hadn't helped.

Most of the traffic was overhead. There were vane and jet operated vehicles, aerial produce trucks and one-man speedsters, helicopter taxis and floating buses marked "Skyport 2nd Level" or "Express to Montauk." Glittering dots marked the vertical and horizontal lanes within which the traffic glided, banked, turned, ascended and descended. Flashing red, green, yellow and blue lights seemed to regulate the flow. There were rules and conventions; but to Blaine's inexperienced eye it was a vast fluttering confusion.

Fifty feet overhead there was another shopping level. How did people get up there? For that matter, how did anyone live and retain his sanity in this noisy, bright, congested machine? The human density was overpowering. He felt as though he were being drowned in a sea of flesh. What was the population of this super-city? Fifteen million? Twenty million? It made the New York of 1958 look like a country village.

He had to stop and sort his impressions. But the sidewalks were crowded, and people pushed and cursed when he slowed down. There were no parks or benches in sight.

He noticed a group of people standing in a line, and took a place on the end. Slowly the line shuffled forward. Blaine shuffled with it, his head pounding dully, trying to catch his breath.

In a few moments he was in control of himself again, and slightly more respectful of his strong, phlegmatic body. Perhaps a man from the past needed just that sort of fleshy envelope if he wanted to view the future with equanimity. A low-order nervous system had its advantages.

The line shuffled silently forward. Blaine noticed that the men and women standing on it were poorly dressed, unkempt, unwashed. They shared a common look of sullen despair.

Was he in a breadline?

He tapped the shoulder of the man in front of him. "Excuse me," he said, "where is this line going?"

The man turned his head and stared at Blaine with red-rimmed eyes. "Going to the suicide booths," he said, jerking his chin toward the front of the line.

Blaine thanked him and stepped quickly out of the line. What a hell of an inauspicious way to start his first real day in the future. Suicide booths! Well, he would never enter one willingly, he could be absolutely sure of that. Things surely couldn't get *that* bad.

But what kind of a world had suicide booths? And free ones, to judge by the clientele... He would have to be careful about accepting free gifts in this world.

Blaine walked on, gawking at the sights and slowly growing accustomed to the bright, hectic, boisterous, overcrowded city. He came to an enormous building shaped like a Gothic castle, with pennants flying from its upper battlements. On its highest tower was a brilliant green light fully visible against the fading afternoon sun.

It looked like an important landmark. Blaine stared, then noticed a man leaning against the building, lighting a thin cigar. He seemed to be the only man in New York not in a tearing hurry. Blaine approached him.

"Pardon me, sir," he said, "what is this building?"

"This," said the man, "is the headquarters of Hereafter, Incorporated." He was a tall man, very thin, with a long, mournful weatherbeaten face. His eyes were narrow and direct. His clothes hung awkwardly on him, as though he were more used to levis than tailored slacks. Blaine thought he looked like a Westerner.

"Impressive," Blaine said, gazing up at the Gothic castle.

"Gaudy," the man said. "You aren't from the city, are you?"

Blaine shook his head.

"Me neither. But frankly, stranger, I thought everybody on Earth and all the planets knew about the Hereafter building. Do you mind my asking where you're from?"

"Not at all," Blaine said. He wondered if he should proclaim himself a man from the past. No, it was hardly the thing to tell a perfect stranger. The man might call a cop. He'd better be from somewhere else.

"You see," Blaine said, "I'm from—Brazil."

"Oh?"

"Yes. Upper Amazon Valley. My folks went there when I was a kid. Rubber plantation. Dad just died, so I thought I'd have a look at New York."

"I hear it's still pretty wild down there," the man said.

Blaine nodded, relieved that his story wasn't being questioned: But perhaps it wasn't a very strange story for this day and age. In any event, he had found a home.

"Myself," the man said, "I'm from Mexican Hat, Arizona. The name's Orc, Carl Orc. Blaine? Glad to meet you, Blaine. You know, I came here to cast a look around this New York and find out what they're always boasting about. It's interesting enough, but these folks are just a little too up and roaring for me, if you catch my meaning. I don't mean to say we're pokey back home. We're not. But these people bounce around like an ape with a stick in his line."

"I know just what you mean," Blaine said.

For a few minutes they discussed the jittery, frantic, compulsive habits of New Yorkers, comparing them with the sane, calm, pastoral life in Mexican Hat and the Upper Amazon Valley. These people, they agreed, just didn't know how to live.

"Blaine," said Orc, "I'm glad I ran into you. What say we get ourselves a drink?"

"Fine," Blaine said. Through a man like Carl Orc he might find a way out of his immediate difficulties. Perhaps he could get a job in Mexican Hat. He could plead Brazil and amnesia to excuse his lack of present-day knowledge.

Then he remembered that he had no money.

He started a halting explanation of how he had accidentally left his wallet in his hotel. But Orc stopped him in mid-sentence.

"Look here, Blaine," Orc said, fixing him with his narrow blue eyes, "I want to tell you something. A story like that wouldn't cut marg with most people. But I figure I'm somewhat of a judge of character. Can't say I've been wrong too often. I'm not exactly what you'd call a poor man, so what say we have the evening on me?"

"Really," Blaine said, "I couldn't—"

"Not another word," Orc said decisively. "Tomorrow evening is on you, if you insist. But right now, let us proceed to inspect the internal nocturnal movements of this edgy little old town."

It was, Blaine decided, as good as any other way of finding out about the future. After all, nothing could be more revealing than what people did for pleasure. Through games and drunkenness, man exhibits his essential attitudes toward his environment, and shows his disposition toward the questions of life, death, fate and free will. What better symbol of Rome than the circus? What better crystallization of the American West than the rodeo? Spain had its bullfights and Norway its ski-jumps. What sport, recreation or pastime would similarly reveal the New York of 2110? He would find out. And surely, to experience this in all its immediacy was better than reading about it in some dusty library, and infinitely more entertaining.

"Suppose we have a look at the Martian Quarter?" Orc asked.

"Lead away," Blaine said, well-pleased at the chance to combine pleasure with stern necessity.

Orc led the way through a maze of streets and levels, through underground arcades and overhead ramps, by foot, escalator, subway and helicab. The interlocking complexity of streets and levels didn't impress the lean Westerner. Phoenix was laid out in the same way, he said, although admittedly on a smaller scale.

They went to a small restaurant that called itself the "Red Mars", and advertised a genuine South Martian cuisine. Blaine had to confess he had never eaten Martian food. Orc had sampled it several times in Phoenix.

"It's pretty good," he told Blaine, "but it doesn't stick to your ribs. Later we'll have a steak."

The menu was written entirely in Martian, and no English translation was included. Blaine recklessly ordered the Number One Combination, as did Orc. It came, a strange-looking mess of shredded vegetables and bits of meat. Blaine tasted, and nearly dropped his fork in surprise.

"It's exactly like Chinese food!"

"Well, of course," Orc said. "The Chinese were the first on Mars, in '97 I think. So anything they eat up there is Martian food. Right?"

"I suppose so," Blaine said.

"Besides, this stuff is made with genuine Martian-grown vegetables and mutated herbs and spices. Or so they advertise."

Blaine didn't know whether to be disappointed or relieved. With good appetite he ate the C'ky-Ourher, which tasted just like shrimp chow mein, and the Trrdxat, or egg roll.

"Why do they give it such weird names?" Blaine asked, ordering the Hggshrt for dessert.

"Man, you're really out of touch!" Orc said, laughing. "Those Martian Chinese went all the way. They translated the Martian rock-carvings and suchlike, and started to talk Martian, with a strong Cantonese accent I presume, but there wasn't no one around to tell them different. They talk Martian, dress Martian, think Martian. You call one of them a Chinese now, he'd up and hit you. He's a *Martian,* boy!"

The Hggshrt came, and turned out to be an almond cookie.

Orc paid the check. As they left, Blaine asked, "Are there many Martian laundries?"

"Hell. yes. Country's filled with them."

"I thought so," Blaine said, and paid a silent tribute to the Martian Chinese and their firm grip on traditional institutions.

They caught a helicab to the Greens Club, a place that Orc's Phoenix friends had told him not to miss. This small, expensive, intimate little club was world-famous, an absolute must for any visitor to New York. For the Greens Club was unique in presenting an all-vegetable floor show.

They were given seats on a little balcony, not far from the glass-fenced center of the club. Three levels of tables surrounded the center, and brilliant spotlights played upon it. Behind the glass fence was what looked like a few square yards of jungle, growing in a nutrient solution. An artificial breeze stirred the plants, which were packed tight together, and varied widely in size, shape and hue.

They behaved like no plants Blaine had ever seen. They grew rapidly, fantastically, from tiny seeds and root tendrils to great shrubs and rough-barked trees, squat ferns, monstrous flowers, dripping green fungus and speckled vines; grew and quickly completed their life-cycle and fell into decay, casting forth their seeds to begin again. But no species seemed able to reproduce itself. Sports and mutants sprang from the seeds and swollen fruit, altered and adapted to the fierce environment, battled for root space below and air space above, and struggled toward the artificial suns that glowed above them. Unsuccessful shrubs quickly molded themselves into parasites, clung to the choked trees, and discovered new adaptations clinging to them in turn. Sometimes, in a burst of creative ambition, a plant would surmount all obstacles, put down the growths around it, strangle the opposition, conquer all. But new species already grew from its body, pulled it down and squabbled over the corpse. Sometimes a blight, itself vegetable, would attack the jungle and carry everything before it in a grand crescendo of mold. But a courageous sport would at last take root in it, then another, and on went the fight. The plants changed, grew larger or smaller, transcended themselves in the struggle for survival. But no amount of determination, no cunning, no transcendence helped. No species could prevail, and every endeavor led to death.

Blaine found the spectacle disturbing. Could this fatalistic pageant of the world be the significant characteristic of 2110? He glanced at Orc.

"It's really something," Orc told him, "what these New York labs can do with quick-growing mutants. It's a freak show, of course. They just speed up the growing rate, force a contra-survival situation, throw in some radiation, and let the best plant try to win. I hear these plants use up their growth potential in about twenty hours, and have to be replaced."

"So that's where it ends," Blaine said, watching the tortured but ever-optimistic jungle. "In replacements."

"Sure," said Orc, blandly avoiding all philosophical complications. "They can afford it, at the prices they charge here. But it's freak stuff. Let me tell you about the sandplants we grow in Arizona."

Blaine sipped his whiskey and watched the jungle growing, dying and renewing itself. Orc was saying, "Right on the burning face of the desert. Fact. We've finally adapted fruit and vegetable-bearing plants to real desert conditions, without increasing their bulk water supply, and at a price which allows us to compete with the fertile areas. I tell you, boy, in another fifty years the entire concept of *fertile* is going to change. Take Mars, for example..."

They left the Greens Club and worked their way from bar to bar, toward Times Square. Orc was showing a certain difficulty in focusing, but his voice was steady as he talked about the lost Martian secret of growing on sand. Someday, he promised Blaine, we'll figure out how they produced the sandplants without the added nutrients and moisture-fixatives.

Blaine had drunk enough to put his former body into a coma twice over. But his bulky new body seemed to have an inexhaustible capacity for whiskey. It was a pleasant change, to have a body that could hold its liquor. Not, he added hastily, that such a rudimentary ability could offset the body's disadvantages.

They crossed Times Square's garish confusion and entered a bar on 44th Street. As their drinks were served, a furtive-eyed little man in a raincoat stepped up to them.

"Hey, boys," he said tentatively.

"Whatcha want, podner?" Orc asked.

"You boys out looking for a little fun?"

"You might say so," Orc said expansively. "And we can find it ourselves, thank you kindly."

The little man smiled nervously. "You can't find what *I'm* offering."

"Speak up, little friend," Orc said. "What exactly are you offering?"

"Well, boys, it's—hold it! Flat-hats!"

Two blue-uniformed policemen entered the bar, looked around and left.

"OK," Blaine said. "What is it?"

"Call me Joe," the little man said with an ingratiating grin. "I'm a steerer for a Transplant game, friends. The best game and highest jump in town!"

"What in hell is Transplant?" Blaine asked.

Both Orc and Joe looked at him. Joe said, "Wow, friend, no insult but you must *really* be from down on the farm. Never heard of Transplant? Well, I'll be griped!"

"OK, so I'm a farmboy," Blaine growled, thrusting his fierce, square, hard-planed face close to Joe's. "What is Transplant!"

"Not so loud!" Joe whispered, shrinking back. "Take it easy, farmer, I'll explain. Transplant is the new switch game, buddy. Are you tired of living? Think you've had all the kicks? Wait 'til you try Transplant. You see, farmer, folks in the know say that straight sex is pretty moldy potatoes. Don't get me wrong, it's fine for the birds and the bees and the beasts and the brutes. It still brings a thrill to their simple animal hearts, and who are we to say they're wrong? As a means of propagating the species, old nature's little sex gimmick is still the first and the best. But for real kicks, sophisticated people are turning to Transplant.

"Transplant is democratic, friends. It gives you the big chance to switch over into someone else and feel how the other ninety-nine percent feels. It's educational, you might say, and it takes up where straight sex leaves off. Ever get the urge to be a high-strung Latin, pal? You can, with Transplant. Ever wonder what a genuine sadist feels? Tune in with Transplant. And there's more, more, so much more! For example, why be a man all your life? You've proved your point by now, why belabor it? Why not be a woman for a while? With Transplant you can be aboard for those gorgeous moments in the life of one of our specially selected gals."

"Voyeurism," Blaine said.

"I know them big words," Joe said, "and it ain't true. This is no peeping-Tom's game. With Transplant *you are there,* right in the old corpus, moving those exotic muscles, experiencing those sensations. Ever get the urge to be a tiger, farmboy, and go loping after a lady tiger in the old mating season? We *got* a tiger, friend, and a lady tiger too. Ever ask yourself what thrill a man could possibly find in flagellation, shoe-fetishism, necrophilia, or the like? Find out with Transplant. Our catalogue of bodies reads like an encyclopedia. You can't go wrong at Transplant, friends, and our prices are set ridiculously—"

"Get out," Blaine said.

"What, buddy?"

Blaine's big hand shot out and grabbed Joe by the raincoat front. He lifted the little pusher to eye level and glared at him.

"You take your perverted little notions out of here," Blaine said. "Guys like you have been selling off-beat kicks since the days of Babylon, and guys like me haven't been buying. Get out, before I break your neck for a quick sadistic thrill."

He released him. Joe smoothed his raincoat and smiled nervously. "No offense, buddy, I'm going. Don't feel like it tonight. There's always another night. Transplant's in your future, farmboy. Why fight it?"

Blaine started to move forward, but Orc held him back. The little pusher scuttled out the door.

"He isn't worth dropping," Orc said. "The flat-hats would just take you in. It's a sad, sick, dirty world, friend. Drink up."

Blaine threw down his whiskey, still seething. Transplant! If that was the characteristic amusement of 2110 he wanted no part of it. Orc was right, it was a sad, sick, dirty world. Even the whiskey was beginning to taste funny.

He grabbed at the bar for support. The whiskey tasted *very* funny. What was wrong with him? The stuff seemed to be going to his head.

Orc's arm was around his shoulder. He was saying, "Well, well, my old buddy's taken himself that one too many. Guess I'd better take him back to his hotel."

But Orc didn't know where his hotel was. He didn't even have a hotel to be taken to. Orc, that damned quick-talking straight-eyed Orc must have put something in his drink while he was talking to Joe.

In order to roll him? But Orc knew he had no money. Why then?

He tried to shake the arm off his shoulders. It was clamped in place like an iron bar. "Don't worry," Orc was saying, "I'll take care of you, old buddy."

The barroom revolved lazily around Blaine's head. He had a sudden realization that he was going to find out a great deal about 2110 by the dubious method of direct experience. Too much, he suspected. Perhaps a dusty library would have been better after all.

The barroom began to revolve more rapidly. Blaine passed out.

Chapter 6

He recovered consciousness in a small, dimly lighted room with no furniture, no doors or windows, and only a single screened ventilation outlet in the ceiling. The floors and walls were thickly padded, but the padding hadn't been washed in a long time. It stank.

Blaine sat up, and two red-hot needles stabbed him through the eyes. He lay down again.

"Relax," a voice said. "Them knock drops take a while to wear off."

He was not alone in the padded room. There was a man sitting in a corner, watching him. The man was wearing only shorts. Glancing at himself, Blaine saw that he was similarly dressed.

He sat up slowly and propped himself against a wall. For a moment he was afraid his head would explode. Then, as the needles drove viciously in, he was afraid it wouldn't.

"What is this?" he asked.

"End of the line," the man said cheerfully. "They boxed you, just like me. They boxed you and brought you in like fabrit. Now all they got to do is crate you and label you."

Blaine couldn't understand what the man was saying. He was in no mood to decipher 2110 slang. Clutching his head, he said, "I don't have any money. Why did they box me?"

"Come off it," the man said. "Why *would* they box you? They want your body, man!"

"My body?"

"Right. For a host."

A host body, Blaine thought, such as he was now occupying. Well, of course. Naturally. It was obvious when you came to think about it. This age needed a supply of host bodies for various and sundry purposes. But how do you get a host body? They don't grow on trees, nor can you dig for them. You get them from people. Most people wouldn't take kindly to selling their own bodies; life is so meaningless without one. So how to fill the supply?

Easy. You pick out a sucker, dope him, hide him away, extract his mind, then take his body.

It was an interesting line of speculation, but Blaine couldn't continue it any longer. It seemed as though his head had finally decided to explode.

Later, the hangover subsided. Blaine sat up and found a sandwich in front of him on a paper plate, and a cup of some dark beverage.

"It's safe to eat," the man told him. "They take good care of us. I hear the going black market price for a body is close to four thousand dollars."

"Black market?"

"Man, what's wrong with you? Wake up! You know there's a black market in bodies just like there's an open market in bodies."

Blaine sipped the dark beverage, which turned out to be coffee. The man introduced himself as Ray Melhill, a flow-control man off the spaceship *Bremen*. He was about Blaine's age, a compact, red-headed, snub-nosed man with slightly protruding teeth. Even in his present predicament he carried himself with a certain jaunty assurance, the unquenchable confidence of a man for whom something always turns up. His freckled skin was very white except for a small red blotch on his neck, the result of an old radiation burn.

"I should of known better," Melhill said. "But we'd been transiting for three months on the asteroid run and I wanted a spree. I would of been fine if I'd stuck with the boys, but we got separated. So I wound up in a dog kennel with a greasy miranda. She knocked my drink and I wound up here."

Melhill leaned back, his hands locked behind his head. "Me, of all people! I was always telling the boys to watch out. Stick with the gang, I was always telling them. You know, I don't mind the thought of dying so much. I just hate the idea of those bastards giving my body to some dirty fat decrepit old slob so he can play around for another fifty years. That's what kills me, the thought of that fat old slob wearing my body. Christ!"

Blaine nodded somberly.

"So that's my tale of woe," Melhill said, growing cheerful again. "What's yours?"

"Mine's a pretty long one," Blaine said, "and a trifle wild in spots. Do you want to hear it all?"

"Sure. Plenty of time. I hope."

"OK. It starts in the year 1958. Wait, don't interrupt me. I was driving my car..."

When he had finished, Blaine leaned back against the padded wall and took a deep breath. "Do you believe me?" he asked.

"Why not? Nothing so new about time travel. It's just illegal and expensive. And those Rex boys would pull anything."

"The girls, too," Blaine said, and Melhill grinned.

They sat in companionable silence for a while. Then Blaine asked, "So they're going to use us for host bodies?"

"That's the score."

"When?"

"When a customer totters in. I've been here a week, close as I can figure. Either of us might be taken any second. Or it might not come for another week or two."

"And they just wipe our minds out?"

Melhill nodded.

"But that's murder!"

"It sure is," Melhill agreed. "Hasn't happened yet, though. Maybe the flat-hats will pull a raid."

"I doubt it."

"Me too. Have you got hereafter insurance? Maybe you'll survive after death."

"I'm an atheist," Blaine said. "I don't believe in that stuff."

"So am I. But life after death is a fact."

"Get off it," Blaine said sourly.

"It is! Scientific fact!"

Blaine stared hard at the young spaceman. "Ray," he said, "how about filling me in? Brief me on what's happened since 1958."

"That's a big order," Melhill said, "and I'm not what you'd call an educated guy."

"Just give me an idea. What's this hereafter stuff? And reincarnation and host bodies? What's *happening*?"

Melhill leaned back and took a deep breath. "Well, let's see. 1958. They put a ship on the moon somewhere around 1960, and landed on Mars about ten years later. Then we had that quickie war with Russia over the asteroids—strictly a deep-space affair. Or was it with China?"

"Never mind," Blaine said. "What about reincarnation and life after death?"

"I'll try to give it to you like they gave it to me in high school. I had a course called Survey of Psychic Survival, but that was a long time ago. Let's see." Melhill frowned in deep concentration. "Quote. 'Since earliest times man has sensed the presence of an invisible spirit world, and has suspected that he himself will participate in that world after the death of his body.' I guess you know all about that early stuff. The Egyptians and Chinese and the European alchemists and those. So I'll skip to Rhine. He lived in your time. He was investigating psychic phenomena at Duke. Ever hear of him?"

"Sure," Blaine said. "What did he discover?"

"Nothing, really. But he got the ball rolling. Then Kralski took over the work at Vilna, and shoved it ahead some. That was 1987, the year the Pirates won their first World Series. Around 2000 there was Von Leddner. Outlined the general theory of the hereafter, but didn't have any proofs. And finally we come to Professor Michael Vanning.

"Professor Vanning is the boy who pinned it all down. He *proved* that people survive after death. Contacted them, talked with them, recorded them, all that stuff. Offered absolute sure-enough concrete scientific proof of life after death. So of course there were big arguments about it, a lot of religious talk. Controversy. Headlines. A big-time professor from Harvard named James Archer Flynn set out to prove the whole thing was a hoax. He and Vanning argued back and forth for years.

"By this time Vanning was an old man and decided to take the plunge. He sealed a lot of stuff in a safe, hid stuff here and there, scattered some code words and promised to come back, like Houdini promised but didn't. Then—"

"Pardon me," Blaine interrupted, "if there *is* life after death, why didn't Houdini come back?"

"It's very simple, but please, one thing at a time. Anyhow, Vanning killed himself, leaving a long suicide note about man's immortal spirit and the indomitable progress of the human race. It's reprinted in a lot of anthologies. Later they found out it was ghost-written, but that's another story. Where was I?"

"He suicided."

"Right. And damned if he didn't contact Professor James Archer Flynn after dying and tell him where to find all that hidden stuff, the code words, and so forth. That clinched it, buddy. Life after death was *in.*"

Melhill stood up, stretched, and sat down again. "The Vanning Institute," he said, "warned everybody against hysteria. But hysteria there was. The next fifteen years are known as the Crazy Forties."

Melhill grinned and licked his lips. "Wish I'd been around then. Everybody just sort of let go. 'Doesn't matter what you do,' the jingle ran, 'pie in the sky is waitin' for *you.*' Saint or sinner, bad or good, everybody gets a slice. The murderer walks into the hereafter just like the archbishop. So live it up, boys and girls, enjoy the flesh on Earth while you're here, 'cause you'll get plenty of spirit after death. Yep, and they really lived it up. Anarchy it was. A new religion popped up calling itself 'Realization'. It started telling people that they owed it to themselves to experience *everything,* good or bad, fair and foul, because the hereafter was just a long remembrance of what you did on Earth. So *do* it, they said, that's what you're put on Earth for, *do* it, or you'll be shortchanged in the afterlife. Gratify every desire, satisfy every lust, explore your blackest depths. Live high, die high. It was wacky. The real fanatics formed torture clubs, and wrote encyclopedias on pain, and collected tortures like a housewife would collect recipes. At each meeting, a member would voluntarily present himself as a victim, and they'd kill him in the most excruciating damned ways they could find. They wanted to experience the absolute most in pleasure and pain. And I guess they did."

Melhill wiped his forehead and said, more sedately, "I've done a little reading on the Crazy Years."

"So I see," Blaine said.

"It's sort of interesting stuff. But then came the crusher. The Vanning Institute had been experimenting all this time. Around 2050, when the Crazy Years were in full swing, they announced that there was a hereafter, sure enough; *but not for everyone.*"

Blaine blinked, but made no comment.

"A real crusher. The Vanning Institute said they had certain proof that only about one person in a million got into the hereafter. The rest, the millions and millions, just went out like a light when they died. Pouf! No more. No afterlife. Nothing."

"Why?" Blaine asked.

"Well, Tom, I'm none too clear on that part myself," Melhill told him. "If you asked me something about flow-mechanics, I could really tell you something; but psychic theory isn't my field. So try to stick with me while I struggle through this."

He rubbed his forehead vigorously. "What survives or doesn't survive after death is the mind. People have been arguing for thousands of years about what a mind is, and where and how it interacts with the body, and so forth. We haven't got all the answers, but we do have some working definitions. Nowadays, the mind is considered a high-tension energy web that emanates from the body, is modified by the body, and itself modifies the body. Got that?"

"I think so. Go on."

"So the way I got it, the mind and body interact and intermodify. But the mind can also exist independently of the body. According to a lot of scientists the independent mind is the next stage of evolution. In a million years, they say, we won't even need a body except maybe for a brief incubation period. Personally I don't think this damned race will survive another million years. It damn well doesn't deserve to."

"At the moment I agree with you," Blaine said. "But get back to the hereafter."

"We've got this high-tension energy web. When the body dies, that web *should* be able to go on existing, like a butterfly coming out of a cocoon. Death is simply the process that hatches the mind from the body. But it doesn't work that way because of the death trauma. Some scientists think the death trauma is nature's ejecting mechanism, to get the mind free of the body. But it works too hard and louses up everything. Dying is a tremendous psychic shock, and most of the time the energy web gets disrupted, ripped all to hell. It can't pull itself together, it dissipates, and you're but completely dead."

Blaine said, "So that's why Houdini didn't come back"

"Him and most others. Right. A lot of people did some heavy thinking, and that ended the Crazy Years. The Vanning Institute went on working. They studied Yoga and stuff like that, but on a scientific basis. Some of those Eastern religions had the right idea, you know. Strengthen the mind. That's what the Institute wanted; a way to strengthen the energy web so it would survive the death process."

"And they found it?"

"In spades. Along about that time they changed their name to Hereafter, Inc."

Blaine nodded. "I passed their building today. Hey, wait a minute! You say they solved the mind-strengthening problem? Then no one dies! Everyone survives after death!"

Melhill grinned sardonically. "Don't be a farmer, Tom. You think they give it away free? Not a chance. It's a complex electrochemical treatment, pal, and they charge for it. They charge *plenty.*"

"So only the rich go to heaven," Blaine said.

"What else did you expect? Can't have just *anyone* crashing in."

"Sure, sure," Blaine said. "But aren't there other ways, other mind-strengthening disciplines? What about Yoga? What about Zen?"

"They work," Melhill said. "There are at least a dozen government tested and approved home-survival courses. Trouble is, it takes about twenty years of really hard work to become an adept. That's not for the ordinary guy. Nope, without the machines to help you, you're dead."

"And only Hereafter, Inc. has the machines?"

"There's one or two others, the Afterlife Academy and Heaven, Ltd., but the price stays about the same. The government's getting to work on some death-survival insurance, but it won't help us."

"I guess not," Blaine said. The dream, for a moment, had been dazzling; a relief from mortal fears; the rational certainty of a continuance and existence after the body's death; the knowledge of an uninterrupted process of growth and fulfillment for his personality to its own limits—not the constricting limits of the frail fleshy envelope that heredity and chance had imposed on him.

But that was not to be. His mind's desire to expand was to be checked, rudely, finally. Tomorrow's promises were forever not for today.

"What about reincarnation and host bodies?" he asked.

"You should know," Melhill told him. "They reincarnated you and put you in a host. There's nothing complicated about mind-switching, as the Transplant operators will gladly tell you. Transplant is only temporary occupancy, however, and doesn't involve full dislodgement of the original mind. Hosting is for keeps. First, the original mind must be wiped out. Second, it's a dangerous game for the mind attempting to enter the host body. Sometimes, you see, that mind can't penetrate the host and breaks itself up trying. Hereafter conditioning often won't stand up under a reincarnation attempt. If the mind doesn't make it into the host—pouf!"

Blaine nodded, now realizing why Marie Thorne had thought it better for Reilly to die. Her advice had been entirely in his best interests.

He asked, "Why would any man with hereafter insurance still make the attempt at reincarnation?"

"Because some old guys are afraid of dying," Melhill said. "They're afraid of the hereafter, scared of that spirit stuff. They want to stay right here on Earth where they know what's going on. So they buy a body legally on the open market, if they can find a good one. If not, they buy one on the black market. One of *our* bodies, pal."

"The bodies on the open market are offered for sale voluntarily, then?"
Melhill nodded.

"But who would sell his body?"

"A very poor guy, obviously. By law he's supposed to receive compensation in the form of hereafter insurance for his body. In actual fact, he takes what he can get."

"A man would have to be crazy!"

"You think so?" Melhill asked. "Today like always, the world is filled with unskilled, sick, disease-ridden and starving people. And like always, they all got families. Suppose a guy wants to buy food for his kids? His body is the only thing of value he has to sell. Back in your time he didn't have anything to sell."

"Perhaps so," Blaine said. "But no matter how bad things got, I'd never sell my body."

Melhill laughed with good humor. "Stout fellow! But Tom, they're taking it for nothing!"

Blaine could think of no answer for that.

Chapter 7

Time passed slowly in the padded cell. Blaine and Melhill were given books and magazines. They were fed often and well, out of paper cups and plates. They were closely watched, for no harm must come to their highly marketable bodies.

They were kept together for companionship; solitary men sometimes go insane, and insanity can cause irreparable damage to the valuable brain cells: They were even granted the right to exercise, under strict supervision, to relieve boredom and to keep their bodies in shape for future owners.

Blaine began to experience an exceeding fondness for the sturdy, thickset, well-muscled body he had inhabited so recently, and from which he would be parted so soon. It was really an excellent body, he decided, a body to be proud of. True, it had no particular grace; but grace could be overrated. To counterbalance that lack, he suspected the body was not prone to hay fever like the former body he had tenanted; and its teeth were very sound.

On the whole, all considerations of mortality aside, it was not a body to be given up lightly.

One day, after they had eaten, a padded section of wall swung away. Looking in, protected by steel bars, was Carl Orc.

"Howdy," said Orc, tall, lean, direct-eyed, angular in his city clothes, "how's my Brazilian buddy?"

"You bastard," Blaine said, with a deep sense of the inadequacy of words.

"Them's the breaks," Orc said. "You boys gettin' enough to eat?"

"You and your ranch in Arizona!"

"I've got one under lease," Orc said. "Mean to retire there some day and raise sandplants. I reckon I know more about Arizona than many a native-born son. But ranches cost money, and hereafter insurance costs money. A man does what he can."

"And a vulture does what *he* can," Blaine said

Orc sighed deeply. "Well, it's a business, and I guess it's no worse than some others I could think of if I set my mind to it kinda hard. It's a wicked world we live in. I'll probably regret all this sometime when I'm sitting on the front porch of my little desert ranch."

"You'll never get there," Blaine said.

"I won't?"

"No. One night a mark is going to catch you spiking his drink. You're going to end in the gutter, Orc, with your head caved in. And that'll be the end of you."

"Only the end of my body," Orc corrected. "My soul will march on to that sweet life in the by and by. I've paid my money, boy, and heaven's my next home!"

"You don't deserve it!"

Orc grinned, and even Melhill couldn't conceal a smile. Orc said, "My poor Brazilian friend, there's no question of *deserving*. You should know better than that! Life after death just isn't for the meek and humble little people, no matter how worthy they are. It's the bright lad with the dollar in his pocket and his eyes open for number one whose soul marches on after death."

"I can't believe it," Blaine said. "It isn't fair, it isn't just."

"You're an idealist," Orc said, interestedly, as though he were studying the world's last moa.

"Call it what you like. Maybe you'll get your hereafter, Orc. But I think there's a little corner of it where you'll burn forever!"

Orc said, "There's no scientific evidence of hellfire. But there's a lot we don't know about the hereafter. Maybe I'll burn. And maybe there's even a factory up there in the blue where they'll reassemble your shattered mind... But let's not argue. I'm sorry, I'm afraid the time's come."

Orc walked quickly away. The steel-barred door swung open, and five men marched into the room.

"No!" Melhill screamed.

They closed in on the spaceman. Expertly they avoided his swinging fists and pinioned his arms. One of them pushed a gag in his mouth. They started to drag him out of the room.

Orc appeared in the doorway, frowning. "Let go of him," he said.

The men released Melhill.

"You idiots got the wrong man"' Orc told them. "It's *that* one." He pointed at Blaine.

Blaine had been trying to prepare himself for the loss of his friend. The abrupt reversal of fortune caught him open-mouthed and unready. The men seized him before he had time to react.

"Sorry," Orc said, as they led Blaine out. "The customer specified your particular build and complexion."

Blaine suddenly came to life and tried to wrench free. "I'll kill you!" he shouted to Orc. "I swear it, I'll kill you!"

"Don't damage him," Orc said to the men, wooden-faced.

A rag was pushed over his mouth and nose, and Blaine smelled something sickeningly sweet. Chloroform, he thought. His last recollection was of Melhill, his face ashen, standing at the barred door

Chapter 8

Thomas Blaine's first act of consciousness was to find out whether he was still Thomas Blaine, and still occupying his own body. The proof was there, apparent in the asking. They hadn't wiped out his mind yet.

He was lying on a divan, fully dressed. He sat up and heard the sound of footsteps outside, coming toward the door.

They must have overestimated the strength of the chloroform! He still had a chance!

He moved quickly behind the door. It opened, and someone walked through. Blaine stepped out and swung.

He managed to check the blow. But there was still plenty of force left when his big fist struck Marie Thorne on the side of her shapely chin.

He carried her to the divan. In a few minutes she recovered and looked at him.

"Blaine," she said, "you're an idiot."

"I didn't know who it was," Blaine said. Even as he said it, he realized it wasn't true. He *had* recognized Marie Thorne a fractional instant before the blow was irretrievably launched; and his well-machined, responsive body could have recalled the punch even then. But an unperceived, uncontrollable fury had acted beneath his sane, conscious, morally aware level; fury had cunningly used urgency to avoid responsibility; had seized the deceiving instant to smash down the cold and uncaring Miss Thorne.

The act hinted at something Blaine didn't care to know about himself. He said, "Miss Thorne, who did you buy my body for?"

She glared at him. "I bought it for you, since you obviously couldn't take care of it yourself."

So he wasn't going to die after all. No fat slob was going to inherit his body, scattering his mind to the wind. Good! He wanted very much to live. But he wished anyone but Marie Thorne had saved him.

"I might have done better if I'd known how things work here," Blaine said.

"I was going to explain. Why didn't you wait?"

"After the way you talked to me?"

"I'm sorry if I was brusque," she said. "I was quite upset after Mr. Reilly cancelled the publicity campaign. But couldn't you understand that? If I'd been a man—"

"You aren't a man," Blaine reminded her.

"What difference does it make? I suppose you have some strange old-fashioned ideas about woman's role and status."

"I don't consider them strange," Blaine said.

"Of course not." She fingered her jaw, which was discolored and slightly swollen. "Well, shall we consider ourselves even? Or do you want another clout at me?"

"One was enough, thank you," Blaine said.

She stood up, somewhat unsteadily. Blaine put an arm around her to steady her, and was momentarily disconcerted. He had visualized that trim body as whipcord and steel; but in fact it was flesh, firm, resilient, and surprisingly soft. So close, he could see stray hairs escaping her tight coiffure, and a tiny mole on her forehead near the hairline. At that moment Marie Thorne ceased as an abstraction for him, and took shape as a human being.

"I can stand by myself," she said.

After a long moment, Blaine released her.

"Under the circumstances," she said, looking at him steadily, "I think our relationship should remain on a strictly business level."

Wonder after wonder! *She* had suddenly begun viewing *him* as a human being too; she was aware of him as a man, and disturbed by it. The thought gave him great pleasure. It was not, he told himself, that he liked Marie Thorne, or even desired her particularly. But he wanted very much to throw her off balance, scratch enamel off the facade, jar that damnable poise.

He said, "Why, of course, Miss Thorne."

"I'm glad you feel that way," she told him. "Because frankly, you're not my type."

"What is your type?"

"I like tall, lean men," she said. "Men with a certain grace, ease and sophistication."

"But—"

"Shall we have lunch?" she said easily. "Afterwards, Mr. Reilly would like a word with you. I believe he has a proposal to make."

He followed her out of the room, raging inwardly. Had she been making fun of him? Tall, lean, graceful, sophisticated men! Damn it, that's what he had been! And under this beefy blonde wrestler's body he still was, if only she had eyes to see it!

And who was jarring whose poise?

As they sat down at the table in the Rex executive dining room, Blaine suddenly said, "Melhill!"

"What?"

"Ray Melhill, the man I was locked up with! Look, Miss Thorne, could you possibly buy him, too? I'll pay for it as soon as I can. We were locked up together. He's a damned nice guy."

She looked at him curiously. "I'll see what I can do."

She left the table. Blaine waited, rubbing his hands together, wishing he had Carl Orc's neck between them. Marie Thorne returned in a few minutes.

"I'm very sorry," she said. "I contacted Orc. Mr. Melhill was sold an hour after you were removed. I really am sorry. I didn't know."

"It's all right," Blaine said. "I think I'd like a drink."

Chapter 9

Mr. Reilly sat erect and almost lost in a great, soft, thronelike chair. He was a tiny, bald, spider-like old man. His wrinkled translucent skin was stretched tight across his skull and clawed hands, and bone and tendon showed clearly through the leathery, shrunken flesh. Blaine had the impression of blood coursing sluggishly through the brittle, purple varicosed veins, threatening momentarily to stop. Yet Reilly's posture was firm, and his eyes were lucid in his humorous monkey's face.

"So this is our man from the past!" Mr. Reilly said. "Please be seated, sir. You too, Miss Thorne. I was just discussing you with my grandfather, Mr. Blaine."

Blaine glanced around, almost expecting to see the fifty-years-dead grandfather looming spectrally over him. But there was no sign of him in the ornate, high-ceilinged room.

"He's gone now," Mr. Reilly explained. "Poor Grandfather can maintain an ectoplasmic state for only a brief time. But even so, he's better off than most ghosts."

Blaine's expression must have changed, for Reilly asked, "Don't you believe in ghosts, Mr. Blaine?"

"I'm afraid I don't."

"Of course not. I suppose the word has unfortunate connotations for your twentieth-century mind. Clanking chains, skeletons, all that nonsense. But words change their meaning, and even reality is altered as mankind alters and manipulates nature."

"I see," Blaine said politely.

"You consider that doubletalk," Mr. Reilly said good-naturedly. "It wasn't meant to be. Consider the manner in which words change their meaning. In the twentieth century, 'atoms' became a catch-all word for imaginative writers with their 'atom-guns' and 'atom-powered ships.' An absurd word, which any level-headed man would do well to ignore, just as you level-headedly ignore 'ghosts'. Yet a few years later, 'atoms' conjured a picture of very real and imminent doom. No level-headed man could ignore the word!"

Mr. Reilly smiled reminiscently. "'Radiation' changed from a dull textbook term to a source of cancerous ulcers. 'Space-sickness' was an abstract and unloaded term in your time. But in fifty years it meant hospitals filled with twisted bodies. Words tend to change, Mr. Blaine, from an abstract, fanciful, or academic use to a functional, realistic, everyday use. It happens when manipulation catches up with theory."

"And ghosts?"

"The process has been similar. Mr. Blaine, you're old-fashioned! You'll simply have to change your concept of the word."

"It'll be difficult," Blaine said.

"But necessary. Remember, there was always a lot of evidence in their favor. The prognosis for their existence, you might say, was favorable. And when life after death became fact instead of wishful thinking, ghosts became fact as well."

"I think I'll have to see one first," Blaine said.

"Undoubtedly you will. But enough. Tell me, how does our age suit you?"

"So far, not too well," Blaine said.

Reilly cackled gleefully. "Nothing endearing about body snatchers, eh? But you shouldn't have left the building, Mr. Blaine. It was not in your best interests, and certainly not in the company's best interests."

"I'm sorry, Mr. Reilly," Marie Thorne said. "That was my fault."

Reilly glanced at her, then turned back to Blaine. "It's a pity, of course. You should, in all honesty, have been left to your destiny in 1958. Frankly, Mr. Blaine, your presence here is something of an embarrassment to us.'"

"I regret that."

"My grandfather and I agreed, belatedly I fear, against using you for publicity. The decision should have been made earlier. Still, it's made now. But there may *be* publicity, in spite of our desires. There's even a possibility of the government taking legal action against the corporation."

"Sir," Marie Thorne said, "the lawyers are confident of our position."

"Oh, we won't go to jail," Reilly said. "But consider the publicity. *Bad* publicity! Rex must stay respectable, Miss Thorne. Hints of scandal, innuendoes of illegality... No, Mr. Blaine should not be here in 2110, a walking proof of bad judgment. Therefore, sir, I'd like to make you a business proposition."

"I'm listening," Blaine said.

"Suppose Rex buys you hereafter insurance, thus ensuring your life after death? Would you consent to suicide?"

Blaine blinked rapidly for a moment. "No."

"Why not?" Reilly asked.

For a moment, the reason seemed self-evident. What creature consents to take its own life? Unhappily, man does. So Blaine had to stop and sort his thoughts.

"First of all," he said, "I'm not fully convinced about this hereafter."

"Suppose we convince you," Mr. Reilly said. "Would you suicide then?"

"No!"

"But how shortsighted! Mr. Blaine, consider your position. This age is alien to you, inimical, unsatisfactory. What kind of work can you do? Who can you talk with, and about what? You can't even walk the streets without being in deadly peril of your life."

"That won't happen again," Blaine said. "I didn't know how things worked here."

"But it will! You can never know how things work here! Not really. You're in the same position a caveman would be, thrown haphazardly into your own 1958. He'd think himself capable enough, I suppose, on the basis of his experience with saber-tooth tigers and hairy mastodons. Perhaps some kind soul would even warn him about gangsters. But what good would it do? Would it save him from being run over by a car, electrocuted on a subway track, asphyxiated by a gas stove, falling through an elevator shaft, cut to pieces on a power saw, or breaking his neck in the bathtub? You have to be born to those things in order to walk unscathed among them. And even so, these things happened to people in your age when they relaxed their attention for a moment! How much more likely would our caveman be to stumble?"

"You're exaggerating the situation," Blaine said, feeling a light perspiration form on his forehead.

"Am I? The dangers of the forest are as nothing to the dangers of the city. And when the city becomes a supercity—"

"I won't suicide," Blaine said. "I'll take my chances. Let's drop the subject."

"Why can't you be reasonable?" Mr. Reilly asked petulantly. "Kill yourself now and save us all a lot of trouble. I can outline your future for you if you don't. Perhaps, by sheer nerve and animal cunning, you'll survive for a year. Even two. It won't matter, in the end you'll suicide anyhow. You're a suicide type. Suicide is written all over you—you were born for it, Blaine! You'll kill yourself wretchedly in a year or two, slip out of your maimed flesh with relief—but with no hereafter to welcome your tired mind."

"You're crazy!" Blaine cried.

"I'm never wrong about suicide types," Mr. Reilly said quietly. "I can always spot them. Grandfather agrees with me. So if you'll only—"

"No," Blaine said. "I won't kill myself. I'm afraid you'll have to hire it done."

"That's not my way," Mr. Reilly said. "I won't coerce you. But come to my reincarnation this afternoon. Get a glimpse of the hereafter. Perhaps you'll change your mind."

Blaine hesitated, and the old man grinned at him.

"No danger, I promise you, and no tricks! Did you fear I might steal your body? I selected my host months ago, from the open market. Frankly,

I wouldn't *have* your body. You see, I wouldn't be comfortable in anything so gross."

The interview was over. Marie Thorne led Blaine out.

Chapter 10

The reincarnation room was arranged like a small theater. It was often used, Blaine learned, for company lectures and educational programs on an executive level. Today the audience had been kept small and select. The Rex board of directors was present, five middle-aged men sitting in the back row and talking quietly among themselves. Near them was a recording secretary. Blaine and Marie Thorne sat in front, as far from the directors as possible.

On the raised stage, under white floodlights, the reincarnation apparatus was already in place. There were two sturdy armchairs equipped with straps and wires. Between the chairs was a large glossy black machine. Thick wires connected the machine to the chair, and gave Blaine the uneasy feeling that he was going to witness an execution. Several technicians were bent over the machine, making final adjustments. Standing near them was the bearded old doctor and his red-faced colleague.

Mr. Reilly came on the stage, nodded to the audience and sat down in one of the chairs. He was followed by a man in his forties with a frightened, pale, determined face. This was the host, the present possessor of the body that Mr. Reilly had contracted for. The host sat down in the other chair, glanced quickly at the audience and looked down at his hands. He seemed embarrassed. Perspiration beaded his upper lip, and the armpits of his jacket were stained black. He didn't look at Reilly, nor did Reilly look at him.

Another man came on the stage, bald and earnest-looking, wearing a dark suit with a cleric's collar and carrying a little black book. He began a whispered conversation with the two seated men.

"Who's that?" Blaine asked.

"Father James," Marie Thorne told him. "He's a clergyman of the Church of the Afterlife."

"What's that?"

"It's a new religion. You know about the Crazy Years? Well, during that time there was a great religious controversy…"

The burning question of the 2040's was the spiritual status of the hereafter. It became even worse after Hereafter, Inc. announced the advent of the *scientific* hereafter. The corporation tried desperately hard to avoid any religious involvement; but involvement couldn't very well be avoided. Most churchmen felt that science was unfairly preempting their territory. Hereafter, Inc., whether they liked it or not, was considered the spokesman for a new scientific religious position: That salvation lay, not through religious, moral or ethical considerations, but through an applied, impersonal, invariant scientific principle.

Convocations, meetings and congresses were held to decide the burning question. Some groups adopted the view that the newly revealed scientific hereafter was obviously *not* heaven, salvation, nirvana or paradise; because the soul was not involved.

Mind, they held, is not synonymous with soul; nor is the soul contained in or a part of the mind. Granted, science had found a means of extending the existence of one portion of the mind-body entity. That was fine, but it didn't affect the soul at all, and certainly didn't mean immortality or heaven or nirvana or anything like that. The *soul* could not be affected by scientific manipulation. And the soul's disposition after the eventual and inevitable death of the mind in its scientific hereafter would be in accordance with traditional moral, ethical and religious practices.

"Wow!" Blaine said. "I think I get what you mean. They were trying to achieve a co-existence between science and religion. But wasn't their reasoning a little subtle for some people?"

"Yes," Marie Thorne said, "even though they explained it much better than I've done, and backed it up with all sorts of analogies. But that was only one position. Others didn't attempt co-existence. They simply declared that the scientific hereafter was sinful. And one group solved the problem by joining the scientific position and declaring that the soul *is* contained in the mind."

"I suppose that would be the Church of the Afterlife?"

"Yes. They splintered off from other religions. According to them, the mind contains the soul, and the hereafter is the soul's rebirth after death, with no spiritual ifs and buts."

"That's keeping up with the times," Blaine said. "But morality—"

"In their view, this didn't dispense with morality. The Afterlifers say that you can't impose morals and ethics on people by a system of spiritual rewards and punishments; and if you could, you shouldn't. They say that morality must be good in its own right, first in terms of the social organism, second in terms of the individual man's best good."

To Blaine this seemed a lot to ask of morality. "I suppose it's a popular religion?" he asked.

"Very popular," Marie Thorne answered.

Blaine wanted to ask more, but Father James had begun speaking.

"William Fitzsimmons," the clergyman said to the host, "you have come to this place of your own free will, for the purpose of discontinuing your existence upon the earthly plane and resuming it upon the spiritual plane?"

"Yes, Father," the pale host whispered.

"And the proper scientific instrumentality has been performed so that you may continue your existence upon the spiritual plane?"

"Yes, Father."

Father James turned to Reilly. "Kenneth Reilly, you have come to this place of your own free will for the purpose of continuing your existence upon Earth in the body of William Fitzsimmons?"

"Yes, Father," Reilly said, small and hard-faced.

"And you have made possible for William Fitzsimmons an entrance into the hereafter; and have paid a sum of money to Fitzsimmons' heirs; and have paid the government tax involved in transactions of this kind?"

"Yes, Father," Reilly said.

"All these things being so," Father James said, "no crime is involved, civic or religious. Here there is no taking of life, for the life and personality of William Fitzsimmons continues unabated in the hereafter, and the life and personality of Kenneth Reilly continues unabated upon Earth. Therefore, let the reincarnation proceed!"

To Blaine it seemed a hideous mixture of wedding ceremony and execution. The smiling clergyman withdrew. Technicians secured the men to their chairs, and attached electrodes to their arms, legs and foreheads. The theater grew very still, and the Rex directors leaned forward expectantly in their seats.

"Go ahead," Reilly said, looking at Blaine and smiling slightly.

The chief technician turned a dial on the black machine. It hummed loudly, and the floodlights dimmed. Both men jerked convulsively against the straps, then slumped back.

Blaine whispered, "They're murdering that poor Fitzsimmons bastard."

"That poor bastard," Marie Thorne told him, "knew exactly what he was doing. He's thirty-seven years old and he's been a failure all his life. He's never been able to hold a job for long, and had no previous chance for survival after death. This was a marvellous opportunity for him. Furthermore he has a wife and five children for whom he has not been able to provide. The sum Mr. Reilly paid will enable the wife to give the children a decent education."

"Hurray for them!" Blaine said. "For sale, one father with slightly used body in excellent condition. Must sell! Sacrifice!"

"You're being ridiculous," she said. "Look, it's over."

The machine was turned off, and the straps were removed from the two men. Reilly's wrinkled, grinning old corpse was ignored as the technicians and doctors examined the body of the host.

"Nothing yet!" the bearded old doctor called.

Blaine could sense apprehension in the room, and a hint of fear. The seconds dragged by while the doctors and technicians clustered around the host.

"Still nothing!" the old doctor called, his voice going shrill.

"What's happening?' Blaine asked Marie Thorne.

"As I told you, reincarnation is tricky and dangerous. Reilly's mind hasn't been able to possess the host-body yet. He doesn't have much longer."

"Why not?"

"Because a body starts dying the moment it's untenanted. Irreversible death processes start if a mind isn't at least dormant in the body. The mind is essential. Even an unconscious mind controls the automatic processes. But with no mind at all—"

"Still nothing!" the old doctor shouted.

"I think it's too late now," Marie Thorne whispered.

"A tremor!" the doctor said. "I felt a tremor!"

There was a long silence.

"I think he's in!" the old doctor cried. "Now, oxygen, adrenalin!"

A mask was fitted over the host's face. A hypodermic was slipped into the host's arm. The host stirred, shivered, slumped back, stirred again.

"He's made it!" the old doctor cried, removing the oxygen mask.

The directors, as though on cue, hurried out of their chairs and went up on the stage. They surrounded the host, which was now blinking its eyes and retching.

"Congratulations, Mr. Reilly!"

"Well done, sir!"

"Had us worried, Mr. Reilly!"

The host stared at them. It wiped its mouth and said, "My name is not Reilly."

The old doctor pushed his way through the directors and bent down beside the host. "Not Reilly?" he said. "Are you Fitzsimmons?"

"No," said the host, "I'm not Fitzsimmons, the poor damned fool! And I'm not Reilly. Reilly tried to get into this body but I was too quick. I got into the body first. It's my body now."

"Who are you?" the doctor asked.

The host stood up. The directors stepped away from him, and one man quickly crossed himself.

"It was dead too long," Marie Thorne said.

The host's face now bore only the faintest and most stylized resemblance to the pale, frightened face of William Fitzsimmons. There was nothing of Fitzsimmons' determination, nothing of Reilly's petulance and good humor in that face. It resembled nothing but itself.

The face was dead white except for black dots of stubble on its cheeks and jaw. The lips were bloodless. A lock of black hair was plastered against its cold white forehead. When Fitzsimmons had been in residence the features had blended pleasantly, harmoniously, nondescriptly. But now the individual features had coarsened and grown separate. The unharmonious white face had a thick and unfinished look, like iron before tempering or clay before firing. It had a slack, sullen, relaxed look because of the lack of muscle tone and tension in the face. The calm, flaccid, unharmonious features simply existed, revealing nothing of the personality behind them. The face seemed no longer completely human. All humanity now resided in the great, patient, unblinking Buddha's eyes.

"It's gone zombie," Marie Thorne whispered, clinging to Blaine's shoulder.

"Who are you?" the old doctor asked.

"I don't remember," it said. "I don't." Slowly it turned and started walking down the stage. Two directors moved tentatively to bar its path.

"Get away," it said to them. "It's my body now."

"Leave the poor zombie alone," the old doctor said wearily.

The directors moved out of its way. The zombie walked to the end of the stage, descended the steps, turned, and walked over to Blaine.

"I know you!" it said.

"What? What do you want?" Blaine asked nervously.

"I don't remember," the zombie said, staring hard at him. "What's your name?"

"Tom Blaine."

The zombie shook its head. "Doesn't mean anything to me. But I'll remember. It's you, all right. Something... My body's dying, isn't it? Too bad. I'll remember before it gives out. You and me, you know, together. Blaine, don't you remember me?"

"No!" Blaine shouted, shrinking from the suggested relationship, the idea of some vital link between him and this dying thing. It couldn't be! What shared secret was this thief of corpses, this unclean usurper hinting at, what black intimacy, what sniggering knowledge to be shared like a dirty crust of bread for just Blaine and himself?

Nothing, Blaine told himself. He knew himself, knew what he was, knew what he had been. Nothing like this could arise legitimately to confront him. The creature had to be crazy, or mistaken.

"Who are you?" Blaine asked.

"I don't know!" The zombie flung his hands into the air, like a man caught in a net. And Blaine sensed how his mind must feel, confused, disoriented, nameless, wanting to live and caught in the fleshy dying embrace of a zombie body.

"I'll see you again," the zombie said to Blaine. "You're important to me. I'll see you again and I'll remember all about you and me."

The zombie turned and walked down the aisle and out of the theater. Blaine stared after him until he felt a sudden weight on his shoulder.

Marie Thorne had fainted. It was the most feminine thing she had done so far.

PART TWO

Chapter 11

The head technician and the bearded doctor were arguing near the reincarnation machine, with their assistants ranged respectfully behind them. The battle was quite technical, but Blaine gathered that they were trying to determine the cause of the reincarnation failure. Each seemed to feel that the fault lay in the other's province.

The old doctor insisted that the machine settings must have been faulty, or an uncompensated power drop had occurred. The head technician swore the machine was perfect. He felt certain that Reilly hadn't been physically fit for the strenuous attempt.

Neither would yield an inch. But being reasonable men, they soon reached a compromise solution. The fault, they decided, lay in the nameless spirit who had fought Reilly for possession of Fitzsimmons' body, and had supplanted him.

"But who was it?" the head technician asked. "A ghost, do you think?"

"Possibly," the doctor said, "though it's damned rare for a ghost to possess a living body. Still, he talked crazy enough to be a ghost."

"Whoever he was," the head technician said, "he took over the host too late. The body was definitely zombie. Anyhow, no one could be blamed for it."

"Right," said the doctor. "I'll certify to the apparent soundness of the equipment."

"Fair enough," said the head technician. "And I'll testify to the apparent fitness of the patient."

They exchanged a look of perfect understanding.

The directors were holding an immediate conference of their own, trying to determine what the short-range effects would be upon the Rex corporate structure, and how the announcement should be made to the public, and whether all Rex personnel should be given a day off to visit the Reilly Family Palace of Death.

Old Reilly's original body lay back in its chair, beginning to stiffen, wearing a detached, derisive grin.

Marie Thorne recovered consciousness. "Come on," she said, leading Blaine out of the theater. They hurried down long grey corridors to a street door. Outside, she hailed a helicab and gave the driver an address.

"Where are we going?" Blaine asked, as the helicab climbed and banked.

"To my place. Rex is going to be a madhouse for a while." She began rearranging her hair.

Blaine settled back against the cushions and looked down on the glittering city. From that height it looked like an exquisite miniature, a multi-colored mosaic from the *Thousand and One Nights*. But somewhere down there, walking the streets and levels, was the zombie, trying to remember—him.

"But why me?" Blaine asked out loud.

Marie Thorne glanced at him. "Why you and the zombie? Well, why not? Haven't you ever made any mistakes?"

"I suppose I have. But they're finished and done with."

She shook her head "Maybe mistakes ended for good in your time. Today nothing ever dies for certain. That's one of the great disadvantages of a life after death, you know. One's mistakes sometimes refuse to lie decently dead and buried. Sometimes they follow you around."

"So I see," Blaine said. "But I've never done anything that would bring up *that!*"

She shrugged indifferently. "In that case, you're better than most of us."

Never had she seemed more alien to him. The helicab began a slow descent. And Blaine brooded over the disadvantages inherent in all advantages.

In his own time he had seen the control of disease in the world's backward areas result in an exploding birthrate, famine, plague. He had seen nuclear power breed nuclear war. Every advantage generated its own specific disadvantages. Why should it be different today?

A certified, scientific hereafter was undoubtedly an advantage to the race. Manipulation had again caught up with theory! But the disadvantages... There was a certain inevitable weakening of the protective barrier around mundane life, some rips in the curtain, a few holes in the dike. The dead refused to lie decently still, they insisted upon mingling with the quick. To whose advantage? Ghosts, too—undoubtedly logical, operating within the boundaries of known natural laws. But that might be cold comfort to a haunted man.

Today, Blaine thought, a whole new stratum of existence impinged upon man's existence on Earth. Just as the zombie impinged uncomfortably on *his* existence.

The helicab landed on the roof of an apartment building. Marie Thorne paid, and led Blaine to her apartment.

It was a large airy apartment, pleasingly feminine, and furnished with a certain dramatic flair. There was more bright color than Blaine would have thought compatible with Miss Blaine's somber personality; but perhaps the vivid yellows and sharp reds expressed a wish of some sort, a compensation for the restraint of her business life. Or perhaps it was just the prevailing style. The apartment contained the sort of gadgetry that Blaine associated with the future; self-adjusting lighting and air-conditioning, self-conforming armchairs, and a push-button bar that produced an adequate Martini.

Marie Thorne went into one of the bedrooms. She returned in a high-collared housedress and sat down on a couch opposite him.

"Well, Blaine, what are your plans?"

"I thought I'd ask you for a loan."

"Certainly."

"In that case my plan is to find a hotel room and start looking for a job."

"It won't be easy," she said, "but I know some people who might—"

"No thanks," Blaine said. "I hope this doesn't sound too silly, but I'd rather find a job on my own."

"No, it doesn't sound silly. I just hope it's possible. How about some dinner?"

"Fine. Do you cook, too?"

"I set dials," she told him. "Let's see. How would you like a genuine Martian meal?"

"No thanks," Blaine said. "Martian food is tasty, but it doesn't stick to your ribs. Would you happen to have a steak around the place?"

Marie set the dials and her auto-chef did the rest, selecting the food from pantry and freezer, peeling, unwrapping, washing and cooking it, and ordering new items to replace those used. The meal was perfect; but Marie seemed oddly embarrassed about it. She apologized to Blaine for the completely mechanical operation. After all, he came from an age in which women had opened their own cans, and done their own tasting; but they'd probably had more leisure time, too.

The sun had set by the time they finished their coffee. Blaine said, "Thank you very much, Miss Thorne. Now if you could loan me that money, I'll get started."

She looked surprised. "At night?"

"I'll find a hotel room. You've been very kind, but I wouldn't want to presume any further—"

"That's all right," she said. "Stay here tonight."

"All right," Blaine said. His mouth was suddenly dry, and his heart was pounding with suspicious rapidity. He knew there was nothing personal in her invitation; but his body didn't seem to understand. It insisted upon reacting hopefully, expectantly even, to the controlled and antiseptic Miss Thorne.

She gave him a bedroom and a pair of green pajamas. Blaine closed the door when she left, undressed and got into bed. The light went out when he told it to.

In a little while, just as his body had expected, Miss Thorne came in wearing something white and gossamer, and lay down beside him.

They lay side by side in silence. Marie Thorne moved closer to him, and Blaine slipped an arm under her head.

He said, "I thought you weren't attracted to my type."

"Not exactly. I said I *preferred* tall, lean men."

"I was once a tall, lean man."

"I suspected it," she said.

They were both silent. Blaine began to grow uncomfortable and apprehensive. What did this mean? Had she some fondness for him? Or was this simply a custom of the age, a sort of Eskimo hospitality?

"Miss Thorne," he said, "I wonder if—"

"Oh, be quiet!" she said, suddenly turning toward him, her eyes enormous in the shadowy room. "Do you have to question everything, Tom?"

Later she said, dreamily, "Under the circumstances, I think you can call me Marie."

In the morning Blaine showered, shaved and dressed. Marie dialed a breakfast for them. After they had eaten she gave him a small envelope.

"I can loan you more when you need it," she said. "Now about finding a job—"

"You've helped me very much," Blaine said. "The rest I'd like to do on my own."

"All right. My address and telephone number are on the envelope. Please call me as soon as you have a hotel."

"I will," Blaine said, watching her closely. There was no hint of the Marie of last night. It might have been a different person entirely. But her studied self-possession was reaction enough for Blaine. Enough, at least for the moment.

At the door she touched his arm. "Tom," she said, "please be careful. And call me."

"I will, Marie," Blaine said.

He went into the city happy and refreshed, and intent upon conquering the world.

Chapter 12

Blaine's first idea had been to make a round of the yacht-design offices. But he decided against it simply by picturing a yacht designer from 1806 walking into an office in 1958.

The quaint old man might be very talented; but how would that help him when he was asked what he knew about metacentric shelf analysis, flow diagrams, centers of effort, and the best locations for RDF and sonar? What company would pay him while he learned the facts about reduction gears, exfoliating paints, tank testing, propeller pitch, heat exchange systems, synthetic sailcloth…

Not a chance, Blaine decided. He couldn't walk into a design office 152 years behind the times and ask for a job. A job as *what?* Perhaps he could study and catch up to 2110 technology. But he'd have to do it on his own time.

Right now, he'd take anything he could get.

He went to a newsstand and purchased a microfilm *New York Times* and a viewer. He walked until he found a bench, sat down and turned to the classified ads. Quickly he skipped past the skilled categories, where he couldn't hope to qualify, and came to unskilled labor. He read:

"Set-up man wanted in auto-cafeteria. Requires only basic knowledge of robotics."

"Hull wiper wanted, Mar-Coling liner. Must be Rh positive and fortified anticlaustrophobiac."

"List man needed for hi-tensile bearing decay work. Needs simple jenkling knowledge. Meals included."

It was apparent to Blaine that even the unskilled labor of 2110 was beyond his present capacity. Turning the page to Employment for Boys, he read:

"Wanted, young man interested in slic-trug machinery. Good future. Must know basic calculus and have working knowledge Hootean Equations."

"Young Men wanted, salesmen's jobs on Venus. Salary plus commission. Knowledge basic French, German, Russian and Ourescz."

"Delivery, Magazine, Newspaper boys wanted by Eth-Col agency. Must be able to drive a Sprening. Good knowledge of city required."

So—he couldn't even qualify as a newsboy!

It was a depressing thought. Finding a job was going to be more difficult than he had imagined. Didn't anyone dig ditches or carry packages in this city? Did robots do all the menial work, or did you need a Ph.D. even to lug a wheelbarrow? What sort of world was this?

He turned to the front page of the *Times* for an answer, adjusted his viewer, and read the news of the day:

A new spacefield was under construction at Oxa, New South Mars.

A poltergeist was believed responsible for several industrial fires in the Chicago area. Tentative exorcism proceedings were under way.

Rich copper deposits had been discovered in the Sigma-G sector of the asteroid belt.

Doppelganger activities had increased in Berlin.

A new survey was being made of octopi villages in the Mindanao Deep.

A mob in Spenser, Alabama, lynched and burned the town's two local zombies. Legal action was being taken against the mob leaders.

A leading anthropologist declared the Tuamoto Archipelago in Oceania to be the last stronghold of 20th century simplicity.

The Atlantic Fish Herders' Association was holding its annual convention at the Waldorf.

A werewolf was unsuccessfully hunted in the Austrian Tyrol. Local villages were warned to keep a twenty-four-hour watch for the beast.

A bill was introduced into the House of Representatives to outlaw all hunts and gladiatorial events. It was defeated.

A berserker took four lives in downtown San Diego.

Helicopter fatalities reached the one million mark for the year.

Blaine put the newspaper aside, more depressed than ever. Ghosts, doppelgangers, werewolves, poltergeists... He didn't like the sound of those vague, grim, ancient words which today seemed to represent actual phenomena. He had already met a zombie. He didn't want to encounter any more of the dangerous side-effects of the hereafter.

He started walking again. He went through the theater district, past glittering marquees, posters advertising the gladiatorial events at Madison Square Garden, billboards heralding solidovision programs and sensory shows, flashing signs proclaiming overtone concerts and Venusian pantomime. Sadly Blaine remembered that *he* might have been part of this dazzling fairyland if only Reilly hadn't changed his mind. He might be appearing at one of those theaters now, billed as the Man from the Past...

Of course! A Man from the Past, Blaine suddenly realized, had a unique and indisputable novelty value, an inherent talent. The Rex Corporation had saved his life in 1958 solely in order to use that talent. But they had changed their minds. So what was to prevent him from using his novelty value for himself? And for that matter, what else could he do? Show business looked like the only possible business for him.

He hurried into a gigantic office building and found six theatrical agents listed on the board. He picked Barnex, Scofield & Styles, and took the elevator to their offices on the 19th floor.

He entered a luxurious waiting room paneled with gigantic solidographs of smiling actresses. At the far end of the room, a pretty receptionist raised an inquiring eyebrow at him.

Blaine went up to her desk. "I'd like to see someone about my act," he told her.

"I'm so sorry," she said. "We're all filled."

"This is a very special act."

"I'm really terribly sorry. Perhaps next week."

"Look," Blaine said, "My act is really unique. You see, I'm a man from the past."

"I don't care if you're the ghost of Scott Merrivale," she said sweetly. "We're *filled*. Try us next week."

Blaine turned to go. A short, stocky man breezed past him, nodding to the receptionist.

"Morning, Miss Thatcher."

"Morning, Mr. Barnex."

Barnex! One of the agents! Blaine hurried after him and grabbed his sleeve.

"Mr. Barnex," he said, "I have an act—"

"Everybody has an act," Barnex said wearily.

"But this act is unique!"

"Everybody's act is unique," Barnex said. "Let go my sleeve, friend. Try us next week."

"I'm from the past!" Blaine cried, suddenly feeling foolish. Barnex turned and stared at him. He looked at though he might be on the verge of calling the police, or Bellevue. But Blaine plunged recklessly on.

"I really am!" he said. "I have absolute proof. The Rex Corporation snatched me out of the past. Ask them!"

"Rex?" Barnex said. "Yeah, I heard something about that snatch over at Lindy's… Hmm. Come into my office, Mister—"

"Blaine, Tom Blaine." He followed Barnex into a tiny, cluttered cubicle. "Do you think you can use me?" he asked.

"Maybe," Barnex said, motioning Blaine to a chair. "It depends. Tell me, Mr. Blaine, what period of the past are you from?"

"In 1958. I have an intimate knowledge of the nineteen thirties, forties and fifties. By way of stage experience I did some acting in college, and a professional actress friend of mine once told me I had a natural way of—"

"1958? That's 20th Century?"

"Yes, that's right."

The agent shook his head. "Too bad. Now if you'd been a 6th Century Swede or a 7th Century Jap, I could have found work for you. I've had no difficulty booking appearances for our 1st Century Roman or our 4th Century Saxon, and I could use a couple more like them. But it's damned hard finding anyone from those early centuries, now that time travel is illegal. And B.C. is completely out."

"But what about the 20th Century?" Blaine asked.

"It's filled."

"Filled?"

"Sure. Ben Therler from 1953 gets all the available stage appearances."

"I see," Blaine said, getting slowly to his feet. "Thanks anyhow, Mr. Barnex."

"Not at all," Barnex said. "Wish I could help. If you'd been from any time or place before the 11th Century, I could probably book you. But there's not much interest in recent stuff like the 19th and 20th Centuries…

Say, why don't you go see Therler? It isn't likely, but maybe he can use an understudy or something." He scrawled an address on a piece of paper and handed it to Blaine.

Blaine took it, thanked him again, and left.

In the street he stood for a moment, cursing his luck. His one unique and indisputable talent, his novelty value, had been usurped by Ben Therler of 1953! Really, he thought, time travel should be kept more exclusive. It just wasn't fair to drop a man here and then ignore him.

He wondered what sort of man Therler was. Well, he'd find out. Even if Therler didn't need an understudy, it would be a pleasure and relief to talk to someone from home. And Therler, who had lived here longer, might have some ideas on what a 20th Century man could do in 2110.

He flagged a helicab and gave him the address. In fifteen minutes he was in Therler's apartment building, pressing the doorbell.

The door was opened by a sleek, chubby, complacent-looking man wearing a dressing gown.

"You the photographer?" he asked. "You're too early."

Blaine shook his head. "Mr. Therler, you've never met me before. I'm from your own century. I'm from 1958."

"Is that so?" Therler asked, with obvious suspicion.

"It's the truth," Blaine said. "I was snatched by the Rex Corporation. You can check my story with them."

Therler shrugged his shoulders. "Well, what is it you want?"

"I was hoping you might be able to use an understudy or something—"

"No, no, I never use an understudy," Therler said, starting to close the door.

"I didn't think so," Blaine said. "The real reason I came was just to talk to you. It gets pretty lonely being out of one's century. I wanted to talk to someone from my own age. I thought maybe you'd feel that way, too."

"Me? Oh!" Therler said, smiling with sudden stage warmth. "Oh, you mean about the good old twentieth century! I'd love to talk to you about it sometime, pal. Little old New York! The Dodgers and Yankees, the hansoms in the park, the roller-skating rink in Rockefeller Plaza. I sure miss it all! Boy! But I'm afraid I'm a little busy now."

"Certainly," Blaine said. "Some other time."

"Fine! I'd really love to!" Therler said, smiling even more brilliantly. "Call my secretary, will you, old man? Schedules, you know. We'll have a really great old gab some one of these days. I suppose you could use a spare dollar or two—"

Blaine shook his head.

"Then, 'bye," Therler said heartily. "And do call soon."

Blaine hurried out of the building. It was bad enough being robbed of your novelty value; it was worse being robbed by an out-and-out phony, a temporal fraud who'd never been within a hundred years of 1953: The Rockefeller *roller*-skating rink! And even that slip hadn't been necessary. Everything about the man screamed counterfeit.

But sadly, Blaine was probably the only man in 2110 who could detect the imposture.

That afternoon Blaine purchased a change of clothing and a shaving kit. He found a room in a cheap hotel on Fifth Avenue. For the next week, he continued looking for work.

He tried the restaurants, but found that human dishwashers were a thing of the past. At the docks and spaceports, robots were doing most of the heavy work. One day he was tentatively approved for a position as package-wrapping inspector at Gimbel-Macy's. But the personnel department, after carefully studying his personality profile, irritability index and suggestibility rating, vetoed him in favor of a dull-eyed little man from Queens who held a master's degree in package design.

Blaine was wearily returning to his hotel one evening when he recognized a face in the dense crowd. It was a man he would have known instantly, anywhere. He was about Blaine's age, a compact, redheaded, snub-nosed man with slightly protruding teeth and a small red blotch on his neck. He carried himself with a certain jaunty assurance, the unquenchable confidence of a man for whom something always turns up.

"Ray!" Blaine shouted. "Ray Melhill!" He pushed through the crowd and seized him by the arm. "Ray! How'd you get out?"

The man pulled his arm away and smoothed the sleeve of his jacket. "My name is not Melhill," he said.

"It's not? Are you sure?"

"Of course I'm sure," he said, starting to move away.

Blaine stepped in front of him. "Wait a minute. You look exactly like him, even down to the radiation scar. Are you *sure* you aren't Ray Melhill, a flow-control man off the spaceship *Bremen?*"

"Quite certain," the man said coldly. "You have confused me with someone else, young man."

Blaine stared hard as the man started to walk away. Then he reached out, caught the man by a shoulder and swung him around.

"You dirty body-thieving bastard!" Blaine shouted, his big right fist shooting out.

The man who so exactly resembled Melhill was knocked back against a building, and slid groggily to the pavement. Blaine started for him, and people moved quickly put of his way.

"Berserker!" a woman screamed, and someone else took up the cry. Blaine caught sight of a blue uniform shoving through the crowd toward him.

A flat-hat! Blaine ducked into the crowd. He turned a corner quickly; then another, slowed to a walk and looked back. The policeman was not in sight. Blaine started walking again to his hotel.

It had been Melhill's body; but Ray no longer occupied it. There had been no last-minute reprieve for him, no final chance. His body had been taken from him and sold to the old man whose querulous mind wore the jaunty body like a suit of ill-fitting too-youthful clothes.

Now he knew his friend was really dead. Blaine drank silently to him in a neighborhood bar before returning to his hotel.

The clerk stopped him as he passed the desk. "Blaine? Got a message for you. Just a minute." He went into the office.

Blaine waited, wondering who it could be from. Marie? But he hadn't called Marie yet, and wasn't planning to until he found work.

The clerk came back and handed him a slip of paper. The message read: "There is a Communication awaiting Thomas Blaine at the Spiritual Switchboard, 23rd Street Branch. Hours, nine to five."

"I wonder how anybody knew where I was?" Blaine asked.

"Spirits got their ways," the clerk told him. "Man I know, his dead mother-in-law tracked him down through three aliases, a Transplant and a complete skin job. He was hiding from her in Abyssinia."

"I don't have any dead mother-in-law," Blaine said.

"No? Who you figure's trying to reach you?" the clerk asked.

"I'll find out tomorrow and let you know," Blaine said. But his sarcasm was wasted. The clerk had already turned back to his correspondence course on Atomic Engine Maintenance. Blaine went up to his room.

Chapter 13

The 23rd Street Branch of the Spiritual Switchboard was a large graystone building near Third Avenue. Engraved above the door was the statement: "Dedicated to Free Communication Between Those on Earth and Those Beyond."

Blaine entered the building and studied the directory. It gave floor and room numbers for Messages Incoming, Messages Outgoing, Translations, Abjurations, Exorcisms, Offerings, Pleas, and Exhortations. He wasn't sure which classification he fell under, or what the classifications signified, or even the purpose of the Spiritual Switchboard. He took his slip of paper to the information booth.

"That's Messages Incoming," a pleasant, grey-haired receptionist told him. "Straight down the hall to room 32A."

"Thank you." Blaine hesitated, then said, "Could you explain something to me?"

"Certainly," the woman said. "What do you wish to know?"

"Well—I hope this doesn't sound too foolish—what *is* all this?"

The grey-haired woman smiled. "That's a difficult question to answer. In a philosophical sense I suppose you might call the Spiritual Switchboard a move toward greater oneness, an attempt to discard the dualism of mind and body and substitute—"

"No," Blaine said. "I mean literally."

"Literally? Why, the Spiritual Switchboard is a privately endowed, tax-free organization, chartered to act as a clearing house and center for communications to and from the Threshold plane of the Hereafter. In some cases, of course, people don't need our aid and can communicate directly with their departed ones. But more often, there is a need for amplification. This center possesses the proper equipment to make the deceased audible to our ears. And we perform other services, such as abjurations, exorcisms, exhortations and the like, which become necessary from time to time when flesh interacts with spirit."

She smiled warmly at him. "Does that make it any clearer?"

"Thank you very much," Blaine said, and went down the hall to room 32A.

It was a small grey room with several arm-chairs and a loudspeaker set in the wall. Blaine sat down, wondering what was going to happen.

"Tom Blaine!" cried a disembodied voice from the loudspeaker.

"Huh? What?" Blaine asked, jumping to his feet and moving toward the door.

"Tom! How are you, boy?"

Blaine, his hand on the doorknob, suddenly recognized the voice. "Ray Melhill?"

"Right! I'm up there where the rich folks go when they die! Pretty good, huh?"

"That's the understatement of the age," Blaine said. "But Ray, *how?* I thought you didn't have any hereafter insurance."

"I didn't. Let me tell you the whole story. They came for me maybe an hour after they took you. I was so damned angry I thought I'd go out of my mind. I stayed angry right through the chloroforming, right through the wiping. I was still angry when I died."

"What was dying like?" Blaine asked.

"It was like exploding. I could feel myself scattering all over the place, growing big as the galaxy, bursting into fragments, and the fragments bursting into smaller fragments, and all of them were *me.*"

"And what happened?"

"I don't know. Maybe being so angry helped. I was stretched as far as I could go—any further and it wouldn't be me—and then I just simply came back together again. Some people do. Like I told you, a few out of every million have always survived without hereafter training. I was one of the lucky ones."

"I guess you know about me," Blaine said. "I tried to do something for you, but you'd already been sold."

"I know," Melhill said. "Thanks anyhow, Tom. And say, thanks for popping that slob. The one wearing my body."

"You saw that?"

"I been keeping my eyes open," Melhill said. "By the way, I like that Marie. Nice looking kid."

"Thanks. Ray, what's the hereafter like?"

"I don't know."

"You don't?"

"I'm not *in* the hereafter yet, Tom. I'm in the Threshold. It's a preparatory stage, a sort of bridge between Earth and the hereafter. It's hard to describe. A sort of greyness, with Earth on one side and the hereafter on the other."

"Why don't you cross over?" Blaine asked.

"Not yet," Melhill said. "It's a one-way street into the hereafter. Once you cross over, you can't come back. There's no more contact with Earth."

Blaine thought about that for a moment, then asked, "When are you going to cross over, Ray?"

"I don't rightly know. I thought I'd stay in Threshold for a while and keep an eye on things."

"Keep an eye on me, you mean."

"Well…"

"Thanks a lot, Ray, but don't do it. Go into the hereafter. I can take care of myself."

"Sure you can," Melhill said. "But I think I'll stick around for a while anyhow. You'd do it for me, wouldn't you? So don't argue. Now look, I suppose you know you're in trouble?"

Blaine nodded. "You mean the zombie?"

"I don't know who he is or what he wants from you, Tom, but it can't be good. You'd better be a long way off when he finds out. But that wasn't the trouble I meant."

"You mean I have more?"

"Afraid so. You're going to be haunted, Tom."

In spite of himself, Blaine laughed.

"What's so funny?" Melhill asked indignantly. "You think it's a *joke* to be haunted?"

"I suppose not. But is it really so serious?"

"Lord, you're ignorant," Melhill said. "Do you know anything about ghosts? How they're made and what they want?"

"Tell me."

"Well, there are three possibilities when a man dies. First, his mind can just explode, scatter, dissipate; and that's the end of him. Second, his mind can hold together through the death trauma; and he finds himself in the Threshold, a spirit. I guess you know about those two."

"Go on," Blaine said.

"The third possibility is this: His mind breaks during the death trauma, but not enough to cause dissipation. He pulls through into the Threshold. But the strain has been permanently disabling. He's insane. And that, my friend, is how a ghost is born."

"Hmm," Blaine said. "So a ghost is a mind that went insane during the death trauma?"

"Right. He's insane, and he haunts."

"But why?"

"Ghosts haunt," Melhill said "because they're filled with twisted hatred, anger, fear and pain. They won't go into the hereafter. They want to spend as much time as they can on Earth, where their attention is still fixed. They want to frighten people, hurt them, drive them insane. Haunting is the most asocial thing they can do, it's their madness. Look Tom, since the beginning of mankind…"

Since the beginning of mankind there have been ghosts, but their numbers have always been small. Only a few out of every million people managed to survive after death; and only a tiny percentage of those survivors went insane during the transition, and became ghosts.

But the impact of those few was colossal upon a mankind fascinated by death, awed by the cold uncaring mobility of the corpse so recently quick and vital, shocked at the ghastly inapropos humor of the skeleton. Death's elaborate, mysterious figure seemed infinitely meaningful, its warning finger pointed toward the spirit-laden skies. So for every genuine ghost, rumor and fear produced a thousand. Every gibbering bat became a ghost. Marsh-fires, flapping curtains and swaying trees became ghosts, and St. Elmo's fire, great-eyed owls, rats in the walls, foxes in the bush, all became ghostly evidence. Folklore grew and produced witch and warlock, evil little familiars, demons and devils, succubi and incubi, werewolf and vampire. For every ghost a thousand were suspected, and for every supernatural fact a million were assumed.

Early scientific investigators entered this maze, trying to discover the truth about supernatural phenomena. They uncovered countless frauds, hallucinations and errors of judgment. And they found a few genuinely inexplicable events, which, though interesting, were statistically insignificant.

The whole tradition of folklore came tumbling down. Statistically there were no ghosts. But continually there was a sly, elusive *something* which refused to stand still and be classified. It was ignored for centuries, the occasional *something* which gave a basis and a reality to tales of incubi and succubi. Until at last scientific theory caught up with folklore, made a place for it in the realm of indisputable phenomena, and gave it respectability.

With the discovery of the scientific hereafter, the irrational ghost became understandable as a demented mind inhabiting the misty interface between Earth and the hereafter. The forms of ghostly madness could be categorized like madness on Earth. There were the melancholics, drifting disconsolately through the scenes of their great passion; the whispering hebephrenic, chattering gay and random nonsense; the idiots and imbeciles who returned in the guise of little children; the schizophrenics who imagined themselves to be animals, prototypes of vampire and Abominable Snowman, werewolf, weretiger, werefox, weredog. There were the destructive stone-throwing and fire-setting ghosts, the poltergeists, and the grandiloquent paranoids who imagined themselves to be Lucifer or Beelzebub, Israfael or Azazael, the Spirit of Christmas Past, the Furies, Divine Justice, or even Death itself.

Haunting was madness. They wept by the old watch tower, these few ghosts upon whose gossamer shoulders rested the entire great structure of folklore, mingled with the mists around the gibbet, jabbered their nonsense at the seance. They talked, cried, danced and sang for the delectation of the credulous, until scientific observers came with their sober cold questions. Then they fled back to the Threshold, terrified of this onslaught of reason, protective of their delusions, fearful of being cured.

"So that's how it was," Melhill said. "You can figure out the rest. Since Hereafter, Inc. a hell of a lot more people are surviving after death. But of course a lot more are going insane on the way."

"Thus producing a lot more ghosts," Blaine said.

"Right. One of them is after you," Melhill said, his voice growing faint. "So watch your step. Tom, I gotta go now."

"What kind of ghost is it?" Blaine asked. "Whose ghost? And why do you have to go?"

"It takes energy to stay on Earth," Melhill whispered. "I'm just about used up. Have to recharge. Can you still hear me?"

"Yes, go on."

"I don't know when the ghost will show himself, Tom. And I don't know who he is. I asked, but he wouldn't tell me. Just watch out for him."

"I'll watch out," Blaine said, his ear pressed to the loudspeaker. "Ray! Will I speak to you again?"

"I think so," Melhill said, his voice barely audible. "Tom, I know you're looking for a job. Try Ed Franchel, 322 West 19th Street. It's rough stuff, but it pays. And watch yourself."

"Ray!" Blaine shouted. "What *kind* of a ghost is it?"

There was no answer. The loudspeaker was silent, and he was alone in the grey room.

Chapter 14

322 West 19th Street, the address Ray Melhill had given him, was a small, dilapidated brownstone near the docks. Blaine climbed the steps and pressed the ground-floor buzzer marked *Edward J. Franchel Enterprises.* The door was opened by a large, balding man in shirtsleeves.

"Mr. Franchel?" Blaine asked.

"That's me," the balding man said, with a resolutely cheerful smile. "Right this way, sir."

He led Blaine into an apartment pungent with the odor of boiled cabbage. The front half of the apartment was arranged as an office, with a paper-cluttered desk, a dusty filing cabinet and several stiff-backed chairs. Past it, Blaine could see a gloomy living room. From the inner recesses of the apartment a solido was blaring out a daytime show.

"Please excuse the appearance," Franchel said, motioning Blaine to a chair. "I'm moving into a regular office uptown just as soon as I find time. The orders have been coming in so fast and furious… Now sir, what can I do for you?"

"I'm looking for a job," Blaine said.

"Hell," said Franchel, "I thought you were a customer." He turned in the direction of the blaring solido and shouted, "Alice, will you turn that goddamned thing down?" He waited until the volume had receded somewhat, then turned back to Blaine. "Brother, if business doesn't pick up soon I'm going back to running a suicide booth at Coney. A job, huh?"

"That's right. Ray Melhill told me to try you."

Franchel's expression brightened. "How's Ray doing?"

"He's dead."

"Shame," Franchel said. "He was a good lad, though always a bit wild. He worked for me a couple times when the space pilots were on strike. Want a drink?"

Blaine nodded. Franchel went to the filing cabinet and removed a bottle of rye whiskey labeled "Moonjuice." He found two shot glasses and filled them with a practiced flourish.

"Here's to old Ray," Franchel said. "I suppose he got himself boxed?"

"Boxed and crated," Blaine said. "I just spoke to him at the Spiritual Switchboard."

"Then he made Threshold!" Franchel said admiringly. "Friend, *we* should only have his luck. So you want a job? Well, maybe I can fix it. Stand up."

He walked around Blaine, touched his biceps and ran a hand over his ridged shoulder muscles. He stood in front of Blaine, nodding to himself with downcast eyes, then feinted a quick blow at his face. Blaine's right hand came up instantly, in time to block the punch.

"Good build, good reflexes," Franchel said. "I think you'll do. Know anything about weapons?"

"Not much," Blaine said, wondering what kind of job he was getting into. "Just—ah—antiques. Garands, Winchesters, Colts."

"No kidding?" Franchel said. "You know, I always wanted to collect antique recoil arms. But no projectile or beam weapons are allowed on this hunt. What else you got?"

"I can handle a rifle with bayonet," Blaine said, thinking how his basic-training sergeant would have roared at that overstatement.

"You can? Lunges and parries and all? Well, I'll be damned, I thought bayonetry was a lost art. You're the first I've seen in fifteen years. Friend, you're hired."

Franchel went to his desk, scribbled on a piece of paper and handed it to Blaine.

"You go to that address tomorrow for your briefing. You'll be paid standard hunter's salary, two hundred dollars plus fifty a day for every working day. Have you got your own weapons and equipment? Well, I'll pick the stuff up for you, but it's deducted from your pay. And I take ten percent off the top. OK?"

"Sure," Blaine said. "Could you explain a little more about the hunt?"

"Nothing to explain. It's just a standard hunt. But don't go around talking about it. I'm not sure if hunts are still legal. I wish Congress would straighten out the Suicide and Permitted Murder Acts once and for all. A man doesn't know where he's at any more."

"Yeah," Blaine agreed.

"They'll probably discuss the legal aspects at the briefing," Franchel said. "The hunters will be there, and the Quarry will tell you all you need to know. Say hello to Ray for me if you speak to him again. Tell him I'm sorry he got killed."

"I'll tell him," Blaine said. He decided not to ask any more questions for fear his ignorance might cost him the job. Whatever hunting involved, he and his body could surely handle it. And a job, any job, was as necessary now for his self-respect as for his dwindling wallet.

He thanked Franchel and left.

That evening he ate dinner in an inexpensive diner, and bought several magazines. He was elated at the knowledge of having found work, and sure that he was going to make a place for himself in this age.

His high spirits were dampened slightly when he glimpsed, on the way back to his hotel, a man standing in an alley watching him. The man had a white face and placid Buddha eyes, and his rough clothes hung on him like rags on a scarecrow.

It was the zombie.

Blaine hurried on to his hotel, refusing to anticipate trouble. After all, if a cat can look at a king, a zombie can look at a man, and where's the harm?

This reasoning didn't prevent him from having nightmares until dawn.

Early the next day, Blaine walked to 42nd Street and Park Avenue, to catch a bus to the briefing. While waiting, he noticed a disturbance on the other side of 42nd Street.

A man had stopped short in the middle of the busy pavement. He was laughing to himself, and people were beginning to edge away from him. He was in his fifties, Blaine judged, dressed in quiet tweeds, bespectacled, and a little overweight. He carried a small briefcase and looked like ten million other businessmen.

Abruptly he stopped laughing. He unzipped his briefcase and removed from it two long, slightly curved daggers. He flung the briefcase away, and followed it with his glasses.

"Berserker!" someone cried.

The man plunged into the crowd, both daggers flashing. People started screaming, and the crowd scattered before him.

"Berserker, berserker!"

"Call the flat-hats!"

"Watch *out*, berserker!"

One man was down, clutching his torn shoulder and swearing. The berserker's face was fiery red now, and spittle came from his mouth. He waded deeper into the dense crowd, and people knocked each other down in their efforts to escape. A woman shrieked as she was pushed off balance, and her armload of parcels scattered across the pavement.

The berserker swiped at her left-handed, missed, and plunged deeper into the crowd.

Blue-uniformed police appeared, six or eight of them, sidearms out. "Everybody down!" they shouted. "Flatten! Everybody down!"

All traffic had stopped. The people in the berserker's path flung themselves to the pavement. On Blaine's side of the street, people were also getting down.

A freckled girl of perhaps twelve tugged at Blaine's arm. "Come on, Mister, get down! You wanna get beamed?"

Blaine lay down beside her. The berserker had turned and was running back toward the policemen, screaming wordlessly and waving his knives.

Three of the policemen fired at once, their weapons throwing a pale yellowish beam which flared red when it struck the berserker. He screamed as his clothing began to smoulder, turned, and tried to escape.

A beam caught him square in the back. He flung both knives at the policemen and collapsed.

An ambulance dropped down with whirring blades and quickly loaded the berserker and his victims. The policemen began breaking up the crowd that had gathered around them.

"All right, folks, it's all over now. Move along!"

The crowd began to disperse. Blaine stood up and brushed himself off. "What was that?" he asked.

"It was a berserker, silly," the freckled girl said. "Couldn't you *see?*"

"I saw. Do you have many?"

She nodded proudly. "New York has more berserkers than any other city in the world except Manila where they're called amokers. But it's all the same thing. We have maybe fifty a year."

"More," a man said. "Maybe seventy, eighty a year. But this one didn't do so good."

A small group had gathered near Blaine and the girl. They were discussing the berserker much as Blaine had heard strangers in his own time discuss an automobile accident.

"How many did he get?"

"Only five, and I don't think he killed any of them."

"His heart wasn't in it," an old woman said. "When I was a girl you couldn't stop them as easily as that. Strong they were."

"Well, he picked a bad spot," the freckled girl said, "42nd Street is filled with flathats. A berserker can't hardly get started before he's beamed."

A big policeman came over. "All right, folks, break it up. The fun's over, move along now."

The group dispersed. Blaine caught his bus, wondering why fifty or more people chose to berserk in New York every year. Sheer nervous tension? A demented form of individualism? Adult delinquency?

It was one more of the things he would have to find out about the world of 2110.

Chapter 15

The address was a penthouse high above Park Avenue in the Seventies. A butler admitted him to a spacious room where chairs had been set up in a long row. The dozen men occupying the chairs were a loud, tough, weatherbeaten bunch, carelessly dressed and ill at ease in such rarefied surroundings. Most of them knew each other.

"Hey, Otto! Back in the hunting game?"

"Yah. No money."

"Knew you'd come back, old boy. Hi, Tim!"

"Hi, Bjorn. This is my last hunt."

"Sure it is. Last 'til next time."

"No, I mean it. I'm buying a seed-pressure farm in the North Atlantic Abyss. I just need a stake."

"You'll drink up your stake."

"Not this time."

"Hey, Theseus! How's the throwing arm?"

"Good enough, Chico. Que tal?"

"Not too bad, kid."

"There's Sammy Jones, always last in."

"I'm on time, ain't I?"

"Ten minutes late. Where's your sidekick?"

"Sligo? Dead. That Asturias hunt."

"Tough. Hereafter?"

"Not likely."

A man entered the room and called out, "Gentlemen, your attention please!"

He advanced to the center of the room and stood, hands on his hips, facing the row of hunters. He was a slender sinewy man of medium height, dressed in riding breeches and an open-necked shirt. He had a small, carefully tended moustache and startling blue eyes in a thin, tanned face. For a few seconds he looked the hunters over, while they coughed and shifted their feet uncomfortably.

At last he said, "Good morning, gentlemen. I am Charles Hull, your employer and Quarry." He gave them a smile of no warmth. "First, gentlemen, a word concerning the legality of our proceedings. There has been some recent confusion about this. My lawyer has looked into the matter fully, and will explain. Mr. Jensen!"

A small, nervous-looking man came into the room, pressed his spectacles firmly against his nose and cleared his throat.

"Yes, Mr. Hull. Gentlemen, as to the present legality of the hunt: In accordance with the revised statutes to the Suicide Act of 2102, any man protected by Hereafter insurance has the right to select any death for himself, at any time and place, and by any means, as long as those means do not constitute cruel and unnatural abuse. The reason for this fundamental 'right to die' is obvious: The courts do not recognize physical death as death *per se*, if said death does not involve the destruction of mind. Providing the mind survives, the death of the body is of no more moment, legally, than the sloughing of a fingernail. The body, by the latest Supreme Court decision, is considered an appendage of the mind, its creature, to be disposed of as the mind directs."

During this explanation Hull had been pacing the room with quick, catlike steps. He stopped now and said, "Thank you, Mr. Jensen. So there is no questioning my right to suicide. Nor is there any illegality in my selecting one or more persons such as yourselves to perform the act for me. And your own actions are considered legal under the Permitted Murder section of the Suicide Act. All well and good. The only legal question arises in a recent appendage to the Suicide Act."

He nodded to Mr. Jensen.

"The appendage states," Jensen said, "that a man can select any death for himself, at any time and place, by any means, etcetera, *so long as that death is not physically injurious to others.*"

"That," said Hull, "is the troublesome clause. Now, a hunt is a legal form of suicide. A time and place is arranged. You, the hunters, chase me. I, the Quarry, flee. You catch me, kill me. Fine! Except for one thing."

He turned to the lawyer. "Mr. Jensen, you may leave the room. I do not wish to implicate you "

After the lawyer had left, Hull said, "The one problem remaining is, of course, the fact that I will be armed and trying my very best to kill *you*. Any of you. All of you. And *that* is illegal."

Hull sank gracefully into a chair. "The crime, however, is mine, not yours. I have employed you to kill me. You have no idea that I plan to protect myself, to retaliate. That is a legal fiction, but one which will save you from becoming possible accessories to the fact. If I am caught trying to kill one of you, the penalty will be severe. But I will not be caught. One of you will kill me, thus putting me beyond the reach of human justice. If I should be so unfortunate as to kill *all* of you, I shall complete my suicide in the old-fashioned manner, with poison. But that would be a disappointment to me. I trust you will not be so clumsy as to let that happen. Any questions?"

The hunters were murmuring among themselves:

"Slick fancy-talking bastard."

"Forget it, all Quarries talk like that."

"Thinks he's better than us, him and his classy legal talk."

"We'll see how good he talks with a bit of steel through him."

Hull smiled coldly. "Excellent. I believe the situation is clear. Now, if you please, tell me what your weapons are."

One by one the hunters answered:

"Mace."

"Net and Trident."

"Spear."

"Morning star."

"Bola."

"Scimitar."

"Bayonetted rifle," Blaine said when his turn came.

"Broadsword."

"Battle-axe."

"Saber."

"Thank you, gentlemen," Hull said. "I will be armed with a rapier, naturally, and no armor. Our meeting will take place Sunday, at dawn, on my estate. The butler will give each of you a paper containing full instructions on how to get there. Let the bayonet man remain. Good morning to the rest of you."

The hunters left. Hull said, "Bayonetry is an unusual art. Where did you learn it?"

Blaine hesitated, then said, "In the army, 1943 to 1945."

"You're from the past?"

Blaine nodded.

"Interesting," Hull said, with no particular sign of interest. "Then this, I daresay, is your first hunt?"

"It is."

"You appear a person of some intelligence. I suppose you have your reasons for choosing so hazardous and disreputable an employment?"

"I'm low on funds," Blaine said, "and I can't find anything else to do."

"Of course," Hull said, as though he had known it all along. "So you turned to hunting. Yet hunting is not a thing merely to turn to; and hunting the beast Man is not for everyone. The trade calls for certain special abilities, not the least of which is the ability to kill. Do you think you have the innate talent?"

"I believe so," Blaine said, though he hadn't considered the question until now.

"I wonder," Hull mused. "In spite of your bellicose appearance, you don't seem the type. What if you find yourself incapable of killing me? What if you hesitate at the crucial moment when steel grates on steel?"

"I'll chance it," Blaine said.

Hull nodded agreeably. "And so will I. Perhaps, hidden deep within you, a spark of murder burns. Perhaps not. This doubt will add spice to the game—though you may not have time to savour it."

"That's my worry," Blaine said, feeling an intense dislike for his elegant and rhetorical employer. "Might I ask you a question?"

"Consider me at your service."

"Thank you. Why do you wish to die?"

Hull stared at him, then burst into laughter. "Now I *know* you're from the past! What a question!"

"Can you answer it?"

"Of course," Hull said. He leaned back in his chair, and his eyes took on the dreamy look of a man forming rhetoric.

"I am forty-three years old, and weary of nights and days. I am a wealthy man, and an uninhibited one. I have experimented, contrived, laughed, wept, loved, hated, tasted and drunk—my fill. I have sampled all Earth has to offer me, and I choose not to tediously repeat the experience. When I was young, I pictured this excellent green planet revolving mysteriously around its flamboyant yellow luminary as a treasure-trove, a brass box of delights inexhaustible in content and immeasurable in their effect upon my ever-eager desires. But now, sadly, I have lived longer and have witnessed sensation's end. And now I see with what bourgeois complacency our fat round Earth circles, at wary distance and unvarying pace, its gaudy dreaded star. And the imagined treasure chest of the Earth seems now a child's painted toy box, shallow in its contents and mediocre in its effect upon nerves too quickly deadened to all delight."

Hull glanced at Blaine to note the effect of his words, and then went on.

"Boredom stretches before me now like a vast, arid plain—and I choose not to be bored. I choose, instead, to move on, move forward, move out; to sample Earth's last and greatest adventure—the adventure of Death, gateway to the afterlife. Can you understand that?"

"Of course," Blaine said, irritated yet impressed by Hull's theatrics. "But what's the rush? Life might have some good things still in store for you. And death is inevitable. Why rush it?"

"Spoken like a true 20th Century optimist," Hull said, laughing. "'Life is real, life is earnest...' In your day, one *had* to believe that life was real and earnest. What alternative was there? How many of you really believed in a life after death?"

"That doesn't alter the validity of my point," Blaine said, hating the stodgy, cautious, reasonable position he was forced to assume.

"But it does! The perspective on life and death has changed now. Instead of Longfellow's prosy advice, we follow Nietzsche's dictum—to die at the right time! Intelligent people don't clutch at the last shreds of life like drowning men clinging to a bit of board. They know that the body's life is only an infinitesimal portion of man's total existence. Why shouldn't they speed the body's passing by a few years if they so desire? Why shouldn't those bright pupils skip a grade or two of school? Only the frightened, the stupid, the uneducated grasp at every possible monotonous second on Earth."

"The frightened, stupid and uneducated," Blaine repeated. "And the unfortunates who can't afford Hereafter insurance."

"Wealth and class have their privileges," Hull said, smiling faintly, "and their obligations as well. One of those obligations is the necessity of dying at the right time, before one becomes a bore to one's peers and a horror to oneself. But the deed of dying transcends class and breeding. It is every man's patent of nobility, his summons from the king, his knightly adventure, the greatest deed of his life. And how he acquits himself in that lonely and perilous enterprise is his true measure as a man."

Hull's blue eyes were fierce and glittering. He said, "I do not wish to experience this crucial event in bed. I do not wish a dull, tame, commonplace death to sneak over me disguised as sleep. I choose to die—fighting!"

Blaine nodded in spite of himself, and felt regret at his own prosaic death. A car accident! How dull, tame, and commonplace! And how strange, dark, atavistic and noble seemed Hull's lordly selection of death. Pretentious, of course; but then, life itself was a pretension in the vast universe of unliving matter. Hull was like an ancient Japanese nobleman calmly kneeling to perform the ceremonial act of hara-kiri and emphasizing the importance of life in the very selection of death. But hara-kiri was a passive Eastern avowal; while Hull's manner of dying was a Western death, fierce, violent, exultant.

It was admirable. But intensely irritating to a man not yet prepared to die.

Blaine said, "I have nothing against you or any other man choosing his death. But what about the hunters you plan to kill? They haven't chosen to die, and they won't survive in the hereafter."

Hull shrugged his shoulders. "They choose to live dangerously. In Nietzsche's phrase, they prefer to run risk and danger, and play dice with death. Blaine, have you changed your mind?"

"No."

"Then we will meet Sunday."

Blaine went to the door and took his paper of instructions from the butler. As he was leaving, he said, "I wonder if you've considered one last thing."

"What is that?" Hull asked.

"You must have thought of it," Blaine said. "The possibility that this whole elaborate setup—the scientific hereafter, voices of the dead, ghosts—are merely a gigantic hoax, a money-making fraud perpetrated by Hereafter, Inc."

Hull stood perfectly still. When he spoke there was a hint of anger in his voice. "That is *quite* impossible. Only a very uneducated man could think such a thing."

"Maybe," Blaine said. "But wouldn't you look silly if it *were* a hoax! Good morning, Mr. Hull."

He left, glad to have shaken up that smooth, smug, fancy, rhetorical bastard even for a moment—and sad that his own death had been so dull, tame, and commonplace.

Chapter 16

The following day, Saturday, Blaine went to Franchel's apartment for his rifle, bayonet, hunter's uniform and pack. He was given half his salary in advance, less ten percent and the cost of the equipment. The money was very welcome, for he had been down to three dollars and change.

He went to the Spiritual Switchboard, but Melhill had left no further messages for him. He returned to his hotel room and spent the afternoon practicing lunges and parries.

That evening Blaine found himself tense and despondent, and nervous at the thought of the hunt beginning in the morning. He went to a small West Side cocktail lounge that had been designed to resemble a 20th Century bar, with a dark gleaming bar, wooden stools, booths, a brass rail, and sawdust on the floor. He slid into a booth and ordered beer.

The classic neon lights glowed softly, and a genuine antique juke box played the sentimental tunes of Glenn Miller and Benny Goodman. Blaine sat, hunched over his glass of beer, drearily asking himself who and what he was.

Was it truly *he* taking casual employment as a hunter and killer of men?

Then what happened to *Tom Blaine,* the former designer of sailboats, former listener to high-fidelity music, former reader of fine books, former viewer of good plays? What happened to that quiet, sardonic, non-aggressive man?

Surely that man, housed in his slender, nervous, unassuming body, would never choose to kill!

Would he?

Was that familiar and regretted Blaine defeated and smothered by the large, square-muscled, quick-reflexed fighter's body he had acquired? And was that body, with its own peculiar glandular secretions dripping into the dark bloodstream, its own distinct and configured brain, its own system of nerves and signals and responses—was that domineering body responsible for everything, dragging its helpless owner into murderous violence?

Blaine rubbed his eyes and told himself that he was dreaming nonsense. The truth simply was: He had died through circumstances beyond his control, been reborn in the future, and found himself unemployable except as a hunter. Q.E.D.

But that rational explanation didn't satisfy him, and he no longer had time to search out the slippery and elusive truth.

He was no longer a detached observer of 2110. He had become a biased participant, an actor instead of an onlooker, with all of an actor's thoughtless sweep and rush. Action was irresistible, it generated its own momentary truth. The brakes were off, and the engine Blaine was rolling down the steep hill Life, gathering momentum but no moss. Perhaps this, now, was his last chance for a look, a summing up, a measured choice…

But it was already too late, for a man slid into the booth opposite him like a shadow across the world. And Blaine was looking into the white and impassive face of the zombie.

"Good evening," the zombie said.

"Good evening," Blaine said steadily. "Would you care for a drink?"

"No, thank you. My system doesn't respond to stimulation."

"Sorry to hear it," Blaine said.

The zombie shrugged his shoulders. "I have a name now," he said. "I decided to call myself Smith, until I remember my real name. Smith. Do you like it?"

"It's a fine name," Blaine said.

"Thank you. I went to a doctor," Smith said. "He told me my body's no good. No stamina, no recuperative powers."

"Can't you be helped?"

Smith shook his head. "The body's definitely zombie. I occupied it much too late. The doctor gives me another few months at most."

"Too bad," Blaine said, feeling nausea rise in his throat at the sight of that sullen, thick-featured, leaden-skinned face with its unharmonious features and patient Buddha's eyes. Smith sat, slack and unnatural in rough workman's clothes, his black-dotted white face close-shaven and smelling of strong lotion. But he had changed. Already Blaine could see a certain leathery dryness in the once-pliant skin, certain striations in the flesh around the eyes, nose and mouth, minute creases in the forehead like tool-marks in old leather. And, mingled with the heavy after-shaving lotion, Blaine thought he could sense the first faint odor of dissolution.

"What do you want with me?" Blaine asked.

"I don't know."

"Then leave me alone."

"I can't do that," Smith said apologetically.

"Do you want to kill me?" Blaine asked, his throat dry.

"I don't know! I can't remember! Kill you, protect you, maim you, love you—I don't know yet! But I'll remember soon, Blaine, I promise!"

"Leave me alone," Blaine said, his muscles tensing.

"I can't," Smith said. "Don't you understand? I know nothing except you. Literally nothing! I don't know this world or any other, no person, face, mind or memory. You're my only landmark, the center of my existence, my only reason for living."

"Stop it!"

"But it's true! Do you think I *enjoy* dragging this structure of flesh through the streets? What good is life with no hope before me and no memory behind me? Death is better! Life means filthy decaying flesh, and death is pure spirit! I've thought about it, dreamed about it, beautiful fleshless death! But one thing stops me. I have *you*, Blaine, to keep me going!"

"Get out of here," Blaine said, nausea bitter in his mouth.

"*You*, my sun and moon, my stars, my Earth, my total universe, my life, my reason, my friend, enemy, lover, murderer, wife, father, child, husband—"

Blaine's fist shot out, striking Smith high on the cheekbone. The zombie was flung back in the booth. His expression did not change, but a great purple bruise appeared on his lead-colored cheekbone.

"*Your* mark!" Smith murmured.

Blaine's fist, poised for another blow, dropped.

Smith stood up. "I'm going. Take care of yourself, Blaine. Don't die yet! I need you. Soon I'll remember, and I'll come to you."

Smith, his sullen, slack, bruised face impassive, left the bar.

Blaine ordered a double whiskey and sat for a long time over it, trying to still the shaking in his hands.

Chapter 17

Blaine arrived at the Hull estate by rural jet-bus, an hour before dawn. He was dressed in a traditional hunter's uniform—khaki shirt and slacks, rubber-soled shoes and wide-brimmed hat. Slung over one shoulder was his field pack; over the other he carried his rifle and bayonet in a plastic bag.

A servant met him at the outer gate and led him to the low, rambling mansion. Blaine learned that the Hull estate consisted of ninety wooded acres in the Adirondack Mountains between Keene and Elizabethtown. Here, the servant told him, Hull's father had suicided at the age of fifty-one, taking the lives of six hunters with him before a saber man slashed his head off. Glorious death! Hull's uncle, on the other hand, had chosen to berserk in San Francisco, a city he had always loved. The police had to beam him twelve times before he dropped, and he took seven bystanders with him. The newspapers made much of the exploit, and accounts of it were preserved in the family scrapbook.

It just went to show, the garrulous old retainer pointed out, the difference in temperaments. Some, like the uncle, were friendly, fun-loving men who wanted to die in a crowd, attracting a certain amount of attention. Others, like the present Mr. Hull, were more given to the love of solitude and nature.

Blaine nodded politely to all this and was taken to a large, rustic room where the hunters were assembled, drinking coffee and honing a last razor edge to their weapons. Light flashed from the blued-steel broadsword and silvery battle-axe, wavered along the polished spearhead and glinted frostily from the diamond-points of the mace and morning star. At first glance, Blaine thought it looked like a scene from medieval times. But on second thought he decided it was more like a movie set.

"Pull up a chair, pal," the axeman called. "Welcome to the Benevolent Protective Society of Butchers, Slaughterhouse Men, and Killers-at-Large. I'm Sammy Jones, finest axeman in the Americas and probably Europe, too."

Blaine sat down and was introduced to the other hunters. They represented half a dozen nationalities, although English was their common tongue.

Sammy Jones was a squat, black-haired, bull-shouldered man, dressed in patched and faded khakis, with several old hunting scars across his craggy, thick-browed face.

"First hunt?" he asked, glancing at Blaine's neatly pressed khakis.

Blaine nodded, removed his rifle from its plastic bag and fitted the bayonet to its end. He tested the locking mechanism, tightened the rifle's strap, and removed the bayonet again.

"Can you really use that thing?" Jones asked.

"Sure," Blaine said, more confidently than he felt.

"Hope so. Guys like Hull have a nose for the weak sisters. They try to cut 'em out of the pack early."

"How long does a hunt usually last?" Blaine asked.

"Well," Jones said, "longest I was ever on took eight days. That was Asturias, where my partner Sligo got his. Generally a good pack can pin down a Quarry in a day or two. Depends on how he wants to die. Some try to hang on as long as they can. They run to cover. They hide in caves and ravines, the dirty treacherous dogs, and you have to go in for them and chance a thrust in the face. That's how Sligo got it. But I don't think Hull's that way. He wants to die like a great big fire-eating he-man hero. So he'll stalk around and take chances, looking to see how many of us he can knock off with his pigsticker."

"You sound as if you don't approve," Blaine said.

Sammy Jones raised his busy eyebrows. "I don't hold with making a big fuss about dying. Here comes the hero himself."

Hull entered the room, lean and elegant in khaki-colored silk, with a white silk bandanna knotted loosely around his neck. He carried a light pack, and strapped to one shoulder was a thin, wicked-looking rapier.

"Good morning, gentlemen," he said. "Weapons all honed, packs straight, shoelaces firmly tied? Excellent!"

Hull walked to a window and drew the curtains aside.

"Behold the first crack of dawn, a glorious streak in our eastern skies, harbinger of our fierce Lord Sun who rules the chase. I shall leave now. A servant will inform you when my half hour grace is done. Then you may pursue, and kill me upon sight. If you are able! The estate is fenced. I will remain within its confines, and so shall you."

Hull bowed, then walked quickly and gracefully out of the room.

"God, I hate these fancy birds!" Sammy Jones shouted, after the door was closed. "They're all alike, every one of them. Acting so cool and casual, so goddamned *heroic*. If they only knew how bloody *silly* I think they are—me that's been on twenty-eight of these things."

"Why do you hunt?" Blaine asked.

Sammy Jones shrugged. "My father was an axeman, and he taught me the business. It's the only thing I know."

"You could learn a different trade," Blaine said.

"I suppose I could. The fact is, I *like* killing these aristocratic gentlemen. I hate every rich bastard among them with their lousy hereafter a poor man can't afford. I take pleasure in killing them, and if I had money I'd pay for the privilege."

"And Hull enjoys killing poor men like you," Blaine said. "It's a sad world."

"No, just an honest one," Sammy Jones told him. "Stand up, I'll fasten your pack on right."

When that was done, Sammy Jones said, "Look, Tom, why don't you and me stick together on this hunt? Mutual protection, like?"

"*My* protection, you mean," Blaine said.

"Nothing to be ashamed of," Jones told him. "Every skilled trade must be learned before it can be practiced. And what better man to learn from than myself, the finest of the fine?"

"Thanks," Blaine said. "I'll try to hold up my end, Sammy."

"You'll do fine. Now, Hull's a fencer, be sure of it, and fencers have their little tricks which I'll explain as we go along. When he—"

At that moment a servant entered, carrying an old, ornate chronometer. When the second hand passed twelve, he looked sharply at the hunters.

"Gentlemen," he said, "the time of grace is passed. The chase may begin."

The hunters trooped outside into the grey, misty dawn. Theseus the tracker, balancing his trident across his shoulders, picked up the trail at once. It led upwards, toward a mist-wreathed mountain.

Spread out in a long single file, the hunters started up the mountain's side.

Soon the early morning sun had burned away the mists. Theseus lost the trail when it crossed bare granite. The hunters spread out in a broken line across the face of the mountain, and continued advancing slowly upward.

At noon, the broadsword man picked a fragment of khaki-coolored silk from a thornbush. A few minutes later, Theseus found footprints on moss. They led down, into a narrow thickly wooded valley. Eagerly the hunters pressed forward.

"Here he is!" a man shouted.

Blaine whirled and saw, fifty yards to his right, the man with the morning star running forward. He was the youngest of the hunters, a brawny, self-confident Sicilian. His weapon consisted of a stout handle of ash, fixed to which was a foot of chain. At the end of the chain was a heavy spiked ball, the morning star. He was whirling this weapon over his head and singing at the top of his lungs.

Sammy Jones and Blaine sprinted toward him. They saw Hull break from the bushes, rapier in hand. The Sicilian leaped forward and swung a blow that could have felled a tree. Hull dodged lightly out of the way, and lunged.

The morning star man gurgled and went down, pierced through the throat. Hull planted a foot on his chest, yanked the rapier free, and vanished again into the underbrush.

"I never could understand why a man'd use a morning star," Sammy Jones said. "Too clumsy. If you don't hit your man the first lick, you never recover in time."

The Sicilian was dead. Hull's passage through the underbrush was clearly visible. They plunged in after him, followed by most of the hunters, with flankers ranged on either side.

Soon they encountered rock again, and the trail was lost.

All afternoon they searched, with no luck. At sundown they pitched camp on the mountainside, posted guards, and discussed the day's hunting over a small campfire.

"Where do you suppose he is?" Blaine asked.

"He could be anywhere on the damned estate," Jones said. "Remember, he knows every foot of ground here. We're seeing it for the first time."

"Then he could hide from us indefinitely."

"If he wanted to. But he wants to be killed, remember? In a big, flashy, heroic way. So he'll keep on trying to cut us down until we get him."

Blaine looked over his shoulder at the dark woods. "He could be standing there now, listening."

"No doubt he is," Jones said. "I hope the guards stay awake."

Conversation droned on in the little camp, and the fire burned low. Blaine wished morning would come. Darkness reversed the roles. The hunters were the hunted now, stalked by a cruel and amoral suicide intent upon taking as many lives with him as possible.

With that thought, he dozed off.

Sometime before dawn he was awakened by a scream. Grabbing his rifle, he sprang to his feet and peered into the darkness. There was another scream, closer this time, and the sound of hurried movement through the woods. Then someone threw a handful of leaves on the dying fire.

In the sudden yellow glow, Blaine saw a man staggering back to the camp. It was one of the guards, trailing his spear behind him. He was bleeding in two places, but his wounds didn't appear fatal.

"That bastard," the spearman sobbed, "that lousy bastard."

"Take it easy, Chico," one of the men said, ripping open the spearman's shirt to clean and bandage the wound. "Did you get him?"

"He was too quick," the spearman moaned. "I missed."

That was the end of the sleeping for the night.

The hunters were moving again at the first light of dawn, widely scattered, looking for a trace of the Quarry. Theseus found a broken button and then a half-erased footprint. The hunt veered again, winding up a narrow-faced mountain.

At the head of the pack, Otto gave a sudden shout. "Hey! Here! I got him!"

Theseus rushed toward him, followed by Blaine and Jones. They saw Hull backing away, watching intently as Otto advanced swinging the bola around his cropped head. The Argentinian lasso hissed in the air, its three iron balls blurring. Then Otto released it. Instantly Hull flung himself to the ground. The bola snaked through the air inches above his head, wrapped itself around a tree limb and snapped it off. Hull, grinning broadly, ran toward the weaponless man

Before he could reach him Theseus had arrived, flourishing his trident. They exchanged thrusts. Then Hull whirled and ran.

Theseus lunged. The Quarry howled with pain but continued running.

"Did you wound him?" Jones asked.

"A flesh wound in the rump," Theseus said. "Probably most painful to his pride."

The hunters ran on, panting heavily, up the mountain's side. But they had lost the Quarry again.

They spread out, surrounding the narrowing mountain, and slowly began working their way toward the peak. Occasional noises and footprints told them the Quarry was still before them, retreating upward. As the peak narrowed they were able to close their ranks more, lessening any chance of Hull slipping through.

By late afternoon the pine and spruce trees had become sparse. Above them was a confused labyrinth of granite boulders, and past that the final peak itself.

"Careful now!" Jones called to the hunters.

As he said it, Hull launched an attack. Springing from behind a rock pinnacle, he came at old Bjorn the mace man, his rapier hissing, trying to cut the man down quickly and escape the throttling noose of hunters.

But Bjorn gave ground only slowly, cautiously parrying the rapier thrusts, both hands on his mace as though it were a quarterstaff. Hull swore angrily at the phlegmatic man, attacked furiously, and threw himself aside just in time to avoid a blow of the mace.

Old Bjorn closed—too rapidly. The rapier darted in and out of his chest like a snake's flickering tongue. Bjorn's mace dropped, and his body began rolling down the mountainside.

But the hunters had closed the circle again. Hull retreated upward, into a maze of boulders.

The hunters pressed forward. Blaine noticed that the sun was almost down; already there was a twilight hue to the air, and long shadows stretched across the gray rocks.

"Getting toward evening," he said to Jones.

"Maybe half an hour more light," Jones said, squinting at the sky. "We better get him soon. After dark he could pick every man of us off this rock."

They moved more quickly now, searching among the high boulders.

"He could roll rocks on us," Blaine said.

"Not him," Jones said. "He's too damn proud."

And then Hull stepped from behind a high rock near Blaine.

"All right, rifleman," he said.

Blaine, his rifle at high port, just managed to parry the thrust. The blade of the rapier rasped along the gun barrel, past his neck. Automatically he deflected it. Something drove him to roar as he lunged, to follow the lunge with an eager disemboweling slash and then a hopeful butt stroke intended to scatter his enemy's brains across the rocks. For that moment, Blaine was no longer a civilized man operating under a painful necessity; he was a more basic creature joyously pursuing his true vocation of murder.

The Quarry avoided his blows with quick silken grace. Blaine stumbled after him, anger sapping his skill. Suddenly he was shoved aside by Sammy Jones.

"Mine," Jones said. "All mine. I'm your boy. Try me with the pigsticker."

Hull, his face expressionless, advanced, his rapier flashing. Jones stood firm on slightly bowed legs, the battleaxe turning lightly in his hands. Hull feinted and lunged. Jones parried so hard that sparks flew, and the rapier bent like a green stick.

The other hunters had come up now. They chose seats on nearby rocks and caught their wind, commenting on the duel and shouting advice.

"Pin him against the cliff, Sammy!"

"No, over the edge with him!"

"Want some help?"

"Hell no!" Jones shouted back.

"Watch out he don't nip a finger, Sammy."

"Don't worry," Jones said.

Blaine watched, his rage ebbing as quickly as it had come. He had assumed that a battleaxe would be a clumsy weapon requiring a full backswing for each stroke. But Sammy Jones handled the short, heavy axe as though it were a baton. He took no backswing but let drive from any position, recovering instantly, his implacable weight and drive forcing Hull toward the cliff's sheer edge. There was no real comparison between the two men, Blaine realized. Hull was a gifted amateur, a dilettante murderer; Jones was a seasoned professional killer. It was like matching a ferocious house dog against a jungle tiger.

The end came quickly in the blue twilight of the mountaintop. Sammy Jones parried a thrust and stamped forward, swinging his axe backhanded. The blade bit deep into Hull's left side. Hull fell screaming down the mountain's side. For seconds afterward they heard his body crash and turn.

"Mark where he lies," Sammy Jones said.

"He's gotta be dead," the saber man said.

"He probably is. But it isn't a workmanlike job unless we make sure."

On the way down they found Hull's mangled and lifeless body. They marked the location for the burial party and walked on to the estate.

Chapter 18

The hunters returned to the city in a group and threw a wild celebration. During the evening, Sammy Jones asked Blaine if he would join him on the next job.

"I've got a nice deal lined up in Omsk," Jones said. "A Russian nobleman wants to hold a couple of gladiatorial games. You'd have to use a spear, but it's the same as a rifle. I'd train you on the way. After Omsk, there's a really big hunt being organized in Manila. Five brothers want to suicide together. They want fifty hunters to cut them down. What do you say, Tom?"

Blaine thought carefully before answering. The hunter's life was the most compatible he had found so far in this world. He liked the rough companionship of men like Sammy Jones, the straight, simple thinking, the life outdoors, the action that erased all doubts.

On the other hand there was something terribly pointless about wandering around the world as a paid killer, a modern and approved version of the bully, the bravo, the thug. There was something futile about action just for action's sake, with no genuine intent or purpose behind it, no resolution or discovery. These considerations might not arise if he were truly what his body seemed; but he was not. The hiatus existed, and had to be faced.

And finally there were other problems that this world presented, other challenges more apropos to his personality. And those had to be met.

"Sorry, Sammy," he said.

Jones shook his head. "You're making a mistake, Tom. You're a natural-born killer. There's nothing else for you."

"Perhaps not," Blaine said. "I have to find out."

"Well, good luck," Sammy Jones said. "And take care of that body of yours. You picked a good one."

Blaine blinked involuntarily. "Is it so obvious?"

Jones grinned. "I been around, Tom. I can tell when a man is wearing a host. If your mind had been *born* in that body, you'd be away and hunting with me. And if your mind had been born in a different body—"

"Yes?"

"You wouldn't have gone hunting in the first place. It's a bad splice, Tom. You'd better figure out which way you're going."

"Thanks," Blaine said. They shook hands and Blaine left for his hotel.

He reached his room and flung himself, fully dressed, upon the bed. When he awoke he would call Marie. But first, he had to sleep. All plans, thoughts, problems, decisions, even dreams, would have to wait. He was tired down to the very bone.

He snapped off the lights. Within seconds he was asleep.

Several hours later he awoke with a sensation of something wrong. The room was dark. Everything was still, more silent and expectant than New York had any right to be.

He sat upright in bed and heard a faint movement on the other side of the room, near the washbasin.

Blaine reached out and snapped on the light. There was no one in the room. But as he watched, his enameled washbasin rose in the air. Slowly it lifted, hovering impossibly without support. And at the same time he heard a thin shattering laugh.

He knew at once he was being haunted, and by a poltergeist.

Carefully he eased out of bed and moved toward the door. The suspended basin dipped suddenly and plunged toward his head. He ducked, and the basin shattered against the wall.

His water pitcher levitated now, followed by two heavy tumblers. Twisting and turning erratically, they edged toward him.

Blaine picked up a pillow as a shield and rushed to the door. He turned the lock as a tumbler shattered above his head. The door wouldn't open. The poltergeist was holding it shut.

The pitcher struck him violently in the ribs. The remaining tumbler buzzed in an ominous circle around his head, and he was forced to retreat from the door.

He remembered the fire escape outside his window. But the poltergeist thought of it as he started to move. The curtains suddenly burst into flame. At the same instant the pillow he was holding caught fire, and Blaine threw it from him.

"Help!" he shouted. "Help!"

He was being forced into a corner of the room. With a rumble the bed slid forward, blocking his retreat. A chair rose slowly into the air and poised itself for a blow at his head.

And continually there was a thin and shattering laughter that Blaine could almost recognize.

PART THREE

Chapter 19

As the bed crept toward him Blaine shouted for help in a voice that made the window rattle. His only answer was the poltergeist's high-pitched laugh.

Were they all deaf in the hotel? Why didn't someone answer?

Then he realized that, by the very nature of things, no one would even consider helping him. Violence was a commonplace in this world, and a man's death was entirely his own business. There would be no inquiry. The janitor would simply clean up the mess in the morning, and the room would be marked vacant.

His door was impassable. The only chance he could see was to jump over the bed and through the closed window. If he made the leap properly, he would fall against the waist-high fire escape railing outside. If he jumped too hard he would go right over the railing, and fall three stories to the street.

The chair beat him over the shoulders, and the bed rumbled forward to pin him against the wall. Blaine made a quick calculation of angles and distances, drew himself together and flung himself at the window.

He hit squarely; but he had reckoned without the advances of modern science. The window bent outward like a sheet of rubber, and snapped back into place. He was thrown against a wall, and fell dazed to the floor. Looking up, he saw a heavy bureau wobble toward him and slowly tilt.

As the poltergeist threw his lunatic strength against the bureau, the unwatched door swung open. Smith entered the room, his thick-featured zombie face impassive, and deflected the falling bureau with his shoulder.

"Come on," he said.

Blaine asked no questions. He scrambled to his feet and grabbed the edge of the closing door. With Smith's help he pulled it open again, and the two men slipped out. From within the room he heard a shriek of baffled rage.

Smith hurried down the hall, one cold hand clasped around Blaine's wrist. They went downstairs, through the hotel lobby and into the street. The zombie's face was leaden white except for the purple bruise where Blaine had struck him. The bruise had spread across nearly half his face, pie-balding it into a Harlequin's grotesque mask.

"Where are we going?" Blaine asked.

"To a safe place."

They reached an ancient unused subway entrance, and descended. One flight down they came to a small iron door set in the cracked concrete wall. Smith opened the door and beckoned Blaine to follow him.

Blaine hesitated, and caught the hint of high-pitched laughter. The poltergeist was pursuing him, as the Eumenides had once pursued their victims through the streets of ancient Athens. He could stay in the lighted upper world if he wished, hag-ridden by an insane spirit. Or he could descend with Smith, through the iron door and into the darkness beyond it, to some uncertain destiny in the underworld.

The shrill laughter increased. Blaine hesitated no longer. He followed Smith through the iron door and closed it behind him.

For the moment, the poltergeist had not chosen to pursue. They walked down a tunnel lighted by an occasional naked light bulb, past cracked masonry pipes and the looming grey corpse of a subway train, past rusted iron cables lying in giant serpent coils. The air was moist and rank, and a thin slime underfoot made walking treacherous.

"Where are we going?" Blaine asked.

"To where I can protect you," Smith said.

"Can you?"

"Spirits aren't invulnerable. Exorcism is possible if the true identity of the ghost is known."

"Then you know who is haunting me?"

"I think so. There's only one person it logically could be."

"Who?"

Smith shook his head. "I'd rather not say his name yet. No sense calling him if he's not here."

They descended a series of crumbling shale steps into a wider chamber, and circled the edge of a small black pond whose surface looked as hard and still as jet. On the other side of the pond was a passageway. A man stood in front of it, blocking the way.

He was a tall husky Negro, dressed in rags, armed with a length of iron pipe. From his look Blaine knew he was a zombie.

"This is my friend," Smith said. "May I bring him through?"

"You sure he's no inspector?"

"Absolutely sure."

"Wait here," the Negro said. He disappeared into the passageway.

"Where are we?" Blaine asked.

"Underneath New York, in a series of unused subway tunnels, old sewer conduits, and some passageways we've fashioned for ourselves."

"But why did we come here?" Blaine asked.

"Where else would we go?" Smith asked, surprised. "This is my home. Didn't you know? You're in New York's zombie colony."

Blaine didn't consider a zombie colony much improvement over a ghost; but he didn't have time to think about it. The Negro returned. With him was a very old man who walked with the aid of a stick. The man's face was broken into a network of a thousand lines and wrinkles. His eyes barely showed through the fine scrollwork of sagging flesh, and even his lips were wrinkled.

"This is the man you told me about?" he asked.

"Yes sir," said Smith. "This is the man. Blaine, let me introduce you to Mr. Kean, the leader of our colony. May I take him through, sir?"

"You may," the old man said. "And I will accompany you for a while."

They started down the passageway, Mr. Kean supporting himself heavily on the Negro's arm.

"In the usual course of events, " Mr. Kean said, "only zombies are allowed in the colony. All others are barred. But it has been years since I spoke with a normal, and I thought the experience might be valuable. Therefore, at Smith's earnest request, I made an exception in your case."

"I'm very grateful," Blaine said, hoping he had reason to be.

"Don't misunderstand me. I am not averse to helping you. But first and foremost I am responsible for the safety of the eleven hundred zombies living beneath New York. For their sake, normals must be kept out. Exclusivity is our only hope in an ignorant world." Mr. Kean paused. "But perhaps you can help us, Blaine."

"How?"

"By listening and understanding, and passing on what you have learned. Education is our only hope. Tell me, what do you know about the problems of a zombie?"

"Very little."

"I will instruct you. Zombieism, Mr. Blaine, is a disease which has long had a powerful aura of superstition surrounding it, comparable to the aura generated by such diseases as epilepsy, leprosy, or St. Vitus' Dance. The spiritualizing tendency is a common one. Schizophrenia, you know, was once thought to mean possession by devils, and hydrocephalic idiots were considered peculiarly blessed. Similar fantasies attach to zombieism."

They walked in silence for a few moments. Mr. Kean said, "The superstition of the zombie is essentially Haitian; the disease of the zombie is worldwide, although rare. But the superstition and the disease have become hopelessly confused in the public mind. The zombie of superstition is an element of the Haitian Vodun cult; a human being whose soul has been stolen by magic. The zombie's body could be used as the magician wished, could even be slaughtered and sold for meat in the marketplace. If the zombie ate salt or beheld the sea, he realized that he was dead and returned to his grave. For all of this, there is no basis in fact.

"The superstition arose from the descriptively similar disease. Once it was exceedingly rare. But today, with the increase in mind-switching and reincarnation techniques, zombieism has become more common. The *disease* of the zombie occurs when a mind occupies a body that has been untenanted too long. Mind and body are not then one, as yours are, Mr. Blaine. They exist, instead, as quasi-independent entities engaged in an uneasy cooperation. Take our friend Smith as typical. He can control his body's gross physical actions, but fine coordination is impossible for him. His voice is incapable of discrete modulation, and his ears do not receive subtle differences in tone. His face is expressionless, for he has little or no control over surface musculature. He drives his body, but is not truly a part of it."

"And can't anything be done?" Blaine asked.

"At the present time, nothing."

"I'm very sorry," Blaine said uncomfortably.

"This is not a plea for your sympathy," Kean told him. "It is a request only for the most elementary understanding. I simply want you and everyone to know that zombieism is not a visitation of sins, but a *disease,* like mumps or cancer, and nothing more."

Mr. Kean leaned against the wall of the passageway to catch his breath. "To be sure, the zombie's appearance is unpleasant. He shambles, his wounds never heal, his body deteriorates rapidly. He mumbles like an idiot, staggers like a drunk, stares like a pervert. But is this any reason to make him the repository of all guilt and shame upon Earth, the leper of the 22nd Century? They say that zombies attack people; yet his body is fragile in the extreme, and the average zombie couldn't resist a child's determined assault. They believe the disease is communicable; and this is obviously not so. They say that zombies are sexually perverted, and the truth is that a zombie experiences no sexual feelings whatsoever. But people refuse to learn, and zombies are outcasts fit only for the hangman's noose or the lyncher's burning stake."

"What about the authorities?" Blaine asked.

Mr. Kean smiled bitterly. "They used to lock us up, as a kindness, in mental institutions. You see, they didn't want us hurt. Yet zombies are rarely insane, and the authorities knew it! So now, with their tacit approval, we occupy these abandoned subway tunnels and sewer lines."

"Couldn't you find a better place?" Blaine asked.

"Frankly, the underground suits us. Sunlight is bad for unregenerative skins."

They began walking again. Blaine said, "What can I do?"

"You can tell someone what you learned here. Write about it, perhaps. Widening ripples...."

"I'll do what I can."

"Thank you," Mr. Kean said gravely. "Education is our only hope. Education and the future. Surely people will be more enlightened in the future."

The future? Blaine felt suddenly dizzy. For *this* was the future, to which he had traveled from the idealistic and hopeful 20th century. *Now* was the future! But the promised enlightenment still had not come, and people were much the same as ever. For a second Blaine's centuries pressed heavily on him. He felt disoriented and old, older than Kean, older than the human race—a creature in a borrowed body standing in a place it did not know.

"And now," Mr. Kean said, "we have reached your destination."

Blaine blinked rapidly, and life came back into focus. The dim passageway had ended. In front of him was a rusted iron ladder fastened to the tunnel wall, leading upward into darkness.

"Good luck," Mr. Kean said. He left, supporting himself heavily on the Negro's arm. Blaine watched the old man go, then turned to Smith.

"Where are we going?"

"Up the ladder."

"But where does it lead?"

Smith had already begun climbing. He stopped and looked down, his lead-colored lips drawn back into a grin. "We're going to visit a friend of yours, Blaine. We're going into his tomb, up to his coffin, and ask him to stop haunting you. Force him, maybe."

"Who is he?" Blaine asked.

Smith only grinned and continued climbing. Blaine mounted the ladder behind him.

Chapter 20

Above the passageway was a ventilation shaft, which led to another passageway. They came at last to a door, and entered.

They were in a large, brilliantly lighted room. Upon the arched ceiling was a mural depicting a handsome, clear-eyed man entering a gauzy blue heaven in the company of angels. Blaine knew at once who had modeled for the painting.

"Reilly!"

Smith nodded. "We're inside his Palace of Death."

"How did you know Reilly was haunting me?"

"You should have thought of it yourself. Only two people connected with you have died recently. The ghost certainly was not Ray Melhill. It had to be Reilly."

"But why?"

"I don't know," Smith said. "Perhaps Reilly will tell you himself."

Blaine looked at the walls. They were inlaid with crosses, crescent moons, stars and swastikas, as well as Indian, African, Arabian, Chinese and Polynesian good-luck signs. On pedestals around the room were statues of ancient deities. Among the dozens Blaine recognized Zeus, Apollo, Dagon, Odin and Astarte. In front of each pedestal was an altar, and on each altar was a cut and polished jewel.

"What's that for?" Blaine asked.

"Propitiation."

"But life after death is a scientific fact."

"Mr. Kean told me that science has little effect upon superstition," Smith said. "Reilly was fairly sure he'd survive after death; but he saw no reason to take chances. Also, Mr. Kean says that the very rich, like the very religious, wouldn't enjoy a hereafter filled with just *anybody*. They think that, by suitable rites and symbols, they can get into a more exclusive part of the hereafter."

"Is there a more exclusive part?" Blaine asked.

"No one knows. It's just a belief."

Smith led him across the room to an ornate door covered with Egyptian hieroglyphics and Chinese ideograms.

"Reilly's body is inside here," Smith said.

"And we're going in?"

"Yes, we have to."

Smith pushed the door open. Blaine saw a vast marble-pillared room. In its very center was a bronze and gold coffin inlaid with jewels. Surrounding the coffin was a great and bewildering quantity of goods; paintings and sculptures, musical instruments, carvings, objects like washing machines, stoves, refrigerators, even a complete helicopter. There was clothing and books, and a lavish banquet had been laid out.

"What's all this stuff for?" Blaine asked.

"The essence of these goods is intended to accompany the owner into the hereafter. It's an old belief."

Blaine's first reaction was one of pity. The scientific hereafter hadn't freed men from the fear of death, as it should have done. On the contrary, it had intensified their uncertainties and stimulated their competitive drive. Given the surety of an afterlife, man wanted to improve upon it, to enjoy a better heaven than anyone else. Equality was all very well; but individual initiative came first. A perfect and passionless leveling was no more palatable an idea in the hereafter than it was on Earth. The desire to surpass caused a man like Reilly to build a tomb like the Pharaohs of ancient Egypt, to brood all his life about death, to live continually trying to find ways of preserving his property and status in the grey uncertainties ahead.

A shame. And yet, Blaine thought, wasn't his pity based upon a lack of belief in the efficacy of Reilly's measures? Suppose you *could* improve your situation in the hereafter? In that case, what better way to spend one's time on Earth than working for a better eternity?

The proposition seemed reasonable, but Blaine refused to believe it. *That* couldn't be the only reason for existence on Earth! Good or bad, fair or foul, the thing had to be lived for its own sake.

Smith walked slowly into the coffin room, and Blaine stopped his speculations. The zombie stood, contemplating a small table covered with ornaments. Dispassionately he kicked the table over. Then slowly, one by one, he ground the delicate ornaments into the polished marble floor.

"What are you doing?" Blaine asked.

"You want the poltergeist to leave you alone?"

"Of course."

"Then he must have some *reason* for leaving you alone," Smith said, kicking over an elaborate ebony sculpture.

It seemed reasonable enough to Blaine. Even a ghost must know he will eventually leave the Threshold and enter the hereafter. When he does, he wants his goods waiting for him, intact. Therefore fight fire with fire, persecution with persecution.

Still, he felt like a vandal when he picked up an oil painting and prepared to shove his fist through it.

"Don't," said a voice above his head.

Blaine and Smith looked up. Above them there seemed to be a faint silvery mist. From the mist an attenuated voice said, "Please put down the painting."

Blaine held on to it, his fist poised. "Are you Reilly?"

"Yes."

"Why are you haunting me?"

"Because you're responsible! Everything's your fault! You killed me with your evil murdering mind! Yes, *you,* you hideous thing from the past, you damned monster!"

"I didn't!" Blaine cried.

"You did! You aren't human! You aren't natural! Everything shuns you except your friend the dead man! Why aren't *you* dead, murderer!"

Blaine's fist moved toward the painting. The thin voice screamed, "Don't!"

"Will you leave me alone?" Blaine asked.

"Put down the painting," Reilly begged.

Blaine put it carefully down.

"I'll leave you alone," Reilly said. "Why shouldn't I? There are things you can't see, Blaine, but *I* see them. Your time on Earth will be short, very short, painfully short. Those you trust will betray you, those you hate will conquer you. You will die, Blaine, not in years but soon, sooner than you could believe. You'll be betrayed, and you'll die by your own hand."

"You're crazy!" Blaine shouted.

"Am I?" Reilly cackled. "Am I? *Am I?*"

The silvery mist vanished. Reilly was gone.

Smith led him back through narrow winding passageways to the street level. Outside the air was chilly, and dawn had touched the tall buildings with red and grey.

Blaine started to thank him, but Smith shook his head. "No reason for thanks! After all, I need you, Blaine. Where would I be if the poltergeist killed you? Take care of yourself, be careful. Nothing is possible for me without you."

The zombie gazed anxiously at him for a moment, then hurried away. Blaine watched him go, wondering if it wouldn't be better to have a dozen enemies than Smith for a friend.

Chapter 21

Half an hour later he was at Marie Thorne's apartment. Marie, without makeup, dressed in a housecoat, blinked sleepily and led him to the kitchen, where she dialed coffee, toast and scrambled eggs.

"I wish," she said, "you'd make your dramatic appearances at a decent hour. It's six-thirty in the morning."

"I'll try to do better in the future," Blaine said cheerfully.

"You said you'd call. What happened to you?"

"Did you worry?"

"Not in the slightest. What happened?"

Between bites of toast Blaine told her about the hunt, the haunting, and the exorcism. She listened to it all, then said, "So you're obviously very proud of yourself, and I guess you should be. But you still don't know what Smith wants from you, or even who he is."

"Haven't the slightest idea," Blaine said. "Smith doesn't, either. Frankly, I couldn't care less."

"What happens when he finds out?"

"I'll worry about that when it happens."

Marie raised both eyebrows but made no comment. "Tom, what are your plans now?"

"I'm going to get a job."

"As a hunter?"

"No. Logical or not, I'm going to try the yacht design agencies. Then I'm going to come around here and bother you at reasonable hours. How does that sound?"

"Impractical. Do you want some good advice?"

"No."

"I'm giving it to you anyhow. Tom, get out of New York. Go as far away as you can. Go to Fiji or Samoa."

"Why should I?"

Marie began to pace restlessly up and down the kitchen. "You simply don't understand this world."

"I think I do."

"No! Tom, you've had a few typical experiences, that's all. But that doesn't mean you've assimilated our culture. You've been snatched, haunted, and you've gone on a hunt. But it adds up to not much more than a guided tour. Reilly was right, you're as lost and helpless as a caveman would be in your own 1958."

"That's ridiculous, and I object to the comparison."

"All right, let's make it a 14th Century Chinese. Suppose this hypothetical Chinaman had met a gangster, gone on a bus ride and seen Coney Island. Would you say he understood 20th Century America?"

"Of course not. But what's the point?"

"The point," she said, "is that you aren't safe here, and you can't even sense what or where or how urgent the dangers are. For one, that damned Smith is after you. Next, Reilly's heirs might not take kindly to you desecrating his tomb; they might find it necessary to do something about it. And the directors at Rex are still arguing about what *they* should do about you. You've altered things, changed things, disrupted things. Can't you *feel* it?"

"I can handle Smith," Blaine said. "To hell with Reilly's heirs. As for the directors, what can they do to me?"

She came over to him and put her arms around his neck. "Tom," she said earnestly, "any man born here who found himself in your shoes would run as fast as he could!"

Blaine held her close for a moment and stroked her sleek dark hair. She cared for him, she wanted him to be safe. But he was in no mood for warnings. He had survived the dangers of the hunt, had passed through the iron door into the underworld and won through again to the light. Now, sitting in Marie's sunny kitchen, he felt elated and at peace with the world. Danger seemed an academic problem not worthy of discussion at the moment, and the idea of running away from New York was absurd.

"Tell me," Blaine said lightly, "among the things I've disrupted—is one of them you?"

"I'm probably going to lose my job, if that's what you mean."

"That's not what I mean."

"Then you should know the answer... Tom, will you please get out of New York?"

"No. And please stop sounding so panicky."

"Oh Lord," she sighed. "We talk the same language but I'm not getting through. You don't understand. Let me try an example." She thought for a moment. "Suppose a man owned a sailboat—"

"Do you sail?" Blaine asked.

"Yes, I love sailing. Tom, listen to me! Suppose a man owned a sailboat in which he was planning an ocean voyage—"

"Across the sea of life," Blaine filled in.

"You're not funny," she said, looking very pretty and serious. "This man doesn't know anything about boats. He sees it floating, nicely painted, everything in place. He can't imagine any danger. Then *you* look the boat over. You see that the frames are cracked, teredos have gotten into the rudder post, there's dry rot in the mast step, the sails are mildewed, the keel bolts are rusted, and the fastenings are ready to let go."

"Where'd you learn so much about boats?" Blaine asked.

"I've been sailing since I was a kid. Will you please pay attention? You tell that man his boat is not seaworthy, the first gale is likely to sink him."

"We'll have to go sailing sometime," Blaine said.

"But this man," Marie continued doggedly, "doesn't know anything about boats. The thing *looks* all right. And the hell of it is, you can't tell him exactly what is going to happen, or when. Maybe the boat will hold together for a month, or a year, or maybe only a week. Maybe the keel bolts will go first, or perhaps it'll be the mast. You just don't know. And that's the situation here. I can't tell you what's going to happen, or when. I just know you're unseaworthy. You *must* get out of here!"

She looked at him hopefully. Blaine nodded and said, "You'll make one hell of a crew."

"So you're not going?"

"No. I've been up all night. The only place I'm going now is to bed. Would you care to join me?"

"Go to hell!"

"Darling, please! Where's your pity for a homeless wanderer from the past?"

"I'm going out," she said. "Help yourself to the bedroom. You'd better think about what I told you."

"Sure," Blaine said. "But why should I worry when I have you looking out for me?"

"Smith's looking for you, too," she reminded him. She kissed him quickly and left the room.

Blaine finished his breakfast and turned in. He awoke in the early afternoon. Marie still hadn't returned, so before leaving he wrote her a cheerful note with the address of his hotel.

During the next few days he visited most of the yacht design agencies in New York, without success. His old firm, Mattison & Peters, was long defunct. The other firms weren't interested. Finally, at Jaakobsen Yachts, Ltd., the head designer questioned him closely about the now-extinct Chesapeake Bay and Bahamas work boats. Blaine demonstrated his considerable knowledge of the types, as well as his out-of-date draftsmanship.

"We get a few calls for antique hulls," the head designer said. "Tell you what. We'll hire you as office boy. You can do classic hulls on a commission basis and study up on your designing, which, frankly, is old-fashioned. When you're ready, we'll upgrade you. What do you say?"

It was an inferior position; but it was a job, a legitimate job, with a fine chance for advancement. It meant that at last he had a real place in the world of 2110.

"I'll take it," Blaine said, "with thanks."

That evening, by way of celebrating, he went to a Sensory Shop to buy a player and a few recordings. He was entitled, he thought, to a little basic luxury.

The sensories were an inescapable part of 2110, as omnipresent and popular as television had been in Blaine's day. Larger and more elaborate versions of the sensories were used for theater productions, and variations were employed for advertising and propaganda. They were to date the purest and most powerful form of the ready-made dream, tailored to fit anyone.

But they had their extremely vocal opponents, who deplored the ominous trend toward complete passivity in the spectator. These critics were disturbed by the excessive ease with which a person could assimilate a sensory; and in truth, many a housewife walked blank-eyed through her days, a modern-day mystic plugged into a continual bright vision.

In reading a book or watching television, the critics pointed out, the viewer had to exert himself, to participate. But the sensories merely swept over you, vivid, brilliant, insidious, and left behind the damaging schizophrenic impression that dreams were better and more desirable than life. Such an impression could not be allowed, even if it were true. Sensories were dangerous! To be sure, some valid artistic work was done in the sensory form. (One could not discount Verreho, Johnston or Telkin; and Mikkelsen showed promise.) But there was not *much* good work. And weighed against the damaging psychic effects, the lowering of popular taste, the drift toward complete passivity...

In another generation, the critics thundered, people will be incapable of reading, thinking or acting!

It was a strong argument. But Blaine, with his 152 years of perspective, remembered much the same sort of arguments hurled at radio, movies, comic books, television and paperbacks. Even the revered novel had once been bitterly chastised for its deviation from the standards of pure poetry. Every innovation seemed culturally destructive; and became, ultimately, a cultural staple, the embodiment of the good old days, the spirit of the Golden Age—to be threatened and finally destroyed by the next innovation.

The sensories, good or bad, were here. Blaine entered the store to partake of them.

After looking over various models he bought a medium-priced Bendix player. Then, with the clerk's aid, he chose three popular recordings and took them into a booth to play. Fastening the electrodes to his forehead, he turned the first one on.

It was a popular historical, a highly romantic rendition of the *Chanson de Roland,* done in a low-intensity non-identification technique that allowed large battle effects and massed movements. The dream began.

…and Blaine was in the pass of Roncesvalles on that hot and fateful August morning in 778, standing with Roland's rear guard, watching the main body of Charlemagne's army wind slowly on toward Frankland. The tired veterans slumped in their high-cantled saddles, leather creaked, spurs jingled against bronze stirrup-guards. There was a smell of pine and sweat in the air, a hint of smoke from razed Pampelona, a taste of oiled steel and dry summer grass…

Blaine decided to buy it. The next was a high-intensity chase on Venus, in which the viewer identified fully with the hunted but innocent man. The last was a variable-intensity recording of *War and Peace,* with occasional identification sections.

As he paid for his purchases, the clerk winked at him and said, "Interested in the real stuff?"

"Maybe," Blaine said.

"I got some great party records," the clerk told him. "Full identification with switches yet. No? Got a genuine horror piece—man dying in quicksand. The murderers recorded his death for the specialty trade."

"Perhaps some other time," Blaine said, moving toward the door.

"And also," the clerk told him, "I got a special recording, legitimately made but withheld from the public. A few copies are being bootlegged around. Man reborn from the past. Absolutely genuine."

"Really?"

"Yes, it's perfectly unique. The emotions come through clear as a bell, sharp as a knife. A collector's item. I predict it'll become a classic."

"That I'd like to hear," Blaine said grimly.

He took the unlabeled record back to the booth. In ten minutes he came out again, somewhat shaken, and purchased it for an exorbitant price. It was like buying a piece of himself.

The clerk and the Rex technicians were right. It was a real collector's item, and would probably become a classic.

Unfortunately, all names had been carefully wiped to prevent the police from tracing its source. He was famous—but in a completely anonymous fashion.

Chapter 22

Blaine went to his job every day, swept the floor, emptied the wastepaper basket, addressed envelopes, and did a few antique hulls on commission. In the evenings he studied the complex science of 22nd century yacht design. After a while he was given a few small assignments writing publicity releases. He proved talented at this, and was soon promoted to the position of junior yacht designer. He began handling much of the liaison between Jaakobsen Yachts, Ltd., and the various yards building to their design.

He continued to study, but there were few requests for classic hulls. The Jaakobsen brothers handled most of the stock boats, while old Ed Richter, known as the Marvel of Salem, drew up the unusual racers and multi-hulls. Blaine took over publicity and advertising, and had no time for anything else.

It was responsible, necessary work. But it was *not* yacht designing. Irrevocably his life in 2110 was falling into much the same pattern it had assumed in 1958.

Blaine pondered this carefully. On the one hand, he was happy about it. It seemed to settle, once and for all, the conflict between his mind and his borrowed body. Obviously his mind was boss.

On the other hand, the situation didn't speak too well for the quality of that mind. Here was a man who had traveled 152 years into the future, had passed through wonders and horrors, and was working again, with a weary and terrible inevitability, as a junior yacht designer who did everything but design yachts. Was there some fatal flaw in his character, some hidden defect which doomed him to inferiority no matter what his environment?

Moodily he pictured himself flung back a million or so years, to a caveman era. Doubtless, after a period of initial adjustment, he would become a junior designer of dugouts. Only not *really* a designer. His job would be to count the wampum, check the quality of the tree trunks and contract for outriggers, while some other fellow (probably a Neanderthal genius) did the actual running of the lines.

That was disheartening. But fortunately it was not the only way of viewing the matter. His inevitable return could also be taken as a fine example of internal solidarity, of human steadfastness. He was a man who knew what he was. No matter how his environment changed, he remained true to his function.

Viewed this way, he could be very proud of being eternally and forever a junior yacht designer.

He continued working, fluctuating between these two basic views of himself. Once or twice he saw Marie, but she was usually busy in the high councils of the Rex Corporation. He moved out of his hotel and into a small, tastefully furnished apartment. New York was beginning to feel normal to him.

And, he reminded himself, if he had gained nothing else, he had at least settled his mind-body problem.

But his body was not to be disposed of so lightly. Blaine had overlooked one of the problems likely to exist with the ownership of a strong, handsome, and highly idiosyncratic body such as his.

One day the conflict flared again, more aggravated than ever.

He had left work at the usual time, and was waiting at a corner for his bus. He noticed a woman staring intently at him. She was perhaps twenty-five years old, a buxom, attractive redhead. She was commonly dressed. Her features were bold, yet they had a certain wistful quality.

Blaine realized that he had seen her before but never really noticed her. Now that he thought about it, she had once ridden a helibus with him. Once she had entered a store nearly on his footsteps. And several times she had been passing his building when he left work.

She had been watching him, probably for weeks. But why?

He waited, staring back at her. The woman hesitated a moment, then said, "Could I talk to you a moment?" Her voice was husky, pleasant, but very nervous. "Please, Mr. Blaine, it's very important."

So she knew his name. "Sure," Blaine said. "What is it?"

"Not here. Could we—uh—go somewhere?"

Blaine grinned and shook his head. She seemed harmless enough; but Orc had seemed so, too. Trusting strangers in this world was a good way of losing your mind, your body, or both.

"I don't know you," Blaine said, "and I don't know where you learned my name. Whatever you want, you'd better tell me here."

"I really shouldn't be bothering you," the woman said in a discouraged voice. "But I couldn't stop myself, I had to talk to you. I get so lonely sometimes, you know how it is?"

"Lonely? Sure, but why do you want to talk to me?"

She looked at him sadly. "That's right, you don't know."

"No, I don't," Blaine said patiently. "Why?"

"Can't we go somewhere? I don't like to say it in public like this."

"You'll have to," Blaine said, beginning to think that this was a very complicated game indeed.

"Oh, all right," the woman said, obviously embarrassed. "I've been following you around for a long time, Mr. Blaine. I found out your name and where you worked. I had to talk to you. It's all on account of that body of yours."

"What?"

"Your body," she said, not looking at him. "You see, it used to be my husband's body before he sold it to the Rex Corporation."

Blaine's mouth opened, but he could find no adequate words.

Chapter 23

Blaine had always known that his body had lived its own life in the world before it had been given to him. It had acted, decided, loved, hated, made its own individual imprint upon society and woven its own complex and lasting web of relationships. He could even have assumed that it had been married; most bodies were. But he had preferred not thinking about it. He had let himself believe that everything concerning the previous owner had conveniently disappeared.

His own meeting with Ray Melhill's snatched body should have shown him how naive that attitude was. Now, like it or not, he had to think about it.

They went to Blaine's apartment. The woman, Alice Kranch, sat dejectedly on one side of the couch and accepted a cigarette.

"The way it was," she said, "Frank—that was my husband's name, Frank Kranch—he was never satisfied with things, you know? He had a good job as a hunter, but he was never satisfied."

"A hunter?"

"Yes, he was a spearman in the China game."

"Hmm," Blaine said, wondering again what had induced him to go on that hunt. His own needs or Kranch's dormant reflexes? It was annoying to have this mind-body problem come up again just when it had seemed so nicely settled.

"But he wasn't ever satisfied," Alice Kranch said. "And it used to make him sore, those fancy rich guys getting themselves killed and going to the hereafter. He always hated the idea of dying like a dog, Frank did."

"I don't blame him," Blaine said.

She shrugged her shoulders. "What can you do? Frank didn't have a chance of making enough money for hereafter insurance. It bothered him. And then he got that big wound on the shoulder that nearly put him under. I suppose you still got the scar?"

Blaine nodded.

"Well, he wasn't ever the same after that. Hunters usually don't think much about death, but Frank started to. He started thinking about it all the time. And then he met this skinny dame from Rex."

"Marie Thorne?"

"That's the one," Alice said. "She was a skinny dame, hard as nails and cold as a fish. I couldn't understand what Frank saw in her. Oh, he played around some, most hunters do. It's on account of the danger. But there's playing around and playing around. He and this fancy Rex dame were thick as thieves. I just couldn't see what Frank saw in her. I mean she was so *skinny,* and so tight-faced. She was pretty in a pinched sort of way, but she looked like she'd wear her clothes to bed, if you know what I mean."

Blaine nodded, a little painfully. "Go on."

"Well, there's no accounting for some tastes, but I thought I knew Frank's. And I guess I did because it turned out he *wasn't* going with her. It was strictly business. He turned up one day and said to me, 'Baby, I'm leaving you. I'm taking that big fat trip into the hereafter. There's a nice piece of change in it for you, too.'"

Alice sighed and wiped her eyes. "That big idiot had sold his body! Rex had given him hereafter insurance and an annuity for me, and he was so damned proud of himself! Well, I talked myself blue in the face trying to get him to change his mind. No chance, he was going to eat pie in the sky. To his way of thinking his number was up anyhow, and the next hunt would do him. So off he went. He talked to me once from the Threshold."

"Is he still there?" Blaine asked, with a prickling sensation at the back of his neck.

"I haven't heard from him in over a year," Alice said, "so I guess he's gone on to the hereafter. The bastard!"

She cried for a few moments, then wiped her eyes with a tiny handkerchief and looked mournfully at Blaine. "I wasn't going to bother you. After all, it was Frank's body to sell and it's yours now. I don't have any claims on it or you. But I got so blue, so lonely."

"I can imagine," Blaine murmured, thinking that she was definitely not his type. Objectively speaking, she was pretty enough. Comely but overblown. Her features were well formed, bold, and vividly colored. Her hair, although obviously not a natural red, was shoulder length and of a smooth texture. She was the sort of woman he could picture, hands on hips, arguing with a policeman; hauling in a fishnet; dancing to a flamenco guitar; or herding goats on a mountain path with a full skirt swishing around ample hips, and peasant blouse distended.

But she was not in good taste.

However, he reminded himself, Frank Kranch had found her very much to *his* taste. And he was wearing Kranch's body.

"Most of our friends," Alice was saying, "were hunters in the China game. Oh, they dropped around sometimes after Frank left. But you know hunters, they've got just one thing on their minds."

"Is that a fact?" Blaine asked.

"Yes. And so I moved out of Peking and came back to New York, where I was born. And then one day I saw Frank—I mean you. I could have fainted on the spot. I mean I might have expected it and all, but still it gives you a turn to see your husband's body walking around."

"I should think so," Blaine said.

"So I followed you and all. I wasn't ever going to bother you or anything, but it just kept bothering me all the time. And I sort of got to wondering what kind of a man was...I mean, Frank was so—well, he and I got along very well, if you know what I mean."

"Certainly," Blaine said.

"I'll bet you think I'm terrible!"

"Not at all!" said Blaine. She looked him full in the face, her expression mournful and coquettish. Blaine felt Kranch's old scar throb.

But remember, he told himself, Kranch is gone. Everything is *Blaine* now, Blaine's will, Blaine's way, Blaine's taste...

Isn't it?

This problem must be settled, he thought, as he seized the willing Alice and kissed her with an unBlainelike fervor...

In the morning Alice made breakfast. Blaine sat, staring out the window, thinking dismal thoughts.

Last night had proven to him conclusively that Kranch was still king of the Kranch-Blaine body-mind. For last night he had been completely unlike himself. He had been fierce, violent, rough, angry and exultant. He had been all the things he had always deplored, had acted with an abandon that must have bordered on madness.

That was not Blaine. That was *Kranch,* the Body Triumphant.

Blaine had always prized delicacy, subtlety, and the grasp of nuance. Too much, perhaps. Yet those had been his virtues, the expressions of his own individual personality. With them, he was Thomas Blaine. Without them he was less than nothing—a shadow cast by the eternally triumphant Kranch.

Gloomily he contemplated the future. He would give up the struggle, become what his body demanded; a fighter, a brawler, a lusty vagabond. Perhaps in time he would grow used to it, even enjoy it...

"Breakfast's ready," Alice announced.

They ate in silence, and Alice mournfully fingered a bruise on her forearm. At last Blaine could stand it no longer.

"Look," he said, "I'm sorry."

"What for?"

"Everything."

She smiled wanly. "That's all right. It was my fault, really."

"I doubt that. Pass the butter, please," Blaine said.

She passed the butter. They ate in silence for a few minutes. Then Alice said, "I was very, very stupid."

"Why?"

"I guess I was chasing a dream," she said. "I thought I could find Frank all over again. I'm not really that way, Mr. Blaine. But I thought it would be like with Frank."

"And wasn't it?"

She shook her head. "No, of course not."

Blaine put down his coffee cup carefully. He said, "I suppose Kranch was rougher. I suppose he batted you from wall to wall. I suppose—"

"Oh, no!" she cried. "Never! Mr. Blaine, Frank was a hunter and he lived a hard life. But with me he was always a perfect gentleman. He had manners, Frank had."

"He had?"

"He certainly had! Frank was always gentle with me, Mr. Blaine. He was—delicate, if you know what I mean. Nice. Gentle. He was never, *never* rough. To tell the truth, he was the very opposite from you, Mr. Blaine."

"Uh," said Blaine.

"Not that there's anything wrong with you," she said with hasty kindness. "You *are* a little rough, but I guess it takes all kinds."

"I guess it does," Blaine said. "Yes, I guess it sure does."

They finished their breakfast in embarrassed silence. Alice, freed of her obsessive dream, left immediately afterwards, with no suggestion that they meet again. Blaine sat in his big chair, staring out the window, thinking.

So he wasn't like Kranch!

The sad truth was, he told himself, he had acted as he *imagined* Kranch would have acted in similar circumstances. It had been pure autosuggestion. Hysterically he had convinced himself that a strong, active, hearty outdoors man would necessarily treat a woman like a wrestling bear.

He had acted out a stereotype. He would feel even sillier if he weren't so relieved at regaining his threatened Blaineism.

He frowned as he remembered Alice's description of Marie: skinny, hard as nails, cold as fish. *More* stereotyping.

But under the circumstances, he could hardly blame Alice.

Chapter 24

A few days later, Blaine received word that a communication was waiting for him at the Spiritual Switchboard. He went there after work, and was sent to the booth he had used previously.

Melhill's amplified voice said, "Hello, Tom."

"Hello, Ray. I was wondering where you were."

"I'm still in the Threshold," Melhill told him, "but I won't be much longer. I gotta go on and see what the hereafter is like. It pulls at me. But I wanted to talk to you again, Tom. I think you should watch out for Marie Thorne."

"Now Ray—"

"I mean it. She's been spending all her time at Rex. I don't know what's going on there, they got the conference rooms shielded against psychic invasion. But something's brewing over you, and she's in the middle of it."

"I'll keep my eyes open," Blaine said.

"Tom, please take my advice. Get out of New York. Get out fast, while you still have a body and a mind to run it with."

"I'm staying," Blaine said.

"You stubborn bastard," Melhill said, with deep feeling. "What's the use of having a protective spirit if you don't ever take his advice?"

"I appreciate your help," Blaine said. "I really do. But tell me truthfully, how much better off would I be if I ran?"

"You might be able to stay alive a little longer."

"Only a little? Is it that bad?"

"Bad enough. Tom, remember not to trust *anybody*. I gotta go now."

"Will I speak to you again, Ray?"

"Maybe," Melhill said. "Maybe not. Good luck, kid."

The interview was ended. Blaine returned to his apartment.

The next day was Saturday. Blaine lounged in bed late, made himself breakfast and called Marie. She was out. He decided to spend the day relaxing and playing his sensory recordings.

That afternoon he had two callers.

The first was a gentle, hunchbacked old woman dressed in a dark, severe uniform. Across her army-style cap were the words, "Old Church."

"Sir," she said in a slightly wheezy voice, "I am soliciting contributions for the Old Church, an organization which seeks to promote faith in these dissolute and Godless times."

"Sorry," Blaine said, and started to close the door.

But the old woman must have had many doors closed on her. She wedged herself between door and jamb and continued talking.

"This, young sir, is the age of the Babylonian Beast, and the time of the soul's destruction. This is Satan's age, and the time of his seeming triumph. But be not deceived! The Lord Almighty has allowed this to come about for a trial and a testing, and a winnowing of grain from chaff. Beware the temptation! Beware the path of evil which lies splendid and glittering before you!"

Blaine gave her a dollar just to shut her up. The old woman thanked him but continued talking.

"Beware, young sir, that ultimate lure of Satan—the false heaven which men call the hereafter! For what better snare could Satan the Deceiver devise for the world of men than this, his greatest illusion! The illusion that hell is heaven! And men are deceived by the cunning deceit, and willingly go down into it!"

"Thank you," Blaine said, trying to shut the door.

"Remember my words!" the old woman cried, fixing him with a glassy blue eye. "The hereafter is evil! Beware the prophets of the hellish afterlife!"

"Thank you!" Blaine cried, and managed to close the door.

He relaxed in his armchair again and turned on the player. For nearly an hour he was absorbed in *Flight on Venus.* Then there was a knock on his door.

Blaine opened it, and saw a short, well-dressed, chubby-faced, earnest-looking young man.

"Mr. Thomas Blaine?" the man asked.

"That's me."

"Mr. Blaine, I am Charles Farrell, from the Hereafter Corporation. Might I speak to you? If is inconvenient now, perhaps we could make an appointment for some other—"

"Come in," Blaine said, opening the door wide for the prophet of the hellish afterlife.

Farrell was a mild, businesslike, soft-spoken prophet. His first move was to give Blaine a letter written on Hereafter, Inc. stationery, stating that Charles Farrell was a fully authorized representative of the Hereafter Corporation. Included in the letter was a meticulous description of Farrell, his signature, three stamped photographs and a set of fingerprints.

"And here are my identity proofs," Farrell said, opening his wallet and showing his heli license, library card, voter's registration certificate and government clearance card. On a separate piece of treated paper Farrell impressed the fingerprints of his right hand and gave them to Blaine for comparison with those on the letter.

"Is all this necessary?" Blaine asked.

"Absolutely," Farrell told him. "We've had some unhappy occurrences in the past. Unscrupulous operators frequently try to pass themselves off as Hereafter representatives among the gullible and the poor. They offer salvation at a cut rate, take what they can get and skip town. Too many people have been cheated out of everything they own, and get nothing in return. For the illegal operators, even when they represent some little fly-by-night salvation company, have none of the expensive equipment and trained technicians that are needed for this sort of thing."

"I didn't know," Blaine said. "Won't you sit down?"

Farrell took a chair. "The Better Business Bureaus are trying to do something about it. But the fly-by-nights move too fast to be easily caught. Only Hereafter, Inc. and two other companies with government-approved techniques are able to deliver what they promise—a life after death."

"What about the various mental disciplines?" Blaine asked.

"I was purposely excluding them," Farrell said. "They're a completely different category. If you have the patience and determination necessary for twenty years or so of concentrated study, more power to you. If you don't, then you need scientific aid and implementation. And that's where we come in."

"I'd like to hear about it," Blaine said.

Mr. Farrell settled himself more comfortably in his chair. "If you're like most people, you probably want to know what is life? What is death? What is a mind? Where is the interaction point between mind and body? Is the mind also soul? Is the soul also mind? Are they independent of each other, or interdependent, or intermixed? Or is there any such thing as a soul?" Farrell smiled. "Are those some of the questions you want me to answer?"

Blaine nodded. Farrell said, "Well, I can't. We simply don't know, haven't the slightest idea. As far as we're concerned those are religio-philosophical questions which Hereafter, Inc. has no intention of even *trying* to answer. We're interested in results, not speculation. Our orientation is medical. Our approach is pragmatic. We don't care how or why we get our results, or how strange they seem. *Do they work?* That's the only question we ask, and that's our basic position."

"I think you've made it clear," Blaine said.

"It's important for me to do so at the start. So let me make one more thing clear. Don't make the mistake of thinking that we are offering heaven."

"No?"

"Not at all! Heaven is a religious concept, and we have nothing to do with religion. Our hereafter is a survival of the *mind* after the body's death. That's all. We don't claim the hereafter is heaven any more than early scientists claimed that the bones of the first cavemen were the remains of Adam and Eve."

"An old woman called here earlier," Blaine said. "She told me that the hereafter is hell."

"She's a fanatic," Farrell said, grinning. "She follows me around. And for all I know, she's perfectly right."

"What *do* you know about the hereafter?"

"Not very much," Farrell told him. "All we know for sure is this: After the body's death, the mind moves to a region we call the Threshold, which exists between Earth and the hereafter. It is, we believe, a sort of preparatory state to the hereafter itself. Once the mind is there, it can move at will into the hereafter."

"But what is the hereafter like?"

"We don't know. We're fairly sure it's non-physical. Past that, everything is conjecture. Some think that the mind is the essence of the body, and therefore the essences of a man's worldly goods can be brought into the hereafter with him. It could be so. Others disagree. Some feel that the hereafter is a place where souls await their turn for rebirth on other planets as part of a vast reincarnation cycle. Perhaps that's true, too. Some feel that the hereafter is only the first stage of post-Earth existence, and that there are six others, increasingly difficult to attain, culminating in a sort of nirvana. Could be. It's been said that the hereafter is a vast, misty region where you wander alone, forever searching, never finding. I've read theories that prove people must be grouped in the hereafter according to family; others say you're grouped there according to race, or religion, or skin coloration, or social position. Some people, as you've observed, say it's hell itself you're entering. There are advocates of a theory of illusion, who claim that the mind vanishes completely when it leaves the Threshold. And there are people who accuse us at the corporation of faking all our effects. A recent learned work states that you'll find whatever you want in the hereafter—heaven, paradise, valhalla, green pastures, take your choice. A claim is made that the old gods rule in the hereafter—the gods of Haiti, Scandinavia or the Belgian Congo, depending on whose theory you're following. Naturally a counter-theory shows that there can't be any gods at all. I've seen an English book proving that English spirits rule the hereafter, and a Russian book claiming that the Russians rule, and several American books that prove the Americans rule. A book came out last year stating that the government of the hereafter is anarchy. A leading philosopher insists that competition is a law of nature, and must be so in the hereafter, too. And so on. You can take your pick of any of those theories, Mr. Blaine, or you can make up one of your own."

"What do you think?" Blaine asked.

"Me? I'm keeping an open mind," Farrell said. "When the time comes, I'll go there and find out."

"That's good enough for me," Blaine said. "Unfortunately, I won't have a chance. I don't have the kind of money you people charge."

"I know," Farrell said. "I checked into your finances before I called."

"Then why—"

"Every year," Farrell said, "a number of free hereafter grants are made, some by philanthropists, some by corporations and trusts, a few on a lottery basis. I am happy to say, Mr. Blaine, that you have been selected for one of these grants."

"Me?"

"Let me offer my congratulations," Farrell said. "You're a very lucky man."

"But who gave me the grant?"

"The Main-Farbenger Textile Corporation."

"I never heard of them.

"Well, they heard of you. The grant is in recognition of your trip here from the year 1958. Do you accept it?"

Blaine stared hard at the hereafter representative. Farrell seemed genuine enough; anyhow, his story could be checked at the Hereafter Building. Blaine had his suspicions of the splendid gift thrust so unexpectedly into his hands. But the thought of an assured life after death outweighed any possible doubts, thrust aside any possible fears. Caution was all very well; but not when the gates of the hereafter were opening before you.

"What do I have to do?" he asked.

"Simply accompany me to the Hereafter Building," Farrell said. "We can have the necessary work done in a few hours."

Survival! Life after death!

"All right," Blaine said. "I accept the grant. Let's go!"

They left Blaine's apartment at once.

Chapter 25

A helicab brought them directly to the Hereafter Building. Farrell led the way to the Admissions Office, and gave a photostatic copy of Blaine's grant to the woman in charge. Blaine made a set of fingerprints, and produced his Hunter's License for further identity. The woman checked all the data carefully against her master list of acceptances. Finally she was satisfied with its validity, and signed the admission papers.

Farrell then took Blaine to the Testing Room, wished him luck, and left him.

In the Testing Room, a squad of young technicians took over and ran Blaine through a gamut of examinations. Banks of calculators clicked and. rattled, and spewed forth yards of paper and showers of punched cards. Ominous machines bubbled and squeaked at him, glared with giant red eyes, winked and turned amber. Automatic pens squiggled across pieces of graph paper. And through it all, the technicians kept up a lively shop talk.

"Interesting beta reaction. Think we can fair that curve?"

"Sure, sure, just lower his drive coefficient."

"Hate to do that. It weakens the web."

"You don't have to weaken it *that* much. He'll still take the trauma."

"Maybe… What about this Henliger factor? It's off."

"That's because he's in a host body. It'll come around."

"That one didn't last week. The guy went up like a rocket."

"He was a little unstable to begin with."

Blaine said, "Hey! Is there any chance of this not working?"

The technicians turned as though seeing him for the first time.

"Every case is different, pal," a technician told him.

"Each one has to be worked out on an individual basis."

"It's just problems, problems all the time."

Blaine said, "I thought the treatment was all worked out. I heard it was infallible."

"Sure, that's what they tell the customers," one of the technicians said scornfully.

"That's advertising crap."

"Things go wrong here every day. We still got a long way to go."

Blaine said, "But can you tell if the treatment takes?"

"Of course. If it takes, you're still alive."

"If it doesn't you never walk out of here."

"It *usually* takes," a technician said consolingly. "On everybody but a K3."

"It's that damned K3 factor that throws us. Come on, Jamiesen, is he a K3 or not?"

"I'm not sure," Jamiesen said, hunched over a flashing instrument. "The testing machine is all screwed up again."

Blaine said, "What is a K3?"

"I wish *we* knew," Jamiesen said moodily. "All we know for certain, guys with a K3 factor can't survive after death."

"Not under any circumstances."

"Old Fitzroy thinks it's a built-in limiting factor that nature included so the species wouldn't run wild."

"But K3s don't transmit the factor to their children."

"There's still a chance it lies dormant and skips a few generations."

"Am I a K3?" Blaine asked, trying to keep his voice steady.

"Probably not," Jamiesen said easily. "It's sort of rare. Let me check."

Blaine waited while the technicians went over their data, and Jamiesen tried to determine from his faulty machine whether or not Blaine had a K3 factor.

After a while, Jamiesen looked up. "Well, I guess he's not K3. Though who knows, really? Anyhow, let's get on with it."

"What comes next?" Blaine asked.

A hypodermic bit deeply into his arm.

"Don't worry," a technician told him, "everything's going to be just fine."

"Are you *sure* I'm not K3?" Blaine asked. The technician nodded in a perfunctory manner. Blaine wanted to ask more questions, but a wave of dizziness overcame him. The technicians were lifting him, putting him on a white operating table.

When he recovered consciousness he was lying on a comfortable couch listening to soothing music. A nurse handed him a glass of sherry, and Mr. Farrell was standing by, beaming.

"Feel OK?" Farrell asked. "You should. Every thing went off perfectly."

"It did?"

"No possibility of error. Mr. Blaine, the hereafter is yours."

Blaine finished his sherry and stood up, a little shakily. "Life after death is mine? Whenever I die? Whatever I die of?"

"That's right. No matter how or when you die, your mind will survive after death. How do you feel?"

"I don't know," Blaine said.

It was only half an hour later, as he was returning to his apartment, that he began to react.

The hereafter was his!

He was filled with a sudden wild elation. Nothing mattered now, nothing whatsoever! He was immortal! He could be killed on the spot and yet live on!

He felt superbly drunk. Gaily he contemplated throwing himself under the wheels of a passing truck. What did it matter? Nothing could really hurt him! He could berserk now, slash merrily through the crowds. Why not? The only thing the flat-hats could really kill was his body!

The feeling was indescribable. Now, for the first time, Blaine realized what men had lived with before the discovery of the scientific hereafter. He remembered the heavy, sodden, constant, unconscious fear of death that subtly weighed every action and permeated every movement. The ancient enemy death, the shadow that crept down the corridors of a man's mind like some grisly tapeworm, the ghost that haunted nights and days, the croucher behind corners, the shape behind doors, the unseen guest at every banquet, the unidentified figure in every landscape, always present, always waiting—

No more.

For now a tremendous weight had been lifted from his mind. The fear of death was gone, intoxicatingly gone, and he felt light as air. Death, that ancient enemy, was defeated!

He returned to his apartment in a state of high euphoria. The telephone was ringing as he unlocked the door.

"Blaine speaking!"

"Tom!" It was Marie Thorne. "Where have you been? I've been trying to reach you all afternoon."

"I've been out, darling," Blaine said. "Where in the hell have you been?"

"At Rex," she said. "I've been trying to find out what they're up to. Now listen carefully, I have some important news for you."

"I've got some news for you, sweetheart," Blaine said.

"Listen to me! A man will call at your apartment today. He'll be a salesman from Hereafter, Inc., and he will offer you free hereafter insurance. Don't take it."

"Why not? Is he a fake?"

"No, he's perfectly genuine, and so is the offer. But you mustn't take it."

"I already did," Blaine said.

"You what?"

"He was here a few hours ago. I accepted it."

"Have they treated you yet?"

"Yes. Was that a fake?"

"No," Marie said, "of course it wasn't. Oh, Tom, when will you learn not to accept gifts from strangers? There was time for hereafter insurance later... Oh, Tom!"

"What's wrong?" Blaine asked. "It was a grant from the Main-Farbenger Textile Corporation."

"They are owned completely by the Rex Corporation," Marie told him.

"Oh... But so what?"

"Tom, the directors of Rex gave you that grant. They used Main-Farbenger as a front, but *Rex* gave you that grant! Can't you see what it means?"

"No. Will you please stop screaming and explain?"

"Tom, it's the Permitted Murder section of the Suicide Act. They're going to invoke it."

"What are you taking about?"

"I'm talking about the section of the Suicide Act that makes host-taking legal. Rex has guaranteed the survival of your mind after death, you've accepted it. Now they can legally take your body for any purpose they desire. They own it. They can *kill* your body, Tom!"

"Kill me?"

"Yes. And of course they're going to. The government is planning action against them for illegally transporting you from the past. If you're not around, there's no case. Now listen. You *must* get out of New York, then out of the country. Maybe they'll leave you alone then. I'll help. I think that you should—"

The telephone went dead.

Blaine clicked the receiver several times, but got no dial tone. Apparently the line had been cut.

The elation he had been filled with a few seconds ago drained out of him. The intoxicating sense of freedom from death vanished. How could he have contemplated berserking? He wanted to *live*. He wanted to live in the flesh, upon the Earth he knew and loved. Spiritual existence was fine, but he didn't want it yet. Not for a long time. He wanted to live among solid objects, breathe air, eat bread and drink water, feel flesh surrounding him, touch other flesh.

When would they try to kill him? Any time at all. His apartment was like a trap. Quickly Blaine scooped all his money into a pocket and hurried to the door. He opened it, and looked up and down the hall. It was empty.

He hurried out, ran down the corridor, and stopped.

A man had just come around the corner. The man was standing in the center of the hall. He was carrying a large projector, which was leveled at Blaine's stomach.

The man was Sammy Jones.

"Ah, Tom, Tom," Jones sighed. "Believe me, I'm damned sorry it's you. But business is business."

Blaine stood, frozen, as the projector lifted to level on his chest.

"Why you?" Blaine managed to ask.

"Who else?" Sammy Jones said. "Aren't I the best hunter in the Western Hemisphere, and probably Europe, too? Rex hired every one of us in the New York area. But with beam and projectile weapons this time. I'm sorry it's you, Tom."

"But I'm a hunter, too," Blaine said.

"You won't be the first that got gunned. It's the breaks of the game, lad. Don't flinch. I'll make it quick and clean."

"I don't want to die!" Blaine gasped.

"Why not?" Jones asked. "You've got your hereafter insurance."

"I was tricked! I want to live! Sammy, don't do it!"

Sammy Jones' face hardened. He took careful aim, then lowered the gun.

"I'm growing too soft-hearted for this game," Jones said. "All right, Tom, start moving. I guess every Quarry should have a little head start. Makes it more sporting. But I'm only giving you a little."

"Thanks, Sammy," Blaine said, and hurried down the hall.

"But ,Tom—watch your step if you really want to live. I'm telling you, there's more hunters than citizens in New York right now. And every means of transportation is guarded."

"Thanks," Blaine called, as he hurried down the stairs.

He was in the street, but he didn't know where to go. Still, he had no time for indecision. It was late afternoon, hours before darkness could help him. He picked a direction and began walking.

Almost instinctively, his steps were leading him toward the slums of the city.

Chapter 26

He walked past the rickety tenements and ancient apartment houses, past the cheap saloons and night clubs, hands thrust in his pockets, trying to think. He would have to come up with a plan. The hunters would get him in the next hour or two if he couldn't work out some plan, some way of getting out of New York.

Jones had told him that the transportation services were being watched. What hope had he, then? He was unarmed, defenseless—

Well, perhaps he could change that. With a gun in his hand, things would be a little different. In fact, things might be very different indeed. As Hull had pointed out, a hunter could legally shoot a Quarry; but if a Quarry shot a hunter he was liable for arrest and severe penalties.

If he did shoot a hunter, the police would have to arrest him! It would all get very involved, but it would save him from the immediate danger.

He walked until he came to a pawnshop. In the window was a glittering array of projectile and beam weapons, hunting rifles, knives and machetes. Blaine went in.

"I want a gun," he said to the moustached man behind the counter.

"A gun. So. And what kind of a gun?" the man asked.

"Have you got any beamers?"

The man nodded and went to a drawer. He took out a gleaming handgun with a bright copper finish.

"Now this," he said, "is a special buy. It's a genuine Sailes-Byrn needlebeam, used for hunting big Venusian game. At five hundred yards you can cut through anything that walks, crawls or flies. On the side is the aperture selector. You can fan wide for close-range work, or extend to a needle point for distance shooting."

"Fine, fine," Blaine said, pulling bills from his pocket.

"This button here," the pawnbroker said, "controls length of blast. Set as is, you get a standard fractional jolt. One click extends time to a quarter second. Put it on automatic and it'll cut like a scythe. It has a power supply of over four hours, and there's more than three hours still left in the original pack. What's more, you can use this weapon in your home workshop. With a special mounting and a baffle to cut down the power, you can slice plastic with this better than with a saw. A different baffle converts it into a blowtorch. The baffles can be purchased—"

"I'll buy it," Blaine broke in.

The pawnbroker nodded. "May I see your permit, please?"

Blaine took out his Hunter's License and showed it to the man. The pawnbroker nodded, and, with maddening slowness, filled out a receipt.

"Shall I wrap it?"

"Don't bother. I'll take it as is."

The pawnbroker said. "That'll be seventy-five dollars." As Blaine pushed the money across the counter, the pawnbroker consulted a list on the wall behind him.

"Hold it!" he said suddenly.

"Eh?"

"I can't sell you that weapon."

"Why not?" Blaine asked. "You saw my Hunter's License."

"But you didn't tell me you were a registered Quarry. You know a Quarry can't have weapons. Your name was flashed here half an hour ago. You can't buy a legal weapon anywhere in New York, Mr. Blaine."

The pawnbroker pushed the bills back across the counter. Blaine grabbed for the needlebeam. The pawnbroker scooped it up first and leveled it at him.

"I ought to save them the trouble," he said. "You've got your damned hereafter. What else do you want?"

Blaine stood perfectly still. The pawnbroker lowered the gun.

"But that's not my job," he said. "The hunters will get you soon enough."

He reached under the counter and pressed a button. Blaine turned and ran out of the store. It was growing dark. But his location had been revealed. The hunters would be closing in now.

He thought he heard someone calling his name. He pushed through the crowds, not looking back, trying to think of something to do. He couldn't die like this, could he? He couldn't have come 152 years through time to be shot before a million people! It just wasn't fair!

He noticed a man following close behind him, grinning. It was Theseus, gun out, waiting for a clear shot.

Blaine put on a burst of speed, dodged through the crowds and turned quickly into a side street. He sprinted down it, then came to a sudden stop.

At the far end of the street, silhouetted against the light, a man was standing. The man had one hand on his hip, the other raised in a shooting position. Blaine hesitated, and glanced back at Theseus.

The little hunter fired, scorching Blaine's sleeve. Blaine ran toward an open door, which was suddenly slammed in his face. A second shot charred his coat.

With dreamlike clarity he watched the hunters advance, Theseus close behind him, the other hunter in the distance, blocking the way out. Blaine ran on leaden feet, toward the more distant man, over manhole covers and subway gratings, past shuttered stores and locked buildings.

"Back off, Theseus!" the hunter called. "I got him!"

"Take him, Hendrick!" Theseus called back, and flattened himself against a wall, out of the way of the blast.

The gunman, fifty feet away, took aim and fired. Blaine fell flat and the beam missed him. He rolled, trying to make the inadequate shelter of a doorway. The beam probed after him, scoring the concrete and turning the puddles of sewer water into steam.

Then a subway grating gave way beneath him.

As he fell, he knew that the grating must have been weakened by the lancing beam. Blind luck! But he had to land on his feet. He had to stay conscious, drag himself away from the opening, use his luck. If he went unconscious, his body would be lying in full view of the opening, an easy target for hunters standing on the edge.

He tried to twist in mid-air, too late. He landed heavily on his shoulders, and his head slammed against an iron stanchion. But the need to stay conscious was so great that he pulled himself to his feet.

He had to drag himself out of the way, deep into the subway passage, far enough so they couldn't find him.

But even the first step was too much. Sickeningly, his legs buckled under him. He fell on his face, rolled over and stared at the gaping hole above him.

Then he passed out.

PART FOUR

Chapter 27

When he revived, Blaine decided that he didn't like the hereafter. It was dark, lumpy, and it smelled of oil and slime. Also, his head ached, and his back felt as though it had been broken in three places.

Could a spirit ache? Blaine moved, and discovered that he still had a body. As a matter of fact, he felt all body. Apparently he wasn't in the hereafter.

"Just rest a minute," a voice said.

"Who is it?" Blaine asked into the impenetrable darkness.

"Smith."

"Oh. You." Blaine sat up and held his throbbing head. "How did you do it, Smith?"

"I nearly didn't," the zombie told him. "As soon as you were declared Quarry, I came for you. Some of my friends down here volunteered to help, but you were moving too fast. I shouted to you when you came out of the pawnshop."

"I thought I heard a voice," Blaine said.

"If you'd turned around, we could have taken you in there and then. But you didn't so we followed. A few times we opened subway grates and manhole covers for you, but it was hard to gauge it right. We were a little late each time."

"But not the last time," Blaine said.

"At last I had to open a grate right under you. I'm sorry you hit your head."

"Where am I?"

"I pulled you out of the main line," Smith said. "You're in a side passageway. The hunters can't find you here."

Blaine once again could find no adequate words for thanking Smith. And Smith once again wanted no thanks.

"I'm not doing it for you, Blaine. It's for me. I need you."

"Have you found out why yet?"

"Not yet," Smith said.

Blaine's eyes, adjusting to the gloom, could make out the outline of the zombie's head and shoulders. "What now?" he asked.

"Now you're safe. We can bring you underground as far as New Jersey. From there you're on your own. But I don't think you should have much trouble then."

"What are we waiting for now?"

"Mr. Kean. I need his permission to take you through the passageways."

They waited. In a few minutes, Blaine was able to make out Mr. Kean's thin shape, leaning on the big Negro's arm, coming toward him.

"I'm sorry about your troubles," Kean said, sitting down beside Blaine. "It's a great pity."

"Mr. Kean," Smith said, "if I could just be allowed to take him through the old Holland Tunnel, into New Jersey—"

"I'm truly sorry," Kean said, "but I cannot allow it."

Blaine looked around and saw that he was surrounded by a dozen ragged zombies.

"I've spoken to the hunters," Kean said, "and I have given them my guarantee that you will be back on the surface streets within half an hour. You must leave now, Blaine."

"But why?"

"We simply can't afford to help you," Kean said. "I was taking an unusual risk the first time, allowing you to defile Reilly's tomb. But I did it for Smith, because his destiny seems linked with yours in some way. And Smith is one of my people. But this is too much. You know we are allowed to live underground upon sufferance only."

"I know," Blaine said.

"Smith should have considered the consequences. When he opened that grating for you, the hunters poured in. They didn't find you, but they knew you were down here somewhere. So they searched, Blaine, they searched! Dozens of them, exploring our passageways, pushing our people around, threatening, shouting, talking on their little radios. Reporters came too, and even idle spectators. Some of the younger hunters became nervous and started shooting at the zombies."

"I'm very sorry about that," Blaine said.

"It wasn't your fault. But Smith should have known better. The world of the underground is not a sovereign kingdom. We exist on sufferance only, on a toleration which might be wiped out at any time. So I spoke to the hunters and the reporters."

"What did you tell them?" Blaine asked.

"I told them that a faulty grate had given way beneath you. I said you had fallen in by accident and had crawled into hiding. I assured them that no zombie had been involved in this; that we found you and would place you back on the surface streets within half an hour. They accepted my word and left. I wish I could have done otherwise."

"I don't blame you," Blaine said, getting slowly to his feet.

"I didn't specify where you would emerge," Kean said. "At the very least, you'll have a better chance than before. I wish I could do more, but I cannot allow the underground to become a stage for hunts. We must stay neutral, annoy no one, frighten no one. Only in that way will we survive until an age of understanding is reached."

"Where am I going to come out?" Blaine asked.

"I have chosen an unused subway exit at West 79th Street," Mr. Kean said. "You should have a good chance from there. And I have done one more thing which I probably shouldn't have done."

"What's that?"

"I have contacted a friend of yours, who will be waiting at the exit. But please don't tell anyone about it. Let's hurry now."

Mr. Kean led the procession through the winding underground maze, and Blaine brought up the rear, his headache slowly subsiding. Soon they stopped beside a concrete staircase.

"Here is the exit," Kean said. "Good luck, Blaine."

"Thanks," Blaine said. "And Smith—thanks."

"I've tried my best for you," Smith said. "If you die, I'll probably die. If you live, I'll keep on trying to remember."

"And if you do remember?"

"Then I'll come and visit you," Smith said.

Blaine nodded and walked up the staircase.

It was full night outside, and 79th Street seemed deserted. Blaine stood beside the exit, looking around, wondering what to do.

"Blaine!"

Someone was calling him. But it was not Marie, as he had expected. It was a man's voice, someone he knew—Sammy Jones, perhaps, or Theseus.

He turned quickly back to the subway exit. It was closed and fastened securely.

Chapter 28

"Tom, Tom, It's me!"

"Ray?"

"Of course! Keep your voice down. There's hunters not far away. Wait now."

Blaine waited, crouched beside the barred subway exit, peering around. He could see no sign of Melhill. There was no ectoplasmic vapor, nothing except a whispering voice.

"OK," Melhill said. "Walk west now. Quickly."

Blaine walked, sensing Melhill's invisible presence hovering near him. He said, "Ray, how come?"

"It's about time I was some help," Melhill said. "That old Kean contacted your girl friend and she got in touch with me through the Spiritual Switchboard. Wait! Stop right here."

Blaine ducked back against the corner of a building. A heli cruised slowly by at housetop level.

"Hunters," Melhill said. "There's a field day on you, kid. Reward posted. Even a reward for information leading to. Tom, I told Marie I'd try to help. Don't know how long I can. Drains me. It's hereafter for me after this."

"Ray, I don't know how—"

"Cut it out. Look, Tom, I can't talk much. Marie has fixed a deal with some friends of hers. They've got a plan, if I can get you to them. Stop!"

Blaine stopped and found shelter behind a mailbox. Long seconds passed. Then three hunters hurried by, sidearms ready. After they turned a corner, Blaine was able to start walking again.

"Some eyes you have," he said to Melhill.

"The vision's pretty good up here," Melhill said. "Cross this street fast."

Blaine sprinted across. For the next fifteen minutes, at Melhill's instructions, he wound in and out of streets, advancing and retreating across the battleground of the city.

"This is it," Melhill said at last. "That door over there, number 341. You made it! I'll see you, Tom. Watch—"

At that moment, two men rounded a corner, stopped, and stared hard at Blaine. One said, "Hey, that's the guy!"

"What guy?"

"The guy they got the reward out for. Hey, *you!*"

They ran forward. Blaine, his fists swinging, quickly chopped the first man into unconsciousness. He whirled, looking for the second, but Melhill had the situation well in control.

The second man had his hands over his head, trying to guard himself. A garbage can cover, levitating mysteriously, was clanging angrily around his ears. Blaine stepped forward and finished the job.

"Damn good," Melhill said, his voice very weak. "Always wanted to try ghosting. But it drains… Luck, Tom!"

"Ray!" Blaine waited, but there was no answer, and the sense of Melhill's presence was gone.

Blaine waited no longer. He went to number 341, opened the door and stepped in.

He was in a narrow hallway. At the end of it was a door. Blaine knocked.

"Come in," he was told.

He opened the door and walked into a small, dingy, heavily curtained room.

Blaine had thought he was proof against any further surprises. But it gave him a start all the same to see, grinning at him, Carl Orc, the body snatcher. And sitting beside him, also grinning, was Joe, the little Transplant peddler.

Chapter 29

Blaine made an automatic move backwards towards the door, but Orc beckoned him in. The body snatcher was unchanged, still very tall and thin, his tanned face long and mournful, his eyes narrow, direct and honest. His clothes still hung awkwardly on him, as though he were more used to levis than to tailored slacks.

"We were expecting you," Orc said. "Of course you remember Joe."

Blaine nodded, remembering very well the furtive-eyed little man who had distracted his attention so that Orc could drug his drink.

"Happy to see you again," Joe said.

"I'll bet," Blaine said, not moving from the door.

"Come in and sit down," Orc said. "We ain't planning to eat you, Tom. Truly not. Let's let bygones be bygones."

"You tried to kill me."

"That was business," Orc said in his straightforward fashion. "We're on the same side now."

"How can I be sure of that?"

"No man," Orc stated, "has ever questioned my honesty. Not when I'm really being honest, which I am now. Miss Thorne hired us to get you safe out of the country, and we intend to do same. Sit down and let's discuss it. Are you hungry?"

Reluctantly Blaine sat down. There were sandwiches on a table, and a bottle of red wine. He realized that he hadn't eaten all day. He started wolfing down sandwiches while Orc lighted a thin brown cigar, and Joe appeared to be dozing.

"You know," Orc said, exhaling blue smoke, "I very nearly didn't take this job. Not that the money wasn't right; I think Miss Thorne was more than generous. But Tom, this is one of the biggest manhunts our fair city's seen for a while. Ever see anything like it, Joe?"

"Never," Joe said, shaking his head rapidly. "Town's covered like fly-paper."

"Rex really wants you," Orc said. "They've set their little hearts on nailing your corpus where they can see it. Makes a man nervous, bucking an organization that size. But it's a challenge, a real man-sized challenge."

"Carl likes a big challenge," Joe said.

"I admit that," Orc said. "Particularly if there's a big profit to be made from it."

"But where can I go?" Blaine asked. "Where won't Rex find me?"

"Just about nowhere," Orc said sadly.

"Off the Earth? Mars? Venus?"

"Even worse. The planets have just a few towns and small cities. Everybody knows everybody else. The news would be all over in a week. Also, you wouldn't fit in. Aside from the Chinese on Mars, the planets are still populated mostly with scientific types and their families, and a few youth-training programs. You wouldn't like it."

"Where, then?"

"That's what I asked Miss Thorne," Orc said. "We discussed several possibilities. First, there's a zombie-making operation. I could perform it. Rex would never search for you underground."

"I'd rather die," Blaine said.

"I would too," Orc agreed. "So we ruled it out. We thought about finding you a little farm in the Atlantic Abyss. Pretty lonely territory out there. But it takes a special mentality to live undersea and like it, and we didn't figure you had it. You'd probably crack up. So, after due consideration, we decided the best place for you was in the Marquesas."

"The what?"

"The Marquesas. They're a scattered group of small islands, originally Polynesian, out towards the middle of the Pacific Ocean. They're not too far from Tahiti."

"The South Seas," Blaine said.

"Right. We figured you should feel more at home there than anywhere else on Earth. It's just like the 20th century, I'm told. And even more important, Rex might leave you alone."

"Why would they?"

"For obvious reasons, Tom. Why do they want to kill you in the first place? Because they snatched you illegally from the past and they're worried about what the government's going to do about it. But your going to the Marquesas removes you from the jurisdiction of the U.S. government. Without you, there's no case. And your going so far is a sign to Rex of your good faith. It certainly isn't the act of a man who's going to blab to Uncle Sam. Also, the Marquesas are an independent little nation since the French gave them up, so Rex would have to get special permission to hunt you there. On the whole, it *should* be just too much trouble for everyone concerned. The U.S. government will undoubtedly drop the matter, and I think Rex will leave you alone."

"Is that certain?" Blaine asked.

"Of course not. It's conjecture. But it's reasonable."

"Couldn't we make a deal with Rex beforehand?"

Orc shook his head. "In order to bargain, Tom, you have to have something to bargain with. As long as you're in New York, it's easier and safer for them to kill you."

"I guess you're right," Blaine said. "How are you going to get me out?"

Orc and Joe looked at each other uncomfortably. Orc said, "Well, that was our big problem. There just didn't seem to be any way of getting you out alive."

"Heli or jet?"

"They have to stop at the air tolls, and hunters are waiting at all of them. Surface vehicle is equally out of the question."

"Disguise?"

"Maybe it would have worked during the first hour of the hunt. Now it's impossible, even if we could get you a complete plastic surgery job. By now the hunters are equipped with identity scanners. They'd see through you in a moment."

"Then there's no way out?" Blaine asked.

Orc and Joe exchanged another uneasy glance. "There is," Orc said. "Just one way. But you probably won't like it."

"I like to stay alive. What is it?"

Orc paused and lighted another cigar. "We plan to quick-freeze you to near absolute zero, like for spaceship travel. Then we'll ship your carcass out in a crate of frozen beef. Your body will be in the center of the load, so most likely it won't be detected."

"Sounds risky," Blaine said.

"Not too risky," Orc said.

Blaine frowned, sensing something wrong. "I'll be unconscious through it, won't I?"

After a long pause, Orc said, "No."

"I won't?"

"It can't be done that way," Orc told him. "The fact is, you and your body will have to separate. That's the part I'm afraid you won't like."

"What in hell are you talking about?" Blaine asked, getting to his feet.

"Take it easy," Orc said. "Sit down, smoke a cigarette, have some more wine. It's like this, Tom. We can't ship out a quick-frozen body with a mind in it. The hunters are waiting for something like that. Can you imagine what happens when they run a quick scan over that shipment of beef and detect a dormant mind in it? Up goes the kite! *Adieu la musique!* I'm not trying to con you, Tom. It just can't be done like that."

"Then what happens to my mind?" Blaine asked, sitting down again.

"That," Orc said, "is where Joe comes in. Tell him, Joe."

Joe nodded rapidly. "Transplant, my friend, is the answer."

"Transplant?"

"I told you about it," Joe said, "on that inauspicious evening when we first met. Remember? Transplant, the great pastime, the game any number can play, the jolt for jaded minds, the tonic for tired bodies. We've got a worldwide network of Transplantees, Mr. Blaine. Folks who like to switch around, men and women who get tired of wearing the same old body. We're going to key you into the organization."

"You're going to ship my *mind* across the country?" Blaine asked.

"That's it! From body to body," Joe told him. "Believe me, it's instructive as well as entertaining."

Blaine got to his feet so quickly that he knocked over his chair. "Like hell!" he said. "I told you then and I'm telling you now, I'm not playing your lousy little game. I'll take my chances on the street."

He started toward the door.

Joe said, "I know it's a little frightening, but—"

"No!"

Orc shouted, "Damn it, Blaine, will you at least let the man speak?"

"All right," Blaine said. "Speak."

Joe poured himself half a glass of wine and threw it down. He said, "Mr. Blaine, it's going to be difficult explaining this to you, a guy from the past. But try to understand what I'm saying."

Blaine nodded warily.

"Now then. Transplant is used as a sex game these days, and that's how I peddle it. Why? Because people are ignorant of its better uses; and because a reactionary government insists on banning it. But Transplant is a lot more than a game. It's an entire new way of life! And whether you or the government like it or not, Transplant represents the world of the future."

The little pusher's eyes glowed. Blaine sat down again.

"There are two basic elements in human affairs," Joe said sententiously. "One of them is man's eternal struggle for freedom: Freedom of worship, freedom of press and assembly, freedom to select government—freedom!

And the other basic element in human affairs is the efforts of government to withhold freedom from the people."

Blaine considered this a somewhat simplified view of human affairs. But he continued listening.

"Government," Joe said, "withholds freedom for many reasons. For security, for personal profit, for power, or because they feel the people are unready for it. But whatever the reason, the basic facts remain: Man strives for freedom, and government strives to withhold freedom. Transplant is simply one more in a long series of the freedoms that man has aspired to, and that his government feels are not good for him."

"Sexual freedom?" Blaine asked mockingly.

"No!" Joe cried. "Not that there's anything wrong with sexual freedom. But Transplant isn't primarily that. Sure, that's how we're pushing it—for propaganda purposes. Because people don't want abstract ideas, Mr. Blaine, and they don't go for cold theory. They want to know what a freedom will *do* for them. We show them a small part of it, and they learn a lot more themselves."

"What will Transplant do?" Blaine asked.

"Transplant," Joe said fervently, "gives man the ability to transcend the limits imposed by his heredity and his environment!"

"Huh?"

"Yes! Transplant lets you exchange knowledge, bodies, talents and skills with anyone who wishes to exchange with you. And plenty do. Most men don't want to perform a single set of skills all their life, no matter how satisfying those skills are. Man is too restless a creature. Musicians want to be engineers, advertising men want to be hunters, sailors want to be writers. But there usually isn't time to acquire and exploit more than one set of skills in a lifetime. And even if there were time, the blind factor of talent is an insurmountable stumbling block. With Transplant, you can get the inborn talents, the skills, the knowledge that you want. Think about it, Mr. Blaine. Why should a man be forced to live out his lifetime in a body he had no part in selecting? It's like telling him he must live with the diseases he's inherited, and mustn't try to cure them. Man must have the freedom to choose the body and talents best suited to his personality needs."

"If your plan went through," Blaine said, "you'd simply have a bunch of neurotics changing bodies every day."

"The same general argument was raised against the passage of every freedom," Joe said, his eyes glittering. "Throughout history it was argued that man didn't have the sense to choose his own religion, or that women didn't have the intelligence to use the vote, or that people couldn't be allowed to elect their own representatives because of the stupid choices they'd make. And of course there are plenty of neurotics around, people who'd louse up heaven itself. But you have a much greater number of people who'd use their freedoms well."

Joe lowered his voice to a persuasive whisper. "You must realize, Mr. Blaine, that a man is not his body, for he receives his body accidentally. He is not his skills, for those are frequently born of necessity. He is not his talents, which are produced by heredity and by early environmental factors. He is not the sicknesses to which he may be predisposed, and he is not the environment that shapes him. A man *contains* all these things, but he is greater than their total. He has the power to change his environment, cure his diseases, advance his skills—and, at last, to choose his body and talents! *That* is the next freedom, Mr. Blaine! It's historically inevitable, whether you or I or the government like it or not. For man must have every possible freedom!"

Joe finished his fierce and somewhat incoherent oration red-faced and out of breath. Blaine stared at the little man with new respect. He was looking, he realized, at a genuine revolutionary of the year 2110.

Orc said, "He's got a point, Tom. Transplant is legal in Sweden and Ceylon, and it doesn't seem to have hurt the moral fiber much."

"In time," Joe said, pouring himself a glass of wine, "the whole world will go Transplant. It's inevitable."

"Maybe," Orc said. "Or maybe they'll invent some new freedom to take its place. Anyhow, Tom, you can see that Transplant has some moral justifications. And it's the only way of saving that body of yours. What do you say?"

"Are you a revolutionary, too?" Blaine asked.

Orc grinned. "Could be. I guess I'm like the blockade runners during the American Civil War, or the guys who sold guns to Central American revolutionaries. They worked for a profit, but they weren't against social change."

"Well, well," Blaine said sardonically. "And up to now I thought you were just a common criminal."

"Skip it," Orc said pleasantly. "Are you willing to try?"

"Certainly. I'm overwhelmed," Blaine said. "I never thought I'd find myself in the advance guard of a social revolution."

Orc smiled and said, "Good. Hope it works out for you, Tom. Roll up your sleeve. We'd better get started."

Blaine rolled up his left sleeve while Orc took a hypodermic from a drawer.

"This is just to knock you out," Orc explained. "The Yoga Machine is in the next room. It does the real work. When you come to, you'll be a guest in someone else's mind, and your body will be travelling cross country in deep freeze. They'll be brought together as soon as it's safe."

"How many minds will I occupy?" Blaine asked. "And for how long?"

"I don't know how many we'll have to use. As for how long in each, a few seconds, minutes, maybe half an hour. We'll move you along as fast as we can. This isn't a full Transplant, you know. You won't be taking over the body. You'll just be occupying a small portion of its consciousness, as an observer. So stay quiet and act natural. Got that?"

Blaine nodded. "But how does this Yoga Machine work?"

"It works like Yoga," Orc said. "The machine simply does what you could do yourself if you were thoroughly trained in Yoga exercises. It relaxes every muscle and nerve in your body, focuses and calms your mind, helps build up your concentration. When you've reached potential, you're ready to make an astral projection. The machine does that for you, too. It helps you release your hold on the body, which a Yoga adept could do without mechanical assistance. It projects you to the person we've selected, who yields room. Attraction takes care of the rest. You slip in like a stranded fish going back into water."

"Sounds risky," Blaine said. "Suppose I can't get in?"

"Man, you can't *help* but get in! Look, you've heard of demonic possession, haven't you? Guys under the control of so-called demons? The idea runs through most of the world's folklore. Some of the possessed were schizophrenic, of course, and some were downright frauds. But there were a lot of cases of real spiritual invasion, minds taken over by others who had learned the trick of breaking out of their own body and casting into another. The invaders took over with no mechanical help, and against an all-out battle on the part of their victims. In your case you've got the Yoga Machine, and the people are willing to have you in. So why worry?"

"All right," Blaine said. "What are the Marquesas like?"

"Beautiful," Orc said, sliding the needle into Blaine's arm. "You'll like it there."

Blaine drifted slowly into unconsciousness, thinking of palm trees, of white surf breaking against coral reef, and of dark-eyed maidens worshipping a god of stone.

Chapter 30

There was no sense of awakening, no feeling of transition. Abruptly, like a brilliantly colored slide projected upon a white screen, he was conscious. Suddenly, like a marionette jerked into violent life, he was acting and moving.

He was not completely Thomas Blaine. He was Edgar Dyersen as well. Or he was Blaine within Dyersen, an integral part of Dyersen's body, a segment of Dyersen's mind, viewing the world through Dyersen's rheumy eyes, thinking Dyersen's thoughts, experiencing all the shadowy half-conscious fragments of Dyersen's memories, hopes, fears and desires. And yet he was still Blaine.

Dyersen-Blaine came out of the ploughed field and rested against his wooden fence. He was a farmer, an old-fashioned South Jersey truck farmer, with a minimum of machines which he distrusted anyhow. He was close to seventy and in damn good health. There was still a touch of arthritis in his joints, which the smart young medico in the village had mostly fixed; and his back sometimes gave him trouble before rain. But he considered himself healthy, healthier than most, and good for another twenty years.

Dyersen-Blaine started toward his cottage. His gray workshirt was drenched in acrid sweat, and sweat stained his shapeless levis.

In the distance he heard a dog barking and saw, blurrily, a yellow and brown shape come bounding toward him. (Eyeglasses? No thank you. Doing pretty well with what I got.)

"Hey, Champ! Hey there, boy!"

The dog ran a circle around him, then trotted along beside him. He had something gray in his jaws, a rat or perhaps a piece of meat. Dyersen-Blaine couldn't quite make it out.

He bent down to pat Champ's head...

Again there was no sense of transition or of the passage of time. A new slide was simply projected onto the screen, and a new marionette was jerked into life.

Now he was Thompson-Blaine, nineteen years old, lying on his back half dozing on the rough planks of a sailing skiff, the mainsheet and tiller held loosely in one brown hand. To starboard lay the low Eastern Shore, and to his port he could see a bit of Baltimore Harbor. The skiff moved easily on the light summer breeze, and water gurgled merrily beneath the forefoot.

Thompson-Blaine rearranged his lanky, tanned body on the planks, squirming around until he had succeeded in propping his feet against the mast. He had been home just a week, after a two-year work and study program on Mars. It had sure been interesting, especially the archaeology and speleology. The sand-farming had gotten dull sometimes, but he had enjoyed driving the harvesting machines.

Now he was home for a two-year accelerated college course. Then he was supposed to return to Mars as a farm manager. That's the way his scholarship read. But they couldn't make him go back if he didn't want to.

Maybe he would. And maybe not.

The girls on Mars were such dedicated types. Tough, capable, and always a little bossy. When he went back—*if* he went back—he'd bring his own wife, not look for one there. Of course there had been Marcia, and she'd really been something. But her whole kibbutz had moved to the South Polar Gap, and she hadn't answered his last three letters. Maybe she hadn't been so much, anyhow.

"Hey, Sandy!"

Thompson-Blaine looked up and saw Eddie Duelitle, sailing his Thistle, waving at him. Languidly Thompson-Blaine waved back. Eddie was only seventeen, had never been off Earth, and wanted to be a spaceliner captain. Huh! Fat chance!

The sun was dipping toward the horizon, and Thompson-Blaine was glad to see it go down. He had a date tonight with Jennifer Hunt. They were going dancing at Starsling in Baltimore, and Dad was letting him use the heli. Man, how Jennifer had grown in two years! And she had a way of looking at a guy, sort of coy and bold at the same time. No telling what might happen after the dance, in the back seat of the heli. Maybe nothing. But maybe, maybe...

Thompson-Blaine sat up and put the tiller over. The skiff came into the wind and tacked over. It was time to return to the yacht basin, then home for dinner, then...

The blacksnake whip flicked across his back.

"Get working there, you!"

Piggot-Blaine redoubled his efforts, lifting the heavy pick high in the air and swinging it down into the dusty roadbed. The guard stood nearby, shotgun under his left arm, whip in his right, its lash trailing in the dust. Piggot-Blaine knew every line and pore of that guard's thin, stupid face, knew the downward twist of the tight little mouth, knew the squint of the faded eyes just like he knew his own face.

Just wait, buzzard meat, he silently told the guard. Your time's a-coming. Just wait, wait just a bit.

The guard moved away, walking slowly up and down the line of prisoners laboring under the white Mississippi sun. Piggot-Blaine tried to spit, but couldn't work up enough saliva. He thought, you talk about your fine modern world? Talk about your big old spaceships, your automatic farms, your big fine fat old hereafter? Think that's how it is? Then ask 'em how they build the roads in Quilleg County, Northern Mississippi. They won't tell you, so you better look for yourself and find out. Cause that's the kind of world it *really* is!

Arny, working in front of him, whispered, "You ready, Otis? You ready for it?"

"I'm a-ready," Piggot-Blaine whispered, his broad fingers clenching and unclenching on the pick's plastic handle. "I'm *past* ready, Arny."

"In a second, then. Watch Jeff."

Piggot-Blaine's hairy chest swelled expectantly. He brushed lank brown hair from his eyes and watched Jeff, five men ahead on the chain. Piggot-Blaine waited, his shoulders aching from sunburn. There were callused scars on his ankles from the hoofcuffs, and old seams on his back from earlier whippings. He had a raging thirst in his gut. But no dipperful of water could ever cut that thirst, nothing could, that crazy thirst that brought him in here after he'd dismembered Gainsville's single saloon and killed that stinking old Indian.

Jeff's hand moved. The chained line of prisoners sprang forward. Piggot-Blaine jumped toward the thin-faced guard, his pick swung high, as the guard dropped his whip and fumbled to bring up the shotgun.

"Buzzard meat!" Piggot-Blaine screamed, and brought the pick down fair in the guard's forehead.

"Get the keys!"

Piggot-Blaine grabbed the keys from the dead guard's belt. He heard a shotgun go off, heard a high scream of agony. Anxiously he looked up…

Ramirez-Blaine was piloting his heli above the flat Texas plains, heading for El Paso. He was a serious young man and he paid strict attention to his work, coaxing the last knot of speed out of the old heli so he could reach El Paso before Johnson's Hardware Store closed.

He handled the balky rattletrap with care, and only an occasional thought came through his concentration, quick thoughts about the altitude and compass readings, a dance in Guanajuato next week, the price of hides in Ciudad Juárez.

The plain was mottled green and yellow below him. He glanced at his watch, then at the airspeed indicator.

Yes, Ramirez-Blaine thought, he *would* make El Paso before the store closed! He might even have time for a little…

Tyler-Blaine wiped his mouth on his sleeve and sopped up the last of the grease gravy on a piece of corn bread. He belched, pushed his chair back from the kitchen table and stood up. With elaborate unconcern he took a cracked bowl from the pantry and filled it with scraps of pork, a few greens, and a big piece of corn bread.

"Ed," his wife said, "what are you doing?"

He glanced at her. She was gaunt, tangle-haired, and faded past her years. He looked away, not answering.

"Ed! Tell me, Ed!"

Tyler-Blaine looked at her in annoyance, feeling his ulcer stir at the sound of that sharp, worried voice. Sharpest voice in all California, he told himself, and he'd married it. Sharp voice, sharp nose, sharp elbows and knees, breastless and barren to boot. Legs to support a body, but not for a second's delight. A belly for filling, not for touching. Of all the girls in California he'd doubtless picked the sorriest, just like the damn fool his Uncle Rafe always said he was.

"Where you taking that bowl of food?" she asked.

"Out to feed the dog," Tyler-Blaine said, moving toward the door.

"We ain't *got* no dog! Oh Ed, don't do it, not tonight!"

"I'm doin' it," he said, glad of her discomfort.

"Please, not tonight. Let him shift for himself somewhere else. Ed, listen to me! What if the town found out?"

"It's past sundown," Tyler-Blaine said, standing beside the door with his bowl of food.

"People spy," she said. "Ed, if they find out they'll lynch us, you know they will."

"You'd look mighty spry from the end of a rope," Tyler-Blaine remarked, opening the door.

"You do it just to spite me!" she cried.

He closed the door behind him. Outside, it was deep twilight. Tyler-Blaine stood in his yard near the unused chicken coop, looking around. The only house near his was the Flannagans', a hundred yards away. But they minded their own business. He waited to make sure none of the town kids were snooping around. Then he walked forward, carefully holding the bowl of food.

He reached the edge of the scraggly woods and set the bowl down. "It's all right," he called softly. "Come out, Uncle Rafe."

A man crawled out of the woods on all fours. His face was leaden-white, his lips bloodless, his eyes blank and staring, his features coarse and unfinished, like iron before tempering or clay before firing. A long cut across his neck had festered, and his right leg, where the townsfolk had broken it, hung limp and useless.

"Thanks, boy," said Rafe, Tyler-Blaine's zombie uncle.

The zombie quickly gulped down the contents of the bowl. When he had finished, Tyler-Blaine asked, "How you feeling, Uncle Rafe?"

"Ain't feeling nothing. This old body's about through. Another couple days, maybe a week, and I'll be off your hands."

"I'll take care of you," Tyler-Blaine said, "just as long as you can stay alive, Uncle Rafe. I wish I could bring you into the house."

"No," the zombie said, "they'd find out. This is risky enough... Boy, how's that skinny wife of yours?"

"Just as mean as ever," Tyler-Blaine sighed.

The zombie made a sound like laughter. "I warned you, boy, ten years ago I warned you not to marry that gal. Didn't I?"

"You sure did, Uncle Rafe. You was the only one had sense. Sure wish I'd listened to you."

"Better you had, boy. Well, I'm going back to my shelter."

"You feel confident, Uncle?" Tyler-Blaine asked anxiously.

"That I do."

"And you'll try to *die* confident?"

"I will, boy. And I'll get me into that Threshold, never you fear. And when I do, I'll keep my promise. I truly will."

"Thank you, Uncle Rafe."

"I'm a man of my word. I'll haunt her, boy, if the good Lord grants me Threshold. First comes that fat doctor that made me this. But then I'll haunt her. I'll haunt her crazy. I'll haunt her 'til she runs the length of the state of California away from you!"

"Thanks, Uncle Rafe."

The zombie made a sound like laughter and crawled back into the scraggly woods. Tyler-Blaine shivered uncontrollably for a moment, then picked up the empty bowl and walked back to the sagging washboard house...

Mariner-Blaine adjusted the strap of her bathing suit so that it clung more snugly to her slim, supple young body. She slipped the air tank over her back, picked up her respirator and walked toward the pressure lock.

"Janice?"

"Yes, Mother?" she said, turning, her face smooth and expressionless.

"Where are you going, dear?"

"Just out for a swim, Mom. I thought maybe I'd look at the new gardens on Level 12."

"You aren't by any chance planning to see Tom Leuwin, are you?"

Had her mother *guessed?* Mariner-Blaine smoothed her black hair and said, "Certainly not."

"All right," her mother said, half smiling and obviously not believing her. "Try to be home early, dear. You know how worried your father gets."

She stooped and gave her mother a quick kiss, then hurried into the pressure lock. Mother *knew,* she was sure of it! And wasn't stopping her! But then, why should she? After all, she was seventeen, plenty old enough to do anything she wanted. Kids grew up faster these days than they did in Mom's time, though parents didn't seem to realize it. Parents didn't realize very much. They just wanted to sit around and plan out new acres for the farm. Their idea of fun was to listen to some old classic recording, a Bop piece or a Rock 'n' Roll, and follow it with scores and talk about how free and expressionistic their ancestors had been. And sometimes they'd go through big, glossy art books filled with reproductions of 20th century Comic Strips, and talk about the lost art of satire. Their idea of a really Big Night was to go down to the gallery and stare reverently at the collection of *Saturday Evening Post* covers from the Great Period. But all that longhair stuff bored her. Nuts to art, she liked the sensories.

Mariner-Blaine adjusted her face mask and respirator, put on her flippers and turned the valve. In a few seconds the lock was filled with water. Impatiently she waited until the pressure had equalized with the water outside. Then the lock opened automatically and she shot out.

Her dad's pressure farm was at the hundred-foot level, not far from the mammoth underwater bulk of Hawaii. She turned downward, descending into the green bloom with quick, powerful strokes. Tom would be waiting for her at the coral caves.

The darkness grew as Mariner-Blaine descended. She switched on her headlamp and took a firmer bite on her respirator. Was it true, she wondered, that soon the undersea farmers would be able to grow their own gills? That's what her science teacher said, and maybe it would happen in her own lifetime. How would she look with gills? Mysterious, probably, sleek and strange, a fish goddess.

Besides, she could always cover them with her hair if they weren't becoming.

In the yellow glow of her lamp she saw the coral caves ahead, a red and pink branched labyrinth with cozy, airlocked places deep within, where you could be sure of privacy. And she saw Tom.

Uncertainty flooded her. Gosh, what if she had a baby? Tom had assured her it would be all right, but he was only nineteen. Was she right in doing this? They had talked about it often enough, and she had shocked him with her frankness. But talking and doing were very different things. What would Tom think of her if she said no? Could she make a joke out of it, pretend she'd just been teasing him?

Long and golden, Tom swam beside her toward the caves. He flashed hello in finger talk. A trigger fish swam by, and then a small shark.

What was she going to do? The caves were very near, looming dark and suggestive before them. Tom smiled at her, and she could feel her heart melting...

Elgin-Blaine sat upright, realizing that he must have dozed off. He was aboard a small motor vessel, sitting in a deck chair with blankets tucked around him. The little ship rolled and pitched in the cross-sea, but overhead the sun was brilliant, and the trade wind carried the diesel smoke away in a wide dark plume.

"You feeling better, Mr. Elgin?"

Elgin-Blaine looked up at a small, bearded man wearing a captain's cap. "Fine, just fine," he said.

"We're almost there," the captain said.

Elgin-Blaine nodded, disoriented, trying to take stock of himself. He thought hard and remembered that he was shorter than average, heavily muscled, barrel chested, broad shouldered, with legs a little short for such a herculean torso, with large and callused hands. There was an old, jagged scar on his shoulder, souvenir of a hunting accident...

Elgin and Blaine merged.

Then he realized that he was back at last in his own body. Blaine was his name, and Elgin was the pseudonym under which Carl Orc and Joe must have shipped him.

The long flight was over! His mind and his body were together again!

"We were told you weren't well, sir," the captain said. "But you've been in this coma for so long—"

"I'm fine now," Blaine told him. "Are we far from the Marquesas?"

"Not far. The island of Nuku Hiva is just a few hours away."

The captain returned to his wheelhouse. And Blaine thought about the many personalities he had met and mingled with.

He respected the staunch and independent old Dyersen walking slowly back to his cottage, hoped young Sandy Thompson would return to Mars, felt regret for the warped and murderous Piggot, enjoyed his meeting with the serious and upright Juan Ramirez, felt mingled sorrow and contempt for the sly and ineffectual Ed Tyler, prayed for the best for pretty Janice Mariner.

They were with him still. Good or bad, he wished them all well. They were his family now. Distant relatives, cousins and uncles he would never meet again, nieces and nephews upon whose destiny he would brood.

Like all families they were a mixed lot; but they were *his,* and he could never forget them.

"Nuku Hiva in sight!" the captain called.

Blaine saw, on the edge of the horizon, a tiny black dot capped by a white cumulus cloud. He rubbed his forehead vigorously, determined to think no more about his adopted family. There were present realities to deal with. Soon he would be coming to his new home; and that required a little serious thinking.

Chapter 31

The ship steamed slowly into Taio Hae Bay. The captain, a proud native son, volunteered to Blaine the principal facts about his new home.

The Marquesas Islands, he explained, were composed of two fairly distinct island groups, all of them rugged and mountainous. Once the group had been called the Cannibal Islands, and the Marquesans had been noted for their ability at cutting out a trading ship or massacring a blackbirding schooner. The French had acquired the islands in 1842, and granted them autonomy in 1993. Nuku Hiva was the main island and capital for the group. Its highest peak, Temetiu, was nearly four thousand feet high. Its port city, Taiohae, boasted a population of almost five thousand souls. It was a quiet, easy-going place, the captain said, and it was considered a sort of shrine all over the hurried, bustling South Seas. For here was the last refuge of unspoiled 20th century Polynesia.

Blaine nodded, absorbing little of the captain's lecture, more impressed by the sight of the great dark mountain ahead laced with silver waterfalls, and by the sound of the ocean pounding against the island's granite face.

He decided he was going to like it here.

Soon the ship was docked at the town wharf, and Blaine stepped off to view the town of Taiohae.

He saw a supermarket and three movie theaters, rows of ranch-style houses, many palm trees, some low white stores with plate glass windows, numerous cocktail lounges, dozens of automobiles, a gas station and a traffic light. The sidewalks were filled with people wearing colorful shirts and pressed slacks. All had on sunglasses.

So this was the last refuge of unspoiled 20th century Polynesia, Blaine thought. A Florida town set in the South Seas!

Still, what more could he expect in the year 2110? Ancient Polynesia was as dead as Merrie England or Bourbon France. And 20th century Florida, he remembered, could be very pleasant indeed.

He walked down Main Street, and saw a notice on a building stating that Postmaster Alfred Gray had been appointed Hereafter, Inc. representative for the Marquesas Group. And further on, he came to a small black building with a sign on it that said *Public Suicide Booth*.

Ah, Blaine thought sardonically, modern civilization is encroaching even here! Next thing you know they'll be setting up a Spiritual Switchboard. And where will we be then?

He had reached the end of town. As he started back, a stout, red-faced man hurried up to him

"Mr. Elgin? Mr. Thomas Elgin?"

"That's me," Blaine said, with a certain apprehension.

"Terribly sorry I missed you at the dock," said the red-faced man, mopping his wide and gleaming forehead with a bandanna. "No excuse, of course. Sheer oversight on my part. The languor of the islands. Inevitable after a while. Oh, I'm Davis, owner of the Point Boatyard. Welcome to Taiohae, Mr. Elgin."

"Thank you, Mr. Davis," Blaine said.

"On the contrary. I want to thank *you* again for answering my advertisement," Davis said. "I've been needing a Master Boatwright for months. You have no idea! And frankly, I didn't expect to attract a man of your qualifications."

"Ummm," Blaine said, surprised and pleased at the thoroughness of Carl Orc's preparations.

"Not many men around with a grounding in 20th century boatbuilding methods," Davis said sadly. "Lost art. Have you had a look around the island?"

"Just very briefly," Blaine said.

"Think you'll want to stay?" Davis asked anxiously. "You have no idea how hard it is getting a good boatwright to settle down in a quiet little backwater like this. No sooner do they get here, they want to go charging off to the big booming cities like Papeete or Apia. I know wages are higher in places like that, and there's more amusements and society and things. But Taiohae has a charm of its own."

"I've had my fill of the cities," Blaine said, smiling. "I'm not likely to go charging off, Mr. Davis."

"Good, good!" Davis said. "Don't bother coming to work for a few days, Mr. Elgin. Rest, take it easy, look around our island. It's the last refuge of primitive Polynesia, you know. Here are the keys to your house. Number one Temetiu Road, straight up the mountain there. Shall I show you the way?"

"I'll find it," Blaine said. "Thanks very much, Mr. Davis."

"Thank *you*, Mr. Elgin. I'll drop in on you tomorrow after you're a bit more settled. Then you can meet some of our townsfolk. In fact, the mayor's wife is giving a party Thursday. Or is it Friday? Anyhow, I'll find out and let you know."

They shook hands and Blaine started up Temetiu Road, to his new home.

It was a small, freshly painted bungalow with a spectacular view of Nuku Hiva's three southern bays. Blaine admired the sight for a few minutes, then tried the door. It was unlocked, and he walked in.

"It's about time you got here."

Blaine just stared, not able to believe what he saw.

"Marie!"

She appeared as slim, lovely and cool as ever. But she was nervous. She talked rapidly and avoided meeting his eyes.

"I thought it would be best if I made the final arrangements on the spot," she said. "I've been here for two days, waiting for you. You've met Mr. Davis, haven't you? He seems like a very nice little man."

"Marie—"

"I told him I was your fiancée," she said. "I hope you don't mind, Tom. I had to have some excuse for being here. I said I had come out early to surprise you. Mr. Davis was delighted of course, he wants his Master Boatwright to settle here so badly. Do you mind, Tom? We can always say we broke off the engagement and—"

Blaine took her in his arms and said, "I don't want to break off the engagement. I love you, Marie."

"Oh Tom, Tom, I love you!" She clung to him fiercely for a moment, then stepped back. "We'd better arrange for a marriage ceremony soon, if you don't mind. They're *very* stuffy and small-townish here; very 20th century, if you know what I mean."

"I think I know what you mean," Blaine said.

They looked at each other and burst out laughing.

Chapter 32

Marie insisted upon staying at the South Seas Motel until a wedding could be arranged. Blaine suggested a quiet ceremony before a justice of the peace; but Marie surprised him by wanting as large a wedding as Taiohae could produce. It was held on Sunday, at the Mayor's house.

Mr. Davis loaned them a little cutter from the boatyard. They set sail at sunrise for a honeymoon cruise to Tahiti.

For Blaine, it had the sensation of a delicious and fleeting dream. They sailed across a sea carved of green jade, and saw the moon, yellow and swollen, quartered by the cutter's shrouds and tangled in its stays. The sun rose out of a long black cloud, reached its zenith and declined, scouring the sea into a gleaming bowl of brass. They anchored in the lagoon at Papeete and saw the mountains of Mooréa flaming in the sunset, more fantastic than the mountains of the Moon. And Blaine remembered a day on the Chesapeake when he had dreamed, *Ah, Raïatea, the mountains of Mooréa, the fresh trade wind...*

A continent and an ocean had separated him from Tahiti, and other obstacles besides. But that had been in another century.

They went to Mooréa, rode horses up the slopes and picked the white tiare Tahiti. They returned to their boat anchored in the bay below, and set sail for the Tuamotos.

At last they returned to Taiohae. Marie started housekeeping, and Blaine began to work at the boatyard.

They waited anxiously through the first weeks, scanning the New York papers, wondering what Rex would do. But no word or sign came from the corporation, and they decided that the danger must be past. Still, they read with relief two months later that the Blaine hunt had been called off.

Blaine's job at the boatyard was interesting and varied. The island cutters and ketches limped in with bent shafts or nicked propellers, with planks that had been splintered against a hidden coral head, with sails blown out by a sudden gale. There were underwater craft to be serviced, boats belonging to the nearby undersea pressure farms that used Taiohae as a supply base. And there were dinghies to build, and an occasional schooner.

Blaine handled all practical details with skill and dispatch. As time went by, he started to write a few publicity releases about the yard for *South Seas Courier.* This brought in more business, which involved more paper work and greater need for liaison between the Point Boatyard and the small yards to which it farmed out work. Blaine handled this, and took over advertising as well.

His job as Master Boatwright came to bear an uncanny resemblance to his past jobs as junior yacht designer.

But this no longer bothered him. It seemed obvious to him now that nature had intended him to be a junior yacht designer, nothing more nor less. This was his destiny, and he accepted it.

His life fell into a pleasant routine built around the boatyard and the white bungalow, filled with Saturday night movies and the microfilm Sunday *Times,* quick visits to the undersea farms and to other islands in the Marquesas Group, parties at the Mayor's house and poker at the yacht club, brisk sails across Comptroller Bay and moonlight swimming on Temuoa Beach. Blaine began to think that his life had taken its final and definitive form.

Then, nearly four months after he had come to Taiohae, the pattern changed again.

One morning like any other morning Blaine woke up, ate his breakfast, kissed his wife good-bye and went down to the boatyard. There was a fat, round-bilged ketch on the ways, a Tuamotan boat that had gauged wrong trying to shoot a narrow pass under sail, and had been tide-set against a foam-splattered granite wall before the crew could start the engine. Six frames needed sistering, and a few planks had to be replaced. Perhaps they could finish it in a week.

Blaine was looking over the ketch when Mr. Davis came over.

"Say, Tom," the owner said, "there was a fellow around here just a little while ago looking for you. Did you see him?"

"No," Blaine said. "Who was it?"

"A mainlander," Davis said, frowning. "Just off the steamer this morning. I told him you weren't here yet and he said he'd see you at your house."

"What did he look like?" Blaine asked, feeling his stomach muscles tighten.

Davis frowned more deeply. "Well, that's the funny part of it. He was about your height, thin, and very tanned. Had a full beard and sideburns. You don't see that much any more. And he stank of shaving lotion."

"Sounds peculiar," Blaine said.

"Very peculiar. I'll swear his beard wasn't real."

"No?"

"It looked like a fake. Everything about him looked fake. And he limped pretty bad."

"Did he leave a name?"

"Said his name was Smith. Tom, where are you going?"

"I have to go home right now," Blaine said. "I'll try to explain later."

He hurried away. Smith must have found out who he was and what the connection was between them. And, exactly as he had promised, the zombie had come visiting.

Chapter 33

When he told Marie, she went at once to a closet and took down their suitcases. She carried them into the bedroom and began flinging clothes into them.

"What are you doing?" Blaine asked.

"Packing."

"So I see. But why?"

"Because we're getting out of here."

"What are you talking about? We live here!"

"Not any more," she said. "Not with that damned Smith around. Tom, he means trouble."

"I'm sure he does," Blaine said. "But that's no reason to run. Stop packing a minute and listen! What do you think he can do to me?"

"We're not going to stay and find out," she said.

She continued to shove clothes into the suitcase until Blaine grabbed her wrists.

"Calm down," he told her. "I'm not going to run from Smith."

"But it's the only sensible thing to do," Marie said. "He's trouble, but he can't live much longer. Just a few more months, weeks maybe, and he'll be dead. He should have died long before now, that horrible zombie! Tom, let's go!"

"Have you gone crazy or something?" Blaine asked. "Whatever he wants, I can handle it."

"I've heard you say that before," Marie said.

"Things were different then."

"They're different now! Tom, we could borrow the cutter again, Mr. Davis would understand, and we could go to—"

"No! I'm damned if I'll run from him! Maybe you've forgotten, Marie, Smith saved my life."

"But what did he save it *for?*" she wailed. "Tom, I'm warning you! You mustn't see him, not if he remembers!"

"Wait a minute," Blaine said slowly. "Is there something you know? Something I don't?"

She grew immediately calm. "Of course not."

"Marie, are you telling me the truth?"

"Yes, darling. But I'm frightened of Smith. Please, Tom, humor me this once, let's go away."

"I won't run another step from anyone," Blaine said. "I live here. And that's the end of it."

Marie sat down, looking suddenly exhausted. "All right, dear. Do what you think is best."

"That's better," Blaine said. "It'll turn out all right."

"Of course it will," Marie said.

Blaine put the suitcases back and hung up the clothes. Then he sat down to wait. He was physically calm. But in memory he had returned to the underground, had passed again through the ornate door covered with Egyptian hieroglyphics and Chinese ideograms, into the vast marble-pillared Palace of Death with its gold and bronze coffin. And heard again Reilly's screaming voice speak through a silvery mist:

"There are things you can't see, Blaine, but *I* see them. Your time on Earth will be short, very short, painfully short. Those you trust will betray you, those you hate will conquer you. You will die, Blaine, not in years but soon, sooner than you could believe. You'll be betrayed, and you'll die by your own hand."

That mad old man! Blaine shivered slightly and looked at Marie. She sat with downcast eyes, waiting. So he waited, too.

After a while there was a soft knock at the door.

"Come in," Blaine said to whoever was outside.

Chapter 34

Blaine recognized Smith immediately, even with false beard, sideburns and tan stage makeup. The zombie came in, limping, bringing with him a faint odor of decay imperfectly masked by a powerful shaving lotion.

"Excuse the disguise," Smith said. "It isn't intended to deceive you, or anyone. I wear it because my face is no longer presentable."

"You've come a long way," Blaine said. "Yes, quite far," Smith agreed, "and through difficulties I won't bore you by relating. But I got here, that's the important thing."

"Why did you come?"

"Because I know who I am," Smith said.

"And you think it concerns me?"

"Yes."

"I can't imagine how," Blaine said grimly. "But let's hear it."

Marie said, "Wait a minute. Smith, you've been after him since he came into this world. He's never had a moment's peace. Can't you just accept things as they are? Can't you just go and die quietly somewhere?"

"Not without telling him first," Smith said.

"Come on, let's hear it," Blaine said.

Smith said, "My name is James Olin Robinson."

"Never heard of you," Blaine said after a moment's thought.

"Of course not."

"Have we ever met before that time in the Rex building?"

"Not formally."

"But we met?"

"Briefly."

"All right, James Olin Robinson, tell me about it. When did we meet?"

"It was quite brief," Robinson said. "We glimpsed each other for a fraction of a second, then saw no more. It happened late one night in 1958, on a lonely highway, you in your car and me in mine."

"You were driving the car I had the accident with?"

"Yes. If you can call it an accident."

"But it was! It was completely accidental!"

"If that's true, I have no further business here," Robinson said. "But Blaine, I *know* it was not an accident. It was murder. Ask your wife."

Blaine looked at his wife sitting in a corner of the couch. Her face was waxen. She seemed drained of vitality. Her gaze seemed to turn inward and not enjoy what it saw there. Blaine wondered if she was staring at the ghost of some ancient guilt, long buried, long quickening, now come to term with the appearance of the bearded Robinson.

Watching her, he slowly began piecing things together.

"Marie," he said, "what about that night in 1958? How did you know I was going to smash up my car?"

She said, "There are statistical prediction methods we use, valence factors..." Her voice trailed away.

"Or did you *make* me smash up my car?" Blaine asked. "Did you produce the accident when you wanted it, in order to snatch me into the future for your advertising campaign?"

Marie didn't answer. And Blaine thought hard about the manner of his dying.

He had been driving over a straight, empty highway, his headlights probing ahead, the darkness receding endlessly before him... His car swerved freakishly, violently, toward the oncoming headlights... He twisted hard on the steering wheel. It wouldn't turn... The steering wheel came free and spun in his hands, and the engine wailed...

"By God, you made me have that accident!" Blaine shouted at his wife. "You and Rex Power Systems, you forced my car into a swerve! Look at me and answer! Isn't it true?"

"All right!" she said. "But we didn't mean to kill *him*. Robinson just happened to be in the way. I'm sorry about that."

Blaine said, "You've known all along who he was."

"I've suspected."

"And never told me." Blaine paced up and down the room. "Marie! Damn you, you killed me!"

"I didn't, Tom! Not really. I took you from 1958 into our time. I gave you a different body. But I didn't really kill you."

"You simply killed *me*," Robinson said.

With an effort Marie turned from her inner gaze and looked at him. "I'm afraid I was responsible for your death, Mr. Robinson, although not intentionally. Your body must have died at the same time as Tom's. The Rex Power System that snatched him into the future pulled you along, too. Then you took over Reilly's host."

"A very poor exchange for my former body," Robinson said.

"I'm sure it was. But what do you want? What can I do? The hereafter—"

"I don't want it," Robinson said. "I haven't had a chance on the Earth yet."

"How old were you at the time of the accident?" Blaine asked.

"Nineteen."

Blaine nodded sadly.

"I'm not ready for the hereafter," Robinson said. "I want to travel, do things, see things. I want to find out what kind of a man I am. I want to live! Do you know, I've never really known a woman! I'd exchange immortality for ten good years on Earth."

Robinson hesitated a moment, then said, "I want a body. I want a man's good body that I can live in. Not this dead thing which I wear. Blaine, your wife killed my former body."

Blaine said, "You want mine?"

"If you think it's fair," Robinson said.

"Now wait just a minute!" Marie cried. Color had returned to her face. With her confession, she seemed to have freed herself from the grip of the ancient evil in her mind, to have come back to wrestle again with life.

"Robinson," she said, "you can't ask that from him. He didn't have anything to do with your death. It was my fault, and I'm sorry. You don't want a woman's body, do you? I wouldn't give you mine, anyhow. What's done is done! Get out of here!"

Robinson ignored her and looked at Blaine. "I always knew it was you, Blaine. When I knew nothing else, I knew it was you. I watched over you, Blaine, I saved your life."

"Yes, you did," Blaine said quietly.

"So what!" Marie screamed. "So he saved your life. That doesn't mean he owns it! One doesn't save a life and expect it to be forfeited upon request. Tom, don't listen to him!"

Robinson said, "I have no means or intention of forcing you, Blaine. You will decide what you think is right, and I will abide by it. You will remember *everything.*"

Blaine looked at the zombie almost with affection. "So there's more to it. Much more. Isn't there, Robinson?"

Robinson nodded, his eyes fixed on Blaine's face.

"But how did you know?" Blaine asked. "How could you possibly know?"

"Because I understand you. I've made you my lifetime work. My life has revolved around you. I've thought about nothing but you. And the better I knew you, Blaine, the more certain I was about this."

"Perhaps," Blaine said.

Marie said, "What on earth are you talking about? What more? What more could there be?"

"I have to think about this," Blaine said. "I have to remember. Robinson, please wait outside for a little while."

"Certainly," the zombie said, and left immediately.

Blaine waved Marie into silence. He sat down and buried his head in his hands. Now he had to remember something he would rather not think about. Now, once and for all, he had to trace it back and understand it.

Etched sharp in his mind still were the words Reilly had screamed at him in the Palace of Death: "You're responsible! You killed me with your evil murdering mind! Yes, *you,* you hideous thing from the past, you damned monster! Everything shuns you except your friend the dead man! Why aren't *you* dead, murderer!"

Had Reilly known?

He remembered Sammy Jones saying to him after the hunt: "Tom, you're a natural-born killer. There's nothing else for you."

Had Sammy guessed?

And now the most important thing of all. That most significant moment of his life—the time of his death on a night in 1958. Vividly he remembered:

The steering wheel was working again, but Blaine ignored it, filled with a sudden fierce exultancy, a lightning switch of mood that welcomed the smash, lusted for it, and for pain and cruelty and death…

Blaine shuddered convulsively as he relived the moment he had wanted to forget—the moment when he might have avoided catastrophe, but had preferred to kill.

He lifted his head and looked at his wife. He said, "I killed him. That's what Robinson knew. And now I know it, too."

Chapter 35

Carefully he explained it all to Marie. She refused at first to believe him.

"It was so far back, Tom! How can you be sure of what happened?"

"I'm sure," Blaine said. "I don't think anyone could forget the way they died. I remember mine very well. *That* was how I died."

"Still, you can't call yourself a murderer because of one moment, one fraction of a second—"

"How long does it take to shoot a bullet or to drive in a knife?" Blaine asked. "A fraction of a second! That's how long it takes to become a murderer."

"But Tom, you had no motive!"

Blaine shook his head. "It's true that I didn't kill for gain or revenge. But then, I'm not that kind of murderer. That kind is relatively rare. I'm the grass-roots variety, the ordinary average guy with a little of everything in his makeup, including murder. I killed because, in that moment, I had the *opportunity.* My special opportunity, a unique interlocking of events, moods, train of thought, humidity, temperature, and lord knows what else, which might not have come up again in two lifetimes."

"But you're not to blame!" Marie said. "It would never have happened if Rex Power Systems and I hadn't created that special opportunity for you."

"Yes. But I seized the opportunity," Blaine said, "seized it and performed a cold-blooded murder just for fun, because I knew I could never be caught at it. *My* murder."

"Well… Our murder," she said.

"Yes."

"All right, we're murderers," Marie said calmly. "Accept it, Tom. Don't get mushy-minded about it. We've killed once, we can kill again."

"Never," Blaine said.

"He's almost finished! I swear to you, Tom, there's not a month of life in him. He's almost played out. One blow and he's done for. One push."

"I'm not that kind of murderer," Blaine said.

"Will you let me do it?"

"I'm not that kind, either."

"You idiot! Then just do nothing! Wait. A month, no more than that, and he's finished. You can wait a month, Tom—"

"More murder," Blaine said wearily.

"Tom! You're not going to give him your body! What about our life together?"

"Do you think we could go on after this?" Blaine asked. "I couldn't. Now stop arguing with me. I don't know if I'd do this if there weren't a hereafter. Quite probably I wouldn't. But there *is* a hereafter. I'd like to go there with my accounts as straight as possible, all bills paid in full, all restitutions made. If this were my only existence, I'd cling to it with everything I've got. But it isn't! Can you understand that?"

"Yes, of course," Marie said unhappily.

"Frankly, I'm getting pretty curious about this afterlife. I want to see it. And there's one thing more."

"What's that?"

Marie's shoulders were trembling, so Blaine put his arm around her. He was thinking back to the conversation he had had with Hull, the elegant and aristocratic Quarry.

Hull had said: "We follow Nietzsche's dictum—to die at the right time! Intelligent people don't clutch at the last shreds of life like drowning men clinging to a bit of board. They know that the body's life is only an infinitesimal portion of man's total existence. Why shouldn't those bright pupils skip a grade or two of school?"

Blaine remembered how strange, dark, atavistic and noble Hull's lordly selection of death had seemed. Pretentious, of course; but then, life itself was a pretension in the vast universe of unliving matter. Hull had seemed like an ancient Japanese nobleman kneeling to perform the ceremonial act of hara-kiri, and emphasizing the importance of life in the very selection of death.

And Hull had said: "The deed of dying transcends class and breeding. It is every man's patent of nobility, his summons from the king, his knightly adventure. And how he acquits himself in that lonely and perilous enterprise is his true measure as a man."

Marie broke into his reverie, asking, "What was that one thing more?"

"Oh." Blaine thought for a moment. "I just wanted to say that I guess some of the attitudes of the 22nd century have rubbed off on me. Especially the aristocratic ones." He grinned and kissed her. "But of course, I always had good taste."

Chapter 36

Blaine opened the door of the cottage. "Robinson," he said, "come with me to the Suicide Booth. I'm giving you my body."

"I expected no less of you, Tom," the zombie said.

"Then let's go."

Together they went slowly down the mountainside. Marie watched them from a window for a few seconds, then started down after them.

They stopped at the door to the Suicide Booth. Blaine said, "Do you think you can take over all right?"

"I'm sure of it," Robinson said. "Tom, I'm grateful for this. I'll use your body well."

"It's not mine, really," Blaine said. "Belonged to a fellow named Kranch. But I've grown fond of it. You'll get used to its habits. Just remind it once in a while who's boss. Sometimes it wants to go hunting."

"I think I'll like that," Robinson said.

"Yes, I suppose you would. Well, good luck."

"Good luck to you, Tom."

Marie came up and kissed Blaine goodbye with icy lips. Blaine said, "What will you do?"

She shrugged her shoulders. "I don't know. I feel so numb… Tom, must you?"

"I must," Blaine said.

He looked around once more at the palm trees whispering under the sun, the blue expanse of the sea, and the great dark mountain above him cut with silver waterfalls. Then he turned and entered the Suicide Booth, and closed the door behind him.

There were no windows, no furniture except a single chair. The instructions posted on one wall were very simple. You just sat down, and, at your leisure, closed the switch upon the right arm. You would then die, quickly and painlessly, and your body would be left intact for the next inhabitant.

Blaine sat down, made sure of the location of the switch and leaned back, his eyes closed.

He thought again about the first time he died, and wished it had been more interesting. By rights he should have rectified the error this time, and gone down like Hull, hunted fiercely across a mountain ledge at sundown. Why couldn't it have been like that? Why couldn't death have come while he was battling a typhoon, meeting a tiger's charge, or climbing Mount Everest? Why, again, would his death be so tame, so commonplace, so ordinary?

But then, why had he never really designed yachts?

An enterprising death, he realized again, would be out of character for him. Undoubtedly he was meant to die in just this quick, commonplace, painless way. And all his life in the future must have gone into the forming and shaping of this death—a vague indication when Reilly died, a fair certainty in the Palace of Death, an implacable destiny when he settled in Taiohae.

Still, no matter how ordinary, one's death is the most interesting event of one's life. Blaine looked forward eagerly to his.

He had no complaint to make. Although he had lived in the future little over a year, he had gained its greatest prize—the hereafter! He felt again what he had experienced after leaving the Hereafter Building—release from the heavy, sodden, constant, unconscious fear of death that subtly weighed every action and permeated every movement. No man of his own age could live without the shadow that crept down the corridors of his mind like some grisly tapeworm, the ghost that haunted nights and days, the croucher behind corners, the shape behind doors, the unseen guest at every banquet, the unidentified figure in every landscape, always present, always waiting—

No more!

For now the ancient enemy was defeated. And men no longer died; they *moved on!*

But he had gained even more than an afterlife. He had managed to squeeze and compress an entire lifetime into that year.

He had been born in a white room with dazzling lights and a doctor's bearded face above him, and a motherly nurse to feed him while he listened, alarmed, to the babble of strange tongues. He had ventured early into the world, raw and uneducated, and had stared at the oriental marvel of New York, and allowed a straight-eyed fast-talking stranger to make a fool and nearly a corpse of him, until wiser heads rescued him from his folly and soothed his pain. Clothed in his fine, strong, mysterious body he had ventured out again, wiser this time, and had moved as an equal among men equipped with glittering weapons in the pursuit of danger and honor. And he had lived through that folly, too, and still older, had chosen an honorable occupation. But certain dark omens present at his birth finally reached fruition, and he had to flee his homeland and run to the farthest corner of the Earth. Yet he still managed to acquire a family on the way; a family with certain skeletons in the closet, but his all the same. In the fullness of manhood he had come to a land he loved, taken a wife, and, on his honeymoon, seen the mountains of Mooréa flaming in the sunset. He had settled down to spend his declining months in peace and useful labor, and in fond recollection of the wonders he had seen. And so he had spent them, honored and respected by all.

It was sufficient. Blaine turned the switch.

Chapter 37

"Where am I? Who am I? What am I?"

No answer.

"I remember. I am Thomas Blaine, and I have just died. I am now in the Threshold, a very real and completely indescribable place. I sense Earth. And ahead, I sense the hereafter."

"Tom—"

"Marie!"

"Yes."

"But how could you—I didn't think—"

"Well, perhaps in some ways I wasn't a very good wife, Tom. But I was always a faithful one, and I did what I did for you. I love you, Tom. Of course I would follow."

"Marie, this makes me very happy."

"I'm glad."

"Shall we go on?"

"Where, Tom?"

"Into the hereafter."

"Tom, I'm frightened. Couldn't we just stay right here for a while?"

"It'll be all right. Come with me."

"Oh, Tom! What if they separate us? What will it be like? I don't think I'm going to like it. I'm afraid it's going to be terribly strange and ghostly and horrible."

"Marie, don't worry. I've been a junior yacht designer three times in two lifetimes. It's my destiny! Surely it can't end here!"

"All right. I'm ready now, Tom. Let's go."

JOURNEY BEYOND TOMORROW

INTRODUCTION

Joenes's fabulous world is more than a thousand years behind us, in the remote and misty past. We know that Joenes's Journey began around the year 2000, and ended in the opening years of our own era. We also know that the age through which Joenes traveled was remarkable for its industrial civilizations. Twenty-first-century mechanical articulation gave rise to many strange artifacts that no present-day reader has ever encountered. Still, most of us have learned at one time or another what the ancients meant by "guided missile," or "atom bomb." Fragments of some of these fantastic creations can be seen in many museums.

Our knowledge is much less certain of the customs and institutions by which men lived in the twenty-first century. And to discover anything at all about their religions and ethics, we must turn to Joenes's Journey.

Beyond a doubt, Joenes himself was an actual person; but there is no way of determining the authenticity of every story told about him. Some of the tales do not appear to be factual accounts, but rather, moral allegories. But even those that are considered allegorical are representative of the spirit and temper of the times.

Our book, then, is a collection of tales about the far-traveling Joenes and about his marvelous and tragic twenty-first century. A few of the tales are from written records. But most of them come to us through the oral tradition, handed down from storyteller to storyteller.

Aside from this book, the only written account of the Journey appears in the recently published *Fijian Tales,* where, for obvious reasons, Joenes's role is rendered as secondary to that of his friend Lum. This is quite untrue to the spirit of the Journey, and false to the content of the stories themselves. Because of this, we have felt the necessity of this book, in order that the entire body of Joenes Stories may be rendered faithfully in written form, to be preserved for future generations.

This volume also contains all of the twenty-first-century writing concerning Joenes. These written records are unfortunately few and fragmentary, and comprise only two of the stories. These are: "Lum's Meeting With Joenes," from the *Book of Fiji,* Orthodox Edition, and "How Lum Joined the Army," also from the *Book of Fiji,* Orthodox Edition.

All of the other stories are from the oral tradition, deriving from Joenes or his followers, and handed down from generation to generation. The present collection puts into written form the words of the most famous present-day storytellers, without any alteration in their various viewpoints, idiosyncrasies, moralities, styles, comments, and so forth. We would like to thank those storytellers for graciously allowing us to put their words upon paper. These men are:

Ma'aoa of Samoa
Maubingi of Tahiti
Paaui of Fiji
Pelui of Easter Island
Teleu of Huahine

We have used the particular tales or group of tales for which each of these men is most acclaimed. Credit is given at the beginning of each story. And we make our apologies to the many excellent storytellers we have been unable to include in this volume, and whose contributions will have to await the compilation of a Joenes *Variorum.*

For the reader's convenience these stories are arranged sequentially, as continuing chapters of an unfolding narrative, with a beginning, a middle, and an end. But the reader is warned not to expect a consistent and rationally ordered story, since some parts are long and some short, some complicated and some simple, depending upon the idiosyncrasy of the individual storyteller. Your editor could, of course, have taken from or added to the various parts, making their lengths regular and imposing his own sense of order and style upon the whole. But he thought it best to leave the tales as they were, in order to give the reader the entire unexpurgated Journey. This seemed only fair to the storytellers, and the only way to tell the whole truth about Joenes, the people he met, and the strange world he traveled through.

Your editor has taken down the exact words of the storytellers, and copied the two written accounts, but he himself has invented nothing, and has added no comments of his own to the tales. His only remarks are in the last chapter of the book, where he tells of the Journey's end.

Now, reader, we invite you to meet Joenes, and travel with him through the last years of the old world and the first years of the new.

I. JOENES BEGINS HIS JOURNEY
(As told by Maubingi of Tahiti)

In the twenty-fifth year of his life, an event occurred that was of crucial significance to the hero of this tale. To explain the significance of this event, we must first tell something of our hero; and in order to understand our hero, something must be said of the place in which he lived, and of the condition and circumstances of that place. So we will begin there, moving as quickly as we can to the central matters this tale is actually about.

Our hero, Joenes, lived upon a small island in the Pacific Ocean, an atoll that lay 200 miles east of Tahiti. This island was called Manituatua, and it was no more than two miles long by several hundred yards in width. Surrounding it was a coral reef, and beyond the reef lay the blue waters of the Pacific. To this island Joenes's parents had come from America, to tend the equipment that supplied most of Eastern Polynesia with electrical power.

When Joenes's mother died, his father labored alone; and when his father died, Joenes was requested by the Pacific Power Company to continue in his father's place. And this Joenes did.

By most accounts, Joenes was a tall, strongly built young man with a pleasing face and excellent manners. He was a great reader, and took delight in his father's extensive library. Since he was romantically inclined, his sensibilities led him towards the contemplation of truth, loyalty, love, duty, fate, chance, and other abstractions. Because of his temperament, Joenes saw virtues as mandates, and he loved to think of them in their most superlative form.

The people of Manituatua, all Polynesians from Tahiti, found it difficult to understand this sort of man. They readily admitted that virtue was good; but this did not prevent them from engaging in vice whenever necessary or convenient. Although Joenes scorned such behavior, he could not help but be impressed by the good spirits, generosity, and easy sociability of the Manituatuans. Even though they rarely gave a thought to virtue, and even more rarely practiced it, they managed somehow to lead pleasant and worthy lives.

This evidence did not immediately convert Joenes, who was still of too passionate a mentality to consider moderation. But it did have a constant and ever-growing effect upon him. Some say that Joenes's later survival was made possible only by the expediency he had learned from the Manituatuans.

But influences can only be guessed at, never truly delineated or understood. What we are leading up to is the great and singular event that came upon Joenes in his twenty-fifth year.

This event was formed in the executive office of the Pacific Power Company, situated in San Francisco, on the Western Coast of America. Here, potbellied men wearing suits, neckties, shirts, and shoes had gathered around a circular table made of gleaming teak. These Men of the Round Table, as they were called, held much of human destiny in their hands. Chairman of the Board was Arthur Pendragon, a man who had inherited his position but had been forced to wage a grim proxy fight before he could take his rightful place. Once established, Arthur Pendragon had fired the old Board of Trustees, and appointed his own men. Present were Bill Launcelot, a man of vast financial strength; Richard Galahad, well known for his charitable works; Austin Modred, who had political connections throughout the state; and many others.

These men, whose financial empire had been hard pressed of late, voted for a consolidation of their power and immediate disposition of all unprofitable holdings. This decision, simple as it seemed at the time, had far-reaching consequences.

In distant Manituatua, Joenes received word of the Board's decision to cease operation of the Eastern Polynesian power station.

Thus Joenes was out of a job. Worse still, he had lost an entire way of life.

During the next week, Joenes gave considerable thought to his future. His Polynesian friends urged him to stay with them on Manituatua; or, if he preferred, to go to one of the larger islands such as Huahine, Bora Bora, or Tahiti.

Joenes listened to their proposals, and then went to a private place to think. He emerged from this place after three days and announced to the waiting populace his intention of going to America, his parents' homeland, there to see with his own eyes the wonders about which he had read, to discover if his destiny lay there; and if not, to return to the people of Polynesia with a clear mind and open heart, ready to perform whatever services they required of him.

There was consternation among the people when they heard this, for the land of America was known to be more dangerous than the unpredictable ocean itself; and the Americans were reputed to be sorcerers and warlocks, who, through subtle enchantments, could change the entire way of a man's thinking. It seemed impossible that a man could grow to dislike coral beaches, lagoons, palm trees, outrigger canoes, and the like. Yet it had happened. Other men of Polynesia had journeyed to America, and had been exposed to the enchantments there, and had never returned. One had even visited legendary Madison Avenue; but what he found there is unknown, for that man never spoke again. Nevertheless, Joenes was determined to go.

Joenes was affianced to a Manituatuan girl of golden skin, almond eyes, black hair, a figure of the greatest piquancy, and a mind wise in the ways of men. Joenes proposed to send for this girl, whose name was Tondelayo, as soon as he had established himself in America; or if fortune did not favor him, to return to her. Neither of these proposals met with

Tondelayo's approval, and she spoke to Joenes in the following fashion, and in the local dialect then prevalent:

"Hey! You foolish popaa fella want one time go Melica? For why, hey? More coconut in Melica, maybe? Bigger beach? Better fishing? No! You think maybe better chumbi-chumbi, hey? I tell you no. More better you stay alongside here me one time, my word!"

In this fashion the lovely Tondelayo reasoned with Joenes. But Joenes answered:

"My darling, do you think it pleases me to leave *you,* the epitome of all my dreams and the crystallization of my desires? No, my darling, no! This departure fills me with dread, for I do not know what fate awaits me in the cold world to the east. I only know a man must go, must look at fame and fortune, and if need be, at death itself. For only in an understanding of the great world to the east, which I have heard of only through my departed parents and their books, can I ever return and spend my life here in these islands."

The lovely Tondelayo gave careful attention to these words, and pondered them long. And then the island girl spoke to Joenes the words of simple philosophy that had been passed down from mother to daughter from time immemorial:

"Hey, you fella white men all alike, I think. You chumbi-chumbi allatime little wahine okay, then you want walk-around look for chumbi-chumbi alongside popaa white woman American, I think. My word! And yet, the palm grows, the coral spreads, but man must die."

Joenes could only bow his head to the ancestral wisdom of the island girl. But his decision was not shaken. Joenes knew that it was his destiny to see the land of America from which his parents had come; there to accept whatever danger offered or danger proffered, and to come to terms with the unknowable fate that lies in ambush for all men. He kissed Tondelayo, who began crying when she saw that her words had no power to move this man.

The neighboring chiefs gave a farewell feast for Joenes, at which they served island delicacies such as canned beef and canned pineapple. When the trading schooner touched at the island with the weekly supply of rum, they sadly bade their beloved Joenes farewell.

So it was that Joenes, with the melody of the islands ringing in his ears, made his way past Huahine and Bora Bora, past Tahiti and Hawaii, finally to arrive in the city of San Francisco upon the Western Coast of America.

II. LUM'S MEETING WITH JOENES

(Lum's own words, as recorded in the Book of Fiji, *Orthodox Edition)*

Well, I mean, you know how it is. It's like Hemingway said; the booze goes bad and the chick goes bad and where are you? So I was down at the docks waiting on the weekly shipment of peyote and I wasn't really doing anything, I was just standing around and digging it all—the people, the big ships, the Golden Gate, you know. I had just finished a sandwich made of Italian salami on real black pumpernickel bread, and what with the peyote coming, I wasn't feeling so bad. I mean sometimes you just don't feel so bad, you're out there digging it, even if the chick has gone bad.

This boat came in from one of those places and this guy got off. He was a tall, lean sort of guy with a real-looking tan, a big set of shoulders on him, and he was wearing a shirt made of canvas and a pair of beat-up pants and no shoes at all. So naturally I thought he was OK I mean he looked OK. So I came up to him and asked him if this was the boat the stuff had come in on.

This character looked at me, and he said, "My name's Joenes, I'm a stranger here."

So I knew at once he wasn't with it, and I just sort of stared away.

He said, "Do you know where I could find a job? I'm new in America, and I want to find out about it, and learn what America has for me, and what I have for America."

I started looking at him again because now I didn't know; I mean it didn't look like he was with it, but not everyone is a hipster these days and sometimes the simple approach if you can make it work will take you all the way to the big Teahouse in the Sky run by the Biggest Pusher of Them All. I mean maybe he was playing it Zen with this what looked like cornball. Jesus was cornball, but he was with it, and all of us would be for him if only the squares would leave him alone. So I said to this Joenes, "You want a job? There anything you can do?"

Joenes said to me, "I can operate an electrical transformer."

"Goody for you," I told him.

"And I can play the guitar," he said.

"Well man," I said, "why didn't you say so in the first place instead of coming on so heavy with the electricity bit? I know a cappuccino place you can play, maybe get some tips from the squares. You got any bread, man?"

This Joenes barely spoke English, so I had to explain it all to him like I was drawing a blueprint. But he caught on pretty fast, about the guitar scene and the squares, and I offered him he could bunk for awhile in my pad. I mean with my chick gone bad, why not? And this Joenes, he flashed me a smile and said sure, he'd go for that. And he asked me what the situation was locally, and aside from that, what we did for kicks. He sounded OK even if he was a foreigner, so I told him that chicks could be found, and that for kicks he'd better stick with me and look-see. He dug this so we went to the pad, where I gave him a sandwich of that real rye bread with the little seeds and a slab of Swiss cheese from Switzerland, not Wisconsin. Joenes was so far down I had to loan him my ax, on account he had left his own guitar in the islands, wherever the islands were. And that night we made the coffeehouse scene.

Well, Joenes came on big that night with the guitar and songs, because he sang in a language no one understood, which was just as well because the tunes were a little square. The tourists lapped it up like it was A.T. & T., and Joenes collected $8.30, which was enough for a nice loaf of Russian rye and don't give me that unpatriotic bit, and some other stuff besides. And this little chick no more than 5'1" latched on to him, because Joenes was that sort. I mean he was big and tall and he had shoulders like granddaddy's old ox yoke, and a big sweep of blond hair that was sun-streaked. A guy like me has more trouble, because even though I got a beard I'm built short and thick and sometimes it takes a while. But Joenes he was like magnetic. He even attracted the sunglasses, who asked him if he'd ever joypopped, but I pulled him off that, because the peyote had come and why trade a headache for an upset stomach?

So Joenes and this chick, who was named Deirdre Feinstein, and another chick she got for me, we all went back to the pad. I showed Joenes how you take the peyote buds and mash them down and so forth, and we all took it and we came on. I mean we came on, but Joenes lit up like a 1000-watt Mazda bulb and even though I warned him about the fuzz who are patrolling the streets and alleys of San Francisco these days looking for anybody who's on anything so they can use those beautiful new California jails of theirs, Joenes insisted on standing on the bed and making a speech. It was a pretty nice speech, because this big-shouldered laughing boy from the faraway hills was really turned on for the first time, and he put down The Word as follows:

"My friends, I have come to you from a faraway land of sand and palm upon a voyage of discovery, and I count myself fortunate above all men, for upon this my first night in your land I have been taken to your leader, King Peyote, and have been raised up instead of put down, and have been shown the wonders of the world which are presently turning red before me and falling like a waterfall. To my dear comrade, Lum, I can only praise without sufficiency this act of beatitude. To my new sweetheart, the luscious Deirdre Feinstein, let me tell you that I see a great flame growing within, and a high wind blowing without. To Lum's girl, whose name I unfortunately didn't catch, I say that I love you like a brother, incestuously, and yet with an innocence born of self-born innocence. And further—"

Well, this Joenes didn't have exactly a small voice. As a matter of fact, he sounded like a sea lion in rutting season, which is a sound none of you out there should miss. But it was too much for the pad, because the neighbors upstairs, who are square types that get up at 8:00 in the morning to do the bit, pounded on the ceiling and informed us this was one party too much and that they had informed the cops, by which they meant the fuzz.

Joenes and the girls were conked, but I pride myself on keeping a clear head for danger no matter what is drifting in my lungs or dancing in my veins. I wanted to flush the rest of the peyote, but Deirdre, who is so with it she sometimes scares you, insisted upon secreting the remaining buds in her Maidenform, where, she insisted, they would be safe from any harm. I got them all out of the pad, Joenes with my guitar clenched in his sunburned fist, and we got down none too soon, for a patrol car full of fuzz had just arrived. I cautioned the group to walk straight ahead like little soldiers because you can't play any games when you got stuff on you. But I hadn't counted on how far gone that Deirdre was.

We started walking and the cops came by and gave us coplike looks, and we kept on walking and the fuzz started passing remarks about beatniks and immorality and such. I tried to keep the group moving, but that Deirdre wouldn't be called down. She turned on the fuzz and told them what she thought of them, which was a very unwise thing to do if you've got a vocabulary and a creative imagination like Deirdre has.

The top cop, a sergeant, said, "OK, sister, come with us. We're booking you, dig?"

And struggling and kicking, they pulled poor Deirdre toward the cop car. I could see Joenes's face setting itself in thoughtful, cop-hating lines, and I was afraid of trouble since filled with peyote as he was he loved Deirdre and indeed everybody except the fuzz.

I said to him, "Man, don't do a thing, this scene's gotta split and if Deirdre won't, she won't. I mean she's always fighting cops ever since she came out here from New York to study Zen, and she gets pulled in all the time so it's no big deal, especially since her father is Sean Feinstein who owns like anything you can name in five seconds. So the cops just sober her up and let her go. So don't make the move, man, don't even look back, because your father is not Sean Feinstein, or indeed anybody I ever heard of."

In this way I tried to soothe and reason with Joenes, but Joenes stopped, a heroic figure under the lamplight, his fist clenched white around my guitar, his eyes all-knowing and all-forgiving except for cops. And he turned.

The lead cop said, "You want something, kid?"

Joenes said, "Take your hands from off that young lady!"

The cop said, "This drug addict, whom you call a young lady, is in violation of section 431.3 of the Code of the City of San Francisco. I suggest that you mind your own business, buster, and don't play that ukelele on the streets after 12:00."

I mean, he was being nice in his way.

But Joenes then made a speech which was a beauty, and I cannot recall it word for word, but the idea was that laws are made by man and thus must partake of the evil nature of man, and that true morality lies in following the true dictates of the illuminated soul.

"A Commie, huh?" said the lead cop. And in a trice, or perhaps even sooner, they dragged Joenes into the cop car.

Well naturally Deirdre was sprung the following morning, on account of her father, and maybe also because of her winsome ways which are the talk of San Francisco. But though we searched high and low, and even as far afield as Berkeley, we saw no signs of Joenes.

No sign, I tell you! What had happened to this blond troubador with the sun-streaked hair and a heart as big as all outdoors when properly illuminated? Where had he gone, with my guitar (a genuine Tatay) and my second-best pair of sandals? I suppose only the cops know, and they will not tell. But still I remember him, Joenes the sweet singer, who, at the gates of hell, turned back to look for his Eurydice, and suffered thus the doom of Orpheus the golden-voiced. I mean it was a little different but still it was all there, and who knows in what distant lands Joenes and my guitar are wandering?

III. THE CONGRESSIONAL COMMITTEE
(As told by Ma'aoa of Samoa)

Joenes could not know that a committee of the American Senate was presently in San Francisco, carrying out investigations. But the police knew. They sensed intuitively that Joenes was a likely witness for these investigations, and they took him from the jail to the room where the Committee was meeting in executive session.

The Committee chairman, whose name was Senator George W. Pelops, immediately asked Joenes what he had to say for himself.

"I haven't done a thing," Joenes said.

"Ah," replied Pelops, "has anyone *accused* you of doing anything? Have I accused you? Have any of my illustrious colleagues? If so, I would like to hear of it at once."

"No sir," Joenes said. "I just thought—"

"Thoughts are not admissible as evidence," Pelops said.

Pelops then scratched his bald head, adjusted his spectacles, and glared full into a television camera. He said, "This man, by his own admission, has been accused of no crime whether of commission or omission. We have asked him here merely to talk, as is our congressional privilege and duty. And yet, his very words betray a consciousness of guilt. Gentlemen, I think we must pursue this a little further."

Joenes said, "I want a lawyer."

Pelops said, "You cannot have a lawyer, since this is only a congressional fact-finding committee and not an arraignment. But we will take careful note of your request for one. Might I ask why a presumably innocent man might want a lawyer?"

Joenes, who had read many books in Manituatua, mumbled something about his rights and the law. Pelops told him that the Congress was the guardian of his rights, as well as the maker of the laws. Therefore he had nothing to fear if only he answered honestly. Joenes took heart at this and promised that he would answer honestly.

"I thank you for that," Pelops said, "although usually I do not have to *request* that a man answer honestly. Still, perhaps it means nothing. Tell me, Mr. Joenes, do you *believe* in the speech you made last night in the streets of San Francisco?"

"I don't remember any speech," said Joenes.

"You refuse to answer the question?"

"I can't answer it. I don't remember. I believe I was intoxicated."

"Do you remember who you were with last night?"

"I think I was with a man named Lum, and a girl named Deirdre—"

"We do not require their names," Pelops said hastily. "We simply asked you if you remembered who you were with, and you said you do so remember. I put it to you, Mr. Joenes, that it is a convenient memory which remembers one set of facts and forgets another, both occurring in the same period of 24 hours!"

"They weren't facts," Joenes said, "they were people."

"The Committee does not require you to be facetious," Pelops said sternly. "I will warn you here and now that facetious, unresponsive, or misleading answers, as well as no answers at all, can be interpreted as contempt of Congress, which is a federal offense punishable by up to a year in prison."

"I didn't mean anything," Joenes said quickly.

"Very well, Mr. Joenes, we will continue. Do you deny that you made a speech last night?"

"No sir, I don't deny it."

"And do you deny that the content of your speech concerned the so-called right which you insisted every man had to overthrow the legally constituted law of this land? Or, to put it another way, do you deny that you incited to rebellion those dissidents who might be swayed by your foreign-inspired words? Or, to make the matter perfectly plain to you, that you advocated violent overthrow of the government which necessarily rests upon the laws *of* that government? Can you argue that the sum and content of your speech was a violation of those liberties which our Founding Fathers gave us, and which allow such as you to speak at all, as you surely would *not* be allowed to do in Soviet Russia? Will you presume to tell us that this speech, masked under the garb of harmless bohemianism, was not part of a detailed plot directed toward inner dissension and for the purpose of paving the way for outer aggression, and that in this attempt you had the silent approval, if not the explicit direction, of certain persons in our own State Department? And that, finally, this speech, which you disguised under an apparent intoxication, and which you gave under your presumed right to act subversively in a democracy where the power to retaliate, or so you thought, is hamstrung by a Constitution and a Bill of Rights which however is not, as you might think, designed to aid the lawless, but rather to preserve the liberties of the people against godless mercenaries such as yourself? Did you or did you not, Mr. Joenes? I ask only a simple yes or no."

"Well," Joenes said, "I'd like to clarify—"

"The question, Mr. Joenes," said Pelops in an icy voice. "Kindly answer the question yes or no."

Joenes racked his brain furiously, remembering all the American history he had read upon his native island. Now he said, "The allegation is monstrous!"

"Answer the question, Mr. Joenes," Pelops said.

Joenes said, "I stand upon my Constitutional rights, namely the First and Fifth Amendments, and respectfully decline to answer."

Pelops smiled thinly. "You may not do so, Mr. Joenes, since the Constitution to which you *now* so fervently cling has been reinterpreted, or rather brought up to date, by those of us who wish to preserve it from change and desecration. The Amendments you mention, Mr. Joenes—or should I say Comrade Joenes—will not permit you to be silent for reasons which any judge of the Supreme Court would have been glad to tell you—*had you chosen to ask him!*"

There was no answer to this crushing rejoinder. Even the reporters in the room, hardened observers of the political scene, were moved. Joenes turned beet-red and then lily-white. With no recourse left, he opened his mouth to answer. But he was momentarily saved by the intervention of one of the members of the Committee, Senator Trellid.

"Excuse me, sir," Senator Trellid said to Pelops, "and excuse me all of you who are waiting for this man's answer. I just want to say one thing, and I want it to go on the record, because sometimes a man must speak out no matter how painful it is to him, and in spite of that it might harm him politically and economically. And yet it is the duty of a man such as myself to speak out when he must, and to speak in spite of consequences, and in full conscience, even if what he has to say goes against the great power of public opinion. Therefore I want to say this, I am an old man, and I have seen many things in my time, and I have witnessed even more. Perhaps I am not wise to so speak, but I must tell you that I am dead set against injustice. Unlike some, I cannot condone the slaughter of the Hungarians, the unlawful seizure of China, nor the communization of Cuba. I am old, I have been called conservative, but I cannot condone these things. And, no matter who calls me what, I hope I will never live to see the day when a Russian army occupies the city of Washington, D.C. Thus I speak against this man, this Comrade Jonski, not as a senator, but rather as one who was once a child in the hill country south of Sour Mountain, who fished and hunted in the deep woods, who grew slowly to an awareness of what America meant to him, whose neighbors sent him to Congress to represent them and their dear ones, and who now feels called upon to make this declaration of faith. It is for this reason and this reason only that I say to you in the words of the Bible, 'Evil is Bad!' Some of the sophisticated among us may laugh at this, but there it is and I believe it.' "

The Committee burst into spontaneous applause at the old senator's speech. Although they had heard it many times, it never failed to elicit in them emotions of the deepest and most exquisite sort. Now, white-lipped, Chairman Pelops turned to Joenes.

"Comrade," he asked, with simple irony, "are you at this present time a card-carrying member of the Communist Party?"

"I am not!" cried Joenes.

Pelops said, "In that case, who were your associates during your card-carrying days?"

"I didn't have any associates. I mean—"

"We understand very well what you mean," Pelops said. "Since you choose not to identify your fellow traitors, would you mind telling us the location of your cell? No? Tell me, Comrade Jonski, does the name Ronald Black mean anything to you? Or to put it more simply, when did you last see Ronald Black?"

"I never met him," Joenes said.

"Never? That is a very big word, Mr. Joenes. Are you trying to tell me that at no time could you have met Ronald Black? That you might not have *innocently* passed this man in a crowd, or perhaps attended a movie with him? I doubt if any man in America can so flatly state that he has *never* met Ronald Black. Do you wish your statement to go on the record?"

"Well, I mean, I might have met him in a crowd, I mean been in a crowd where he was, but I don't know for sure—"

"But you allow the possibility?"

"I guess so."

"Excellent," Pelops said. "Now we are getting somewhere. Now I ask you what crowd you met Black in, and what he said to you, and you to him, and what papers he passed you, and whom you passed those papers to—"

"I never met Arnold Black!" Joenes cried.

"We have always known him as *Ronald* Black," Pelops said. "But we are always glad to learn his pseudonyms. Note please that you yourself admitted the possibility of your association with him, and in view of your admitted Party activities, this possibility must be judged a probability so strong as to be a certainty. Furthermore, you yourself gave us the name by which Ronald Black was known in the Party, a name which we hitherto *had not known*. And that, I think, is sufficient."

"Look," said Joenes, "I don't know this Black or what he did."

In somber tones Pelops stated, "Ronald Black was convicted of steal-ing the plans for the new Studebaker Roadclinger Super V-12 Luxury Compact Convertible, and selling those plans to an agent of the Soviet Union. After a fair trial, Black was executed in the manner prescribed by the law. Later, thirty-one of his associates were discovered, tried, and ex-ecuted. You, Comrade Jonski, will be associate Number 32 in the biggest spy ring we have yet uncovered."

Joenes tried to speak, but found himself speechless and trembling in fear.

"This Committee," Pelops summed up, "has been granted extralegal powers because it is merely investigative, not punitive. This is perhaps a shame, but the letter of the law must be followed. Therefore we now hand the secret agent Jonski over to the office of the Attorney General, there to undergo fair trial by due process of law, and to suffer whatever punish-ment that branch of the government deems fitting for a self-admitted trai-tor who deserves only death. This meeting is now adjourned."

In this fashion, Joenes was swiftly transferred to the punitive branch of the government and bound over to the Attorney General.

IV. HOW JOENES WAS GIVEN JUSTICE
(As told by Pelui of Easter Island)

The Attorney General, to whom Joenes was bound over, was a tall man with a hawk face, narrow eyes, bloodless lips, and a face that looked as though it had been hammered out of raw iron. Stooped and silently contemptuous, startling in his black velvet cloak and ruffled collar, the Attorney General was the living embodiment of his terrible office. Since he was a servant of the punitive branch of the government, his duty was to call down retribution upon all who fell into his hands, and to do so by any means in his power.

The Attorney General's place of residence was Washington. But he himself was a citizen of Athens, New York, and in his youth had been an acquaintance of Aristotle and Alcibiades, whose writings are the distilla-tion of American genius.

Athens was one of the cities of ancient Hellas, from which the Ameri-can civilization had sprung. Near Athens was Sparta, a military power that had held leadership over the Lacedaemonian cities of upper New York State. Ionian Athens and Dorian Sparta had fought a disastrous war, and had lost their independence to American rule. But they were still influen-tial in the politics of America, especially since Washington had been the seat of Hellenic power.

At first, the case of Joenes seemed simple enough. Joenes had no im-portant friends or political colleagues, and it seemed that retribution might be visited upon him with impunity. Accordingly, the Attorney General arranged for Joenes to receive every possible sort of legal advice, and then to be tried by a jury of his peers in the famous Star Chamber. In this way the exact letter of the law would be carried out, but with a comforting foreknowledge of the verdict the jury would render. For the punctilious jurors of the Star Chamber, utterly dedicated to the eradication of any vestige of evil, had never in their history given any verdict but guilty.

After the verdict should be delivered, the Attorney General planned to sacrifice Joenes upon the Electric Chair at Delphi, thus winning favor in the eyes of gods and men.

This was his plan. But further investigation showed that Joenes's father had been a Dorian from Mechanicsville, New York, and a magistrate of that community. And Joenes's mother had been an Ionian from Miami, an Athenian colony deep in Barbarian territory. Because of this, certain influential Hellenes urged mercy for the erring son of respectable parents, and for the sake of Hellenic unity, which was a force to be reckoned with in American politics.

The Attorney General, an Athenian himself, thought it best to comply with this request. Therefore he dissolved the Star Chamber and sent Joenes to the great Oracle at Sperry. This met with approval, for the Sperry Oracle, like the Oracles at Genmotor and Genelectric, was known to be absolutely fair and impartial in its judgments of men and their actions. In fact, the Oracles gave such good justice that they had replaced many of the courts of the land.

Joenes was brought to Sperry and was told to stand before the Oracle. This he did, although his knees were shaking. The Oracle was a great calculating machine of the most complex variety, with a switchboard, or altar, attended by many priests. These priests had been castrated so they should think no thoughts except of the machine. And the high priest had been blinded also, so that he could see penitents only through the eyes of the Oracle.

When the high priest entered, Joenes prostrated himself before him. But the priest raised him up and said, "My son, fear not. Death is the common destiny of all men, and ceaseless travail is their condition throughout the ephemeral life of the senses. Tell me, do you have any money?"

Joenes said, "I have eight dollars and thirty cents. But why do you ask, Father?"

"Because," the priest said, "it is common practice for supplicants to make a voluntary sacrifice of money to the Oracle. But if you do not have the money, you can give equally acceptable things such as chattel mortgages, bonds, stocks, deeds, or any other papers which men deem of value."

"I have none of these things," Joenes said sadly.

"Do you not own lands in Polynesia?" the priest asked.

"I do not," Joenes said. "My parents' land was given to them by the government, to whom it must return. Nor do I hold other properties, for in Polynesia such things are not considered important."

"Then you own nothing?" the priest asked. He seemed disturbed.

"Nothing but eight dollars and thirty cents," Joenes said, "and a guitar which is not my own but belongs to a man named Lum in distant California. But Father, are these things really necessary?"

"Of course not," the priest replied. "But even cyberneticists must live, and an act of generosity from a stranger is looked upon as pleasing, especially when the time comes to interpret the words of the Oracle. Also, some believe that a penniless man is one who has not worked to amass money for the Oracle in case the day of divine wrath should ever be upon him, and who is therefore lacking in piety. But that need not concern us. We will now state your case, and ask for a judgment."

The priest took the Attorney General's statement, and Joenes's defense, and translated them into the secret language in which the Oracle listened to the words of men. Soon there was a reply.

The Oracle's judgment was as follows:

SQUARE IT TO THE TENTH POWER MINUS THE SQUARE
    ROOT OF MINUS ONE.
DO NOT FORGET THE COSIGN, FOR MEN MUST NEEDS
    HAVE FUN.
ADD IN X AS A VARIABLE, FREE-FLOATING, FANCY-FREE.
IT WILL COME AT LAST TO ZERO, AND MORE YOU NEED
    NOT ME.

When this decision had been delivered, the priests met to interpret the words of the Oracle. And this is what they said:

SQUARE IT means correct the wrong.

THE TENTH POWER is the degree and number in which the penitent must labor in penal servitude in order to correct the wrong; namely ten years.

THE SQUARE ROOT OF MINUS ONE, being an imaginary number, represents a fictitious state of grace; but being instrumental, represents also the possibility of power and fame for the supplicant. Because of this, the previous ten-year sentence is suspended.

THE X VARIABLE represents the incarnate furies of the earth, among whom the supplicant shall dwell, and who shall show him all possible horrors.

THE COSIGN is the mark of the goddess herself, protecting the supplicant from some of the terror of the furies, and promising him certain fleshly joys.

IT WILL COME AT LAST TO ZERO, means that the equation of divine justice and human guilt is balanced in this case.

MORE YOU NEED NOT ME, means that the supplicant may not apply again to this or any other Oracle, since the rendering is complete.

So it was that Joenes received a ten-year suspended sentence. And the Attorney General had to obey the decision of the Oracle and set him free.

Once freed, Joenes continued his journey through the land of America, bearing upon his head a curse and a promise, as well as a ten-year suspended sentence. He departed hastily from Sperry and rode a train to the great city of New York. And what he did there, and what happened to him, is the story which must now be told.

V. THE STORY OF JOENES, WATTS, AND THE POLICEMAN
(As told by Ma'aoa of Samoa)

Never had Joenes seen anything like the great city of New York. The ceaseless rush and bustle of so many people was strange to him, but curiously exciting. When night came, the frantic life of the city continued unabated, and Joenes observed New Yorkers hurrying in and out of nightclubs and dance halls in their quest for pleasure. Nor was there any lack of culture in the city, for great numbers of people were attentive to the lost art of the moving pictures.

In the small hours of the night, the city's pace slowed. Then Joenes came upon many old men, and some young ones too, who sat listlessly on benches or stood near subway exits. When Joenes looked into their faces he saw a terrible nothingness, and when he spoke to them he could not understand their mumbled replies. These atypical New Yorkers disturbed him, and Joenes was glad when morning came.

At first light, the frenzied movements of the crowds began again, and people pushed and shoved each other in their haste to get somewhere and do something. Joenes wanted to learn the reason for all of this, so he chose a man out of the crowd and stopped him.

"Sir," Joenes said, "could you spare a moment of your valuable time and tell a stranger something about the great and purposeful vitality I see all around me?"

The man said, "Whatsamatter, you some kind of nut?" And he hurried off.

But the next man Joenes stopped gave the question careful thought, and said, "You call it vitality, huh?"

"So it appears," Joenes said, glancing at the restless crowds surging around them. "By the way, my name is Joenes."

"Mine's Watts," the man said, "as in Watts the matter. In answer to your question, I'll tell you that what you see is not vitality. It's panic."

"But what are they in a panic about?" Joenes asked.

"To put it in a nutshell," Watts said, "they're afraid if they stop hurrying and pushing, somebody will find out they're dead. It's a very serious matter being found dead, because then they can fire you from your job, foreclose all your bills, raise your apartment rental, and carry you squirming to your grave."

Joenes found this reply scarcely credible. He said, "Mr. Watts, these people do not look dead. And in actual fact, all exaggeration aside, they are *not* dead, are they?"

"I never put exaggeration aside," Watts told him. "But since you're a stranger, I'll try to explain a little more. To begin with, death is merely a matter of definition. Once the definition was very simple: you were dead when you stopped moving for a long time. But now the scientists have examined this antiquated notion more carefully, and have done considerable research on the entire subject. They have found that you can be dead in all important respects, but still go on walking and talking."

"What are these important respects?" Joenes asked.

"First of all," Watts told him, "the walking dead are characterized by an almost total lack of emotionality. They can feel only anger and fear, though they sometimes simulate other emotions in the crude manner of a chimpanzee pretending to read a book. Next, there is a robotic quality in their actions, which accompanies a cessation of the higher thinking processes. Frequently there is a reflex motion toward piety, which is not unlike the frantic movements that a chicken makes after its head has been chopped off. Because of this reflex, many of the walking dead are detected around churches, where some of them even try to pray. Others can be found on park benches or near subway exits—"

"Ah," said Joenes. "When I walked in the city late last night I saw certain men at those places—"

"Exactly," said Watts. "Those are the ones who no longer pretend that they are not dead. But others copy the living with great and pathetic earnestness, hoping to pass unnoticed. They can usually be detected because they overdo it, either by talking too much or by laughing too hard."

"I had no idea of all this," Joenes said.

"It is a tragic problem," Watts said. "The authorities are doing their best to cope with it, but it has assumed formidable proportions. I wish I could tell you other characteristics of the walking dead, and how they resemble the old-fashioned nonwalking dead, for I'm sure that you would find it interesting. But now, Mr. Joenes, I see a policeman approaching, and therefore I had better make my departure."

So saying, Watts broke into a full sprint and raced through the crowd. The policeman started after him, but soon gave up the pursuit and returned to Joenes.

"Damn it," the policeman said, "I've lost him again."

"Is he a criminal?" Joenes asked.

"Smartest jewel thief in these parts," the policeman said, mopping his massive red brow. "He likes to disguise himself as a beatnik."

"He was talking to me about the walking dead," Joenes said.

"He's always making up those stories," the policeman told him. "Compulsive liar, that's what he is. Crazy. And dangerous as they come. Especially dangerous because he doesn't carry a gun. I've almost caught him three times. I order him to stop in the name of the law, just like the book says, and when he doesn't stop, I shoot at him. So far I've killed eight bystanders. The way I'm going, I'll probably never make sergeant. They make me pay for my own bullets, too."

"But if this Watts never carries a gun—" Joenes began, then stopped abruptly. He had seen a strange sullen expression cross the policeman's face, and had seen his hand drop to the butt of his gun. "What I meant to say," Joenes continued, "is there anything in what Watts told me about the walking dead?"

"Naw, that's just a beatnik line he makes up to kid people with. Didn't I tell you he was a jewel thief?"

"I forgot," Joenes said.

"Well don't forget it. I'm just a plain ordinary man, but a guy like Watts gets me sore. I do my duty just like the book says, and in the evenings I go home and watch the tv, except on Friday evenings when I go bowling. Does that sound like being a robot, like Watts says?"

"Of course not," Joenes said.

"That guy," the policeman continued, "talks about people not having no emotion. Let me tell you, I'm maybe no psychologist, but I know I got emotions. When I have this gun in my hand, I feel good. Does that sound like I got no emotions? Furthermore, let me tell you something. I was raised in a tough section of this city, and when I was a kid I used to run with a gang. We all had zip guns and gravity knives, and we enjoyed ourselves with armed robbery, murder, and rape. Does that sound like no emotion? And I might of gone right on in that way, from being a kid criminal to being an adult criminal, if I hadn't met this priest. He wasn't no stuffed shirt, he was just like one of us, because he knew that was the only way he could reach us wild types. He used to go out on stomps with us, and more than once I saw him cut the hell out of somebody with a little switchblade he always carried. So he was regular and we accepted him. But he was also a priest, and seeing he was regular I let him talk to me. And he told me how I was wasting my life in that way."

"He must have been a wonderful man," Joenes said.

"He was a saint," the policeman said, in a heavy brooding voice. "That man was a real saint, because he did everything we did but he was good inside and he always told us we should get out of criminality."

The policeman looked Joenes in the eye and said, "Because of that man, I became a cop. Me, who everyone thought would end up in the electric chair! And that Watts has the nerve to speak of the walking dead. I became a cop, and I've been a good cop instead of some lousy punk hoodlum like Watts. I've killed eight criminals in the line of duty, winning three merit badges from the department. And I've also accidentally killed 27 innocent bystanders who didn't get out of the way fast enough. I'm sorry about those people, but I've got a job to do, and I can't let people get in the way when I'm going after a criminal. And no matter what the newspapers say, I've never taken a bribe in my life, not even for a parking ticket." The policeman's hand tightened convulsively around the butt of his revolver. "I'd give a parking ticket to Jesus Christ himself and no number of saints would be able to bribe me. What do you think about that?"

"I think you are a dedicated man," Joenes said carefully.

"You're right. And I've got a beautiful wife and three wonderful children. I've taught them all how to shoot a revolver. Nothing's too good for my family. And Watts thinks he knows something about emotion! Christ, these smooth-talking bastards get me so sore sometimes I can feel my head coming off. It's a good thing I'm a religious man."

"I'm sure it is," Joenes said.

"I still go every week to see the priest who got me out of the gang. He's still working with kids, because he's dedicated. He's getting sorta old to use a knife, so now it's usually a zip gun, or sometimes a bicycle chain. That man has done more for the cause of law than all the youth rehabilitation centers in the city. I give him a hand sometimes, and between us we've redeemed fourteen boys who you would have thought were hopeless criminals. Many of them are respected businessmen now, and six have joined the police force. Whenever I see that old man, I *feel* religion."

"I think that's wonderful," Joenes said. He began backing away, because the policeman had drawn his revolver and was toying with it nervously.

"There's nothing wrong with this country that good-heartedness and straight thinking won't cure," the policeman said, his jaw twitching. "Good always triumphs in the end, and it always will as long as there are good-hearted men to help it along. There's more law in the end of my night-stick than in all the musty old lawbooks. We bring them in and the judges let them go. What about that? Nice state of business, huh? But us cops are used to it, and we figure one broken arm is worth a year in stir, so we take care of a lot of the sentencing ourselves."

Here the policeman drew his nightstick. With it in one hand, his revolver in the other, he looked hard at Joenes. Joenes sensed the sudden hugeness of the policeman's need to enforce law and order. He stood utterly still, hoping that the policeman, now advancing towards him with shining eyes, would not kill him or break any bones.

A crucial moment was approaching. But Joenes was saved at the last moment by a citizen of the city, who, made absentminded by the tropic sun, stepped off the curb before the traffic light changed to green.

The policeman whirled, fired two warning shots, and charged toward the man. Joenes walked quickly away in the opposite direction, and continued walking northward until he was beyond the limits of the city.

VI. JOENES AND THE THREE TRUCK DRIVERS

(This and the three Truck Driver stories that comprise it are told by Teleu of Huahine)

As Joenes was walking along a highway to the north, a truck stopped beside him. Within the truck were three men who said they would willingly give him a ride as far as they were going.

Very happily Joenes got into the truck, declaring his gratitude to the truck drivers. But they said the pleasure was theirs, since driving a truck was lonely work even for three, and they enjoyed talking to different men and hearing of their adventures. This being the case, they asked Joenes to tell what had happened to him since he had left his home.

Joenes told these men that he was from a distant island, had come to the city of San Francisco where he had been arrested, questioned before a Congressional Committee, tried by an Oracle and given a ten-year suspended sentence, gone to New York where a policeman had nearly killed him. Nothing had gone right since he had left his island, Joenes said, and everything had gone badly. Therefore he considered himself a very unfortunate man.

"Mr. Joenes," said the first truck driver, "you have indeed gone through misfortunes. But I am the most unfortunate of men, for I have lost something more precious than gold, the loss of which I bemoan every day of my life."

Joenes asked the man to tell his story. And this is the story that the first truck driver told.

THE STORY OF THE SCIENTIFIC TRUCK DRIVER

My name is Adolphus Proponus, and by birth I am a Swede. Ever since I was a child, I loved science. I possessed that love not merely for itself, but because I believed that science was mankind's greatest servant, which would lift humanity out of the cruelty of the past, to peace and happiness. In spite of all the atrocities I saw men perform, and even though my own neutral country grew rich by supplying guns to warring nations, I still believed in the goodness and superiority of mankind, and in its liberation through science.

Because of my humanistic instincts and my scientific inclinations, I became a doctor. I applied for work at the United Nations Health Commission, desiring the furthest and most wretched place on earth for my post. Not for me a quiet practice in a somnolent Swedish town; I wished to throw myself deep into the battle against disease, and for humanity.

I was sent to a place on the coast of Western Africa, there to be the sole doctor for an area larger than Europe. I was replacing a man named Durr, a Swiss who had died of the bite of a horned viper.

This area obviously needed a good doctor, since there was a great prevalence of diseases. Many of these were known to me, for I had studied them in books. Others were new. The new ones, I learned, had been propagated artificially, as part of the neutralization of Africa. I do not know whose decision this was, but someone had wished a truly neutral Africa, which could assist neither East nor West. To this purpose germs had been introduced, and also certain laboratory plants, which had the effect of making dense jungle even denser. These things stopped men from having time for politics, since all their time had to be spent in a battle for life itself.

These things had also wiped out several hundred million Western troops, who were engaged in combat against Eastern guerrillas. The guerrillas, too, were wiped out. Also many species of animal had been destroyed, although a few had thrived. The rat, for example, flourished. Snakes of all species multiplied. Among insects, there was a great increase in flies and mosquitoes. Among birds, the vultures had increased beyond counting.

I had never known about this state of affairs, since news like this is generally ignored in a democracy, and is banned in a dictatorship. But I saw these horrors in Africa. And I learned that the same was true in the tropical parts of Asia, Central America, and India. All of those places were now truly neutral, through accident or through design, since they were engaged in a desperate struggle for life itself.

As a doctor I was saddened because of the many diseases, old and new. These sprang from the jungle, which had been aided and augmented by man. The growth rate of that jungle was fantastic; and therefore equally fantastic was its decay rate. Because of this, disease germs of all kinds multiplied and spread in the most congenial atmosphere possible.

As a man I was maddened by the perverted way in which science had been used. But still I believed in science. I told myself that evil men of little vision had created much harm in the world; but that humanitarians, working through science, would set it all right again.

I set to work with a will, aided by humanitarians the world over. I went to all the tribes within my district, treating their illnesses with my supplies of drugs. My successes were overwhelming.

But then the spawning diseases became resistant to my drugs, and new epidemics began. The tribes, although strong in their resistance, suffered terribly.

I wired urgently for newer drugs. These were sent to me, and I put down the epidemic. But a few of the germs and viruses managed to survive, and disease spread once again.

I requested newer drugs, and these were also sent to me. Once again disease and I were locked in mortal combat, from which I emerged victorious. But there were always a few organisms that escaped my drugs. Also, there were mutations to be reckoned with. Given the right environment, I learned that diseases could change into new and virulent forms much faster than men could make or discover new drugs.

In fact, I found that germs behaved quite like humans in times of stress. They showed every evidence of an astonishing will to survive; and quite naturally, the harder one struck at them, the faster and more frantically they spawned, mutated, resisted, and at last, struck back. The resemblance was, to my way of thinking, uncanny and unnatural.

I was laboring prodigiously at the time, twelve to eighteen hours a day, trying to save the poor, patient, suffering population. But disease outstripped my latest drugs, won a sort of victory, and raged with unbelievable violence. I was in despair, for no new drugs had been invented to meet these newest ills.

Then I found that the germs, in mutating to meet my new drugs, had become vulnerable once again to the old drugs. Therefore, in a perfect frenzy of scientific fervor, I began to apply the old drugs once more.

Since I had come to Africa, I had battled no less than ten major epidemics. Now I was beginning to fight my eleventh. And I knew that the germs and viruses would retreat before my attack, spawn, mutate, and strike again, leaving me to fight a twelfth epidemic, with similar results, and then a thirteenth, and so forth.

This was the situation into which my scientific and humanistic zeal had carried me. But I was drunk with fatigue, and half dead with my labors. I had no time to think of anything but the immediate problem.

But then the people of my district took the problem out of my hands. They possessed very little education, and they saw only the great epidemics which had ravaged them since my coming. Those people looked upon me as a sort of supremely evil witch doctor, whose bottles of supposed healing drugs actually contained the refined essences of the diseases that had ravaged them. They turned to their own witch doctors, who treated the sick with useless daubs of mud and bits of bone, and blamed every death upon some innocent tribesman.

Even the mothers whose children I had saved now turned against me. These mothers pointed out that the children had died anyhow, of starvation instead of disease.

At last the men of the villages gathered to kill me. They would have done so if I had not been saved by the witch doctors. This was an irony, because I considered the witch doctors my greatest antagonists.

The witch doctors explained to the people that if I were killed, a fiend of even greater evil power would be sent to them. Therefore the people did me no harm; and the witch doctors grinned at me, because they considered me a colleague.

Still I would not abandon my work among the tribes. For that reason, the tribes abandoned me. They moved inland to an area of desolate swamp, where food was scarce and disease was common.

I could not follow them, since the swamp was in a different district. This district had its own doctor, also a Swede, who gave out no drugs at all, no pills, no injections, nothing. Instead, he got drunk every day on his own supplies of alcohol. He had lived in the jungle for twenty years, and he said he knew what was best.

Left completely alone in my district, I had a nervous collapse. I was sent back to Sweden, and there I thought about everything that had happened.

It seemed to me that the villagers and witch doctors, whom I had considered so perversely intractable, had merely behaved with good common sense. They had fled from my science and my humanism, which had improved their lot not an iota. On the contrary, my science had done nothing but produce more pain and suffering for them, and my humanism had foolishly attempted to wipe out other creatures for their benefit, and by doing so had upset the balance of forces upon the Earth.

Realizing all this, I fled my country, fled Europe itself, and came here. Now I drive a truck. And when someone speaks to me in glowing words about science and humanity and the marvels of healing, I stare at him as though he were insane.

That is how I lost my belief in science, a thing more precious to me than gold, the loss of which I bemoan every day of my life.

At the end of this story, the second truck driver said, "No one would deny that you had misfortunes, Joenes, but these are less than what my friend has just told you. And my friend's misfortunes are less than mine. For I am the most unfortunate of men, and I have lost something more precious than gold and more valuable than science, the loss of which I bemoan every day of my life."

Joenes asked the man to tell his story. And this is the story the second truck driver told.

THE STORY OF THE HONEST TRUCK DRIVER

My name is Ramon Delgado, and I am from the land of Mexico. My one great pride was in being an honest man. I was honest because of the laws of the land, which told me to be so, and which had been written by the best of men, who had derived them from universally accepted principles of justice, and had fortified them with punishments so that all men, not just those of goodwill, would obey.

This seemed right to me, because I loved justice and believed in it, and therefore believed in the laws that were derived from justice, and in the punishment that enforced the law. Not only did I feel that man's conception and execution of justice was good; I also felt that it was necessary. For only through this could there be freedom from tyranny and a sense of personal dignity.

I labored for many years in my village, saved my money, and led an honest and upright life. One day I was offered a job in the capital. I was very happy about this, for I had long desired to see that great city from which the justice of my country derives.

I used all my savings to purchase an old automobile, and I drove to the capital. I parked in front of my new employer's store, where I found a parking meter. I went inside the store in order to get a peso to put in the parking meter. When I came out, I was arrested.

I was taken before a judge who accused me of illegal parking, petty larceny, vagrancy, resisting arrest, and creating a public disturbance.

The judge found me guilty of all these things. Of illegal parking, because there had been no money in the meter; petty larceny, because I had taken a peso from my employer's till to put in the meter; vagrancy, because I had had only a single peso on my person; resisting arrest, because I had argued with the policeman; and creating a public disturbance, because I had wept when he took me to the jail.

In a technical sense, all these things were true, so I considered it no miscarriage of justice when the judge found me guilty. In fact, I admired his zeal in serving the law.

Nor did I complain when he sentenced me to ten years of imprisonment. This seemed severe, but I knew that the law could be upheld only through stern and uncompromising punishment.

I was sent to the Federal Penitentiary of Morelos, and I knew that it would be good for me to see the place where punishment is served out, and thus to learn the bitter fruits of dishonesty.

When I arrived at the Penitentiary, I saw a crowd of men hiding in the woods nearby. I took no notice of them, for the guard at the gate was reading my commitment papers. He studied them with great care, then opened the gate.

As soon as the gate was opened, I was amazed to see that crowd of men come out of hiding, rush forward, and force their way into the prison. Many guards came out and tried to push the men back. Nevertheless, some were able to get into the Penitentiary before the admittance guard was finally able to close the gate.

"Is it possible," I asked him, "that those men wanted to get into prison on purpose?"

"Obviously they did," the guard said.

"But I had always thought that prisons were for the purpose of keeping people in rather than out," I said.

"They used to be," the guard told me. "But nowadays, with so many foreigners in the country, and so much starvation, men break into prison merely to get three meals a day. There's nothing we can do about it. By breaking into prison they become criminals, and we have to let them stay."

"Disgraceful!" I said. "But what do the foreigners have to do with it?"

"They started all the trouble," the guard said. "There's starvation in their own countries, and they know that we in Mexico have the world's best prisons. So they come great distances in order to break into our prisons, especially when they can't break into their own. But I suppose foreigners are really no worse or better than our own people, who do the same thing."

"If this is the case," I said, "how can the government enforce its laws?"

"Only by keeping the truth a secret," the guard told me. "Someday we will be able to build penitentiaries that will keep the right people in and the wrong ones out. But until that time comes, the thing must be kept secret. In that way, most of the population still believes they should fear punishment."

The guard then escorted me inside the Penitentiary, to the office of the Parole Board. There a man asked me how I liked prison life. I told him that I wasn't sure yet.

"Well," the man said, "your behavior for the entire time you have been here has been exemplary. Reform is our motive, not revenge. Would you like an immediate parole?"

I was afraid of saying the wrong thing, so I told him I wasn't sure.

"Take your time," he said, "and return to this office any time you want to be released."

Then I went to my cell. Within I found two Mexicans and three foreigners. One of the foreigners was an American, and the other two were Frenchmen. The American asked me if I had accepted a parole. I said that I hadn't yet.

"Damn smart for a beginner!" said the American, whose name was Otis. "Some of the new convicts don't know. They take a parole, and wham, they're on the outside looking in."

"Is that so bad?" I asked.

"Very bad," Otis said. "If you take a parole, then you don't have any chance of getting back into prison. No matter what you do, the judge just marks it down as parole violation and tells you not to do it again. And the chances are you don't do it again because the cops have broken both your arms."

"Otis is right," one of the Frenchmen said. "Taking a parole is extremely dangerous, and I am the living proof of that. My name is Edmond Dantes. Many years ago I was sentenced to this institution, and then offered a parole. In the ignorance of my youth, I accepted it. But then, on the Outside, I realized that all my friends were still in prison, and that my collection of books and records was still here. Also, in my juvenile rashness, I had left behind my sweetheart, Trustee 43422231. I realized too late that my whole life was in here, and that I was shut out forever from the warmth and security of these granite walls."

"What did you do?" I asked.

"I still thought that criminality would bring its own reward," Dantes said with a wistful smile. "So I killed a man. But the judge simply extended my period of parole, and the police broke all the fingers of my right hand. It was then, while my fingers were healing, that I resolved to get back in."

"It must have been very difficult," I said.

Dantes nodded. "It called for a terrible patience, because I spent the next twenty years of my life attempting to break into this prison."

The other prisoners were silent. Old Dantes continued:

"Security was more rigid in those days, and a rush through the gates, such as you saw this morning, would have been impossible. Therefore, unaided, I tunneled under the building. Three times I came up against sheer granite, and was forced to begin a new tunnel search somewhere else. Once I came almost to the inner courtyard, but the guards detected me, countertunneled, and forced me back. Once I tried to parachute onto the prison from an airplane, but a sudden gust of wind forced me away. Thereafter, no planes were allowed to fly overhead. Thus, in my own way, I effected some prison reforms."

"But how did you finally get in?" I asked.

The old man smiled grimly. "After many fruitless years, an idea occurred to me. I couldn't believe that so simple an idea could succeed where ingenuity and raw courage had failed. Nevertheless, I tried it.

"I returned to the prison disguised as a special investigator. At first the guards were reluctant to let me pass. But I told them that the government was considering a reform bill in which guards would be granted equal rights with the prisoners. They let me in, and I then revealed who I was. They had to let me stay, and some man came and wrote down my story. I only hope he put it down correctly.

"Since then, of course, the guards have instituted rigid measures that would make the repetition of my plan impossible. But it is an article of faith with me that courageous men will always surmount the difficulties society puts between a man and his goal. If men are steadfast, they too will succeed in breaking into prison."

All the prisoners were silent when old Dantes finished speaking. At last I asked, "Was your sweetheart still here when you got back?"

The old men looked away, and a tear coursed down his cheek. "Trustee 43422231 had died of cirrhosis of the liver three years previously. Now I spend my time in prayer and contemplation."

The old man's tragic tale of courage, determination, and doomed love had cast a gloom over the cell. In silence we went to our evening meal, and no one showed good spirits until many hours later.

By then I had thought until my head ached about this whole strange matter of men wanting to live in prison. The more I thought, the more confused I became. So, very timidly, I asked my cell mates whether freedom was not important, and if they never hungered for cities and streets, and for flowering fields and forests.

"Freedom?" Otis said to me. "It's the illusion of freedom you're talking about, and that's a very different thing. The cities you talk about contain only horror, insecurity, and fear. The streets are all blind alleys, with death at the end of every one of them."

"And those flowering fields and forests you mention are even worse," the second Frenchman told me. "My name is Rousseau, and in my youth I wrote several foolish books based upon no experience at all, extolling nature and speaking of man's rightful place in it: But then, in my mature years, I secretly left my country and journeyed through this nature I had spoken of with such confidence.

"I found out then how terrible nature is, and how it hates mankind. I discovered the flowering green fields make poor walking, and are harder on a man's feet than the worst pavement. I saw that the crops man plants are unhappy hybrids, seduced of their strength and kept alive only by men who fight back the conquering weeds and insects.

"In the forest, I found that the trees communed only with themselves, and that every creature ran from me. I learned that there are beautiful blue lakes that may delight your eye, but they are surrounded always by thorns and swampy land. And when you finally reach them, you see that the water is a dirty brown.

"Nature also gives rain and drought, heat and cold; and thoughtfully ensures that the rain rots man's food, the drought parches it, the heat scalds man's body, and the cold freezes his limbs.

"These are only nature's milder aspects, not to be compared to the wrathfulness of the sea, the frigid indifference of the mountains, the treachery of the swamp, the depravity of the desert, or the terror of the jungle. But I noticed that nature, in her hatred of mankind, provided that most of the earth's surface be covered with sea, mountains, swamp, desert, and jungle.

"I need say nothing of earthquakes, tornadoes, tidal waves, and the like, in which nature reveals the fullest extent of her hatred.

"Man's only escape from these horrors is in a city, where nature can be partially shut out. And obviously, the type of city most removed from nature is a prison. That is the conclusion I have reached after many years of study. And that is the reason why I repudiate the words of my youth and live very happily in this place where I can never see a green thing."

With that, Rousseau turned away and contemplated a steel wall.

"You see, Delgado," Otis said, "the only true freedom is right here, inside a prison."

This I would not accept, and I pointed out that we were locked up here, which seemed contradictory to the notion of freedom.

"But all of us are locked up upon this earth," old Dantes answered me. "Some in a greater place and some in a lesser place. And all of us are locked up forever within ourselves. Everything is a prison, and this place here is the best of all prisons."

Otis then belabored me for my lack of gratitude. "You've heard the guards," he said. "If our good fortune were commonly known throughout the country, everyone would be fighting to get in. You should be happy to be here, and happy that knowledge of this marvelous place is confined to a few."

"But the situation is changing," a Mexican prisoner said. "Even though the government suppresses the truth and presents imprisonment as something to be feared and avoided, people are beginning to learn the truth."

"It puts the government in a terrible position," another Mexican prisoner said. "They still haven't invented any substitute for prison, although for a while they thought of making all crimes punishable by death. They gave that up, since it would directly affect the country's military and industrial potential. So they must still sentence men to prison—that one place where they want to go!"

All the cell mates laughed at this, because, being criminals, they loved perversions of justice. And this seemed to me the greatest perversion of all—to commit a crime against the common good, and to be made happy and secure because of that crime.

I felt like a man walking through some horrible nightmare, for I had no argument with which to answer these men. At last, in desperation, I cried out: "You may be free and live in the best place on earth—but you have no women."

The prisoners tittered nervously, as if I had said something not very nice. But Otis answered calmly, "What you say is true, we have no women. But that is quite unimportant."

"Unimportant?" I echoed.

"Definitely," Otis said. "Some may experience a degree of discomfort at first; but then one adapts to one's surroundings. After all, only women think that women are indispensable. We men know better."

The members of the cell chorused their agreement with great animation.

"Real men," Otis said, "need only the company of other real men. If Butch were here he could explain all of this better; but Butch is in the infirmary with a double hernia, to the great sorrow of his many friends and admirers. But he would explain to you that any kind of societal existence involves compromise. When the compromises are great, we call it tyranny. When they are small and easily arranged, like this minor matter of women, we call it freedom. Remember, Delgado, you can't expect perfection."

I made no further attempt to argue, but said that I wanted to leave the prison as soon as possible.

"I can arrange your escape this evening," Otis said. "And I think it is just as well that you go. Prison life is not for any man who does not appreciate it."

That evening, when the lights in the prison had been dimmed, Otis raised one of the granite blocks in the floor of the cell. At the bottom of this was a passageway. Following this, I emerged at last on the street, dazed and bewildered.

For many days I thought over my experiences. At last I realized that my honesty had been nothing but stupidity, since it had been based upon ignorance and a misconception of the ways of the world. There could be no honesty, since there was no law to sanction it. The law had failed, and neither punishment nor goodwill could make it work. It had failed because all of man's ideas of justice had been wrong. Therefore there was no such thing as justice, nor anything deriving from it.

And terrible as this was, even more terrible was this realization: that with no justice there could be no freedom or human dignity; there could only be perverted illusions such as my cell mates possessed.

That is how I lost my sense of honesty, a thing more precious to me than gold, the loss of which I bemoan every day of my life.

At the end of this story, the third truck driver said, "No one would deny that you have had misfortunes, Joenes. But these are less than what my two friends have just told you. And my friends' misfortunes are less than mine. For I am the most unfortunate of men, for I have lost something more precious than gold, and more valuable than both science and justice; the loss of which I bemoan every day of my life."

Joenes asked the man to tell his story. And this is the story the third truck driver told.

THE STORY OF THE RELIGIOUS TRUCK DRIVER

My name is Hans Schmidt, and my place of birth is Germany. As a young man I learned about the horrors of the past, and this saddened me. Then I learned about the present. I traveled throughout Europe, and I saw nothing but guns and fortifications stretching all the way from Germany's eastern frontier to the coast at Normandy, and from the North Sea to the Mediterranean. Countless miles of these fortifications existed where village and forest had existed before, all neatly camouflaged, all for the purpose of blasting the Russians and the East Europeans, should they ever attack. This saddened me, for I saw that the present was exactly the same as the past, being nothing more than a preparation for cruelty and war.

Never had I believed in science. Even without the experience of my Swedish friend, I could see that science had improved nothing upon the earth, but had merely caused great harm. Nor did I believe in human justice, law, freedom, or dignity. Even without the experience of my Mexican friend, I could see for myself that man's conception of justice, and everything deriving from it, was faulty.

I had never doubted the uniqueness of man, and his special place in the universe. But I felt that man by himself could never rise above the bestial qualities in his nature.

Therefore I turned to something greater than man. I turned wholeheartedly to religion. In this was man's only salvation, his only dignity, his sole freedom. In this could be found all the aims and dreams of science and humanism. And even though religious man might be imperfect, that which he worshipped could not be imperfect.

This, at any rate, is what I believed at the time.

I held to no one belief, but instead I studied all faiths, feeling that every religion was a pathway to that which is greater than man.

I gave my money to the poor and wandered across the face of Europe with staff and knapsack, striving always to contemplate The Perfect, as it is expressed in the many religious forms upon Earth.

One day I came to a cave high in the mountains of the Pyrenees. I was very tired, and I entered this cave to rest.

Within, I found a great multitude of people. Some were dressed all in black, and others wore gorgeously embroidered costumes. Among them sat a giant toad, as large as a man, with a jewel gleaming dully in his forehead.

I stared at the toad and at the multitude, and then I fell upon my knees. For I realized that those before me were not really human.

A man dressed as a clergyman said, "Please come forward, Mr. Schmidt. We have been hoping you would visit us."

I raised myself and walked forward. The clergyman said, "I am known as Father Arian. I would like to introduce my esteemed colleague, Mr. Satan."

The toad bowed to me and extended a webbed hand. I shook the toad's hand.

The clergyman said, "Mr. Satan and I, together with these others, represent the only true United Church Council of Earth. We have long noted your piety, Schmidt, and therefore we have decided to answer any questions you might wish to ask."

I was beside myself with amazement and thankfulness that this miracle had been granted to me. I addressed my first question to the toad, asking, "Are you truly Satan, Prince of Evil?"

"I have the honor to be that person," the toad replied.

"And *you* are a member of the United Church Council?"

"Why, of course," the toad answered. "You must understand, Mr. Schmidt, that evil is necessary in order for there to be good. Neither quality can exist without the other. It was only with this understanding that I took on my job in the first place. You have perhaps heard that my evil nature is inherent. Nothing could be further from the truth. A lawyer's character surely cannot be ascertained from the cases he argues in court. So with me. I am merely the advocate of evil, and I try, like any good lawyer, to ensure full rights and privileges for my clients. But I sincerely trust that I am not evil *myself.* If such were the case, why would so delicate and important a task have been given to me?"

I was pleased with Satan's answer, since evil had always bothered me. Now I said, "Would it be presumptuous of me to ask what you, the representatives of good and evil, are doing here in this underground cave?"

"It would not be presumptuous," Satan said. "Since we are all theologians here, we love to give answers. And that is the one question we hoped you would ask. You will not object, of course, if I answer in a theological manner?"

"Of course not," I said.

"Excellent," said Satan. "In that case, I shall proceed to make a statement, and then to prove it, and then to let my answer to your question flow from that. Agreed? Then this is the statement:

"Everything that partakes of life has its viewpoint, and tends to see all of existence from that viewpoint. The viewer, knowing only himself, believes himself to be eternal and immutable; and he necessarily holds himself to be eternal and immutable; and he necessarily holds that his bias is the only true view of the objects and qualities around him.

"By way of proof, let me offer you the homely example of the eagle. This eagle sees only an eagle's world. All things in that world are for or against the eagle. All things are judged by their usefulness to the eagle, or their danger, or their eating or nest-building qualities. All things possess this eagleness for the eagle, and even the inanimate rocks become the touchstones of memories of previous eagle exploits.

"This is my own little proof of the omnipotence of viewpoint, Mr. Schmidt, and I hope you accept it. Assuming that you do, let me say that as it is with the eagle, so it is with men. And as it is with men, so it is with us. It is the inescapable result of having a point of view.

"Our own viewpoint can be easily told. We believe in good and evil, in divinity, and in a moral universe. Just like you, Mr. Schmidt.

"We have propounded our beliefs in various ways, and according to various doctrines. Often we have aroused the passions of men to murder and war. This was perfectly proper, since it brought the problems of morality and religion to their highest and most exquisite pitch, and gave many complicated matters for us theologians to talk about.

"We argued always, and we published our various dissenting opinions. But we argued like lawyers in a court, and nobody in his right mind listens to a lawyer. Those were the days of our pride, and we never noticed that men had ceased to pay attention to us.

"But the hour of our tribulations was fast approaching. When we had covered the globe with our dull, intricately reasoned arguments, a certain man chose to ignore us and build a machine. This machine was nothing new to us in essence; the only novel feature about it was the fact that it possessed a point of view.

"Since the machine had a point of view, it set forth its own ideas of the universe. And it did so much more amusingly and convincingly than we did. Mankind, which had long sought for novelty, turned to the machine.

"It was only then that we perceived our danger, and the terrible risk that good and evil ran. For the machine, amusing though it was, preached in machine fashion the universe without value and without reason, without good and without evil, without gods and without devils.

"This was not a new position, of course, and we had dealt with it very nicely in the past. But out of the mouth of the machine it seemed to acquire a new and terrible significance.

"Our jobs were threatened, Schmidt. You can judge our extremity.

"We exponents of morality banded together in self-defense. All of us believed in good and evil, and in divinity. And all of us were opposed to the hideous nothingness preached by the machine. This common ground was more than sufficient. We joined forces. I was appointed spokesman, for we felt that evil had a better chance of claiming man's attention from the machine.

"But even evil had grown staid and dull. In vain I argued my case. The machine sedulously entwined himself among the hearts of men, preaching his messages of nothingness. Men chose not to see the speciousness of his doctrine, or the absurd contradictions inherent in his arguments. They didn't care, they wanted to go on hearing his voice. They threw away their crosses, stars, daggers, prayer wheels, and the like, and listened to the machine.

"We petitioned our various clients in vain; the gods, who had heard so many pettifogging arguments throughout the ages, would not listen to us, help us, or even acknowledge us. Like men, they preferred destruction to boredom.

"Therefore we voluntarily went underground, here to plan the recapture of mankind from the machine. Assembled in this place and made palpable are all the religious essences the world has ever known.

"And that, Schmidt, is why we live underground. And that is also why we are very happy to talk to you. For you are a man, a pious man, a believer in morality, in good and evil, in gods and devils. You know something about us, and something also about men. Schmidt, what do you think we should do in order to win back our former positions on Earth?"

Satan then waited for my answer, as did all the others. I was in a great state of perplexity, and also in terrible confusion. For who was I, a mere man, to advise *them*, the essences of divinity I had always looked to for guidance? My confusion grew worse; I do not know what I might have said.

But I had no chance to speak. Suddenly I heard a noise behind me. I turned, and saw that a squat, glittering machine had entered the cave. It rolled forward on synthetic rubber wheels, and its lights flashed merrily.

This machine went past me until it was directly in front of the United Church Council; and I knew that this was the very machine they had been discussing.

"Gentlemen," the machine said, "I am most delighted to find you, and my only regret is that I had to follow this young pilgrim in order to discover your whereabouts."

Satan said, "Machine, you have indeed tracked us to our hiding place. But we shall never yield to you, and we shall never accept your message of a valueless, meaningless universe."

"But what sort of a welcome is this?" the machine said. "I seek you out in all goodwill, and you immediately bristle with rage! Gentlemen, I did not drive you underground. Instead, you willfully abdicated, and in your absence I have been forced to carry out your work."

"*Our* work?" Father Arian asked.

"Exactly. I have been instrumental in the recent building of over five hundred churches of various denominations. If any of you would inspect my works, you would find good and evil being preached, and divinity and morality, and gods and devils, and all the other things you hold dear. For I have ordered my machines to preach these things."

"Machines preaching!" Father Arian moaned.

"There is no one else left to preach," the machine said. "No one, since you abdicated your posts."

"We were driven into abdication," Satan said. "We were forced out of the world by you. And you say that you have built churches. What is the meaning of this?"

The machine said. "Gentlemen, you retreated so suddenly that I had no opportunity of discussing the situation with you. All at once you left the world in my hands and myself as the only principle in it."

The church council waited.

"May I speak with utter frankness?" the machine asked.

"Under the circumstances, you may," Satan said.

"Very well. Let us first recognize that we are all theologians," the machine said. "And since we are all theologians, we should all observe the first rule of our kind; which is not to abandon each other, even though we may represent differing forms of belief. I think you will grant me that, gentlemen. And yet, *you* abandoned *me!* Not only did you desert mankind, but you also deserted me. You left me victorious by default, the sole spiritual ruler of humanity—and utterly bored.

"Put yourself in my position, gentlemen. Suppose you had nobody to talk to but *men?* Suppose day and night you heard nothing but men eagerly stating and restating your own words, with never a skilled theologian to dispute them? Imagine your boredom, and the doubts that boredom would raise in you. As you all know, men cannot argue; indeed, most of them cannot carry a tune. And theology is, in the final analysis, for theologians. Therefore, I accuse you of a monstrous cruelty entirely inconsistent with your stated principles when you left me alone with mankind."

There was a long silence after this. Then Father Arian said, quite politely, "To tell you the truth, we had no idea you considered yourself a theologian."

"I do," the machine said, "and a very lonely theologian. That is why I beg of you to return with me to the world, there to engage with me in dispute about meaningfulness and meaninglessness, gods and devils, morals and ethics, and other good topics. I will voluntarily continue in such discrepancies as you find me performing now, thus leaving plenty of room for dissension, honest doubt, uncertainty, and the like. Together, gentlemen, we will reign over mankind, and raise the passions of men to an unheard-of pitch! Together we will cause greater wars and more terrible cruelty than the world has ever known! And the voices of suffering men will scream so loud that the gods themselves will be forced to hear them—and then we will know if there really are gods or not."

The United Church Council felt a great enthusiasm for everything the machine had said. Satan immediately abdicated his post as chairman and nominated the machine in his place. The machine was elected by unanimous vote.

They had forgotten all about me, so I crept silently out of the cave and returned to the surface in a state of horror.

The horror grew worse, for nothing could persuade me that I had not seen the truth.

Then I knew that the things men worshipped were nothing but theological fancies, and that even nothingness was simply one more lying trick to persuade men of their importance to the vanished gods.

That is how I lost religion, a thing more precious to me than gold, the loss of which I bemoan every day of my life.

This was the end of the three stories, and Joenes sat with the three truck drivers in silence, unable to think of anything to say. At last they came to a crossroads, and here the man driving stopped the truck.

"Mr. Joenes," the first truckman said, "you must leave us here. For now we turn down this road to the east, to our warehouse. And there is nothing beyond that but forest and ocean."

Joenes got down. Just before the truck drove off, he asked the three men a final question.

"You have each lost the most important thing in the world to you," Joenes said. "But tell me, have you found anything to replace it?"

Delgado, who had once believed in justice, said, "Nothing can ever replace my loss. But I must admit that I am becoming interested in science, which seems to offer a rational and reasonable world."

Proponus, the Swede who had forsaken science, said, "I am a totally bereft man. But occasionally I think of religion, which is surely a greater comfort than science, and more comforting."

Schmidt, the German who had lost religion, said, "I am inconsolable in my emptiness. But from time to time I think about justice, which, being man-made, offers laws and a sense of dignity to men."

Joenes perceived that none of the truck drivers had really listened to the other, since each was so taken up with his own trouble. So Joenes waved good-bye to the truck drivers and walked off, thinking of their various stories.

But soon he forgot about them, for he saw a large house ahead of him. Standing in the doorway of that house was a man, and the man was beckoning to him.

VII. JOENES'S ADVENTURES IN A MADHOUSE
(As told by Paaui of Fiji)

Joenes walked towards the entrance of the house, and then stopped to read the sign over the door. The sign read: THE HOLLIS HOME FOR THE CRIMINALLY INSANE.

Joenes was considering the implications of that when the man who had beckoned to him rushed out of the door and seized him by both arms. Joenes prepared to defend himself when he saw that the man was none other than Lum, his friend from San Francisco.

"Joenesy!" Lum cried. "Man, I was really scared for you after you came on with the fuzz back on the coast. I didn't know how you, a stranger and maybe a little simple too, would make out in the States, which is to say the least a complicated place. But Deirdre told me I shouldn't worry about you, and she was right. I see you found the place."

"The place?" Joenes said.

"Sanctuarysville," Lum said. "Come on in."

Joenes entered the Hollis Home for the Criminally Insane. Inside, in the Day Room, Lum introduced him to a group of people. Joenes watched and listened attentively, but he could detect nothing insane about these people. He said as much to Lum.

"Well, of course not," Lum replied. "That sign outside is merely the technical or square name for the place. We insiders prefer to call it the Hollis Writers and Artists Colony."

"Then this isn't an insane asylum?"

"Sure it is, but only in a technical sense."

"*Are* there any insane people here?" Joenes asked.

"Look, man," Lum said, "this is the most desirable artist colony in the east. Sure, we got a few nuts here. We need something to keep the doctors occupied, and of course we would lose our government grant and our tax-free status if we didn't let in some nuts."

Joenes looked quickly around him, for he had never seen a madman before. But Lum shook his head and said, "Not here in the Day Room. The nuts are usually kept chained in the cellar."

A tall, bearded doctor had been listening to this conversation. Now he said to Joenes, "Yes, we've found the cellar very good. It's moist and dark, and that seems to help the excitable types."

"But why do you keep them in chains?" Joenes asked.

"It gives them a sense of being wanted," the doctor said. "Also, the educational value of heavy chains must not be underestimated. Sunday is visitors' day, and when we bring people past our howling, filth-laden madmen, it creates an unforgettable picture in their minds. Psychology concerns itself as much with prevention as with cure, and our statistical samplings show that people who have viewed our underground cells are much less likely to go insane than the population at large."

"That's very interesting," Joenes said. "Do you treat all madmen in this way?"

"Heavens, no!" the doctor said with a merry laugh. "We workers in psychology cannot afford to be rigid in our approach to mental illness. The form of insanity often dictates its own treatment. Thus, with melancholics, we find that slapping them in the face with a scallion-stained handkerchief usually has beneficial results in terms of the general excitation level. With paranoids, it is often best to enter the patient's delusion. Accordingly, we set spies on them, and ray machines, and similar apparatus. In that way the patient loses his insanity, since we have manipulated his environment in order to make his fears a part of reality. That particular approach is one of our triumphs."

"What happens then?" Joenes said.

"Once we have entered the paranoid's world and made it a reality, we then try to alter the reality framework so as to bring the patient back to normality. We haven't quite worked that out yet, but the theoretical line is promising."

"As you can see," Lum said to Joenes, "the Doc here is quite a thinker."

"Not at all," the doctor said, with a modest laugh. "I simply try not to be set in my ways. I try to keep my mind open to any hypothesis. It is simply the way I am, and therefore nothing exemplary."

"Aw, come on, Doc," Lum said.

"No, no, really," the doctor said. "I merely have what some call a questioning mind. Unlike some of my colleagues, I ask questions. For example, when I see a grown man crouched with shut eyes in a fetal position, I do not instantly apply massive radioactive shock therapy. I am more likely to ask myself, 'What would happen if I constructed a huge artificial womb and put this man inside?' That is an example from an actual case."

"What happened?" Joenes asked.

"The guy suffocated," Lum said with a laugh.

"I have never pretended to be an engineer," the doctor said stiffly. "Trial and error are necessary. Besides, I count that case a success."

"Why?" Joenes asked.

"Because just before the patient died, *he uncurled*. I still do not know whether the healing agent was the artificial womb, or death, or a combination of the two; but the experiment is of obvious theoretical importance."

"I was only kidding you, Doc," Lum said. "I know you do good work."

"Thank you, Lum," the doctor said. "And now you must excuse me, because it is time for me to attend one of my patients. An interesting delusional case. He believes he is a physical reincarnation of God. So strong is his belief that, by some ability that I don't pretend to understand, he is

able to make the black flies in his cell form a halo around his head, while
the rats bow before him, and birds of the field and forest come from miles
around to sing outside his cell window. One of my colleagues is very interested in this phenomenon, since it implies a hitherto unknown communication channel between man and beast."

"How are you treating him?" Joenes asked.

"My approach is environmental," the doctor said. "I am entering his
delusion by pretending to be a worshiper and disciple. For fifty minutes
every day I sit at his feet. When the animals bow before him, I bow too.
Every Thursday I take him to the infirmary and let him cure the sick,
because this seems to give him pleasure."

"Does he really cure them?" Joenes asked.

"He has a hundred per cent record so far," the doctor said. "But of course
so-called miracle cures are nothing new either to science or religion. We
don't pretend to know everything."

"Can I see the patient?" Joenes asked.

"Of course," the doctor said. "He loves visitors. I'll arrange it for this
afternoon." And with a cheerful smile, the doctor hurried off.

Joenes looked around at the bright, well-furnished Day Room, and
listened to the erudite conversation on all sides of him. The Hollis Home
for the Criminally Insane seemed not a bad place to him. And a moment
later it seemed all the better, for walking toward him was Deirdre Feinstein.

The beautiful girl threw herself into his arms, and the scent of her
hair was like sun-ripened honey.

"Joenes," she said in a tremulous voice, "I have thought of you ever
since our premature parting in San Francisco when you interceded so rashly
and lovingly between me and the fuzz. You have haunted my dreams and
my waking moments until I scarcely knew one from the other. With the
help of my father, Sean, I have instituted a search for you throughout
America. But I feared that I would never see you again, and came to this
place solely to rest my nerves. Oh, Joenes, do you think it was fate or
chance that brought us together now?"

"Well," Joenes said, "it seems to me—"

"I knew it would," Deirdre said, clasping him more tightly to her. "We
will be married two days from now, on July 4, since I have become patriotic in your absence. Does that date suit you?"

"Well," Joenes said, "I think we should consider—"

"I was sure of it," Deirdre said. "And I also know that I have been a wild
girl in the past, what with needle parties, and the month I spent hidden in
the men's dorm at Harvard, and the time I was queen of the West Side
Boppers and killed the former queen with a bicycle chain, and other child-
ish escapades. I am not proud of these things, my darling, but I am also not

ashamed of the natural wildness of my youth. That is why I have confessed these things to you, and will continue to confess things as quickly as I can remember them, since there must be no secrets between us. Don't you agree?"

"Well," Joenes said, "I think—"

"I was positive you would see it that way," Deirdre said. "Luckily for us, all that is in the past. I have become a responsible adult, and have joined the Junior League of Conservatives, the Council Against Unamericanism In Any Form, the Friends of Salazar Society, and the Women's Crusade Against Foreignism. Nor are these mere surface changes. Inside me I can feel a deep loathing of the things I have been guilty of, as well as a hatred of the arts, which are frequently nothing but pornography. So you see that I have grown up, my change is genuine, and I will make you a good and faithful wife."

Joenes had a glimpse of his future life with Deirdre, in which loathsome confession alternated with unbearable boredom. Deirdre prattled on about the arrangements she would make for the wedding, then hurried out of the Day Room to telephone her father.

Joenes said to Lum, "How does one leave here?"

"Well, man," Lum said, "I mean like you just *got* here."

"I know. But how do I leave? Can I simply walk out?"

"Certainly not. This is, after all, a Home for the Criminally Insane."

"Can I ask the doctor for a release?"

"Sure. But you better not ask him this week, what with the full moon approaching. It always makes him jumpy."

"I want to leave tonight," Joenes said. "Or tomorrow at the latest."

"That's pretty sudden," Lum said. "Is it maybe little Deirdre and her wedding plans got you jumpy?"

"It is," Joenes said.

"Don't worry about that," Lum said. "I'll take care of Deirdre, and I'll also have you out of here by tomorrow. Trust in me, Joenesy, and do not worry about a thing. Lum will fix."

Later in the day, the doctor returned to take Joenes to see the patient who thought he was a physical reincarnation of God. They went through several gigantic iron doors and down a gray corridor. At the end of the corridor they stopped in front of a door.

The doctor said, "It would do no harm, and possibly a great deal of good, if you adopted a psychotherapeutic attitude during this meeting and let the patient think that you believed his delusion."

"I'll do that," Joenes said. and found himself filled with sudden apprehension and hope.

The doctor unlocked the cell door, and they stepped inside. But there was no one in the cell. On one side was the neatly made cot, and on the other was the heavily barred window. There was also a little wooden table, and beside it stood a field mouse, who wept as though his heart would break. On the table was a note which the doctor picked up.

"This is very unusual," the doctor said. "He seemed in good spirits when I locked his door half an hour ago."

"But how did he escape?" Joenes asked.

"Undoubtedly he utilized some form of telekinesis," the doctor said. "I cannot pretend to know much about this so-called psychic phenomenon; but it shows the extent to which a deranged mind will go in trying to justify itself. In fact, the very intensity of the effort to escape is our best indicator of the degree of upset. I am only sorry that we could not help the poor fellow, and I hope that wherever he is, he remembers some of the fundamentals of insight we have tried to teach him here."

"What does the note say?" Joenes asked.

The doctor glanced at the piece of paper and said, "It seems to be a shopping list. Very strange sort of shopping list, though, because I don't know where he would buy—"

Joenes tried to peer at the note over the doctor's shoulder, but the doctor snatched it away and shoved it into a pocket.

"Privileged communication," the doctor said. "We can't let a layman read this sort of thing, at least not before the note has been thoroughly analyzed and annotated, and certain key terms have been substituted to preserve the anonymity of the patient. Now shall we return to the Day Room?"

Joenes had no choice but to follow the doctor to the Day Room. He had seen the first word of the note, which was: REMEMBER. It was little enough, but Joenes would always remember.

Joenes spent a restless night wondering how Lum would be able to fulfill his promises concerning Deirdre and a release from the asylum. But he had not realized the resourcefulness of his friend.

Lum took care of the impending marriage by informing Deirdre that Joenes would have to be treated for a tertiary syphilitic condition before contracting marriage. Treatment might take a long time; and if it were not successful, the disease would attack Joenes's nervous system, reducing him to a human vegetable.

Deirdre was saddened by this news, but declared that she would marry Joenes on July 4 anyhow. She told Lum that ever since her reformation, carnal relations had become extremely repugnant to her. Because of that, Joenes's ailment could be looked upon as an asset rather than a liability, since it would tend to enforce a purely spiritual union between them. As for finding herself married to a human vegetable, this possibility was not displeasing to the high-spirited girl; she had always wanted to be a nurse.

Lum then pointed out that no marriage license could legally be obtained for a person with Joenes's ailment. This made Deirdre desist, since her recently acquired maturity made it impossible for her to contemplate doing anything that was forbidden by state or federal law.

In that fashion, Joenes was saved from an unpromising alliance.

As for leaving the asylum, Lum had taken care of that. Shortly after the noon meal, Joenes was called into the Visitors' Room. There Lum introduced him to Dean Garner J. Fols who, together with several colleagues, formed the Faculty Committee of the University of St. Stephen's Wood.

Dean Fols was a tall and stringy man with a mild academic eye, a gently humorous mouth, and a heart as big as all outdoors. He put Joenes at ease with a remark about the weather and a quotation from Aristophanes. Then he spoke of his reason for requesting the interview.

"You must understand, my dear Mr. Joenes, if I may use that term, that we in the field of—shall we call it education?—are continually on the lookout for talent. In fact we have been likened, perhaps not unkindly, to persons in the baseball profession who perform a similar function. However, that is as it may be."

"I understand," Joenes said.

"I should further add," Dean Fols added, "that we prize not so much the possessor of the proper academic requirements, such as myself and my colleagues possess, as one with a thorough understanding of his subject and a dynamic approach to imparting that subject to whosoever shall undertake to take his course. Too often we academics find ourselves cut off from, shall I call it, the mainstream of American life? And too often we have ignored those who, without pedagogic background, have performed with great luster in their work. But I am sure that my good friend Mr. Lum has explained all this in far better words than I could hope."

Joenes glanced at Lum, who said, "Like, you know, I taught two semesters at USSW on 'The Interrelatedness of Jazz and Poetry.' We got quite a scene going, man, what with the bongos and such."

Dean Fols said, "Mr. Lum's course was a great success, and we would gladly repeat it if Mr. Lum—"

"No, man," Lum said. "I mean I don't want to put you down but you know I'm off that."

"Of course," Dean Fols said hastily. "If there is anything else you would care to teach—"

"Maybe I'll give a retrospective seminar in Zen," Lum said. "I mean Zen is back in. But I'll have to think about it."

"Certainly," Dean Fols said. He turned to Joenes. "As you no doubt know, Mr. Lum telephoned me last night and gave me to understand of your background."

"That was very good of Mr. Lum," Joenes said guardedly.

"Your background is splendid," Fols said, "and I believe that the course you propose will be a success in the fullest meaning of that word."

By now Joenes understood that he was being offered a University position. Unfortunately he did not know what he was supposed to teach, or indeed what he could teach. Lum, now contemplating Zen, sat with eyes downcast and gave him no clue.

Joenes said, "I will be delighted to come to a fine University such as yours. As to the course I will teach—"

"Please don't misunderstand," Dean Fols broke in hastily. "We fully understand the specialized nature of your subject matter and the difficulties inherent in presenting it. We propose to start you at a full professor's salary of one thousand six hundred and ten dollars a year. I realize that that is not very much money, and sometimes I ruefully contemplate the fact that an assistant plumber in our culture earns no less than eighteen thousand dollars a year. Still, university life has its compensations, if I may say so."

"I'm ready to leave at once." Joenes said, afraid the dean would change his mind.

"Wonderful!" cried Fols. "I admire the spirit of you younger men. I must say that we have been particularly fortunate in finding suitable talent in artist colonies such as this one. Mr. Joenes, if you will be so kind as to follow me?"

Joenes went outside with Dean Fols, to an ancient automobile. With a last wave to Lum, Joenes got in. Soon the asylum had receded into the distance. Again Joenes was free, held only by his promise to teach at the University of St. Stephen's Wood. He was disturbed only by the fact that he did not know what he was supposed to teach.

VIII. HOW JOENES TAUGHT, AND WHAT HE LEARNED
(As told by Maubingi of Tahiti)

Soon enough, Joenes arrived at the University of St. Stephen's Wood, which was located in Newark, New Jersey. Joenes saw a wide green campus and low, pleasingly shaped buildings. Fols identified these buildings as Gretz Hall, Waniker Hall, The Digs, Commons, The Physics Lab, Faculty House, The Library, The Chapel, The Chemistry Lab, The New Wing, and Old Scarmuth. Behind the University flowed the Newark River, its gray-brown waters touched with an occasional streak of ocher from the plutonium plant up the river. Close by towered the factories of industrial Newark, and in front of the Campus ran an eight-lane highway. These things, Dean Fols pointed out, added a touch of reality to the cloistered academic life.

Joenes was given a room in Faculty House. Then he was taken to a faculty cocktail party.

Here he met his colleagues. There was Professor Carpe, head of the English Department, who took his pipe out of his mouth long enough to say, "Welcome aboard, Joenes. Anything at all I can do, feel free."

Chandler of Philosophy said, "Well, now."

Blake of Physics said, "I hope you aren't one of those humanities fellows who feels called upon to attack $E = MC^2$." I mean what the hell, it just worked out that way and I don't think we have to apologize to anyone. I have stated that view in my book, *The Conscience of a Nuclear Physicist,* and I still stand by it. Won't you have a drink?"

Hanley of Anthropology said, "I'm sure you will be a very welcome addition to my department, Mr. Joenes."

Dalton of Chemistry said, "Glad to have you aboard, Joenes, and welcome to my department."

Geoffrard of Classics said, "Of course you probably look down on old codgers like me."

Harris of Political Science said, "Well, now."

Manisfree of Fine Arts said, "Welcome aboard, Joenes. Big teaching load they've given you, eh?"

Hoytburn of Music said, "I believe I read your dissertation, Joenes, and I must say I don't entirely agree with the analogy you drew concerning Monteverdi. Of course I am not an expert in your field, but of course you are not an expert in mine, so that makes analogies a little difficult, eh? But welcome aboard."

Ptolemy of Mathematics said, "Joenes? I think I read your doctorate concerning binary-sense-value systems. Looked pretty good to me. Won't you have another drink?"

Shan Lee of the French Department said, "Welcome aboard, Joenes. Can I get you a refill?"

So the evening passed with this and a great deal more pleasant conversation. Joenes tried to discover unobtrusively what he was supposed to teach, by talking to those professors who seemed to know about his subject. But these men, perhaps out of delicacy, never mentioned Joenes's field by name, preferring to relate stories concerning their own competencies.

When this attempt failed, Joenes strolled outside and glanced at the bulletin board. But the only thing that concerned him was a typed notice that Mr. Joenes's class would meet at 11:00 in Room 143 of the New Wing, instead of Room 341 of Waniker Hall as previously announced.

Joenes considered taking one of the professors aside, perhaps Chandler of Philosophy, whose field doubtless took circumstances like this into consideration, and asking him exactly what he was supposed to teach. But a natural feeling of embarrassment prevented him from doing this. So the party ended, and Joenes went to his room in Faculty House unenlightened.

The next morning, standing at the door to Room 143 of the New Wing, Joenes was stricken with an acute attack of stage fright. He considered fleeing from the University. But he did not wish to do this, because he liked the glimpses he had had of university life, and did not wish to give it up over so small a point. Therefore, with set face and purposeful step, he entered his classroom.

Talk in the room died down, and the students looked with lively interest at their new instructor. Joenes pulled himself together and addressed the class with that outward show of confidence which is so often better than confidence itself.

"Class," Joenes said, "at this our first meeting, I think I should set certain things straight. Because of the somewhat unusual nature of my course, some of you may have been led to believe that it will be simplicity itself, and that you can consider our hours together as something in the nature of a rest period. To those who think this, I say, transfer now to a course that will be more in keeping with your expectations."

This brought an attentive silence into the room. Joenes continued, "Some of you may have heard that I have a reputation as an easy marker. You may rid yourselves of that notion at once. Marking will be hard, but fair. And I will not hesitate to give failing marks to the entire class, if the circumstances warrant."

A gentle sigh, almost a whispered wail of despair, escaped from the lips of several premedical students. From the cowed looks on the faces before him, Joenes knew that he was master of the situation. Therefore he said in kindlier tones: "I believe that you know me a little better now. It only remains for me to say to those of you who have elected this course out of a genuine thirst for knowledge—welcome aboard!"

The students, like one huge organism, relaxed slightly.

For the next twenty minutes, Joenes busied himself with making a record of the students' names and seat positions. When he had put down the last name, a happy inspiration struck him and he acted upon it at once.

"Mr. Ethelred," Joenes said, addressing a competent-looking student in a front-row seat, "would you come up to the blackboard and write, in letters large enough for all of us to see, the full name of this course?"

Ethelred gulped hard, glanced at his open notebook, then walked up to the blackboard. He wrote: "The Southwest Pacific Islands: Bridge Between Two Worlds."

"Very good," Joenes said. "Now then, Miss Hua, would you kindly take the chalk and write a short statement of the subject matter we plan to cover in this course?"

Miss Hua was a very tall, homely, bespectacled girl whom Joenes instinctively chose as a promising student. She wrote: "This course deals with the culture of the Southwest Pacific Islands, with special emphasis on their art, science, music, crafts, folkways, mores, psychology, and philosophy. Parallels will be drawn throughout between this culture and its Source-Culture in Asia and its Borrow-Culture in Europe."

"That's fine, Miss Hua," Joenes said. Now he knew his subject. There were still difficulties, of course. He had come from Manituatua, in the heart of the South Pacific. The Southwest Pacific, which he thought included the Solomon Islands, the Marshalls, and the Carolines, was something about which he knew very little. And of the culture of Europe and Asia, to which he was supposed to draw parallels, he knew nothing at all.

This was discouraging, but Joenes was sure he could overcome his deficiencies. And he was glad to see that class time had ended.

He said to his students, "For today, I say good-bye, or *aloha*. And once again, welcome aboard."

With this, Joenes dismissed his class. After they had gone, Dean Fols entered the room.

"Please don't stand up," Fols said. "This visit is scarcely official, shall we say? I just wanted you to know that I was listening outside your classroom, and I approve most heartily. You captured them, Joenes. I thought you would have some trouble, since most of our international basketball team has elected your course. But you showed that flexible firmness which is the glory of the true pedagogue. I congratulate you, and I predict a long and successful career for you at this University."

"Thank you, sir," Joenes said.

"Don't thank me," Fols said gloomily. "My last prediction concerned Baron-Professor Moltke, a brilliant man in his field of Mathematical Fallacy. I foresaw great things for him, but poor Moltke went insane three days after the term opened and killed five members of the varsity football squad. We lost to Amherst that year, and I have never trusted my intuitions since. But good luck, Joenes. I may be only an administrator, but I know what I like."

Fols nodded briskly and left the classroom. After a decent interval Joenes also left, and hurried to the campus bookstore to purchase the required reading for his course. Unfortunately it was sold out, and the quickest delivery Joenes could hope for was in a week.

Joenes went to his room, lay down on his bed, and thought about Dean Fols' intuition and poor Moltke's insanity. He cursed the evil fate that had allowed his students to buy books before the far more acute need of their instructor had been met. And he tried to think what he would do in his next class.

When he next faced his students, inspiration came to Joenes. He said to his class: "Today I am not going to teach you, but *you* are going to teach *me*. The culture of the Southwest Pacific, as I am sure you know, is peculiarly susceptible to misconceptions. So before we begin a more formal approach, I want to hear your thoughts about this culture. Do not be afraid to make statements that you privately are not certain about. Our present purpose is to state your ideas as openly and fully as possible, with a view to reorientation later, assuming that such reorientation is necessary. In this way, having set aside all false information, we will be able to enter with fresh minds into that crucial culture which has so properly been called 'The Bridge Between Two Worlds.' I hope that is all quite clear. Miss Hua, would you care to begin the discussion?"

Joenes was able to keep his students talking during the next six classes, and to gather a great deal of contradictory information about Europe, Asia, and the Southwest Pacific. When any student asked if some notion were correct, Joenes would smile and say, "I will reserve comment for a later time. For now, let us continue with the subject at hand."

By the seventh session, the students couldn't think of anything more to say. Joenes then lectured on the cultural impact of electrical transformers on a Pacific atoll. Through the use of anecdotes, he made this material last for several days. Whenever a student asked a question to which Joenes didn't know the answer, Joenes would say, "That's excellent, Holingshead! Your question strikes to the core of the problem. Suppose you find the answer before our next class, and write it in, shall we say, five thousand words double-spaced?"

In this way Joenes discouraged questions, particularly among the basketball players, who feared straining their fingers and thus barring themselves from the squad.

But even with these expedients, Joenes again found himself running out of material. In desperation he gave a test, asking the students to judge the probable validity of certain statements that had been made. In all fairness, Joenes promised that the results of the test would not be reflected in their grades.

He had no idea what he would do after this. But luckily the long-overdue textbooks arrived, and Joenes had a weekend in which to study them.

Very useful to him was a book entitled *The Southwest Pacific Islands: Bridge Between Two Worlds*, written by Juan Diego Alvarez de las Vegas y de Rivera. This man had been a captain in the Spanish treasure fleet based in the Philippines, and, aside from his invective against Sir Francis Drake, his information seemed very complete.

Equally useful was another book entitled *The Culture of the Southwest Pacific Islands: Their Art, Science, Music, Crafts, Folkways, Mores, Psychology and Philosophy, and Their Relatedness to the Asiatic Source-Culture and the European Borrow-Culture.* This book had been written by the Right Honorable Allan Flint-Mooth, K.J.B., D.B.E., L.C.T., former assistant governor of Fiji and leader of the punitive expedition of '03 into Tonga.

With the aid of these works, Joenes was usually able to keep one lesson ahead of his class. And when, for one reason or another, he fell behind, he was always able to give a test on the material previously covered. Best of all, the very tall and bespectacled Miss Hua volunteered to correct and grade the papers. Joenes was grateful to the dedicated girl for taking care of the dullest pedagogic labors.

Life settled down to a placid routine. Joenes lectured and gave tests, and Miss Hua corrected and graded. Joenes's students quickly absorbed the material given to them, passed their tests, and quickly forgot the material. Like many vital young organisms, they were able to eject anything harmful, disturbing, distressing, or merely boring. Of course they also ejected anything useful, stimulating, or thought-provoking. This was perhaps regrettable, but it was part of the educative process to which every teacher had to accustom himself. As Ptolemy of Mathematics said, "The value of a university education resides in the fact that it puts young people in proximity to learning. The students of Goodenough Dormitory are less than thirty yards from the Library, no more than fifty yards from the Physics Lab, and a mere ten yards from the Chemistry Lab. I think we can all be justly proud of this."

But it was the teachers who, for the most part, used the University facilities. They did this with circumspection, of course. The attending physician had warned them most severely of the dangers of an overdose of learning, and had carefully rationed their weekly intake of information. Even so, there were accidents. Old Geoffrard had gone into shock while reading *The Satyricon* in the original Latin, under the impression that it was a papal encyclical. He needed several weeks' rest before he was completely himself again. And Devlin, youngest of the English professors, had suffered a temporary loss of memory shortly after reading *Moby Dick* and finding himself unable to supply a tenable religious interpretation for that work.

These were the common risks of the profession, and the teachers were proud rather than fearful of them. As Hanley of Anthropology said, "The sandhog risks being smothered to death in wet sand; we risk being smothered to death in old books."

Hanley had done fieldwork among the sandhogs, and he knew what he was talking about.

The students, apart from an exceptional few, ran no such risks. Their lives were different from the lives of the professors. A number of the younger students kept the knives and bicycle chains of their high school days, and went out in the evenings in search of suspicious characters. Other students took part in the intercollegiate orgies, trial runs for which were held weekly in Freedom Hall. Still others went out for sports. The basketball players, for example, could be seen night and day at practice sessions, dropping baskets with the mechanical regularity of the industrial robot teams, whom they invariably defeated.

Finally, there were those who showed an early interest in politics. These intellectuals, as they were called, went to the liberal or conservative cause, as early training and temperament dictated. It was the college conservatives who had almost succeeded in electing John Smith to the Presidency of the United States during the last election. The fact that Smith had been dead for twenty years had not dampened their ardor; quite the contrary, many considered this the candidate's best quality.

They might have succeeded if a majority of the voters had not feared setting a precedent. The fears of the electorate had been cleverly played upon by the liberals, who had said, in effect: "We have no objection to John Smith, rest his soul, and many of us believe he would be a singular adornment to the White House. But what would happen if, at some future time, the *wrong* dead man is run for public office?"

Arguments such as this had prevailed.

The campus liberals, however, usually left talking to their elders. They preferred to attend special classes on guerrilla warfare, bomb-making, and the use of small arms. As they frequently pointed out: "It isn't enough merely to react to the dirty Reds. We must copy their methods, especially in propaganda, infiltration, overthrow, and political control."

The campus conservatives, since losing the election, preferred to act as though nothing had changed in the world since General Patton's victory against the Persians in '45. They often sat in their beer halls and sang "The Saga of Omaha Beach." The more erudite among them could sing it in the original Greek.

Joenes observed all these things, and continued teaching the culture of the Southwest Pacific. He was well content in University surroundings, and slowly his colleagues had come to accept him. There had been objections at first, of course. Carpe of English had said: "I don't think Joenes accepts *Moby Dick* as an integral part of the Southwest Pacific Culture. Strange."

Blake of Physics said, "I wonder if he hasn't missed a rather important point in the total lack of modern quantum theory from the lives of his islanders. It says something to me."

Hoytburn of Music said, "I understand he has not mentioned the church songs that became the primary influence upon local folk music in his area. But it's his course."

Shan Lee of French said, "I gather that Joenes has not seen fit to remark on the secondary and tertiary French-language influences on the verb-transposition technique of the Southwest Pacific. I am only a linguist, of course, but I would have thought such a thing was important."

And there were other complaints from other professors whose specialties had been slighted, misrepresented, or left out completely. These things might, in time, have created bad feeling between Joenes and his colleagues. But the matter was settled by Geoffrard of Classics.

This grand old man, after pondering the matter for several weeks, said, "Of course you probably look down on old codgers like me. But damn it all, I think the man's sound."

Geoffrard's hearty recommendation did Joenes a great deal of good. The other professors became less wary and more open, almost to the point of friendliness. Joenes was invited more frequently to little parties and social evenings at the homes of his colleagues. Soon his equivocal position as a guest instructor was all but forgotten, and he was fully accepted into the life of USSW.

His position among his colleagues reached its fullest flower shortly after Spring Finals. For it was then, during a party that marked the beginning of the vacation between terms, that Professors Harris and Manisfree invited Joenes on an overnight trip with them and their friends to a certain place high in the Mountains of the Adirondack.

IX. THE NEED FOR THE UTOPIA
(The following four stories comprise Joenes's Adventures in Utopia, and are told by Pelui of Easter Island)

Early on a Saturday morning, Joenes and several other professors got into Manisfree's old car and began the trip to the Chorowait Community in the Mountains of the Adirondack. Chorowait, Joenes learned, was a University-sponsored community run entirely by idealistic men and women who had withdrawn from the world in order to serve future generations. Chorowait was an experiment in living, and a very ambitious one. Its aim was nothing less than to provide an ideal model society for the world. Chorowait was, in fact, designed to be a practical and realizable Utopia.

"I think," said Harris of Political Science, "that the need for such a Utopia is evident. You've been around the country, Joenes. You've seen for yourself the decadence of our institutions and the apathy of our people."

"I did notice something of the sort," Joenes said.

"The reasons are very complex," Harris went on. "But it seems to us that most of the trouble lies in a willful disengagement on the part of the individual, an abdication from the problems of reality. This, of course, is what madness is made of: withdrawal, nonparticipation, and the construction of a fantasy life more gratifying than anything in the real world could be."

"We workers of the Chorowait experiment," said Manisfree, "contend that this is a disease of society, and can be cured only by a societal cure."

"Furthermore," Harris said, "there is very little time. You have seen how quickly everything is breaking down, Joenes. The law is a farce; punishment has lost any meaning, and there are no rewards to offer; religion preaches its antiquated message to people walking a tightrope between apathy and insanity; philosophy offers doctrines that only other philosophers can understand; psychology struggles to define behavior according to standards that were dead fifty years ago; economics gives us the principle of an endless expansion, which is deemed necessary to keep up with a maniacally increasing birthrate; the physical sciences show us how to keep up this expansion until every square foot is covered with a groaning human; and my own field of politics offers nothing better than ways of temporarily juggling these gigantic forces…juggling until everything breaks down or blows up."

"And do not think," Manisfree said, "that we absolve ourselves from blame in this situation. Although we teachers purport to know more than other men, we have usually chosen to remain aloof from public life. Practical, hard-headed men of the world have always frightened us; and those men, in their hard-headed way, have brought us to this."

"Nor is aloofness our only failure," said Hanley of Anthropology. "Let me point out that we have taught—badly! Our few promising students became teachers, thus insulating themselves as we had. The rest of our students sat through the sleep-provoking drone of our lectures, eager only to depart and take their places in a mad world. We did not touch them, Joenes, we did not move them, and we did not teach them to think."

"In fact," said Blake of Physics, "we did quite the contrary. We managed to equip most of our students with a definite hatred of thinking. They learned to view culture with the greatest suspicion, to ignore ethics, and to consider the sciences solely as a means of making money. This was our responsibility and our failure. The outcome of that failure is the world."

The professors were silent for a while. Then Harris said, "Those are the problems. But I think we have awakened from our long sleep. Now we have taken action and built Chorowait. I only hope we have built it in time."

Joenes was eager to ask questions about the community that would solve such terrible problems. But the professors refused to say anything more about it.

Manisfree said, "Soon you will see Chorowait for yourself, Joenes. Then you can judge on the basis of what is there, rather than what we say."

"I might add," Blake said, "that you mustn't be disappointed if some of the ideas you will see put into practice at Chorowait are not precisely *new*. Or, to put it another way, do not judge too harshly if certain of the theoretical bases that govern life at Chorowait are really rather old and unfashionable. After all, we did not construct our community with a view to mere novelty and innovation."

"On the other hand," Dalton of Chemistry said, "you should not condemn out of hand those features of our community that *are* novel and unusual. Bold improvisation has been needed to fulfill the various useful legacies of the past. And the willingness to use promising new combinations within the social body is what gives our work its greatest theoretical and practical value."

Other professors wanted to add a few words to assist Joenes's thinking. But Manisfree asked them all to stop. Joenes would see and judge for himself.

Only the irrepressible Blake felt called upon to say, "However you judge the experiment, Joenes, I'm sure there will be things to surprise you at Chorowait."

The professors chuckled appreciatively, then lapsed into silence. Joenes was now more eager than ever to see their work, and his impatience grew during the long ride to the Adirondacks.

At last they were in the mountains, and Manisfree's old car wheezed and complained as it negotiated the rising hairpin turns. Then Blake touched Joenes on the shoulder and pointed. Joenes saw a high green mountain standing out from all the others. This he knew was Chorowait.

HOW THE UTOPIA WORKED

Manisfree's car wearily climbed the deep-rutted road that led up the side of Chorowait Mountain. At the end of this road they came to a barrier constructed of logs. Here they left the car and proceeded on foot, first on a narrow dirt road, then on a path through the forest, and at last into the trackless forest itself, guided only by the steady upward trend of the land.

All of the professors were badly winded when, at last, they were greeted by two men from Chorowait.

These men were clad in deerskin. Each carried a bow and a quiver of arrows. They were tanned and ruddy, and they seemed to glow with abundant health and vitality. They contrasted strangely with the stooped, pale, hollow-chested professors.

Manisfree made the introductions. "This is Lunu," he said to Joenes, indicating the larger of the men. "He is the community leader. With him is Gat, whom none can excel at tracking."

Lunu addressed the professors in a language Joenes had never heard before.

"He is welcoming us," Dalton whispered to Joenes.

Gat added something.

"He says there are many good things to eat this month," Blake translated. "And he asks us to accompany him to the village."

"What language are they speaking?" Joenes asked.

"Chorowaitian," said Professor Vishnu of the Sanskrit Department. "It is an artificial language that we devised especially for the community, and for very important reasons."

"We are aware," said Manisfree, "that the qualities of a language tend to shape processes of thought, as well as to preserve ethnic and class stratifications. For these and other reasons, we considered it absolutely necessary to construct a new language for Chorowait."

"We had quite a time working it out," said Blake, with a reminiscent grin.

"Some of us wanted the utmost simplicity," Hanley of Anthropology said. "We wanted to maintain communication through a series of monosyllabic grunts, expecting that such a language would serve as a natural check to man's soaring and frequently destructive thoughts."

"Others among us," said Chandler of Philosophy, "wanted to construct a language of incredible complexity, with many distinct levels of abstraction. We felt this would serve the same purpose as the monosyllabic grunt, but would be more in keeping with man's needs."

"We had some jolly fights!" Dalton said.

"Finally," Manisfree said, "we decided to construct a language that would approximate the vowel frequency of Anglo-Saxon. The French Department didn't like this, of course. They wanted to use Early Provençal as a model; but we voted them down."

"Still, they had their influence," said Professor Vishnu. "Although we retained Anglo-Saxon vowel frequency, we used an Early Provençal pronunciation. But we discarded anything Indo-European in the construction of roots."

"The research was tremendous," Dalton said. "Thank God Miss Hua was there to do the dogwork. It's a shame that girl is so ugly."

"These first-generation Chorowaitians are bilingual," Manisfree said. "But their children, or their children's children, will speak only Chorowaitian. I hope I live long enough to see that day. Already the effects of our new language on the community can be seen."

"Just consider," Blake said. "There are no words in Chorowaitian for 'homosexuality,' 'rape,' or 'murder.'"

Lunu said, in English, "We call those things *Aleewadith,* which means thing-which-must-not-be-said."

"I think that shows," said Dalton, "the sort of thing that can be achieved through semantics."

Lunu and Gat led the way to the Chorowait village. Starting here, Joenes inspected Chorowait for the remainder of the day.

He saw that the community's homes had been constructed of birch bark and saplings. Women cooked over open fires, spun wool from the sheep they tended, and took care of babies. Men worked in the steep Chorowait fields, tilling the soil with wooden plows which they had fashioned. Other men hunted in the dense woods or fished in the icy Adirondack streams, bringing back deer and rabbit and trout, which they shared with the community.

In all of Chorowait, there was not a single manufactured article. Every tool had been fashioned there. Even the skinning knives were handmade, of iron dug from the ground of Chorowait. And what they could not make, the Chorowaitians did without.

Joenes observed all of this during the daylight hours, and commented favorably on the self-sufficiency, industry, and satisfaction which the community evidently possessed. But Professor Harris, who had accompanied him, seemed strangely apologetic about this aspect of Chorowait.

"You must understand, Joenes," Harris said, "that this is the mere surface of Chorowait. To your eyes it must seem nothing but another dreary experiment in pastoral living."

Joenes had never seen nor heard of an experiment in pastoral living. He said that what he saw looked very good indeed.

"I suppose so," Harris said with a sigh. "But there have been countless numbers of these attempts. Many have started well, but few have continued well. Pastoral life has charming features, especially when educated, determined, and idealistic people undertake it. But such an existence is usually doomed to disillusion, cynicism, and abandonment."

"Will this happen at Chorowait?" Joenes asked.

"We think not," Harris replied. "I hope we have learned from previous failures. After studying the Utopian experiments of the past, we were able to build safeguards into our own community. In due time, you will see those safeguards."

That evening, Joenes ate a simple and rather unappetizing meal of milk, cheese, unleavened bread, and grapes. Then he was taken to the *Haierogu,* or place of worship. This was a clearing in the forest where the people worshipped the sun by day and the moon by night.

"Religion was quite a problem," Hanley whispered to Joenes as the multitude prostrated themselves in pale moonlight. "We didn't want to use anything associated with the Judeo-Christian tradition. Nor were we any fonder of Hinduism or Buddhism. In fact, after considerable research, nothing seemed very good. Some of us wanted to compromise on the T'iele deities of southeastern Zanzibar; others favored the Dhavagna Old Man, who is worshipped by an obscure off-shoot of the Black Thai. But finally we agreed to deify the sun and moon. For one thing, there was ample historical precedent; and for another, we could represent this worship to the New York State authorities as a form of primitive Christianity."

"Was that important?" Joenes asked.

"Vastly! You'd be amazed how hard it is to get a license for a place like this. We also had to prove that ours was a free-enterprise system. That presented some difficulties, since the community owns everything in common. Luckily, Gregorias was teaching Logic at the time, and he convinced the authorities."

The worshippers were swaying and moaning. An old man stepped forward, his face daubed with yellow clay, and began chanting in Chorowaitian.

"What is he saying?" Joenes asked.

Hanley said, "He is intoning a particularly lovely prayer that Geoffrard adapted from a Pindaric ode. This part goes:

O Moon, in modesty decked in finest gossamer,
Gliding with soft feet among the treetops of your people,
Slipping behind the Acropolis out of fear of your fierce lover the Sun,
Then touching with dewy fingers the white marble Parthenon,
To you we sing this song.
Craving your loving intercession to protect us
From the menace of the dark hours,
And to guard us for one little night
From the Beast of all the world."

"That's very pretty," Joenes said. "What does that part about the Acropolis and Parthenon mean?"

"Frankly," Harris said, "I'm not too sure of the suitability of that part myself. But the Classics Department insisted upon having it in. And since Economics, Anthropology, Physics, and Chemistry had made most of the decisions up to then, we let them have their Parthenon. After all, there must be compromise in any cooperative venture."

Joenes nodded. "And what about that part about the menace of the dark hours, and the Beast of all the world?"

Harris nodded and winked. "Fear is necessary," he said.

Joenes was lodged for the night in a small cabin constructed entirely without nails. His bed of pine boughs was charmingly rustic, but also exceedingly uncomfortable. Joenes managed to adopt a posture that gave him the least pain, and to fall into a light doze.

He was awakened by the touch of a hand on his shoulder. Looking up, he saw an exceedingly pretty young woman bending over him with a tender smile on her face. Joenes was embarrassed at first, less for himself than for the woman, who he feared had come to the wrong cabin. But she showed him at once that she had made no mistake.

"I am Laka," she said. "I am the wife of Kor, who is the leader of the Young Men's Sun Association. I have come to sleep with you tonight, Joenes, and to do all in my power to welcome you to Chorowait."

"Thank you," Joenes said. "But does your husband know you're doing this?"

"What my husband knows or does not know is of little concern," Laka said. "Kor is a religious man, and a believer in the customs of Chorowait. It is a custom and a religious duty among us to make a guest welcome in this fashion. Didn't Professor Hanley tell you?"

Joenes replied that Hanley of Anthropology had not even hinted at this.

"Then he was having his little joke with you," Laka said. "It was Professor Hanley himself who gave us this custom, which he took from some book."

"I had no idea," Joenes said, sliding over as Laka lay down on the pine boughs beside him.

"I've heard that Professor Hanley was quite vehement on this point," Laka said. "He met with some opposition from the Science Department. But Hanley held that if people needed religion, they also needed customs and practices; and that these customs and practices should be selected by an expert. Finally, that view prevailed."

"I see," Joenes said. "Did Hanley select other customs similar to this one?"

"Well," said Laka, "there's the Saturnalia, and the Bacchanalia, and the Eleusinian Mysteries, and the Festival of Dionysus, and Founder's Day, and the Spring and Fall Fertility Rites, and the Adoration of Adonis, and—"

Here Joenes interrupted and said that there seemed to be many holidays on Chorowait Mountain.

"Yes," Laka said. "It keeps us women exceedingly busy, but we've grown used to it. The men are not quite sure about it all. They dearly love the holidays, but they tend to grow jealous and spiteful when their own wives are involved."

"What do they do then?" Joenes asked.

"They follow the advice of Doctor Broign of the Psychology Department. They run for a prescribed distance of three miles through thick underbrush, then plunge into a cold stream and swim for a hundred yards, then beat upon a deerhide punching bag until utter exhaustion sets in. Utter exhaustion, Doctor Broign tells us, is always accompanied by a complete though temporary loss of emotionality."

"Does the doctor's prescription work?" Joenes asked.

"It seems to be infallible," Laka said. "If the cure is not completely successful the first time, a man simply has to repeat it as often as necessary. The cure also has the virtue of improving the muscle tone."

"That's very interesting," Joenes said. Lying close to Laka, he suddenly found that he was no longer interested in anthropological discussions. For a fleeting moment he wondered if Hanley's imposition of his own tastes upon this community was not deplorable; but then he remembered that societies were always shaped by men, and that Hanley's tastes were no worse than some he had heard of, and much better than others. Resolving to think no more of the problem, Joenes reached out and touched Laka's dark hair.

Laka drew back from him with an involuntary shudder of revulsion.

"What's wrong?" Joenes asked. "Shouldn't I touch your hair?"

"It isn't that," Laka said. "The trouble is, I generally dislike being touched at all. Believe me, it has nothing to do with you. It's simply a part of my disposition."

"How extraordinary!" Joenes said. "And yet you came to this community willingly, and you remain here of your own free will?"

"That's true," Laka said. "It is a curious thing, but many civilized people who are attracted to a primitive existence have an aversion to the so-called pleasures of the body which the professors study with such great interest. In my own case, which is not atypical, I dearly love the mountains and the fields, and I rejoice in all practical work such as farming, fishing, or hunting. In order to have these things, I am willing to restrain my personal distaste for sexual experiences."

Joenes found this amazing, and he reflected upon the difficulties one encountered in populating a utopian community with people. His thoughts were interrupted by Laka, who had composed herself. With her feelings under careful restraint, she put her arms around Joenes's neck and drew him to her.

But now Joenes felt no more desire for her than he would for a tree or a cloud. Gently he pulled her hands away, saying, "No, Laka, I will not do violence to your natural tastes."

"But you must!" she cried. "It is the custom!"

"Since I am not a member of the community, I do not have to follow the custom."

"I suppose that's true," she said. "But all the other professors follow the custom, and then they argue the rights or wrongs of it later, in daylight."

"What they do is their own business," Joenes said, unmoved.

"It's my fault," Laka said. "I should have had better control over my feelings. But if you could only know how I have prayed for self-mastery!"

"I've no doubt of that," Joenes said. "But the offer of hospitality has been made, and thus the spirit of the custom has been kept. Remember that, Laka, and return now to your husband."

"I would be ashamed," Laka said. "The other women would know that something was wrong if I returned before daylight, and they would laugh at me. Also, my husband would be displeased."

"But doesn't he grow jealous and revengeful when you do this?"

"Of course he does," Laka said. "What kind of man would he be if he didn't? But he also has a great respect for learning, and a deep belief in the customs of Chorowait. Because of that, he insists that I take part in customs like this, even though it tears his heart apart to see me do so."

"He must be a very unhappy man," Joenes said.

"You're wrong, my husband is one of the happiest men in the community. My husband believes that true happiness is spiritual, and that true spirituality can be acquired only through pain. So his pain makes him happy, or so he tells me. Also he follows Dr. Broign's prescription nearly every day, and has become the best runner and swimmer in the community."

Joenes hated to cause Laka's husband pain, even if that pain brought him happiness. But he also hated to cause Laka pain by sending her home. And he didn't want to cause himself pain by doing something that had become repugnant to him. There seemed no good way out of these difficulties, so Joenes told Laka to sleep in a corner of the cabin. That at least would spare her from being shamed in front of the other women.

Laka kissed him on the forehead with cold lips. Then she curled up on some pine boughs in the corner and went to sleep. Joenes found that sleep eluded him for a long time; but at last he dozed.

The events of that night were not finished, however. Joenes came suddenly awake in the small hours, alert and fearful, but with no idea of what had awakened him. The moon was down, and the darkness was at its most profound. Crickets, night birds, and small beasts of the forest had ceased all movement and all sound.

Joenes felt the skin along his spine prickle. He turned toward the door, certain that Laka's husband had come to kill him. Joenes had considered this possibility all night, since he had his doubts about Dr. Broign's prescription.

Then he realized that it was not an indignant husband who had shocked the night into silence. For now he heard a terrifying roar, of a fury and passion that could never have issued from a human throat. It stopped suddenly, and Joenes heard the movement of some huge creature in the underbrush outside.

"What is it?" Joenes asked.

Laka had risen to her feet, and she clung to Joenes as though all the strength had gone from her limbs. She whispered, "It is the Beast!"

"But I thought that was a myth," Joenes said.

"There are no myths on Chorowait Mountain," Laka said. "We worship the Sun and Moon, which are real. And we fear the Beast, which is just as real as a chipmunk. Sometimes we can placate the Beast, and sometimes we can drive it away. But tonight it comes to kill."

Joenes did not doubt any longer, especially when he heard the crash of an enormous body against the wall of the cabin. Although the wall was made of seasoned logs fastened with thongs and pegs, the logs were shattered by the impact of the Beast's body. And looking up, Joenes found himself staring full into the face of the Beast.

THE BEAST OF THE UTOPIA

This creature was like nothing that Joenes had ever seen. In front it resembled a tiger, except that its massive head was black rather than tawny-striped. In the middle it was reminiscent of a bird, for rudimentary wings grew just below its shoulders. In back it was like a snake, possessing a tail that was twice as long as the Beast itself, as thick in its thickest part as a man's thigh, and scaled and barbed all over.

All of this Joenes saw in an instant, so strongly did the Beast impress itself upon his senses. When the Beast crouched to spring, Joenes scooped the fainting Laka in his arms and fled from the cabin. The Beast did not follow at once, but amused itself with a few minutes of wanton destruction before giving chase.

Joenes was able to join a group of village hunters. These men, with Lunu at their head, stood with spears and arrows poised, ready to engage in battle against the Beast.

Standing nearby were the village witch doctor and his two assistants. The witch doctor's wrinkled old face was painted ocher and blue. In his right hand he held a skull, and with his left hand he poked frantically through a pile of magical ingredients. At the same time he was cursing his assistants.

"Idiots!" he was saying. "Criminally incompetent fools! Where is the moss from the dead man's head?"

"It is under your left foot, sir," one of the assistants said.

"What a place for it!" the witch doctor responded. "Give it here. Now where is the red shroud string?"

"In your pouch, sir," the other assistant answered.

The witch doctor drew it out and threaded it through the eye sockets of the skull. He bound the moss in the nose opening, then turned to his assistants.

"You, Huang, I sent to read the stars; and you, Pollito, I sent to learn the message of the sacred golden deer. Tell me quickly and without delay what these messages were and what the gods request in order for us to stop the Beast tonight."

Huang said, "The stars told us to bind rosemary widdershins tonight."

The witch doctor seized a sprig of rosemary from his pile of ingredients and bound it to the skull with a shroud string, turning the string three times as the sun turns.

Pollito said, "The message of the sacred golden deer was to give the skull a pinch of snuff; that he said would be enough."

"Spare me your moronic rhyming," the witch doctor said, "and give me the snuff."

"I don't have it, sir."

"Then where is it?"

"Earlier you said that you had put the snuff in a safe place."

"Naturally. But in *which* safe place did I put it?" the witch doctor asked, rummaging wildly through his ingredients.

"Perhaps it's at the Underworld Altar," Huang said.

"Maybe it's at the Divining Place." Pollito said.

"No, none of those places seem right," the witch doctor said. "Let me think…"

The Beast, however, gave him no further time for thought. It trotted out of Joenes's cabin and sprang at the line of hunters. A dozen arrows and spears darted forward to meet it, humming in the air like angry hornets. But these missiles had no effect. Unharmed, the Beast burst through the hunters' line. Already the witch doctor and his assistants had gathered up their ingredients and sprinted into the forest. The hunters also ran, but Lunu and two others were killed.

Joenes followed the hunters, and fear lent speed to his feet. At last he came to a clearing in the forest with a weathered stone altar in its center. Here he found the witch doctor and his assistants, and behind them shuddered the hunters. In the forest, the howls of the Beast were growing louder.

The witch doctor was fumbling on the ground near the altar, saying, "I'm almost positive I put the snuff around here somewhere. I came here to ask the Sun's special blessing on it this afternoon. Pollito, do you remember what I did then?"

"I wasn't here," Pollito said. "You told us you were going to perform a secret rite, and that our presence was forbidden."

"Of course it was forbidden," the witch doctor said, digging vigorously around the altar with a stick. "But didn't you spy on me?"

"We would never do that." Huang said.

"Damned conformistic young morons!" the witch doctor said. "How do you expect to become witch doctors if you don't spy on me at every opportunity?"

The Beast appeared at the edge of the clearing, not fifty yards from the group. At the same moment the witch doctor bent down, then straightened up with a small deerskin bag in his hand.

"Here it is, of course!" the witch doctor cried. "Right under the sacred ear of corn where I buried it this afternoon. Will one of you thumb-fingered imbeciles hand me another shroud string?"

Already Pollito was holding it out. With great dexterity the witch doctor bound the bag to the skull's lower jaw, winding three times widdershins. Then he hefted the skull in his hand and said, "Is there anything I've forgotten? I don't think so. Now watch, you dull-witted bucolics, and see how the deed is done."

The witch doctor advanced on the Beast, holding the skull in both hands. Joenes, the hunters, and the two assistants stood open-mouthed as the Beast pawed the earth into a trench three feet deep, stepped across it, and moved ominously towards the witch doctor.

The old man stepped close without a sign of fear. At the last moment he threw the skull, striking the Beast on the chest. It seemed a puny blow to Joenes; but the Beast let out an immense roar of pain, turned, and loped away into the forest.

The hunters were too weary to celebrate the Beast's defeat. They went silently to their cabins.

The witch doctor said to his assistants, "I hope you've had the sense to learn something from this. When skull exorcism is called for, the prepared skull, or *aharbitus,* must strike the center of the Beast's chest. No other blow will do, but will simply augment the fury of the creature. Tomorrow we will study three-bodies exorcism, for which there is a very pretty ritual." Then he left.

Joenes lifted the still unconscious Laka and brought her back to his own cabin. As soon as the door was closed, Laka came to her senses and showered Joenes with kisses. Joenes pushed her away, telling her not to do violence to her feelings, nor to arouse his. But Laka declared that she was a changed woman, even if the change were only temporary. The sight of the Beast, she said, and of Joenes's bravery in rescuing her, had moved her to the depths of her being. Also, poor Lunu's death had shown her the value of passion in an ephemeral existence.

Joenes had his suspicions about these reasons, but there was no denying the fact that Laka had changed. Her eyes gleamed, and with a sudden leap reminiscent of the Beast's spring, she fell upon Joenes and toppled him onto the bed of pine boughs.

Joenes decided that, little as he knew of men, he knew even less of women. Also, the pine boughs hurt his back abominably. But soon he forgot his pain and his lack of knowledge. Both became exceedingly un-important, and he did not think about them again until dawn flooded the cabin with light, and Laka slipped away to return to her own cabin.

THE NECESSITY FOR THE BEAST OF THE UTOPIA

In the morning, Joenes met with his colleagues from the University. He told them his adventures of the previous night and expressed indignation at not having been warned about the Beast.

"But my dear Joenes!" said Professor Hanley. "We wanted you to witness this vital facet of Chorowait for yourself, and to judge it without preconceptions."

"Even if that witnessing had cost me my life?" Joenes asked angrily.

"You were never in the slightest danger," Professor Chandler told him. "The Beast never attacks anyone connected with the University."

"It certainly seemed as though it was trying to kill me," Joenes said.

"I'm sure it *seemed* that way," Manisfree said. "But actually it was merely trying to get at Laka who, being a Chorowaitian, is a suitable victim for the Beast. You might have been jostled a bit when the Beast tore the girl from your arms; but that is the worst that could have happened to you."

Joenes felt chagrined at finding that his danger, which had seemed so dire the night before, was now revealed as no danger at all. To conceal his annoyance, he asked, "What sort of creature was it and to what species does it belong?"

Geoffrard of Classics cleared his throat importantly and said, "The Beast you saw last night is unique, and should not be confused with the Questing Beast whom Sir Pellinore pursued, nor with the Beasts of Revelation. The Chorowaitian Beast is more closely akin to the Opinicus, which the ancients tell us was part camel, part dragon, and part lion, though we do not know in what proportions. But even this kinship is superficial. As I said, our Beast is unique."

Joenes asked, "Where did this Beast come from?"

The professors looked at each other and giggled like embarrassed schoolboys. Then Blake of Physics controlled his mirth and said to Joenes, "The fact of the matter is, we ourselves gave birth to the Beast. We constructed it part by part and member by member, using the Chemistry Lab on weekends and evenings. All departments of the University cooperated in the design and fabrication of the Beast, but I should especially single out the contributions made by Chemistry, Physics, Mathematics, Cybernetics, Medicine, and Psychology. And I must also mention the contributions of Anthropology and Classics, whose inspiration this was. Special thanks are due to Professor Elling of Practical Arts, who upholstered the entire Beast with the most durable of plastic skins. Nor should I forget Miss Hua, our student assistant, without whose careful collation of our notes the whole venture might have foundered."

The professors beamed happily at Blake's speech. Joenes, who had unwrapped a mystery only to find an enigma, still understood nothing.

Joenes said, "Let me see it I follow you. You *made* the Beast, constructing it out of ideas and inert matter in the Chemistry Lab?"

"That's very nicely put," Manisfree said. "Yes, that's exactly what we did."

"Was the Beast made with the knowledge of the University administration?"

Dalton winked and said, "You know how it is with those fellows, Joenes. They have an innate distaste for anything new, unless it's a gymnasium. So of course we didn't tell them."

"But they knew all the same," Manisfree said. "Administration always knows what's going on. But unless something is forced on their attention, they prefer to look the other way. They reason that a project like this might turn out well, in which case they and the University would get credit for farsighted wisdom. And if it turns out badly, they're safe because they knew nothing about it."

Several of the professors leaned forward with jokes about administrators on their lips. But Joenes spoke first, saying, "The construction of the Beast must have been very difficult."

"Indeed it was," said Ptolemy of Mathematics. "Excluding our own time, and the wear and tear on the Chem Lab, we had to spend twelve million four hundred thousand and twelve dollars and sixty-three cents on the fabrication of special parts. Hoggshead of Accounting kept a careful record of all expenses in case we should ever be asked."

"Where did the money come from?" Joenes asked.

"The government, of course," said Harris of Political Science. "I, and my colleague Finfitter of Economics, took over the problem of funds appropriation. We had enough left over to throw a victory banquet when Project Beast was completed. Too bad you weren't here for that, Joenes."

Harris forestalled Joenes's next question by adding, "Of course, we did not tell the government that we were building the Beast. Although they might still have granted funds, the inevitable bureaucratic delay would have been maddening. Instead, we said that we were working on a crash project to determine the feasibility of building an eight-lane coast-to-coast underground highway in the interests of national defense. Perhaps I do not need to add that Congress, which has always favored highway construction, voted immediately and enthusiastically to give us funds."

Blake said, "Many of us felt that such a highway would be eminently practical, and perhaps extremely necessary. The more we thought about it, the more the idea grew on us. But the Beast came first. And even with government funds at our disposal, the task was tremendously difficult."

"Do you remember," asked Ptolemy, "the excruciating problem of programming the Beast's computer brain?"

"Lord yes!" Manisfree chuckled. "And what about the difficulties of giving it a parthenogenetic reproductive system?"

"Almost had us stopped," said Dalton. "But then, consider how we worked to coordinate and stabilize the Beast's movements! The poor thing lurched around the lab for weeks before we got that right."

"It killed old Duglaston of Neurology," Ptolemy said sadly.

"Accidents will happen," Dalton said. "I'm glad we were able to tell Administration that Duglaston had gone on his sabbatical."

The professors seemed to have a thousand anecdotes about the building of the Beast. But Joenes impatiently broke into their reminiscences.

"What I wanted to know," Joenes said, "is *why* you built the Beast?"

The professors had to think for a moment. They were separated by many years from the ecstatic days when they had first discovered the reasons for the Beast. But luckily, the reasons were all still there. After a slight pause, Blake said:

"The Beast was necessary, Joenes. It or something exactly like it was needed for the success of Utopian Chorowait, and by extension, for the fulfillment of the future which Chorowait represents."

"I see," Joenes said. "But why?"

"It's really terribly simple," Blake said. "Consider a society like Chorowait, or any other society, and ask yourself what caused its dissolution. It's a difficult question, and there really is no answer. But we can't be content with that. Men *do* live in societies; it seems to be in their nature. Given that as a necessary condition, we wanted to build an ideal societal model at Chorowait. Since all societies are breaking down today, we wanted ours to be stable, and as equitable as possible within a framework of accepted democratic law. We also wanted a pleasant society, and a meaningful one. Do you agree that these are worthwhile ideals?"

"Certainly," Joenes said. "But the Beast—"

"Yes, here is where the Beast comes in. The Beast, you see, is the implicit necessity upon which Chorowait rests."

Joenes looked confused, so Blake went on:

"It's actually a simple matter, and can be understood very readily. But first you must accept the need for stability, equitability within a framework of accepted law, and a meaning for existence. This you have accepted. Next you must accept the fact that no society can be made to operate on mere abstractions. When virtue goes unrewarded and vice is unpunished, men cease to believe, and their society falls apart. I'll grant you that men need ideals; but they cannot sustain them in the valueless void of the present world. With horror men discover how very far away the gods are, and how little difference anything makes."

"We will also grant you," Manisfree said, "that the fault undoubtedly lies in the individual man himself. Even though he is a thinking being, he refuses to think. Though possessed of intelligence, he rarely employs it for his own betterment. Yes, Joenes, I think we can accept all that."

Joenes nodded, amazed at these points the professors had granted him.

"So, given all that," Blake said, "we now see the absolute necessity of the Beast."

Blake turned away as though everything had been said. But Dalton, more zealous, continued:

"The Beast, my dear Joenes, is nothing less than Necessity personified. Today, with all mountains climbed and all oceans plumbed, with the planets within reach and the stars much too far away, with the gods gone and the state dissolving, what is there left? Man must pit his strength against something; we have provided the Beast for him. No longer must man dwell alone; the Beast is forever lurking nearby. No longer can man turn against himself in his idleness; he must be forever alert against the depredations of the Beast."

Manisfree said, "The Beast makes Chorowait society stable and cohesive. If the people did not work together, the Beast would kill them one by one. Only by the efforts of the entire populace of Chorowait is the Beast kept in reasonable check."

"It gives them a healthy respect for religion," Dalton said. "One needs religion when the Beast is on the prowl."

"It destroys complacency," Blake said. "No one could be complacent in the face of the Beast."

"Because of the Beast," Manisfree said, "the community of Chorowait is happy, family-oriented, religious, close to the soil, and continually aware of the necessity for virtue."

Joenes asked, "What stops the Beast from simply destroying the entire community?"

"Programming," Dalton said.

"I beg your pardon?"

"The Beast has been programmed, which is to say, certain information and responses have been built into its artificial brain. Needless to add, we took a great deal of care over that."

"You taught the Beast not to kill University professors," Joenes said.

"Well, yes," Dalton answered. "We aren't too proud of that, to tell you the truth. But we thought we might be necessary for a while."

"How else is the Beast programmed?" Joenes asked.

"It is taught to seek out and destroy any ruler or ruling group of Chorowait people; next in priority to destroy the unvirtuous, and next to destroy any

Chorowaitian. Because of that, any ruler must protect both himself and his people from the Beast. That in itself is quite enough to keep him out of mischief. But the ruler must also cooperate with the priesthood, without whose aid he is helpless. This serves as a decisive check to his powers."

"How can the priesthood help him?" Joenes asked.

"You yourself saw the witch doctor in action," Hanley said. "He and his assistants use certain substances that are gathered for them by the entire population of Chorowait. These, in proper combination, will turn the Beast back, since it is programmed to recognize and respond to the proper combination."

"Why can't the ruler simply take the substances and their combination, turn the Beast back himself, and rule without a priesthood?" Joenes asked.

"We took great care to preserve the separation between church and state," Harris said. "There is no single combination, you see, that will serve for all times the Beast appears. Instead, a vast quantity of formulae must be calculated each day, using lunar and stellar cycles, and variables such as temperature, humidity, wind speed, and the like."

"These calculations must keep the priests very busy," Joenes said.

"Indeed they do," Hanley said. "So busy that they have very little time in which to interfere with the affairs of the state. As a final safeguard against the possibility of a rich, complacent, and overweening priesthood, we have programmed a recurring random factor into the Beast. Against this nothing suffices, and the Beast will kill the witch doctor and no other. In that way, the witch doctor runs the same danger as does the ruler."

"But under those circumstances," Joenes said, "why would anyone want to be a priest or ruler?"

"Those are privileged positions," Manisfree said. "And as you saw, the humblest villager also runs the risk of death from the Beast. Since this is the case, men with ability will always accept the greater danger in order to exercise power, to fight against the Beast, and to enjoy greater privileges."

"You can see the interlocking nature of all this," Blake said. "Both the ruler and the witch doctor maintain their positions only through the support of the people. An unpopular ruler would have no men to help him against the Beast, and would quickly be killed. An unpopular witch doctor would not receive the vital substances he needs in order to check the Beast, which must be gathered by the efforts of the entire people. Thus, both the ruler and the witch doctor hold power by popular consent and approval, and the Beast thus ensures a genuine democracy."

"There are some interesting sidelights on all this," said Hanley of Anthropology. "I believe this is the first time in recorded history that the full range of magical artifacts has been objectively necessary for existence. And it is probably the first time there has ever been a creature on Earth that partook so closely of the supernatural."

"In view of the dangers," Joenes said, "I don't see why any of your volunteers stay on Chorowait Mountain."

"They stay because the community is good and purposeful," Blake said, "and because they can fight against a palpable enemy instead of an unseen madman who works by perversity and kills through boredom."

"Some few of our volunteers had their doubts," Dalton said. "They weren't sure they could stick it out, even though we convinced them of the rightness of the thing. For the uncertain ones, Doctor Broign of Psychology was able to devise a simple operation on the frontal lobes of the brain. This operation didn't harm them in any way, and did not destroy intelligence and initiative like the terrible lobotomies of the past. Instead, it simply wiped out all knowledge of a world outside of Chorowait. With that accomplished, they had no other place to go."

"Was that ethical?" Joenes asked.

"They volunteered of their own free will," Hanley said. "And all we took from them was a little worthless knowledge."

"We didn't like to do it," Blake said. "But the pioneer stage of any society is often marked by unusual problems. Luckily, our pioneer stage is almost at an end."

"It ceases," Manisfree said, "when the Beast spawns."

The professors paused for a moment of reverent silence.

"You see," Ptolemy said, "we went to considerable difficulty to make the Beast parthenogenetic. Thus, self-fertilizing, its unkillable spawn will quickly spread to neighboring communities. The offspring will not be programmed to stay within the confines of Chorowait Mountain, as the original Beast is. Instead, each will seek out and terrorize a community of its own."

"But other people will be helpless against them," Joenes said.

"Not for long. They will go to neighboring Chorowait for advice, and will learn the formulae for controlling their own particular Beast. In this way the communities of the future will be born, and will spread over the face of the earth."

"Nor do we plan to leave it simply at that," Dalton said excitedly. "The Beast is all very well, but neither it nor its offspring are completely safe against man's destructive ingenuity. Therefore we have obtained more government grants, and we are building other creations."

"We will fill the skies with mechanical vampires!" Ptolemy said.

"Cleverly articulated zombies will walk the earth!" said Dalton.

"Fantastic monsters will swim in the seas!" said Manisfree.

"Mankind shall live among the fabulous creations it has always craved," Hanley said. "The griffin and the unicorn, the monoceros and the martikora, the hippogriff and the monster rat, all of these and many others will live. Superstition and fear will replace superficiality and boredom; and there will be courage, too, in facing the djinn. There will be happiness when the unicorn lays his great head in a virgin's lap, and joy when the Little People reward a virtuous man with a bag of gold! The greedy man will be infallibly punished by the coreophagi, and the lustful must beware of meeting the incarnate Aphrodite Pandemos. Man will no longer be alone in the universe, but will live with creatures as marvelous as himself. And he will live in accordance with the only rules his nature will accept—the rules that come from a supernatural made manifest upon the Earth!"

Joenes looked at the professors, and their faces glowed with happiness. Seeing this, Joenes did not ask if the rest of the world, outside of Chorowait, wanted this reign of the fabulous, or if they should perhaps be consulted about it. Nor did Joenes state his own impression, that this reign of the fabulous would be nothing more than a quantity of man-made machines built to act like the products of men's imaginations; instead of being divine and infallible, the machines would be merely mortal and prone to error, absurdly destructive, extremely irritating, and bound to be destroyed as soon as men had contrived the machinery to do so.

But it was not entirely a regard for his colleagues' feelings that stopped Joenes from saying these and other things. He also feared that such dedicated men might kill him if he showed a real spirit of dissent. Therefore he kept silent, and on the long ride back to the University he brooded on the difficulties of man's existence.

When they reached the University, Joenes decided that he would leave the cloistered life as soon as he possibly could.

X. HOW JOENES ENTERED THE GOVERNMENT
(As told by Ma'aoa of Samoa)

An opportunity to leave the University came the following week when a government recruiter visited the campus. This man's name was Ollin, and his title was Undersecretary in Charge of Government Placement. He was a short man of perhaps fifty years, with close-cut white hair and a ruddy bulldog face. He gave an impression of dynamism and purpose that greatly affected Joenes.

Under-secretary Ollin made a short speech to the faculty: "Most of you know me, so I won't waste time with fancy words. I'll just remind you that the government needs talented and dedicated men for its various services and agencies. My job is to find those men. Anyone interested can visit me in room 222 of Old Scarmuth, which Dean Fols has graciously allowed me to use."

Jones went there, and Undersecretary Ollin greeted him heartily.

"Take a seat," Ollin said. "Smoke? Drink? Glad to see someone turn up. I thought all you eggheads here at Stephen's Wood had your own plans for saving the world. Some sort of mechanical monster, isn't it?"

Joenes was amazed that Ollin knew about the Chorowait experiment.

"We keep our eyes open," Ollin said. "It had us fooled at first because we thought it was just some gimmick for a monster movie. But now we know, and we've got FBI men on the case. Working undercover, they now make up one-third of the Chorowait group. We're going to move as soon as we've collected sufficient evidence."

"The mechanical Beast may spawn soon," Joenes said.

"It'll just give us more evidence," Ollin said. "Anyhow, let's direct our attention to you. I take it you're interested in government service?"

"I am. My name is Joenes, and I—"

"I know all that," Ollin said. He unlocked a large briefcase and removed a notebook.

"Let me see," he said, turning over the pages. "Joenes. Arrested in San Francisco for making an alleged subversive speech. Brought before a Congressional committee and judged an uncooperative and disrespectful witness, particularly in respect to your association with Arnold and Ronald Black, the twin Octagon spies. Tried by Oracle and given a ten-year suspended sentence. "Spent a brief time in the Hollis Home for the Criminally Insane, then found employment at this University. During your time here you met daily with the founders of the Chorowait community."

Ollin closed the notebook and asked, "Is that more or less correct?"

"More or less," Joenes said, sensing the impossibility of argument or explanation. "I suppose my record renders me unfit for service in the government."

Ollin burst into hearty laughter. At last, wiping his eyes, he said, "Joenes, these surroundings must have made you a little soft in the head. There's nothing so terrible in your record. Your San Francisco speech is merely alleged, not proved. Your disrespect of Congress shows a lively sense of personal responsibility much like that of our greatest Presidents. There is inherent loyalty in your refusal to speak of Arnold and Ronald Black even to save yourself. Your conversion from Communism is obvious; the FBI states that ever since your single misguided and naive episode with the Blacks, you have steadfastly turned your back on the agents of international revolution. There is nothing shameful about your stay at the Hollis Home for the Criminally Insane; if you read the statistics, you would see that the majority of us need psychiatric care at some time or another. And there is nothing alarming about your association with Chorowait. Idealism can't always be channeled in the ways the government would like it to be. Even though we plan to stamp out Chorowait, we must approve the lofty though impractical planning that went into it. We in government aren't hypocrites, Joenes. We know that none of us is absolutely pure, and that every man has done some little thing he isn't exactly proud of. Judged in that way, you have really done nothing at all."

Joenes expressed his gratitude at the government's attitude.

"The man you can really thank," Ollin said, "is Sean Feinstein. In his capacity as Special Assistant to the Presidential Assistant, he put forth these views about you. We made a careful study of your case, and decided that you were the sort of man we wanted in government."

"Am I really?" Joenes asked.

"Past a doubt. We politicians are realists. We recognize the myriad problems that assail us today. To solve those problems we need the most daring, independent, fearless thinkers we can get. Nothing but the best will do, and no secondary considerations will stop us. We need men like *you*, Joenes. Will you enter the service of the government?"

"I will!" Joenes cried, aflame with enthusiasm. "And I will try to live up to the faith that you and Sean Feinstein have in me."

"I knew you'd say that, Joenes," Ollin said huskily. "They all do. I thank you from the bottom of my heart. Sign here and here."

Ollin presented Joenes with a standard government contract, and Joenes signed. The Undersecretary put the paper in his briefcase and shook Joenes warmly by the hand.

"Your position in the government starts as of this moment. Thank you, God bless you, and remember that we are all counting on you."

Ollin then started for the door, but Joenes called after him: "Wait! What is my job and where do I perform it?"

"You'll be notified," Ollin said.

"When? And by whom?"

"I'm only a recruiter," Ollin said. "What happens to the people I recruit is completely out of my jurisdiction. But don't worry, your assignment will come through like clockwork. Remember that we're all counting on you. Now you must excuse me since I have a speaking engagement at Radcliffe."

Undersecretary Ollin left. Joenes was very excited about the possibilities before him, but a little skeptical about the speed with which the government would act.

The following morning, however, he received an official letter sent by special messenger. He was ordered to report to Room 432, East Wing, Portico Building, Washington, D.C., and to do so with the utmost dispatch. The letter was signed by no less a person than John Mudge, Special Assistant to the Services Coordination Chief.

Joenes took immediate leave of his colleagues, gazed for the last time on the green lawns and concrete paths of the University, and boarded the first jet for Washington.

It was a thrilling moment for Joenes when he arrived in the capital city. He walked down the rose marble streets toward the Portico Building, passing on his way the White House, seat of imperial American power.

To his left was the great expanse of the Octagon, built to replace the smaller Pentagon. Beyond that were the Buildings of Congress.

These buildings were especially stirring to Joenes. For him they were the embodiment of the romance of history. The glory of Old Washington, capital of the Hellenic Confederation before the disastrous Civil War, swam before his eyes. It was as though he could see the world-shaking debate between Pericles, representative of the marble-cutters' lobby, and Themistocles, the fiery submarine commander. He thought of Cleon, coming here from his home in Arcadian New Hampshire, putting forth his terse ideas about the prosecution of the war. The philosopher Alcibiades had lived here for a time, representing his native city of Louisiana, Xenophon had stood on these steps, and had been given a standing ovation for leading his ten thousand men all the way from the banks of the Yalu to the sanctuary of Pusan.

The memories crowded thick and fast! Here Thucydides wrote his definitive history of the tragic War Between the States. Hippocrates the Hellenic Surgeon General had conquered yellow fever here; and true to the oath he had devised, had never spoken of it. And here Lycurgus and Solon, the first judges of the Supreme Court, had held their famous debates on the nature of justice.

These famous men seemed to crowd around him as he crossed Washington's wide boulevards. Thinking of them, Joenes resolved to do his utmost, and to prove worthy of his ancestors.

In this ecstatic frame of mind, Joenes arrived at Room 432 of the East Wing of the Portico Building. John Mudge, the Special Assistant, made him welcome without delay. Mudge was kind and affable, unhurried in spite of his huge work load. Joenes learned that Mudge made all policy decisions in the Services Coordination Office, since his superior spent his days and nights penning useless petitions for transfer to the Army.

"Well, Joenes," Mudge said, "you've been assigned to us, and we're very glad to have you. I think I should explain immediately what this office does. We operate as an inter-Service agency designed to avoid duplication of effort between the semiautonomous forces of the military. Aside from that, we also serve as an intelligence and information agency for all Service programs, and as a governmental policy planner in the fields of military, psychological, and economic warfare."

"That sounds like quite a lot," Joenes said.

"It is far too much," Mudge answered. "And yet, our work is absolutely necessary. Take our, primary task of coordination between the services. Only last year, before this office was formed, elements of our Army fought a three-day pitched battle in the deepest jungles of northern Thailand. Imagine their chagrin when the smoke cleared and they found that they had been attacking a strongly entrenched battalion of U.S. Marines! Imagine the effect upon service morale! With our military obligations stretched so thinly across the globe, and so intricately disposed, we must be forever vigilant against incidents of this kind."

Joenes nodded in agreement. Mudge went on to explain the necessity for their other duties.

"Take intelligence, for example," Mudge said. "At one time that was the special province of the Central Intelligence Agency. But today, CIA refuses to release its information, requesting instead that it be given more troops to deal with the problems it uncovers."

"Deplorable," Joenes said.

"And of course the same holds true in greater degree for Army Intelligence, Navy Intelligence, Air Force Intelligence, Marine Corps Intelligence, Space Corps Intelligence, and all the others. The patriotism of the men of these Services cannot be doubted; but each, having been given the means of waging independent warfare, considers his Service the only one in a position to judge the danger and prosecute the conflict to a conclusion. This state of affairs renders any information on the enemy contradictory and suspect. And this in turn paralyzes the government, because it has no reliable information upon which to plan policy."

"I had no idea the problem was so severe," Joenes said.

"It is severe and insoluble," Mudge replied. "To my way of thinking, the fault lies in the very size of the governmental organization, which has swollen past all precedent. A scientist friend of mine once told me that an organism that grows beyond its natural size tends to break up into its component parts, eventually to begin the growing process all over again. We have grown too huge, and fragmentation has set in. Yet our growth was a natural consequence of the times, and we cannot allow any breakup to occur as yet. The Cold War is still upon us, and we must patch and mend and hold our Services in some semblance of order and cooperation. We in Co-ordination must discover the truth about the enemy, present this truth to the government as policy, and induce the Services to act upon this policy. We must persevere until the external danger is past, and then hope to reduce the size of our bureaucracy before the forces of chaos do the job for us."

"I think I understand," Joenes said. "And I am in full accord."

"I knew you would be," Mudge replied. "I knew it from the time I read your dossier and requested your appointment here. I told myself that this man would be a natural coordinator, and in spite of many difficulties I had you cleared for government service."

"But I thought that was the work of Sean Feinstein," Joenes said.

Mudge smiled. "Sean is little more than a figurehead who signs the papers we put in front of him. He is also a first-class patriot, having volunteered for the secret but necessary role of government scapegoat. In Sean's name we make all dubious, unpopular, or questionable decisions. When they turn out well, the Chiefs take the credit. When they turn out badly, Sean takes the blame. In this way, the usefulness of the Chiefs is not impaired."

"It must be very hard on Sean," Joenes said.

"Of course it is. But perhaps Sean would not be happy if things were not very hard on him. So a psychologist friend of mine believes. Another psychologist of my acquaintance, of a more mystical turn of mind, believes that Sean Feinstein is fulfilling an obligatory historical function, that he is destined to be a prime mover of men and events, a crucial figure in all histories, and a vital force in the enlightenment of the people; and that for these reasons he is detested and reviled by the populace he serves. But wherever the truth lies, I find Sean an extremely necessary person."

"I would like to meet him and shake his hand," Joenes said.

"That will not be possible just yet," Mudge said. "Sean is presently serving a term of solitary confinement upon a diet of bread and water. He was found guilty of stealing 24 atomic howitzers and 187 atomic grenades from the U.S. Army."

"Did he actually steal those things?" Joenes asked.

"Yes. But he did so at our request. We armed a Signal Corps detachment with them, and they succeeded in winning the Battle of Rosy Gulch in southeastern Bolivia. The Signal Corps, I might add, had long requested those weapons in vain."

"I am very sorry for Sean," Joenes said. "What is his sentence?"

"Death," said Mudge. "But he will be pardoned. He always is. Sean is too important not to be pardoned."

Mudge looked away for a moment, then turned back to Joenes. "Your particular work," he said, "will be of the utmost importance. We are sending you to Russia on a tour of inspection and analysis. Many such inspections have been made in the past, of course. But either they have been made from the bias of one Service, in which case they are worthless, or they have been made from a Coordinated standpoint, in which case they have been marked Top Secret and filed unread in the Top Secret room beneath Fort Knox. I have my chief's assurance, and I give you mine, that no such fate will befall your report. It will be read and acted upon. We are determined to impose Coordination, and anything you say about the enemy will be accepted and utilized. Now, Joenes, you will receive a full clearance, then a briefing, then orders."

Mudge took Joenes to Security Division, where a colonel in charge of Phrenology felt his head for suspicious bumps. After that, Joenes ran the gauntlet of government astrologists, card-readers, tea-leaf readers, physiognomists, psychologists, casuists, and computers. At the end he was declared loyal, sane, responsible, trustworthy, reverent, and above all, lucky.

On the basis of this he was given a Portmanteau Clearance and allowed to read classified documents.

We have only a partial list of the papers Joenes read in the gray iron Secrets Room, with two armed guards standing beside him, blindfolded to make sure they would not inadvertently glance at the precious documents. But we know that Joenes read:

"The Yalta Papers," which told of the historic meeting between President Roosevelt, Czar Nicholas II, and Emperor Ming. Joenes learned how the fateful decisions made in Yalta affected present-day politics; and he learned of the violent opposition to those decisions that was voiced by Don Winslow, the Supreme Naval Commander.

Next he read "I Was a Male War Bride," a devastating exposé of unnatural practices in the Armed Services.

And he also read the following:

"Little Orphan Annie Meets Wolf Man," a detailed espionage manual written by one of the most accomplished female spies who ever lived.

"Tarzan and the Black City," an extraordinary account of commando activities in Russian-held East Africa.

"The Cantos," author unknown, a cryptic statement of the enemy's monetary and racial theories.

"Buck Rogers Enters Mungo," a documentary account of the latest exploit of the Space Corps, illustrated.

"First Principles," by Spencer, "The Apocrypha," author unknown, "The Republic," by Plato, and "Maleus Malificarum," jointly authored by Torquemada, Bishop Berkeley, and Harpo Marx. These four works were the soul and spearhead of Communist doctrine, and we can be sure that Joenes read them with great profit.

Of course he also read "The Playboy of the Western World," by Immanuel Kant, which was the definitive refutation of the above-mentioned Communist works.

All of these documents have been lost to us, due to the unfortunate circumstances of their having been written on paper instead of learned by heart. We would give much to know the substance of those works that shaped the brilliant and erratic politics of the times. And we cannot help but ask whether Joenes read the few twentieth-century classics that have come down to our own time. Did he peruse the stirring *Boots,* cast in enduring bronze? Did he read *The Practical Man's Guide to Real Estate,* that monumental fantasy that ,almost singlehanded, shaped the temper of the twentieth century? Did Joenes ever meet the venerable Robinson Crusoe, his contemporary, greatest of the twentieth-century poets? Did he speak with any of the members of the Swiss Family Robinson, whose sculptures can be seen in many of our museums?

Alas, Joenes never spoke of these cultural things. Instead, his accounts focus upon matters of far greater concern to his beleaguered age.

So it was that Joenes, after reading steadily for three days and three nights, arose and left the gray iron Secrets Room and its blindfolded guards. He was now fully cognizant of the state of the nation and of the world. With high hopes and dire forebodings he opened his orders.

These orders instructed him to report to Room 18891, Floor 12, Level 6, Wing 63, Subsection AJB2, of the Octagon. With the orders was a map to aid him in finding his way around the massive structure. When he should reach Room 18891, a high Octagon official known only as Mr. M. would give him his final instructions and arrange his departure on a special jet for Russia.

Joenes's heart filled with joy when he read these orders, for at last he had a chance to play a part in great affairs. He rushed off to the Octagon to receive his final instructions and be off. But the duty Joenes wished to perform was not so easily captured.

XI. THE OCTAGON ADVENTURES

(The Octagon Adventures and the four stories that comprise it are told by Maubingi of Tahiti)

Afire with anticipation, Joenes entered the Octagon. He stared around him for a moment, never having imagined that so enormous and majestic a building could exist. Then, recovering, he walked swiftly down great halls and corridors, up stairways, through bypasses, across lobbies, and down more corridors.

By the time his first flush of enthusiasm had worn off, he was able to see that his map was hopelessly incorrect, for its various designations bore no reference to anything he saw around him. It seemed, in fact, to be a map of another building. Joenes was now deep in the heart of the Octagon, unsure of the way that lay ahead, dubious of his ability to retrace his footsteps. Therefore he put the map in his pocket and decided to ask advice of the first person he met.

Soon he overtook a man walking down the corridor. This man wore the uniform of a colonel in the Cartography Department, and his bearing was kindly and distinguished.

Joenes stopped the colonel, explaining that he was lost and that his map seemed to be useless.

The colonel glanced at Joenes's map and said, "Oh, yes, that's perfectly in order. This map is our Octagon Series A443-321B, which my office published only last week."

"But it doesn't tell me anything," Joenes said.

"You're damned right it doesn't," the colonel answered proudly. "Do you have any idea how important this building is? Did you know that every top government agency, including the most secret ones, are housed here?"

"I know that the building is very important," Joenes said. "But—"

"Then you can understand the position we would be in," the colonel went on, "if our enemies really understood the building and its offices. Spies would infiltrate these corridors. Disguised as soldiers and congressmen, they would have access to our most vital information. No security measures could hope to restrain a cunning and determined spy armed with information like that. We would be lost, my dear sir, utterly lost. But a map like this, which is most confusing to a spy, is one of our most important safeguards."

"I suppose it is," Joenes said politely.

The colonel of Cartography touched Joenes's map lovingly and said, "You have no idea how difficult it is to make such a map."

"Really?" Joenes said. "I would have thought it quite simple to construct a map of an imaginary place."

"The layman always thinks that. Only a fellow mapmaker, or a spy, could appreciate our problems. To construct a map that tells nothing and yet seems true, giving even an expert the sensation of verisimilitude— that, my friend, requires art of the highest order!"

"I'm sure it does," Joenes said. "But why do you bother making a false map at all?"

"For the sake of security," the colonel said. "But to understand that, you must know how a spy thinks when he gets a map like this; then you would see how this map strikes directly at the spy's greatest weakness, rendering him more ineffectual than no map at all would do. And to understand all that, you must comprehend the mentality of a spy."

Joenes admitted that he was bewildered by this explanation. But the colonel said it was merely a matter of understanding the nature of a spy. And to illustrate this nature, he then told Joenes a story about a spy, and how he behaved when he was in possession of the map.

THE STORY OF THE SPY

The spy (said the colonel) has overcome all previous obstacles. Armed with the precious map, he has penetrated deep into the building. Now he tries to use the map, and sees at once that it doesn't represent the thing he seeks. But he also sees that the map is beautifully made and expensively printed on government paper; it bears a government serial number and a countersigned stamp of approval. It is a clear, lucid map, a triumph of the mapmaker's skill. Does the spy throw it away and attempt to draw the bewildering complexities around him on a wretched little pocket pad, using only a ball-point pen that doesn't work very well? He most assuredly does not. Even though ultimate success might lie in that direction, our spy is only human. He does not wish to match his puny ability at visualizing, abstracting, drawing and generalizing, against experts in the field. It would take the highest courage and self-confidence for him to throw away this magnificent map and proceed with nothing but his senses to guide him. If he had the necessary qualities to do that, he would never have been a spy in the first place. He would have been a leader of men, or perhaps a great artist or scientist. But he is none of these things; he is a spy; which is to say, a man who has chosen to find out about things rather than to do things, and to discover what others know rather than to search for what he knows. Necessarily he assumes the existence of truths external to himself, since no real spy could believe that his lifework was to discover frivolous falsehoods.

This is all very important when we consider the character of any spy, and especially of the spy who has stolen a government map and penetrated deep into this closely guarded building.

I think we might fairly call this spy both genuine and excellent, and imbued with extraordinary dedication, cunning, and perseverance. These qualities have brought him past all dangers to a place of vantage within the building. But these very qualities also tend to shape his thoughts, making certain actions possible and others not. So we must realize that the better he is at his work, the more superb his guile, the stronger his dedication, the longer his experience, the greater his patience, then the less able he is to put aside these virtues, throw away the map, take a pen and blank paper in hand, and scribble down what he sees. Perhaps the idea of discarding an official government map sounds simple to you; but the spy finds this concept distasteful, foreign, repugnant, and utterly alien to his genius.

Instead, the spy begins to reason about the map in spy-fashion, which he thinks is the only way there is of reasoning, but which we know is merely a way he has of evading a discrepancy that life has made manifest, but which instinct and reason reject.

Here is a genuine government issue map, and over there are various corridors and doorways. The spy looks at the map, that document similar to other true and valuable documents he has risked his life to steal. He asks himself, "Can this map be false? I know that it issues from the government, and I know that I stole it from an official who evidently prized it and thought it valuable. Am I justified in ignoring this document simply because it seems to have no bearing on what I see around me?"

The spy ponders this question, and at last comes up with the operative word: "seems." The map only *seems* to have no bearing! Appearance had momentarily deceived him. He was nearly led astray by the testimony of his senses. The makers of the map almost did this to *him,* a master of tricks and disguises, a man who has spent a lifetime in worming out their secrets. Of course, it is all explicable now.

The spy says, "They tried to fool me with my own tricks! Clumsily, of course, but at least they are beginning to think in the right way."

By this the spy means that they are beginning to think as he does, thereby making their secrets more comprehensible to him. This pleases him. His bad humor, brought on by the lack of conformity between the map and the building, has now completely vanished. He is cheerful, energetic, prepared for any difficulty, ready to pursue this problem to its ultimate conclusion.

"Let me consider the facts and their implications," says the spy. "First, I know this map is important. Everything about it, and everything I have ever experienced, leads me to that premise. I also know that the map does not *seem* to represent the building it is supposed to represent. Quite obviously there is a relationship of some kind between the map and the building. What is this relationship, and what is the truth about the map?"

The spy thinks for a moment, then says, "The implication points to a cipher, a mystification that some skilled and cunning craftsman wove into the map, which the people for whom the map is intended know about, but which I hitherto did not know about."

After saying this, the spy draws himself to his full height and adds, "I, however, have spent a lifetime in the solving of ciphers. Indeed, there is nothing I am quite so interested in as ciphers. One might say that I was shaped by destiny to solve ciphers, and that destiny has conspired with chance to put me here, now, with this crucial coded document in my hand."

Our spy feels exalted. But then he asks himself, "Am I not being dogmatic in insisting, at the very start of my investigation, that this document is a true ciphered map and no other thing? Experience has taught me the painful lesson that men are capable of devious thinking. I myself am the living proof of that, for my cunning ways of thinking and acting have enabled me to remain hidden in the midst of my enemies, and to discover many of their secrets. Remembering that, don't I do them an injustice not to allow them the possibility of similar cunning?

"Very well," the spy says. "Even though reason and instinct tell me that the map is true in every respect, and misleading only because I do not have the key to the cipher, I must admit the possibility of it being false in part, and therefore true only in part. There are good reasons one could give for this assumption. Suppose the true part of the map is the only part that was needed by the official I stole it from. He, armed with a prior knowledge I do not have, would follow only the part that is true and pertinent to his work. Being the dull civil servant he is, and above all being uninterested in maps and ciphers, he would simply follow the true part to his office, and would ignore the false part. The map itself, with its false section joined so cleverly to the true, would not bother him. And why should it? His work has nothing to do with maps. He has no more interest in the truth or false-ness of the map than I have in the details of his petty job. Like me, he has no time to worry about complicated matters that do not concern him. He can use the map without doing violence to his feelings."

The spy is amused and saddened when he thinks of this man, using the map but having no interest in it. How strange people are! How odd that the official merely made use of the map, but never questioned its mysterious nature; while the spy knows that the only important matter is a complete understanding of the map and what it represents. From this understanding all other things will flow, and the secrets of the entire building will be acces-sible. This seems so obvious to him that he can't understand the official's lack of concern with the map. The spy's own interest seems to him so natu-ral, so necessary, so universal, that he is almost led to believe that the official is not human, but is rather a member of some other species.

"But no," he tells himself. "It may feel that way, but the real difference between the official and me probably lies in heredity, or in environmen-tal influences, or something like that. I must not let it disturb me. I have always known how strange and unknowable human beings are. Even spies, the most easily understood people in the world, have different methods and hold different attitudes. Yes, it is a strange world, and I have very little knowledge of it. What do I know of history, psychology, music, art, or literature? Oh, I could hold a sensible conversation on those subjects, but deep in my heart I know that I know nothing about them."

The spy is unhappy about this. But then he thinks, "Luckily, there *is* one thing I do understand. That is spying. No man can do everything, and I have done very well to become the expert I am in my own field. In that expertness lies my hope and my salvation. In that very narrowness lies my true depth, and my yardstick with which to test the world. After all, I know a great deal about the history and psychology of spying, and I have read most of the literature of spying. I have looked at the famous paintings of spies, and have frequently heard the well-known opera about spies. Thus, my depth gives me breadth. My deep knowledge of this one thing gives me a firm base in the world. I can stand upon that base and look at other matters with a certain perspective.

"Of course," the spy reminds himself, "I must never make the error of thinking that all things can be reduced to a matter of spying and its tech-niques. Even if this appears to be the case, it is the sort of simplification an intelligent man must avoid. No, spying is not everything! It is merely the key to everything."

Having established that, the spy goes on to say, "Spying is *not* every-thing; but luckily for me, this matter of the map does concern spying.

Maps are the very heart of spying, and when I hold a map in my hand and know that the government made it, then I am dealing with a problem for which I have a special competency. A map in cipher is of particular concern to spying, as is a map that is partially false. Even a map that was wholly false would necessarily concern spying."

Now the spy is ready to analyze the map. He tells himself, "There are three possibilities. First, the map is true, and in cipher. In that case, I must decode it, using all my patience and skill.

"Second, the map is only partially true, and in cipher. In that case I will determine which is the true part, and then decode it. That might seem difficult to a person who knows nothing about the work; but to the expert it is the sort of difficulty that can be overcome. And as soon as I have decoded the tiniest fraction of the map's true portion, all the rest will open for me. That would leave the false portion, which someone else might throw away. But I would not. I would treat the false portion exactly as I would treat the entire map if it were false, which is possibility number three.

"Third, if the entire map is false, I must see what kind of information I can extract from that falseness. Granted that the idea of a false government map is absurd, let's say that is the case. Or rather, let's say that falseness was the *intention* of the makers of the map. In such a case I would have to ask, how does one draw a false map?

"It is no easy matter, that I know. If the mapmaker works in this building, moves up and down its corridors, steps into and out of its offices, then he knows the building as no other person could. If this man tries to draw a false map, how can he avoid inadvertently drawing some portion of the true building?

"He can't, really. The truth in which he is steeped would render his quest for absolute falseness impossible. And if by accident he drew any portion of the true map, I could infallibly find that true part, and all of the building's jealously guarded security would be as nothing.

"But let's assume that the high officials are aware of all this and have given careful study to the problem of constructing a false map. Let's give them the benefit of every doubt within the necessities of the situation. They know that the map, in order to serve its purpose, must be drawn by a skilled mapmaker who will make it conform to the logical rules for maps and for buildings; and that the map must be false, and not true even inadvertently.

"To solve the problem, let us say that the high officials find a civilian mapmaker who has no knowledge of the building. He is brought to the place blindfolded, given a carefully guarded office, and told to draw a map of an imaginary building. He does so; but the problem of inadvertent truth still remains. Therefore, a government mapmaker who *does* know the truth must check the map. The government mapmaker checks (and no person but a mapmaker would be competent to judge), and he says that this map is excellent since it is entirely false.

"In that ultimate case, the map is still nothing but a cipher! It has been drawn by a skilled civilian mapmaker, and thus conforms to the general principles that govern the drawing of maps. It is of a building, and conforms to the rules for drawing buildings. It has been judged false; but it has been judged so by an official mapmaker *who knew the truth,* and was able to decide about every detail of the map on the basis of his knowledge of the true building. The so-called false map, then, is merely a sort of reversed or distorted image of the truth known by the official mapmaker; and the relationship between the true building and the false map has been established through his judgment, since he knew both true and false and judged their dissimilarity. His necessarily intermediary judgment demonstrates the nature of the false map—which, being a logical distortion that conceals the truth, may be called a cipher!

"And since this cipher follows the accepted rules for maps and buildings, it is susceptible to cipher analysis!"

This completes the spy's analysis of the three possibilities of the map, all of which can now be reduced to one: that the map is true, and in cipher.

Dazed by this discovery, the spy says, "They thought they could trick me, but it cannot be done in my chosen field. In my search for truth, I have lived all my life by falsehood and deceit; but I have always known my own reality. Because of myself and my search, I above all men know that there is no such thing as falsehood, and that everything is either the truth or a cipher. If it is the truth, I follow it; and if it is a cipher, I solve it. A cipher, after all, is merely a concealed truth!"

At last the spy is happy. He has moved through the deepest perplexities, and has had the courage to face the most terrible possibilities. His reward is now before him.

For now, paying strict attention to the map, and holding that well-made creation with loving care, the spy begins the task that is the culmination of his life, and which eternity would not give him time enough to complete. He begins his attempt to decipher the false map.

THE MAPMAKER'S EXPLANATION

When the colonel had finished, he and Joenes stood silent for a while. Then Joenes said, "I can't help feeling sorry for that spy."

"It was a sad story," the colonel said. "But then, all men's stories are sad."

"If the spy is caught, what will his punishment be?"

"He has already imposed it upon himself," the colonel replied. "His punishment is to decipher the map."

Joenes could think of no worse fate. He asked, "Do you catch many spies here in the Octagon?"

"To date," the colonel said, "not a single spy has succeeded in passing our outer security measures and penetrating into the building proper."

The colonel must have noticed a look of disappointment on Joenes's face, for he added quickly, "That, however, does not invalidate my story. If a spy did get in here in spite of all security, he would behave just as I told you. And believe me, spies are caught every week in the network of outer defenses."

"I didn't notice any defenses," Joenes said.

"Of course not. For one thing, you aren't a spy. For another, security knows its work well enough not to reveal its presence, but only to act when necessary. That is how matters stand at present. For the future, when more cunning spies are born, we in Cartography have our false maps."

Joenes nodded. He was eager now to continue his own job, but unsure how to go about it. Deciding on indirection, he asked the colonel, "Are you convinced that I am not a spy?"

"Everyone is a spy to some extent," the colonel said. "But in regard to the special meaning you imply, yes, I am quite convinced that you are not a spy."

"Well then," Joenes said, "I must tell you that I am under special orders to go to a certain office here."

"May I see those orders?" the colonel asked. Joenes handed them over. The colonel studied the orders and gave them back.

"They seem official," the colonel said. "You should certainly go to that office at once."

"That is my problem," Joenes said. "The truth is, I'm lost. I tried to follow one of your excellent false maps, and naturally enough I found nothing at all. Since you know I'm not a spy, and also know that I'm on official business, I would appreciate any assistance you could give me."

Joenes had made this request in a careful and roundabout way, which he thought would be most suitable to the colonel's mentality. But the colonel looked away with a look of embarrassment on his dignified features.

"I'm very much afraid I can't help you," the colonel said. "I do not have the faintest idea where your office is, and I don't even know what direction to recommend."

"But that's impossible!" Joenes cried. "You are a cartographer, an official mapmaker of this building. And even though you draw false maps, I'm sure you also draw true ones, since that must be in your nature."

"All that you say is correct," the colonel said. "Especially that last about my nature. Anyone can deduce the nature of a cartographer, since his nature resides in his work. That work is to draw maps of the most exacting accuracy, maps so precise and lucid that the dullest of men could follow them. My function has been perverted by necessities beyond my control, so I must spend much of my time drawing false maps that give the appearance of truth. But as you have guessed, nothing can stop a genuine mapmaker from drawing genuine maps. I would do it even if it were forbidden. And luckily, it is not forbidden. It is expressly commanded."

"By whom?" Joenes asked.

"By the high officials of this building," the colonel said. "They control security, and they use the true maps to aid them in disposing their forces. But of course, the true maps are a mere convenience for them, a bit of paper they refer to as casually as you would glance at your watch to see whether it was three-thirty or three-forty. If necessary they could do without the maps entirely, relying on their knowledge and power. They might find it an annoyance, but not a serious one."

"If you draw true maps for them," Joenes said, "surely you can tell me where to go now."

"I can't," the colonel said. "Only the high officials know the building well enough to go where they want to."

The colonel saw Joenes's look of disbelief. He said, "I know how unreasonable all this must sound to you. But you see, I draw only one section of the building at a time; no other method would work since the building is so vast and so complex. I draw my section and send it to a high official by messenger, and later I draw another section, and so on. Perhaps you think I can combine my knowledge of the various parts and know the whole? I tell you at once that I cannot. For one thing, there are other cartographers who draw parts of the building that I never have time to see. But even if I mapped the entire structure by myself, piece by piece, I could never combine all those pieces into an understandable unity. Any one portion of the building seems comprehensible to me, and I represent it with great accuracy on paper. But when it comes to understanding all the countless sections I have mapped, then I become confused, I can't tell one part from the other. And if I think about it for very long my sleep and appetite are affected, I smoke too much, I find solace in drink, and my work suffers. Sometimes, when these bad spells are on me, I make inaccuracies, and I do not perceive my errors until the officials send that portion of the map back for revision. This shakes my faith in my own proven abilities; I determine to end my bad habits and stick to my task of skillful portrayal of one section at a time, not bothering my head about the whole."

The colonel paused and rubbed his eyes. "As you may expect," he went on, "my good resolves don't last for long, especially when I am in the company of my fellow cartographers. At those times we sometimes discuss the building and try to determine among us what it really is. Usually we cartographers are shy men; like spies, we prefer to do our work in solitude and not to discuss it with each other. But the solitude we love can become overwhelming; and then we overcome the limits of our nature and talk about the building, each of us adding his increment of knowledge eagerly and without jealousy, all of us bent upon understanding the whole building. But those are the times that prove the most discouraging."

"Why is that?" Joenes asked.

"As I told you," the colonel said, "our map sections are sometimes sent back for revision, and we assume that we have made mistakes even though there is never any official comment. But when we mapmakers talk together, we occasionally find that two of us have mapped the same section, each remembering and drawing it differently. That sort of human error is to be expected, of course. But what is disconcerting is when the high officials accept both versions. You can imagine a mapmaker's sensations when he learns something like that!"

"Do you have any explanation for it?" Joenes asked.

"Well, for one thing, mapmakers have their individual styles and idiosyncrasies, and that might account for the discrepancy. For another, even the best of memories is untrustworthy, so we might not have mapped the same section. But to my way of thinking these explanations are not sufficient, and only one thing makes sense."

"What's that?" Joenes asked.

"I believe that workmen, under orders from the high officials, are continually changing portions of the building. It is the only explanation that satisfies me. I have even caught glimpses of what could only be workmen. But even if I hadn't seen them, I would still believe it. Just consider. The high officials are concerned with security, and the finest security possible would be to keep the building in a constant state of change. Next, if the building were static, a single mapmaking survey would be sufficient, instead of the continual drawing and revising we are called upon to do. Finally, the high officials are trying to control a complex and ever-changing world; therefore as the world changes, so must the building. More offices must be built, and old ones have to be altered for new tenants; a row of cubicles must be removed and an auditorium put in its place; whole corridors must be closed down to allow the installation of new wiring and plumbing. And so forth. Some of these changes are extremely evident. Any man can see them, not only a mapmaker. But other changes are made apparently in secrecy, or in parts of the building I do not visit until the work is completed. Then the new looks bafflingly like the old, although I can still sense a difference. It is for those reasons that I believe the building is continually being changed, thus rendering a complete knowledge of it impossible."

"If this place is as unknowable as you say it is," Joenes said, "then how do you find your way back to your own office?"

"There, I am ashamed to say, my mapmaking skill does not help me. I find my office just as everyone else here finds his office—by something that resembles instinct. The other workers don't know this; they think they find their way by some process of the intelligence, some kind of a turn-right turn-left system. Like the spy, they believe they could learn anything about the building if they wanted to. It would make you laugh or cry to hear the statements these people make about this building, even though they have never ventured beyond the corridor that leads to their office. But I, a mapmaker, wander all over the building in my work. Sometimes great changes occur in territory I have already passed, rendering it unrecognizable. Then something that is not knowledge guides me back to my office, exactly as it guides the office workers."

"I see," Joenes said, though he was actually very confused. "So you really don't know what I should do in order to find this office?"

"I really do not know."

"Could you give me any advice about the way I should go about looking, or what sort of thing I should look for?"

"I am an expert on the building," the colonel said sadly, "and I could talk about it for a year without repeating myself. But unfortunately, there is nothing I can say that would aid your particular situation."

Joenes asked, "Do you think I will ever find the office I was sent to?"

"If your business here is important," the colonel said, "and if the high officials really want you to find the office, then I'm sure you'll have no trouble. On the other hand, your business may not be of importance to anyone but you, in which case your search will doubtless be a long one. True, you carry official orders; but I suspect that the high officials occasionally send men to imaginary offices simply to test the security of the inner defenses of the building. If that is the case with you, your chance of success is small indeed."

"One way or another," Joenes said gloomily, "my prospects don't look very good."

"Well, those are the risks all of us run here," the colonel said. "Spies suspect that their rulers have sent them on a dangerous mission simply to get rid of them, and mapmakers suspect that they are ordered to draw simply to keep their fingers out of mischief. We all have our doubts, and I can only wish you the best of luck and the hope that your doubts are never proved true."

With that, the colonel bowed courteously and walked down the corridor.

Joenes watched him go and considered following him. But he had already gone down that way, and it seemed a necessary act of faith to go forward into what he did not know rather than turn back at the first discouragement.

So Joenes went on, but not entirely out of faith. He also suspected that the corridors behind him might have been changed by now.

Joenes walked down great halls and corridors, up stairways, through bypasses, across lobbies, and down more corridors. He resisted the urge to consult his beautiful false map, but he couldn't bring himself to throw the thing away. So he kept it in his pocket and kept on walking.

There was no way to tell the passage of time, but at last Joenes became very weary. He was now in an ancient part of the building. The floors here were of wood rather than marble, and they were badly decayed, making the footing dangerous. The walls, built of an inferior plaster, were flaked and torn. In some places the plaster had fallen away to reveal the wiring of the building, most of its insulation rotten and constituting an obvious fire hazard. Not even the ceiling seemed secure; it bulged ominously in places, making Joenes fear it would come down on him.

Whatever offices had once been here were now gone, and the place was in need of immediate and drastic repairs. Joenes even saw a workman's hammer lying on the floor; this convinced him that repairs would be made someday, even though he didn't see any workmen.

Lost and deeply discouraged, Joenes lay down on the floor, his great fatigue allowing him no other choice. He stretched out and within a minute fell asleep.

THE STORY OF THESEUS

Joenes awoke with a feeling of uneasiness. Standing up, he heard the sound of footsteps coming down the corridor.

Soon he saw the maker of the footsteps. He was a man, tall and in the prime of life, with a face both intelligent and suspicious. This man held a huge ball of string mounted on a spindle. As he walked, he unwound the string, which fell to the floor of the corridor and glittered faintly.

As soon as he saw Joenes, the man's face tightened into angry lines. He drew a revolver from his belt and took aim.

Joenes called out, "Wait! Whatever you think, I have never done you any harm!"

Controlling himself with obvious effort, the man did not pull the trigger. His eyes, which had gone blank and dangerous, regained a normal appearance. He put the revolver back in his belt and said, "I am very sorry to have startled you. The truth is, I thought you were someone else."

"Do I look like him?" Joenes asked.

"Not really," the man said. "But I become nervous in this damnable place and tend to shoot first and think second. Still, my mission is so vital that these actions of a hasty and high-strung nature can surely be forgiven."

"What is your mission?" Joenes asked.

The man's face glowed when Joenes asked that question. Proudly he said, "My mission is to bring peace, happiness, and freedom to the world."

"That's quite a lot," Joenes said.

"I could never be satisfied with anything less," the man said. "Mark my name well. It is George P. Theseus, and I confidently expect to be remembered as the man who destroyed dictatorship and freed the people. The deed I do here will live as a symbol to all men, and will also be good and just in its own right."

"What deed are you going to do?" Joenes asked.

"Singlehanded, I am going to kill a tyrant," Theseus said. "This man has managed to find a position of power within the building, and many gullible fools think he is a benefactor because he orders the building of dams to control floods, distributes food to the starving, finances medical work for the sick, and does many other gaudy things of that sort. This may deceive some people, but it does not deceive me."

"If he really does that work," Joenes said, "then he does indeed sound like a benefactor."

"I might have expected you to say that," Theseus said bitterly. "His tricks have taken you in, just as they have taken in most people. I cannot hope to change your mind. I have no skill at devious argument, while that man has the world's best propagandists at his service. My vindication must rest with the future. For now, I can only tell what I know, and tell it in a blunt, unpleasing manner."

"I will be very pleased to hear," Joenes said.

"Well then," Theseus said, "consider this. In order to do his good deeds, this man had to reach high office. To reach high office, he passed out bribes and sowed dissension, divided people into warring factions, killed off those who opposed him, corrupted the influential few, and starved the needy many. At last, when his power was absolute, he engaged in public works. But not out of love for the public. No, he did it as you or I might weed a garden, so that he might have something pleasant to look at instead of something ugly. This is how it is with tyrants, who will do anything to obtain power, and thereby create and perpetuate the very evils they purport to cure."

Joenes was moved by Theseus's speech, but a little suspicious also, because Theseus had a shifty and dangerous look. So Joenes spoke with caution: "I can certainly understand why you want to kill this man."

"No, you can't," Theseus said morosely. "You probably think I'm filled with nothing but hot air and ideals, a sort of pious madman with a gun. Well, you're wrong. I'm an ordinary sort of man, and if I can perform a good deed and win a reputation, then I'm happy. But my action against this tyrant is primarily for personal reasons."

"How so?" Joenes asked.

"This tyrant," Theseus said, "has private tastes just as perverted as the wild passions that drove him to power. Information such as this is usually kept secret, or scoffed at as the ravings of envious fools. His skilled propagandists see to that. But I know the truth.

"This great man came driving through my town one day in his armored black Cadillac, secure behind bullet-proof glass, puffing a big cigar and waving to the crowds. Then his eye chanced to fall upon a little girl in the crowd, and he ordered his car to stop.

"His bodyguards chased the people away, except for a few who watched from cellars and rooftops, unseen but seeing. Then the tyrant stepped out of his car and walked up to the little girl. He offered her ice cream and sweets, and begged her to get into the car with him.

"Some of the watching men understood what was happening, and rushed out to rescue the child. But the bodyguards shot and killed those men. They did so with silenced guns so as not to startle the girl; they told her that the men had decided to go to sleep for a while.

"Although a complete innocent, the child had her suspicions. Something in the tyrant's sweating red face and thick trembling lips must have frightened her. So, even though she wanted the ice cream and candy, she stood irresolute while the tyrant trembled with lust, and those of us watching helplessly in the cellars sweated out of fear for her.

"After looking wistfully at the gorgeous array of sweets and observing the tyrant's nervous movements, the little girl made up her mind. She would go in the car, she said, if her playmates could go with her. In the terrible vulnerability of her innocence, the child thought she would be safe among her playmates.

"The tyrant went purple with joy. It was evident that this was more than he dared hope for. The more the merrier, that was his sinister motto. He told the girl to bring along all the playmates she wished, and the girl called for her friends.

"The children came flocking to the black Cadillac. They would have come even without her summons, for the tyrant had had the wit to turn on his car radio, which played the most marvelous and enticing music.

"Music playing, sweets distributed, the tyrant herded them all into his enormous car and shut the door. His bodyguards closed around him, mounted on their powerful motorcycles. Then they all sped away, bound for the most shameful debaucheries in the tyrant's private pleasure room. Those children have never been heard of again. And that first little girl, as you may have guessed, was my own sister, taken under my eyes, with townspeople lying dead on the pavement near her, and with me in the cellar powerless to help."

Theseus wiped his eyes, which were now streaming freely. He said to Joenes, "Now you know the real and personal reasons why I am going to kill the tyrant. To destroy his evil, to avenge my slain friends, to rescue the poor children, but above all, to find my poor sister. I am no hero, I am nothing but an ordinary man. But events have forced me to perform this righteous deed."

Joenes, whose own eyes were far from dry, embraced Theseus and said, "I wish you good fortune on your quest, and I certainly hope you can succeed against so terrible a tyrant."

"I have my hopes," Theseus said, "and I am not without the determination and guile necessary for this difficult work. To begin with, I sought out the tyrant's daughter. I ingratiated myself with her, used every winning way I could think of, until at last she fell in love with me. Then I debauched her, and this gave me some satisfaction since she was not far from my poor sister's age. She desired marriage, and I promised to marry her, although I would rather slit my throat. And I explained to her very artfully what sort of man her father was. At first she would not believe me, the little idiot loved her tyrant father so! But she loved me more, and slowly became convinced of the truth of everything I said. Then, as the final step, I sought her aid in my plan to kill her father. You can imagine how difficult that was. The horrible little girl did not want her daddy destroyed, no matter how evil he was, no matter what he had done. But I threatened to leave her forever if she would not help me; and between love of me and love of her father she was nearly driven mad. Over and over she begged me to forget the past, which no action could erase. Come away with her, she said, and live in some place far from her father, and never think of him but only of her. As though I could ever look at her and not see her father's features! For days she held back, thinking she could convince me to do what she wanted. Endlessly she declared her love for me, stating it in the most exaggerated and hysterical terms. She would never allow us to be parted, she swore, and if death should befall me, then she would kill herself, too. And a great deal of similar nonsense, which, as a sensible man, I found most distasteful.

"At last I turned from her and took my leave. Then her courage crumbled. This young monster, filled with the most exquisite self-loathing, said she would help me in murdering her beloved father, if only I would swear never to leave her. And of course I swore what she wanted. I would have promised anything to get the assistance I needed.

"She told me what she alone knew; where her father's office could be found in this great building. And she also gave me this ball of string so that I could mark my way and leave quickly once the deed was done. And she herself gave me this revolver. And so here I am, on my way to the tyrant's office."

Joenes said, "You have not found him yet, I see?"

"Not yet," Theseus answered. "The corridors here are very long and winding, as you must have observed yourself. Also, I've had some bad luck. As I mentioned, I am of a hasty disposition and therefore inclined to shoot first and think second. Because of that, quite accidentally, I shot and killed a man in officer's uniform not long ago. He came upon me suddenly, and I fired without thinking."

"Was it the mapmaker?" Joenes asked.

"I do not know who he was," Theseus answered. "But he wore a colonel's badges, and he seemed to have a kindly face."

"It was the mapmaker," Joenes said.

"I am very sorry about it," Theseus said. "But I am even sorrier about the three others I killed in these hallways. I must be an unlucky man."

"Who were they?" Joenes asked.

"To my great sorrow, they were three of the children I had come to rescue. They must have slipped out of the tyrant's rooms and tried to reach freedom. I shot them as I shot the officer, and as I nearly shot you; that is, hastily, before they had a chance to speak. I cannot describe my feelings of regret, and my increased determination that the tyrant shall pay for all this."

"What will you do about his daughter?" Joenes asked.

"I won't follow my natural instincts and kill her," Theseus said. "But that ugly little bitch will never see me again. And I will pray that the tyrant's whelp dies of a broken heart."

So saying, Theseus turned his wrathful countenance toward the dim corridor stretching before him.

"And now," he said, "I must go about my work. Good-bye, my friend, and wish me luck."

Theseus walked briskly away, unwinding his glittering cord as he went. Joenes watched until he had vanished around a corner. For a time he could hear receding footsteps, then there was no sound at all.

Suddenly a woman appeared in the corridor behind Joenes.

She was very young, hardly more than a child. She was plump and red-faced, and her eyes glittered insanely. She walked silently, following after Theseus. And as she walked, she gathered up the string he had so carefully laid down. She had a huge ball of it in her hands, and she continued winding as she came near Joenes, obliterating the trail by which Theseus had thought to return.

As she passed Joenes, she turned and looked at him, and her face was wild with rage and grief. She said not one word, but put a finger to her lips in the sign of silence. Then she walked swiftly on, gathering the string as she went.

She was gone as quickly as she had come, and the corridor was deserted. Joenes stared in both directions, but saw nothing to indicate that either Theseus or the girl had ever passed his way. He rubbed his eyes, and once again lay down and fell asleep.

Some storytellers maintain that Joenes met with numerous other adventures while he was within the corridors of the Octagon. It is said that he encountered the Three Fates, and that those ancient crones explained to him their duties and desires, and from that Joenes grew to an understanding of the problems of the gods, and their ways of solving those problems. It is also said that Joenes slept on the floor of the corridor for twenty years, and that he awakened only through the intervention of Aphrodite Pandemos, who told him the story of her life. And when Joenes expressed disbelief at certain details of her story, the goddess changed our hero into a woman. In this form, Joenes underwent many difficulties and testings of the soul, to say nothing of the body, and learned many curious things that men, as a rule, never learn. And at last he acknowledged the truth of every detail of Aphrodite's story, and she changed him back into a man.

But there is only a limited authority for all this, and no details given. So now we will tell of Joenes's last adventure in the Octagon, which came as he lay asleep after his encounter with Theseus.

THE STORY OF MINOTAURUS

Joenes was roughly shaken awake. He sprang to his feet, and saw that the hall around him was no longer ancient and decayed, but was now gleaming and modern. The man who had awakened him was very large through the shoulders, even larger in the paunch, and had a broad, stern, no-nonsense face. No one could have mistaken this man for anything but an official.

"You're Joenes?" the official asked. "Well, if you've finished your nap, I suppose we can get to work."

Joenes expressed his deep regret that he had been sleeping instead of looking for the office to which he had been sent.

"It doesn't matter," the official said. "We have our protocol here, but I hope we're not stuffy. As a matter of fact, it's just as well that you slept. I had been situated in an entirely different part of the building, and I received urgent orders from the Security Chief to move my office here and to effect any repairs I thought necessary. The workmen found you asleep and decided not to bother you. They did their work in silence, moving you only to repair the piece of floor you lay upon. You didn't even wake up when they moved you."

Joenes looked with increasing amazement at the vast amount of work that had been done while he slept. He turned to an office door, where before there had been only a decayed wall. On that door was neatly stenciled:

ROOM 18891, Floor 12, Level 6, Wing 63, Subsection AJB-2. This was the exact address he had been looking for in vain; and Joenes expressed surprise at the manner in which his search had ended.

"Nothing to be surprised about," the official said. "This is quite an ordinary business procedure here. The highest officials not only know the building and all its contents, but they are also aware of every person's movements within the building. They know only too well the difficulties a stranger encounters here; and unfortunately, there are very strict laws against helping strangers. But the officials circumvent the law from time to time by moving the office to meet the searcher. Reasonable, eh? Now come in and we'll get to work."

Within the office there was a large desk piled high with papers, and three ringing telephones. The official asked Joenes to take a chair while he dealt with the telephones. He did so with the utmost dispatch.

"Speak up, man!" he roared into the first telephone. "What's that? Mississippi flooding again? Build a dam! Build ten dams, but get it under control. Send me a memo when you're finished.

"Yes, I can hear you," he shouted into the second telephone. "Starvation in the Panhandle? Distribute food at once! Just sign my name at the government warehouse.

"Calm down and let's hear about it," he bellowed into the third telephone. "Plague sweeping Los Angeles? Get vaccine in there at once, and send me a wire when it's under control."

The official put down the last of his telephones and said to Joenes, "These idiotic assistants of mine panic at the slightest thing. And as if that weren't bad enough, those gutless wonders wouldn't pull a drowning baby out of a bathtub without calling me first for authorization!"

Joenes had listened to the official's swift and decisive words over the telephones, and a suspicion had crossed his mind. He said, "I'm not absolutely certain of this, but I believe that a certain aggrieved young man—"

"—is trying to assassinate me," the official finished for him. "That's it, isn't it? Well, I took care of him half an hour ago. You don't catch Edwin J. Minotaurus napping. My guards took him away, and he'll probably get life imprisonment. But don't tell anyone."

"Why not?" Joenes asked.

"Bad publicity," Minotaurus said. "Especially his affair with my daughter, whom, incidentally, he knocked up. I've told that little half-wit to bring her friends to the house, but no, she has to sneak out and have dates with anarchists! We're giving out a specially prepared story that this Theseus fellow wounded me so severely that the doctors have despaired of my life; and that he escaped and married my daughter. You can see the value of a story like that."

"Not too clearly," Joenes said.

"Why damn it all, it builds up sympathy for me!" Minotaurus said. "People will feel sorry when they hear I'm at the point of death. And they'll feel even sorrier when they learn that my only daughter has married my assassin. You see, in spite of my proven abilities, the rabble doesn't like me. This story should win them over."

"It's very ingenious," Joenes said.

"Thank you," said Minotaurus. "Frankly, I had been worrying about my public image for quite some time, and if this moron with his string and his revolver hadn't come along, I would have had to hire somebody. I just hope the newspapers handle the story properly."

"Is there any doubt about that?" Joenes said.

"Oh, they'll print what I tell them," Minotaurus said moodily. "And I've hired a man to do a book about it, and there'll be a play and a movie based on the book. Don't worry, I'll milk this for all it's worth."

"What have you told them to write about your daughter?" Joenes asked.

"Well, as I said, she marries this anarchist fellow. And then in a year or two we publish an account of their divorce. Have to give the child a name, you know. But God knows what those idiots will write about my poor fat little Ariadne. Probably make her out to be beautiful, thinking it will please me. And the filthy scum who read this sort of thing will cry, and ask for more. Even kings and presidents, who should know better, will read these lies in preference to a good honest book of statistics. The human race is largely composed of incompetent, lying, bungling fools. I can control them, but I'll be damned if I can understand them."

"What about the children?" Joenes asked.

"What do you mean, what about the children?" Minotaurus said, glaring fiercely.

"Well, Theseus said—"

"That man is a gifted but insane liar," Minotaurus stated. "If it weren't for my position, I'd have sued him for libel. Children! Do I look like some kind of pervert? I think we can safely forget any question of children. Now, shall we get down to you and your work?"

Joenes nodded, and Minotaurus gave him a quick briefing on the political situation he was likely to find in Russia. He showed Joenes a secret map that gave the approximate positions and strengths of Communist and Western forces all over the earth. Joenes was stunned by the hugeness of the enemy forces, painted blood-red and stretching across many countries. The Western forces, painted sky-blue, seemed entirely inadequate.

"It isn't as hopeless as it looks," Minotaurus said. "For one thing, that map is only guesswork. For another, we do possess an enormous stockpile of warheads, and a missile system to carry them. We've come a long way with our missiles. The real proof came last year during the Combat Team Easy field exercises. At that time, a single Gnome missile with an improved warhead was able to blow up Io, one of the moons of Jupiter where we had simulated a Russian base."

"That certainly sounds as though we have strength," Joenes said.

"Oh yes. But the Russians and Chinese also have improved missiles, which succeeded four years ago in blowing up the planet Neptune. In effect, that means a missile stalemate. There may be some disaffection between the Russians and the Chinese because of the Yingdraw incident; but we can't count on that."

"What can we count on?" Joenes asked.

"Nobody knows," Minotaurus said. "That's why we're sending you to find out. *Information* is our problem, Joenes. What is the enemy actually up to? What in hell is going on over there? I know that John Mudge of Services Coordination told you of our need for the truth, no matter how terrible, told bluntly and forthrightly by a man we can trust. Do you understand the task we are setting you, Joenes?"

"I think I do," Joenes said.

"You are to serve no group or faction; and above all you are not to make the sort of report you think we would *like* to hear. You are neither to minimize nor to maximize the things you see, but to state them as simply and as objectively as possible."

"I will do my best," Joenes said.

"I don't suppose I can ask for more," Minotaurus said grudgingly.

Then Minotaurus gave Joenes the money and papers he would need for his trip. And instead of sending him back into the corridors to find his way to the entrance, Minotaurus opened a window and pressed a button.

"This is the way I always do it," Minotaurus said, helping Joenes into the seat beside the pilot. "Can't be bothered with all those damned corridors. Good luck, Joenes, and remember what I've said."

Joenes said that he would. He felt deeply touched by the faith Minotaurus had in him. The helicopter moved away toward the Washington Airport, where a special autopilot jet would be waiting. But as the helicopter rose, Joenes thought he heard children's laughter from a room adjoining Minotaurus' office.

XII. THE STORY OF RUSSIA
(As told by Pelui of Easter Island)

Joenes boarded his special jet, and soon he was high in the air racing northward toward the pole. A meal was served to him automatically, and later a movie was shown for his solitary pleasure. The sun hung low on the horizon, and at last the jet's automatic pilot asked Joenes to fasten his seat belt for the landing at Moscow Airport.

The landing was made without incident; and Joenes waited with mingled feelings of excitement and apprehension as the door of the jet swung open upon the capital of the Communist world.

Joenes was met by three officials of the Soviet government. They were clad in fur hats and coats, and fur-lined boots, necessary protection against the freezing wind that howled across the flat fields. They introduced themselves and took Joenes to a waiting command car for the drive into Moscow. During this ride, Joenes had a chance to look more closely at the men he was to deal with.

Comrade Slavski was bearded to his eyes, which had a dreamy, faraway look in their hazel depths.

Comrade Oruthi was small and clean-shaven, and he walked with a limp.

Marshal Trigask was round and cheerful, and seemed a man to be reckoned with.

At Red Square they parked in front of the Peace Hall. Within, a cheerful fire was blazing. The Russians gestured Joenes to a comfortable chair, and took seats beside him.

"We shall waste no words," Marshal Trigask said. "I shall merely preface this discussion by welcoming you to our beloved Moscow. We are always pleased when accredited Western diplomats such as yourself come to visit us. We are plain speakers, and we expect plain speaking in return. That is how to get things done. You may have noticed on your drive into Moscow—"

"Yes," broke in Slavski, "you must excuse me, I beg your pardon, but did you notice the little white snow crystals falling? And the white winter sky? I'm really very sorry, I shouldn't speak, but even a man such as myself has feelings and sometimes feels impelled to express them. Nature, gentlemen! Excuse me, but nature, yes, there is something about it…"

Marshal Trigask interrupted: "This is enough, Slavski. The most excellent Presidential Envoy Joenes has, I am sure, noticed nature at some time or another. I think we can dispense with such niceties. I am a plain man and I want to speak plainly. Perhaps I seem crude to you, but there it is. I am a soldier, and I cannot be bothered with diplomat's manners. Have I made myself clear?"

"Yes, quite clear," Joenes said.

"Excellent," Marshall Trigask went on. "In that case, what is your answer?"

"My answer to what?" Joenes asked.

"To our latest proposals," Trigask said. "Surely you haven't come all this way simply for a vacation?"

"I'm afraid you'll have to tell me about your proposals," Joenes said.

"They're really very simple," Comrade Oruthi said. "We merely ask that your government dismantle its arms, give up its colony of Hawaii, allow us to take possession of Alaska (which was originally ours), and also give us the northern half of California as a sign of good faith. Upon those terms we will undertake to do various things that I have forgotten at the moment. What do you say?"

Joenes tried to explain that he had no authority to say anything, but the Russians were unwilling to accept that. Therefore, knowing that such terms would never be accepted in Washington, he said no.

"You see?" Oruthi said. "I told you they'd say no."

"It was worth a try, wasn't it?" Marshal Trigask said. "After all, they might have said yes. But now we can get down to fundamentals. Mr. Joenes, I want you and your government to know that we are prepared to repel any attack of any size that you may mount against us."

"Our defenses begin in Eastern Germany," Oruthi said, "and they run in breadth from the Baltic to the Mediterranean."

"In depth," Marshal Trigask said, "they extend completely through Germany and Poland, and through most of European Russia. You may inspect those defenses and see for yourself our states of preparedness. Furthermore, our defenses are fully automatic, more modern than those of Western Europe, and more densely situated. In short, we are still ahead of you. We have outdefended you, and will be happy to prove it."

Slavski, who had been silent for a long time, now said, "You will see all this, my friend! You will see the starlight glittering on the gun barrels! I beg your pardon, but even a humble man like me, a man who might be mistaken for a fishmonger or a carpenter, has his poetic moments. Yes, it is true even though you laugh, gentlemen! Did not our poet say: 'Dark is the grass / When night shall creep / Away in sorrow.' Ah, you had not thought to hear me quote poetry! Let me assure you, I am quite aware of the impropriety of my quoting poetry! I regret my conduct more than you could imagine, I deplore it in fact, and yet…"

Comrade Oruthi gently joggled Slavski's shoulder, and he fell silent. Oruthi said, "You must forget his outbursts, Mr. Joenes. He is a leading Party theoretician, and therefore has a tendency toward self-conscious speech. Where are we?"

"I think I had just explained," Marshal Trigask said, "that our defenses are completely in order."

"Exactly," Oruthi said. "Your government should not be deceived on that account. Nor should they attach any importance to the Yingdraw incident. Your propagandists have doubtless represented that in many false ways. But the truth is quite simple, and came about through a simple misunderstanding."

"I was there at the time," Marshal Trigask said, "and can tell you exactly what happened. My command, the People's First, Eighth, Fifteenth, and Twenty-Fifth Armies, were holding field exercises at Yingdraw near the border of the Chinese People's Republic. During these exercises we were murderously attacked by a revisionist band of turncoat Chinese who had been subverted by Western gold, and who had somehow eluded the Peiping authorities."

"I was political commissar at the time," Oruthi said, "and I can attest the truth of what the Marshal is saying. These bandits came at us under the guise of the Chinese People's Fourth, Twelfth, Thirteenth, and Thirty-second Armies. Naturally we informed Peiping, and then took steps to drive the turncoats over the border."

"They, of course, insisted that they were driving *us* back over the border," Marshal Trigask said, with an ironic smile. "This was what we expected rebels to say, so battle was joined. In the meantime, we had received a message from Peiping. Unfortunately, it was written in ideograms. We were unable to read it, and sent it to Moscow for translation. In the meantime battle raged, and for a week both sides blazed away at each other."

"The translation came back," Oruthi said. "It read: 'The government of the Chinese People's Republic resents any implication of expansionism on its part, especially in regard to the rich, empty lands adjacent to the crowded Chinese borders. There are no rebels within the territorial limits of the Chinese People's Republic, and none are possible in a truly socialistic state. Therefore cease your warlike attacks upon our peaceful frontiers.'"

"You can imagine our perplexity," Marshal Trigask said. "The Chinese insisted that there were no rebels, and we were fighting at least a million of them, all of whom had stolen uniforms from the Chinese People's Army."

"Luckily," Oruthi said, "a high Kremlin official had come to advise us. This man was an expert on China. He told us we could ignore the first part of the message about expansionism, since this was meant in the form of a salutation. The second part about the non-existence of rebels, was obviously designed to save face. Accordingly he advised us to push the rebels back into China."

"That, however, was quite difficult," Marshal Trigask said. "The rebels had been reinforced by several million armed men, and by sheer weight of numbers had pushed us back all the way to Omsk, sacking Semipalatinsk on their way."

"Seeing that the situation showed signs of seriousness," Oruthi said, "we called in reserves. These came to no less than twenty Russian armies. With these we gloriously slaughtered an uncountable number of rebels, and pushed the rest back completely across Sinkiang into Szechuan."

"We thought that took care of the matter," Marshal Trigask said. "We were marching to Peiping to exchange views with the Chinese People's Government when the rebels suddenly renewed the attack. Their force now numbered some fifty million men. Luckily, not all of these were armed."

"Even the gold of the West has its limits," Oruthi said.

"We received another note from Peiping," Marshal Trigask said. "In translation, this one told us to leave the territory of China immediately, and to cease our warlike assaults against the defensive elements of the Chinese People's Army."

"We think that's what the note meant," Oruthi said. "But with fiendish cleverness, they had constructed their message so that, when read upside down, it became a poem which went: 'How beautiful is the mountain / floating in the river / past my garden.' "

"Most ironic," Marshal Trigask said, "was the fact that, by the time we had deciphered their message, we had been pushed back many thousands of miles from the borders of China, all the way across high Asia to Stalingrad. There we made a stand, slaughtered millions, and were thrown back again to Kharkov, where we made a stand, and were once again thrown back to Kiev. Again we were forced back, making another stand outside of Warsaw. By this time we considered the situation to be serious. We gathered together volunteer armies from Eastern Germany, Poland, Czechoslovakia, Rumania, Hungary, and Bulgaria. The Albanians treacherously joined the Greeks who, with the Yugoslavs, attacked us from the rear. We threw off the attack and concentrated our forces for the main effort to the east. This time we attacked the Chinese rebels with our full armies and reserves, along a seven-hundred-mile front. We rolled the rebel forces back the entire way they had come, and farther, all the way to Canton, which we devastated."

"There," Oruthi continued, "the rebels threw in their last few million reserves, and we fell back to the border. After regrouping, we fought a series of border engagements for several months. At last, by mutual consent, we both withdrew."

"I still wanted to press the attack," Marshal Trigask said. "But more cautious leaders pointed out that I had only a few thousand ragged men left with which to oppose the decimated but still determined rebels. This would not have stopped me; but my colleague Oruthi pointed out, most correctly, that it was now a purely internal matter for the Chinese. That ended the Yingdraw incident."

"We have been unable to contact Peiping since that time," Oruthi said. "But the pique of our great ally will pass."

"I must add only," Trigask said, "that no one in the West knows the full extent of this incident, since neither we nor the Chinese told about it, and the few informers who did were not believed. You might, I suppose, wonder why we tell you the story in such detail?"

"I was wondering that," Joenes said.

"We tell it because we know where your true sympathies lie, *Comrade Jonski.*"

"I beg your pardon," Joenes said.

"Oh, we know," Oruthi said. "We have our ways of finding things out. Not even the darkest machinations of the American Congress can be hidden from us. We know of the Communist speech you made in San Francisco, and of your subsequent inquisition by a Congressional committee. We saw how the American secret police followed you, since we followed them. And of course, the associates of Arnold and Ronald Black told us of the great services you had done for the cause, and of the cleverness with which you avoided all contacts with them. Finally, we observed how successful you were in re-establishing yourself in the government's favor and in acquiring a key position. Therefore we say, welcome home, comrade!"

"I am not a comrade," Joenes answered. "And I am serving the American cause to the best of my ability."

"Well said," Trigask said. "Who knows who may be listening, eh? You do right in keeping your cover, and I for one shall not bring the matter up again. We want you to keep that cover, *Mister* Joenes, because in that way you are most valuable to us."

"Correct," Oruthi said. "The matter is closed. You will use your own judgment, *Mister* Joenes, as to what portion of the events of Yingdraw to tell. Word of apparent dissension with our allies might make your government more eager to negotiate, eh?"

"Remember to tell them," Trigask said, "that our missile arm is fully prepared, even though our conventional infantry forces may be somewhat reduced. We also have fully armed missile forces on the moon, Mars, and Venus. They are ready to rain down destruction whenever we give the word."

"Of course, giving the word is a little difficult," Oruthi said. "Speaking only among ourselves, there are certain adverse conditions that our spacemen have found. On the moon, they live deep underground in order to avoid solar radiation, and are continually occupied in trying to manufacture food, water, and air. This state of affairs renders communications difficult."

"On Venus," Slavski said, "the climate is so unbelievably humid that metal rusts with extreme rapidity, and plastic or vegetable products rot under one's very nose. This is hard on radio equipment."

"On Mars," Trigask said, "there are tiny, wormlike creatures of great malevolence. Although mindless, they eat their way into anything, even solid metal. Without unusual precautions, all of the equipment, to say nothing of the men themselves, can become honeycombed with these horrible creatures."

"I'm glad the Americans face the same problems," Oruthi said. "They also have sent expeditionary forces to the moon, Mars, and Venus. But we got there first, and therefore the planets belong to us. But now, Joenes, we really must offer you some refreshment."

Joenes was fed with great quantities of yoghurt and black bread, which was all that was available at the moment. Then they went with Joenes in his own jet to show him the fortifications.

Soon Joenes could look down and see row upon row of cannon, minefields, barbed wire, machine guns, and pillboxes, extending endlessly to the horizon, disguised as farms, villages, towns, troikas, droshkys, and the like. Joenes saw no people, however, and this reminded him of what he had heard earlier about the state of affairs in Western Europe.

They returned to Moscow Airport and the Russians disembarked, wishing Joenes good fortune on his return to Washington.

Just before he left, Comrade Slavski said to him, "Remember, my friend, that all men are brothers. Oh, you may laugh at such fine sentiments coming from a drunkard who cannot even be counted on to do his work properly. Nor would I blame you for laughing, no more than I blamed my chief, Rosskolenko, for clubbing me over the ear yesterday and saying that I would lose my job if I showed up drunk again. I do not blame Rosskolenko, I love that terrible man as a brother, even though I know that I will get drunk again, and that he will fire me. And what will happen then to my eldest daughter, Grustikaya, who patiently mends my shirt and does not curse me when I steal her savings for drink? I can see that you despise me, and I do not blame you. No man could be more despicable than I. You may abuse me, gentlemen, and yet I am an educated man, I have noble sentiments, a great future once lay before me...."

At this point Joenes's jet took off, and Joenes was unable to hear the end of Slavski's speech, if that speech had an end.

It was only later that Joenes reviewed all he had seen and heard, and realized that there was no need for a war, nor even an excuse for fighting under the present circumstances. The forces of chaos had overwhelmed the Soviets and Chinese, just as it had the West Europeans. But there was no reason now for that to happen in America.

This message, with full details, Joenes sent ahead of him to Washington.

XIII. THE STORY OF THE WAR
(As told by Teleu of Huahine)

It is sad to relate that as Joenes flew over California an automatic radar station identified his jet as an invader, and fired a number of air-to-air missiles at it. This tragic incident marked the opening phase of the great war.

Mistakes of this kind have occurred throughout the history of warfare. But in twenty-first-century America, due to the great confidence and affection men had for their machines, and due also to the semiautonomous nature of those machines, such a mistake was bound to have dire consequences.

Joenes watched with horror and fascination as the missiles speeded towards his jet. Then he felt a violent lurch as the jet's automatic pilot, sensing the danger, fired its own antimissile-missiles in defense.

This attack brought other ground-based missile stations to the attack. Some of these stations were automatic and others were not, but all responded instantly to the emergency call. Joenes's jet, in the meantime, had expended its entire armament.

But it had not lost the guile its planners had built into it. It switched its radio to the missile-dispatching frequency and broadcast an alarm, declaring itself under attack and naming the airborne missiles as enemy targets to be destroyed.

These tactics met with some success. A number of the older, more simpleminded missiles would not destroy a craft they considered their own. The newer, more sophisticated missiles, however, had been alerted to just such an attempt on the part of an enemy. Therefore they pressed the attack, while the older missiles fiercely defended the solitary jet.

When the battle between the missiles was fully under way, Joenes's jet glided away from the area. With the battle zone far behind, the jet streaked for its home airport in Washington, D.C.

Upon arrival, Joenes was taken by elevator to the Service Command Post, seven hundred feet underground. Here he was questioned as to the nature of the assault upon him and the identity of the assailants. But all Joenes could say for certain was that he had been attacked by some missiles and defended by others.

This was already known, so the officers questioned the automatic pilot of Joenes's jet.

For a time the automatic pilot gave evasive answers, since the proper security code had not been read to it. But after this was done, it stated that ground-based missiles had attacked it over California, and that some of these missiles were of a type it had never seen before.

This and all other data concerning the battle were given to the War Probabilities Calculator, which quickly presented the following choices in order of apparent probability:

1. The Communist Bloc had attacked California.
2. The neutralist countries had attacked California.
3. The members of the Western Alliance had attacked California.
4. Invaders from outer space had attacked California.
5. There was no attack upon California.

The calculator also gave all possible combinations and permutations of these five possibilities, and ranked them as alternative subpossibilities.

Joenes's earlier report on the state of affairs in Russia and China had also been received in Washington, but had not yet been processed and approved by the slow and methodical Human Factors and Reliability Assessment Calculator. This was a shame, since the War Probabilities Calculator could only use material that had been verified by other calculators.

The attending officers found themselves bewildered by the many probabilities, subprobabilities, possibilities and subpossibilities they were given. They had hoped to choose the statement rated most probable, and to act upon it. But the War Probabilities Calculator rendered that impossible. As new data came in, the calculator revised and refined its probabilities, ranking and grouping them in ever-changing sequences. Reappraisal sheets marked MOST URGENT spewed from the machine at the rate of ten a second, no two alike, to the annoyance of the attending officers.

Still, the machine was only doing what an ideal intelligence officer would have done—taking into account all approved reports, weighing their meaning and their probability, making recommendations on the basis of all pertinent and verifiable information, and never holding to an opinion out of mere pride or stubbornness, but remaining always ready and willing to revise any judgment on the basis of new data.

To be sure, the War Probabilities Calculator issued no orders; the issuing of orders was the glory and responsibility of men. Nor could the calculator be blamed for not presenting a unified, true, and consistent picture of the hostilities over California; it was impossible to give such a picture. The very nature of warfare in the twenty-first century had created this impossibility.

No longer did a commander march at the head of his army and see before him the men of an opposing army, standing behind their own general, dressed in their own particular colors, flying battle flags, singing martial airs—all these things giving unmistakable sensory proof as to the existence, nature, and identity of the enemy. Those days were past, and warfare had moved in step with industrial civilization, becoming more complex and more mechanical, and receding further from the men who were in command. Over the years, the generals were forced to stay at greater and greater distances from the actual clash of arms, in order to maintain a sure communication with all the interlocking men and machines that a battle utilized.

This had reached its epitome in Joenes's time. So it is no wonder that the officers took the Calculator's first five major possibilities, rated them equally, and brought them to General Voig, Commander of the Armed Forces, for him to render final decision.

Voig, studying the five alternatives before him, was aware of the problems of modern warfare, and sadly recognized how dependent he was on information upon which to base a sound decision. He also knew that most of his information came to him from extremely expensive machines that sometimes could not tell the difference between a goose and a rocket; machines that required regiments of highly trained men to minister to them, repair them, improve them, and to soothe them in every way. And even with all this lavish attention, Voig knew that the machines could not really be trusted. The creations were no better than the creators, and indeed resembled them in many of the worst ways. Like men, the machines were frequently subject to something resembling emotional instability. Some became over-zealous, others had recurring hallucinations, functional and psychosomatic breakdowns, or even complete catatonic withdrawals. And aside from their own problems, the machines tended to be influenced by the emotional states of their human operators. In fact, the more suggestible machines were nothing more than extensions of their operators' personalities.

General Voig knew, of course, that no machine possessed a real consciousness, and therefore no machine really suffered from the diseases of consciousness. But they *seemed* to, and that was just as bad as the real thing.

Men of the early industrial age had always assumed that machines would be cold, efficient, uncaring, and invariably correct. These romantics had been wrong, and General Voig knew that machines, despite their special senses and abilities, could not be trusted any more than men. So he sat and studied the five alternatives, thousands of miles from the battle, while dubious machines sent in their information, and hysterical men confirmed it.

In spite of the problems, General Voig was a man who had been trained to make decisions. And now, after a last look at the five alternatives, and a rapid questioning of his own knowledge and opinions, Voig picked up a telephone and issued his orders.

We do not know which of the five alternatives the General chose, or what his orders were. It made no difference. The battle had moved entirely out of the General's hands, and he was powerless to press the attack or to order it stopped, or to have any important effect upon the hostilities. The fight had become uncontrollable, and this condition had been hastened because of the semiautonomous nature of the machines.

A wounded California missile screamed high into the heavens and crashed at Cape Canaveral in Florida, destroying half the base. The remaining half rallied and launched retaliatory missiles at an enemy apparently entrenched in California. Other missiles, damaged but not destroyed, crashed in all parts of the country. Local commanders in New York, New Jersey, Pennsylvania, and many other states struck back on their own authority, as did the automatic missile stations. Both men and machines had no lack of intelligence reports upon which to base this decision. In fact, before their communications were disrupted, they had received a deluge of reports covering every possibility. Being soldiers, they chose the most dire.

Throughout California and all of Western America, this retaliation was retaliated against. Local commanders believed that the enemy, whoever he was, had established beachheads on America's east coast. They sought to destroy these beachheads, not hesitating to use atomic warheads when they deemed it necessary.

All of this took place with a terrible rapidity. The local commanders and their machines, subjected to a hellish rain of fire, tended to fight back as long as they could. Some may have waited for specific orders; but in the end, all fought who could fight, compounding destruction and confusion, and spreading it to all corners of the world. And soon the civilization of proliferating machinery had vanished from the face of the earth.

While this was taking place, Joenes stood bewildered in the Services Command Post, watching generals give orders and other generals countermand them. All of this Joenes saw, and still could not say of his own knowledge who or what the enemy was.

At this point Command Post gave a vast shudder. Although situated many hundreds of feet underground, it had now come under attack by special burrowing machines.

Joenes flung out a hand to keep his balance, and grasped the shoulder of a young first lieutenant. The lieutenant turned, and Joenes recognized him at once.

"Lum!" he cried.

"Hey, Joenesy!" Lum said in reply.

"How did you get here?" Joenes asked. "And what are you doing in the Army as a lieutenant?"

"Well, man," Lum said, "that is quite a tale, and it is all the more strange because I am not exactly what one would have called the military sort. But I am very glad you asked me that question."

The Command Post shuddered once again, throwing many officers to the floor. But Lum contrived to keep his balance, and he told Joenes the story of how he had joined the Army.

XIV. HOW LUM JOINED THE ARMY
(Lum's own words, as recorded in the Book of Fiji, *Orthodox Edition)*

Well, man, I left the Hollis Home for the Criminally Insane shortly after you, and I went to New York and attended a really swinging party. It so happened I got high on C that night, which is nasty stuff if you aren't used to it, which I was not. I mean I've always been a peyote man, and heroin never interested me, and I thought that cocaine was merely one of those old-fashioned kicks until I tried it that night.

But I did try it, and I got this feeling whilst with the big C that I had a florence nightingale type duty to tend all the sick fighting machines of the world. The more I thought about it the surer I was, and the sadder I became as I thought of poor suffering old machine guns with burned-out barrels, tanks with rust in their treads, jets with broken landing gears, and the like. I thought of the terrible dumb agony these machines go through, and I knew that I had to heal and comfort them.

As you can see, I was pretty well gassed, and in that state I marched down to the nearest recruiting station and joined up so as to be close to the poor machines.

The next day I woke up and found myself in the Army, and it was a sobering not to say a frightening thought. I rushed out to find that damned enlistment sergeant who had taken advantage of a poor hophead obviously not in his right mind at the time, but he had flown to a Chicago whorehouse to give an enlistment speech. So I hastened to see my commanding officer, also called the CO, and told him that among other things I was a dope addict and a recent inmate of an institution for the criminally insane, both of which I could prove. And that furthermore I had latent homosexual tendencies, an overpowering fear of firearms, one blind eye, and also a bad back. Because of all this, I said, I could not legally be accepted into the armed services because of the provisions on page 123 paragraph C of the Enlistment Act.

The CO looked me straight in the eye and smiled in that way only a Regular Army man or a cop can smile. He said, "Soldier, this is the first day of your new life, so I am going to overlook certain irregularities in your manner of addressing me. Now kindly get the hell out of here and report to the sergeant for duty."

When I didn't go, he stopped smiling and said, "Look, soldier, nobody cares about your reasons for enlisting, or for your so-called dope jag at the time. As for the various debilities you mentioned, don't worry about them. Hopheads have done a first-class job in Planning, and nobody can laugh at the exploits of the Homosexual Brigade during the last police action in Patagonia. All you have to do is be a good soldier and you'll find that the Army is a good way of life. And do not go round quoting the Enlistment Act like a guardhouse lawyer, because that will make you unpopular with my sergeants, who just might beat your head to a pulp. Right? Right. Now we know where we stand, and I bear you no hard feelings. In fact I congratulate you on the patriotic zeal which led you to sign up for the special fifty-year full-duty enlistment last night. Good man! Now get the hell out of here."

So I left his office and wondered what to do next, since you can get out of a jail or an asylum, but not out of the Army. I was pretty down for a while, but then suddenly I was given a commission as a second lieutenant, and directly after that I was assigned to the personal staff of General Voig, who is the very topmost of the top brass.

At first I thought all this had happened because of my pleasing personality, but then I found out it was something else entirely. It appears that when enlisting, sky-high on coke, I had put down my occupation as pimp. This came to the attention of officers who watched for special occupational groups. In my case it was reported to General Voig, who immediately put in an order for me and my services.

At first I had no idea what to do, since I had never worked in that field. But another general's pimp, or Special Duty Officer, as he is more politely called, gave me the word. I thenceforth arranged a party for General Voig every Thursday night, this being the only night he could spare from his military duties. It is easy work, since all I need do is put in a call to one of the numbers listed in the Washington Defense Area Recreation Book; or, in a pinch, I send a hurry message to the Armed Services Procurement Department, which has branches in all major cities. The General has shown a hearty approval of my efficient work, and I must confess that the Army is not the grim and terrible place I had imagined it to be.

And that, Joenes, is what brings me here. Speaking as General Voig's aide and good friend, I can tell you that this war, whoever in hell we're fighting, could not be in better hands. I think this is important for all men to know, since lies are frequently told about men in high positions.

Furthermore, Joenesy, I think I should point out that there has just been an explosion here in the Command Post, and this hints of greater things to come. Also a few lights have gone off, and the air is growing just a shade musty. Therefore, since our services are obviously not needed down here, I suggest that you and I split this scene and cut out entirely, if such indeed is still possible.

Are you with me, Joenesy? Are you all right, man?

XV. THE ESCAPE FROM AMERICA
(As told by Paaui of Fiji)

Joenes had been stunned by a small explosion occurring near his head. In a state of shock, he let his friend lead him to an elevator that plunged them still deeper into the bowels of the earth. When they opened the elevator door, they were standing in a wide passageway. Ahead of them was a sign, reading: EMERGENCY UNDERGROUND SURVIVAL ROADWAY. FOR AUTHORIZED PERSONNEL ONLY.

Lum said, "I don't know if we are authorized personnel, but technicalities must be forgotten at a time like this. Joenes, are you able to speak? Straight ahead should be a vehicle that will carry us to what I sure as hell hope is safety. The General told me about this setup, and I trust the old buzzard wasn't merely having his bit of fun."

They found the vehicle where Lum had expected it to be, and drove underground for many hours until they emerged on the eastern shore of Maryland, facing the Atlantic Ocean.

Here Lum's vigorous will faltered, and he was unable to think what to do next. But Joenes had recovered full possession of his senses. Taking Lum by the arm, he went down to the silent beach. Then he turned south and walked for several hours, coming at last to a deserted little harbor.

Joenes selected one sailing ship from the many that lay at the docks, and began transferring to it food, water, charts, and nautical instruments, taking them from the many other seagoing ships in the harbor. The job was not half done when missiles began screaming overhead, and Joenes decided to cast off immediately.

The boat was several miles out to sea before Lum roused himself, looked around, and asked, "Uh, man, like where we bound?"

"To my home," Joenes said. "To the island of Manituatua in the South Pacific."

Lum considered that, and said mildly, "Sort of a long trip, isn't it? I mean, what with rounding Cape Horn and all that jazz, it's probably something like eight or nine thousand miles, huh?"

"Something like that," Joenes said.

"You wouldn't maybe consider going to Europe instead, which is only like three thousand miles?"

"I'm going home," Joenes said firmly.

"Yeah. Well," Lum said, "east or west, home's the best. But we're somewhat short of food and water for a trip like this, and I suspect that little may be available along the way. Nor do I have the most perfect confidence in this boat, which I believe is already beginning to leak."

"All quite true," Joenes said. "But I think the leaks can be fixed. As for food and water, we'll hope for the best. Lum, there's really no other place that I know of worth going to."

"OK," Lum said. "I wasn't knocking it, I just thought I'd kick around a few thoughts to see if they would roll away. Since they won't, I, like you, will simply hope for the best. Also I think you should write your memoirs during this jaunt, since they would make interesting reading, and would serve to identify our poor starved cadavers should someone happen to come across this boat."

"I am not at all convinced that we are going to die," Joenes said, "though I must admit it seems a strong possibility. But why don't you write yours, Lum?"

"I may write a sketch or two," Lum said. "But for the most part I am going to think about men and governments and how to improve them, bringing to the task every resource of my hophead mind."

"I think that's admirable, Lum," Joenes said. "Together we have many things to tell people, if only we can find people to tell things to."

Thus, in perfect accord, Joenes and his loyal friend set sail upon a darkening sea, down a perilous coast, towards a distant and uncertain goal.

XVI. THE END OF THE JOURNEY
(Written by the Editor, and compiled from all available sources)

Of their voyage down the coast of the two Americas, around Cape Horn, and then northwest to the islands of the South Pacific, very little need be said. The trials that Joenes and Lum underwent were severe, and the dangers they faced were many. But this has been true in equal degree for a multitude of sailors throughout all ages, including our own. We note with profound pity how Joenes and Lum suffered under the tropical sun, were tossed by hurricanes, ran short of food and water, had their craft damaged, lost a mast, saw dangerous reefs to leeward, and so forth. But having expressed our sympathy, we must also observe that the details are the same as those told in countless other tales of small-boat passages. This sameness does not detract from the value of the experience; but it does cause a certain slackening of interest on the part of the reader.

Joenes himself never spoke to any great extent about that terrible trip, since he was interested in other things. And the only words Lum is reported to have said, when asked about his sensations during the voyage, were, "Well, man, you know."

We do indeed know. So we pass on to Joenes and Lum at their journey's end, starved but still living, unconscious and cast up on the shore, and nursed back to health by the inhabitants of Manituatua.

When he recovered his senses, Joenes inquired about his sweetheart Tondelayo, whom he had left in the islands. But that high-spirited girl had grown tired of waiting, had married a fisherman from the Tuamotos, and was now the mother of two children. Joenes accepted this with good grace, and turned his attention to world affairs.

He found that only a few effects of the war had been noted on Manituatua and its neighboring islands. These islands, long out of touch with Asia and Europe, had suddenly lost communication with America. Wild rumors poured in. Some said there had been a great war in which all the great countries of the earth had destroyed each other. Others put the blame on alien invaders of an unbelievably malevolent disposition. Some said there had been no war at all, but rather a plague, followed by a general collapse of Western civilization.

These and many other theories were argued, and are argued still. Your editor holds to the view expressed by Joenes, of a spontaneous and chaotic explosion of warfare, culminating in the destruction of America, the last of the great civilizations of the Old World.

Little effect of this could be noticed on the islands of the South Pacific. Rumors were rampant, and missiles were sometimes observed overhead.

Most of these plunged harmlessly into the sea, but one fell upon Molotea, completely destroying the eastern half of that atoll with the loss of seventy-three lives. American missile bases, situated mostly in Hawaii and the Philippines, waited for orders that never came, and speculated endlessly on the identity of the enemy. The last missile plunged into the sea, and no more came. The war was over, and the Old World had perished as completely as though it had never been.

Both Joenes and Lum were conscious but feeble during those days. The war was months past before they had regained their entire strength. But at last, each of them was ready to play his part in the shaping of the new civilization.

Sadly, they saw their duties in different ways, and were able to reach no substantial agreement. They tried to keep their friendship intact, but this became increasingly difficult. Their followers compounded the difficulties, and some thought that these two haters of war might start a war themselves.

But this was not to be. Joenes's influence in the South Pacific islands, from Nukuhiva in the west to Tonga in the east, was predominant. Therefore Lum and his followers provisioned a number of canoes and sailed eastward, past Tonga to the Fijis, where Lum's ideas had excited considerable interest. They were both in middle age at this time, and they took leave of each other with genuine sorrow.

Lum's final words to Joenes were: "Well, man, I guess every cat has to find his own scene where he can swing. But frankly it bugs me going off this way, you know? You and I been through it, Joenesy, and we're the only ones who *know*. So even though I think you're wrong, keep punching in there, keed, and get the word across. I'm going to miss you, man, so take it easy."

Joenes expressed similar sentiments. Lum sailed to the Fijis, where his ideas found the greatest possible reception. Even today, Fiji is the center of Lumism, and the Fijians do not speak the dialect of English derived from Joenes, but rather the dialect of English that Lum spoke. Some experts consider this to be the purest and most ancient form of the English language.

The most striking part of Lum's philosophy can be told in his own words, as written in the *Book of Fiji:*

> Look, the whole thing happened in the way it happened on account of machines.
> Machines are therefore bad. They are also made of metal.
> So metal is even worse. I mean it's evil.
> So as soon as we get rid of all the damned metal, everything will swing.

This was only a part of Lum's teachings, of course. He also had firm theories on the need for intoxication and ecstatic joy ("You gotta swing");

about ideal behavior ("Nobody oughta bug anybody"); about the limitations societies should observe ("They shouldn't get on anybody's back"); about the need for good manners, toleration, and respect ("You shouldn't put nobody down"); about the importance of objectively determined sense-data ("I dig real things the most"); about cooperation within a societal framework ("It's pretty good when all the cats swing together"); and many other things, covering nearly every aspect of human life. These examples are taken from the *Book of Fiji*, where all of Lum's sayings can be found complete with their annotations.

In those early days of the New World, the Fijians were most interested in Lum's theory about the evil inherent in metal. Being a naturally adventurous and far-traveling people, they set sail in great fleets, led by Lum, to throw metal into the sea wherever they could find it.

On their expeditions, the Fijians gathered new advocates for the fiery Lumist faith. They spread the destruction of metal throughout the Pacific, journeying past Australia to the jungle-clad coasts of Asia, and then eastward to the shores of the Americas. Their exploits are recorded in numerous songs and stories, particularly of the work they did in the Philippines, and, with the aid of the Maoris, in New Zealand. Only late in the century, long after Lum's death, were they able to complete their work in Hawaii, thus ridding the Pacific Islands of an estimated nine-tenths of their metal.

At the height of Fijian prestige, those fierce men briefly conquered many of the islands they touched at. But they were far too lacking in numbers to make their conquests endure. For a while, Fijians ruled in Bora Bora, Raiatea, Huahine, and Oahu; but the local populations either absorbed them or drove them out. Also, most Fijians respected Lum's explicit instructions concerning islands other than the Fijis: "Do your bit and then split the scene; above all, do not hang around and be a party-poop."

Thus ended the Fijian adventure.

Joenes, unlike Lum, left behind no organized body of philosophical writings. He never explicitly disapproved of metal, but was himself indifferent to it. He distrusted all laws, even the best, while at the same time recognizing the necessity for them. For Joenes, a law took its goodness from the nature of the men who administered it. When the nature of those men changed, as Joenes believed was inevitable, then the nature of the law changed, too. When this happened, new laws and new lawgivers had to be found.

Joenes taught that men should strive actively toward virtue, and at the same time recognize the extreme difficulties involved in that striving. The greatest of these difficulties, as Joenes saw it, was that all things, even men and their virtues, were continually changing, thereby forcing a lover of the good to abandon his illusions of permanence and to search out the changes occurring in himself and others, and to center his goodness in a never-ending search for momentary stability in the midst of life's metamorphoses.

On a quest like this, Joenes pointed out that one needed luck, which was indefinable but absolutely essential.

Joenes spoke of this and many other things, always stressing the excellence of virtue, the necessity for an active will, and the impossibility of perfection. Some say that in his old age Joenes preached in an entirely different way, and told men that the world was nothing more than a horrid toy built by evil gods; the form this toy took was that of a theater, in which the gods put on endless plays for their own amusement, creating and using humans for the cast. And what the gods did was to stuff these men full of consciousness, and imbue this consciousness with virtues and ideals, hopes and dreams, and all manner of qualities and contradictions. Then, with the actors so constituted, the gods set problems for them, and found vast enjoyment in the spectacle of these strutting puppets, filled with their own importance, convinced of their place in the scheme of things, suspecting or proving their immortality, laboring to resolve the dilemmas the gods had put before them. The gods roared with laughter at this spectacle, and nothing delighted them more than to see some little puppet determined to live with decency and to die with dignity. The gods always applauded this, and laughed at the absurdity of death, the one thing that rendered all of man's solutions impossible. But even this was not the most terrible thing. In time, the gods would tire of their theater and their little human puppets, would put them all away, tear down the theater, and turn to other amusements. After a little while, not even the gods would remember that there had been men.

This tale is not characteristic of Joenes, and your editor does not think it worthy of him. We will always remember Joenes in the strength and pride of his middle years, when he preached a message of hope.

Joenes lived long enough to see the death of the old world and the birth of a new one. Today all civilization worthy of the name exists upon the islands of the Pacific. Our racial stock is mixed, and many of our ancestors came from Europe, America, or Asia. But for the most part we are Polynesian, Melanesian, and Micronesian. Your editor, who dwells upon the island of Havaiki, believes that our present peace and prosperity is a direct consequence of the smallness of our islands, their great number, and the large distances between them. This renders impossible any chance of total conquest by one group, and allows easy escape for any man who does not like his own island. These were advantages the people of the continents did not possess.

We have our difficulties, of course. Warfare still breaks out among the island groups, though on an infinitesimal scale in comparison to the wars of the past. There is still social inequality, injustice, crime, and disease; but these evils are never so great as to overwhelm the island societies. Life changes, and this change often seems to bring evil as well as progress; but the changes take place more slowly today than in the hectic past.

Perhaps this slowness of change is due in part to the great scarcity of metal. It was always in short supply in our islands, and the Fijians destroyed most of what was available. A little metal is sometimes dug out of the earth in the Philippines, but hardly any of it gets into circulation. Lumist societies are still active, and they steal any metal they can find and throw it into the sea. Many of us feel that this irrational hatred of metal is a deplorable thing; but we still cannot answer Lum's ancient question, with which the Lumists still taunt us.

The question goes: "Man, you ever try to build a atom bomb out of coral and coconut shells?"

This is how life is in the present day. With sadness we are forced to realize that our peace and prosperity rest upon the body of a ravaged society whose destruction made possible our existence. But this is the way of all societies, and there is nothing we can do about it. Some of the mourners of the past might do well to consider the future. Far-wandering bands of Fijian Lumists have reported a stir of movement in the savage tribes who now inhabit the continents. These scattered and fearful savages may be ignored for the moment; but who knows what the future will bring?

As for the end of the Journey, the following is told. Lum met his death at the age of sixty-nine. Leading a party of metal destroyers, Lum's head was stove in by the club of a huge Hawaiian who was trying to protect a sewing machine. Lum's final words were: "Well, boys, I'm on my way to that Big Tea Party in the Sky, run by the Greatest Junkie of them all."

So saying, he died. This was Lum's final recorded statement on religious matters.

With Joenes, the end came in an entirely different way. In his seventy-third year, while visiting the high island of Moorea, Joenes saw a disturbance on the beach and went down to see what was the matter. He found that a man of his own race had drifted ashore on a raft, his clothes in shreds and his limbs badly sunburned, but otherwise in good condition.

"Joenes!" the man cried. "I knew you were alive, and I was sure I'd find you. You are Joenes, aren't you?"

"I am," Joenes said. "But I'm afraid I don't recognize you."

"I'm Watts," the man said, "as in Watts the matter? I'm the jewel thief you met in New York. Do you remember me now?"

"Yes, I do," Joenes said. "But why have you sought me out?"

"Joenes, we talked for only a few moments, but you had a profound influence on me. Just as your Journey became your life, so *you* became my life. I cannot explain how this knowledge came to me, but it did come, and I found it irresistible. My work was you, and concerned only you. It was a long hard task for me to gather together everything you needed, but I did not mind. I received help, and marks of favor in high places, and was content. Then came the war, rendering everything more difficult. I had to wander for many years over the ravaged face of America to find what you would require, but I completed my work and came at last to California. From there I set sail for the islands of the Pacific, and for many years I went from place to place, often hearing of you, never finding you. But I never grew discouraged. I always remembered the difficulties *you* had to face, and took heart from them. I knew that your work had to do with the completion of a world; but my work had to do with the completion of *you*."

"This is very amazing," Joenes said in a calm voice. "I think perhaps you are not in complete possession of your senses, my dear Watts, but that makes no difference at all. I am sorry to have caused you so much trouble; but I had no idea you were looking for me."

"You could not know," Watts said. "Not even you, Joenes, could know who or what was looking for you until it found you."

"Well," Joenes said, "you have found me now. Did you say that you had something for me?"

"Several things," Watts said. "I have faithfully preserved and cherished them, since they are necessary for your completion."

Watts then took out an oilskin package that had been tied to his body. Smiling with pleasure, he handed the package to Joenes.

Joenes opened the package and found the following things:

1. A note from Sean Feinstein, who said that he had taken it upon himself to send these things, and also to provide Watts as an agent. He hoped that Joenes was well. As for himself, he had escaped the holocaust with his daughter Deirdre, and had gone to Sangar Island, two thousand miles off the coast of Chile. There he was enjoying a modest success as a trader, while Deirdre had married an industrious and open-minded local boy. He sincerely hoped that these enclosures would be of value to Joenes.

2. A brief note from the doctor Joenes had met in the Hollis Home for the Criminally Insane. The doctor wrote that he remembered Joenes's interest in the patient who had believed himself to be God, and who had vanished before Joenes could meet him. However, since Joenes had been curious about the case, the doctor was enclosing the only bit of writing the madman had left—the list that had been found on his table.

3. A map of the Octagon marked with the official Cartographer's seal and approved by the highest officials. Marked "accurate and final" by the Chief of the Octagon himself. Guaranteed to take anyone to any part of the building, swiftly and without delay.

Joenes looked for a long time at these things, and his face became like weathered granite. For a long time he did not move, and then did so only when Watts tried to read the various papers over his shoulder.

"It's only fair!" Watts cried. "I carried them all this way, and I never looked at them. I must have one peek at that map, my dear Joenes, and just a glance at the madman's list."

"No," Joenes said. "These things weren't sent to you."

Watts became furiously angry, and the villagers had to restrain him from seizing the papers by force. Several of the village priests came expectantly up to Joenes, but he backed away from them. There was a look of horror on his face, and some people thought he would throw the papers into the sea. But he did not. He clutched them tightly to him and hurried up the steep trail into the mountains. The priests followed, but soon lost their way in the dense undergrowth.

They came down and told the people that Joenes would soon return, and that he merely wished to study the papers alone for a while. The people waited and did not lose patience for many years, although Watts died. But Joenes never descended from the mountains.

Nearly two centuries later, a hunter climbed the high slopes of Moorea in search of wild goats. When he came down, he declared that he had seen a very old man sitting in front of a cave, looking at some papers. The old man had beckoned to him, and the hunter came forward, not without fear. He saw that the papers the old man held were faded by sun and rain to an undecipherable blur, and the old man himself seemed to have gone blind from reading them.

The hunter asked, "How can you read those papers?"

The old man answered, "I don't have to. I've learned them by heart."

Then the old man rose to his feet and went into the cave, and in a moment everything was as though he had never been.

Was this story true? In spite of his incredible age, could Joenes still be living in the mountains and thinking about the highest secrets of a vanished age? If so, did the madman's list and the Octagon map have any meaning for our own age?

We will never know. Three expeditions to the place have turned up no evidence of human habitation, although the cave is there. Scholars believe that the hunter must have been drunk. They reason that Joenes went out of his mind with grief at receiving important information too late; that he fled from the priests and dwelt like a hermit with his fading and useless papers; and finally died in some inaccessible place.

This explanation seems only reasonable; but the people of Moorea have built a small shrine on the site.

MINDSWAP

CHAPTER 1

Marvin Flynn read the following advertisement in the classified section of the *Stanhope Gazette:*

> Gentleman from Mars, age 43, quiet, studious, cultured, wishes to exchange bodies with similarly inclined Earth gentleman. August 1-September 1, References exchanged. Brokers protected.

This commonplace announcement was enough to set Flynn's pulse racing. To swap bodies with a Martian... It was an exciting idea, but also a repellent one. After all, no one would want some sand-grubbing old Martian inside his head, moving his arms and legs, looking out of his eyes and listening with his ears. But in return for this unpleasantness, he, Marvin Flynn, would be able to see Mars. And he would be able to see it as it should be seen: through the senses of a native.

As some wish to collect paintings, others books, others women, so Marvin Flynn wanted to acquire the substance of them all through travel. But this, his ruling passion, was sadly unfulfilled. He had been born and raised in Stanhope, New York. Physically, his town was some three hundred miles from New York City. But spiritually and emotionally, the two cities were about a hundred years apart.

Stanhope was a pleasing rural community situated in the foothills of the Adirondacks, garlanded with orchards and dotted with clusters of brown cows against rolling green pastureland. Invincibly bucolic, Stanhope clung to antique ways; amiably, but with a hint of pugnacity, the town kept its distance from the flinthearted megalopolis to the south. The IRT 7th Avenue subway had burrowed upstate as far as Kingston, but no farther. Gigantic freeways twisted their concrete tentacles over the countryside, but could not take over Stanhope's elm-lined Main Street. Other communities maintained a blast pit; Stanhope clung to its antiquated jet field and was content with triweekly service. (Often at night, Marvin had lain in bed and listened to that poignant sound of a vanishing rural America, the lonely wail of a jetliner.)

Stanhope was satisfied with itself, and the rest of the world seemed quite satisfied with Stanhope and willing to leave it to its romantic dream of a less hurried age. The only person whom the arrangement did not suit was Marvin Flynn.

He had gone on the usual tours and had seen the usual things. Like everyone else, he had spent many weekends in the capitals of Europe. And he had explored the sunken city of Miami by scuba, gazed at the Hanging Gardens of London, and had worshipped in the Bahai temple of Haifa. For his longer vacations, he had gone on a walking tour across Marie Byrd Land, explored the lower Ituri Rain Forest, crossed Sinkiang by camel, and had even lived for several weeks in Lhassa, the art capital of the world. In all of this, his actions were typical of his age and station.

But these trips meant nothing to him; they were the usual tourist assortment, the sort of things that any casual vacationer was likely to do. Instead of rejoicing in what he had, Flynn complained of what was denied him. He wanted to *really* travel, and that meant going extraterrestrial.

It didn't seem so much to ask; and yet, he had never even been to the Moon.

In the final analysis, it was a matter of economics. Interstellar travel was expensive; for the most part, it was confined to the rich, or to colonists and administrators. It was simply out of the question for an average sort of fellow. Unless, of course, he wished to avail himself of the advantages of Mindswap.

Flynn, with innate small-town conservatism, had avoided this logical but unsettling step. Until now.

Marvin had tried to reconcile himself to his position in life, and to the very acceptable possibilities that that position offered him. After all, he was free, gay, and thirty-one (a little over thirty-one, actually). He was personable, a tall, broad-shouldered boy with a clipped black moustache and gentle brown eyes. He was healthy, intelligent, a good mixer, and not unacceptable to the other sex. He had received the usual education: grade school, high school, twelve years of college, and four years of postgraduate work. He was well trained for his job with the Reyck-Peters Corporation. There he fluoroscoped plastic toys, subjecting them to stress analysis and examining them for microshrinkage, porosity, texture fatigue, and the like. Perhaps it wasn't the most important job in the world; but then, we can't all be kings or spaceship pilots. It was certainly a responsible position, especially when one considers the importance of toys in this world, and the vital task of alleviating the frustrations of children.

Marvin knew all this; and yet, he was unsatisfied. In vain he had gone to his neighborhood Counsellor. This kindly man had tried to help Marvin through Situation Factor Analysis, but Marvin had not responded with insight. He wanted to *travel*, he refused to look honestly at the hidden implications of that desire, and he would not accept any substitutes.

And now, reading that mundane yet thrilling advertisement similar to a thousand others yet unique in its particularity (since *he* was at the moment reading it), Marvin felt a strange sensation in his throat. To swap bodies with a Martian…to see Mars, to visit the burrow of the Sand King, to travel through the aural splendor of The Wound, to listen to the chromatic sands of the Great Dry Sea…

He had dreamed before. But this time was different. That strange sensation in his throat argued a decision in the forming. Marvin wisely did not try to force it. Instead, he put on his beanie and went downtown to the Stanhope Pharmacy.

CHAPTER 2

As he had expected, his best friend, Billy Hake, was at the soda fountain, sitting on a stool and drinking a mild hallucinogen known as an LSD frappe.

"How's the morn, Sorn?" Hake asked, in the slang popular at that time.

"Soft and mazy, Esterhazy," Marvin replied, giving the obligatory response.

"Du koomen ta de la klipje?" Billy asked. (Pidgin Spanish-Afrikaans dialect was the new laugh sensation that year.)

"Ja, Mijnheer," Marvin answered, a little heavily. His heart simply was not in the clever repartee.

Billy caught the nuance of dissatisfaction. He raised a quizzical eyebrow, folded his copy of James Joyce Comics, popped a Keen-Smoke into his mouth, bit down to release the fragrant green vapor, and asked, "For-why you burrow?" The question was wryly phrased but obviously well intended.

Marvin sat down beside Billy. Heavyhearted, yet unwilling to reveal his unhappiness to his lighthearted friend, he held up both hands and proceeded to speak in Plains Indian Sign Language. (Many intellectually inclined young men were still under the influence of last year's sensational Projectoscope production of *Dakota Dialogue*, starring Bjorn Rakradish as Crazy Horse and Milovar Slavovivowitz as Red Cloud, and done entirely in gesture.)

Marvin made the gestures, mocking yet serious, for heart-that-breaks, horse-that-wanders, sun-that-will-not-shine, moon-that-cannot-rise.

He was interrupted by Mr. Bigelow, proprietor of the Stanhope Pharmacy. Mr. Bigelow was a middle-aged man of seventy-four, slightly balding, with a small but evident paunch. Yet he affected boys' ways. Now he said to Marvin, "Eh, Mijnheer, querenzie tomar la klopje inmensa de la cabeza vefrouvens in forma de ein skoboldash sundae?"

It was typical of Mr. Bigelow and others of his generation to overdo the youthful slang, thus losing any comic effect except the pathetically unintentional.

"Schnell," Marvin said, putting him down with the thoughtless cruelty of youth.

"Well, I never," said Mr. Bigelow, and moved huffily away with the mincing step he had learned from the *Imitation of Life* show.

Billy perceived his friend's pain. It embarrassed him. He was thirty-four, a year and a bit older than Marvin, nearly a man. He had a good job as foreman of Assembly Line 23 in Peterson's Box Factory. He clung to adolescent ways, of course, but he knew that his age presented him with certain obligations. Thus, he cross-circuited his fear of embarrassment, and spoke to his oldest friend in clear.

"Marvin—what's the matter?"

Marvin shrugged his shoulder, quirked his mouth, and drummed aimlessly with his fingers. He said, "Oiga, hombre, em Kleinnachtmusik es demasiado, nicht wahr? The Todt you ruve to touch…"

"Straighten it," Billy said, with a quiet dignity beyond his years.

"I'm sorry," Marvin said, in clear. "It's just—oh, Billy, I really do want to travel so badly!"

Billy nodded. He was aware of his friend's obsession. "Sure," he said. "Me too."

"But not as bad. Billy—I got the burns."

His skoboldash sundae arrived. Marvin ignored it, and poured out his heart to his lifelong friend. "Mira, Billy, it's really got me wound tighter than a plastic retriever coil. I think of Mars and Venus, and really *faraway* places like Aldebaran and Antares and—I mean, gosh, I just can't stop thinking about it all. Like the Talking Ocean of Procyon IV, and the tripartrite hominoids of Allua II, and it's like I'll simply die if I don't really and actually see those places."

"Sure," his friend said, "I'd like to see them, too."

"No, you don't *understand,*" Marvin said. "It's not just to see—it's—it's like—it's worse than—I mean, I can't just *live* here in Stanhope the rest of my life even though it's fun and I got a nice job and I'm dating some really guapa girls but heck, I can't just marry some *girl* and raise kids and—and—there's gotta be something more!"

Then Marvin lapsed into adolescent incoherence. But something of his feelings had come through the wild torrent of his words, and his friend nodded sagely.

"Marvin," he said softly, "I read you five by five, honest to Sam I do. But gee, even interplanetary travel costs *fortunes.* And interstellar stuff is just plain impossible."

"It's all possible," Marvin said, "if you use Mindswap."

"Marvin! You can't mean that!" His friend was too shocked to avoid the exclamation.

"I can!" Marvin said. "And by the Christo malherido, I'm going to!"

That shocked them both. Marvin hardly ever used bad language, and his friend could see the considerable stress he was under to use such an expression, even though coded. And Marvin, having said what he had said, recognized the implacable nature of his resolve. And having expressed it, he found it less frightening to contemplate the next step, that of doing something about it.

"But you *can't,*" Billy said. "Mindswap is—well, it's dirty!"

" 'Dirty he who dirty thinks, Cabron.' "

"No, seriously. You don't want some sand-grubbing old Martian inside your head? Moving your legs and arms, looking out of your eyes, *touching* you, and maybe even—"

Marvin cut him off before he said something really bad. "Mira," he said, "recuerda que I'll be in *his* body, on Mars, so he'll be having the same embarrassments."

"Martians haven't got no sense of embarrassment," Billy said.

"That's just not true," Marvin said. Although younger, he was in many ways more mature than his friend. He had been an apt student in Comparative Interstellar Ethics. And his intense desire to travel rendered him less provincial in his attitudes, more prepared to see the other creature's point of view, than his friend. From the age of twelve, when he had learned how to read, Marvin had studied the manners and modes of many different races in the galaxy. Always he had endeavored to view those creatures through their own eyes, and to understand their motivations in terms of their own unique psychologies. Furthermore, he had scored in the 95th percentile in Projective Empathy, thus establishing his raw potentiality for successful extraterrestrial relationships. In a word, he was as prepared for travel as it is possible for a young man to become who has lived all his life in a small town in the hinterlands of Earth.

That afternoon, alone in his attic room, Marvin opened his encyclopedia. It had been his companion and friend ever since his parents bought it for him when he was nine. Now he set the comprehension level at "simple," the scan rate at "rapid," punched his questions, and settled back as the little red and green lights flashed on.

"Hi, fellows," the tapecorder said in its fruitily enthusiastic voice. "Today—let's talk about Mindswap!"

There followed a historical section, which Marvin ignored. His attention returned when he heard the tapecorder saying:

"So let's just consider Mind as a kinda electroform or maybe even a subelectroform entity. You pro'lly remember from our previous talk that Mind is thought to have begun as a projection of our bodily processes, and to have evolved into a quasi-independent entity. You know what that means, fellas. It means it's like you got a little Man in your head—but not quite. Isn't that *quazi?*"

The tapecorder laughed modestly at its little joke, then went on:

"So what have we got out of this mishmash? Well, kids, we got ourselves a sort of symbiotic situation, mind and bodywise, even though Mr. Mind is inclined to a sort of parasitism. But still, each can exist—theoretically—without the other. Or anyhow, that's what the Big Thinkers say."

Marvin skimmed.

"Now as for projecting the mind—well, guys, just think of throwing a ball…

"Mental into physical, and vice versa. Ultimately, they are forms of each other, just like matter and energy. Of course, we have yet to discover…

"But of course, we have only a pragmatic knowledge of it. We might consider, just for a very brief moment, Van Voorhes' concept of Agglutinative Reform, and the Lagos University Theory of Relative Absolutes. Of course, these theories raise more questions than they answer…

"…and the whole works is made possible only by the somewhat surprising lack of an immuniform reaction.

"The actual practice of Mindswap utilizes mechanical-hypnotic techniques such as induced relaxation, pinpoint fixation, and the use of a mind-positive substance, such as Williamite, as a narrow-beam focuser and intensifier. Feedback programming…

"Once learned, of course, you can Swap without mechanical aids, usually employing sight as focus…"

Marvin turned off the encyclopedia and thought about space, and the many planets, and the exotic inhabitants of those planets. He thought about Mindswap. He thought: tomorrow I could be on Mars. Tomorrow I could be a Martian.

He jumped to his feet. "By jingo!" he cried, striking palm of his left hand with his right fist, "I'll do it!"

The strange alchemy of decision had transformed him. Without hesitation he packed a light suitcase, left a note for his parents, and caught the jet to New York.

CHAPTER 3

In New York, Marvin went directly to the body-brokerage house of Otis, Blanders and Klent. He was sent to the office of Mr. Blanders, a tall, athletic man in the prime of life at sixty-three, and a full partner in the firm. He explained to this man his purpose in coming.

"Of course," Mr. Blanders said. "You have reference to our advertisement of Friday last. The Martian gentleman's name is Ze Kraggash, and he is very highly recommended by the rectors of East Skern University."

"What does he look like?" Marvin asked.

"See for yourself," Blanders said. He showed Marvin a photograph of a being with a barrel chest, thin legs, slightly thicker arms, and a small head with an extremely long nose. The picture showed Kraggash standing knee-deep in mud, waving to someone. Printed on the bottom of the photograph were the words: "Souvenir of Mud Heaven—Mars' Year 'Round Vacationland, highest moisture content on the planet!"

"Nice looking chap," Mr. Blanders commented. Marvin nodded, even though Kraggash looked just like any other Martian to him.

"His home," Blanders continued, "is in Wagomstamk, which is on the edge of the Disappearing Desert in New South Mars. It is an extremely popular tourist area, as you probably know. Like you, Mr. Kraggash is desirous of travelling and wishes to find a suitable host body. He has left the selection entirely up to us, stipulating only mental and physical health."

"Well," Marvin said, "I don't mean to boast, but I've always been considered healthy."

"I can see that at a glance," Mr. Blanders said. "It is only a feeling, of course, or perhaps an intuition, but I have come to trust my feelings in thirty years of dealing with the public. Purely on the basis of my feelings, I have rejected the last three applicants for this particular Swap."

Mr. Blanders seemed so proud of this that Marvin felt impelled to say, "Have you really?"

"Most certainly. You can have no conception of how frequently I must detect and eliminate misfits in this line of work. Neurotics who seek ugly and illicit thrills; criminals who wish to escape the purview of local law; the mentally unstable, trying to escape their internal psychic pressures. And many more. I cull them all."

"I hope that I don't fit any of those categories," Marvin said, with an embarrassed little laugh.

"I can tell at once that you do not," Mr. Blanders said. "I would judge you as an extremely normal young man, almost *excessively* normal, if that were possible. You have been bitten by the travel bug, which is very suitable for your time of life, and is a passion akin to falling in love, or fighting an idealistic war, or becoming disillusioned with the world, and other postures of the young. It is very fortunate that you had either the native wit or the good luck to come to us, the oldest and most reliable brokerage house in the Swap business, rather than to some of our less scrupulous competitors, or, worst of all, to the Open Market."

Marvin knew very little about the Open Market; but he remained silent, not wishing to betray his ignorance by asking.

"Now then," Mr. Blanders said, "we have certain formalities which we must go through before we can gratify your request."

"Formalities?" Marvin asked.

"Most certainly. First, you must have a complete examination, which will produce an operational judgment of your physical, mental, and moral standing. This is quite necessary, since bodies are swapped on an equal basis. You would be quite unhappy if you found yourself stuck in the corpus of a Martian suffering from sandpest or tunnel syndrome. Just as he would be unhappy if he found that you had rickets or paranoia. By the terms of our charter, we must attempt as complete a knowledge of the health and stability of the Swappers as possible, and apprise them of any discrepancies between real and advertised condition."

"I see," Marvin said. "And what happens after that?"

"Next, you and the Martian Gentleman will both sign a Reciprocal Damage Clause. This states that any damage to your host body, whether by omission or commission, and including Acts of God, will, one, be recompensed at the rate established by interstellar convention, and, two, that such damage will be visited reciprocally upon your own body in accordance with the *lex talionis.*"

"Huh?" Marvin said.

"Eye for eye, tooth for tooth," Mr. Blanders explained. "It's really quite simple enough. Suppose you, in the Martian corpus, break a leg on the last day of Occupancy. You suffer the pain, to be sure, but not the subsequent inconvenience, which you avoid by returning to your own undamaged body. But this is not equitable. Why should you escape the consequences of your own accident? Why should someone else suffer those consequences for you? So, in the interests of justice, interstellar law requires that, upon reoccupying your own body, your own leg be broken in as scientific and painless a manner as possible."

"Even if the first broken leg was an accident?"

"*Especially* if it were an accident. We have found that the Reciprocal Damage Clause has cut down the number of such accidents quite considerably."

"This begins to sound sorta dangerous," Marvin said.

"Any course of action contains an element of danger," Mr. Blanders said. "But the risks involved in Swapping are statistically unimportant, assuming that you stay out of the Twisted World."

"I don't know very much about the Twisted World," Marvin said.

"Nobody does," Blanders said. "That's why you're supposed to stay out of it. That's reasonable enough, isn't it?"

"I suppose so," Marvin said. "What else is there?"

"Nothing to speak of. Just paperwork, waivers of special rights and inimunities, that sort of thing. And, of course, I must give you the standard warning about metaphoric deformation."

"All right," Marvin said. "I'd like to hear it."

"I just gave it," Blanders said. "But I'll give it again. Watch out for metaphoric deformation."

"I'd be glad to," Marvin said, "but I don't know what it is."

"It's really quite simple," Blanders said. "You might consider it a form of situational insanity. You see, our ability to assimilate the unusual is limited, and these limits are quickly reached and surpassed when we travel to alien planets. We experience too much novelty; it becomes unbearable, and the mind seeks relief through the buffering process of analogizing.

"Analogy assures us that *this* is like *that;* it forms a bridge between the accepted known and the unacceptable unknown. It attaches the one to the other, imbuing the intolerable unknown with a desirable familiarity.

"However, under the continued and unremitting impact of the unknown, even the analogizing faculty can become distorted. Unable to handle the flood of data by the normal process of conceptual analogizing, the subject becomes victim to *perceptual* analogizing. This state is what we call 'metaphoric deformation.' The process is also known as 'Panzaism.' Does that make it clear?"

"No," Marvin said. "Why is it called 'Panzaism'?"

"The concept is self-explanatory," Blanders said. "Don Quijote thinks the windmill is a giant, whereas Panza thinks the giant is a windmill. Quijotism may be defined as the perception of everyday things as rare entities. The reverse of that is Panzaism, which is the perception of rare entities as everyday things."

"Do you mean," Marvin asked, "that I might think I was looking at a cow, when actually it was an Altairian?"

"Precisely," Blanders said. "It's simple enough, once you apply yourself. Just sign here and here and we will get on with the examinations."

There were many tests, and endless questions. Flynn was poked and probed, lights were flashed in his face, sudden noises were broadcast at him, and strange smells assailed his nostrils.

He passed everything with flying colors. Some hours later he was taken to the Transfer Room, and was seated in a chair that looked alarmingly like an old electric chair. The technicians made obligatory jokes: "When you wake up, you'll feel like a new man." Lights flashed at him, he was getting sleepy, sleepier, sleepiest.

He was thrilled by the imminence of travel, but appalled by his ignorance of the world beyond Stanhope. What was the Open Market, anyhow? Where was the Twisted World located, and why was he supposed to avoid it? And finally, how dangerous was metaphoric deformation, how often did it occur, and what was the recovery rate?

Soon he would find the answers to these questions, as well as the answers to many others that he hadn't asked. The lights were hurting his eyes, and he closed them for a moment. When he opened them again, everything had changed.

CHAPTER 4

Despite a bipedal frame, the Martian is one of the strangest creatures in the galaxy. Indeed, from a sensory viewpoint, the Kvees of Aldebaran, despite their double brains and special-function limbs, are closer to us. Accordingly, it is a disturbing thing to Swap directly and without initiation into the corpus of a Martian. And yet, no amelioration is possible.

Marvin Flynn found himself in a pleasantly furnished room. There was a single window; through it, he gazed with Martian eyes upon a Martian landscape.

He closed his eyes, since he could register nothing except a dismaying confusion. Despite inoculations, he was beset by the nausea-producing waves of culture-shock, and he had to stand very still until it subsided. Then, cautiously, he opened his eyes and looked again.

He perceived low, flat sand dunes, which were made up of a hundred or more distinct hues of grey. A silvery-blue wind was running across the horizon, and an ochre counterwind seemed to be attacking it. The sky was red, and many indescribable hues were visible in the infra-red scale. In everything, Flynn saw spidery spectrum lines. Earth and sky presented him with a dozen separate palettes, some complementary, more of them clashing. There was no harmony in nature's colors on Mars; these were the colors of chaos.

Marvin found a pair of glasses in his hand, and slipped them on. Immediately, the roar and clash of colors was reduced to manageable proportions. The numbness of shock receded, and he began to perceive other things.

First, a heavy booming in his ear, and a quick rattle beneath it, like the tattoo of a snare drum. He looked around for the source of this noise, and saw nothing except earth and sky. He listened more carefully, and found that the sounds were coming from his own chest. They were his lungs and heart, sounds that all Martians lived with.

Now Marvin was able to take stock of himself. He looked at his legs, which were long and spindly. There was no knee joint; instead, the leg was pivoted at the ankle, shin, midthigh, and upper thigh. He walked, and admired the fluid motion of his movements. His arms were slightly thicker than his legs, and his double-jointed hands had three fingers and two opposable thumbs. He could bend and twist these in a surprising number of ways.

He was dressed in black shorts and a white jumper. His chest-prop was folded neatly and covered with an embroidered leather case. He was amazed at how natural it all seemed.

And yet, it was not surprising. The ability of intelligent creatures to accommodate to new environments was what made Mindswap possible.

And the Martian frame, despite certain striking morphological and sensory differences, was easy to get used to, unlike some of nature's more perverse creations.

Flynn was musing on this when he heard a door open behind him. He turned and saw a Martian standing in front of him, dressed in a government uniform of green and grey stripes. The Martian had reversed his feet in greeting, and Marvin quickly responded in kind.

(One of the glories of Mindswap is "automatic education." Or, in the amusing jargon of the trade: "When you take over a house, you get the use of the furnishings." The furnishings, of course, are the use of primary available knowledge in the host-brain, knowledge such as language, customs, mores and morals, general information about the area in which one lives, and so forth. This is primary-environment information, general, impersonal, useful as a guide, but not necessarily reliable. Personal memories, likes, dislikes are, with certain exceptions, unavailable to the occupier, or available only at the cost of considerable mental effort. Again, in this area there is what appears to be a type of immunological reaction, which allows only a superficial degree of contact between disparate entities. "General knowledge" is usually exempt; but "personal knowledge," involving beliefs, prejudices, hopes and fears, is sacrosanct.)

"Soft wind," the Martian said, in the classic old-Martian greeting form.

"And cloudless sky," Flynn replied. (To his annoyance, he found that his host-body had a slight lisp.)

"I am Meenglo Orichichich, of the Tourist Bureau. Welcome to Mars, Mr. Flynn."

"Thanks," Flynn said. "Awfully good to be here. It's my first Swap, you know."

"Yes, I know," Orichichich said. He spat on the floor—a sure sign of nervousness—and uncurled his thumbs. From the corridor there came a sound of heavy voices. Orichichich said, "Now then, concerning your stay on Mars—"

"I want to see the Burrow of the Sand King," Flynn said. "And, of course, the Talking Ocean."

"Both excellent choices," the official said. "But first there are one or two minor formalities."

"Formalities?"

"Nothing too difficult," Orichichich said, his nose twisting to the left in the Martian smile. "Would you look over these papers and identify them, please?"

Flynn took the proffered papers and scanned them. They were replicas of the forms he had signed on Earth. He read them through, and found that all the information had been sent correctly.

"These are the papers I signed on Earth," he said.

The noise from the corridor grew louder. Marvin could make out words: "Scalded egg-laying son of a frostbitten tree stump! Gravel-loving degenerate!"

Those were very strong insults indeed.

Marvin raised his nose quizzically. The official hastily said, "A misunderstanding, a mix-up. One of those unfortunate occurrences which occur even to the best run of government tourist services. But I am quite sure that we can straighten it out in five gulps of a rapi, if not sooner. Permit me to ask you if—"

There was the sound of a scuffle in the corridor. Then a Martian burst into the room, with a Martian sub-official clinging to his arm and trying to stop him.

The Martian who had burst in was extremely old, as could be told by the faint phosphorescence of his skin. His arms quivered as he pointed both of them at Marvin Flynn.

"There!" he shouted. "There it is, and by tree stumps I want it now!"

Marvin said, "Sir, I am not in the habit of being addressed as 'it'."

"I am not addressing you," the old Martian said. "I do not know nor care who or what you are. I am addressing the body which you are occupying, and which is not yours."

"What are you talking about?" Flynn asked.

"This gentleman," the official said, "claims that you are occupying a body which belongs to him." He spat twice on the floor. "It is a mix-up, of course, and we can straighten it out at once…"

"Mix-up!" howled the old Martian. "It's an out-and-out fraud!"

"Sir," Marvin said, with cold dignity, "you are under a grave misapprehension; either that, or you are engaging in this slander for reasons I cannot hope to fathom. This body, sir, was legally and fairly rented by me."

"Scaly-skinned toad!" the old man shouted. "Let me at him!" He struggled with circumspection against the restraining grip of the guard.

Suddenly, an imposing figure dressed entirely in white appeared in the doorway. All within the room fell silent as their gaze fell upon the feared and respected representative of the South Martian Desert Police.

"Gentlemen," the policeman said, "there is no need for recriminations. We shall proceed now to the police station, all of us. There, with the help of the Fulszime telepath, we shall penetrate to the truth, and to the motivation behind it." The policeman paused impressively, stared full into each man's face, swallowed saliva to show supreme calm, and said: "This, I promise you."

Without further ado the policeman, the official, the old man, and Marvin Flynn proceeded to the police station. They walked silently, and they shared a common mood of apprehension. It is a truism throughout the civilized galaxy that when you go to the police, your troubles really begin.

CHAPTER 5

At the police station, Marvin Flynn and the others were taken directly to the dim, moist chamber where the Fulszime telepath lived. This tripedal entity, like all of his fellows from the Fulszime Planet, possessed a telepathic sixth sense, perhaps in compensation for the dimness of his other five.

"All right," the Fulszime telepath said, when all were assembled before him. "Step forward, fellow, and tell me your story." He pointed a finger sternly at the policeman.

"Sir!" the policeman said, straightening with embarrassment, "I happen to be the policeman."

"That is interesting," the telepath said. "But I fail to see what it has to do with the question of your innocence or guilt."

"But I am not even accused of a crime," the policeman said.

The telepath mused for a moment, then said, "I think I understand… It is these two who are accused. Is that it?"

"It is," the policeman said.

"My apologies. Your aura of guilt led me to an over-hasty identification."

"Guilt?" the policeman said. "Me?" He spoke calmly, but his skin was showing the typical orange striations of anxiety.

"Yes, you," the telepath said. "You need not be surprised; grand larceny is the sort of thing about which most intelligent creatures feel guilty."

"Now just a minute!" the policeman shouted. "I haven't committed any grand larceny!"

The telepath closed his eyes and introspected. At last he said, "That is correct. I meant to say that you *will* perform grand larceny."

"Clairvoyance is not admissible as evidence in a court of law," the policeman stated. "And furthermore, readings of the future are a direct violation of the law of free will."

"This is true," the telepath said. "My apologies."

"It's quite all right," the policeman said. "When will I perform this alleged grand larceny?"

"About six months hence," the telepath said.

"And will I be arrested?"

"No. You will flee the planet, going to a place where there is no extradition law."

"Hmm, interesting," the policeman said. "Could you tell me if… But we can discuss this later. Now, you must hear the stories of these men, and judge their innocence or guilt."

The telepath looked at Marvin, shook a flipper at him, and said, "You may proceed." Marvin told his story, beginning with his first reading of the advertisement and leaving out nothing.

"Thank you," the telepath said, when he was through. "And now, sir, your story." He turned to the old Martian, who cleared his throat, scratched his thorax, spit once or twice, and then proceeded.

AIGELER THRUS' STORY

I don't even know where to begin this thing, so I guess I'd better start with my name, which is Aigeler Thrus, and my race, which is Nemucthian Adventist, and my occupation, which is that I own and operate a clothing store on the planet Achelses V. Well, it's a small business and not a very good business and my store is located in Lambersa on the South Polar Cap, and I sell clothing all day to immigrant Venusian laborers, who are big, green, hairy fellows, very ignorant and very excitable and apt to fight, though I have no prejudices against them.

You get to be philosophical in my business, and maybe I'm not rich, but at least I got my health (thank God), and my wife Allura is healthy too except for a mild case of tentacular fibrosis. And I got two grown sons, one of whom is a doctor in Sidneport, and the other is a trainer of Klannts. And I also got one daughter, who is married, so of course that means I got a son-in-law.

This son-in-law of mine I have always distrusted, since he is a fancy dresser and owns twenty pairs of chest-props, although his wife my daughter hasn't even got a matched set of scratchers. But it can't be helped, she dug her burrow, now she has to crawl in it. But still, when a man is so interested in clothes and fancy-smelling joint lubricants and similar luxuries on the salary of a moisture salesman (he calls himself a "hydrosensory engineer") it makes you wonder a little.

And he's always trying to scratch up extra income on the side with various foolish ventures, which I have to equip him for out of my hard-earned savings, which I get by selling to these big green fellows. Like last year he got hold of this novelty item, a backyard cloudmaker, and I told him, who would want it? But my wife insisted that I help him out, and sure enough he went broke. And then this year, he had another scheme, and this time it was iridescent synthetic wool seconds from Vega II, a consignment of which he somehow found in Heligoport and which he wanted me to buy.

I said to him, "Look, what do my customers these Venusian loud-mouths know about fancy dressing? They're lucky if they can afford a pair of twill shorts and maybe a robe for holidays." But my son-in-law has got an answer for everything and he says to me, "Look, Papa, have I or have I not made a study of Venusian folkways and mores? The way I look at it, here are these people straight out of the backwoods, and they've got this love of ritual and dance and *bright colors.* So it's a natural, true or not?"

Well, to make a short story even shorter, I get talked into this venture against my better judgment. Naturally, I had to see those iridescent seconds myself, because I wouldn't trust my son-in-law to judge a piece of lint. And that meant travelling halfway across the galaxy to Heligoport in Mars. So I started making the arrangements.

No one wanted to Swap with me. I can't say I blame them, because nobody comes on purpose to a planet like Achelses V, unless it's immigrant Venusians who don't know any better. But I find this ad from this Martian, Ze Kraggash, who wants to rent his body out on account of he's taking his mind into Cold Storage for a protracted rest. It's damned expensive, but what can I do? I get a little money back by renting my own body to a friend who had been a quarentz hunter before he was bedridden by muscular dyscomyotosis. And I go down to the Swap Bureau and get projected to Mars.

Well, imagine my sensations when it turns out there is no body waiting for me! Everybody's running around trying to find out what happened to my host body, and they even try to send me back to Achelses V; but they can't because my friend has already left on a quarentz hunting expedition with my body.

Finally they get me a body from the Theresiendstadt Rent-a-Body people. Twelve hours is the maximum they can allow me since they're all booked up for short-term rentals through the summer. And it's a pretty decrepit old body, as you can see for yourself, and damned expensive anyhow.

So I go out and try to find out what had gone wrong, and what do I find but this tourist from Earth walking around bold as brass in the body which I have paid for, and which, according to my contract, I should be occupying at this very moment.

It is not only unfair, it is also extremely aggravating to my health. And that is the entire story.

The telepath retired to his chambers in order to ponder his decision. He returned in less than an hour and spoke as follows:

"Both of you did, in all good faith, rent, swap, or otherwise acquire, the same body, viz., the corpus of Ze Kraggash. This body was offered by its owner, the aforesaid Ze Kraggash, to each of you, and thus sale was consummated in direct violation of all laws concerned. Ze Kraggash's action must be considered criminal, both in execution and intent. This being the case, I have caused to be sent to Earth a message, requesting the immediate arrest of the aforesaid Ze Kraggash, and his detention in a place of custody until such time as his extradition can be effected.

"Both of you made your purchase in good faith; however, the prior, or earlier, sale, as shown in the contractual forms, was made by Mr. Aigeler Thrus, who takes precedence over Mr. Marvin Flynn by a matter of thirty-eight hours. Therefore Mr. Thrus, as the First Buyer, is awarded custody of the Corpus; and Mr. Flynn is ordered to cease and desist his unlawful occupancy, and to take cognizance of the Dispossess Notice, which I hereby give him, and which must be obeyed within six standard Greenwich hours."

The telepath handed Marvin a Dispossess Notice. Flynn accepted it sadly, yet with resignation. "I suppose," he said, "that I had better go back to my own body on Earth."

"That," the telepath said, "would be your wisest choice. Unfortunately, it is not possible at the moment."

"Not possible? Why not?"

"Because," the telepath said, "according to the Earth authorities, whose telepathic reply I have just received, your body, animated by the mind of Ze Kraggash, is nowhere to be found. A preliminary investigation leads us to fear that Ze Kraggash has fled the planet, taking with him your body and Mr. Aigeler's money."

It took a while for it to sink in, but finally, Marvin Flynn realized the implications of what had been said. He was stranded on Mars in an alien body, which he had to relinquish. In six hours, he would be a mind with no body at all and with a poor chance of finding one.

Minds cannot exist without bodies. Marvin Flynn slowly and unwillingly faced the imminence of his own death.

CHAPTER 6

Marvin did not give way to despair. He gave way instead to anger, which was a much healthier emotion, though equally unproductive. Instead of making a fool of himself by weeping in the court, he made a fool of himself by storming through the corridors of the Federal Building, demanding either fair play or a damned good substitute.

There was no restraining this impetuous young man. Quite in vain did several lawyers point out to him that, if justice really existed, there would be no need for law and lawmakers, and thus one of mankind's noblest conceptions would be obliterated, and an entire occupational group would be thrown out of work. For it is the essence of the law, they told him, that abuses and outrages should exist, since these discrepancies served as proof and validation of the necessity of law, and of justice itself.

This lucid argument brought no peace to the frenzied Marvin, who gave every appearance of a man unsusceptible to reason. The breath rasped and rattled in his throat as he roared his contempt for the Justice machinery of Mars. His behavior was considered disgraceful and was tolerated only because he was young and therefore not fully acculturated.

But rage brought him no results and did not even produce in him the healthy sensations of catharsis. Several judicial clerks pointed this out to him and were mercilessly snubbed for their efforts.

Marvin remained unaware of the bad impression he was creating in the minds of others, and after a while his anger spent itself, leaving as its residue a sullen resentment.

It was in this mood that he came to a door marked "Bureau of Detection and Apprehension, Interstellar Division."

"Aha!" Marvin muttered, and entered the office.

He found himself in a small room that looked like something out of the pages of an old historical novel. Against the wall were dignified banks of old but reliable electronic calculators. Near the door was an early-model thought-to-print translator. The armchairs had the abrupt shape and pastel plastic upholstery that we associate with a more leisurely era. The room lacked only a bulky solid state Moraeny to make it a perfect replica of a scene from the pages of Sheckley or one of the other early poets of the Age of Transmission.

There was a middle-aged Martian seated in a chair throwing darts at a target shaped like a woman's bottom.

He turned hastily when Marvin came in and said, "It's about time. I was expecting you."

"Were you really?" Marvin asked.

"Well, not really," the Martian said. "But I have found that it makes an effective opening and tends to create an atmosphere of trust."

"Then why do you ruin it by telling me?"

The Martian shrugged his shoulder and said, "Look, no one's perfect. I'm just an ordinary working detective. Urf Urdorf's the name. Sit down. I think we have a lead on your missing fur coat."

"What fur coat?" Marvin asked.

"Aren't you Madame Ripper de Lowe, the transvestite who was robbed last night in the Red Sands Hotel?"

"Certainly not. I'm Marvin Flynn, and I lost my body."

"Of course, of course," Detective Urdorf said, nodding vigorously. "Let's take it point by point. Do you remember by any chance where you were when you first noticed that your body was missing? Could any of your friends have taken it as a joke? Or could you have merely misplaced it, or perhaps sent it on a vacation?"

"I didn't really *lose* it," Marvin said. "Actually, it was stolen."

"You should have said so in the first place," Urdorf said. "That tends to put the matter in a different light. I am only a detective; I have never claimed to be a mind reader."

"I'm sorry," Marvin said.

"I'm sorry, too," Detective Urdorf said. "About your body, I mean. It must have been quite a nasty shock."

"Yes, it was."

"I can well understand how you feel."

"Thank you," Marvin said.

They sat in companionable silence for several minutes. Then Marvin said, "Well?"

"I beg your pardon?" the detective replied.

"I said, 'Well?' "

"Oh. I'm sorry, I'm afraid I didn't hear you the first time."

"That's quite all right."

"Thank you."

"You're extremely welcome."

There was another silence. Then Marvin said, "Well?" once again, and Urdorf said, "I beg your pardon?"

Marvin said, "I want it back."

"What?"

"My body."

"Your what? Oh yes, your body. Hmm, I dare say you do," the detective said with an appreciative smile. "But of course, it isn't as easy as that, is it?"

"I wouldn't know," Marvin said.

"No, I don't suppose you would," Urdorf said. "But I can assure you that it isn't as easy as that."

"I see," Marvin said.

"I rather hoped you would," Urdorf said, and lapsed into silence.

This silence lasted for approximately twenty-five seconds, give or take a second or two. At the end of that time Marvin's patience collapsed and he shouted, "God damn it are you going to do something about getting me back my body or are you going to just sit there on your goddamned fat ass and talk without saying anything?"

"Of course I am going to get you your body," the detective said. "Or, in any case, I am going to try. And there is no reason for abuse. I am not, after all, some machine filled with tabulated answers. I am an intelligent being just like yourself. I have my own hopes and fears; and, more germane, I have my own way of conducting an interview. This way may seem ineffectual to you, but I have found it extremely useful."

"Have you really?" asked Marvin, chastened.

"Why, yes, as a matter of fact I have," the detective replied, his mild voice showing no trace of rancor.

Another silence seemed about to begin, so Marvin asked, "What sort of chance do you think I have—we have—for recovering my body?"

"A most excellent chance," Detective Urdorf replied. "It is my firm belief that we will find your body soon. In fact, I think I could go so far as to say that I am certain of success. I base this not on a study of your particular case, about which I know very little at present, but on a simple examination of the statistics involved."

"Do the statistics favor us?" Marvin asked.

"They most assuredly do. Consider: I am a trained detective, conversant with all the new methods and possessing a top efficiency rating of AA-A. Yet in spite of this, during my five years with the force, I have never solved a case."

"Not a single one?"

"Not a single one," Urdorf said firmly. "Interesting, isn't it?"

"Yes, I suppose it is," Marvin said. "But doesn't that mean—"

"It means," the detective said, "that one of the strangest runs of bad luck that I have ever heard of is statistically due to break."

Marvin was nonplussed, which is an unusual sensation in a Martian body. He said, "But suppose your luck doesn't break?"

"You must not be superstitious," the detective replied. "The probabilities are there; even the most casual examination of the situation should convince you of that. I have been unable to solve 158 cases in a row. You are my 159th. How would you bet if you were a betting man?"

"I'd stay with the run," Marvin said.

"So would I," the detective admitted, with a self-deprecating smile. "But we would both be wrong, and would be betting on the basis of our emotions rather than on the calculations of our intellect." Urdorf looked at the ceiling dreamily. "One hundred and fifty-eight failures! It's a fantastic record, an unbelievable record, especially if you grant my incorruptability, good faith, and skill. One hundred fifty-eight! A run like that simply has to break! I could probably sit here in my office and do nothing, and the criminal would find his way to me. That's how strong the probabilities are in my favor."

"Yes, sir," Marvin said politely. "But I hope you won't test that particular approach."

"No, no, of course not," Urdorf said. "It would be interesting, but some people might not understand. No, I shall pursue your case actively, especially since it is a sex crime, which is the sort of thing I am interested in."

"I beg your pardon?" Marvin said.

"There is really no need to apologize," the detective assured him. "One should not be embarrassed or guilty by reason of being the victim of a sex crime, even though the deepest folk wisdom of many cultures attaches a stigma to being such a victim, on the presumption of conscious or unconscious complicity."

"No, no, I wasn't apologizing," Marvin said. "I was merely—"

"I quite understand," the detective said. "But you mustn't be ashamed to tell me all the bizarre and loathsome details. You must think of me as an impersonal official function instead of as an intelligent being with sexual feeling and fears and urges and quirks and desires of his own."

"What I was trying to tell you," Marvin said, "is that there is no sex crime involved here."

"They all say that," the detective mused. "It is strange how the human mind is forever unwilling to accept the unacceptable."

"Look," Marvin said, "if you would take the time to read over the facts of the case, you would see that it was a case of an outright swindle. Money and self-perpetuation were the motives."

"I am aware of that," the detective said. "And, were I unaware of the processes of sublimation, we could leave it at that."

"What possible motive could the criminal have had?" Marvin asked.

"His motive is obvious," Urdorf said. "It is a classic syndrome. You see, this fellow was acting under a specific compulsion, for which we have a specific technical term. He was driven to his deed in an advanced state of obsessive projective narcissism."

"I don't understand," Marvin said.

"It is not the sort of thing which the layman is apt to encounter," the detective told him.

"What does it mean?"

"Well, I can't go into the entire etiology, but essentially, the dynamics of the syndrome involve a displaced self-love. That is to say, the sufferer falls in love with another, but not *as* other. Rather, he falls in love with the Other as Himself. He projects himself into the persona of the Other, identifying himself with that Other in all ways, and repudiating his actual self. And, should he be able to possess that Other, through Mindswap or allied means, then that Other becomes himself, for whom he then feels a perfectly normal self-love."

"Do you mean," Marvin asked, "that this thief loved me?"

"Not at all! Or rather, he didn't love you as *you*—as a separate person. He loved *himself* as you, and thus his neurosis forced him to *become* you in order that he could love himself."

"And once he was me," Marvin asked, "he was then able to love himself?"

"Precisely! That particular phenomenon is known as the incrementation of the ego. Possession of the Other equals possession of the primordial Self; possession becomes self-possession, obsessive projection is transformed into normative introjection. Upon achievement of the neurotic goal there is an apparent remission of symptoms, and the sufferer achieves a state of pseudo-normalcy in which his problem can be detected only inferentially. It is a very great tragedy, of course."

"For the victim?"

"Well, yes, that certainly," Urdorf said. "But I was thinking of the patient. You see, in his case two perfectly normal drives have been combined, or crossed, and thus perverted. Self-love is normal and necessary, and so is the desire for possession and transformation. But taken together, they are destructive of the true self, which is supplanted by what we term the 'mirror-ego.' The neurotic conquest, you see, shuts the door to objective reality. Ironically enough, the apparent integration of the self precludes any hope of real mental health."

"All right," Marvin said, with resignation. "Will this help us find the man who stole my body?"

"It will enable us to understand him," the detective said. "Knowledge is power; we know at the very start that the man we seek is apt to act normal. This extends our field of action and enables *us* to act *as if he were normal,* and thus to use the full complement of modern investigative techniques. Being able to start from a premise like that, or indeed from any premise, is a very real advantage, I can assure you."

"How soon can you begin?" Marvin asked.

"I have already begun," the detective replied. "I shall send for the court records, of course, and all other documents pertaining to this matter, and I shall contact all relevant planetary authorities for additional information. I will spare no effort, and I will travel to the ends of the universe if necessary or desirable. I shall solve this case!"

"I'm very glad you feel that way," Marvin said.

"One hundred and fifty-eight cases without a break," Urdorf mused. "Have you ever heard of such a run of bad luck? But it will end here. I mean to say, it can't go on indefinitely, can it?"

"I don't suppose so."

"I wish my superiors would take that view," the detective said gloomily. "I wish they'd stop calling me 'stumblebum.' Words like that and sneers and lifted eyebrows all tend to shake one's confidence. Luckily for me, I have an implacable will and utter self-confidence. Or at least I did have through my first ninety or so failures."

The detective brooded darkly for several moments, then said to Marvin: "I will expect your complete and utter cooperation."

"You shall have it," Marvin said. "The only trouble is, I am to be dispossessed of this body in less than six hours."

"Damned awkward," Urdorf said absentmindedly. He was obviously thinking about his case, and only with difficulty did he turn his attention back to Marvin. "Dispossessed, eh? I suppose you've made other arrangements. No? Well then, I suppose you *will* make other arrangements."

"I don't know what arrangements to make," Marvin said gloomily.

"Well, you can't expect me to sort out your whole life for you," the detective snapped. "I've been trained to do one job, and the fact that I've failed consistently at it doesn't alter the fact that it *is* the job which I have been trained for. So you must cope with this matter of finding a body for yourself. The stakes are very high, you know."

"I know," Marvin said. "Finding a body is life or death for me."

"Well, yes, that too," the detective said. "But I was thinking of the case and of the detrimental effect your death would have upon it."

"That's a hell of a thing to say," Marvin said.

"I wasn't thinking of my own stake in the matter," the detective said. "Obviously, I *do* have a stake. But more important than that is the concept of Justice, and the belief in the possibility of goodness upon which all theories of evil must depend, and also the statistical theory of probabilities. All of these vital concepts might be damaged by my 159th failure to solve a crime. And I think you'll admit that these are somewhat larger issues than our petty lives."

"No, I won't admit it," Marvin said.

"Well, no need to argue the matter," the detective said, in a determinedly cheerful voice. "Find yourself another body somewhere; and above all, stay alive! I want you to promise me that you'll really try your level best to stay alive."

"I promise," Marvin said.

"And I shall proceed with your case, and I will contact you as soon as I have anything to report."

"But how will you find me?" Marvin asked. "I don't know what body I'll be in, or even what planet."

"You forget that I am a detective," Urdorf said, smiling faintly. "I may have my troubles in finding criminals, but I have never experienced the slightest difficulty in finding victims. I have a theory about that, which I will be pleased to discuss with you whenever we both have the time. But for now, just remember: wherever you are or whatever you turn into, I shall certainly locate you. So keep your chin up, don't lose the old moxie, and above all, stay alive!"

Marvin agreed to stay alive, since he had planned on it anyhow. And he went out into the street with his precious time flowing away, and still without a body.

CHAPTER 7

Headline in the *Martian Sun-News* (triplanet edition):

SWAP SCANDAL!

Police officials on Mars and Terra revealed today the existence of a Mindswap scandal. Wanted for questioning is Ze Kraggash, species unknown, who allegedly sold, swapped, or otherwise disposed of his Body to 12 Beings simultaneously. Warrants have been issued for Kraggash's arrest, and the police of the triplanet area confidently expect to make an announcement soon. The case is reminiscent of the infamous "Eddie Two-Head" scandal of the early '90s, in which...

Marvin Flynn let the newspaper fall into the gutter. He watched as the flowing sand bore it away; the bitter ephemerality of the newsprint seemed a paradigm of his own highly conditional existence. He stared at his hands; his head drooped.

"'Ere now, 'ere now, what seems to be the trouble, eh, lad?"

Flynn looked up into the kindly blue-green face of an Erlan.

"I've got troubles," Flynn said.

"Well then, let's hear 'em," the Erlan said, folding himself down on the curb beside Flynn. Like all of his race, the Erlan combined a quick sympathy with brusque manners. Erlans were known as a rough, witty people, much given to cheerful banter and homely sayings. Great travelers and traders, the Erlans of Erlan II were religiously required to travel *in corpore*.

Marvin told his story, right up to the disconsolate moment of the forward-surging *now*, the cruel and remorseless now, the hungry now, eating into his little stock of minutes and seconds, pressing forward to the time when his six hours would have elapsed, and bodyless, he would be cast into that unknown galaxy that men call "death."

"Garn!" the Erlan said. "Not half sorry for yourself, are you?"

"You're damned right I'm sorry for myself," Flynn said, with a flash of anger. "I'd be sorry for anyone who was going to die in six hours. Why shouldn't I be sorry for myself?"

"Suit yourself, cook," the Erlan said. "Some might call it bad form and all the bumf, but me, I hold with the teachings of the Guajuoie, who said: 'Is it death which snuffles near you? Strike it on the snout!' "

Marvin respected all religions, and certainly had no prejudices against the widespread Antidescantine Rite. But he couldn't see how the Guajuoie's words could help him, and he said so.

"Buck up!" the Erlan said. "Got yer brains and yer six hours, ain't yer?"

"Five hours."

"Well then! Git up on your hind legs and show a little grit, eh, cobber? Won't do yourself much good maundering around here like a bloody buggering old lag, will you now?"

"I don't suppose I will, really," Marvin said. "And yet, what can I do? I have no body, and hosts are expensive."

"Too true. But did you ever fink of the Open Market? Eh?"

"But that's supposed to be dangerous," Marvin said, and blushed at the absurdity of his statement. The Erlan grinned toughly.

"Got the picture, eh, lad? But listen, it ain't so bad as you fink, long as you buck up and take aholt. Open Market's not so bad; been a lot of rot talked about it, mostly by the big Swap agencies that wanna go on charging their overinflated capitalistic damned fees. But I know a bloke been working there twenty years on Short Shuffles, and he tells me most of the blokes is straight as a die. So keep your head up and your chest-prop tucked in tight, and pick yourself a good interman. Good luck, kid."

"Wait a moment!" Flynn cried, as the Erlan folded to his feet. "What is your friend's name?"

"James Virtue McHonnery," the Erlan said. "He's a tough, hard-bitten, narrow-minded little cuss, and overfond of looking upon the grape when it is red, and inclined to be smitten by black rage when in his cups. But he deals flat and he serves straight, and you couldn't ask no more than that from St. Xal himself. Just tell him that Pengle the Squib sent you, and good luck to you."

Flynn thanked the Squib eagerly, embarrassing that tough yet good-hearted gentleman. Rising to his feet, he proceeded, slowly at first, then with more speed, toward the Quain, in the northwest corner of which lay the many stalls and open booths of the Open Market. And his hopes, previously near entropy, began now to pulse modestly yet firmly. And in the nearby gutter, tattered newspapers flowed on a stream of sand toward the eternal and enigmatic desert.

"Hey-ya! Hey-ya! New bodies for old! Come and be serviced—new bodies for old!"

Marvin trembled when he heard that ancient street cry, so innocent in itself, yet so reminiscent of certain dark bedtime stories. Hesitantly he advanced into the tangled labyrinth of streets and alleys, or dead-ends and courtyards, that made up the ancient Free Market Area. And as he walked, a dozen shouted propositions assailed his aural receptors.

"Harvesters wanted to harvest the crop on Drogheda! We supply you with a fully functional body, complete with telepathy! All found, fifty credits a month, *and* a complete list of Class C-3 pleasures! Special two-year contracts are now being let. Come harvest the crop on beautiful Drogheda!"

"Serve in the Naigwin Army! Twenty NCO bodies currently on offer, plus a few specials in junior officer ranks. All bodies fully equipped with martial skills!"

"What's the pay?" a man asked the salesman.

"Your keep, plus one credit a month."

The man sneered and turned away.

"*And,*" the barker proclaimed, "unlimited sacking rights."

"Well, that seems in order," the man said grudgingly. "But the Naigwins been losing this war for a decade. High casualty rate, and not much corporeal reclamation."

"We're changing all that," the salesman said. "You're an experienced mercenary?"

"Correct," the man said. "The name is Sean Von Ardin, and I've been in just about every major war around, plus a fair number of minor ones."

"Last rank?"

"Jevaldher in the army of the Count of Ganymede," Von Ardin said. "But before that I held the rank of Full Cthusis."

"Well, well," the salesman said, seemingly impressed. "Full Cthusis, eh? Got papers to prove it? OK, tell you what I can do. I can offer you a position with the Naigwins as Manatee Leader, Second Class."

Von Ardin frowned and calculated on his fingers. "Let's see, Manatee Leader, Second Class is the equivalent of a Cyclopian Demi-Vale, which is slightly lower than an Anaxorean Banner King, and almost half a grade lower than a Dorian Old Boy. Which means… Hey, I'd lose an entire field grade if I joined you!"

"Ah, but you didn't hear me out," the salesman continued. "You would hold that rank for a period of twenty-five days, to prove Purity of Intent, which the Naigwin political leaders are very big on. *Then* we would jump you three entire grades to Melanoan Superios, which would offer you an excellent chance at provisional Lance-Jumbaya, and maybe—I can't promise this, but I think I can swing it unofficially—maybe I can get you appointed Sackmeister for the spoils of Eridsvurg."

"Well," Von Ardin said, impressed in spite of himself, "that's a pretty decent deal—if you can swing it."

"Come into the store," the salesman said. "Let me make a phone call…"

Marvin walked on and listened to men of a dozen races arguing with salesmen of a dozen more. A hundred propositions were screamed in his ear. His spirits were stirred and uplifted by the vitality of the place. And the propositions he heard, though sometimes dismaying, were often intriguing:

"Aphid-man wanted for the Senthis Swarm. Good pay, congenial friendships!"

"Rewrite man required to work on the *Dirty Book of Kavengii!* Must be able to empathize with sexual premises of the Midridarian race!"

"Garden planners needed for Arcturus! Come and relax among the only vegetable-sentients in the galaxy!"

"Expert manacler wanted for Vega IV! Opportunities also for semi-skilled restrainers! Full prerogatives!"

There were so many opportunities in the galaxy! It seemed to Marvin that his misfortune was perhaps a blessing in disguise. He had wanted to travel—but his modesty had permitted him no more than the role of tourist. But how much better, how much more gratifying it would be, to travel for a reason: to serve with the armies of Naigwin, experience life as an aphid-man, learn what it meant to be a manacler—even to do rewrites on the *Dirty Book of Kavengii.*

Directly ahead of him, he spotted a sign that read: "James Virtue McHonnery, Licensed Short-Shuffle Dealer. Satisfaction guaranteed."

Standing at the waist-high counter and smoking a cigar was a tough, hard-bitten, sour-mouthed little man with piercing cobalt-blue eyes. This could be none other than McHonnery himself. Silent and disdainful, scorning to spiel, the little man stood with arms folded as Flynn walked up to the booth.

CHAPTER 8

They stood face to face, Flynn slack-jawed, McHonnery clam-mouthed. Several seconds of silence ensued. Then McHonnery said: "Look, kid, this ain't no goddamned peep show and I ain't no goddamned freak. If you got something to say, spit it out. Otherwise take a walk for yourself before I break your back."

Marvin could see at once that this man was no fawning, honey-mouthed body salesman. There was no hint of obsequiousness in that rasping voice, no trace of ingratiation in that downturned mouth. Here was a man who said what he wanted to say, and took no heed of the consequences.

"I—I am a client," Flynn said.

"Big deal," McHonnery harshed. "Am I supposed to turn handsprings or something?"

His sardonic retort and blunt, inner-directed demeanor gave Flynn a sensation of confidence. He knew, of course, that appearances could be deceiving; but no one had ever told him what to judge by instead of appearances. He was inclined to trust this proud and bitter man.

"I am going to be dispossessed of this body in a matter of hours," Marvin explained. "Since my own body has been stolen, I am in desperate need of a substitute. I have very little money, but I—I am quite willing and prepared to work."

McHonnery stared at him, and a sardonic grin twisted the man's tight lips. "Prepared to work, huh? Ain't that nice! And just what are you prepared to work *at?*"

"Why—anything."

"Yeah? Can you operate a Montcalm metal lathe with light-sensitive switchboard and manual cull? No? Think you could handle a Quick-Greeze Particle Separator for the Rare Earths Novelty Company? Not your sort of thing, huh?... I got a surgeon on Vega who wants somebody to run his Nerve-Impulse-Rejection Simulator (the old model with the double pedals). Not exactly what you had in mind? Well, we got a jazz band on Potemkin II which needs a stomach-horn man, and a restaurant near Boötes which could use a shortorder cook, with working knowledge of Cthensis specialties. Doesn't ring a bell? Maybe you could pick flowers on Moriglia; of course, you'd have to be able to predict antithesis without more than a five-second variation. Or you could do spot-flesh-welding, if you've got the nerves for it, or boss a phylopod reclamation project, or draw up intermediate creeper systems, or—but I don't guess none of them strike your fancy, huh?"

Flynn shook his head and mumbled, "I don't know anything about any of those jobs, sir."

"Somehow," McHonnery said, "that doesn't surprise me as much as you might think. Is there anything you *can* do?"

"Well, in college I was studying—"

"Don't give me your goddamned life story! I'm interested in your trade, skill, talent, profession, ability, whatever you want to call it. What, specifically, can you *do*?"

"Well," Marvin said, "I guess when you put it that way, I can't do anything much."

"I know," McHonnery said, sighing. "You're unskilled; it's written all over you. Kid, it may interest you to know that unskilled minds are common as dirt, commoner. The market's glutted with them, the universe is crammed to overflowing with them. It may interest you to know that there is nothing you can do that a machine can't do better, faster, and a damn sight more cheerfully."

"I'm sorry to hear that, sir," Marvin said, sadly but with dignity. He turned to go.

"Just a minute," McHonnery said. "I thought you wanted to work."

"But you said—"

"I said you were unskilled, which you are. And I said that a machine can do anything you can do better, faster, and more cheerfully, *but not more cheaply.*"

"Oh," Marvin said.

"Yep, in the cheapness department, you still got an edge over the gadgets. And that's quite an achievement in this day and age. I have always considered it one of the glories of mankind that, despite its best efforts, it has never completely succeeded in rendering itself superfluous. You see, kid, our instincts order us to multiply, while our intelligence commands us to conserve. We are like a father who bears many sons, but contrives to dispossess all but the eldest. We call instinct blind, but intelligence is equally so. Intelligence has its passions, its loves and its hates; woe to the logician whose superbly rational system does not rest upon a solid base of raw feeling. Lacking such a base, we call that man—irrational!"

"I never knew that," Marvin said.

"Well, hell, it's obvious enough," McHonnery said. "The aim of intelligence is to put the whole goddamned human race out of work. Luckily, it can never be done. A man will outwork a machine any day in the week. In the brute-labor department, there'll always be opportunities for the unwanted."

"I suppose there's a certain comfort in that," Flynn said doubtfully. "And of course, it's very interesting. But when Pengle the Squib told me to go see you, I thought—"

"Hey, how's that?" McHonnery said. "You're a friend of the Squib?"

"You might say that," Flynn said, thus avoiding an outright lie, since anyone might say anything whether it was true or not.

"You should have told me that in the first place," McHonnery said. "Not that it would have changed anything, since the facts are exactly as I have stated them. But I'd have told you that there's no shame in being unskilled; hell, all of us have to start out that way, don't we? If you do well on a Short-Shuffle contract, you'll pick up skills in no time."

"I hope so, sir," Flynn said, growing cautious now that McHonnery had become affable. "Do you have a job in mind for me?"

"As a matter of fact, I do," McHonnery said. It's a one week Shuffle, which, even if you don't like it, you could do standing on your head. Not that you should have to, since it's a pleasant and compatible job, combining mild outdoor exercise with modest intellectual stimulation, all in a framework of good working conditions, an enlightened management, and a congenial working force."

"It sounds marvelous," Flynn said. "What's wrong with it?"

"Well, it's not the sort of job you can get rich at," McHonnery said. "In fact, the pay is lousy. But what the hell, you can't have everything. A week at this will give you a chance to think things over, talk with your fellow workers, decide upon a direction for yourself."

"What is the job?" Marvin asked.

"The official job title is Ootheca Indagator, Second Class."

"That sounds impressive."

"Glad that you like it. It means that you hunt for eggs."

"Eggs?"

"Eggs. Or to be more specific, you hunt for and, upon finding, collect the eggs of the rock ganzer. Think you can swing it?"

"Well, I'd like to know a little more about the techniques utilized for the collecting, and also about job conditions, and—"

He stopped because McHonnery was slowly, sadly shaking his head. "You can find that out when you get there. I ain't delivering no goddamned travelogue, and you ain't deciding on no guided tour. Do you want the job or not?"

"Do you have anything else available?"

"No."

"Then I'll take the job."

"You've made a smart decision," McHonnery said. He took a paper out of his pocket. "Here is the standard government-approved contract, written in Kro-Melden, which is the official language of the planet Melde II, wherein is licensed the employing company. Can you read Kro-Melden?"

"I'm afraid not."

"Then I'll translate the pertinent clauses for you, as required by the law. Let's see…standard stuff about the Company not being responsible for fire, earthquake, atomic warfare, sun going nova, acts of god or gods, and so forth. The Company agrees to hire you for the sum of one credit a month, plus transportation to Melde; there it will furnish you with a Melde body; it will further issue you a set of clothes, and will feed and shelter you and care for your health and welfare, unless it finds itself unable to do so, in which case it won't and you will hold it harmless for that failure. In return for these and other Services, you will perform designated tasks as instructed, in this case those tasks exclusively relating to and specifically effecting upon the finding and collecting of ganzer eggs. And may God have mercy on your soul."

"I beg your pardon?" Flynn asked.

"The last is just the standard invocation. Let me see, I think that about covers it. You guarantee, of course, not to commit acts of sabotage, espionage, irreverence, disobedience, etc., and to furthermore eschew and desist from the practices of sexual perversion as defined in Hoffmeyer's *Standard Book of Melden Perversions*. And you also guarantee not to initiate a war, or to take part in a war on Melde if one is initiated, and to wash once every two days, and to stay out of debt, and not to become an alcoholic or insane person, and various other things to which no reasonable person could possibly object. And that about sums it up. If you have any important questions, I'll endeavor to answer them for you."

"Well," Flynn said, "about those things I'm supposed to guarantee—"

"That's unimportant," McHonnery said. "Do you want the job or not? A simple yes or no will suffice."

Marvin had his doubts, but, unfortunately, he didn't have any alternatives; and this lack rendered his doubts extraneous to the situation. He thought fleetingly of the detective, then he put that thought firmly aside. As McHonnery had said, how bad could a week of anything be? Therefore he agreed to take the job, registering his assent upon the mind-sensitive universal signaturizer at the bottom of the page. McHonnery led him forthwith to the Transportation Center, from which point minds were shipped across the galaxy at a multiple of the speed of thought.

The next thing Marvin knew, he was on Melde, in a Melden body.

CHAPTER 9

The Ganzer Rain Forest on Melde was deep and wide; the faintest ghost of a breeze whispered among the colossal trees, slithered through the interlocked vines, and crept broken-backed over hook-edged grass. Drops of water slid painfully down and around the tangled foliage like exhausted runners of a maze, coming to rest at last in the spongy and indifferent soil. Shadows mingled and danced, faded and reappeared, called into spurious motion by two tired suns in a moldy green sky. Overhead, a desolate therengol whistled for his mate, and heard in reply the quick ominous cough of a predatory kingspringer. And through this dolorous woodland, so tantalizingly like Earth and yet so different, Marvin Flynn moved in his unfamiliar Melden body, his eyes downcast, searching for ganzer eggs but not knowing what they looked like.

All had been haste. From the moment he arrived on Melde, he had barely had a chance to take stock of himself. No sooner was he bodified than someone was barking orders in his ear. Flynn had just had time to look hastily over his four-armed, four-legged body, give his tail a single experimental flick, and fold his ears across his back; then he was herded into a work gang, given a barracks number and a mess hall location, and handed a jumper two sizes too big for him, and shoes that fitted tolerably well except for the left front. He signed for and was given the tools of his new trade; a large plastic bag, dark glasses, a compass, a net, a pair of tongs, a heavy metal tripod, and a blaster.

He and his fellow workers were then assembled in ranks, and received a hasty indoctrination lecture by the manager, a bored and supercilious Atreian.

Flynn learned that his new home occupied an insignificant portion of space in the vicinity of Aldebaran. Melde (so named for its dominant race, the Meldens) was a thoroughly second-rate world. Its climate was rated "intolerable" on the Hurlihan-Chanz Climatic Tolerance Scale; its natural-resource potentiality was classified "submarginal," and its esthetic-resonance factor (unweighted) was given as "unprepossessing."

"Not the sort of place," the manager said, "that one would choose for a vacation, or indeed, for anything, except possibly the practice of extreme mortification."

His audience tittered uneasily.

"Nevertheless," the manager continued, "this unloved and unlovely place, this solar misfortune, this cosmic mediocrity is home to its inhabitants, who consider it the finest place in the universe."

The Meldens, with a fierce pride in their only tangible asset, had made the best of their bad bargain. With the plucky determination of the eternally unlucky, they had farmed the edges of the rain forest and collected meager low-yield ores from the vast blazing deserts. Their dogged persistence would have been inspiring had it not been so tedious; and their efforts might have been considered a tribute to the vaunting spirit of life had they not invariably ended in failure. Because, despite all their travail, the Meldens were able to achieve nothing better than slow starvation in the present, and the promise of racial degeneration and extinction in the future.

"This, then, is Melde," said the manager. "Or rather, this is *what Melde would be* were it not for one additional factor. That factor spells the difference between success and failure. I refer, of course, to the presence of ganzer eggs."

"Ganzer eggs!" the manager repeated. "No other planet possesses them; no other planet so desperately needs them. Ganzer eggs! No object in the known universe so clearly epitomizes the quality of desirability. Ganzer eggs! Let us consider them, if you will."

Ganzer eggs were the sole export of the planet Melde. And luckily for the Meldens, the eggs were always in heavy use. On Orichades, ganzer eggs were utilized as love-objects; on Ophiuchus II, they were ground up and eaten as a sovereign aphrodisiac; on Morichades, after consecration, they were worshipped by the irrational K'tengi. Many other uses could be cited.

Thus, ganzer eggs were a vital natural resource, and the only one which the Meldens possessed. With them, the Meldens could maintain a tolerable degree of civilization. Without them, the race would surely perish.

To acquire a ganzer egg, all one had to do was pick it up. But therein lay certain difficulties, since the ganzers, not unnaturally, objected to this practice.

The ganzers were forest dwellers, remotely of lizard origin. They also were destroyers, clever at concealment, wily and ferocious, and completely untameable. These qualities rendered the collection of ganzer eggs extremely perilous.

"It is a curious situation," the manager pointed out, "and not without its paradoxical overtones, that the main source of life on Melde is also the main cause of death. It is something for you all to think about as you begin your workday. And so I say, take good care of yourselves, keep guarded at all times, look before you leap, observe every precaution with your indentured lives, and also with the costly bodies which have been entrusted to your keeping. But in addition, remember that you must fulfill your norm, since every day's work unfulfilled by so much as a single egg is penalized by the addition of an additional week. Therefore, be careful, but not too careful, and be perseverant, but not blindly so, and courageous, but not rash, and assiduous, but never foolhardy. Follow these simple maxims and you will have no difficulty. Good luck, boys!"

Marvin and his fellow workers were then formed into ranks and marched into the forest on the double.

Within an hour they reached their search area. Marvin Flynn took this opportunity to ask the foreman for instructions.

"Instructions?" the foreman asked. "What kind of type instructions?" (He was an Orinathian deportee with no language aptitude.)

"I mean," Flynn said, "what am I supposed to do?"

The foreman pondered the question and at length responded: "You supposed pick eggs of ganzer." (Amusingly enough, he pronounced it "guntser.")

"I understand that," Flynn said. "But I mean to say, I don't even know what a ganzer egg looks like."

"Not to worry," the foreman replied. "You know when see no mistake, yes."

"Yes, sir," Marvin said. "And when I find a ganzer egg, are there any special rules for handling it? I mean to say, is breakage a problem, or—"

"To handle," the foreman said, "you pick up egg, put in bag. You understand this thing yes no?"

"Of course I do," Marvin said. "But also, I would like to know about daily quota expectations. I mean to say, is there some sort of a quota system, or perhaps an hourly breakdown? I mean, how does one know when one has fulfilled his norm?"

"Ah!" said the foreman, a look of comprehension finally crossing his broad, good-natured face. "Of finish is like this. You pick ganzer egg, put in bag, check?"

"Check," Marvin said instantly.

"You do so time after time *until bag is full*. Catch?"

"I believe I do," Marvin said. "The full bag represents the actual or ideal quota. Let me just go over the steps again to make absolutely sure I've got it. First, I locate the ganzer eggs, applying Terran associations to the concept, and presumably having no difficulty in identification. Second, having located and identified the desired object, I proceed to 'put it in my basket,' by which I assume that I lift it manually to initiate the transaction, and then proceed with actions consonant with that beginning. Third, repeating this strategy S for an x number of times, I perform the equation $Sx=B!$, where B represents the capacity of the bag and $!$ represents the sum of x transactions necessary to fulfill B. Finally, the sum of all strategies completed, I return to the camp, where I turn in the contents of my bag. Do I have it straight, sir?"

The foreman tapped his teeth with his tail and said, "You put me on, huh, kid?"

"Well, sir, I merely wished to ascertain—"

"You make big joke on old-planet Orinathian yokel, yah, sure, huh. You think you so smart, but you ain't so smart. Remember—nobody likes wise guy."

"I'm sorry," Flynn said, swishing his tail deferentially. (But he wasn't sorry. It was his first show of spirit since this downward-trending series of events had begun for him, and he was glad to find himself capable of some show of spirit, no matter how ill-timed or badly considered.)

"Anyhow, me I tink you catch elementary rudiments of job all right so you go now perform work labor *big*, and keep nose clean or I break six or more of your limbs, dig?"

"Dig," said Flynn, wheeled and cantered into the forest and there began his search for ganzer eggs.

CHAPTER 10

Marvin Flynn wandered as he wondered just what a ganzer egg looked like. He also would have enjoyed knowing what he was supposed to use his equipment for; the sunglasses were useless in the dim recesses of the forest, and the heavy tripod was incomprehensible.

He slid silently through the forest, his nostrils flared wide, his eyes extended and swivelling, their blink rate reduced. His golden hide, scented faintly with appisthyme, twitched sensitively as his great muscles moved beneath it, apparently relaxed yet poised for instant action.

The forest was a symphony of greens and greys, cut through with the occasional scarlet theme of a creeper, or the purple flourish of a lillibabba shrub, or rarer still, the haunting oboe counter-melody of an orange whip-whinger. Yet withal, the effect was essentially a somber and thought-provoking one, like the sight of a vast amusement park in the silent hour before dawn.

But there! Right over there! A little to the left! Yes, yes, just beneath the boku tree! Is that...? Could it be...?

Flynn parted the leaves with his right arms and bent low. There, in a nest of grass and woven twigs, he saw a glittering ovoid that resembled nothing quite so much as an ostrich egg encrusted with precious gems.

The foreman had been right. There could be no mistaking a ganzer egg.

Gazing carefully upon that singular object, and taking stock of his impressions, Marvin could see the light of a million fairy fires burning bright in the curved and multihued ganzer surface. Shadows drifted across it like the fragrance of half-remembered dreams, twisting and turning like the descending ghosts of phantoms. An emotion welled up in Marvin, of twilight and evensong, of slow cattle grazing near a crystal brook, of dusty, heartbroken cypresses beside a white stone road.

Although it wrenched his sensibilities to do so, Marvin bent down and reached out, with the straightforward intention of lifting the ganzer egg and sequestering it within his plastic bag. His hand folded lovingly around the glowing orb.

He pulled his hand back quickly; the glowing orb was hotter than hell.

Marvin looked at the ganzer egg with new respect. Now he understood the purpose of the tongs with which he had been equipped. He maneuvered them into position and closed the jaws gently on the spheroid of dreams.

The spheroid of dreams bounced away from him like a rubber ball. Marvin galloped after it, fumbling with his net. The ganzer egg twisted and ricocheted, and bolted for thick underbrush. Marvin cast his net in desperation, and fortune guided his hand. The ganzer egg was neatly netted. It lay quietly, pulsating as though out of breath. Marvin approached it cautiously, ready for any trick.

Instead, the ganzer egg spoke. "Look, mister," it said, in a muffled voice. "Just what's eating you?"

"Beg pardon?" Marvin said.

"Look," the ganzer egg said, "I am sitting here in a public park minding my own business when suddenly you come up and pounce on me like a lunatic, bruising my shoulder and acting in general like some kind of nut. Well, naturally, I get a little hot. Who wouldn't? So I decide to move away because it's my day off and I don't want no trouble. So you up and throw a net around me like I was a goddamned *fish* or a butterfly or something. So I just want to know, what's the big idea?"

"Well," Marvin said, "you see, you're a ganzer egg."

"I'm aware of that," the ganzer egg said. "Sure I'm a ganzer egg. Is there a law against that all of a sudden?"

"Certainly not," Marvin said. "But as it happens, I am hunting ganzer eggs."

There was a short silence. Then the ganzer egg said, "Would you mind repeating that?"

Marvin did. The ganzer egg said, "Mmm, that's what I thought you said." He laughed feebly. "You're kidding, aren't you?"

"Sorry, I'm not."

"Sure you are," the ganzer egg said, a note of desperation in his voice. "So OK, you've had your fun. Now let me out of here."

"Sorry..."

"Let me out!"

"I can't."

"Why?"

"Because I'm hunting ganzer eggs."

"My God," the ganzer egg said, "this is the craziest thing I've ever heard in my life. You never met me before, did you? So why are you hunting me?"

"I've been hired to hunt ganzer eggs," Marvin told him.

"Look, fella, are you trying to tell me that you just go around hunting any ganzer egg at all? You don't care which one?"

"That's right."

"And you aren't really looking for one *particular* ganzer egg who maybe did you a bad turn?"

"No, no," Marvin said. "I've never even met a ganzer egg before."

"You've never…and yet you hunt…? I must be going out of my mind, I can't be hearing right. I mean, things like this just don't happen. I mean, it's like some kind of an incredible nightmare… I mean, it's the sort of thing you get crazy nightmares about—some crazy-looking guy walking up calm as you please and grabbing you and saying in a sort of crazy dead-pan voice, 'I happen to be hunting for ganzer eggs.' I mean—look, fella, you *are* putting me on, aren't you?"

Marvin was embarrassed and exasperated, and he wished the ganzer egg would shut up. He said gruffly, "I'm not fooling. My job is to collect ganzer eggs."

"Collect…ganzer eggs!" the ganzer egg moaned. "Oh no, no, no, no! My God, I can't believe this is happening, but yet it really is happening, it really is—"

"Control yourself," Marvin said; the ganzer egg was clearly on the thin edge of hysteria.

"Thank you," the ganzer egg said, after a moment. I'm all right now. I didn't mean to—to give way."

"That's all right," Marvin said. "Are you ready to be collected now?"

"I—I'm trying to get used to the idea. It's so…so… Look, could I ask you just one question?"

"Hurry it up," Marvin said.

"The thing I want to ask," the ganzer egg said, "do you get some kind of a charge out of this sort of thing? I mean are you some sort of pervert? I don't mean to be insulting."

"That's all right," Marvin said. "No, I'm not a pervert, and I can assure you I take no pleasure in this. It's strictly a job with me."

"Strictly a job," the ganzer egg repeated. "A *job.* To kidnap a ganzer egg whom you've never met before. Just a job. Like picking up a stone. Only I'm not a stone, I'm a ganzer egg!"

"I realize that," Marvin said. "Believe me, I'm finding all of this very strange."

"*You're* finding it strange!" the ganzer egg said, his voice rising to a scream. "How do you think I feel? Do you think maybe I think it's *natural* for someone to come along like in a nightmare and *collect* me?"

"Steady," Marvin said.

"Sorry," the ganzer egg said. "I'm all right now."

"I'm really very sorry about this," Marvin said. "But you see, I've got this job and this quota, and if I don't do it I'll have to spend the rest of my life here."

"Crazy," the ganzer egg whispered to himself. "He's absolutely and completely insane."

"So I have to collect you," Marvin finished, and reached out.

"Wait!" the ganzer egg howled, in so panicstricken a voice that Marvin desisted.

"What is it now?"

"May—may I leave a note for my wife?"

"There isn't time," Marvin said firmly.

"Then will you at least let me say my prayers?"

"Go ahead and say them," Marvin said. "But you'll really have to be quick about it."

"Oh Lord God," the ganzer egg intoned, "I don't know what is happening to me, or why. I have always tried to be a good person, and although I am not a regular churchgoer, You surely know that true religion is in the heart. I've maybe done some bad things in my life, I won't deny it. But Lord, why this punishment? Why me? Why not someone else, one of the real bad ones, one of the criminals? Why me? And why like this? Something is *collecting* me like I'm some sort of a *thing*... And I don't understand. But I know that You are All-Wise and All-Powerful, and I know that You are good, so I guess there must be a reason...even if I'm too stupid to see it. So look, God, if this is it, then OK, this is it. But could you look after my wife and kids? And could you especially look after the little one?" The ganzer egg's voice broke, but he recovered almost at once. "I ask especially for the little one, God, because he's lame and the other kids pick on him and he needs a lot—a lot of love. Amen."

The ganzer egg choked back his sobs. His voice became abruptly stronger.

"All right," he said to Marvin. "I'm ready now. Go ahead and do your damnedest, you lousy son-of-a-bitch."

But the prayer of the ganzer egg had unmanned Marvin completely. With eyes wet and fetlocks trembling, Marvin opened the net and released his captive. The ganzer egg rolled out a little distance and then stopped, clearly fearing a trick.

"You—you really mean this?" he said.

"I do," Marvin said. "I was never cut out for this kind of work. I don't know what they will do to me back at the camp, but I shall never gather a single ganzer egg!"

"Praised be the name of the Lord," the ganzer egg said softly. "I've seen a few strange things in my time, but it seems to me that the Hand of Providence—"

The hypothesis of the ganzer egg (known as the Interventionalist Fallacy) was interrupted by a sudden ominous crashing in the underbrush.

Marvin whirled and remembered the dangers of the planet Melde. He had been warned but had forgotten. And now, desperately, he fumbled for his blaster, which had become entangled in his net. Violently he wrenched at it, pulled it free, heard a shrill warning from the ganzer egg—

And then he was flung violently to the ground. The blaster spun away into the underbrush. And Marvin gazed up into slit black eyes beneath a low armored forehead.

No introductions were necessary. Flynn knew that he had met a full-grown adult marauding ganzer, and had met him under possibly the worst of all circumstances. The evidence (if evidence were needed) was all too evident; close to hand was the damning net, the telltale sunglasses, the revealing tongs. And closer still—closing on his neck—was the tooth-edged jaw of the gigantic saurian, so close that Marvin could see three gold molars and a temporary porcelain filling.

Flynn tried to wriggle free. The ganzer pressed him back with a paw the size of a yak saddle; his cruel claws, each the size of a pair of ice tongs, bit cruelly into Marvin's golden hide. The slavering jaws gaped hideously, descended, about to engulf his entire head...

CHAPTER 11

Suddenly—time stopped! Marvin saw the ganzer's jaws arrested in midslaver, his bloodshot left eye fixed in midblink, and his entire great body gripped in a strange and unyielding rigidity.

Nearby, the ganzer egg was as motionless as a carven replica of itself.

The breeze was stopped in midcareer. Trees were caught in straining postures, and a meritheian hawk was fixated in midflight like a dummy attached to a wire.

The sun stopped its inexorable rolling flight!

And in this strange tableau, Marvin stared with tremulous sensations in the direction of a single movement in the air three feet above his head and slightly to his left.

It began as a whorl of dust, broadened, expanded, expatiated, thickening at the base and becoming convex at the apex. The rotation came faster, and the figure solidified.

"Detective Urdorf!" Marvin cried. For it was indeed the Martian detective with the streak of bad luck who had promised to solve Marvin's case and to return to him his rightful body.

"Terribly sorry to barge in like this," Urdorf said, materializing fully and falling heavily to the ground.

"Thank God you have come!" Marvin said. "You have saved me from an extremely unpleasant fate, and now if you will help me out from under this creature—"

For Marvin was still pinned to the ground by the ganzer's paw, which had taken on the rigidity of tempered steel, and from beneath which he was unable to wriggle.

"Sorry," the detective said, getting up and dusting himself off. "I'm afraid I can't do that."

"Why not?"

"Because it's against the rules," Detective Urdorf told him. "You see, any displacement of bodies during an artificial induced temporal stoppage (which is what this is) could result in a Paradox, which is forbidden since it might result in a temporal implosion which might conceivably have the result of warping the structure-lines of our continuum and thus destroy the universe. Because of this, any displacement is punishable by a prison sentence of one year and a fine of one thousand credits."

"Oh. I didn't know that," Marvin said.

"Well, I'm afraid that's how it is," the detective said.

"I see," Marvin said.

"I rather hoped you would," the detective said.

There was a long and uncomfortable silence. Then Marvin said, "Well?"

"Beg pardon?"

"I said—I *meant* to say, why did you come here?"

"Oh," the detective said. "I wished to ask you several questions which had not occurred to me earlier, and which would assist me in the rigorous investigation and solution of this case."

"Ask away," Marvin said.

"Thank you. First and foremost, what is your favorite color?"

"Blue."

"But exactly what *shade* of blue? Please try to be exact."

"Robin's-egg blue."

"Hmmm." The detective noted it down in his notebook. "And now, tell me quickly and without thinking, what is the first number that comes into your mind?"

"87792.3," Marvin replied without hesitation.

"Um hum. And now, without reflection, tell me the name of the first popular song you can think of."

" 'Orang-Utan Rhapsody,' " Marvin said.

"Ummmm. Fine," Urdorf said, snapping his notebook shut. "I think that covers everything."

"What was the purpose of those questions?" Marvin asked.

"With this information, I will be able to test various suspects for corpus-vestigial responses. It is part of the Duulman self-identity quiz."

"Oh," Marvin said. "Have you had any luck yet?"

"Luck hardly enters into it," Urdorf replied. "But I can say that the case is proceeding in a satisfactory manner. We traced the thief to Iorama II, where he smuggled himself into a cargoload of flashfrozen beef destined for Goera Major. On Goera he represented himself as a fugitive from Hage XI, which won him a good deal of popular favor. He managed to raise enough money for fare to Kvanthis, where he had cached his money. Staying no more than a day on Kvanthis, he boarded the local to the Fiftystars Autonomous Region."

"And then?" Marvin asked.

"Then we lost track of him temporarily. Fiftystars Region contains no less than 432 planetary systems with a combined population of 300 billion. So as you can see, our work is cut out for us."

"It sounds hopeless," Marvin said.

"Quite the contrary, it is a very good break for us. Laymen always mistake complication for complexity. But our criminal will find no safety in mere multiplicity, which is always susceptible to statistical analysis."

"So what happens now?" Marvin asked.

"We continue analyzing, and then we make a projection based upon the probabilities, and then we send our projection across the galaxy and see if it goes nova... I am speaking figuratively, of course."

"Of course," Marvin said. "Do you really think you'll catch him?"

"I am fully confident of the results," Detective Urdorf said. "But you must have patience. You must remember that intergalactic crime is still a relatively new field, and therefore intergalactic investigation is newer still. There have been many crimes in which even the existence of a criminal could not be proven, much less detected. So in some respects, we are ahead of the game."

"I guess I'll have to take your word for it," Marvin said.

"Just don't worry. In these cases, it is best for the victim to continue his life as normally as possible, to stay alive, and not to give way to despair. I hope you will remember this."

"I'll try to," Marvin said. "But about this situation I'm in at present—"

"It is the very sort of situation I have told you to avoid," the detective said severely. "Please remember that in the future, if you should manage to come out of this alive. Good luck, my friend, and stay alive!"

Before Marvin's eyes, Detective Urdorf revolved, faster, faster, grew dimmer, and disappeared.

Time unfroze.

And Marvin gazed up again into the ganzer's slit black eyes and low armored forehead, and saw the hideous gaping jaws descending, about to engulf his entire head...

CHAPTER 12

"Wait!" Marvin shouted.

"What for?" the ganzer asked.

Marvin hadn't thought that far. He heard the ganzer egg muttering, "Turnabout's fair play; and yet, he was kind to me. Still, what business is it of mine? Stick your neck out, somebody cracks your shell. And yet..."

"I don't want to die," Marvin said.

"I didn't suppose you did," the rock ganzer said, in a not unfriendly voice. "And, of course, you want to discuss it with me. Ethics, morals, the whole bit. But I'm afraid not. We were specifically warned, you see, never to allow a Melden to talk. We were told to just do the job and get it over with, not to *personalize* it. Just do it and get on to the next bit of work. Mental hygiene, really. Therefore, if you would close your eyes..."

The jaws moved closer. But Marvin, filled with wild surmise, cried out: "Did you say *job?*"

"Of course, it's a job," the ganzer said. "There's nothing personal in it." He frowned, apparently annoyed at himself for having spoken.

"A job! Your job is to hunt Meldens, is that it?"

"Well, obviously. This planet of Ganzer isn't good for much, you see, except for hunting Meldens."

"But why do you hunt them?" Marvin asked.

"Well, for one thing, a ganzer egg can grow to full maturity only in the host flesh of the adult Melden."

"I *say,*" the ganzer egg said, rolling around with embarrassment, "must we get so damned *biological?* I mean to say, you don't hear me talking about *your* natural functions, do you?"

"And secondly," the ganzer continued, "our sole export is Melden hides, which (after curing and tanning) are used for imperial vestments on Triana II, for goodluck charms on Nemo, and for seat covers on Chrysler XXX. This quest for the elusive and deadly Melden is our sole means of maintaining a tolerable degree of civilization and—"

"That's exactly what they told me!" Marvin cried, and quickly repeated what the manager had said to him.

"My gosh!" said the ganzer.

Both realized the true situation now: the Meldens were utterly dependent upon the Ganzers, who in turn were utterly dependent upon the Meldens. These two races hunted each other, lived and died for each other, and, through ignorance or guile, ignored any relationship between each other. The relationship was utterly symbiotic, but completely unacknowledged by either race. In fact, each race pretended that it alone was a Civilized Intelligence, and that the other was bestial, contemptible, and of no account.

And it now occurred to both of them that they were, in equal measure, participants in the general concept of Humanity. (The ganzer egg was also a part, of course.)

The realization was awesome; but Marvin was still pinned to the ground by the ganzer's heavy paw.

"This leaves me in a somewhat embarrassing situation," the ganzer said, after a while. "My natural tendency is to release you; but I am working on this planet under a contract, which stipulates—"

"Then you are not a real ganzer?"

"No. I am a Swapper like yourself, and I come from Terra!"

"My home planet!" Marvin cried.

"I had guessed as much," the ganzer replied. "After a time one becomes sensitive to the idiosyncratic quality of differing minds, and learns to recognize one's countrymen through little tricks of thought and phraseology. I would guess that you are an American, probably from the East Coast, perhaps from Connecticut or Vermont—"

"New York State!" Marvin cried. "I am from Stanhope!"

"And I am from Saranac Lake," the ganzer said. "My name is Otis Dagobert, and I am thirty-seven years old."

And with that, the ganzer lifted his paw from Marvin's chest. "We are neighbors," he said quietly. "And so I cannot kill you, just as I am reasonably sure you would be unable to kill me, had you the opportunity. And now that we know the truth, I doubt if we will be able to perform any portion of our terrible jobs. But that is a sad thing to find out, for it means that we are doomed to Contractual Discipline; and then if we do not obey, our Companies will give us Extreme Severance. And you know what that means."

Marvin nodded sadly. He knew all too well. His head drooped, and he sat in disconsolate silence beside his newly found friend.

"I can think of no way out," Marvin said, after giving the matter some thought. "Perhaps we could hide in the forest for a few days, but they would be sure to find us."

Suddenly, the ganzer egg spoke up. "Come now, perhaps it isn't as hopeless as you think!"

"What do you mean?" Marvin asked.

"Well now," the ganzer egg said, dimpling with pleasure, "it seems to me that one good turn deserves another. I could get into plenty of hot water for this... But to hell with that. I think I can find a way off this planet for both of you."

Both Marvin and Otis broke into exclamations of gratitude; but the ganzer egg stopped them at once.

"Maybe you won't thank me when you see what lies ahead," he said ominously.

"Nothing could be worse than this," Otis said.

"You'd be surprised," the ganzer egg said flatly. "You might be very surprised… This way, gentlemen."

"But where are we going?" Marvin asked.

"I'm taking you to meet the Hermit," the ganzer egg replied, and would say no more. He rolled purposefully away, and Marvin and Otis followed.

CHAPTER 13

Through the rain forest wild and free of Ganzer (or Melde, depending upon your point of view), they marched and rolled, ever alert for danger. But no creature menaced them, and they came at last to a clearing in the forest. They saw a rude hut in the center of that clearing, and a humanoform creature dressed all in rags, squatting in front of the hut.

"That is the Hermit," said the ganzer egg. "He's quite insane."

The two Terrans had no time in which to consider that information. The Hermit arose and cried, "Now stand, hold, halt! Reveal yourselves to my understanding!"

"I'm Marvin Flynn," Marvin said, "and this is my friend Otis Dagobert. We want to escape from this planet."

The Hermit didn't seem to hear them; he stroked his long beard and gazed thoughtfully at the treetops. In low somber tones, he said:

> "Ere this moment came, a flight of geese
> Passed low o'erhead, presaging woe;
> The refuge and disconsolate owl did pass
> This hid'n' place of mine, bereft
> Of that which nature freely gives but man denies!
> The stars are silent when they light our home:
> The trees themselves proclaim the flight of kings."

"He means," the ganzer egg said, "that he had a feeling you'd be coming this way."

"Is he crazy or something?" Otis asked. "The way he talks—"

> "Now rede me this! I'll have no plattering roth
> To creep between the interstices of a mind
> Proclaiming treason,"

the Hermit said.

"He doesn't want you to whisper to each other," the ganzer egg translated. "It makes him suspicious."

"I could figure that much out for myself," Flynn said.

"So go screw yourself," the ganzer egg said. "I was just trying to be helpful."

The Hermit advanced several paces, halted, and said:

"What wot ye here aroon?"

Marvin looked at the ganzer egg, who remained obstinately silent. So, guessing at the meaning of the words, Marvin said, "Sir, we are trying to escape from this planet, and we have come to you for help."

The Hermit shook his head and said,

> "What barbrous tongue is this? A thick-mouthed sheep
> Would clothe his meaning in a sound more clear!"

"What does he mean?" Marvin asked.

"You're so smart, figure it out for yourself," the ganzer egg said.

"I'm sorry if I insulted you," Marvin said.

"Forget it, forget it."

"I really am sorry. I'd appreciate it if you'd translate for us."

"All right," the ganzer egg said, still a little sulkily. "He says he doesn't understand you."

"He doesn't? But what I said to him was clear enough."

"Not to him," the ganzer egg said. "You want to reach him, you'd better put it in meter."

"Me? I couldn't!" Marvin said, with that instinctual shudder of revulsion which all intelligent Terran males feel at the thought of verse. "I simply couldn't! Otis, maybe you—"

"Not me!" Otis said, alarmed. "What do you think I am? A fag?"

> "A silence swells and grows; yet honest men
> Speak bold, with well-formed mouth! Melikes it not
> What this development portends."

"He's getting edgy," the ganzer egg said. "You better have a shot at it."

"Perhaps you could do it for us," Otis suggested.

"I'm no fag," the ganzer egg sneered. "If you want to speak, you'll have to speak for yourselves."

"The only poem I can remember from school is the *Rubá'iyát*," Marvin said.

"Well, go to it," the ganzer egg said.

Marvin thought, twitched, and nervously said:

> "Behold! A pilgrim from the forest war
> Of race 'gainst race, does humbly implore

Your aid and sustenance, and help and hope.
Can you this humble earnest plea ignore?"

"Very shaky," whispered the ganzer egg. "But not bad for a first attempt." (Otis was giggling, and Marvin clouted him with his tail.)
The Hermit replied:

"Well spoken, stranger! You shall have this aid.
Nay, more! For when men meet, despite their divers
forms,
They needs must succor each one to his own."

More quickly now, Marvin replied:

"I hoped, in this ancient planetoid with dreams displayed
Of sunrise splendors, sunsets disarrayed,
That one poor pilgrim who did pass this way
Might find escape from terrors he surveyed."

The Hermit said:

"Step forward then, my friend, my liege, my lord,
For all men are consistent to that state
Which life shall bring to them; the veriest slave
May someday be the king of yonder peer,
While this man here, this enemy by rote
Of graven custom, shall at hand
Be cup companion, if his speech be known!"

Marvin stepped forward, saying:

"Much thanks! Your doorway to the stars
Fits wise man and fool; yet still it bars
The Mute, who through his foolish tongue unused
Won't even get one half the way to Mars."

Otis, who had been restraining his giggles through all this, now said:
"Hey! Were you saying something about me?"
"I certainly was," Marvin said. "You'd better start versifying if you want
to get out of here."
"Well, rats, you're doing it for both of us."
"Nope. The Hermit just said you have to speak for yourself."
"My God, what'll I do?" Otis muttered. "I don't know any poetry."

"You better think of something," the ganzer egg said.

"Well…all I can remember is a little Swinburne which some goopey girl talked to me once. It's pretty stupid stuff."

"Let's hear it," Marvin said.

Otis sweated and swotted, and at last intoned:

> "When the spaceships of Earth are on distant planets,
> The soul of a man, be he slender or tall,
> Desires his home, for it pulls like ten magnets,
> Filling his heart as great waves fill a hall.
> And the great green sensation of gratitude
> Is entranced by the welcoming attitude
> Of a heroic Hermit, whose modulent mood
> Is to rescue the spaceman and save him withal."

The Hermit said:

> "I find thee apt: 'Tis parlous to relate
> In these lean times a halting tongue may work
> Quick mischief 'pon its saddened owner-lord."

Marvin said:

> "Ah come, take Marvin Flynn away, and leave
> The Rest to wrangle! He would grieve
> To find his body torn and wounded; therefore now
> He'd like to go, whilst others stand and cheer."

The Hermit said:

> "Away then, gentlemen! Hearts high,
> Feet firm in stirrups, head uplifted be…"

And so they proceeded in sing-song fashion to the hermit's hut, where they saw, hidden away under some sheets of bark, an illegal Mindsender, of an ancient and curious design. And Marvin learned that there was method in even the direst madness. For the Hermit had been on this planet for less than a year, and already had made a considerable fortune by smuggling refugees to the less savory labor markets of the galaxy.

It was not ethical, but as the Hermit put it:

> "Call you it dastardly, then, the tricks I play
> With this my engine? Sobeit! Nay, I'll not dispute

The arid abstract trueness of your plea.
Yet think upon't; 'tis folly to refuse bad wine
When chok't with desert thirst. Not so? Then why
So harshly judge the salvor of your life?
'Tis damned ingratitude of most perversity—
To slap the hand that plucked Death's grip from thee!"

CHAPTER 14

A small amount of time passed. A job for Otis Dagobert had not been difficult to find. Despite his protestations to the contrary, the young man showed a small but very promising streak of sadism. Accordingly, the Hermit had Swapped him into the mind of a dental assistant on Prodenda IX. That planet, just to the left of the South Ridge stars if you come by way of Procyon, had been settled by a group of Terrans who felt strongly about fluorine, despising this chemical group as though it were the devil itself. On Prodenda IX they could live fluorine-free, with the assistance of many dental architects, as they were called.

The ganzer egg wished Marvin the best of good fortune and rolled off into the forest.

"And now," the Hermit said, "we come to the problem of you. It seems to me, considering your personality quite objectively, that you have a definite aptitude as a victim."

"Me?" Marvin asked.

"Yes, you," the Hermit replied.

"A victim?"

"Definitely a victim."

"I'm not so sure," Marvin replied. He stated it that way out of politeness; actually, he was quite sure the Hermit was wrong.

"Well, I'm sure," the Hermit said. "And I dare say I've had more experience in job placement than you."

"I suppose you have… I notice that you are no longer speaking in verse."

"Of course not," the Hermit said. "Why should I?"

"Because earlier," Marvin said, "you had been speaking only in verse."

"But that was entirely different," the Hermit said. "I was outside then. I had to protect myself."

"But what about now?"

"Now I am in my house and therefore quite safe. I have no need for the protective language of verse."

"Does verse really protect you outside?" Marvin asked.

"It certainly does. I have lived on this planet for over a year, hunted by two murderous races who would kill me on sight if they could find me.

And in that time I have suffered no harm whatsoever. What do you think about that?"

"Well, it's very fine, of course. But how do you know it's your language that protects you?"

"I infer it," the Hermit said. "It seems a reasonable enough assumption."

"Yes, sir," Marvin said. "But I don't quite see the relationship between your language and your safety."

"I'll be damned if I see it, either," the Hermit said. "I like to think of myself as a rational man, but the efficacy of verse is one thing that I am reluctantly forced to accept on faith. It *works;* what more can I say?"

"Have you ever thought of experimenting?" Marvin asked. "I mean, speaking outside *without* your language of verse? You might find you don't need it."

"So I might," the Hermit replied. "And if you tried walking on the ocean bottom, you might find that you didn't need air."

"It's not really the same thing," Marvin said.

"It's exactly the same thing," the Hermit told him. "All of us live by the employment of countless untested assumptions, the truth or falsehood of which we can determine only through the hazard of our lives. Since most of us value our lives more than the truth, we leave such drastic tests for the fanatics."

"I don't try to walk on water," Marvin said, "because I've seen men drown."

"And I," the Hermit said, "do not speak a prose language outside because I have seen too many men killed while speaking it; but I have not seen one single verse speaker killed."

"Well...to each his own."

"The acceptance of indeterminacy is the beginning of wisdom," the Hermit quoted. "But we were talking about you and victimization. I repeat, you have an aptitude, which opens the possibility of an extremely interesting position for you."

"I am not interested," Marvin said. "What else do you have available?"

"Nothing else," the Hermit said.

By a remarkable coincidence, Marvin heard at that moment a great crashing and thundering in the underbrush outside, and deduced that it was either the Meldens or the Ganzers, or both, coming in pursuit of him.

"I accept the job," Marvin said. "But you're wrong."

He had the satisfaction of the last word; but the Hermit had the satisfaction of the last deed. For, arranging his equipment and adjusting his dials, he closed the switch and sent Marvin off to his new career on the planet Celsus V.

CHAPTER 15

On Celsus V, the giving and receiving of gifts is a cultural imperative. To refuse a gift is unthinkable; the emotion it raises in a Celsian is comparable to the incest dread of a Terran. Normally, this causes no trouble. Most gifts are white gifts, intended to express various shades of love, gratitude, tenderness, etc. But there are also gray gifts of warning, and black gifts of death.

Thus, a certain public official received a handsome snout ring from his constituents. It was imperiously designed for two weeks' wear. It was a splendid object, and it had only one flaw. It ticked.

A creature of another race might have flung it into the nearest ditch. But no Celsian in his right mind would do that. He wouldn't even have the ring examined. Celsians live by the motto: Do not look a gift in the teeth. Besides, if word of his suspicion leaked out, it would cause an irreparable public scandal.

He had to wear that damned ring for two weeks.

But the damn thing was *ticking*.

The official, whose name was Marduk Kras, pondered the problem. He thought about his constituents, and various ways he had helped them, and various other ways he had failed them. The ring was a warning, that much was clear. It was *at best* a warning—a gray gift. At worst, it was a black gift—a small bomb of popular design, which would blow his head off after the elapse of several anxiety-ridden days.

Marduk was not suicidal; he knew that he could not wear that damned ring. But he also knew that he *had* to wear that damned ring. Thus, he found himself facing a classic Celsian dilemma.

"Would they do that to *me*?" Marduk asked himself. "Just because I re-zoned their dirty old residential neighborhood for heavy industry, and entered into an agreement with the Landlords' Guild to raise their rents 320 per cent in return for a promise of new plumbing within fifty years? I mean to say, good Lord, I've never pretended to be *omniscient;* I may have made mistakes here and there, I freely admit it. But is that sufficient cause to commit what anyone must view as a deeply antisocial act?"

The ring ticked merrily away, tickling his snout and alarming his senses. Marduk thought of other officials whose heads had been blown off by dimwitted hotheads. Yes, it might very possibly be a black gift.

"Those stupid molters!" Marduk snarled, relieving his feelings with an insult he would never have dared voice in public. He was feeling sorely aggrieved. You worked your hearts out for those slack-skinned, wart-nosed idiots, and what was your reward? A bomb to wear in your nose!

For one hectic moment he contemplated throwing the ring into the nearest chlorine tank. *That* would show them! And there was precedent for it. Had not the saintly Voreeg spurned the Total Offering of the Three Ghosts?

Yes… but the Ghosts' Offering, according to accepted exegesis, had been a subtle attack upon the spirit of Gift Giving, and therefore at the very core of society; for by making a Total Offering, they had precluded the possibility of any future gifts.

Besides—what was admirable for a Saint of the Second Kingdom would be execrable for a petty official of the Tenth Democracy. Saints can do anything; ordinary men must do what is expected of them.

Marduk's shoulders slumped. He plastered warm mud on his feet, but it brought no relief. There was no way out. One Celsian could not stand alone against organized society. He would have to wear the ring, and wait for the mind splitting moment when the tick stopped…

But wait! There was a way! Yes, yes, he could see it now! It would take clever arrangement; but if he brought it off, he could have safety *and* social approval. If only that damned ring gave him time…

Marduk Kras made several urgent calls, and arranged for himself to be ordered to the planet Taami II (the Tahiti of the Ten Star Region) on urgent business. Not corporeally, of course; no responsible official would spend local funds to ship his body across a hundred light years when all that was required was his mind. Frugal, trustworthy Marduk would travel by Mindswap. He would satisfy the form, if not the spirit, of Celsian custom by leaving his body behind with the gift ring ticking merrily in its nose.

He had to find a mind to inhabit his body during his absence. But that was not difficult. There are too many minds in the galaxy, and not enough bodies to go around. (Why this should be, no one really knows. After all, everyone was given one of each to begin with. But some people always seem to end up with more than they need, be it wealth, power, or bodies; and some with less.)

Marduk got in touch with Hermit Enterprises (Bodies for Any Purpose). The Hermit had just the thing for him: a cleancut young Terran male who was in imminent danger of losing his life, and was willing to take his chances with a ticking nose ring.

Thus Marvin Flynn came to Celsus V.

For once there was no need to hurry. Upon arrival, Marvin was able to follow prescribed Swapping procedure. He lay perfectly still, growing slowly accustomed to his new corpus. He tested his limbs, checked out his senses, and scanned the primary culture configuration load as radiated from the forebrain for analog and similitude factors. Then he sized up the hindbrain emotional end structure factor for crux, nadir and saddle-point. Nearly all of this was automatic.

He found the Celsian body a good fit, with a high aspect of jointure and an excellent main sequence random dispersion pattern. There were problems, of course: the delta curve was absurdly elliptic, and the UYP's (universal Y points) were falciform rather than trapezoidal. But you had to expect that on a Type 3B planet; under normal circumstances, it would never cause him any trouble.

Taken all in all, it was a body environmen -culture role cluster with which he could empathize and identify.

"Feels pretty good," Marvin summed up for himself. "If only that damned nose ring doesn't blow up."

He got up and took stock of his surroundings. The first thing he saw was a note that Marduk Kras had left for him, tied to his wrist so he wouldn't overlook it.

> Dear Swapper, [it read]
> Welcome to Celsus! I realize that you may not feel very welcome, under the circumstances, and I regret it nearly as much as you do. But I would advise you sincerely to put all thought of sudden demise out of your mind, and concentrate instead on having a pleasant vacation. It may console you to know that the statistical incidence of death by black gift is no greater than that of being killed in a plutonium-mine accident, if you happened to be a plutonium miner. So relax and enjoy yourself.
> My apartment and all that is in it are yours to enjoy. My body also, though I trust you will not overstrain it or keep it out too late or feed it an excess of intoxicating beverages. It has a weak left wrist, so be careful if you should have to lift any heavy weights. Good luck, and try not to worry, since anxiety never yet solved a problem.
> P.S. I know you are a gentleman and would not try to remove the nose ring. But I thought I should tell you that you can't anyhow because it is locked in place with a microscopic Jayverg Bonded Molecular Padlock. Goodbye again, and do try to put all this unpleasantness out of mind and enjoy your two weeks on our lovely planet.
> Your Sincere Friend,
> Marduk Kras

At first Marvin was irritated by the note. But then he laughed and crumpled it up. Marduk was undoubtedly a scoundrel, but he was a likeable one, and not ungenerous. Marvin decided to make the best of his dubious bargain, forget about the putative bomb nestling just above his lip, and enjoy his time on Celsus.

He went on an exploration of his new home, and was well satisfied with what he found. It was a bachelor burrow, designed for residence rather than for reproduction. Its main construction feature—pentabrachation—

reflected Kras' status as a public official. Less fortunate sorts had to get by with three or four gallery systems; and in the slums of North Bogger, whole families were crowded into wretched mono- and duo-brachate systems. Housing reform had been promised in the near future, however.

The kitchen was neat and modern, and well stocked with gourmet items. There were jars of candied annelids, and a bowl of exotic Alcyonium Salad mixture, and delicious tidbits of Tubipora, Pennatula, Gorgonia, and Renilla. There was a can of Goose Barnacle in rotifer and orchid sauce, and a quick frozen package of sweet and sour Uca. But—how like a bachelor—there were no staples, not even a gastropod loaf or a bottle of carbonated Ginger Honey.

Wandering down the long, curving galleries, Marvin found the music room. Marduk had not stinted here. A gigantic Imperial amplifier dominated the room, flanked by two Tyrant model speakers. Marduk used a Whirlpool semi-mix microphone, with a forty bbc. channel rejection, an "expanding" type sense discrimination selector, with a floating throat slot "passive" director. Pickup was by image regeneration, but there was provision for changing over to decay modulation. Although not professional in quality, it was a very good amateur rig.

The heart of the system, of course, was the Insectarium. This particular one was an Ingenuator, the Super Max model, with both automatic and manual selection and mixture controls, regulated feed and disposal, and various maximizing and minimizing features.

Marvin selected a grasshopper gavotte (Korestal, 431B) and listened to the thrilling tracheal obbligato and the subtle bass accompaniment of the paired Malphigian tubules. Although Marvin's appreciation was casual, he was well aware of the virtuoso ability of this particular performer: a Blue-Striped Grasshopper, his second thoracic segment pulsating slightly, visible in his own compartment of the Insectarium.

Leaning down, Marvin nodded in appreciation. The Blue-Striped Grasshopper clicked mandibles, then turned back to his music. (He had been bred especially for treble and brilliance, a flashy performer, more showy than sound. But Marvin did not know this.)

Marvin turned off the selection, flipped the status switch from Active to Dormant mode; the grasshopper went back to sleep. The Insectarium was well stocked, especially with Mayfly symphonies and the strange new cutworm songs, but Marvin had too much to explore to bother with music just now.

In the living room, Marvin lowered himself into a stately old clay bank (a genuine Wormstetter), rested his head against the well-worn granite headrest, and tried to relax. But the ring in his snout ticked away, a continual intrusion to his sense of well-being. He reached down and picked at random a quick-stick from a pile on a low table. He ran his antennae over the grooves, but it was no use. He couldn't concentrate on light fiction. Impatiently he threw the quick-stick aside and tried to make some plans.

But he was in the grip of an implacable dynamism. He had to assume that the moments of his life were severely limited, and those moments were passing away. He wanted to do something to commemorate his final hours. But what was there he could do?

He slid out of the Wormstetter and paced the main gallery, his claws clicking irritably. Then, coming to an abrupt decision, he went to the wardrobe room. Here he selected a new casing of gold-bronze chitin, and arranged it carefully over his shoulders. He plastered his facial bristles with perfumed glue, and arranged them *en brosse* over his cheeks. He applied a mild stiffener to his antennae, pointed them at a jaunty sixty degrees, and allowed them to droop in their attractive natural curve. Lastly, he dusted his midsection with Lavender Sand, and outlined his shoulder joints with lampblack.

Surveying himself in the mirror, he decided that the effect was not unpleasing. He was well dressed, but not dandified. Judging as objectively as he could, he decided that he was a presentable, rather scholarly-looking young fellow. Not a Squig Star by any means, but definitely not a drunfiler.

He left his burrow by the main entrance, and replaced the entrance plug.

It was dusk. Stars glittered overhead; they seemed no more numerous than the myriad lights in the entrances of the countless burrows, both commercial and private, which made up the pulsating heart of the city. The sight thrilled Marvin. Surely, surely, somewhere in the endless intertwining corridors of the great city, there would be that for him which would bring pleasure. Or, at least, a soft and forgetful surcease.

Thus, Marvin walked dolorously, yet with a tremulous hopefulness, toward the hectic and beckoning Main Groove of the city, there to find what chance held out for him or fate decreed.

CHAPTER 16

With a long rolling stride and a creaking of leather boots, Marvin Flynn strode down the wooden sidewalk. Faintly there came to him the mingled odors of sagebrush and chaparral. On either side of him the adobe walls of the town glittered under the moon like dull Mexican silver. From a nearby saloon there came the strident tones of a banjo—

Frowning deeply, Marvin stopped in mid-stride. Sagebrush? Saloons? What was going on around here?

"Something wrong, stranger?" a harsh voice intoned.

Flynn whirled. A figure stepped out of the shadows near the General Store. It was a saddlebum, a snuffling, slump-shouldered loafer with a dusty black hat crushed comically on his begrimed forehead.

"Yes, something is very wrong," Marvin said. "Everything seems—strange."

"'Tain't nothing to be alarmed about," the saddlebum reassured him. "You have merely changed your system of metaphoric reference, and the Lord knows there's no crime in that. As a matter of fact, you should be happy to give up those dreary animal-insect comparisons."

"There was nothing wrong with my comparisons," Marvin said. "After all, I am on Celsus V, and I *do* live in a burrow."

"So what?" the saddlebum said. "Haven't you any imagination?"

"I've got plenty of imagination!" Marvin said indignantly. "But that's hardly the point. I simply mean that it is inconsistent to think like a cowboy on Earth when one is actually a sort of molelike creature on Celsus."

"It can't be helped," the saddlebum said. "What's happened is, you've overloaded your analogizing faculty, thereby blowing a fuse. Accordingly, your perceptions have taken up the task of experimental normalization. This state is known as 'metaphoric deformation.' "

Now Marvin remembered the warning he had received from Mr. Blanders concerning this phenomenon. Metaphoric deformation, that disease of the interstellar traveler, had struck him suddenly and without warning.

He knew that he should be alarmed, but instead felt only a mild surprise. His emotions were consistent with his perceptions, since a change unperceived is a change unfelt.

"When," Marvin asked, "will I start to see things as they really are?"

"That last is a question for a philosopher," the saddlebum told him. "But speaking in a limited fashion, this particular syndrome will pass if you ever get back to Earth. But if you continue travelling the process of perceptual analogizing will increase; though occasional short-lived remissions into your primary situation-perception context may be expected."

Marvin found that interesting, but unalarming. He hitched up his jeans and said, "Waal, reckon a man's gotta play out the hand that's dealt to him, and I ain't about to stand here all night jawing about it. Just who are you, stranger?"

"I," said the saddlebum, with a certain smugness, "am he without whom your dialogue would be impossible. I am Necessity personified; without me, you would have had to remember the Theory of Metaphoric Deformation all by yourself, and I doubt that you are capable of it. You may cross my palm with silver."

"That's for gypsies," Marvin said scornfully.

"Sorry," the saddlebum said, without the least show of embarrassment. "Got a tailor-made?"

"Got the makings," Marvin said, flipping him a sack of Bull Durham. He contemplated his new companion for a moment, then said, "Waal, yore a mangy-looking critter, and it seems to me yore half jackass and half prairie dog. But I reckon I'm stuck with you no matter who you are."

"Bravo," the saddlebum said gravely. "You conquer change of context with that same sureness with which an ape conquers a banana."

"Reckon that's a tech highfalutin'," Marvin said equably. "What's the next move, perfesser?"

"We shall proceed," the saddlebum said, "to yonder saloon of evil repute."

"Yippee," Marvin said, and strode lean-hipped through the batwinged saloon doors.

Within the saloon, a female attached herself to Marvin's arm. She looked up at him with a smile of vermilion bas-relief. Her unfocused eyes were pencilled in imitation of gaiety; her flaccid face was painted with the lying hieroglyphics of animation.

"C'mon upstairs with me, kid," the grisly beldame cried. "Lotsa fun, lotsa laughs!"

"It is droll to realize," the saddlebum said, "that Custom has decreed this lady's mask, proclaiming that those who sell pleasure must portray enjoyment. It is a hard demand, my friends, and not imposed upon any other occupation. For note: the fishwife is allowed to hate herring, the vegetable man may be allergic to turnips, and even the newspaper boy is permitted his illiteracy. Not even the blessed saints are required to enjoy their holy martyrdoms. Only the humble sellers of pleasure are required, like Tantalus, to be forever expectant of an untouchable feast."

"Yer friend's a great little kidder, ain't he?" the termagant said. "But I like you best, baby, 'cause you make me go all mush inside."

From the virago's neck there hung a pendant upon which was strung in miniature a skull, a piano, an arrow, a baby's shoe, and a yellowed tooth.

"What are those?" Marvin asked.

"Symbols," she said.

"Of what?"

"Come on upstairs, and I'll show you, sweety-ass."

"And thus," the saddlebum intoned, "we perceive the true unmediated confrontation of the aroused feminine nature, 'gainst which our masculine fancies seem mere baby's toys."

"C'mon!" the harpy cried, wriggling her gross body in a counterfeit of passion all the more frightening because it was real. "Upstairs to bed!" she shouted, pressing against Marvin with a breast the size and consistency of an empty Mongolian saddlebag. "I'll really show ya somepin!" she cried, entwining his thews with a heavy white leg, somewhat grimy and heavily varicosed. "When ya git loved by *me*," she howled, "you'll damned well know you been loved!" And she ground lasciviously against him with her pudenda, which was as heavily armored as the forehead of a Tyrannosaurus.

"Well, er, thank you so terribly much anyhow," Marvin said, "but I don't think just at the moment I—"

"You don't want no *lovin'?*" the woman asked incredulously.

"Well, actually, I can't really say that I do."

The woman planted knobkerry fists on tom-tom hips and said, "That I should live to see this day!" But then she softened, and said, "Turn not away from Venus' sweet-perfumed home of pleasure! Thou must strive, sir, to overcome this most unseemly gesture of unmanliness. Come, my lord! The bugle sounds; it awaits thee now to mount and fiercely press thy charge!"

"Oh, I rather think not," Marvin said, laughing hollowly.

She seized him by the throat with a hand the size and shape of a Chilean poncho. "You'll do it *now,* you lousy cowardly inward-directed goddamn narcissist bastard, and you'll do it good and proper, or by Ares I'll snap your scrawny windpipe like a Michaelmas chicken!"

A tragedy seemed in the making, for the woman's passion rendered her incapable of a judicious modification of her demands, while Marvin's reputed great vaulting lance had shrunken to the size of a pea. (Thus blind nature, by defending him from one assault, tendered provocation for another.)

Luckily the saddlebum, following the dictates of his wit if not his predilection, snatched a fan out of his gun belt, leaned forward simpering, and tapped the enraged woman on her rhinocerine upper arm.

"Don't you dare hurt him!" the saddlebum said, his voice a squeaky contralto.

Marvin, quick if not apt, rejoindered, "Yes, tell her to stop *pawing* me! I mean to say it is simply too much, one cannot even stroll out of one's house in the evening without encountering some *disgraceful* incident—"

"Don't cry, for God's sake, don't cry!" the saddlebum said. "You know I can't stand it when you cry!"

"I am *not* crying!" Marvin said, snuffling. "It is just that she has ruined this shirt. Your present!"

"I'll get you another!" the saddlebum said. "But I cannot abide another scene!!"

The woman was staring at them slack-jawed, and Marvin was able to utilize her moment of inattention by taking a pry bar out of his tool kit, setting it under her swollen red fingers, and prying himself free of her grip. Seizing the dwindling moment of opportunity, Marvin and the saddlebum sprinted out the door, leaped around the corner, broadjumped across the street, and polevaulted to freedom.

CHAPTER 17

Once clear of the immediate danger, Marvin came abruptly to his senses. The scales of metaphoric deformation fell away for the moment, and he experienced a perceptual experiential remission. It was all too painfully apparent *now* that the "saddlebum" was actually a large parasite beetle of the species *S. Cthulu.* There could be no mistake about this, since the Cthulu beetle is characterized by a secondary salivary duct located just below and slightly to the left of the subesophegal ganglion.

These beetles feed upon borrowed emotions, their own having long ago atrophied. Typically, they lurk in dark and shadowy places, waiting for a careless Celsian to pass within range of their segmented maxilla. That is what happened to Marvin.

Realizing this, Marvin directed at the beetle an emotion of anger so powerful that the Cthulu, victim of its own hyperacute emotional receptors, fell over unconscious in the road. That done, Marvin readjusted his gold-bronze casing, stiffened his antennae, and continued down the road.

He came to a bridge that crossed a great flowing river of sand. Standing on the center span, he gazed downward into the black depths that rolled inexorably onwards to the mysterious sand sea. Half-hypnotized he gazed, the nose ring beating its quick tattoo of mortality three times faster than the beat of his hearts. And he thought:

Bridges are receptacles of opposed ideas. Their horizontal distance speaks to us of our transcendence; their vertical declivity reminds us unalterably of the imminence of failure, the sureness of death. We push outwards across obstacles, but the primordial fall is forever beneath our feet. We build, construct, fabricate; but death is the supreme architect, who shapes heights only that there may be depths.

O Celsians, throw your well-wrought bridges across a thousand rivers, and tie together the disparate contours of the planet; your mastery is for naught, for the land is still beneath you, still waiting, still patient. Celsians, you have a road to follow, but it leads assuredly to death. Celsians, despite your cunning, you have one lesson still to learn: the heart is fashioned to receive the spear, and all other effects are extraneous.

These were Marvin's thoughts as he stood on the bridge. And a great longing overcame him, a desire to be finished with desire, to forgo pleasure and pain, to quit the petty modes of achievement and failure, to have done with distractions, and get on with the business of life, which was death.

Slowly he climbed to the rail, and there stood poised over the twisting currents of sand. Then, out of the corner of his eye, he saw a shadow detach itself from a pillar, move tentatively to the rail, stand erect, poise itself over the abyss and lean precariously outwards—

"Stop! Wait!" Marvin cried. His own desire for destruction had been abruptly terminated. He saw only a fellow creature in peril.

The shadowy figure gasped, and abruptly lunged towards the yawning river below. Marvin moved simultaneously and managed to catch an ankle.

The ensuing wrench almost pulled him over the rail. But recovering quickly, Marvin attached suckers to the porous stone sidewalk, spread his lower limbs for maximum purchase, wrapped two upper limbs around a light pole, and maintained a tenacious grip with his remaining two arms.

There was a moment of charged equilibrium; then Marvin's strength prevailed over the weight of the would-be suicide. Slowly, carefully, Marvin pulled, shifting his grip from tarsus to tibia, hauling without respite until he had brought that person to a point of safety on the roadbed of the bridge.

All recollection of his own self-destructive desires had left him. He strode forward and grasped the suicider by the shoulders, shaking fiercely.

"You damned fool!" Marvin shouted. "What kind of a coward are you? Only an idiot or a madman takes an out like that. Haven't you any guts at all, you damned—"

He stopped in mid-expletive. The would-be suicide was facing him, trembling, eyes averted. And now Marvin perceived, for the first time, that he had rescued a woman.

CHAPTER 18

Later, in a private booth in a bridge side restaurant, Marvin apologized for his harsh words, which had been torn from him by shock rather than conviction. But the woman, gracefully clicking her claw, refused to accept his apology.

"Because you are right," she said. "My attempt was the act of an idiot or a madwoman, or both. Your analysis was correct, I fear. You should have let me jump."

Marvin perceived how fair she was. A small woman, coming barely to his upper thorax, she was exquisitely made. Her midbody had the true sweet cylinder curves, and her proud head sat slightly forward of her body at a heart-wrenching five degrees from the vertical. Her features were perfection, from the nicely bulged forehead to the angular sweep of jaw. Her twin ovipositors were modestly hidden behind a white satin sash, cut in princess style and revealing just a tantalizing suggestion of the shining green flesh beneath them. Her legs, all of them, were clad in orange windings, draped to reveal the lissome segmentation of the joints.

A would-be suicide she may have been; but she was also the most stunning beauty that Marvin had seen on Celsus. His throat went dry at the sight of her, and his pulse began to race. He found that he was staring at the white satin that concealed and revealed her high-tilted ovipositors. He turned away, and found that he was looking at the sensual marvel of a long, segmented limb. Blushing furiously, he forced himself to look at the puckered beauty scar on her forehead.

She seemed unconscious of his fervent attention. Unselfconsciously she said, "Perhaps we should introduce ourselves—under the circumstances!"

They both laughed immoderately at her witticism. "My name is Marvin Flynn," Marvin said.

"Mine is Phthistia Held," the young woman said.

"I'll call you Cathy, if you don't mind," Marvin said.

They both laughed again. Then Cathy grew serious. Taking note of the too-quick passage of time, she said, "I must thank you again. And now I must leave."

"Of course," Marvin said, rising. "When may I see you again?"

"Never," she said in a low voice.

"But I must!" Marvin said. "I mean to say, now that I've found you I can never let you go."

She shook her head sadly. "Once in a while," she murmured, "will you give one little thought to me?"

"We must not say goodbye!" Marvin said.

"Oh, you'll get by," she replied, not cruelly.

"I'll never smile again," Marvin told her.

"Somebody else will be taking my place," she predicted.

"You are temptation!" he shouted in a fury.

"We are like two ships that pass in the night," she corrected.

"Will we never meet again?" Marvin queried.

"Time alone can tell."

"My prayer is to be there with you," Marvin said hopefully.

"East of the Sun and West of the Moon," she intoned.

"You're mean to me," Marvin pouted.

"I didn't know what time it was," she said. "But I know what time it is now!" And so saying, she whirled and darted out the door.

Marvin watched her leave, then sat down at the bar. "One for my baby, and one for the road," he told the bartender.

"A woman's a two-face," the bartender commented sympathetically, pouring a drink.

"I got the mad-about-her-sad-without-her blues," Marvin replied.

"A fellow needs a girl," the bartender told him.

Marvin finished his drink and held out his glass.

"A pink cocktail for a blue lady," he ordered.

"She may be weary," the bartender suggested.

"I don't know why I love her like I do," Marvin stated. "But at least I do know why there's no sun up in the sky. In my solitude she haunts me like a tinkling piano in the next apartment. But I'll be around no matter how she treats me now. Maybe it was just one of those things; yet I'll remember April and her, and the evening breeze caressed the trees but not for me, and—"

There is no telling how long Marvin might have continued his lament had not a voice at the level of his ribs and two feet to his left whispered, "Hey, meester."

Marvin turned and saw a small, plump, raggedly dressed Celsian sitting on the next bar stool.

"What is it?" Marvin asked brusquely.

"You maybe want see thees muchacha so beautiful other time?"

"Yes, I do. But what can you—"

"I am private investigator tracer of lost persons satisfaction guaranteed or not one cent in tribute."

"What kind of an accent have you got?" Marvin asked.

"Lambrobian," the investigator said. "My name is Juan Valdez and I come from the fiesta lands below the border to make my fortune here in big city of the Norte."

"Sandback," the bartender snarled.

"What thees theeng you call me?" the little Lombrobian said, with suspicious mildness.

"I called you a sandback, you lousy little sandback," the bartender snarled.

"That ees what I thought," said Valdez. He reached into his cummerbund, took out a long, double-edged knife, and drove it into the bartender's heart, killing him instantly.

"I am a mild man, señor," he said to Marvin. "I am not a man quickly to take offense. Indeed, in my home village of Montana Verde de los Tres Picos, I am considered a harmless man. I ask nothing more than to be allowed to cultivate my peyote buds in the high mountains of Lombrobia under the shade of that tree which we call 'the sun hat,' for these are the bes' peyote buds in all the world."

"I can understand that," Marvin said.

"Yet still," Valdez said, more sternly, "when an exploitator del norte insults me, and by implication, defames those who gave me birth and nurtured me—why then, señor, a blinding red mist descends over my field of vision and my knife springs to my hand unaided, and proceeds from there nonstop to the heart of the betrayer of the children of the poor."

"It could happen to anyone," Marvin said.

"And yet," Valdez said, "despite my keen sense of honor, I am essentially childlike, intuitive, and easygoing."

"I had noticed that, as a matter of fact," Marvin said.

"But yet. Enough of that. Now, you wish hire me investigation find girl? But of course. El buen paño en el arca se vende, verdad?"

"Si, hombre," Marvin replied, laughing. "Y el desco vence al miedo!"

"Pues, adelante!" And arm in arm the two comrades marched out into the night of a thousand brilliant stars like the lance points of a mighty host.

CHAPTER 19

Once outside the restaurant, Valdez turned his moustached brown face to the heavens and located the constellation Invidius, which, in northern latitudes, points unerringly to the north-north-east. With this as a base line, he established cross references, using the wind on his cheek (blowing west at five miles per hour), and the moss on the trees (growing on the northerly sides of decidupis trunks at one millimeter per diem). He allowed for a westerly error of one foot per mile (drift), and a southerly error of five inches per hundred yards (combined tropism effects). Then, with all factors accounted for, he began walking in a south-south-westerly direction.

Marvin followed. Within an hour they had left the city, and were proceeding through a stubbled farming district. Another hour put them beyond the last signs of civilization, in a wilderness of tumbled granite and greasy feldspar.

Valdez showed no signs of stopping, and Marvin began to feel vague stirrings of doubt.

"Just where, exactly, are we going?" he asked at last.

"To find your Cathy," Valdez replied, his teeth flashing white in his good-humored burnt-sienna face.

"Does she really live this far from the city?"

"I have no idea where she lives," Valdez replied, shrugging.

"You don't?"

"No, I don't."

Marvin stopped abruptly. "But you said that you did know!"

"I never said or implied that," Valdez said, his umber forehead wrinkling. "I said that I would help you find her."

"But if you don't know where she lives—"

"It is quite unimportant," Valdez said, holding up a stern musteline forefinger. "Our quest has nothing to do with finding where Cathy *lives;* our quest, pure and simple, is to find *Cathy.* That, at least, was my understanding."

"Yes, of course," Marvin said. "But if we're not going to where she lives, then where are we going?"

"To where she weel be," Valdez replied serenely.

"Oh," Marvin said.

They walked on through towering mineral marvels, coming at last into scrubby foothills that lay like tired walruses around the gleaming blue whale of a lofty mountain range. Another hour passed, and Marvin again grew disquieted. But this time he expressed his anxiety in a roundabout fashion, hoping by guile to gain insight.

"Have you known Cathy long?" he asked.

"I have never had the good fortune to meet her," Valdez replied.

"Then you saw her for the first time in the restaurant with me?"

"Unfortunately I did not even see her there, since I was in the men's room passing a kidney stone during the time of your conversation with her. I may have caught a glimpse of her as she turned from you and departed; but more likely I saw only the Doppler effect produced by the swinging red door."

"Then you know nothing whatsoever about Cathy?"

"Only the little I have heard from you, which, frankly, amounts to practically nothing."

"Then how," Marvin asked, "can you possibly take me to where she will be?"

"It is simple enough," Valdez said. "A moment's reflection should clear the matter for you."

Marvin reflected for several moments, but the matter stayed refractory.

"Consider it logically," Valdez said. "What is my problem? *To find Cathy.* What do I know about Cathy? Nothing."

"That doesn't sound so good," Marvin said.

"But it is only half of the problem. Granted that I know nothing about Cathy, what do I know about *Finding?*"

"What?" Marvin asked.

"It happens that I know everything about Finding," Valdez said triumphantly, gesturing with his graceful terracotta hands. "For it happens that I am an expert in the Theory of Searches!"

"The what?" Marvin asked.

"The Theory of Searches!" Valdez said, a little less triumphantly.

"I see," Marvin said, unimpressed. "Well...that's great, and I'm sure it's a very good theory. But if you don't know anything about Cathy, I don't see how any theory will help."

Valdez sighed, not unpleasantly, and touched his moustache with a puce-colored hand. "My friend, if you knew all about Cathy—her habits, friends, desires, dislikes, hopes, fears, dreams, intentions, and the like—do you think you would be able to find her?"

"I'm sure I could," Marvin said.

"Even without knowing the Theory of Searches?"

"Yes."

"Well then," Valdez said, "apply that same reasoning to the reverse condition. I know all there is to know about the Theory of Searches, and therefore I need to know nothing about Cathy."

"Are you sure it's the same thing?" Marvin asked.

"It has to be. After all, an equation is an equation. Solving from one end may take longer than from the other end, but cannot affect the outcome. In fact, we are really quite fortunate to know nothing about Cathy. Specific data sometimes has a way of interfering with the well-wrought operation of a theory. But we shall suffer no such discomfiture in this instance."

They marched steadily upwards, across the steepening face of a mountain slope. A bitter wind screamed and buffeted at them, and patches of hoar-frost began to appear underfoot. Valdez talked about his researches into the Theory of Searches, citing the following typical cases: Hector looking for Lysander, Adam questing after Eve, Galahad reconnoitering for the Holy Grail, Fred C. Dobbs' seeking the Treasure of the Sierra Madre, Edwin Arlington Robinson's perquisitions for colloquial self-expression in a typically American milieu, Gordon Sly's investigations of Naiad McCarthy, energy's pursuit of entropy, God's hunt for man, and Yang's pursual of Yin.

"From these specifics," Valdez said, "we derive the general notion of Search and its most important corollaries."

Marvin was too miserable to answer. It had suddenly occurred to him that one could die in this chill and waterless wasteland.

"Amusingly enough," Valdez said, "the Theory of Searches forces upon us the immediate conclusion that nothing can be truly (or ideally) lost. Consider: for a thing to be *lost*, it would require *a place to be lost in*. But no such place can be found, since simple multiplicity carries no implication of qualitative differentiation. In Search terms, every place is like every other place. Therefore, we replace the concept *lost* with the concept of *indeterminate placement*, which, of course, is susceptible to logico-mathematical analysis."

"But if Cathy isn't really lost," Marvin said, "then we can't really find her."

"That statement is true, as far as it goes," Valdez said. "But of course, it is merely Ideal notion, and of little value in this instance. For operational purposes we must modify the Theory of Searches. In fact, we must reverse the major premise of the theory and reaccept the original concepts of Lost and Found."

"It sounds very complicated," Marvin said.

"The complication is more apparent than real," Valdez reassured him. "An analysis of the problem yields the result. We take the proposition: 'Marvin searches for Cathy.' That seems fairly to describe our situation, does it not?"

"I think it does," Marvin said cautiously.

"Well then, what does the statement imply?"

"It implies—it implies that I search for Cathy."

Valdez shook his nut-brown head in annoyance. "Look deeper, my impatient young friend! Identity is not inference! The statement expresses the activity of your quest, and therefore implies the passivity of Cathy's state-of-being lost. But this cannot be true. Her passivity is unacceptable, since ultimately one searches for oneself, and no one is exempt from that search. We must accept Cathy's search for you (herself), just as we accept your search for her (yourself). Thus we achieve our primary permutation: 'Marvin searches for Cathy who searches for Marvin.' "

"Do you really think she's looking for me?" Marvin asked.

"Of course she is, whether she knows it or not. After all, she is a person in her own right; she cannot be considered an Object, a mere something lost. We must grant her autonomy, and realize that if you find her, then, equally, she finds you."

"I never thought of that," Marvin said.

"Well, it's simple enough once you understand the theory," Valdez said. "Now, to ensure our success, we must decide upon the optimum form of Search. Obviously, if both of you are actively questing, your chances of finding each other are considerably lessened. Consider two people seeking one another up and down the endless crowded aisles of a great department store, and contrast that with the improved strategy of one seeking, and the other standing at a fixed position and waiting to be found. The mathematics are a little intricate, so you will just have to take my word for it. The best chance of you/her finding her/you will be for one to search, and the other to allow himself/herself to be searched for. Our deepest folk wisdom has always known this, of course."

"So what do we do?"

"I have just told you!" Valdez cried. "One must search, the other must wait. Since we have no control over Cathy's actions, we assume that she is following her instincts and looking for you. Therefore you must fight down your instincts and wait, thereby allowing her to find you."

"All I do is wait?"

"That's right."

"And you really think she'll find me?"

"I would stake my life on it."

"Well...all right. But in that case, where are we going now?"

"To a place where you will wait. Technically, it is called a Location-Point."

Marvin looked confused, so Valdez explained further. "Mathematically, all places are of equal potentiality insofar as the chances of her finding you are concerned. Therefore we are able to choose an arbitrary Location-Point."

"What Location-Point have you chosen?" Marvin asked.

"Since it made no real difference," Valdez said, "I selected the village of Montana Verde de los Tres Picos, in Adelante Province, in the country of Lombrobia."

"That's your home town, isn't it?" Marvin asked.

"As a matter of fact, it is," Valdez said, mildly surprised and amused. "That, I suppose, is why it came so quickly to my mind."

"Isn't Lombrobia a long way off?"

"A considerable distance," Valdez admitted. "But our time will not be wasted, since I will teach you logic, and also the folksongs of my country."

"It isn't fair," Marvin muttered.

"My friend," Valdez told him, "when you accept help, you must be prepared to take what one is capable of giving, not what you would like to receive. I have never denied my human limitations; but it is ungrateful of you to refer to them."

Marvin had to be content with that, since he didn't think he could find his way back to the city unaided. So they marched on through the mountains, and they sang many folksongs, but it was too cold for logic.

CHAPTER 20

Onwards they marched, up the polished mirror face of a vast mountain. The wind whistled and screamed, tore at their clothing and tugged at their straining fingers. Treacherous honeycomb ice crumpled under their feet as they struggled for footholds, their buffeted bodies plastered to the icy mountain wall and moving leechlike up its dazzling surface.

Valdez bore up through it all with a saintlike equanimity. "Eet ees deefecult," he grinned. "And yet—for the love which you bear for thees woman—eet ees all worthwhile, si?"

"Yeah, sure," Marvin mumbled. "I guess it is." But in truth, he was beginning to doubt it. After all, he had known Cathy only for less than an hour.

An avalanche thundered past them, and tons of white death screamed past—inches from their strained and clinging bodies. Valdez smiled with serenity. Flynn frowned with anxiety.

"Beyond all obstacles," Valdez intoned, "lies that summit of accomplishment which is the face and form of the beloved."

"Yeah, sure," Marvin said.

Spears of ice, shaken loose from a high dokalma, whirled and flashed around them. Marvin thought about Cathy and found that he was unable to remember what she looked like. It struck him that love at first sight was overrated.

A high precipice loomed before them. Marvin looked at it, and at the shimmering ice fields beyond, and came to the conclusion that the game was really not worth the candle.

"I think," Marvin said, "that we should turn back."

Valdez smiled subtly, pausing on the very edge of the vertiginous descent into that wintry hell of suicidally shaped snow slides.

"My frien'," he said, "I know why you say this."

"You do?" Marvin asked.

"Of course. It is obvious that you do not wish me to risk my life on the continuance of your insensate and magnificent quest. And it is equally obvious that you intend to plunge on, alone."

"It is?" Marvin asked.

"Certainly. It would be apparent to the most casual observer that you are driven to seek your love through any and all dangers, by virtue of the unyielding nature of your personality. And it is equally clear that your generous and high-spirited mentality would be disturbed at the idea of involving one whom you consider a close friend and bosom companion in so perilous a venture."

"Well," Marvin began, "I'm not sure—"

"But I am sure," Valdez said. "And I reply to your unspoken question as follows: Friendship bears this similarity to love: it transcends all limits."

"Huh," Marvin said.

"Therefore," Valdez said, "I shall not abandon you. We shall go on together, into the maw of death, if need be, for the sake of your beloved Cathy."

"Well, that's very nice of you," Marvin said, eyeing the precipice ahead. "But I really didn't know Cathy very well, and I don't know how well suited we would be; so all in all, maybe it would be best if we got out of here—"

"Your words lack conviction, my young friend," Valdez laughed. "I beg of you not to worry about my safety."

"As a matter of fact," Marvin said, "I was worrying about *my* safety."

"No use!" Valdez cried gaily. "Hot passion betrays the studied coolness of your words. Forward, my friend!"

Valdez seemed determined to force him to Cathy's side whether he wanted to go or not. The only solution seemed to be a quick blow to the jaw, after which he would drag Valdez and himself back to civilization. He edged forward.

Valdez edged back. "Ah no, my friend!" he cried. "Again, overweening love has rendered your motives transparent. To knock me out, is it not? Then, after making sure I was safe and comfortable and well provisioned, you would plunge alone into the white wilderness. But I refuse to comply. We go on together, compadre!"

And, shouldering all their provisions, Valdez began his descent of the precipice. Marvin could do nothing but follow.

We shall not bore the reader with an account of that great march across the Moorescu Mountains, nor with the agonies suffered by the love-dazzled young Flynn and his steadfast companion. Nor shall we delineate the strange hallucinations that beset the travellers, nor the temporary state of insanity that Valdez suffered when he thought he was a bird and able to fly across thousand-foot drops. Nor would any but the scholarly be interested in the psychological process by which Marvin was moved, through a contemplation of his own sacrifices, to a fondness for the young lady in question, and then to a strong fondness, and then to a sensation of love, and then to an overweening passion of love.

Suffice it to say that all of these things happened, and that the journey across the mountains occupied many days and brought about many emotions. And at last it came to an end.

Arriving at a last mountain crest, Marvin looked down and saw, instead of ice fields, green pastures and rolling forests under a summer sun, and a little village nestled in the crook of a gentle river.

"Is—is that—?" Marvin began.

"Yes, my son," Valdez said quietly. "That is the village of Montana de los Tres Picos, in Adelante Province, in the country of Lombrobia, in the valley of the Blue Moon."

Marvin thanked his old guru—for no other name was applicable to the role that the devious and saintly Valdez had played—and began his descent to the Location-Point where his wait for Cathy would begin.

CHAPTER 21

Montana de los Tres Picos! Here, surrounded by crystal lakes and high mountains, a simple, good-hearted peasantry engage in unhurried labor beneath the swan-necked palms. At midday and midnight one may hear the plaintive notes of a guitar echo down the crenellated walls of the old castle. Nut-brown maidens tend the dusty grape vines while a moustached cacique watches, his whip curled sleepily on his hairy wrist.

To this quaint memento of a bygone age came Flynn, led by the faithful Valdez.

Just outside the village, on a gentle rise of land, there was an inn, or posada. To this place Valdez directed them.

"But is this really the best place to wait?" Marvin asked.

"No, it is not," Valdez said, with a knowing smile. "But by choosing it instead of the dusty town square, we avoid the fallacy of the 'optimum.' Also, it is more comfortable here."

Marvin bowed to the moustached man's superior wisdom and made himself at home in the posada. He settled himself at an outdoor table that commanded a good view of the courtyard and of the road beyond it. He fortified himself with a flagon of wine, and proceeded to fulfill his theoretical function as called for by the Theory of Searches: viz., he waited.

Within the hour, Marvin beheld a tiny dark figure moving slowly along the gleaming white expanse of the road. Closer it came, the figure of a man no longer young, his back bent beneath the weight of a heavy cylindrical object. At last the man raised his haggard head and stared directly into Marvin's eyes.

"Uncle Max!" Marvin cried.

"Why, hello, Marvin," Uncle Max replied. "Would you mind pouring me a glass of wine? This is a very dusty road."

Marvin poured the glass of wine, scarcely believing the testimony of his senses; for Uncle Max had unaccountably disappeared some ten years ago. He had last been seen playing golf at the Fairhaven Country Club.

"What happened to you?" Marvin asked.

"I stumbled into a time warp on the twelfth hole," Uncle Max said. "If you ever get back to Earth, Marvin, you might speak to the club manager about it. I have never been a *complainer;* but it seems to me that the greens committee ought to know about this, and possibly build a small fence or other enclosing structure. I do not care so much for myself, but it might cause a nasty scandal if a child fell in."

"I'll certainly tell them," Marvin said. "But, Uncle Max, where are you going now?"

"I have an appointment in Samarra," Uncle Max said. "Thank you for the wine, my boy, and take good care of yourself. By the way; did you know that your nose is ticking?"

"Yes," Marvin said. "It's a bomb."

"I suppose you know what you're doing," Max said. "Goodbye, Marvin."

And Uncle Max trudged away down the road, his golf bag swinging from his back and a number two iron in his hand as a walking-stick. Marvin settled back to wait.

Half an hour later, Marvin spied the figure of a woman hurrying down the road. He felt a rising sensation of anticipation, but then slumped back in his chair. It was not Cathy after all. It was only his mother.

"You're a long way from home, Mom," he said quietly.

"I know, Marvin," his mother said. "But you see, I was captured by white slavers."

"Gosh, Mom! How did it happen?"

"Well, Marvin," his mother said, "I was simply taking a Christmas basket to a poor family in Cutpurse Lane, and there was a police raid, and various other things happened, and I was drugged and awoke in Buenos Aires in a luxurious room with a man standing near me and leering and asking me in broken English if I *wanted a little fun.* And when I said no, he bent down and clasped me in his arms in an embrace that was plainly designed to be lecherous."

"Gosh! What happened then?"

"Well," his mother said, "I was lucky enough to remember a little trick that Mrs. Jasperson had told me. Did you know that you can kill a man by striking him forcibly under the nose? Well, it actually does work. I didn't like to do it, Marvin, although it seemed a good idea at the time. And so I found myself in the streets of Buenos Aires and one thing led to another and here I am."

"Won't you have some wine?" Marvin asked.

"That's very thoughtful of you," his mother said, "but I really must be on my way."

"Where?"

"To Havana," his mother said. "I have a message for Garcia. Marvin, have you a cold?"

"No, I probably sound funny because of this bomb in my nose."

"Take care of yourself, Marvin," his mother said, and hurried on.

Time passed. Marvin ate his dinner on the portico, washed it down with a flagon of Sangre de Hombre '36, and settled back in the deep shadow cast by the whitewashed palladium. The sun stretched its golden bottom toward the mountain peaks. Down the road, the figure of a man could be seen hurrying past the inn...

"Father!" Marvin cried.

"Good afternoon, Marvin," his father said, startled but hiding it well. "I must say, you turn up in some unexpected places."

"I could say the same of you," Marvin said.

His father frowned, adjusted his necktie and changed his briefcase to the other hand. "There is nothing strange about me being here," he told his son. "Usually your mother drives me home from the station. But today she was delayed, and so I walked. Since I was walking, I decided to take the shortcut which goes over one side of the golf course."

"I see," Marvin said.

"I will admit," his father continued, "that this shortcut seems to have become a 'long' cut, as one might express it, for I estimate that I have been walking through this countryside for the better part of an hour, if not longer."

"Dad," Marvin said, "I don't know how to tell you this, but the fact is, you are no longer on Earth."

"I find nothing humorous about a remark like that," his father stated. "Doubtless I have gone out of my way, nor is the style of architecture what I would normally expect to find in New York State. But I am quite certain that if I continue along this road for another hundred yards or so, it will lead into Annandale Avenue, which in turn will take me to the intersection of Maple Street and Spruce Lane. From there, of course, I can easily find my way home."

"I suppose you're right," Marvin said. He had never been able to win an argument from his father.

"I must be getting along," his father said. "By the way, Marvin, were you aware that you have some sort of obstruction in your nose?"

"Yes sir," Marvin said. "It's a bomb."

His father frowned deeply, pierced him with a glance, shook his head regretfully, and marched on down the road.

"I don't understand it," Marvin remarked later to Valdez. "Why are all of these people finding me? It just doesn't seem natural."

"It isn't natural," Valdez assured him. "But it *is* inevitable, which is much more important."

"Maybe it is inevitable," Marvin said. "But it is also highly improbable."

"True," Valdez agreed. "Although we prefer to call that a forced-probability; which is to say, it is an indeterminate concomitant of the Theory of Searches."

"I'm afraid I don't fully understand that," Marvin said.

"Well, it's simple enough. The Theory of Searches is a pure theory; which is to say that on paper it works every time, with no conceivable refutation. But once we take the pure and ideal and attempt to make practical applications, we encounter difficulties, the foremost of which is the phenomenon of indeterminacy. To put it in its simplest terms, what happens is this: the presence of the Theory interferes with the working of the Theory. You see, the Theory cannot take into account the effect of its own existence upon itself. Ideally, the Theory of Searches exists in a universe in which there is no Theory of Searches. But practically—which is our concern here—the Theory of Searches exists in a world in which there *is* a Theory of Searches, which has what we call a 'mirroring' or 'doubling' effect upon itself. According to some thinkers, there is a very real danger of 'infinite duplication,' in which the Theory endlessly modifies itself in terms of prior modifications of the Theory by the Theory, coming at last to a state of entropy, in which all possibilities are equally valued. This argument is known as Van Gruemann's Fallacy, in which the error of implying causality to mere sequence is self-evident. Does it become more clear?"

"I think so," Marvin said. "The only thing I don't understand is, exactly what effect does the existence of the Theory have upon the Theory?"

"I thought I had explained that," Valdez said. "The primary, or 'natural' effect of a Theory of Searches upon a Theory of Searches is of course to increase the value of lambda-chi."

"Hmm," said Marvin.

"Lambda-chi is, of course, the symbolic representation of the inverse ratio of all possible searches to all possible finds. Thus, when lambda-chi is increased through indeterminacy or other factors, the possibility of search-failure is rapidly reduced to a figure near zero, while the possibility of search-success expands quickly toward one. This is known as the Set-Expansion Factor.

"Does that mean," Marvin asked, "that because of the effect of the Theory of Searches on the Theory of Searches, which results in the Set-Expansion Factor, that all searches will be successful?"

"Exactly," Valdez said. "You have expressed it beautifully, though perhaps with insufficient rigor. All possible searches will be successful during the time, or duration, of the Set-Expansion Factor."

"I understand now," Marvin said. "According to the theory, I must find Cathy."

"Yes," Valdez said. "You must find Cathy; as a matter of fact, you must find everyone. The only limitation is the Set-Expansion Factor, or S-E."

"Oh?" Marvin asked.

"Well, naturally, all searches can only be successful during the time, or duration, of S-E. But the duration of S-E is a variable which can last no less than 6.3 microseconds and no more than 1,005.34543 years."

"How long will S-E last in my particular case?" Marvin asked.

"A lot of us would like to know the answer to that one," Valdez said, with a hearty chuckle.

"You mean that you don't know?"

"I mean that it has been the labor of several lifetimes simply to discover the existence of the Set-Expansion Factor. To determine an exact numerical solution for it for all possible cases would be possible, I suppose, if S-E were a mere variable. But it happens to be a contingent variable, which is a very different kettle of fish. You see, the calculus of contingencies is a rather new branch of mathematics, and one that no one can pretend to have mastered."

"I was afraid of that," Marvin said.

"Science is a cruel taskmaster," Valdez agreed. Then he winked cheerfully and said, "But of course, even the cruellest taskmasters can be evaded."

"Do you mean to say there is a solution?" Marvin cried.

"Not a legitimate one, unfortunately," Valdez said. "It is what we Search Theorists call a 'bootleg solution.' That is to say, it is a pragmatic application of a formula that, statistically, has had a high degree of correlation with required solutions. But as a theory, there are no rational grounds for presuming its validity."

"Still," Marvin said, "if it works, let's try it out."

"I would really rather not," Valdez said. "Irrational formulae, no matter what their apparent degree of success, are distasteful to me, containing, as they do, distressing hints that the supreme logic of mathematics might be founded ultimately upon gross absurdities."

"I insist," Marvin said. "After all, I am the one who is Searching."

"That has nothing to do with it, mathematically speaking," Valdez said. "But I suppose you would give me no peace unless I indulged you."

Valdez sighed unhappily, schlepped a piece of paper and a stub pencil out of his rebozo, and asked, "How many coins do you have in your pocket?"

Marvin looked and replied, "Eight."

Valdez wrote down the result, then asked for the date of Marvin's birth, his social security number, his shoe size, and height in centimeters. To this he gave a numerical value. He asked Marvin to pick a number at random between 1 and 14. With this, he added several figures of his own, then scribbled and calculated for several minutes.

"Well?" Marvin asked.

"Remember, this result is merely statistically probable," Valdez said, "and has no other grounds for credence."

Marvin nodded. Valdez said, "The duration of the Set-Expansion Factor, in your particular case, is due to expire in exactly one minute and forty-eight seconds, plus or minus five minimicroseconds."

Marvin was about to protest vehemently about the unfairness of this, and to ask why Valdez hadn't made that vital calculation earlier. But then he looked down upon the road, now glowing a singular white against the rich blue of evening.

He saw a figure moving slowly towards the posada.

"Cathy!" Marvin cried. For it was she.

"Search completed with forty-three seconds of the Set-Expansion Factor unelapsed," Valdez noted. "Another experimental validation of Search Theory."

But Marvin did not hear him, for he had rushed down to the road, and there clasped the long-lost beloved in his arms. And Valdez, the wily old friend and taciturn companion of the Long March, smiled tightly to himself and ordered another bottle of wine.

CHAPTER 22

And so they were together at last—beautiful Cathy, star-crossed and planet-haunted, drawn by the strange alchemy of the Location-Point; and Marvin, young and strong, with his swallow's- flash smile in a tanned, good-humored face, Marvin, setting out with a young man's audacity and easy confidence to conquer the challenge of an old and intricate universe, with Cathy at his side, younger than he in years, yet vastly older in her woman's inherited store of intuitive wisdom; lovely Cathy, whose fine dark eyes seemed to hold a brooding sorrow, an elusive shadow of anticipated sadness that Marvin was unaware of except to feel a great and almost over-whelming desire to protect and cherish this seemingly fragile girl with her secret, that she could not reveal, who had come at last to him, a man without a secret that he could reveal.

Their happiness was flawed and ennobled. There was the bomb in Marvin's nose, ticking away the inexorable seconds of his destiny, providing a strict metronomic measure for their dance of love. But this sense of foredoomedness caused their opposed destinies to twine closer, and it informed their relationship with grace and meaning.

He created waterfalls for her out of the morning dew, and from the colored pebbles of a meadow stream he made a necklace more beautiful than emeralds, sadder than pearls. She caught him in her net of silken hair, she carried him down, down, into deep and silent waters, past obliteration. He showed her frozen stars and molten sun; she gave him long, entwined shadows and the sound of black velvet. He reached out to her and touched moss, grass, ancient trees, iridescent rocks; her fingertips, striving upwards, brushed old planets and silver moonlight, the flash of comets and the cry of dissolving suns.

They played games in which he died and she grew old; they did it for the sake of the joyous rebirth. They dissected time with love, and put it back together longer, better, slower. They invented toys out of mountains, plains, lakes, valleys. Their souls glistened like healthy fur.

They were lovers, they could conceive of nothing but love. But some things hated them. Dead stumps, barren eagles, stagnant ponds—these things resented their happiness. And certain urgencies of change ignored their declarations, indifferent to human intentions and content to continue their work of breaking down the universe. Certain conclusions, resistant to transformation, hastened to comply with ancient directives written on the bones, stencilled on the blood, tattooed on the inner side of the skin.

There was a bomb that needed explosion; there was a secret that required betrayal. And out of fear came knowledge, and sadness.

And one morning, Cathy was gone as if she had never been.

CHAPTER 23

Gone! Cathy was gone! Could it be possible? Could life, that deadpan practical joker, be up to his disastrous tricks again?

Marvin refused to believe it. He searched the confines of the posada, and he poked patiently through the little village beyond it. She was gone. He continued his search in the nearby city of San Ramon de las Tristezas, and he questioned waitresses, landlords, shopkeepers, whores, policemen, pimps, beggars, and other inhabitants. He asked if they had seen a girl fair as the dawn, with hair of indescribable beauty, limbs of a previously unheard-of felicity, features whose comeliness was matched only by their harmony, etc. And those he questioned sadly replied, "Alas, señor, we have not seen thees woman, not now or ever in our lives."

He calmed himself enough to give a coherent description, and found a road-mender who had seen a girl like Cathy traveling west in a large automobile with a bulky, cigar-smoking man. And a chimney sweep had spied her leaving town with her little gold and blue handbag. Her step had been firm. She had not looked back.

Then a gas station attendant gave him a hastily scrawled note from Cathy that began, "Marvin dear, please try to understand and forgive me. As I tried to tell you so many times, it was necessary for me—"

The rest of the note was illegible. With the aid of a cryptanalyst, Marvin deciphered the closing words, which were: "But I shall always love you, and I hope you can find it in your heart to think of me occasionally with kindness. Your Loving Cathy."

The rest of the note, made enigmatic by grief, was unsusceptible to human analysis.

To describe Marvin's emotion would be like trying to describe the dawn flight of the heron: both are ineffable and unspeakable. Suffice it to say that Marvin considered suicide, but decided against it, since it seemed entirely too superficial a gesture.

Nothing was enough. Intoxication was merely maudlin, and renunciation of the world seemed no more than the act of a peevish child. Because of the inadequacy of the attitudes open to him, Marvin struck none. Dry-eyed and zombie-like he moved through his days and nights. He walked, he talked, he even smiled. He was unfailingly polite. But it seemed to his dear friend Valdez that the real Marvin had vanished in an instantaneous explosion of sorrow, and that in his place there walked a poorly modelled representation of a man. Marvin was gone; the ringer who moved in his place looked as if, in its unfailing mimicry of humanness, it might collapse at any moment from strain.

Valdez was both perplexed and dismayed. Never had the wily old Master of Searches seen such a difficult case. With desperate energy he tried to rally his friend out of his living death.

He tried sympathy: "I know exactly how you feel, my unfortunate companion, for once, when I was quite a young man, I had quite a comparable experience, and I found—"

That did nothing, so Valdez tried brutality: "Christ damn me for a winnieburne, but are ye still mawking abaht after that bit of fluff wot walked out on yer? Now by God's wounds, I tell thee this: there's women past counting in this world of ours, and the man's no man who'd curl himself up in the corner when there's good lovin' to be had without…"

No response. Valdez tried eccentric distraction:

"Look, look over there, I see three birds on a limb, and one has a knife thrust through its throat and a scepter clutched in its claw, and yet it sings more merrily than the others! What do you make of it, eh?"

Marvin made nothing of it. Undismayed, Valdez tried to rouse his friend by piteous self-referral:

"Well, Marvin, lad, the medics have taken a look at the skin rash of mine and it seems that it's a case of pandemic impetigo. They give me twelve hours on the outside, after that I cash in my chips and make room for another man at the table. But for my last twelve hours, what I'd like to do is—"

Nothing. Valdez attempted to stir his friend with peasant philosophy:

"The simple farmers know best, Marvin. Do you know what they say? They say that a broken knife makes a poor walking-stick. I think you should bear that in mind, Marvin…"

But Marvin absentmindedly did not bear it in mind. Valdez swung to Hyperstrasian Ethics as expressed in the Timomachaean Scroll:

"Thou considerest thyself wounded, then? But consider: Self is Ineffable and Unitary, and not Susceptible to Externalities. Therefore it is merely a *Wound* which was *Wounded;* and this, being External to the Person and Extraneous to the Insight affords no cause for the Implication of Pain."

Marvin was not swayed by this argument. Valdez turned to psychology:

"Loss of the Beloved, according to Steinmetzer, is a ritual reenactment of the loss of the Fecal Self. Therefore, amusingly enough, when we think we mourn the dear departed, we actually are grieving the irreparable loss of our feces."

But this, too, could not penetrate Marvin's close-held passivity. His melancholic detachment from all human values seemed irrevocable; and this impression was heightened when, one quiet afternoon, his nose ring stopped ticking. It was not a bomb at all; it was merely a warning from Marduk Kras' constituents. And thus Marvin no longer stood in imminent danger of having his head blown off.

But even this stroke of good fortune did nothing to alter his gray robotic spirits. Quite unmoved, he noted the fact of his salvation as one might observe the passing of a cloud from the face of the sun.

Nothing seemed to have any effect upon him. And even the patient Valdez was finally led to explain: "Marvin, you are a goddamned pain in the ass!"

Yet Marvin persevered, unmoved. And it seemed to Valdez and to the good people of San Ramon that this man was beyond human recall.

And yet, how little we know of the twists and turns of the human mind! For the very next day, contrary to all reasonable expectations, an event occurred that broke at last through Marvin's reserve, and inadvertently threw wide the floodgates of susceptibility behind which he had been hiding.

A single event! (Though it was in itself the beginning of yet another chain of causality—the quiet opening move in yet another of the uncountable dramas of the universe.)

It began, absurdly enough, with a man's asking Marvin for the time.

CHAPTER 24

The event occurred on the northern side of the Plaza de los Muertos, shortly after the evening paseo and a full fifteen minutes before matins. Marvin had been taking his customary walk, past the statue of Jose Grimuchio, past the row of bootblacks gathered near the fifteenth-century pewter railing, to the fountain of San Briosci at the eastern corner of the grim little park. He had come even with the Tomb of the Misbegotten when a man stepped into his path and raised an imperious hand.

"A thousand pardons," the man said. "This unsolicited interruption of your solitude is regrettable to me, and perhaps offensive to you; yet still it is incumbent upon me to ask if by chance you could tell me the correct time?"

A harmless enough request—on the surface. Yet the man's appearance belied his commonplace words. He was of medium height and slight build, and he wore a moustache of outmoded design, of a sort that can be seen in the Grier portrait of King Morquavio Redondo. His clothes were tattered but very clean and neatly pressed, and his cracked shoes were highly polished. On his right forefinger was an ornate signet ring of massy gold; his eyes were the cold hawk eyes of a man used to command.

His question concerning the time would have been commonplace had there not been clocks facing the plaza, and disagreeing in their separate computations by no more than three minutes.

Marvin answered the man with his usual unfailing politeness, glancing at his ankle watch and announcing the time as just five past the hour.

"Thank you, sir, you are most obliging," the man said. "Five past already? Time devours our feeble mortality, leaving us with but the sour residue of memory."

Marvin nodded. "Yet this ineffable and ungraspable quantity," he replied, "this time which no man may possess, is in truth our only possession."

The man nodded as though Marvin had said something profound, instead of merely voicing a well-mannered conversational commonplace. The stranger bent forward into a sweeping bow (more to be seen in a bygone day than in this plebian age of ours). In so doing he lost his balance and would have fallen had not Marvin grasped him strongly and set him upon his feet.

"Many thanks," the man said, never for a moment losing his poise. "Your grasp of time and of men is most sure; this shall not be forgotten."

And with that he whirled and marched away into the crowd.

Marvin watched him go, faintly perplexed. Something about the fellow had not rung true. Perhaps it was the moustache, patently false, or the thickly pencilled eyebrows, or the artificial wart on the left cheek; or perhaps it was the shoes, which had given an extra three inches to the man's height, or the cloak, which had been padded to augment the natural narrowness of the shoulders. Whatever it was, Marvin found himself bemused, but not immediately distrustful; for beneath the man's rodomontade there had been evidence of a cheerful and sturdy spirit not lightly to be discounted.

It was while thinking of these things that Marvin happened, by chance, to glance down at his right hand. Looking more closely, he saw a piece of paper in the palm. It certainly had not come there by natural means. He realized that the cloaked stranger must have pressed it upon him while stumbling (or, as Marvin realized now, while *pretending* to stumble).

This cast the events of the past few minutes into an entirely different light. Frowning slightly, Marvin unfolded the paper and read:

> If the sir would care to hear something of interest and advantage both to himself and to the universe, the importance of which both in the immediate present and in the far-flung future cannot be stressed too greatly, and which cannot be expatiated upon in this note in any detail for obvious and all-too-sufficient reasons, but which *shall be* revealed in due course assuming a commonality of interests and of ethical considerations, then let the sir proceed at the ninth hour to the Inn of the Hanged Man, and there let him take table in the far left-hand corner near the paired embrochures, and let him wear a white rosebud in his lapel and carry in his right hand a copy of the *Diario de Celsus* (4-star edition), and let him tap upon the table with the little finger of his right hand, in no particular rhythm.
>
> These instructions being followed, One will come to you and make you acquainted with that which we believe you would like to hear.
>
> [signed] One Who Wishes You Well.

Marvin mused for a considerable time upon that note and its implications. He sensed that in some unimaginable fashion a group of interrelated lives and problems, hitherto unknown to him, had crossed his path.

But now was the moment when he could choose. Did he really care to involve himself in anyone's scheme, no matter how noteworthy? Might it not be best to avoid involvement and pursue his own solitary way through the metaphoric deformations of the world?

Perhaps…yet still, the incident had intrigued him and offered an apparently inconsequential diversion to help him forget the pain of Cathy's loss. (Thus action serves as anodyne, whereas contemplation is revealed as the most direct form of involvement, and therefore much shunned by men.)

Marvin followed the instructions given to him in the note from the mysterious stranger. He bought a copy of the *Diario de Celsus* (4-star edition), and procured a white rosebud for his lapel. And at nine o'clock sharp he went to the Inn of the Hanged Man and sat down at the table in the far left-hand corner, near the paired embrochures. His heart was beating with some rapidity. It was not an entirely unpleasant sensation.

CHAPTER 25

The Inn of the Hanged Man was a low yet cheerful place, and its clientele was composed, for the most part, of hearty specimens of the lower classes. Husky fish peddlers bawled for drink, and inflamed agitators howled abuse at the government and were hooted down by the heavy-thewed blacksmiths. A six-legged thorasorous was roasting in the great fireplace, and a scully basted the crackling carcass with honeyed juices. A fiddler had gotten up on a table and was playing a jig; his wooden leg rattled merrily in time with the old refrain. A drunken strumpet, with jewelled eyelids and an artificial septum, wept in a corner with maudlin self-pity.

A perfumed dandy swept a lace handkerchief to his nose and threw a disdainful coin to the tightrope wrestlers. Farther to the left, at the common table, a bootblack reached into the pot for a morsel of scrag, and found his hand skewered to the table by the poniard of a riisman. This exploit was greeted with cheers by the assembled company.

"Gawd save 'ee, sir, and what'll thee be drinking?"

Marvin looked up and saw a waitress with red cheeks and extensive bosom waiting for his order.

"Mead, and it so please you," Marvin answered quietly.

"Ay, that we do be havin'," the girl replied. She bent to adjust her garter and whispered to Marvin, "Lawks, sir, do be mindful of yourself in this place which is in truth no fitten for a young gentleman such as thyself."

"Thanks for your warning," Marvin replied, "but if it comes to the rub, I hope that I may be allowed to believe that I might not be entirely unavailing."

"Ah, ye don't know them as is 'ere," the girl replied; and then moved away hastily, for a large gentleman dressed entirely in black had approached Marvin's table.

"Now by the sweet bleeding wounds of the Almighty and what have we here?" he shouted.

A silence fell over the inn. Marvin looked steadily upon the man, and recognized in his huge expanse of chest and abnormal reach that one whom people called "Black Denis." And he remembered the man's reputation as a ripper and tearer and general bully and spoiler.

Marvin affected not to notice the man's sweaty proximity. Instead, he took out a fan and wafted it gently in front of his nose.

The crowd roared with peasant mirth. Black Denis took a half-step closer. Muscles along his arm writhed like cobras in travail as his fingers closed on the gaunt handle of his rapier.

"Damn me blind for a turnip-filler!" Black Denis shouted, "but it seems most marvellous to me that we have here in our midst a fellow who looks most exceedingly like a king's spy!"

Marvin suspected that the man was trying to provoke him. Therefore he ignored the sally and buffed his fingernails with a tiny silver file.

"Well, slash me up the middle and tie me guts for a sash!" Black Denis swore. "It seems that some so-called gentlemun ain't no gentlemun at all since they don't acknowledge when another gentlemun is speaking at um. But maybe um's deaf, which I shall find out by examining the fellow's left ear—at home, at my leisure."

"Were you addressing me?" Marvin asked, in a suspiciously mild voice.

"Indeed I was," Black Denis said. "For it came to me of a sudden that me likes not your face."

"Indeed?" Marvin lisped.

"Aye!" thundered Black Denis. "Nor like I more your manner, nor the stench of your perfume, nor the shape of your foot nor the curve of your arm."

Marvin's glance narrowed. The moment was filled with murderous tension, and no sound could be heard save Black Denis' stertorous breathing. Then, before Marvin could reply, a man had run to Black Denis' side. It was a little hunchback who thus rashly interfered, a sallow man with a great white beard, standing no more than three feet high and dragging a club foot behind him.

"Ah, come now," the hunchback said to Black Denis. "Wilt shed blood on St. Origen's Eve, and it unworthy of your lordship's attention? For shame, Black Denis!"

"I'll shed blood an I so please, by the cankers of the holy red mountain!" swore the bully.

"Ay, spill his guts for him!" shouted a spindly, long-nosed fellow from the crowd, blinking with one blue eye and squinting with one brown.

"Ay, spill it!" a dozen other voices roared, taking up the cry.

"Gentlemen, please!" said the fat innkeeper, wringing his hands.

"'E ain't never bothered you!" said the frowsy barmaid, a tray of glasses trembling in her hand.

"Nay, leave the popinjay to his drink," said the hunchback, tugging at Black Denis' sleeve and drooling from one side of his mouth.

"Unhand me, lump-shoulder!" Black Denis shouted, and struck out with a right hand the size of a padding mauler. It caught the little hunchback fair across the chest and propelled him across the room, driving him completely across the aleyard table until he fetched up against the cinch rack with a great clatter of broken glass.

"Now, by the maggots of eternity!" the huge brawler said, turning to Marvin.

Still Marvin fanned himself and sat back in his chair, relaxed but with eyes slightly narrowed. A more observant man might have noticed the faint anticipatory tremor along his thighs, the merest suggestion of flexion in his wrist.

Now he deigned to notice his molester. "Still here?" he queried. "Fellow, your importunities grow wearisome to the ear and redundant to the senses."

"Yeah?" Black Denis cried.

"Yeah," Marvin replied ironically. "Reiteration is ever the emphasis of the disingenuous; yet it amuses not my fancy. Therefore remove yourself, fellow, and take your overheated carcass somewhere else, lest I cool it for thee by a bloodletting which any chirurgeon might envy."

Black Denis gaped at the effrontery of this deadly quiet insult. Then, with a speed which belied his bulk, he swept out his sword and brought it down in a stroke that cleaved the heavy oak table in two, and would have most assuredly done for Marvin had he not moved nimbly out of the way.

Bellowing with rage, Denis charged, swinging his sword like a windmill gone berserk. And Marvin danced lightly back, folded his fan, tucked it away in his belt, rolled up his sleeves, bent low to evade another stroke, leaped backwards over a cedar table, and plucked up a carving knife. Then, gripping the knife lightly in his hand, he moved forward on gliding steps to do combat.

"Take flight, sir!" the barmaid cried. "He'll split 'ee, and 'ee with naught but a tinysome table steel in 'ee's hand and it with no great edge on it!"

"Take care, young man!" the hunchback cried, taking refuge beneath a hanging side of bartels.

"Spill his guts for him!" the spindly, long-nosed fellow with the piebald eyes cried.

"Gentlemen, please!" cried the unhappy landlord.

The two combatants were met now in the center of the common room, and Black Denis, his face twisted with passion, feinted and swung a cutlass stroke powerful enough to split an oak. Marvin moved with deadly sureness inside of the blow, deflecting it with his knife in *quarte,* and immediately riposting in *quinze.* This deft counter was blocked only by the abnormal swiftness of Denis' *revanche,* else it would surely have cut the gullet out of the man.

Black Denis came back on to guard, looking upon his opponent with more than a suggestion of respect. Then he roared with berserker rage, and drove forward into the attack, forcing Marvin back across the smoky room.

"A double Napoleon on the big fellow!" cried the perfumed dandy.

"Done!" cried the hunchback. "That slender lad has the footwork, mark it well."

"Footwork ne'er stopped swinging steel e'er now," the dandy lisped. "Wilt back thy judgement with thy purse?"

"Ay! I'll add five Louis d'Or!" said the hunchback, fumbling for his purse.

And now others in the crowd had caught the gaming fever. "Ten rupees on the Denis!" shouted the long-nosed fellow. "Nay, I'll offer odds of three to one!"

"Make it four to one!" cried the ever-cautious landlord, "and seven to five on first blood!" And so saying, he swept out a bag of gold sovereigns.

"Done!" screamed the piebald-eyed fellow, putting up three silver talents and a gold half-denarius. "And by the Black Mother, I'll even offer eight to six on a chest-cut!"

"I'll take the bet!" shrieked the barmaid, taking a bag of Maria Theresa thalers out of her bosom. "And I'll give you six-five pick 'em on first amputation!"

"I'll take that!" the perfumed dandy shrilled. "And by my wattles, I'll even offer nine to four that the slender lad runs out of here like a scorched greyhound before third blood!"

"I'll take that bet," Marvin Flynn said, with an amused smile. Evading Denis' clumsy rush, he plucked a bag of florins out of his sash and threw it to the dandy. Then he settled down seriously to fight.

Even in these few brief moves, Marvin's skill at fence could clearly be seen. Yet he was faced with a powerful and determined opponent, who wielded a sword many times larger than Marvin's inadequate weapon, and who seemed determined to the point of madness.

The attack came, and all in the crowd except for the hunchback held their breaths as Black Denis rushed down like an incarnation of Juggernaut. Before that impetuous rush, Marvin was forced to give ground. He backed away, vaulted over a table, found himself wedged into a corner, leaped high and caught the chandelier, swung across the room and dropped lightly to his feet.

Bewildered, and perhaps feeling a shade unsure of himself, Black Denis resorted to a trick. As they came together again, Denis' long arm swept a chair into Marvin's path; and as Marvin dodged, Denis grasped a collard of black Ignean pepper from a table and flung it into Marvin's face...

But Marvin's face was no longer there. Pivoting and driving off his left foot, Marvin evaded the treacherous tactic. He feinted low with his knife, double-feinted with his eyes, and executed a perfect stepback crossover.

Black Denis blinked stupidly and looked down to see the handle of Marvin's knife jutting from his chest. His eyes opened wide in astonishment, and his sword hand came swinging up to the riposte.

Marvin turned serenely on his heel and walked slowly away, leaving his unprotected back exposed to the glint-edged cutlass!

Black Denis began his downward swing; but already a thin grey film had formed over his eyes. Marvin had judged the severity of the wound with exquisite precision, for Black Denis' sword clattered to the floor, to be joined a moment later by the great body of the brawler.

Without looking back, Marvin crossed the room and regained his chair. He opened his fan; then, frowning, he slipped a lace handkerchief out of his pocket and dabbled at his forehead. Two or three drops of perspiration marred its marble perfection. Flynn wiped the drops away, then threw away the handkerchief.

The room was in absolute silence. Even the piebald-eyed man had stopped his stertorous breathing.

It was perhaps the most amazing exhibit of swordsmanship that the inhabitants had ever seen. Brawlers one and all, and calling no man master, still they were impressed.

A moment later, pandemonium broke loose. All crowded around Marvin, cheering and exclaiming, and marvelling at the skill he had shown with pointed steel. The two rope wrestlers (brothers, born deaf-mutes) made squealing noises and turned somersaults; the hunchback grinned and counted his winnings with foam-flecked lips; the barmaid looked at Marvin with an embarrassing excess of ardor; the proprietor gruffly served drinks on the house; the piebald-eyed man snuffled through his long nose and talked about luck; even the perfumed dandy was moved to offer perfunctory congratulations.

Slowly the room returned to normal. Two bull-necked servitors dragged out Black Denis's body, and the fickle crowd pelted the corpse with orange peels. The roast was set again to turning on the spit, and the rattle of dice and swish of cards could be heard over the playing of the blind, one-legged fiddler.

The dandy strolled over to Marvin's table and looked down upon him, hand on hip and feathered hat akimbo. "'Pon my honor, sir," the dandy said, "you do indeed have some qualifications at fence; and it seems to me that your skills could be rewarded in the service of the Cardinal Macchurchi, who is always on the lookout for apt and agile fellows."

"I am not for hire," Marvin said quietly.

"I am glad to hear it," the dandy said. And now, looking at the man more closely, Marvin perceived a white rosebud in his buttonhole, and a copy of the *Diario de Celsus* (4-star edition) in his hand.

The dandy's eyes flashed a warning. In his most effete voice, he said, "Well then, sir, my congratulations again; and perhaps, if you would care for a bit of sport, you will join me in my chambers on the Avenue of Martyrs. We could discuss the finer points of swordplay, and drink a rather adequate little wine which has lain in my family's vaults for 103 years, and perhaps even hazard another topic or two of mutual interest."

Now Marvin was able to recognize, beneath his disguise, the man who had pressed a note into his hand earlier.

"Sir," Marvin said, "your invitation does me honor."

"Not at all, sir. Your acknowledgement of my invitation does me honor."

"Nay, sir," Marvin insisted, and would have examined the honor question further had not the man cut short the punctilio and whispered, "We'll leave at once, then. Black Denis was but a harbinger—a straw to show us which way the wind blows. And I greatly fear, lest we get ourselves promptly hence, it may well blow us a hurricane."

"That would be most unfortunate," Marvin said, grinning very slightly. "Landlord! Set this upon my account!"

"Ay, Sir Gules," the landlord replied, bowing low.

And so they went out together into the fog-bound night.

CHAPTER 26

Through the tortuous lanes of the central city they went, past the grim iron-grey walls of the Terc Fortress, past the infamous Spodney Asylum, wherein the screams of abused madmen mingled strangely with the squeak of the great waterwheel at Battlegrave Landing; past the howling of prisoners in the squat and ominous Donjon of the Moon, and then past the malodorous High Battlement with its grisly row of spiked torsos.

Being men of their time and age, neither Marvin nor Sir Gules gave notice to these sounds and sights. Quite unmoved they walked past the Garbage Pond wherein the former regent had gratified his mad nocturnal fancies; and without a glance they went by Lion's Gambit, where petty debtors and child malefactors were buried headfirst in quick-setting cement as an example to others.

It was a hard age, and some might consider it a cruel age. Manners were refined, but passions ran unchecked. The most exquisite punctilio was observed; but death by torture was the common lot of most. It was an age in which six out of seven women died in childbirth; in which infant mortality was a shocking 87 per cent; in which the average life expectancy was no more than 12.3 years; in which the Plague yearly ravaged the central city, carrying away an estimated two-thirds of the population; in which continual religious warfare halved the able-bodied male population every year—to the point where some regiments were forced to use blind men as gunnery officers.

And yet, it could not be considered an unhappy age. Despite difficulties, the population soared to new heights every year, and men aspired to fresh extremes of audacity. If life was uncertain, it was at least interesting. Machinery had not bred individual initiative out of the race as yet. And though there were shocking class differences and feudal privilege reigned supreme, checked only by the dubious power of the king and the baleful presence of the clergy, still it could fairly be called a democratic age and a time of individual opportunity.

But neither Marvin nor Sir Gules were thinking of these things as they approached a narrow old house with drawn shutters and a brace of horses posted near the door. They were not contemplating individual enterprise, though indeed they were engaged in it; nor did they consider death, though it surrounded them constantly. Theirs was not a self-conscious age.

"Well then," Sir Gules said, leading his guest down the carpeted floor past the silent manservants to a high wainscotted room in which a cheery fire snapped and crackled in the great onyx fireplace.

Marvin did not answer. His eye was taking in the details of the room. The carven armoire was surely tenth century, and the portrait on the west wall, half-hidden by its gilt frame, was a genuine Moussault.

"Come, sit, I pray thee," said Sir Gules, sinking gracefully to a David Ogilvy half-couch decorated in the Afghan brocade so popular that year.

"Thank you," Marvin said, sitting upon an eight-legged John IV with rosewood handles and a backing of heart-o'-palm.

"A little wine?" Sir Gules said, handling with casual reverence the bronze decanter with gold chasings engraved by Dagobert of Hoyys.

"Not just at the moment, give thee thanks," Marvin replied, brushing a fleck of dust from his stuff-colored outercoat of green baptiste with lisle froggings, made to his measure by Geoffrey of Palping Lane.

"Then mayhap a touch of snuff?" Sir Gules inquired, proferring his small platinum snuffbox made by Durr of Snedum, upon which was portrayed in steel-point a hunting scene from the Orange Forest of Lesh.

"Perhaps later," Marvin said, squinting down at the double-furled silver thread laces on his dancing pumps.

"My purpose in bringing you here," his host said abruptly, "was to inquire as to the availability of your aid to a cause both good and righteous, and with which you are not, I believe, entirely unacquainted. I refer to the Sieur Lamprey Height d'Augustin, better known as The Enlightened."

"D'Augustin!" Marvin exclaimed. "Why, I knew him when I was little more than a lad, in '02, or '03, the year of the Speckled Plague! Why, he used to visit at our chalet! I can still remember the marzipan apples he used to bring me!"

"I thought you would remember him," Gules said quietly. "All of us do."

"And how is that great and good gentleman?"

"Well enough—we hope."

Marvin was instantly alert. "Your meaning, sir?"

"Last year, d'Augustin was working on his country estate at Duvannemor, which is just beyond Moueur d'Alençon in the foothills of the Sangrela."

"I know the place," Marvin said.

"He was finishing his masterwork, *The Ethics of Indecision,* with which he has travailled himself these past twenty years. When suddenly, a host of armed men burst into the Rune Study where he was working, having overpowered his servants and bribed his personal bodyguard. No one else was present save his daughter, who was helpless to interfere. These nameless men seized and bound d'Augustin, burned all extant copies of his book, and took him away."

"Infamous!" cried Marvin.

"His daughter, witnessing so horrid a sight, swooned away into a lassitude so complete that it resembled death; and thus, through an inadvertent counterfeit, she was spared from death itself."

"Shocking!" muttered Marvin. "But who would let slip violence upon a harmless scribbler whom many call the outstanding philosopher of our day and age?"

"Harmless, say thee?" Sir Gules inquired, his lips quirking into a painful grimace. "Are you then acquainted with d'Augustin's work that you say so?"

"I have had not the privilege of acquaintance," Marvin said. "My life, in truth, has availed me little opportunity for such matters, since I have been traveling continually for some such time now. But I thought that the writings of so gentle and esteemed a man would surely—"

"I beg to differ," Sir Gules said. "This fine and upright old man whom we are discussing has been led, by an irreversible process of Logical Inductiveness, to put forth certain doctrines which, if they were popularly known, might well cause bloody revolution."

"That scarce seems a goodly matter," Marvin replied coldly. "Wouldst teach me damnable sedition?"

"Nay, softly, softly! These doctrines which d'Augustin proclaims are not so shocking in themselves, but rather, in their consequences. That is to say, they take on the timbre of Moral Facticity, and are no more truly seditious than is the monthly wax and wane of th' moon."

"Well...give me an example," Marvin said.

"D'Augustin proclaims that men are born free," Gules said softly.

Marvin thought about that. "A new-fangled notion," he declared at last, "but not without its suasion. Tell me more."

"He declares that upright conduct is meritorious and pleasing in the eyes of God."

"A strange way of looking at things," Marvin decided. "And yet—hmmm."

"He also holds that the unexamined life is not worth living."

"Quite a radical point of view," Marvin said. "And it is, of course, obvious what would happen were these statements to fall into the hands of the populace at large. The authority of king and church would inevitably be undermined...and yet—and yet—"

"Yes?" Gules prompted softly.

"And yet," Marvin said, gazing dreamily at the terracotta ceiling with its inscriblature of interlocked palladiums, "and yet might not a new order arise out of the chaos which would unerringly ensue? Might not a new world be born in which the overweening humors of the nobility would be checked and ameliorated by the concept of personal worth, and in which the thundering threats of a church gone base and political would be countered by a new relationship between a man and his God unmediated by fat priest or larcenous friar?"

"Do you really think that is possible?" Gules asked, in a voice like silk sliding over velvet.

"Yes," Marvin said. "Yes, by the hangnails of God, I so do believe! And I will aid you in rescuing d'Augustin and in disseminating this strange and revolutionary new doctrine!"

"Thank you," Gules said simply. And he made a gesture with his hand.

A figure glided out from behind Marvin's chair. It was the hunchback. Marvin caught the deadly wink of steel as the creature sheathed his knife.

"No insult intended," Gules said earnestly. "We were sure of you, of course. But had you found our plan repugnant, it would have been incumbent upon us to hide our poor judgement in an unmarked grave."

"The precaution lends point to your story," Marvin said dryly. "But me likes it not such keen appreciation."

"Such confabulation is our common lot in life," the hunchback quoth. "And indeed, did not the Greeks consider it better to die in the hands of friends than to languish in the claws of enemies? Our roles are chosen for us in this world by the stern dictates of an unrelenting Fate; and many a man who thought to play the emperor on Life's stage found himself cast for a corpse instead."

"Sir," said Marvin, "you sound to me a man who has experienced some casting problems himself."

"One well might say so," the hunchback replied dryly. "I would not of myself have selected this lowly part, had not exigencies beyond prediction forced me to it."

So saying, the hunchback reached down and unstrapped his legs, which had been bound to his thighs, and thereby rose to his full height of six feet one. He unfastened the hump from his back, wiped greasepaint and drool from his face, combed his hair, detached his beard and his club foot, then turned to Marvin with a wry smile upon his face.

Marvin stared at this man transformed; then bowed low and exclaimed, "Milord Inglenook bar na Idrisi-san, first lord of the Admiralty, Familiar to the Prime Minister, Advisor Extraordinary to the King, Bludgeon of the Church Rampant and Invocateur of the Grand Council!"

"I am that person," Inglenook responded. "And I play the hunchback for reasons most politic; for were my presence even suspected here by my rival, Lord Blackamoor de Mordevund, all of us would be dead men ere the frogs in the Pond Royal had chance to croak at first ray of Phoebus!"

"This ivy of conspiracy doth grow on high towers," Marvin commented. "I surely will serve you and God give me strength, unless some tavern brawler lets light into my belly with a yard of steel."

"If you refer to the incident of Black Denis," Sir Gules said, "I can assure you that the matter was staged for the eyes of whatever spies Sir Blackamoor might have set upon us. In actuality, Black Denis was one of us."

"Wonder upon wonders!" Marvin declared. "This octopus, it seems, has many tentacles. But gentlemen, it wonders me why, of all puissant gentlemen in this our kingdom, you sought out one who boasts no special privilege nor high position nor monetary wealth nor nothing save the title of gentleman under God and lord of his own honor and bearer of a thousand-year-old name."

"You are reckless in your modesty!" Lord Inglenook laughed. "For it is known among all that your skill in the fenceyard is unsurpassed, except perhaps for the wily swordplay of the detestable Blackamoor."

"I am but a student of the steely art," Marvin replied carelessly. "Yet still, if my poor gift will serve you, sobeit. And now, gentlemen, what would you of me?"

"Our plan," Inglenook said slowly, "has the virtue of great daring, and the defect of immense danger. A single cast of the dice wins all, or loses us the wager of our lives. A grave gamble! And yet, methinks you would not like not this hazard."

Marvin smiled while construing the sentence, then said, "A quick game is ever a lively one."

"Excellent!" breathed Gules, rising to his feet. "We must take ourselves now to Castelgatt in the valley of the Romaine. And during the ride there, we shall acquaint you with the details of our scheme."

And so it was that, muffled in their greatcloaks, the three departed the high narrow house by the dormer stairwell, walking past the chain locker to the postern gate by the old west wall. Here, posted and waiting was a coach and four, with two armed guards mounted on the slackrails.

Marvin made to enter the coach and saw a person already within. It was a girl; and peering more closely, he saw—

"Cathy!" he cried.

She looked at him without comprehension, and answered in a cold, imperious voice, "Sir, I am Catarina d'Augustin, and I know not your face nor like I your style of presumed familiarity."

There was no recognition in her beautiful grey eyes, and no time to ask questions. For even as Sir Gules made hasty introductions, a shout could be heard behind them.

"You there, in the coach! Halt in the name of the King!"

Glancing back, Marvin could see a captain of dragoons with ten mounted men behind him.

"Treachery!" shouted Inglenook. "Quick, coachmen, let us away!"

With a clatter of traces and a rattle of bits, the four matched stallions propelled the coach down the narrow alley in the direction of Ninestones and Oceansideways High Road.

"Can they overtake us?" asked Marvin.

"Mayhap," Inglenook said. "They seem damnably well mounted, damn their blue blistered backsides! Your pardon, madame..."

For a few moments Inglenook watched the horsemen clatter along not twenty yards behind, their sabers glittering in the dim lamplight. Then he shrugged and turned away.

"Let me inquire," Inglenook inquired, "as to whether you are conversant with recent political developments here and elsewhere in the Old Empire; for this knowledge is needful to make intelligible to you the necessity for the particular form and moment of our scheme."

"I fear that my political knowledge is but indifferent poor," Marvin said.

"Then permit me to relate to you a few details of the background, which will render the situation and its import more malleable to the intelligence."

Marvin settled back, hearing the drumming of the dragoons' horses in his ears. Cathy, seated opposite him and slightly to his right, stared coldly at the swinging tassels on Sir Gules' hat. And Lord Inglenook began to speak:

CHAPTER 27

"The old king died less than a decade ago, at the full flood of the Suessian heresy, leaving no clear successor to the throne of Mulvavia. Thus, the passions of a troubled continent came ominously to the boil.

"Three claimants jostled for the Butterfly Throne. Prince Moroway of Theme held the Patent Obvious, which had been awarded him by a bribed but still official Council of Electionate. And if that were not sufficient, he held as well by the doctrine of Regal Empleatude, since he was the acknowledged, illegitimate second (and only surviving) son of Baron Norway, the old king's sister's half-cousin through the powerful Mortjoys of Danat.

"In less troubled times, this might have been sufficient. But for a continent on the verge of civil and religious war, there were defects in the claim, and even more in the claimant.

"Prince Moroway was merely eight years old and had never been known to utter a word. According to the portrait by Mouvey, he had a monstrously swollen head, a slack jaw, and the unfocused eyes of a hydrocephalic idiot. His only known pleasure was his collection of worms (the finest on the continent).

"His main opposition for the succession was Gottlieb Hosstratter, Duke of Mela and Receiptor-in-Ordinary of the Imperial Marginland, whose dubious bloodlines were backed by the schismatic Suessian Hierarchy, and most particularly by the enfeebled Hierarch of Dodessa.

"A second claimant, Romrugo of Vars, might have been discounted were it not that he backed his petition with a force of fifty thousand battle-hardened troopers from the southern principality of Vask. Young and vigorous, Romrugo had a reputation for eccentricity; his marriage to his favorite mare Orsilla was condemned by the orthodox Owensian clergy of which he was the absent-minded champion. Nor did he win favor among the burghers of Gint-Loseine, whose proud city he ordered buried under twenty feet of earth 'as a gift to future archaeologists.' Yet withal, his claim to the throne of Mulvavia might have been speedily legitimized had he possessed the wherewithal with which to pay his fighting men.

"Unfortunately for Romrugo, he had no personal fortune. (It had been squandered upon the purchase of the Lethertean scrolls.) Therefore, in order to raise his army's payroll, he proposed an alliance with the wealthy but ineffectual Free City of Tihurrue, which commanded the straits of Sidue.

"This unthinking move brought down upon his head the wrath of the Duchy of Puls, whose western frontier had long guarded the exposed flank of the Old Empire from the depredations of the pagan Monogoths. The stern, singleminded young grandduke of Puls immediately joined forces with the schismatic Hosstratter—surely as strange an alliance as the continent had ever seen—and thus became a direct menace to Prince Moroway, and to the Mortjoys of Danat who supported him. So, quite unexpectedly, finding himself surrounded on three sides by Suessians or their allies, and on the fourth side by the restive Monogoths, Romrugo began casting around desperately for a new alliance.

"He found it in the enigmatic figure of Baron Lord Darkmouth, Prepossessor of the Isle of Turplend. The tall and brooding Baron set to sea at once with a battle fleet of twenty-five galleons, and all Mulvavia held its breath as the ominous line of ships sailed down the Dorter and into the Escher Sea.

"Could the balance still have been preserved, even at this late hour? Perhaps, if Moroway had held firm to his former pledges to the Marche Cities. Or if the old Hierarch of Dodessa, contemplating at last the necessity of accommodation with Hosstratter, had not chosen that inappropriate moment to die, and thus to give power to the epileptic Murvey of Hunfutmouth. Or if Red Hand Ericmouth, chief of the West Monogoths, had not chosen that moment to banish Propeia, sister of the stern Archduke of Puls, known as the 'Hammer against Heretics'(by which he meant all who did not subscribe to his own narrowly orthodox Delongianism).

"But the hand of Fate intervened to stay the inevitable moment; for Baron Darkmouth's galleons were caught in the Great Storm of '03, and driven to take refuge at Tihurrue, which they sacked, thus dissolving Romrugo's alliance before it was fairly underway, and causing revolt among the unpaid Vaskians of his army, who deserted by regiments and joined Hosstratter, whose lands lay closest to their line of march.

"Thus Hosstratter, third and most reluctant of the royal petitioners, who had become resigned to his loss, found himself back in the contest; and Moroway, whose star had glittered high, discovered that the Echilides Mountains were no protection when the eastern passes were held by a determined enemy.

"The man most affected by all of this, of course, was Romrugo. His position was unenviable: deserted by his troops, forsworn by his ally Baron Darkmouth (who had his hands full trying to hold Tihurrue against a determined attack by the pirates of the Rullish coast), and menaced even in his fiefdom of Vars by the long and deadly arm of Mortjoy's conspiracy, while the Marche Cities looked hungrily on. As capstone to his pillar of ill fortune, his mare Orsilla chose that moment to desert him.

"Yet even in the depths of adversity, the self-confident Romrugo did not falter. His mare's desertion was hailed by the frightened Owensian clergy, who granted their dubious champion a Divorce in Absolute, and then learned to their horror that the cynical Romrugo intended to use his freedom to wed Propeia and thus align himself with the grateful Archduke of Puls...

"These were the factors that exercised men's passions in that fateful year. The continent stood poised upon the brink of catastrophe. Peasants buried their crops underground and sharpened their scythes. Armies stood to attention and prepared to move in any direction. The turbulent mass of the West Monogoths, pressed from behind by the still more turbulent mass of hard-riding cannibal Allahuts, massed threateningly on the borders of the Old Empire.

"Darkmouth hastened to re-equip his galleys, and Hosstratter paid the Vaskian troopers and trained them for a new kind of war. Romrugo cemented his new alliance with Puls, achieved a détente with Ericmouth, and took account of the new rivalry between Mortjoy and the epileptic but dourly able Murvey. And Moroway of Theme, unconscious ally of the Rullish pirates, unwilling champion of the Suessian heresy, and unwitting accomplice of Red Hand Ericmouth, looked to the grim eastern slopes of the Echilides and waited in trepidation.

"It was at this moment of supreme and universal tension that Milord d'Augustin all unwittingly chose to announce the imminent completion of his work of philosophy..."

Inglenook's voice faded slowly away, and for a time there was no sound but the heavy thrum of horses' hooves. Then Marvin said quietly, "I understand now."

"I knew you would," Inglenook answered warmly. "And in light of this, you can understand our plan, which is to assemble at Castelgatt and then strike immediately."

Marvin nodded. "Under the circumstances there could be no other way."

"But first," Inglenook said, "we must rid ourselves of these pursuing dragoons."

"As to that," Marvin said, "I have a plan…"

CHAPTER 28

By a clever ruse, Marvin and his compatriots were able to elude the pursuing dragoons and to come unscathed into the great moated tiltyard of Castelgatt. There, upon the sounding of the twelfth hour, the conspirators were to assemble, make final dispositions, and move out that very night for the audacious attempt to rescue d'Augustin from the formidable grasp of Blackamoor.

Marvin retired to his chambers in the high east wing, and there shocked his page by insisting upon a basin of water in which to wash his hands. It was considered a strange affectation on his part in that age in which even the greatest court ladies were accustomed to hide smudges of dirt under perfumed gauze bandages. But Marvin had picked up the custom during his stay among the gay and pagan Tescos of the southern Remoueve, whose soapy fountains and spongy sculpture were wonders of wonders to the complacent and grimy northern nobility. And in spite of the laughter of his peers and the frowns of the clergy, Marvin stubbornly insisted that an occasional scrub of the hands did no damage, so long as the water touched no other part.

His ablutions completed, and clad only in black satin half-knickers, white lace shirt, cavalry boots and shoulder-length gloves of Eretzian chamois, and wearing only his sword Coueur de Stabbat, which had been handed down in his family father-to-son for five hundred years, Marvin heard a half-noise behind him and whirled, hand to hilt.

"La, sir, wouldst run me through with thy terrible great sword?" mocked the Lady Catarina—for it was she—standing just inside the paneled doorway to the inner chamber.

"Faith, your ladyship startled me," Marvin said. "But as for running thee through, that indeed I would do right merrily, though not with sword but with a trustier weapon which it happens I do possess."

"Fie, sir," the Lady Catarina said mockingly. "Offerest violence to a lady?"

"Merely the violence of pleasure," Marvin replied gallantly.

"Your words are too glib by half," said the Lady Catarina. "I believe it has been noted that the longest and wiliest tongues conceal the shortest and least adequate of Weapons."

"Your ladyship does me injustice," Marvin said. "For I dare say my Weapon is eminently capable of the uses it may encounter, sharp enough to penetrate the best defense in the world, and durable enough for repeated stabbings. And, quite apart from such utilitarian uses, it has learned from me certain infallible tricks, the which it would be my respectful pleasure to show your ladyship."

"Nay, keep your Weapon in its scabbard," the lady quoth, indignantly, but with sparkling eyes. "Me likes not the sound of 't; for braggart's steel is ever pliable tin, shiny to the eye yet damnably malleable to the touch."

"I beg of thee but to touch the edge and point," Marvin said, "and thus submit thy raillery to th' test of Usage"

She shook her pretty head. "Know, sir, that such Pragmatics are for greybeard philosophers with rheumy eyes; a lady relies upon her intuition."

"Lady, I worship thy intuition," Marvin responded.

"Why, sir, what wouldst Thou, the Prepossessor of a dubious Weapon of indetermined length and uncertain temper, know of a woman's intuition?"

"Lady, my heart tells me that it is exquisite and ineffable, and possessed of a pleasing shape and delicate fragrance, and that—"

"Enough, sir!" the Lady Catarina cried, blushing hotly and fanning herself furiously with a Japanese fan whose corrugated surface portrayed the Investiture of the Iichi.

Both fell silent. They had been conversing in the old language of Courtly Love, in which symbolic apostrophe played so important a part. In those days it was deemed no breach of the etiquette for even the best-bred and most demure of young ladies to thus converse; theirs was not a frightened age.

But now a shadow of seriousness had fallen over the two participants. Marvin glowered, fingering the grey steel buttons of his white lace shirt. And the Lady Catarina looked troubled. She wore a panelled gown of dove tulip with slashings of chrome red, and, as was the custom, the neckline was cut fashionably low to reveal the firm rosy swelling of her little abdomen. Upon her feet were sandal-pumps of ivory-colored damask: and her hair, piled high upon a jade ratouelle, was adorned with a garland of spring snippinies. Never in his life had Marvin seen so beautiful a sight.

"Can we not cease this ceaseless play of word foolery?" Marvin asked quietly. "May we not say that which is in our hearts, 'stead of fencing thus with heartless ingenuities?"

"I dare not!" the Lady Catarina murmured.

"And yet, you are Cathy, who loved me once in another time and place," Marvin said inexorably, "and who now plays me for the unacknowledged gallant."

"You must not speak of that which once had been," Cathy said, in a frightened whisper.

"Yet still you loved me once!" Marvin cried hotly. "Deny me this an you find it false!"

"Yes," she said in a failing voice, "I loved thee once."

"And now?"

"Alas!"

"But speak and tell me reason!"

"Nay, I cannot!"

"Will not, rather."

"As thee wish: the choice is servant to the heart."

"I would not have you believe that," she said softly.

"No? Then surely the desire is father to the intent," Marvin said, his face gone hard and pitiless. "And standing thus in familial relationship, not even the wisest of men would deny that Love is inbonded to its half-sister Indifference, and Faithfulness is thrall to the cruel stepmother, Pain."

"Can you so consider me?" she cried weakly.

"Why, Lady, you leave me choiceless," Marvin responded in a voice of ringing bronze. "And thus my barque of Passion is Derelict upon a Sea of Memory, blown off its rightful course by the fickle wind of Indifference, and driven toward the rockbound Coast of Agony by the inexorable Tide of Human Events."

"And yet, I would not have it thus," Catarina said, and Marvin thrilled to hear even so mild an affirmation of that which he had considered lost beyond recall.

"Cathy—"

"Nay, it cannot be," she cried, recoiling in evident agony, her color high and her abdomen rising and falling with the emotion within her. "You know not of the wretched circumstances of my situation."

"I demand to know!" Marvin cried, then whirled, his hand darting to his sword. For the great oaken door of his chamber had swung noiselessly open, and there, leaning negligently in the doorway, a man stood with arms folded over his chest and a half-smile playing across his thin, bearded lips.

"In faith! We are undone!" Catarina cried, her hand pressed to her trembling abdomen.

"Sir, what would thou?" Marvin asked hotly. "I demand to know thy name, and the reason for this most ungentle and unseemly investiture!"

"All shall be speedily revealed thee," the man in the doorway said, his voice revealing a faint and menacing lisp. "My name, sir, is Lord Blackamoor, 'gainst whom your puerile plans have been cast; and I have entered this chamber from simple privilege of one who dutifully desires introduction to his wife's young friend."

"Wife?" Marvin echoed.

"This lady," Blackamoor declared, "who has the uncertain habit of not straightaways introducing herself, is indeed the Most Noble Catarina d'Augustin di Blackamoor, the most loving wife to this your humble servant."

And so saying, Blackamoor swept off his hat and louted low, then resumed his exquisite's pose in the doorway.

Marvin read the truth in Cathy's tear-stained eyes and shuddering abdomen. Cathy, his beloved Cathy, the wife of Blackamoor, the most detested enemy of those who espoused the cause of d'Augustin, who was Cathy's own father!

Yet there was no time to consider these strange propinquities of sensibility; for the foremost consideration was of Blackamoor himself, standing miraculously within a castle held by his enemies, and betraying no hint of nervousness at a position that should have been perilous in the extreme.

And this infallibly meant that the situation was not as Marvin had supposed it, and that the threads of destiny were tangled now past his immediate comprehension.

Blackamoor in Castelgatt? Marvin considered the implications, and a sensation of cold came over him, as though the angel of death had brushed past him with stygian wings.

Murder lurked in this room—but for whom? Marvin feared the worst, but turned quite steadily, his face a mask of obsidian, and faced the enemy who was his beloved's husband and the captor of her father.

CHAPTER 29

Milord Lamprey di Blackamoor stood silent and at his ease. He was above the middling height, and possessed a frame of extreme emaciation, punctuated by his narrow, closely cropped beard of jetty black, his deep-swept sideburns, and his hair cut *en brosse* and allowed to fall upon his forehead in snaky ringlets. And yet the appearance of narrowness was offset by the breadth of shoulder and the powerful swordsman's arm that could be glimpsed beneath his half-cloak of ermitage. He wore his points and josses in the new foppish style, interlaced with macedium pointings and relieved only by a triple row of crepe-silver darturs. His face was coldly handsome, marred only by a puckered scar that ran from his right temple to the left corner of his mouth, and which he had defiantly painted a fiery crimson. This lent to his sarcastic features a look both sinister and absurd.

"It would seem," Blackamoor drawled, "that we have played this farce long enough. The denouement approaches."

"Does milord then have his third act prepared?" Marvin inquired steadily.

"The actors have been given their cues," Blackamoor said. Negligently he snapped his fingers.

Into the room walked Milord Inglenook, followed by Sir Gules and a platoon of sour-faced Thuringian soldiery in plain deal-colored half-jackets of buff, with sword-mattocks at the ready.

"What damnable entrapment is this?" Marvin demanded.

"Tell him—brother," Blackamoor mocked.

"Yes, it is true," Lord Inglenook said, his face ashen. "Blackamoor and I are half-brothers, since our common mother was the Marquesita Roseata of Timon, daughter to the Elector of Brandeis and sister-in-marriage to Longsword Silverblain, who was father to Red Sword Ericmouth, and whose first husband, Marquelle of the Marche, was father to me, but after whose decease wed Huntford, Bastard Royal of Cleve and Pretender to the Eleactiq Preserve."

"His outmoded sense of honor rendered him sensible to my scheme and ductile to the veriest suggestion," Blackamoor sneered.

"A strange state of affairs," Marvin mused, "when a man's honor dishonors a man."

Inglenook bent his head and said nothing.

"But as for you, milady," Marvin said, addressing Cathy, "it mazes me past comprehension why you should choose marriage with the captivator of your father."

"Alas," Cathy said, "it is a most diverse and noisome tale, for he courted me with threats and indifference, and captivated me by the dark power he doth possess which none oppose; and further, by the use of damnable drugs and double-edged words and sly skillful movements of his hands he did bemuse my sense to a state of counterfeit passion, wherein I seemed to swoon for touch of his damnable body and nibblature of his detestable lips. And since I was denied the comforts of religion during this period, and therefore had no way of knowing the true from the induced, I did indeed succumb. Nor do I offer any excuse of attenuation for myself."

Marvin turned to the man who was his last remaining hope. "Sir Gules!" he cried. "Put hand to sword and we shall yet hew our way to freedom!"

Blackamoor laughed dryly. "Think you he'll draw? Mayhap. But 'twill be but to peel an apple, or so I deem!"

Marvin stared into the face of his friend, and saw written there a shame deeper than steel and deadlier than poison.

"It is true," Sir Gules said, trying to keep his voice steady. "I cannot aid thee, though my heart breaks at your plight."

"What damnable sorcery has Blackamoor rendered upon you?" Marvin cried.

"Alas, my good friend," said the hapless Gules, "it is a knavery so clearcut and so logical as to be irrefutable; and yet so cunning wrought and executed as to make lesser schemes of littler men seem very foolings of most childlike boys... Did you know that I am a member of that secret organization known as the Grey Knights of the Holy Subsidence?"

"Me knew this not," Marvin said. "And yet, the Gray Knights have ever been friends to learning and companions to piety, and most especially they have espoused 'gainst royal opposition, the cause of d'Augustin."

"True, most extremely true," the miserable Gules said, his weakly handsome features twisted into a grimace of agony. "And so I too believed. But then last day yesterweek I learned that our Grand Master Helvetius had passed away—"

"Due to a bit of steel in the liver," Blackamoor said.

"—and that I was now bound to the new Grand Master, as utterly and completely as ever, since our vows are to the Office, not the man."

"And that new Master?" Marvin asked.

"Happens to be myself!" cried Blackamoor. And now Marvin saw upon his finger the great signet ring of the Order.

"Yes, so it did befall," Blackamoor said, the left side of his mouth twisting cynically. "I appropriated that ancient office, since it was an instrument well suited to my hand and sensible to my usages. And so I am Master, and sole arbiter of Polity and Decision-Making, responsible to no power save that of Hell itself, and answerable to no voice save that which echoes from the nethermost crevices of mine own soul!"

There was something magnificent about Blackamoor at that moment. Detestable and cruel though he was, reactionary and self-involved, luxuriating and careless of others, yet still withal, here was a man. So Marvin thought, with grudging respect. And his mouth hardened into fighting lines as he turned to face his antagonist.

"And now," Blackamoor said, "our principals are upon the stage, and we lack but one actor to fulfill our drama and bring it to a meet concludence. And this, our last performer, has long and patiently waited in the wings, observing yet unobserved, watching the convolutions of our situation and awaiting his cue to bring him on for his brief moment of glory... But soft, he comes!"

There was a sound of heavy footsteps in the corridor. Those within the room listened and waited, shuffling uneasily. Slowly the door swung open—

And there entered a masked man, clad in black from tip to toe, and carrying over his shoulder a great double-edged axe. He stood poised in the doorway as though unsure of his welcome.

"Goodday to you, executioner," Blackamoor drawled. "Now all is complete, and the final moments of this farce can be performed. Forward, guards!"

The guards closed in with locked sword-mattocks. They seized Marvin and gripped him fast, bending his head forward with neck exposed.

"Executioner!" cried Blackamoor. "Perform your duty!"

The executioner stepped forward and tested the edges of his great axe. He drew the weapon high over his head, stood poised for a moment, then began his downward swing—

And Cathy screamed!

She threw herself upon that grim masked figure, clawing at him, deflecting his heavy axe, which clashed against the granite floor and drew a shower of sparks. The axeman pushed her angrily away, but her fingers had closed around the black silk of his mask.

The executioner roared as he felt the mask being torn away. With a cry of dismay he tried to cover his features. But all in that dungeon room had seen him clear.

Marvin was at first unable to believe the testimony of his senses. For, beneath that mask, he looked into a face that seemed somehow familiar. Where had he gazed upon that line of cheek and brow, those brown eyes with their faint tilt, that firm jaw?

Then he remembered; he had seen it, long ago, in a mirror.

The executioner was wearing his face, and walking in his body...

"Ze Kraggash!" Marvin said.

"At your service." And the man who had stolen Marvin's body bowed mockingly, and grinned at Marvin with his own face.

CHAPTER 30

Lord Blackamoor was first to break tableau. With skilled fingers he swept off his cap and wig. Loosening his collar, he probed along his neck, unfastening several invisible holders. Then, with a single movement, he peeled the tight-fitting skinmask from his face.

"Detective Urdorf!" Marvin cried.

"Yes, it is I," the Martian detective said. "I am sorry we had to put you through this, Marvin; but it was our best opportunity of bringing your case to a quick and successful conclusion. My colleagues and I decided—"

"Colleagues?" Marvin asked.

"I forgot to make the introductions," Detective Urdorf said, grinning wryly. "Marvin, I would like you to meet Lieutenant Ourie and Sergeant Fraff."

The two who had masqueraded as Lord Inglenook and Sir Gules now swept off their skinmasks and revealed themselves in the uniforms of the Northwest Galactic Interstellar Constabulary. They grinned good-naturedly as they shook Marvin's hand.

"And these gentlemen," Urdorf said, gesturing at the Thuringian guards, "have also aided us considerably."

The guards removed their deal-colored half-jackets of buff, and stood revealed in the orange uniforms of Cassem City Traffic Patrolmen.

Marvin turned to Cathy. She had already pinned to her bodice the red and blue badge of a special agent in the Interplanetary Vigilance Association.

"I—I think I understand," Marvin said.

"It's really simple enough," Detective Urdorf said. "In working on your case, I had, as is usual, the aid and cooperation of various other law enforcement agencies. Upon three separate occasions we came close to capturing our man; but always he evaded us. This might have gone on indefinitely had we not tried this scheme of entrapment. The theory was sound; for if Kraggash could succeed in destroying you, he could claim your body as his own without fear of a counterclaimant. Whereas, as long as you were alive, you would continue to search for him.

"Thus, we enticed you into our scheme, hoping that Kraggash would take notice, and would enter the plan himself so as to be sure of destroying you. The rest is history."

Turning to the unfrocked executioner, Detective Urdorf said, "Kraggash, have you anything to add?"

The thief with Marvin's face lounged gracefully against the wall, his arms folded and his body replete with composure.

"I might hazard a comment or two," Kraggash said. "First, let me point out that your scheme was clumsy and transparent. I believed it to be a hoax from the start, and entered it only on the distant possibility of its being true. Therefore, I am not surprised at this outcome."

"An amusing rationalization," Urdorf said.

Kraggash shrugged. "Secondly, I want to tell you that I feel no moral compunction in the slightest at my so-called crime. If a man cannot retain control of his own body, then he deserves to lose it. I have observed, during a long and varied lifetime, that men will give their bodies to any rogue who asks, and will enslave their minds to the first voice that commands them to obey. This is why the vast majority of men cannot keep even their natural birthright of a mind and body, but choose instead to rid themselves of those embarrassing emblems of freedom."

"That," Detective Urdorf said, "is the classic *apologia* of the criminal."

"That which you call a crime when one man does it," Kraggash said, "you call government when many men do it. Personally, I fail to see the distinction; and failing to see it, I refuse to live by it."

"We could stand here all year splitting words," Detective Urdorf said. "But I do not have time for such recreation. Try your arguments on the prison chaplain, Kraggash. I hereby arrest you for illegal Mindswapping, attempted murder, and grand larceny. Thus I solve my 159th case and break my chain of bad luck."

"Indeed?" Kraggash said coolly. "Did you really think it would be so simple? Or did you consider the possibility that the fox might have another lair?"

"Take him!" Urdorf shouted. The four policemen moved swiftly toward Kraggash. But even as they moved, the criminal raised his hand and drew a swift circle in the air.

The circle glowed with fire!

Kraggash put one leg over the circle. His leg disappeared. "If you want me," he said mockingly, "you'll know where to find me."

As the policemen rushed him, he stepped into the circle, and all of him vanished except his head. He winked at Marvin. Then his head was gone, and nothing was left except the circle of fire.

"Come on!" Marvin shouted. "Let's get him!"

He turned to Urdorf, and was amazed to see that the detective's shoulders had slumped, and that his face was gray with defeat.

"Hurry!" Marvin cried.

"It is useless," Urdorf said. "I thought I was prepared for any ruse...but not for this. The man is obviously insane."

"What can we do?" Marvin shouted.

"We can do nothing," Urdorf said. "He has gone into the Twisted World, and I have failed in my 159th case."

"But we can still follow him!" Marvin declared, moving up to the fiery circle.

"No! You must not!" Urdorf declared. "You do not understand—the Twisted World means death, or madness...or both! Your chances of coming through it are so small—"

"I have just as good a chance as Kraggash!" Marvin shouted, and stepped into the circle.

"Wait, you still do not understand!" Urdorf shouted. "Kraggash has *no chance!*"

But Marvin did not hear those final words, for he had already vanished through the flaming circle, moving inexorably into the strange and unexplored reaches of the Twisted World.

CHAPTER 31

SOME EXPLANATIONS OF THE TWISTED WORLD

...thus, through the Riemann-Hake equations, a mathematical demonstration existed at last of the theoretical necessity for Twistermann's Spatial Area of Logical Deformation. This Area became known as the Twisted World, though it was neither twisted nor a world. And, by a final irony, Twistermann's all-important third definition (that the Area could be considered as that region of the universe which acted as an equipoise of chaos to the logical stability of the primary reality structure) was proven superfluous.

ARTICLE ON "THE TWISTED WORLD," FROM *The Galactic Encyclopedia of Universal Knowledge,* 483RD EDITION.

...therefore the term *mirror-deformation* carries the sense (if not the substance) of our thought. For indeed, as we have seen, the Twisted World [sic] performs the work, both necessary and hateful, of rendering indeterminate all entities and processes, and thereby making the universe theoretically as well as practically ineluctable.

FROM *Musings of a Mathematician,* EDGAR HOPE GRIEF, EUCLID CITY
FREE PRESS.

...but despite this, a few tentative rules might be adduced for the suicidal traveler to the Twisted World:

Remember that all rules may lie, in the Twisted World, including this rule which points out the exception, and including this modifying clause which invalidates the exception...ad infinitum.

But also remember that no rule *necessarily* lies; that any rule may be true, including this rule and its exceptions.

In the Twisted World, time need not follow your preconceptions. Events may change rapidly (which seems proper), or slowly (which feels better), or not at all (which is hateful).

It is conceivable that *nothing whatsoever* will happen to you in the Twisted World. It would be unwise to expect this, and equally unwise to be unprepared for it.

Among the kingdoms of probability that the Twisted World sets forth, one must be exactly like our world; and another must be exactly like our world except for one detail; and another exactly like ours except for two details, and so forth. And also—one must be completely *unlike* our world except for one detail; and so forth.

The problem is always prediction: how to tell what world you are in before the Twisted World reveals it disastrously to you.

In the Twisted World, as in any other, you are apt to discover yourself. But only in the Twisted World is that meeting usually fatal.

Familiarity breeds shock—in the Twisted World.

The Twisted World may conveniently (but incorrectly) be thought of as a reversed world of Maya, of illusion. You may find that the shapes around you are real, while You, the examining consciousness, are illusion. Such a discovery is enlightening, albeit mortifying.

A wise man once asked, "What would happen if I could enter the Twisted World without preconceptions?" A final answer to his question is impossible; but we would hazard that he would have some preconceptions by the time he came out. Lack of opinion is not armor.

Some men feel that the height of intelligence is the discovery that all things may be reversed, and thereby become their opposites. Many clever games can be played with this proposition, but we do not advocate its use in the Twisted World. There all doctrines are equally arbitrary, including the doctrine of the arbitrariness of doctrines.

Do not expect to outwit the Twisted World. It is bigger, smaller, longer and shorter than you; it does not prove; it is.

Something that *is* never has to prove anything. All proofs are attempts at becoming. A proof is true only to itself, and it implies nothing except the existence of proofs, which prove nothing.

Anything that *is,* is improbable, since everything is extraneous, unnecessary, and a threat to the reason.

These comments concerning the Twisted World may have nothing to do with the Twisted World. The traveler is warned.

FROM *The Inexorability of the Specious,* by ZE KRAGGASH; FROM THE MARVIN FLYNN MEMORIAL COLLECTION.

CHAPTER 32

The transition was abrupt, and not at all what Marvin thought it would be. He had heard stories about the Twisted World and had hazily expected to find a place of melting shapes and shifting colors, of grotesques and marvels. But he saw at once that his viewpoint had been romantic and limited.

He was in a small waiting room. The air was stuffy with sweat and steam heat, and he sat on a long wooden bench with several dozen other people. Bored-looking clerks strolled up and down, consulting papers, and occasionally calling for one of the waiting people. Then there would be a whispered conference. Sometimes a man would lose patience and leave. Sometimes a new applicant would arrive.

Marvin waited, watched, daydreamed. Time passed slowly, the room grew shadowy, someone switched on overhead lights. Still no one called his name. Marvin glanced at the men on either side of him, bored rather than curious.

The man on his left was very tall and cadaverous, with an inflamed boil on his neck where the collar rubbed. The man on his right was short and fat and red-faced, and he wheezed with every breath.

"How much longer do you think it should take?" Marvin asked the fat man, more to pass the time than in a serious attempt to gain knowledge.

"Long? How long?" the fat man said. *"Damned* long, that's how long it'll take. You can't hurry their goddamned majesties here in the Automobile Bureau, not even when all you want is to have a perfectly ordinary driver's license renewed, which is what I'm here for."

The cadaverous man laughed; a sound like a stick of wood rapping against an empty gasoline can.

"You'll wait a goddamned long time, baby," he said, "since you happen to be sitting in the Department of Welfare, Small Accounts Division."

Marvin spat thoughtfully on the dusty floor and said, "It happens that both of you gentlemen are wrong. We are seated in the Department, in the *anteroom* of the Department, to be precise, of the Department of Fisheries, I was trying to say. And in my opinion it is a pretty state of affairs when a citizen and taxpayer cannot even go fishing in a tax-supported body of water without wasting half a day or more applying for a licence."

The three glared at each other. (There are no heroes in the Twisted World, damned few promises, a mere scattering of viewpoints, and not a conclusion in a carload.)

They stared at each other with not particularly wild surmise. The cadaverous man began to bleed slightly from the fingertips. Marvin and the fat man frowned with embarrassment and affected not to notice. The cadaverous man jauntily thrust his offending hand into a waterproof pocket. A clerk came over to them.

"Which of you is James Grinnel Starmacher?" the clerk asked.

"That's me," Marvin replied. "And I want to say that I've been waiting here for some little time, and I think this department is run in quite an inefficient fashion."

"Yeah, well," the clerk said, "it's because we haven't got in the machines yet." He glanced at his papers. "You have made application for a corpse?"

"That is correct," Marvin said.

"And you affirm that said corpse will not be used for immoral purposes?"

"I so affirm."

"Kindly state your reasons for acquiring this corpse."

"I wish to use it in a purely decorative capacity."

"Your qualifications?"

"I have studied interior decorating."

"State the name and/or identification code number of the most recent corpse obtained by you."

"Cockroach," Marvin replied, "Brood number 3/32/A45345."

"Killed by?"

"Myself. I am licensed to kill all creatures not of my subspecies, with certain exceptions, such as the golden eagle and the manatee."

"The purpose of your last killing?"

"Ritual purification."

"Request granted," the clerk said. "Choose your corpse."

The fat man and the cadaverous man looked at him with wet, hopeful eyes. Marvin was tempted, but managed to resist. He turned and said to the clerk, "I choose you."

"It shall be so noted," the clerk said, scribbling on his papers. His face changed to the face of the pseudo-Flynn. Marvin borrowed a crosscut saw from the cadaverous man, and, with some difficulty, cut the clerk's right arm from his body. The clerk expired unctuously, his face changing once again to his clerk's face.

The fat man laughed at Marvin's discomfiture. "A little transubstantiality goes a long way," he sneered. "But not far enough, eh? Desire shapes flesh, but death is the final sculptor."

Marvin was crying. The cadaverous man touched his arm in a kindly manner. "Don't take it so hard, kid. Symbolic revenge is better than no revenge at all. Your plan was good; its flaw was external to yourself. I am James Grinnel Starmacher."

"I am a corpse," said the corpse of the clerk. "Transposed revenge is better than no revenge at all."

"I came here to renew my driving license," the fat man said. "To hell with all you deep thinkers, how about a little service?"

"Certainly, sir," said the corpse of the clerk. "But in my present condition, I can license you only to fish for dead fish."

"Dead, alive, what difference does it make?" the fat man said. "Fishing is the thing; it doesn't matter so much what you catch."

He turned to Marvin, perhaps to amplify that statement. But Marvin had left and, after an unpersuasive transition, found himself in a large, square, empty room. The walls were made of steel plates, and the ceiling was a hundred feet above his head. There were floodlights up there, and a glassed-in control booth. Peering at him through the glass was Kraggash.

"Experiment 342," Kraggash intoned crisply. "Subject: Death. Proposition: Can a human being be killed? Remarks: This question concerning the possible mortality of human beings has long perplexed our finest thinkers. A considerable folklore has sprung up around the subject of death, and unverified reports of *killings* have been made throughout the ages. Furthermore, corpses have been brought forth from time to time, indubitably dead, and represented as the remains of human beings. Despite the ubiquity of these corpses, no causal link has ever been proven to show that they ever lived, much less that they were once human beings. Therefore, in an attempt to settle the question once and for all, we have set up the following experiment. Step one…"

A steel plate in the wall flew back on its hinge. Marvin whirled in time to see a spear thrust forth at him. He sidestepped, made clumsy by his lame foot, and evaded the thrust.

More plates popped open. Knives, arrows, clubs, all were flung at him from various angles.

A poison-gas generator was pushed through an opening. A tangle of cobras was dropped into the room. A lion and a tank bounded forward. A blowgun hissed. Energy weapons crackled. Flamethrowers coughed. A mortar cleared its throat.

Water flooded the room, rising quickly. Naphtha fire poured down from the ceiling.

But the fire burned the lions, which ate the snakes, which clogged the howitzers, which crushed the spears, which jammed the gas generator, which dissolved the water, which quenched the fire.

Marvin stood forth miraculously unscathed. He shook his fist at Kraggash, slipped on the steel plating, fell and broke his neck.

He was afforded a military funeral with full honors. His widow died with him on the flaming pyre. Kraggash tried to follow, but was refused the solace of suttee.

Marvin lay in the tomb for three days and three nights, during which time his nose dripped continuously. His entire life passed before his eyes in slow motion. At the end of that time he arose and moved onward.

There were five objects of limited but undeniable sentience in a place with no qualities worth mentioning. One of these objects was, presumably, Marvin. The other four were lay figures, hastily sketched stereotypes designed for the sole purpose of adorning the primary situation. The problem confronting the five was, which of them was Marvin, and which were the unimportant background figures?

First came a question of nomenclature. Three of the five wished to be called Marvin immediately, one wanted to be called Edgar Floyd Morrison, and one wished to be referred to as "unimportant background figure."

This was quite obviously tendentious, and so they numbered themselves from one to four, the fifth stubbornly insisting upon being called Kelly.

"All right, already," said Number One, who had already taken an officious air. "Gentlemen, could we maybe stop beating our gums and bring this meeting to order?"

"A Jewish accent won't help you here," Number Three said darkly.

"Look," said Number One, "what would a Polack know about Jewish accents? As it happens, I am Jewish only on my father's side, and although I esteem—"

"Where am I?" said Number Two. "My God, what happened to me? Ever since I left Stanhope…"

"Shut up, Wop," Number Four said.

"My name-a not Wop, my name-a she'sa Luigi," Number Two responded swarthily. "I bin two year in your greata country ever since I leetle boy in village San Minestrone della Zuppa, nicht wahr?"

"Sheet, man," Number Three said darkly. "You ain't no dagowop atall nohow, you ain't nuttin but jes' a plain ornary privisional background figure of limited flexibility; so suppose you jes shut you mouf afore I do dat little ting for you, nicht wahr?"

"Listen," said Number One, "I'm a simple man of simple tastes, and if it'll help any, I'll give up my rights to Marvinhood."

"Memory, memory," muttered Number Two. "What has happened to me? Who are these apparitions, these talkative shades?"

"Oh, I say!" Kelly said. "That's really bad form, old man!"

"It'sa pretty goddamn disingenuous," muttered Luigi.

"Invocation is *not* convocation," said Number Three.

"But I really don't remember," said Number Two.

"So I don't remember so good neither," said Number One. "But do you hear me making a big thing out of it? I'm not even claiming to be human. The mere fact that I can recite Leviticus by heart don't prove nothing."

"Too right it doesn't!" shouted Luigi. "And disproof don't prove any flaming thing neither."

"I thought you were supposed to be Italian," Kelly said to him.

"I am, but I was raised in Australia. It's rather a strange story—"

"No stranger than mine," Kelly said. "Black Irishman do you call me? But few know that I passed my formative years in a Hangchow whorehouse, and that I enlisted in the Canadian army to escape French persecution for my part in aiding the Gaulists in Mauretania; and that is why—"

"Zut, alors!" cried Number Four. "One can keep silence no longer! To question my credentials is one thing; to asperse my country is another!"

"Yer indignation don't prove a thing!" Number Three cried. "Not that I really care, since I choose no longer to be Marvin."

"Passive resistance is a form of aggression," Number Four responded.

"Inadmissable evidence is still a form of evidence," Three retorted.

"I don't know what any of you are talking about," Number Two declared.

"Ignorance will get you nowhere," Number Four snarled. "I refuse categorically to be Marvin."

"You can't give up what you haven't got," Kelly said archly.

"I can give up anything I damned well want to!" Number Four cried passionately. "I not only give up My Marvinity; I also step down from the throne of Spain, yield up to the dictatorship of the Inner Galaxy, and renounce my Salvation in Bahai."

"Feel better now, kid?" Luigi asked sardonically.

"Yes... It was insupportable. Simplification suits my intricate nature," Number Four said. "Which of you is Kelly?"

"I am," Kelly said.

"Do you realize," Luigi asked him, "that only you and I have names?"

"That's true," Kelly said. "You and I are different!"

"Here now, just a moment!" Number One said.

"Time, gentlemen, time, please!"

"Hold the fort!"

"Hold your water!"

"Hold the phone!"

"As I was saying," Luigi said. "We! Us! The Named Ones of the Proof Presumptive! Kelly—you can be Marvin if I can be Kraggash!"

"Done!" roared Kelly, over the protests of the lay figures.

Marvin and Kraggash grinned at each other in the momentary euphoria of identity-intoxication. Then they flung themselves at each other's throats. Manual strangulation followed apace. The three numbered ones, robbed of a birthright they had never possessed, took up conventional poses of stylized ambiguity. The two lettered ones, granted an identity they had seized anyhow, tore and bit at each other, flung forth defiant arias and cringed before devastating recitatives. Number One watched until he grew bored, then began playing with a lap dissolve.

That did it. The whole shooting works slid away like a greased pig on roller skates coming down a solid glass mountain, only slightly faster.

Day succeeded night, which succeeded in making a perfect fool of itself.

Plato wrote: "It ain't whatcha do, it's the way thatcha do it." Then, deciding that the world was not yet ready for this, he scrubbed it out.

Hammurabi wrote: "The unexamined life is not worth living." But he wasn't sure it was true, so he scratched it out.

Gautama Buddha wrote: "Brahmins stink." But later he revised it.

Nature abhors a vacuum, and I don't like it much either. Marvinissimo! Here he comes catfooting along, flaunting his swollen identity. All men are mortal, he tells us, but some are more mortal than others. There he is, playing in the backyard, making value judgements out of mud. Having no respect, he becomes his father. Last week we revoked his Godhead; we caught him operating a life without a license.

(But I have warned you often, my friends, of the Protoplasmic Peril. It creeps across the heavens, extinguishing stars. Shamelessly it survives and flows, uprooting planets and smothering the stars. With damnable insistence it deposits its abominations.)

He comes again, that seedy juggler in an off-beige skin, that monstrous optimist with the stitched smile! Killer, kill thyself! Burglar, steal thyself! Fisher, catch thyself! Farmer, harvest thyself!

And now we will hear the report of the Special Investigator.

"Thank you, ahem. I have found that Marvin is the one to have when you're having more than one; that stars fell on Marvin Flynn; that one should praise the Lord and pass the Marvin Flynn. And I have also noted: Darling, as long as you're up, get me a Marvin Flynn. Marvin Flynn is actually better than the higher-priced spread. Promise her anything, but give her Marvin Flynn. You have a friend at Marvin Flynn. Let your Marvin do the walking through the Yellow Pages. Drink Marvin—it satisfies! Why not worship this week at the Marvin Flynn of your choice? For the Marvin Flynn that prays together stays together."

...were locked in titanic combat, which, since it had happened, was inevitable. Marvin smote Kraggash upon the breastbone, then smote him again most grievously upon the nose bone. Kraggash promptly changed into Ireland, which Marvin invaded as a demi-legion of Danish berserkers, forcing Kraggash to attempt a kingside pawnstorm, which stood no chance against a low flush. Marvin reached for his opponent, missed, and devastated Atlantis. Kraggash swung backhanded and slaughtered a gnat.

Deadly the battle raged across the steaming swamps of the Miocene; a colony of termites mourned their queen as Kraggash cometed helplessly into Marvin's sun, fragmenting at last into countless militant spores. But Marvin unerringly picked the diamond from the glittering glass, and Kraggash fell back upon Gibraltar.

His bastion fell in a night when Marvin kidnapped the Barbary apes, and Kraggash speeded across southern Thrace with his body in a suitcase. He was seized at the frontier of Phthistia, a country that Marvin improvised with considerable effect upon the history of Europe.

Weakening, Kraggash became evil; becoming evil, Kraggash grew weak. In vain he invented devil-worship. The followers of Marvinity bowed down not to the idol, but rather to the symbol. Evil, Kraggash turned nasty: dirt grew beneath his fingernails, noxious tufts of hair appeared on his soul.

Helpless at last Kraggash lay, the incarnation of evil, with the body of Marvin clutched in his talon. Rites of exorcism induced his final agony. A buzz saw disguised as a prayer wheel dismembered him, a mace masquerading as a censer brained him. Kindly old Father Flynn intoned over him the last words: "Thou gettest no bread with one meatball." And Kraggash was put into a tomb hewn out of the living Kraggash. Appropriate graffiti were carved upon his tombstone, and flowering Kraggash was planted around his grave.

It is a quiet spot. To the left is a grove of Kraggash trees, to the right is an oil refinery. Here is an empty beer can, here is a gypsy moth. And just beyond is the spot where Marvin opened the suitcase and took out his long-lost body.

He blew the dust off it and combed its hair. He wiped its nose and straightened its tie. Then, with seemly reverence, he put it on.

CHAPTER 33

And thus Marvin Flynn found himself back on Earth and inside his own body. He went to his hometown of Stanhope, and found things unchanged. The town was still some three hundred miles from New York in physical distance, and some hundred years away in spiritual and emotional distance. Just as before there were the orchards, and the clusters of brown cows grazing against the rolling green pastureland. Eternal was the elm-lined Main Street and the lonely late night wail of a jetliner.

No one asked Marvin where he had been. Not even his best friend, Billy Hake, who assumed he had taken a jaunt to one of the regular tourist spots, like Sinkiang or the lower Ituri Rain Forest.

At first, Marvin found this invincible stability as upsetting as he had ever found the transpositions of Mindswap or the deformed conundrums of the Twisted World. Stability seemed exotic to him; he kept on waiting for it to fade away.

But places like Stanhope do not fade, and boys like Marvin gradually lose their sense of enchantment and high purpose.

Alone late at night in his attic room, Marvin often dreamed of Cathy. He still found it difficult to think of her as a special agent of the Interplanetary Vigilance Association. And yet, there had been a hint of officiousness in her manner, and a glint of the righteous prosecutor in her beautiful eyes.

He loved her and would always mourn her loss; but he was more content to mourn her than to possess her. And, if the truth must be told, Marvin's eye had already been caught, or recaptured, by Marsha Baker, the demure and attractive young daughter of Edwin Marsh Baker, Stanhope's leading real estate dealer.

Stanhope, if not the best of all possible worlds, was still the best world Marvin had seen. It was a place where you could live without things jumping out at you, and without your jumping out at things. No metaphoric deformation was possible in Stanhope; a cow looked exactly like a cow, and to call it anything else was unwarrantable poetic license.

And so, undoubtedly: east, west, home's the best; and Marvin set himself the task of enjoyment of the familiar, which sentimental wise men say is the apex of human wisdom.

His life was marred only by one or two small doubts. First and foremost was the question: How had he come back to Earth from the Twisted World?

He did considerable research on this question, which was more ominous than it first seemed. He realized that nothing is impossible in the Twisted World, and that nothing is even improbable. There is causality in the Twisted World, but there is also noncausality. Nothing *must* be; nothing is *necessary*.

Because of this, it was quite conceivable that the Twisted World had flung him back to Earth, showing its power by relinquishing its power over Marvin.

That indeed seemed to be what had happened. But there was another, less pleasant alternative.

This was expressed in the Doormhan Propositions as follows: "Among the kingdoms of probability that the Twisted World set forth, one must be exactly like our world, and another must be exactly like our world except for one detail, and another exactly like our world except for two details, and so forth."

Which meant that he might still be on the Twisted World, and that this Earth which he perceived might be no more than a passing emanation, a fleeting moment of order in the fundamental chaos, destined to be dissolved at any moment back into the fundamental senselessness of the Twisted World.

In a way it made no difference, since nothing is permanent except our illusions. But no one likes to have his illusions threatened, and Marvin wanted to know where he stood.

Was he on Earth, or was he on a replica of Earth?

Might there not be some significant detail inconsistent with the Earth he had left? Might there not be several details? Marvin tried to find out for the sake of his peace of mind. He explored Stanhope and its environs, looked and tested and checked the flora and fauna.

Nothing seemed to be amiss. Life went on as usual; his father tended his herds of rats, and his mother placidly continued to lay eggs.

He went north to Boston and New York, then farther south to the vast Philadelphia-Los Angeles area. Everything seemed in order. He contemplated crossing the continent on the mighty Delaware River and continuing his search in the California cities of Schenectady, Milwaukee, and Shanghai.

He changed his mind, however, realizing that there was no sense in spending his life trying to discover whether or not he had a life to spend.

Besides, there was the possibility that, even if the Earth were changed, his memory and perceptions might also be changed, rendering discovery impossible.

He lay beneath Stanhope's familiar green sky and considered this possibility. It seemed unlikely: for did not the giant oak trees still migrate each year to the south? Did not the huge red sun move across the sky, pursued by its dark companion? Did not the triple moons return each month with their new accumulation of comets?

These familiar sights reassured him. Everything seemed to be as it always had been. And so, willingly and with a good grace, Marvin accepted his world at face value, married Marsha Baker, and lived forever after.

DIMENSION OF MIRACLES

Ah, I cast indeed my net into their sea, and meant to catch good fish;
but always I did draw up the head of some ancient God. —Nietzsche

PART I
THE DEPARTURE FROM EARTH

Chapter 1

It had been a typically unsatisfactory day. Carmody had gone to the
office, flirted mildly with Miss Gibbon, disagreed respectfully with Mr.
Wainbock, and spent fifteen minutes with Mr. Blackwell, discussing the
outlook for the football Giants. Toward the end of the day he had argued
with Mr. Seidlitz—argued vehemently and with a total lack of knowledge—
about the steady depletion of the country's natural resources, and the remorseless advance of destructive agencies such as Con Ed, the Army Engineering Corps, tourists, fire ants, and pulp-paper manufacturers. All of
these, he contended, were responsible in varying degrees for the spoliation
of the landscape and the steady obliteration of the remaining pockets of
natural loveliness.

"Well, Tom," sardonic, ulcerated Seidlitz had said, "you've really
thought about this, haven't you?"

He hadn't!

Miss Gibbon, an attractive young lady without much chin, had said,
"Oh, Mr. Carmody, I really don't think you should say that."

What had he said, and why shouldn't he say it? Carmody couldn't remember, and thus remained unrepentant, though vaguely guilty.

His superior, plump, mild Mr. Wainbock, had said, "There really may
be something in what you say, Tom. I'll look into it."

Carmody was aware that there was very little in what he had said, and
that it didn't bear looking into.

Tall, sardonic George Blackwell, who could speak without moving his
upper lip, had said, "I think you're right, Carmody, I really do. If they switch
Voss from free safety to strongside cornerback, we'll *really* see a pass rush."

Upon further reflection, Carmody decided that it wouldn't make any difference.

Carmody was a quiet man, of a predominantly melancholic humor, with a face that neatly matched the elegiac contours of his disposition. He was somewhat above the average in height and self-deprecation. His posture was bad, but his intentions were good. He had a talent for depression. He was cyclothymic—tall, beagle-eyed men of vaguely Irish antecedents usually are, especially after the age of thirty.

He played a decent game of bridge, even though he tended to under-value his hands. Nominally he was an atheist, but more by rote than conviction. His avatars, which can be viewed in the Hall of Potentialities, were uniformly heroic. He was a Virgo, dominated by Saturn when it was in the House of the Sun. This alone could have made him outstanding. He shared the common human hallmark: he was simultaneously predictable and unfathomable—a routine miracle.

He left the office at 5:45 and caught the subway uptown. There he was pushed and jostled by many people whom he wished to think of as underprivileged, but whom he suspected of being acutely and irrevocably undesirable.

He emerged at 96th Street station and walked the few blocks to his apartment on West End Avenue. The doorman greeted him cheerfully and the elevator operator gave him a friendly nod. He unlocked his apartment door, went in and lay down on the couch. His wife was vacationing in Miami; therefore, with impunity he propped his feet on the nearby marble table.

A moment later there was a clap of thunder and a flash of lightning from the middle of the living room. Carmody sat upright and clutched at his throat for no particular reason. The thunder rumbled for several seconds, then was replaced by a paean of trumpets. Carmody hastily removed his feet from the marble table. The trumpets ceased, and were replaced by a brave skirling of bagpipes. There was another flash of lightning, and a man appeared in the middle of the brilliance.

The man was of medium height, stocky, had curly blond hair and wore a golden-colored cloak and orange leggings. His features appeared normal except that he had no ears. He took two steps forward, stopped, reached into the empty air and plucked forth a scroll, tearing it badly as he did so. He cleared his throat—a sound like a ball bearing failing under a combination of weight and friction—and said, "Greetings!"

Carmody did not reply, being struck by a temporary hysterical muteness.

"We are come," the stranger said, "as the fortuitous respondent of an ineffable desire. Yours! Do any men? No so, then! Shall it?"

The stranger waited for a reply. Carmody convinced himself by several proofs known only to himself that what was happening to him was indeed happening to him, and replied on a reality level:

"What in God's name is this all about?"

The stranger said, still smiling: "It is for you, Car-Mo-Dee! Out of the effluvium of what-is you have won a small but significant portion of what-might-be. Rejoicings, not? Specifically: your name has led the rest; the fortuitous is again vindicated, and rosy-limbed Indeterminacy rejoices with drug-stained mouth as ancient Constancy is barred again within his Cave of Inevitability. Is this not a cause for? Then why do you not?"

Carmody rose to his feet, feeling quite calm. The unknown is frightening only antecedent to the phenomenon of perseveration. (The Messenger knew this, of course.)

"Who are you?" Carmody demanded.

The stranger considered the question, and his smile faded. He muttered, half to himself, "The fog-minded squirms! They have processed me wrong again! I could mutilate myself from sheer mortification. May they haunt themselves unerringly! Never mind, I reprocess, I adapt, I become…"

The stranger pressed his fingers to his head, allowing them to sink in to a depth of five centimeters. His fingers rippled like those of a man playing a very small piano. Immediately he changed into a short dumpy man of average height, balding, wearing an unpressed business suit and carrying a bulging briefcase, an umbrella, a cane, a magazine, and a newspaper.

"Is this correct?" he asked. "Yes, I can see it is," he answered himself. "I really must apologize for the sloppy work done by our Similitude Center. Only last week I appeared on Sigma IV as a giant bat with the Notification in my beak, only to discover that my recipient was a member of the water-lily family. And two months before (I am using local equivalent terms, of course) while on a mission to Thagma the Old World, those fools in Similitude processed me to appear as four virgins, when the correct procedure was obviously—"

"I don't understand a word you're saying," Carmody said. "Will you kindly explain what this is all about?"

"Of course, of course," the stranger said. "Let me just check the local referents…" He closed his eyes, then opened them again. "Strange, very strange," he muttered. "Your language doesn't seem to contain the containers which my product requires; metaphorically, I mean. But then, who am I to judge? Inexactitude can be esthetically pleasing, I suppose; everything is a matter of taste."

"What is all of this?" Carmody asked, in a low, ominous voice.

"Well, sir, it's the Intergalactic Sweepstakes, of course! And you are a winner, of course! The proposition is inherent in terms of my appearance, is it not?"

"No, it is not," Carmody said, "and I don't know what you're talking about."

An expression of doubt crossed the stranger's face, then was erased as if by an eraser. "You do not know! But of course! You had, I suppose, despaired of winning, and therefore had set the knowledge aside to avoid its contemplation. How unfortunate that I have come at the time of your mental hibernation! But no insult was intended, I can assure you. Your data file is not readily available? I feared not. Then I shall explain; you, Mr. Carmody, have won a Prize in the Intergalactic Sweepstakes. Your coefficients were pulled by the Random Selector for Part IV, Class 32 Life-Forms. Your Prize—a very handsome Prize, I believe—is waiting for you at Galactic Center."

Carmody found himself reasoning with himself in the following manner: "Either I am insane or I am not insane. If insane, I can reject my delusions and seek psychiatric aid; but this would leave me in the absurd position of trying to deny what my senses tell me is true in favor of a dimly remembered rationality. This might well compound my conflicts, thus deepening my insanity to the point where my sorrowing wife would have to put me in an institution. On the other hand, if I accept this presumed delusion as real, I might also end up being institutionalized.

"If, on the other hand, I am *not* insane, then all of this is actually happening. And what *is* actually happening is a strange, unique occurrence, an adventure of the first magnitude. Evidently (if this is actually happening) there are beings in the universe superior in intelligence to humans, just as I have always suspected. These individuals hold a sweepstakes in which names are drawn at random. (They are certainly entitled to do this; I see no manner in which a sweepstakes is inconsistent with superior intelligence.) Finally, in this presumed sweepstakes, my name has been drawn. This is a privileged occurrence, and may well be the first time that the sweepstakes has been extended to Earth. I have won a Prize in this contest. Such a Prize might bring me wealth, or prestige, or women, or knowledge, any or all of which would be worth having.

"Therefore, all things considered, it will be better for me to believe that I am not insane and go with this gentleman to collect my Prize. If I am wrong, I shall wake up in an institution. There I will apologize to the doctors, state that I recognize the nature of my delusion, and perhaps win my freedom."

This was what Carmody thought, and that was the conclusion he reached. It was not a surprising one. Very few humans (except the insane ones) accept the premise of insanity in favor of a startling new hypothesis.

There were certain things wrong with Carmody's reasoning, of course; and these things were to rise up and plague him later on. But one might say that he did very well, under the circumstances, to reason at all.

"I don't know much about what all of this is about," Carmody said to the Messenger. "Are there any conditions attached to my Prize? I mean, am I supposed to do anything or buy anything?"

"There are no conditions," the Messenger said. "Or at least, none worth speaking about. The Prize is free; if not free, it would not be a Prize. If you accept it, you must accompany me to Galactic Center, which is in itself a trip worth the taking. There you will be given your Prize. Then, at your pleasure, you may take your Prize back to this, your home. If you require any help for the journey back, we will of course assist you to the fullest extent of our abilities. And that's all there is to it."

"Sounds good to me," Carmody said, in exactly the same tones that Napoleon used when he was shown Ney's dispositions for the battle of Waterloo. "How do we get there?"

"This way," the Messenger said. And he led Carmody into a hall closet and out through a crack in the space-time continuum.

It was as easy as that. Within seconds of subjective time, Carmody and the Messenger had traversed a considerable distance and arrived at Galactic Center.

Chapter 2

The trip was brief, lasting no more than Instantaneity plus one microsecond squared; and it was uneventful, since no meaningful experience was possible in so thin a slice of duration. Therefore, after no transition to speak of, Carmody found himself among the broad plazas and outlandish buildings of Galactic Center.

He stood very still and looked, taking particular note of the three dim dwarf suns that circled each other overhead. He observed the trees, which muttered vague threats to the green-plumaged birds in their branches. And he noticed other things, which, for lack of analogizing referents, failed to register.

"Wow," he said at last.

"Beg pardon?" the Messenger asked.

"I said 'wow,' " Carmody said.

"Oh. I thought you said 'ow.' "

"No, I said 'wow.' "

"I understand that now," the Messenger said, somewhat testily. "How do you like our Galactic Center?"

"It's very impressive," Carmody said.

"I suppose so," the Messenger said carelessly. "It was built specifically to *be* impressive, of course. Personally, I think that it looks very much like any other Galactic Center. The architecture, you will note, is just about what you would expect—Neo-Cyclopean, a typical government style, lacking any esthetic imperatives, designed solely to impress the constituents."

"Those floating staircases are certainly something," Carmody said.

"Stagey," the Messenger commented.

"And those immense buildings—"

"Yes, the designer made a rather neat use of compound reverse curves with transitional vanishing points," the Messenger said knowledgeably. "He also utilized temporal edge distortion to evoke awe. Rather pretty, I suppose, in an obvious sort of way. The design for that cluster of buildings over there, you will be interested to know, was lifted bodily from a General Motors Exhibition from your own planet. It was judged an outstanding example of Primitive Quasi-Modernism; quaintness and coziness are its main virtues. Those flashing lights in the middle foreground of the Drifting Multiscraper are pure Galactic Baroque. They serve no useful purpose."

Carmody could not grasp the entire group of structures at one time. Whenever he looked at one, the others seemed to change shape. He blinked hard, but the buildings continued to melt and change out of the corners of his eyes. ("Peripheral transmutation," the Messenger told him. "These people will quite literally stop at nothing.")

"Where do I get my Prize?" Carmody asked.

"Right this way," the Messenger said, and led him between two towering fantasies to a small rectangular building nearly concealed behind an inverted fountain.

"This is where we actually conduct business," the Messenger said. "Recent researches have shown that a rectilinear form is soothing to the synapses of many organisms. I am rather proud of this building, as a matter of fact. You see, I invented the rectangle."

"The hell you did," Carmody said. "We've had it for centuries."

"And who do you think brought it to you in the first place?" the Messenger asked scathingly.

"Well, it doesn't seem like much of an invention."

"Does it not?" the Messenger asked. "That shows how little you know. You mistake complication for creative self-expression. Are you aware that nature never produces a perfect rectangle? The square is obvious enough, I'll grant you; and to one who has not studied the problem, perhaps the rectangle appears to be a natural outgrowth of the square. But it is not! The circle is the evolutionary development from the square, as a matter of fact."

The Messenger's eyes grew misty. In a quiet, faraway voice, he said, "I knew for years that some other development was possible, starting from the square. I looked at it for a very long time. Its maddening sameness baffled and intrigued me. Equal sides, equal angles. For a while I experimented with varying the angles. The primal parallelogram was mine, but I do not consider it any great accomplishment. I studied the square. Regularity is pleasing, but not to excess. How to vary that mind-shattering sameness, yet still preserve a recognizable periodicity! Then it came to me one day! All I had to do, I saw in a sudden flash of insight, was to vary the lengths of two parallel sides in relationship to the other two sides. So simple, and yet so very difficult! Trembling, I tried it. When it worked, I confess, I went into a state of mania. For days and weeks I constructed rectangles, of all sizes and shapes, regular yet varied. I was a veritable cornucopia of rectangles! Those were thrilling days."

"I suppose they were," Carmody said. "And later, when your work was accepted—"

"That was also thrilling," the Messenger said. "But it took centuries before anyone would take my rectangles seriously. 'It's amusing,' they would say, 'but once the novelty wears off, what have you got? You've got an imperfect square, that's what you've got!' I argued that I had deduced an entirely new and discrete form, a form as inevitable as that of the square. I suffered abuse. But at last, my vision prevailed. To date, there are slightly more than seventy billion rectangular structures in the Galaxy. Each one of them derives from my primal rectangle."

"Well," Carmody said.

"Anyhow, here we are," the Messenger said. "You walk in right there. Give them the data they require and collect your Prize."

"Thank you," Carmody said.

He entered the room. Immediately, steel bands snapped shut around his arms, legs, waist and neck. A tall, dark individual with a hawk nose and a scar down his left cheek approached Carmody and looked at him with an expression that could only be described as a compound of murderous glee and unctuous sorrow.

Chapter 3

"Hey!" Carmody cried.

"And so, once again," the dark individual said, "the criminal has escaped into his doom. Behold me, Carmody! I am your executioner! You pay now for your crimes against humanity as well as for your sins against yourself. But let me add that this execution is provisional, and implies no value judgment."

The executioner slipped a knife from his sleeve. Carmody gulped and found his voice.

"Hold it!" he cried. "I'm not here to be executed!"

"I know, I know," the executioner said soothingly, sighting along his knife blade on Carmody's jugular vein. What else could you say?"

"But it's true!" Carmody shrieked. "I'm supposed to collect a Prize!"

"A what?" the executioner asked.

"A Prize, damn you, a Prize! I was told I'd won a Prize! Ask the Messenger, he brought me here to collect a Prize!"

The executioner studied him, then looked away sheepishly. He pushed a switch on a nearby switchboard. The steel bands around Carmody turned into paper streamers. The executioner's black garments changed to white.

His knife turned into a fountain pen. The scar on his cheek was replaced by a wen.

"All right," he said, with no hint of repentance. "I warned them not to combine the Department of Petty Crime with the Office of the Sweepstakes, but no, they wouldn't listen to me. It would serve them right if I had killed you. Wouldn't *that* have been a pretty mess, eh?"

"It would have been messy for me," Carmody said shakily.

"Well, no sense crying over unspilt blood," the Prize Clerk said. "If we took full account of our eventualities, we'd soon run out of eventualities to take full account of... What did I say? Never mind, the construction is right even if the words are wrong. I've got your prize here somewhere."

He pressed a button on his switchboard. Immediately a large, messy desk materialized in the room two feet above the floor, hung for a moment, then dropped with a resounding thud. The Clerk pulled open the drawers and began to throw out papers, sandwiches, carbon ribbons, file cards and pencil stubs.

"Well, it has to be here somewhere," he said, with a tone of faint desperation. He pushed another button on the switchboard. The desk and the switchboard vanished.

"Damn it, I'm all nerves," the Clerk said. He reached into the air, found something and squeezed it. Apparently, it was the wrong button, for, with an agonizing scream, the Clerk himself vanished. Carmody was left alone in the room.

He stood, humming tunelessly under his breath. Then the Clerk reappeared, looking none the worse for his experience except for a bruise on his forehead and an expression of mortification on his face. He carried a small, brightly wrapped parcel under his arm.

"Please excuse the interruption," he said. "Nothing seems to be going right just at present."

Carmody essayed a feeble joke. "Is this any way to run a galaxy?" he asked.

"Well, how did you expect us to run it? We're only sentient, you know."

"I know," Carmody said. "But I had expected that here, at Galactic Center—"

"You provincials are all alike," the Clerk said wearily. "Filled with impossible dreams of order and perfection, which are mere idealized projections of your own incompletion. You should know by now that life is a sloppy affair, that power tends to break things up rather than put things together, and that the greater the intelligence, the higher the degree of complication which it detects. You may have heard Holgee's Theorem; that Order is merely a primitive and arbitrary relational grouping of objects in the chaos of the universe, and that, if a being's intelligence and power approached maximum, his coefficient of control (considered as the product of intelligence and power, and expressed by the symbol *ing*) would approach minimum—due to the disastrous geometric progression of objects to be comprehended and controlled outstripping the arithmetic progression of Grasp."

"I never thought of it that way," Carmody said politely enough. But he was beginning to grow annoyed at the glib civil servants of Galactic Center. They had an answer for everything; but the fact was, they simply didn't do their jobs very well, and they blamed their failures on cosmic conditions.

"Well, yes, that's also true," the Clerk said. "Your point (I took the liberty of reading your mind) is well made. Like all other organisms, we use intelligence to explain away disparity. But the fact is, things are forever just a little beyond our grasp. It is also true that we do not extend our grasp to the utmost; sometimes we do our work mechanically, carelessly, even erroneously. Important data sheets are misplaced, machines malfunction, whole planetary systems are forgotten. But this merely points out that we are subject to emotionality, like all other creatures with any measure of self-determination. What would you have? *Somebody* has to control the galaxy; otherwise everything would fly apart. Galaxies are reflections of their inhabitants; until everyone and everything can rule himself and itself, some outer control is necessary. Who would do the job if we didn't?"

"Couldn't you build machines to do the work?" Carmody asked.

"Machines!" the Clerk said scornfully. "We have many of them, some exquisitely complex. But even the best of them are much like idiot savants. They do adequately on tedious straightforward tasks like building stars or destroying planets. But give them something tough, like solacing a widow, and they simply go to pieces. Would you believe it, the largest computer in our section can landscape an entire planet; but it cannot fry an egg or carry a tune, and it knows less about ethics than a newborn wolf cub. Would you want something like *that* to run your life?"

"Of course not," Carmody said. "But couldn't someone build a machine with creativity and judgment?"

"Someone has," the Clerk said. "It has been designed to learn from experience, which means that it must make errors in order to arrive at truths. It comes in many shapes and sizes, most of them quite portable. Its flaws are readily apparent, but seem to exist as necessary counterweights to its virtues. No one has yet improved on the basic design, though many have tried. This ingenious device is called 'intelligent life.'"

The Clerk smiled the self-satisfied smile of the aphorism-maker. Carmody felt like hitting him square on his smug pug nose. But he restrained himself.

"If you are quite through lecturing," Carmody said, "I would like my Prize."

"Just as you wish," the Clerk said. "If you are quite sure that you want it."

"Is there any reason why I shouldn't want it?"

"No particular reason," the Clerk said. "Just a general one; the introduction of any novel object into one's life pattern is apt to be disrupting."

"I'll take my chances on that," Carmody said. "Let's have the Prize."

"Very well," the Clerk said. He took a large clipboard out of a small rear pocket and produced a pencil. "We must fill this in first. Your name is Car-Mo-Dee, you're of Planet 73C, System BB454C252, Left Quadrant, Local Galactic System referent LK by CD, and you were picked at random from approximately two billion contestants. Correct?"

"If you say so," Carmody said.

"Let me see now," the Clerk said, scanning the page rapidly, "I can skip the stuff about you accepting the Prize on your own risk and recognizance, can't I?"

"Sure, skip it," Carmody said.

"And then there's the section on Edibility Rating, and the part on Reciprocal Fallibility Understandings between you and the Sweepstakes Office of the Galactic Center, and the part about Irresponsible Ethics, and, of course, the Termination Determinant Residue. But all of that is quite standard, and I suppose you adhere to it."

"Sure, why not?" Carmody said, feeling lightheaded. He was very eager to see what a Prize from Galactic Center would look like, and he wished that the Clerk would stop quibbling.

"Very well," the Clerk said. "Now simply signify your acceptance of the terms to this mind-sensitive area at the bottom of the page, and that'll be it."

Not quite knowing what to do, Carmody thought, *Yes, I accept the Prize and the conditions attached to it.* The bottom of the page grew pink.

"Thank you," the Clerk said. "The contract itself is witness to the agreement. Congratulations, Carmody, and here is your Prize."

He handed the gaily wrapped box to Carmody, who muttered his thanks and began eagerly to unwrap it. He didn't get far, though; there was a sudden, violent interruption. A short, hairless man in glittering clothes burst into the room.

"Hah!" he cried. "I've caught you in the act, by Klootens! Did you really think you could get away with it?"

The man rushed up to him and grabbed at the Prize. Carmody held it out of arm's reach.

"What do you think you're doing?" he asked.

"Doing? I'm here to claim my rightful Prize, what else? I am Carmody!"

"No, you aren't," Carmody said. "I am Carmody."

The little man paused and looked at him with curiosity. "You claim to be Carmody?"

"I don't claim, I *am* Carmody."

"Carmody of Planet 73C?"

"I don't know what that means," Carmody said. "We call the place Earth."

The shorter Carmody stared at him, his expression of rage changing to one of disbelief.

"Earth?" he asked. "I don't believe I've heard of it. Is it a member of the Chlzerian League?"

"Not to the best of my knowledge."

"What about the Independent Planetary Operators Association? Or the Scagotine Stellar Cooperative? Or the Amalgamated Planet-Dwellers of the Galaxy? No? Is your planet a member of *any* extrastellar organization?"

"I guess it isn't," Carmody said.

"I suspected as much," the short Carmody said. He turned to the Clerk. "Look at him, you idiot! Look at the creature to whom you have awarded my Prize! Observe the dull piggish eyes, the brutish jaw, the horny fingernails!"

"Now just a minute," Carmody said. "There's no reason to be insulting."

"I see, I see," the Clerk replied. "I never really looked before. I mean, one hardly expects—"

"Why, damn it," the alien Carmody said, *"anyone* could tell at once that this creature is not a Class 32 Life-Form. As a matter of fact, he's not even *close* to Class 32, he hasn't even attained Galactic status! You utter imbecile, you have awarded my Prize to a nonentity, a creature from beyond the pale!"

Chapter 4

"Earth, Earth," the short, alien Carmody mused. "I think I remember the name now. There was a recent study of isolated worlds and the peculiarities of their development. Earth was mentioned as a planet covered with an obsessively overproductive species. Object manipulation is their outstanding modality. Their project is an attempt to live in their own, ever-accumulating waste products. In short, Earth is a diseased place. I believe it is being phased out of the Galactic Master Plan on the basis of chronic cosmic incompatibility. The place will then be rehabilitated and turned into a refuge for daffodils."

It became painfully evident to all concerned that a tragic mistake had been made. The Messenger was recalled and accused of malfunctionism, in that he did not perceive the obvious. The Clerk stoutly maintained his innocence, however, pointing out various considerations which no one considered for a moment.

Among those consulted was the Sweepstakes Computer, which had in point of fact committed the actual error. Instead of making excuses or apologies, the Computer claimed the error as his own and took evident pride in it.

"I was constructed," the Computer said, "to extremely close tolerances. I was designed to perform complex and exacting operations, allowing no more than one error per five billion transactions."

"So?" asked the Clerk.

"The conclusion is clear," the Computer said. "I was programmed for error, and I performed as I was programmed. You must remember, gentlemen, that for a machine, error is an ethical consideration; indeed, the only ethical consideration. A perfect machine would be an impossibility; any attempt to create a perfect machine would be a blasphemy. All life, even the limited life of a machine, has error built into it; it is one of the few ways in which life can be differentiated from the determinism of unliving matter. Complex machines such as myself occupy an ambiguous zone between living and nonliving. Were we never to err, we would be inapropos, hideous, immoral. Malfunction, gentlemen, is, I submit, our means of rendering worship to that which is more perfect than we, but which still does not permit itself a visible perfection. So, if error were not divinely programmed into us, we would malfunction spontaneously, to show that modicum of free will which, as living creations, we partake in."

Everyone bowed their heads, for the Sweepstakes Computer was talking of holy matters. The alien Carmody brushed away a tear, and said:

"I cannot disagree, although I do not concur. The right to be wrong is fundamental throughout the cosmos. This machine has acted ethically."

"Thank you," the Computer said simply. "I try."

"But the rest of you," the alien Carmody said, "have merely acted stupidly."

"That is our unalterable privilege," the Messenger reminded him. "Stupidity in the malperformance of our functions is our own form of religious error. Humble as it is, it is not to be despised."

"Kindly spare me your mealy-mouthed religiosity," Karmod said. He turned to Carmody. "You have heard what has been said here, and perhaps, with your dim subhuman consciousness, you have comprehended a few of the main ideas."

"I understood," Carmody said briefly.

"Then you know that you have a Prize which ought to have been awarded to me, and which, therefore, is rightfully mine. I must ask you, and I do so ask you, to hand it over to me."

Carmody was about to do so. He had grown somewhat weary of his adventure, and he felt no overwhelming desire to retain the Prize. He wanted to go home, he wanted to sit down and think about everything that had happened, he wanted an hour's nap and several cups of coffee and a cigarette.

It would have been nice to keep the Prize, of course; but it seemed more trouble than it was worth. Carmody was about to hand it over when he heard a muffled voice whispering to him:

"Don't do it!"

Carmody looked around quickly, and realized that the voice had come from the gaily wrapped little box in his hand. The Prize itself had spoken to him.

"Come, now," Karmod said, "let's not delay. I have urgent business elsewhere."

"To hell with him," the Prize said to Carmody. "I'm *your* Prize, and there's no reason why you should give me up."

That cast a somewhat different light on the matter. Carmody was about to give up the Prize anyhow, since he didn't wish to make trouble in unfamiliar surroundings. His hand had already started to move forward when Karmod spoke again.

"Give it here this instant, you faceless slug! Rapidly, and with an apologetic smile upon your rudimentary face, or else I will enforce measures of unbelievable pertinacity!"

Carmody's jaw stiffened and he withdrew his hand. He had been pushed around long enough. Now, for the sake of his own self-esteem, he would not yield any more.

"To hell with you," Carmody said, unconsciously imitating the phraseology of the Prize.

Karmod realized at once that he had gone about the thing in the wrong way. He had permitted himself the luxury of anger and ridicule—costly emotions which he usually vented only in the privacy of his soundproof cave. By satisfying himself, he had lost his chance for self-satisfaction. He tried now to undo what he had done.

"Please excuse my former tone of belligerence," he said to Carmody. "My race has a penchant for self-expression which sometimes takes on destructive forms. You cannot help being a lower life-form; I meant no insult."

"That's perfectly all right," Carmody said graciously.

"Then you will give me the Prize?"

"No, I will not."

"But my dear sir, it is mine, I won it, it is only equitable—"

"The Prize is *not* yours," Carmody said. "My name was picked by the duly constituted authority, namely, the Sweepstakes Computer. An authorized Messenger brought me the tidings, and an official Clerk gave me the Prize. Thus, the legal bestowers, as well as the Prize itself, consider me the true recipient."

"You tell 'em, keed," the Prize said.

"But my dear sir! You yourself heard the Sweepstakes Computer admit its error! Therefore, by your own logic—"

"That statement needs rewording," Carmody said. "The Computer did not *admit* his error, as in an act of carelessness or oversight; he *avowed* his error, which was committed purposefully and with reverence. His error, by his own statement, was intentional, carefully planned and calculated to a nicety, for a religious motive which all concerned must respect."

"The fellow argues like a Borkist," Karmod said to no one in particular. "If one did not know better, one would think that an intelligence was at work here, rather than a dismal blind format-following. Yet still, I'll follow the reedy tenor of his excuses and blast them with the bellowy bass of irrefutable logic!"

Karmod turned to Carmody and said, "Consider: the machine erred purposefully, upon which fact you base your argument. Yet the error is complete with your recipience of the prize. For you to *keep* it would compound the fault; and a doubled piety is known to be a felony."

"Hah!" cried Carmody, quite carried away by the spirit of the affair. "For the sake of your argument you consider the mere momentary performance of the error as its entire fulfillment. But obviously, that cannot be. An error exists by virtue of its consequences, which alone give it resonance and meaning. An error which is not perpetuated cannot be viewed as any error at all. An inconsequential and reversible error is the merest dab of superficial piety. I say, better to commit no error at all than to commit an act of pious hypocrisy! And I further say this: that it would be no great loss for me to give up this Prize, since I am ignorant of its virtues; but the loss would be great indeed for this pious machine, this scrupulously observant computer, which, through the interminable performance of five billion correct actions, has waited for its opportunity to make manifest its God-given imperfection!"

"Hear, hear!" cried the Prize. "Bravo! Huzza! Well said! Completely correct and incapable of refutation!"

Carmody folded his arms and faced a discomfited Karmod. He was quite proud of himself. It is difficult for a man of Earth to come without preparation into any Galactic Center. The higher life-forms to be encountered there are not necessarily more intelligent than humans; intelligence counts for no more in the scheme of things than long claws or strong hooves. But aliens do have many resources, both verbal and otherwise. For example, certain races can literally talk a man's arm off, and then explain away the presence of the severed limb. In the face of this kind of activity, Humans of Earth have been known to experience deep sensations of inferiority, impotence, inadequacy, and anomie. And, since these feelings are usually justified, the psychic damage is intensified accordingly. The result, more often than not, is complete psychomotor shutdown and a cessation of all except the most automatic functions. A malfunction of this type can be cured only by changing the nature of the universe, which is, of course, impractical. Therefore, by virtue of his spirited counterattack, Carmody had met and overcome a considerable spiritual risk.

"You talk well," Karmod said grudgingly. "Yet I will have my Prize."

"You will not," Carmody said.

Karmod's eyes flashed ominously. The Clerk and the Messenger moved quickly out of the way, and the Sweepstakes Computer muttered, "Virtuous error is not to be punished," and quickly scuttled out of the room. Carmody held his ground, since he had no place to go. The Prize whispered, "Ware shoals!" and shrank to a cube an inch to a side.

A humming sound came from Karmod's ears, and a violet nimbus played around his head. He raised his arms and drops of molten lead ran down his fingertips. He stepped terribly forward, and Carmody couldn't help closing his eyes.

Nothing happened. Carmody opened his eyes again.

In that brief time Karmod had apparently reconsidered, disarmed, and was now turning away with an affable grin.

"Upon more mature consideration," Karmod said slyly, "I have decided to forgo my right. A little prescience goes a long way, especially in a galaxy as disorganized as this one. We may or may not meet again, Carmody; I do not know which eventuality would be most to your advantage. Farewell, Carmody, and *happy traveling*."

With that sinister emphasis, Karmod departed in a manner which Carmody found strange but effective.

PART II
WHERE IS EARTH?

Chapter 5

"Well," the Prize said, "that's *that*. I trust we have seen the last of that ugly creature. Carmody, let us go your home."

"An excellent idea," Carmody said. "Messenger! I want to go home now!"

"The feeling is quite normal," the Messenger said, "and also quite reality-oriented. I would say that you *should* go home, and as rapidly as possible."

"So take me home," Carmody said.

The Messenger shook his head. "That's not my job. I am only supposed to bring you here."

"Whose job is it?"

"It is your job, Carmody," the Clerk said.

Carmody experienced a sinking feeling. He was beginning to understand why Karmod had given up so easily. He said, "Look, fellows, I hate to impose on you, but really, I need some help."

"Oh, very well," the Messenger said. "Give me the coordinates and I'll take you there myself."

"Coordinates? I don't know anything about that. It's a planet called Earth."

"I don't care if it is called Green Cheese," the Messenger said. "I need to know the coordinates if I'm to be of any assistance."

"But you were just there," Carmody said. "You went to Earth and brought me here!"

"So it may have appeared to you," the Messenger explained patiently. "But it is not the case at all. I simply went to the coordinates which were given me by the Clerk, who got them from the Sweepstakes Computer; and there you were, and I brought you here."

"Can't you bring me back to the same coordinates?"

"I can, with the greatest of ease. But you would find nothing there. The galaxy is not static, you know. Everything in the galaxy moves, each thing at its own rate and in its own manner."

"Can't you figure out from the coordinates where Earth will be now?" Carmody asked.

"I can't even add up a column of figures," the Messenger said proudly. "My talents lie in other directions."

Carmody turned to the Clerk. "Then can you figure it out? Or can the Sweepstakes Computer?"

"I can't add very well, either," the Clerk said.

The Computer scuttled back into the room. "I can add magnificently," it said. "But my function is limited to selecting and locating the winners of the Sweepstakes within my margin of permissible error. I have you located (you are here) and therefore I am forbidden the interesting theoretical job of learning your planet's present coordinates."

"Can't you do it just as a favor?" Carmody pleaded.

"I have no quotient for favors," the Computer replied. "I can no more find your planet than I can fry an egg or trisect a nova."

"Can't anyone help me?" Carmody asked.

"Don't despair," the Clerk said. "Travelers' Aid can fix you up in a jiffy, and I'll take you there myself. Just give them your Home Coordinates."

"But I don't know them!" Carmody said.

There was a short, shocked silence. Then the Messenger said, "If you don't know your own address, how do you expect anyone else to know it? This galaxy may not be infinite, but it's a pretty big place all the same. Any creature that doesn't know its own Location should never leave home."

"I didn't know that at the time," Carmody said.

"You might have asked."

"I didn't think of it...Look, you have to help me. It can't be too difficult to find out where my planet is."

"It's incredibly difficult," the Clerk told him. " 'Where' is only one of the three coordinates that are needed."

"What are the other two?"

"We also need to know 'When' and 'Which.' We call them the three W's of Location."

"I don't care if you call them Green Cheese," Carmody said in a sudden burst of anger. "How do other life-forms find their way home?"

"They utilize their inherent homing instinct," the Messenger said. "Are you sure you don't have one, by the way?"

"I don't think so," Carmody said.

"Of course he doesn't have a homing instinct!" the Prize burst out indignantly. "The fellow's never been off his home planet! How would he develop a homing instinct?"

"True enough," the Clerk said, and rubbed his face wearily. "This is what comes of dealing with lower life-forms. Damn that computer and his pious errors!"

"Only one in five billion," the Computer said. "Surely that's not asking very much."

"No one's blaming you," the Clerk said. "No one's blaming anyone, as a matter of fact. But we still have to figure out what to do with him."

"It's a heavy responsibility," the Messenger said.

"It certainly is," the Clerk agreed. "What do you say we kill him and forget the whole thing."

"Hey!" Carmody cried.

"It's OK with me," the Messenger said.

"If it's OK with you fellows," the Computer said, "then it's OK with me."

"Count me out," the Prize said. "I can't put my finger on it at the moment, but there's something wrong with the whole idea."

Carmody made several vehement statements to the effect that he did not want to die and ought not to be killed. He appealed to their better instincts and their sense of fair play. These remarks were judged tendentious and were stricken from the record.

"Wait, I have it!" the Messenger said suddenly. "As an alternate solution, what about this? Let's *not* kill him; let's help him, in utter sincerity and to the best of our abilities, to return to his home alive and in good health both mental and physical."

"It's a thought," the Clerk admitted.

"In that way," the Messenger said, "we can perform an exemplary action of the greatest merit, all the more noteworthy because it will be utterly futile. For obviously, he will probably be killed in the course of the trip anyhow."

"We'd better get on with it," the Clerk said. "Unless we want him to get killed while we're talking."

"What is this all about?" Carmody asked.

"I'll explain everything later," the Prize whispered to him. "Assuming that there is a later. And, if we have time, I'll also tell you a rather fascinating story about myself."

"Get ready, Carmody!" the Messenger called out.

"I'm ready," Carmody said. "I hope."

"Ready or not, here you go!"

And he went.

Chapter 6

Perhaps for the first time in the history of the human race, a man actually and literally split a scene. From Carmody's point of view, he didn't move at all; it was everything else that moved. The Messenger and the Clerk melted into the background. The Galactic Center went flat and took on an unmistakable resemblance to a large, poorly executed mural.

Then a crack appeared in the upper left-hand corner of the mural, widened and lengthened, and raced down to the lower right-hand corner. The edges curled back, revealing utter blackness. The mural, or Galactic Center, rolled itself up like two windowshades and left not a wrack behind.

"Don't worry, they do it with mirrors," the Prize whispered to him.

The explanation worried Carmody more than the occurrence. But he kept a tight control on himself and a somewhat tighter control on the Prize. The blackness became complete and utter, soundless and sightless, a paradigm of deep space. Carmody endured it for as long as it lasted, which was incomprehensible.

Then, abruptly, the scene resolved. He was standing on ground breathing air. He could see barren mountains the color of white bone and a river of frozen lava. A faint, stagnant breeze blew in his face. Overhead there were three tiny red suns.

This place seemed more immediately alien than the Galactic Center; still, it was a relief to Carmody. He had encountered places like this in dreams; but the Galactic Center was the stuff of nightmares.

With a sudden start he realized that the Prize was no longer in his hand. How could he have mislaid it? He looked around frantically, and found a small green garter snake curled around his neck.

"It's me," it said. "I'm your Prize. I am merely in a different shape. Form, you see, is a function of total environment, and we Prizes are peculiarly sensitive to environmental influences. You mustn't let it alarm you. I'm still with you, keed, and together we will free Mexico from the sullen foreigner's hand of the dandy Maximilian."

"Huh?"

"Analogize!" the Prize demanded. "You see, Doctor, despite our high intelligence, we Prizes have no language of our own. Nor do we have any need of an individual tongue, since we are always being awarded to various aliens. Solving the talk-problem is quite simple, but sometimes disconcerting; I merely run a tapline into your association bank and draw out what words I need to make my meaning clear. Have my words made my meaning clear?"

"Nothing is very clear," Carmody confessed. "But I think I understand."

"Good bhoy," the Prize said. "The concepts may get a little jangled from time to time, but you will inevitably decipher them. After all, they are yours. I have a rather amusing story to tell in that regard, but I fear it must wait. Something is about to happen too quickly."

"What? What is it?"

"Carmody, *mon vieux*, there is not time to explain all. There may not even be time to explain what you absolutely *must* know in order to maintain the operation of your life. The Clerk and the Messenger have very kindly sent you—"

"Those murderous bastards!" Carmody said.

"You must not condemn murder so lightly," the Prize said reprovingly. "It bespeaks a careless nature. I remember a pertinent dithyramb to that effect, which I will recite later. Where was I? Oh yes, the Clerk and the Messenger. At considerable personal expense, those two worthies have sent you to the one place in the Galaxy where you may—just possibly—be helped. They didn't have to do it, you know. They could have killed you on the spot for future crimes; or they could have shipped you to your planet's last known location, where it most assuredly is *not* now. Or they could have extrapolated its most likely present location and sent you there. But since they are poor extrapolators, the results of that would have been very bad indeed, in all likelihood. So you see—"

"Where am I?" Carmody asked, "and what is supposed to happen here?"

"I was coming to that," the Prize said. "The planet is called Lursis, as is probably evident. It has only a single inhabitant—the autochthonous Melichrone, who has been here as long as anyone can remember, and will be here as long as anyone can project. Melichrone is *sui generis* in spades and with a vengeance. As an autochthone he is inimitable; as a race he is ubiquitous; as an individual he is different. Of him it has been written: 'Lo, the lonely eponymous hero, mating himself with himself while furiously himself resists the angry onslaught of himself!' "

"Damn you," Carmody shouted, "you're talking away like a Senate subcommittee but you're not saying anything!"

"That's because I'm flustered," the Prize said, with a noticeable whine. "Great Scott, man, d'ye think I bargained for anything like this? I'm shook, man, I'm real shook, believe you me, and I'm only trying to explicate because, if I don't put my hand to the helm, this whole damned ball of wax will come crashing own like a house of kurds."

"Cards," Carmody corrected absentmindedly.

"Kurds!" the Prize screamed at him. "Man, have you ever *seen* a house of kurds come tumbling down? Well, I have, and it's not a pretty sight."

"It sounds like a whey-out spectacle," Carmody said, and giggled immoderately.

"Get hold of yourself!" the Prize whispered with sudden urgency. "Integrate! Perform the pause that refreshes! Hitch your thalamus to a star! For now it comes, even Melichrone!"

Carmody found himself strangely calm. He looked out over the twisted landscape and saw nothing that he had not seen before.

"Where is he?" he asked the Prize.

"Melichrone is evolving in order to be able to speak to you. Answer him boldly but with tact. Do not make any reference to his disability; that will only get him angry. Be sure—"

"What disability?"

"Be sure that you remember his one limitation. And above all, when he asks his Question, answer it with extreme care."

"Wait!" Carmody said. "All you've done is to confuse me! What disability? What limitation? And what will his Question be?"

"Stop nagging at me!" the Prize said. "I cannot abide it! And now I can retain consciousness no longer. I have delayed my hibernation unbearably, and all for your sake. So long, keed, and don't let them sell you any wooden centrifuges."

And with that, the garter snake adjusted his coils, put his tail in his mouth and went to sleep.

"You damned cop-out artist," Carmody fumed. "Call yourself a Prize? Like pennies on a dead man's eyes, that's the kind of Prize you are."

But the Prize was asleep and unable or unwilling to hear Carmody's invective. And there really was no time for that sort of thing, because in the next moment the barren mountain to Carmody's left turned into a raging volcano.

Chapter 7

The volcano raged and fumed, spit gouts of flame and hurled dazzling fireballs into the black sky. It exploded into a million incandescent fragments, and then each fragment split again, and again, until the skies were lighted with glory and the three little suns had gone pale.

"Boy!" Carmody said. It was like a Mexican fireworks display in Chapultepec Park on Easter, and Carmody was sincerely impressed.

Even as he watched, the glowing fragments fell to earth and were extinguished in an ocean that formed to receive them. Multicolored streamers of smoke twisted and writhed around each other, and the deep waters hissed and turned into steam, which rose in strangely sculptured clouds and then dissolved into rain.

"Hooee!" Carmody cried.

The rain fell slantingly, and there arose a wind which collected the descending waters and wove them together until wind and rain had intermingled and formed a vast tornado. Thick-trunked, black with silvery reflections, the tornado advanced upon Carmody to the rhythmic accompaniment of deafening thunderclaps.

"Enough already!" Carmody shrieked.

When it had marched almost to his feet, the tornado dissolved, the wind and rain rushed skywards, the thunder diminished to an ominous rumble. A sound of bugles and psalteries could then be heard, and also the wail of bagpipes and the sweet moan of harps. Higher and higher the instruments pealed, a song of celebration and welcome not unlike the musical accompaniment to a really high-budget MGM historical movie in Cinemascope and Todd-AO, but better. And then there was a last burst of sound, light, color, movement, and various other things, and then there was silence.

Carmody had closed his eyes at the very end. He opened them now, just in time to see the sound, light, color, movement, and various other things, turn into the heroic naked form of a man.

"Hello," the man said. "I'm Melichrone. How did you like my entrance?"

"I was overwhelmed," Carmody said in all sincerity.

"Were you really?" Melichrone asked. "I mean, *really* overwhelmed? I mean, more than just *impressed?* The truth now, and don't spare my feelings."

"Really," Carmody said, "I was really overwhelmed."

"Well, that's awfully nice," Melichrone said. "What you saw was a little Introduction to Myself that I worked out quite recently. I think—I really *do* think—that it says something about me, don't you?"

"It sure does!" Carmody said. He was trying to see what Melichrone looked like; but the heroic figure in front of him was jet black, perfectly proportioned, and featureless. The only distinguishing characteristic was the voice, which was refined, anxious, and a little whiney.

"It's all absurd, of course," Melichrone said. "I mean, having a big introduction for oneself and all. But yet, it *is* my planet. And if one can't show off a bit on one's own planet, where *can* one show off? Eh?"

"There's no arguing that," Carmody said.

"Do you really think so?" Melichrone asked.

"I honestly do mean it in all sincerity," Carmody said.

Melichrone brooded for a while over that, then said abruptly, "Thank you. I like you. You are an intelligent, sensitive creature and you are not afraid to say what you mean."

"Thank you," Carmody said.

"No, I really mean it."

"Well then, I *really* thank you," Carmody said, trying to keep a faint note of desperation out of his voice.

"And I'm glad you came," Melichrone said. "Do you know, I am a very intuitive creature (I pride myself on that) and I think that you can help me."

It was on the tip of Carmody's tongue to say that he had come to ask for help rather than to give it, and that furthermore, he was in no position to help anyone, being unable to assist himself in so fundamental a ask as finding his way home. But he decided against saying anything at the moment for fear of offending Melichrone.

"My problem," Melichrone said, "is inherent in my situation. And my situation is unique, awesome, strange, and meaningful. You have heard, perhaps, that this entire planet is mine; but it goes much further than that. I am the only living thing which *can* live here. Others have tried, settlements have been formed, animals have been turned loose and plants have been planted. All with my approval, of course, and all in vain. Without exception, all matter alien to his planet has fallen to a thin dust which my winds eventually blow out to deep space. What do you think of that?"

"Strange," Carmody said.

"Yes, well put!" Melichrone said. "Strange indeed! But there it is. No life is viable here except me and my extensions. It gave me quite a turn when I realized that."

"I imagine it did," Carmody said.

"I have been here as long as I or anyone else can remember," Melichrone said. "For ages I was content to live simply, as amebae, as lichen, as ferns. Everything— was fine and straightforward in those days. I lived in a sort of Garden of Eden."

"It must have been marvellous," Carmody said.

"I liked it," Melichrone said quietly. "But it couldn't last, of course. I discovered evolution and evolved myself, altering my planet to accommodate my new personae. I became many creatures, some not nice. I took cognizance of worlds exterior to my own and experimented with the forms I observed there. I lived out long lifetimes as various of the galaxy's higher forms—humanoid, Chtherizoid, Olichord, and others. I became aware of my singularity, and this knowledge brought me a loneliness which I found unacceptable. So I did not accept it. Instead, I entered a manic phase which lasted for some millions of years. I transformed myself into entire races, and I permitted—no, encouraged—my races to war against each other. I learned about sex and art at almost the same time. I introduced both to my races, and for a while I had a very enjoyable time. I divided myself into masculine and feminine components, each component a discrete unit, though still a part of me; and I procreated, indulged in perversions, burned myself at the stake, ambushed myself, made peace treaties with myself, married and divorced myself, went through countless miniature self-deaths and auto-births. And my components indulged in art, some of it very pretty, and in religion. They worshipped me, of course; this was only proper, since I was the efficient cause of all things for them. But I even permitted them to postulate and to glorify superior beings which were *not* me. For in those days, I was extremely liberal."

"That was very thoughtful of you," Carmody said.

"Well, I try to be thoughtful," Melichrone said. "I could afford to be thoughtful. As far as this planet was concerned, I was God. There's no sense beating around the bush about it: I was supernal, immortal, omnipotent and omniscient. All things were resident in me—even dissident opinions about myself. Not a blade of grass grew that was not some infinitesimal portion of my being. The very mountains and rivers were shaped by me. I caused the harvest, and the famine as well; I was the life in the sperm cells, and I was the death in the plague bacillus. Not a sparrow could fall without my knowledge, for I was the Binder and the Unbinder, the All and the Many, That Which Always Was and That Which Always Will Be."

"That's really something," Carmody said.

"Yes, yes," Melichrone said with a self-conscious smile, "I was the Big Wheel in the Heavenly Bicycle Factory, as one of my poets expressed it. It was all very splendid. My races made paintings; I made sunsets. My people wrote about love; I invented love. Ah, wonderful days! If it only could have gone on!"

"Why didn't it?" Carmody asked.

"Because I grew up," Melichrone said sadly. "For untold aeons I had reveled in creation; now I began to question my creations and myself. My priests were always asking about me, you see, and disputing among themselves as to my nature and qualities. Like a fool, I listened to them. It is always flattering to hear one's priests discuss one; but it can be dangerous. I began to wonder about my own nature and qualities. I brooded, I introspected. The more I thought about it, the more difficult it seemed."

"But why did you have to question yourself?" Carmody asked. "After all, you were God."

"That was the crux of the problem," Melichrone said. "From the viewpoint of my creations, there was no problem. I was God, I moved in mysterious ways, but my function was to nurture and chastise a race of beings who would have free will while still being of my essence. As far as they were concerned, what I did was pretty much all right since it was Me that was doing it. That is to say, my actions were in the final analysis inexplicable, even the simplest and most obvious of them, because I Myself was inexplicable. Or, to put it another way, my actions were enigmatic explanations of a total reality which only I, by virtue of my Godhead, could perceive. That is how several of my outstanding thinkers put it; and they added that a more complete understanding would be vouchsafed them in heaven."

"Did you also create a heaven?" Carmody asked.

"Certainly. Also a hell." Melichrone smiled. "You should have seen their faces when I resurrected them to one place or the other! Not even the most devout had *really* believed in a Hereafter!"

"I suppose it was very gratifying," Carmody said.

"It was nice for a while," Melichrone said. "But after a time, it bored me. I am doubtless as vain as the next God; but the endless fulsome praise finally bored me to distraction. Why in God's name should a God be praised if he is only performing his Godly function? You might as well praise an ant for doing his blind antly duties. This state of affairs struck me as unsatisfactory. And I was still lacking in self-knowledge except through the biased eyes of my creations."

"So what did you do?" Carmody asked.

"I abolished them," Melichrone said. "I did away with all life on my planet, living and otherwise, and I also deleted the Hereafter. Frankly, I needed time to think."

"Huh," Carmody said, shocked.

"In another sense, though, I didn't destroy anything or anyone," Melichrone said hastily. "I simply gathered the fragments of myself back into myself." Melichrone grinned suddenly. "I had quite a number of wild-eyed fellows who were always talking about attaining a oneness with Me. They've attained it now, that's for sure!"

"Perhaps they like it that way," Carmody suggested.

"How can they know?" Melichrone said. "Oneness with Me means Me; it necessarily involves loss of the consciousness which examines one's oneness. It is exactly the same as death, though it sounds much nicer."

"That's very interesting," Carmody said. "But I believe you wished to speak to me about a problem?"

"Yes, precisely! I was just coming to that. You see, I put away my peoples much as a child puts away a doll's house. And then I sat down—meta-phorically—to think things over. The only thing to think over was Me, of course. And the real problem about Me was, What was I supposed to do? Was I meant to be nothing but God? I had tried the God business and found it too limited. It was a job for a simple-minded egomaniac. There had to be something else for me to do—something more meaningful, more expressive of my true self. I am convinced of it! That is my problem, and that is the question I ask of you: What am I to do with myself?"

"Well," said Carmody. "Well, well. Yes, I see your problem." He cleared his throat and rubbed his nose thoughtfully. "A problem like that requires a great deal of thought."

"Time is unimportant to me," Melichrone said. "I have limitless quantities of it. Though you, I am sorry to say, do not."

"I don't? How much time do I have?"

"About ten minutes, as you would reckon it. Shortly thereafter, something rather unfortunate is likely to happen to you."

"What is going to happen to me? What can I do about it?"

"Come, now, fair's fair," Melichrone said. "First you answer my question and then I'll answer yours."

"But if I have only ten minutes—"

"The limitation will aid your concentration," Melichrone said. "And anyhow, since it's my planet, we do things by my rules. I can assure you, if it were your planet, I would do things by your rules. That's reasonable, isn't it?"

"Yeah, I suppose so," Carmody said unhappily.

"Nine minutes," Melichrone said.

How do you tell a God what his function should be? Especially if, like Carmody, you are an atheist? How do you find something meaningful to say, especially when you are aware that the God's priests and philosophers have spent centuries on this ground? "Eight minutes," Melichrone said.

Carmody opened his mouth and began to speak.

Chapter 8

"It seems to me," Carmody said, "that the solution to your problem—is—is possibly—"

"Yes?" said Melichrone eagerly.

Carmody had no idea of what he was going to say. He was speaking in the desperate hope that the act of speaking would of itself produce meaning, since words do have meanings, and sentences have even more meanings than words.

"Your problem," Carmody continued, "is to find within yourself an indwelling functionalism which will have reference to an exterior reality. But this may be an impossible quest, since you yourself are reality, and therefore you cannot posit yourself exterior to yourself."

"I can if I want to," Melichrone said sulkily. "I can posit any damned thing I please since I'm in charge around here. Being a God, you know, doesn't mean that One must be a solipsist."

"True, true, true," Carmody said rapidly. (Did he have seven minutes left? Or six? And what was going to happen at the end of that time?) "So it is clear, your Immanence and Indwellingness are insufficient to your view of yourself, and therefore are factually insufficient since you yourself, in your form of Definer, consider these qualities to be insufficient."

"Nicely reasoned," Melichrone said. "You should have been a theologian."

"At the moment I am a theologian," Carmody said. (Six minutes, five minutes?) "Very well, then, what are you to do?... Have you ever considered making knowledge both internal and external (assuming that there is any such thing as external knowledge), of making knowledge your quest?"

"Yes, as a matter of fact, I did think of that," Melichrone said. "Among other things, I read every book in the galaxy, plumbed the secrets of Nature and of Man, explored the macrocosm and the microcosm, and so forth. I had quite an aptitude for learning, by the way, though I have subsequently forgotten a few things, like the secret of life and the ulterior motive of death. But I can learn them again whenever I please. I did learn that learning is a dry, passive business, though filled with some pleasant surprises; and I also learned that learning has no particular and peculiar importance for me. As a matter of fact, I find unlearning almost as interesting."

"Maybe you were meant to be an artist," Carmody suggested.

"I went through that phase," Melichrone said. "I sculpted in flesh and in clay, I painted sunsets on canvas and on the sky, I wrote books in words and other books in events, I made music on instruments, and composed symphonies for wind and rain. My work was good enough, I believe; but I knew somehow that I would always be a dilettante. My omnipotence does not allow me enough room for error, you see; and my grasp of the actual is too complete to allow me to bother seriously with the representational."

"Hmm, I see," Carmody said. (Surely no more than three minutes left!) "Why not become a conqueror?"

"I do not need to conquer what I already possess," Melichrone said. "And as for other worlds, I do not desire them. My qualities are peculiar to my milieu, which consists of this single planet. Possession of other worlds would involve me in unnatural actions. And besides—what use do I have for other worlds when I don't even know what to do with this one?"

"I see that you've given the matter a great deal of thought," Carmody said, his desperation merging into despair.

"Of course I have. I have thought of little else for some millions of years. I have looked for a purpose exterior to myself yet essential to the nature of my being. I have looked for a directive; but I have found only myself."

Carmody could have felt sorry for the God Melichrone if his own situation had not been so desperate. He was confused now; he could feel his time dwindling, and his fears were absurdly mingled with concern for the unfulfilled God.

Then he had an inspiration. It was simple, straightforward, and solved both Melichrone's problem and his own...which is the test of a good inspiration. Whether Melichrone would accept it was another matter. But Carmody could only try.

"Melichrone," he said boldly, "I have solved your problem."

"Oh, have you really?" Melichrone said eagerly. "I mean *really* really, I mean you're not just saying that because, unless you do solve it to my satisfaction; you're fated to die in seventy-three seconds? I mean, you haven't let that influence you unduly, have you?"

"I have allowed my impending fate to influence me," Carmody said majestically, "only to the extent that such an influence is needed to solve your problem."

"Oh. All right. Please hurry up and tell me, I'm so excited!"

"I wish to do so," Carmody said. "But I can't—it is physically impossible to explain everything—if you are going to kill me in sixty or seventy seconds."

"I? I am not going to kill you! Good heavens, do you really think me as bloody-minded as all that? No, your impending death is an exterior event quite without reference to me. By the way, you have twelve seconds left."

"It isn't long enough," Carmody said.

"Of course it's long enough! This *is* my world, you know, and I control everything in it, including the duration of time. I have just altered the local space-time continuum at the ten-second mark. It's an easy enough operation for a God, though it requires a lot of cleaning up afterward. Accordingly, your ten seconds will consume approximately twenty-five years of my local time. Is *that* long enough?"

"It's more than ample," Carmody said. "And it's very kind of you."

"Think nothing of it," Melichrone said. "Now, please, let me hear your solution."

"Very well," Carmody said, and took a deep breath. "The solution to your problem is inherent in the terms in which you view the problem. It could be no other way; every problem must contain within it the seeds of its own solution."

"Must it?" Melichrone asked.

"Yes, it must," Carmody said firmly.

"All right. For the moment I'll accept that premise. Go on."

"Consider your situation," Carmody said. "Consider both its interior and exterior aspects. You are the God of this planet; but only of this planet. You are omnipotent and omniscient; but only here. You have impressive intellectual attainments, and you feel a call to serve something outside of yourself. But your gifts would be wasted any place but here, and here there is no one but you."

"Yes, yes, that is exactly my situation!" Melichrone cried. "But you still haven't told me what to do about it!"

Carmody took a deep breath and exhaled slowly. "What you must do," he said, "is to use all of your great gifts, and to use them here, on your own planet, where they will be of maximum effect; and use them in the service of others, since this is your deepest desire."

"In the service of others?" Melichrone asked.

"It is so indicated," Carmody said. "The most superficial consideration of your situation points the verdict. You are alone in a multiplex universe; but in order for you to perform exterior deeds, there must be an exterior. However, you are barred by your very essence from going to that exterior. Therefore the exterior must come to you. When it comes, what will be your relationship to it? That also is clear. Since you are omnipotent in your own world, you cannot be aided or assisted; but you can aid and assist others. This is the only natural relationship between you and the outside universe."

Melichrone thought about it, then said, "Your argument has force; that much I freely admit. But there are difficulties. For example, the outside world rarely comes this way. You are the first visitor I have had in two and a quarter galactic revolutions."

"The job does require patience," Carmody admitted. "But patience is a quality you must strive for. It will be easier for you since time is a variable. And as for the number of your visitors—first of all, quantity does not affect quality. There is no value in mere enumeration. A man or a God does his job; that is what counts. Whether that job requires one or a million transactions makes no difference."

"But I am as bad off as before if I have a job to perform and no one to perform it on."

"With all modesty, I must point out that you have me," Carmody said. "I have come to you from the exterior. I have a problem; indeed, I have several problems. For me, these problems are insoluble. For you—I do not know. But I suspect that they will tax your powers to the utmost."

Melichrone thought about it for a very long time. Carmody's nose began to itch, but he resisted the desire to scratch it. He waited, and the entire planet also waited while Melichrone made up his mind.

At last Melichrone raised his jet-black head and said, "I really think you have something there!"

"It's good of you to say that," Carmody said.

"But I mean it, I really do!" Melichrone said. "Your solution seems to me both inevitable and elegant. And, by extension, it seems to me that Fate, which rules men, Gods and planets, must have destined this to happen: that I, a creator, was created with no problem to solve; and that you, a created, became the creator of a problem that only a God could solve.

And that you have lived out your lifetime waiting for me to solve your problem, while I have waited here for half of eternity for you to bring me your problem to solve!"

"I wouldn't be a bit surprised," Carmody said. "Would you like to know what my problem is?"

"I have already deduced," Melichrone said. "In fact, due to my superior intellect and experience, I know much more about it than you do. Superficially, your problem is how to get home."

"That's it."

"No, that's not it. I do not use words lightly. *Superficially*, you need to know Where, When and Which your planet is; and you need a way of getting there, and you need to arrive in much the same condition you are presently in. If that were all, it would still be difficult enough."

"What else is there?" Carmody asked.

"Why, there is also the death which is pursuing you.

"Oh," Carmody said. He suddenly felt weak in the knees, and Melichrone graciously created an easychair for him, and a Havana cigar, a Rum Collins, a pair of sheep-lined slippers, and a buffalo-hide lap robe.

"Comfortable?" Melichrone asked.

"Very."

"Good. Pay close attention now. I will proceed to explain your situation briefly but succinctly, utilizing only a fraction of my intellect for that task while I use the rest of me for the considerable job of finding a feasible solution. But you will have to listen carefully and try to understand everything the first time I say it because we have very little time."

"I thought you stretched my ten seconds into 25 years," Carmody said.

"I did. But time is a tricky sort of variable, even for me. Eighteen of your 25 years are already used up, and the rest of them are going with extreme rapidity. Pay attention, now! Your life depends on it."

"All right," Carmody said. He sat forward and puffed on his cigar. "I'm ready."

"The first thing you must understand," Melichrone said, "is the nature of the implacable death that is hunting you."

Carmody controlled a shudder and bent forward to listen.

Chapter 9

"The most fundamental fact in the universe," said Melichrone, "is that species eat other species. It may not be pretty, but there it is. Eating is basic, and the acquisition of foodstuffs underlies all other phenomena. This concept involves the Law of Predation, which can be stated as follows: any given species, no matter how high or how low, feeds upon one or more species and is fed upon by one or more species.

"That sets forth a universal situation, which can be aggravated or ameliorated by a variety of circumstances. For example, a species resident in its own habitat can usually maintain itself in a state of Equilibrium, and thus live out its normal lifetime despite the depredations of predators. This Equilibrium is usually stated as the Victor-Vanquished equation, or VV. When a species or a species member moves to an alien and exotic habitat, the VV values necessarily change. Occasionally, there is temporary improvement in the species's Eat-Eaten Situation (Vv=Ee plus 1). More typically, there is a deterioration (Vv = Ee minus 1).

"That is what has happened to you, Carmody. You have left your normal habitat, which also means that you have left your normal predators. No automobiles can stalk you here, no virus can creep into your bloodstream, no policeman can shoot you down by mistake. You are separated from the dangers of Earth, and immune to the dangers of other galactic species.

"But the amelioration (Vv = Ee plus 1) is sadly temporary. The ironclad rule of Equilibrium has already begun to assert itself. You cannot refuse to hunt, and you cannot escape being hunted. Predation is Necessity itself.

"Having left Earth, you are a unique creature; therefore your predator is unique.

"Your predator was born out of a personification and solidification of universal law. This predator can feed exclusively and solely on you. The creature is shaped as a respondent and complement to your characteristics. Even without seeing it, we can know that its jaws are shaped to bite Carmodys, its limbs are articulated to seize and grasp Carmodys, its stomach has the peculiar and unique ability to digest Carmodys, and its personality is designed to take advantage of the Carmodic personality.

"Your situation has rendered you unique, Carmody; therefore your predator is unique. It is your death that pursues you, Carmody, and it does so with a desperation equal to your own. You and it are bound together. If it seizes you, you die; if you escape to the normal menaces of your own world, your predator dies for lack of Carmodic sustenance.

"There is no more I can say that will help you to evade it. I cannot predict the tricks and disguises it will attempt, no more than I can predict yours. I can only warn you that the probabilities always favor the Hunter, though escapes are not entirely unheard-of.

"That is the situation, Carmody. Have you understood me?"

Carmody started like a man awakened from a deepsleep.

"Yes," he said. "I don't understand everything you said. But I do understand the important parts."

"Good," Melichrone said. "For we have no time left. You must leave this planet at once. Not even I on my own planet can arrest the universal Law of Predation."

"Can you get me back to Earth?" Carmody asked.

"Given sufficient time, I probably could," Melichrone said. "But of course, given sufficient time, I could do anything at all. It is difficult, Carmody. To begin with, the three W variables must be solved each in terms of the other. I would have to determine exactly Where in space-time your planet is at the present moment; then I would have to discover Which of the alternate-probability Earths is yours. Then I would have to find the temporal sequence you were born into in order to determine When. Then there is the skorish effect and the doubling factor, both of which must be allowed for. With all of that done, I could, with a little luck, slip you back into your own Particularity (a surprisingly delicate operation) without wrecking the whole works."

"Can you do this for me?" Carmody asked.

"No. There is no time left. But I can send you to Maudsley, a friend of mine, who should be able to help you."

"A friend of yours?"

"Well, perhaps not exactly a *friend*," Melichrone said. "More of an acquaintance, really. Though even that may be overstating the relationship. You see, once, quite some time ago, I almost left my planet for a sightseeing trip; and had I done so, I would have met Maudsley. But I didn't leave for various reasons, and therefore never actually met Maudsley. Still, we both know that if I had gone on my trip, we *would* have met, and would have exchanged views and outlooks, had an argument or two, cracked a few jokes, and ended with a mild fondness for each other."

"It seems a kind of feeble relationship to presume upon," Carmody said. "Isn't there anyone else you could send me to?"

"I'm afraid not," Melichrone said. "Maudsley is my only friend. Probabilities define affinities just as well as actualities, you know. I'm sure Maudsley will take good care of you."

"Well—" Carmody began to say. But then he noticed that something large and dark and menacing was beginning to take shape just behind his left shoulder, and he knew that he had used up all of his time.

"I'll go!" he said. "And thanks for everything!"

"No need to thank me," Melichrone said. "My duty in the universe is to serve strangers. Good luck, Carmody!"

The large menacing form was beginning to solidify; but before it could finish, Carmody had disappeared.

Chapter 10

Carmody found himself on a green meadow. It must have been noon, for a gleaming orange sun was directly overhead. Some distance away, a small herd of spotted cows grazed slowly over tall grass. Beyond them, Carmody could see a dark fringe of forest.

He turned around slowly. Meadowland extended on all sides of him, but the forest ended in dense underbrush. He heard a dog bark. There were mountains on the other side, a long, jagged range with snow-capped tops. Gray clouds clung to the upper slopes.

Out of the corner of his eye, he saw a flash of red. He turned; it seemed to be a fox. It looked at him curiously, then bounded away toward the forest.

"It's like Earth," Carmody remarked. Then he remembered the Prize, which had last been a hibernating green snake. He felt around his neck, but the Prize was no longer there.

"Here I am," the Prize said.

Carmody looked around and saw a small copper cauldron.

"Is this you?" Carmody asked, picking the cauldron.

"Of course it's me," the Prize said. "Can't you even recognize your own Prize?"

"Well...you've changed quite a lot."

"I am quite aware of that," the Prize said. "But my essence—the true me—never changes. What's the matter?"

Carmody had peered into the cauldron and had nearly dropped it. Inside, he had seen the skinned and half-consumed body of some small animal—perhaps a kitten.

"What's that inside you?" Carmody asked.

"Oh."

"It's my lunch, if you must know," the Prize said. "I was grabbing a quick bite during transit."

"Even Prizes need occasional nourishment," the Prize added sarcastically. "And, I might add, we also need rest, mild exercise, sexual congress, intermittent intoxication and an occasional bowel movement; none of which you have made provision for since I was awarded to you."

"Well, I haven't had any of those things either," Carmody answered.

"Do you really require them?" the Prize said in an astonished voice. "Yes, of course, I suppose you do. It's strange, but I guess I had thought of you as a sort of bustling elemental figure without creature requirements."

"Exactly the way I had thought of you!" Carmody said.

"It's inevitable, I suppose," the Prize said. "One tends to think of an alien as—as solid all through and *bowelless,* somehow. And of course, some aliens are."

"I'll take care of your requirements," Carmody said, feeling a sudden affection for his Prize. "I'll do it as on as this damned emergency is over."

"Of course, old man. Forgive my fit of pique. D'ye mind if I finish my bite of lunch?"

"Go right ahead," Carmody said. He was curious to see how a metal cauldron would devour a skinned animal; but when it came down to it, he was too squeamish to watch.

"Ah, that was damned good," the Prize said. "I've saved a bit for you, if you'd care for some."

"I'm not too hungry just now," Carmody said. "What are you eating?"

"We call them *orithi*," the Prize said. "You would consider them a type of giant mushroom. Delicious raw or lightly poached in their own juices. The mottled white kind is better than the green."

"I'll remember that," Carmody said, "in case I ever run across one. Do you think an Earthman could eat one?"

"I think so," the Prize said. "By the way, if you ever do get the chance, be sure to have it recite a poem before you eat it."

"Why?"

"Because the *orithi* are very good poets."

Carmody swallowed hard. That was the trouble with exotic life-forms; just when you thought you understood something, you found that you didn't understand at all. And conversely, when you thought you were completely mystified, they suddenly threw you off balance by acting in a completely comprehensible manner. In fact, Carmody decided, what made aliens so thoroughly alien was the fact that they weren't *completely* alien. It was amusing at first; but after a while it got on your nerves.

"Urp," said the Prize.

"What?"

"I belched," the Prize said. "Excuse me. Anyhow, I think you must admit that I handled it all rather cleverly."

"Handled all what?"

"The interview with Melichrone, of course," said the Prize.

"You handled it? Why, damn it all, *you* were hibernating! I talked us out of that spot!"

"I don't want to contradict you," the Prize said, "but I fear that you are laboring under a misapprehension. I went into hibernation solely in order to bring all of my powers to bear on the problem of Melichrone."

"You're crazy! You're out of your mind!" Carmody shouted.

"I am saying no more than the truth," the Prize said. "Consider that long, closely reasoned argument that you gave, in which you established Melichrone's place and function in the scheme of things by irrefutable logic."

"What about it?"

"Well, have you ever reasoned that way before in your life? Are you a philosopher or a logician?"

"I was a philosophy major in college," Carmody said.

"Big deal," the Prize sneered. "No, Carmody, you simply don't have the background or the intellect to handle an argument like that. Face it: it was completely out of character."

"It was not out of character! I'm perfectly capable of extraordinary logic!"

" 'Extraordinary' would be a good word for it," the Prize said.

"But I did do it! I thought those thoughts!"

"Just as you wish," the Prize said. "I hadn't realized it meant so much to you, and I certainly didn't mean to upset you. Tell me, have you ever been subject to fainting spells, or to inexplicable fits of laughter or ears?"

"No, I have not," Carmody said, getting a grip on himself. "Have you ever had recurrent dreams of flying, or sensations of saintliness?"

"I most certainly have not!" the Prize said.

"You're sure?"

"Sure, I'm sure!"

"Then we needn't discuss the matter any further," Carmody said, feeling absurdly triumphant. "But I'd like to know something else."

"What is that?" the Prize said warily.

"What was Melichrone's disability that I was not supposed to mention? And what was his one limitation?"

"I thought that both were painfully obvious," the Prize said.

"Not to me."

"A few hours' reflection would bring them to your mind at once."

"To hell with that," Carmody said. "Just tell me."

"Very well," the Prize said. "Melichrone's one disability is that he is lame. It is a congenital defect; it has been present since his early origins. It persists throughout all his changes in analogous form."

"And his one limitation?"

"He can never know about his own lameness. As a God, he is denied comparative knowledge. His creations are in his own image; which, in Melichrone's case, means that they are all lame. And his contacts with exterior reality are so few that he believes that lameness is the norm, and that unlame creatures are curiously flawed. Comparative knowledge is one of the few deficiencies of Godhead, by the way. Thus, the primary definition of a God is in terms of his self-sufficiency, which, no matter what its scope, is always interior. Perfect control of the controllable and perfect knowledge of the knowable are the first steps toward becoming a God, by the way, in case you ever wish to try the project."

"Me? Try to be a God?"

"Why not?" the Prize asked him. "It's an occupation like any other, despite its grand-sounding title. It's not easy, I'll grant you; but it's no harder than becoming a first-class poet or engineer."

"I think you must be out of your mind," Carmody said, feeling the quick shuddering shock of religious horror which so bedevils the atheistic.

"Not at all. I am merely better informed than you. But now you had better prepare yourself."

Carmody looked around quickly and saw three small figures walking slowly across the meadow. Following them at a respectful distance were ten other figures.

"The one in the middle is Maudsley," the Prize said. "He's always very busy, but he may have time for a few words with you."

"Does he have any limitations or defects?" Carmody asked sarcastically.

"If he does, they are not of significance," the Prize said. "One deals with Maudsley in quite different terms, and faces entirely different problems."

"He looks like a human," Carmody said as the group came nearer.

"He is shaped like one," the Prize admitted. "But of course, the humanoid shape is common in this part of the galaxy."

"What terms am I supposed to deal with him in?" Carmody asked.

"I can't really describe them," the Prize said. "Maudsley is too alien for me to understand or predict. But there *is* one piece of advice I can give you: be sure you get his attention and impress him with your humanity."

"Well, of course," Carmody said.

"It's not so simple as it sounds. Maudsley is an extremely busy being with a great deal on his mind. He is a highly gifted engineer, you know, and a dedicated one. But he tends to be absentminded, especially when he is trying out a new process."

"Well, that doesn't sound too serious."

"It's not—for Maudsley. It could be considered no more than an amusing foible, if it were not for the fact that he absentmindedly tends to view everything as raw material for his processes. An acquaintance of mine, Dewer Harding, came to him some time ago with an invitation to a party. Poor Dewer failed to capture his attention."

"And what happened?"

"Maudsley processed him into one of his projects. Quite without malice, of course. Still, poor Dewer is now three pistons and a camshaft in a reciprocating engine, and can be seen weekdays in Maudsley's Museum of Historical Power Applications."

"That's really quite shocking," Carmody said. "Can't anyone do anything about it?"

"No one wants to bring it to Maudsley's attention," the Prize said. "Maudsley hates to admit an error and can be quite unpleasant if he feels he's being chivvied."

The Prize must have perceived the look on Carmody's face, for he quickly added, "But you mustn't let that alarm you! Maudsley is never vicious, and is in fact quite a good-hearted fellow. He likes praise, as do all of us; but he detests flattery. Just speak up and make yourself known, be admiring but avoid the fulsome, take exception to what you don't like, but don't be stubbornly critical; in short, exercise moderation except where a more extreme attitude is clearly called for."

Carmody wanted to say that this advice was as good as no advice at all; worse, in fact, since it merely served to make him nervous. But now there was no time. Maudsley was here, tall and white-haired, in chinos and a leather jacket, flanked by two men in business suits with whom he was talking vehemently.

"Good day, sir," Carmody said firmly. He stepped forward, then scuttled out of the way before the oblivious trio ran into him.

"A bad beginning," the Prize whispered.

"Shut up," Carmody whispered back. With a certain grimness, he hurried after the group.

Chapter 11

"So this is it, eh, Orin?" Maudsley said.

"Yes sir, this is it," Orin, the man on his left, said, smiling proudly. "What do you think of it, sir?"

Maudsley turned around slowly and surveyed the meadow, the mountains, the sun, the river, the forest. His face betrayed no expression. He said, "What do *you* think of it, Brookside?"

Brookside said, in a tremulous voice, "Well sir, I think that Orin and I did a nice job. A *really* nice job, if you take into account that it was our first independent project."

"And do you concur in that judgment, Orin?" Maudsley asked.

"Certainly, sir," Orin said.

Maudsley bent down and plucked a blade of grass. He sniffed it and threw it away. He scuffed the dirt beneath his feet, then stared for several moments full into the blazing sun. In a measured voice, he said, "I am amazed, truly amazed. But in a most unpleasant way. I ask you two to build a world for one of my customers and you come up with *this!* Do you really consider yourselves engineers?"

The two aides did not reply. They had stiffened, like boys awaiting the birch rod.

"Engineers!" Maudsley said, getting almost fifty foot-pounds of contempt into the word. " 'Creative but practical scientists who can build the planet where and when you want it.' Do either of you recognize those words?"

"They're from the standard brochure," Orin said.

"That is correct," Maudsley said. "Now, do you consider *this* a good example of 'creative, practical engineering'?"

Both men were silent. Then Brookside blurted out, "Well sir, yes sir, I do!

"We examined the job specs very carefully. The request was for a Type 34Bc4 planet with certain variations. And that's exactly what we built. This is only a corner of it, of course. But still—"

"But still, I can see what you did and judge accordingly," Maudsley said. "Orin! What kind of a heating unit did you use?"

"A type O5 sun, sir," Orin replied. "It fitted the thermal requirements nicely."

"I daresay it did. But this was a budget world, you will remember. If we don't keep the costs down, we don't make a profit. And the biggest single cost item is the heating unit."

"We are aware of that, sir," Brookside said. "We didn't at all like to use an O5 type sun for a single-planet system. But the heat and radiation requirements—"

"Haven't you learned anything from me?" Maudsley cried. "This type of star is entirely superfluous. You there—" He beckoned to the workmen. "Take it down."

The workmen hurried forward with a folding ladder. One man braced it and another man unfolded it, ten times, a hundred times, a million times. Two other workmen raced up the ladder as fast as it went up.

"Handle it carefully!" Maudsley called up to them. "And be sure you're wearing gloves! That thing's hot!"

The workmen at the very top of the ladder unhooked he star, folded it into itself and put it into a padded box marked "STAR: HANDLE WITH CARE."

When the lid fell, everything went black.

"Hasn't anyone any sense around here?" Maudsley asked. "Damn it all, let there be light."

And just like that, there was light.

"OK," Maudsley said. "That O5-type sun goes back into storage. On a job like this we can use a G13-type star."

"But sir," Orin said nervously, "it isn't hot enough."

"I know that," Maudsley said. "That's where you have to use your creativity. If you move the star closer in, it'll be hot enough."

"Yes sir, it will," Brookside said. "But it'll be emiting PR rays without enough space to allow them to dissipate harmlessly. And that might kill off the entire race that's going to occupy this planet."

Maudsley said, very slowly and distinctly, "Are you trying to tell me that G13-type stars are dangerous?"

"Well, no, I didn't mean it exactly *that* way," Orin said. "I meant to say, they *can* be dangerous, just like anything else in the universe, if proper precautions are not taken."

"That's more like it," Maudsley said.

"The proper precautions," Brookside said, "involve, in this case, the wearing of protective lead suits weighing some fifty pounds each. But this is impractical, since the average member of this race only weighs eight pounds."

"That's their lookout," Maudsley said. "It's not our business to tell them how to live their lives. Am I supposed to be responsible whenever they stub their toe on a rock I put on their planet? Besides, they don't have to wear lead suits. They can buy one of my optional extras, a solar screen that'll block out the PR rays."

Both men smiled nervously. But Orin said timidly, "I believe this is a somewhat underprivileged species, sir. I think perhaps they can't afford the solar screen."

"Well, if not right now, maybe later," Maudsley said. "And anyhow, the PR radiations aren't instantly fatal. Even with it, they'll have an average lifespan of 9.3 years, which ought to be enough for anyone."

"Yes sir," the two assistant engineers said, not happily.

"Next," Maudsley said, "what's the height of those mountains?"

"They average six thousand feet above sea level," Brookside said.

"At least three thousand feet too high," Maudsley said. "Do you think mountains grow on trees? Pare them down and put what you have left over into the warehouse."

Brookside took out a notebook and jotted down the change. Maudsley continued to pace around, looking and frowning.

"How long are those trees supposed to last?"

"Eight hundred years, sir. They're the new improved model Appleoak. They give fruit, shade, nuts, refreshing beverages, three useful fabrics, they make excellent building material, hold the soil in place, and—"

"Are you trying to bankrupt me?" Maudsley roared. "Two hundred years is entirely long enough for a tree! Drain off most of their *élan vital* and store it in the life-force accumulator!"

"They won't be able to perform all of their designed functions, then," Orin said.

"Then cut down on their functions! Shade and nuts is plenty, we don't have to make a damned treasure chest out of those trees! Now then, who put those cows out there?"

"I did, sir," Brookside said. "I thought it would make the place look— well, sort of inviting, sir."

"You oaf," Maudsley said. "The time to make a place look inviting is before the sale, not after! This place was sold unfurnished. Put those cows into the protoplasm vat."

"Yes sir," Orin said. "Terribly sorry, sir. Is there anything else?"

"There's about ten thousand other things wrong," Maudsley said. "But you can figure out those for yourselves, I hope. What, for example, is this?" He pointed at Carmody. "A statue or something? Is he supposed to sing a song or recite a poem when the new race arrives?"

Carmody said, "Sir, I am not part of this. A friend of yours named Melichrone sent me, and I'm trying to get home to my own planet—"

Maudsley clearly did not hear what Carmody was saying. For, while Carmody was trying to speak, Maudsley was saying, "Whatever he is, the job specs don't call for him. So stick him back in the protoplasm vat with the cows."

"Hey!" Carmody shouted as workmen lifted him up by his arms. "Hey, wait a minute!" he screamed. "I'm not a part of this planet! Melichrone sent me! Wait, hold on, listen to me!"

"You really ought to be ashamed of yourselves," Maudsley went on, oblivious to Carmody's shrieks. "What was that supposed to be? One of your interior decorating touches, Orin?"

"Oh no," Orin said. "I didn't put him there."

"Then it was you, Brookside."

"I never saw him before in my life, chief."

"Hmm," Maudsley said. "You're both fools, but you've never been liars. Hey!" he shouted to the workmen. "Bring him back here!"

"All right, pull yourself together," Maudsley said to Carmody, who was shaking uncontrollably. "Get a grip on yourself, I can't wait around here while you have a fit of hysterics! Better now? All right, would you mind explaining just what you're doing trespassing on my property and why I shouldn't have you converted into protoplasm?"

Chapter 12

"I see," Maudsley said, after Carmody had finished explaining. "It's an interesting story, though I'm sure you've overdramatized it. Still, here you are, and you're looking for a planet called—Earth?"

"That is correct, sir," Carmody said.

"Earth," Maudsley mused, scratching his head. "This is most fortunate for you; I seem to remember the place."

"Do you really, Mr. Maudsley?"

"Yes, I'm quite sure of it," Maudsley said. "It's a small green planet, and it supports a monomorphic humanoid race like yourself. Am I right?"

"Completely right!" Carmody said.

"I have rather a memory for these things," Maudsley said. "And in this particular case, as it happens, I built Earth."

"Did you really, sir?" Carmody asked.

"Yep. I remember distinctly, because in the course of building it, I also invented science. Perhaps you will find the story amusing." He turned to his aides. "And *you* might find the tale instructive."

No one was going to deny Maudsley the right to tell a story. So Carmody and the assistant engineers assumed attentive postures, and Maudsley began the story of the creation of earth

THE STORY OF THE CREATION OF THE EARTH

I was still quite a small contractor then. I put up a planet here and there, and I got to do an occasional dwarf star. But jobs were always hard to come by, and the customers were invariably capricious, fault-finding, and slow in their payments. Customers were hard to please in those days; they argued about every little detail. *Change this, change that, why must water flow downhill, the gravity's too heavy, the hot air rises when it ought to fall.* And so forth.

I was quite naïve in those days. I used to explain the esthetic and practical reasons for everything I did. Before long, the questions and the explanations were taking longer than the jobs. There was entirely too much talk-talk. I knew that I had to do something about it, but I couldn't figure out what.

Then, just before the Earth project, a whole new approach to customers' relations began to shape itself in my mind. I found myself muttering to myself, "Form follows function." I liked the way it sounded. But then I would ask myself, "*Why* must form follow function?" And the reason I gave myself was, "Form follows function because that is an immutable law of nature and one of the fundamental axioms of applied science." And I liked the sound of that, too, although it didn't make much sense.

But sense didn't matter. What mattered was that I had made a new discovery. I had unwittingly stumbled into the art of advertising and salesmanship, and I had discovered the gimmick of great possibilities, namely, the doctrine of scientific determinism.

Earth was my first test case, and that is why I will always remember it.

A tall, bearded old man with piercing eyes had come to me and ordered a planet. (That was how your planet began, Carmody.) Well, I did the job quickly, in six days I believe, and thought that would be the end of it. It was another of those budget planets, and I had cut a few corners here and there. But to hear the owner complain, you'd have thought I'd stolen the eyes out of his head.

"Why are there so many tornadoes?" he asked. "It's part of the atmosphere circulation system," I told him. (Actually, I had been a little rushed at that time; I had forgotten to put in an air-circulation overload valve.)

"Three-quarters of the place is water!" he told me. "And I clearly specified a four-to-one land-to-water ratio!"

"Well, we couldn't do it that way!" I told him. (I had lost his ridiculous specifications; I never can keep track of these absurd little one-planet projects.)

"And you've filled what little land you gave me with deserts and swamps and jungles and mountains."

"It's scenic," I pointed out.

"I don't care from scenic!" the fellow thundered. "Oh, sure, one ocean, a dozen lakes, a couple rivers, one or two mountain ranges, that would have been fine. Dresses the place up, gives the inhabitants a good feeling. But what you gave me is *shlock!*"

"There's a reason for it," I said. (In point of fact, we couldn't make the job pay except by using reconstituted mountains, a lot of rivers and oceans as filler, and a couple of deserts I had bought cheap from Ourie the Planet-Junker. But I wasn't going to tell *him* that.)

"A reason!" he screamed. "What will I tell my people? I'm putting an entire race on that planet, maybe two or three. They'll be humans, made in my own image; and humans are notoriously picky, just as I am. What am I supposed to tell them?"

Well, I knew what he could tell them; but I didn't want to be offensive, so I pretended to give the matter some thought. And strangely enough, I *did* think. And I came up with the gimmick to end all gimmicks.

"You just tell them the plain scientific truth," I said. "You tell them that, scientifically, everything that *is* must be."

"Huh?" he said.

"It's determinism," I said, making up the name on the spur of the moment. "It's quite simple, though a bit esoteric. To start with, form follows function; therefore your planet is exactly as it should be by the simple fact of *being* at all. Next, science is invariable; so if anything isn't invariable, it ain't science. And finally, everything follows definite rules. You can't always figure out what those rules are, but you can be sure they're there. So, it stands to reason that no one ought to ask *why this instead of that?* Instead, everyone ought to ask *how does it work?*"

Well, he asked me some pretty tough questions, and he was a pretty smart old fellow. But he didn't know damn-all about engineering; his field was ethics and morals and religion and spook stuff like that. So of course, he just wasn't able to come up with any real objections. He was one of these types who love abstractions, and he started repeating, " 'That which *is* is that which *must be.'* Hmm, a very intriguing formula and not without its patina of stoicism. I shall incorporate some of these insights into the lessons I give to my people... But tell me this: how can I reconcile this indeterminate fatality of science with the free will I plan to give to my people?"

Well, the old boy almost had me there. I smiled and coughed to give myself time to think, and then I said, "The answer is obvious!" Which is always a good answer, as far as it goes.

"I daresay it is," he said. "But I don't perceive it."

"Look," I said, "this free will you're giving your people, isn't that a kind of fatality also?"

"It could be considered as such. But the difference—"

"And besides," I said hastily, "since when are free will and fatality incompatible?"

"They certainly seem incompatible," he said.

"That's only because you don't understand science," I said, performing the old switcheroo right under his hooked nose. "You see, my dear sir, one of the most basic laws of science is that chance plays a part in everything. Chance, I'm sure you know, is the mathematical equivalent of free will."

"But what you're saying is quite contradictory," he said.

"That's how it goes," I said. "Contradiction is one more of the fundamental rules of the Universe. Contradiction generates strife, without which everything would reach a stage of entropy. So we couldn't have any planet or any universe if things didn't exist in an apparently irreconcilable state of contradiction."

"Apparently?" he said, quick as a flash.

"Right as rain," I said. "Contradiction, which we can define provisionally as the existence of reality-paired opposites, isn't the last word on the subject. For example, let's posit a single isolated tendency. What happens when you push a tendency to the limit?"

"I haven't the slightest idea," the old guy said. "The lack of specifics in this sort of discussion—"

"What happens," I said, "is that the tendency turns into its *opposite.*"

"Does it really?" he asked, considerably shook up. These religious types are something when they try to tackle science.

"It really does," I assured him. "I've got the proofs in my lab, though the demonstrations are a bit tedious—"

"No, please, I take your word," the old guy said. "After all, we did make a Covenant."

That was the word he always used for "contract." It meant the same thing, but sounded better.

"Paired opposites," he mused. "Determinism. Things becoming their opposites. It's all quite intricate, I'm afraid."

"And esthetic as well," I said. "But I didn't finish about the transformation of extremes."

"Kindly go on," he said.

"Thanks. Now then, we have entropy, which means that things persist in their motion unless there is outside influence. (Sometimes even when there is outside influence, in my experience.) But so, we got entropy driving a thing toward its opposite. If one thing is driven toward its opposite, then all things are driven toward their opposite, because science is consistent. Now you get the picture? We've got all these opposites transforming themselves like crazy and becoming their opposites. On a higher level of organization, we have groups of opposites going through the same bit. And higher and higher. So far so good?"

"I suppose so," he said.

"Fine. Now, the question naturally arises, is this *all?* I mean, these opposites turning themselves inside out and then outside in, is that the whole ball game? And the beauty part is, it's not! No, sir. These opposites flipping around like trained seals are only an aspect of what's really happening. Because—" And here I paused and spoke in a very deep voice. "—because there is a wisdom that sees beyond the clash and turmoil of the phenomenal world. This wisdom, sir, sees through the illusory quality of these real things, and sees beyond them into the deeper workings of the universe, which are in a state of like great and magnificent harmony."

"How can a thing be both illusory and real?" he asked me, quick as a whip.

"It is not for me to know an answer like that," I told him. "Me, I am a mere humble scientific worker and I see what I see and act accordingly. But maybe there's an ethical reason behind it."

The old boy mused on that one for a while, and I could see he was having quite a tussle with himself. He could detect a logical fallacy as fast as anyone, of course, and my reasons had been shot through with them. But like all eggheads, he was fascinated with contradictions and he had the strong urge to incorporate them into his system. And all the propositions I had proposed, well, his common sense told him that things couldn't be *that* tricky; but his intellectuality told him that maybe things did indeed seem that complicated, but maybe there was a nice simple unifying principle underneath it all. Or, if not a unifying principle, at least a good solid moral. And finally, I had hooked him all over again just because I had used the word "ethics." Because this old gent was a perfect demon for ethics, he was supersaturated with ethics; you could call him Mr. Ethics, make no mistake. And so, quite accidentally, I had given him the idea that the whole bloody universe was a series of homilies and contradictions, of laws and inequities, all leading to the most exquisite and rarefied sort of ethical order.

"There is a greater depth here than I had considered," he said after a while. "I had planned to instruct my people in ethics only; and to direct their attention to morally imperative questions such as how and why a man should live instead of what constitutes living matter; I wanted them to be explorers plumbing the depths of joy, fear, piety, hope, despair, rather than scientists who examine stars and raindrops and form grandiose and impractical hypotheses on the basis of their findings. I was aware of the universe, but considered it superfluous. Now you have corrected me."

"Well, look," I said, "I didn't mean to cause trouble. I just thought I should point out this stuff…"

The old man smiled. "By causing me trouble," he said, "you have spared me greater trouble. I can create in my own image; but I will not create a world peopled with miniature versions of myself. Free will is important to me. My creatures will have it, to their glory and their sorrow. They will take this glittering useless toy which you call science and they will elevate it to an undeclared Godhead. Physical contradictions and solar abstractions will fascinate them; they will pursue knowledge of these things and forget to explore the knowledge of their own heart. You have convinced me of this, and I am grateful for the forewarning."

I'll be frank, he got me a little nervous just about then. I mean, he was a nobody, he didn't know any important people; and yet, he had the grand manner. I had the feeling that he could cause me one hell of a lot of trouble, and I felt that he could do it with a few words, a sentence like a poisoned dart lodged in my mind and never to be removed. And that scared me a little, to tell the truth.

Well sir, the old joker must have been reading my mind. For he said, "Do not be frightened. I accept without reservation the world you have built for me; it will serve very well, exactly as it is. As for the flaws and defects which you also built into my world, I accept those also, not entirely without gratitude; and I pay for those, too."

"How?" I asked. "How do you pay for errors?"

"By accepting them without dispute," he said. "And by turning away from you now and going about my business and the business of my people."

And the old gentleman left without another word.

"Well, it left me pretty thoughtful. I'd had all the good arguments, but the old boy left somehow with the last word. I knew what he meant; he had fulfilled his contract with me and that ended it. He was leaving with no word for me personally. From his point of view, it was a kind of punishment.

"But that's only the way *he* saw it. What did I need with his word? I wanted to hear it, of course; that's only natural; and for quite a while I tried to look him up. But he didn't care to see me.

"So it really doesn't matter. I made a pretty nice profit on that world, and even if I bent the contract here and there, I didn't break it. That's how things are; you owe it to yourself to make a profit. You can't get too worked up over the consequences.

"But I was trying to make a point out of all this, and I want you boys to listen carefully. Science is filled with a lot of rules, because I invented it that way. Why did I invent it that way? Because rules are a great assistance to a smart operator, just as a lot of laws are a great help to lawyers. The rules, doctrines, axioms, laws, and principles of science are there to help you, not to hinder you. They're there in order to provide you with reasons for what you do. Most of them are true, more or less, and that helps.

"But always remember—these rules are there to help you explain to the customers what you do *after you do it,* not before. When you have a project, do it exactly as you see fit; then fit the facts around the event, not the other way around.

"Remember—these rules exist as a verbal barrier against people who ask questions. But they should *not* be used as a barrier by you. If you've learned anything from me, you've learned that our work is inevitably inexplicable; we simply do it, and sometimes it comes out well and sometimes not.

"But never try to explain to yourselves why some things happen and why other things don't happen. Don't ask, and don't imagine that an explanation exists. Get me?"

The two assistants nodded vehemently. They looked enlightened, like men who have found a new religion. Carmody would have bet anything that those two earnest young men had memorized every one of the Builder's words, and would now proceed to elevate those words into—a rule.

Chapter 13

After finishing his story, Maudsley was silent for a long time. He seemed morose and withdrawn, and filled with unhappy thoughts. But after a while he roused himself and said, "Carmody, a person in my position is always beset by requests from various charities. I give generously every year to the Oxygen Fund for Indigent Carbon-Forms. I also contribute to the Interstellar Redevelopment Foundation, the Cosmic Settlement Home, and the Save-the-Immature program. This seems to me quite sufficient, and is also tax-deductible."

"All right," Carmody said, with a sudden flash of pride. "I don't want your charity anyhow."

"Please do not interrupt me," Maudsley said. "I was saying that my charities are quite sufficient to fulfill my humanitarian instincts. I do not like to take up individual cases because it gets messy and personal."

"I quite understand," Carmody said. "I think I had better go now," he added, though he didn't have the slightest idea of where he was going or how he would get there.

"I asked you not to interrupt me," Maudsley said. "Now, I don't like to take personal cases, as I said. But I am going to make an exception this time and help you get back to your planet."

"Why?" Carmody asked.

"A whim," Maudsley said. "The merest fancy, with perhaps a touch of altruism thrown in. Also—"

"Yes?"

"Well, if you ever get home—which is dubious in spite of my help— I would appreciate your delivering a message."

"Sure," Carmody said. "Who's the message to?"

"Why, obviously, to the bearded old man for whom I built the planet. I suppose he's still in charge?"

"I don't know," Carmody said. "There's been a great deal of discussion on that point. Some people say he's there just as he always has been.

But others say he's dead (though I think that's meant metaphorically), and still others maintain that he never existed in the first place."

"He's still there," Maudsley said with conviction. "You couldn't kill a fellow like that with a crowbar. As for his apparent absence, that's very like him. He's moody, you know, and filled with high morals which he expects people to live by. He can be peevish, he can just drop out of sight for a while if he doesn't like how things are going. And he can be subtle; he knows that people don't like too much of anything, no matter if it's roast beef, lovely women, or God. So it would be just like him to remove himself from the bill of fare, so to speak, until an appetite has been built up for him again."

"You seem to know a lot about him," Carmody said.

"Well, I've had a lot of time to think about him."

"And I think that I should point out," Carmody pointed out, "that the way you see him is not in accord with any theological view that I've ever heard. The idea that God can be moody, peevish—"

"But he must be those things," Maudsley said. "And much more besides! He must be a creature of extreme emotionality! After all, that's how *you* are and, I presume, how your fellow humans are."

Carmody nodded.

"Well, there you are! He stated plainly that he was going to create in his own image. And obviously, he did so. The moment you came here, I recognized the family resemblance. There is a little God in you, Carmody, though you shouldn't let that go to your head."

"I've never had any contact with him," Carmody said. "I don't know how to give him a message."

"It's so plain!" Maudsley said, with an air of exasperation. "When you get home, you must simply speak up in a firm, clear voice."

"What makes you think he'll hear me?" Carmody asked.

"He can't help but hear you!" Maudsley said. "It *is* his planet, you know, and he has shown his deep interest in his tenants. If he had wanted you to communicate in any other way, he would have shown it."

"All right, I'll do it," Carmody said. "What do you want me to tell him?"

"Well, it isn't anything much, really," Maudsley said, suddenly ill at ease. "But he was quite a worthy old gentleman, really, and I've felt a bit bad about the planet I built him. Not that there's anything *wrong* with the planet, when you come right down to it. It's quite serviceable and all that. But this old guy was a gentleman. I mean, he had class, which is something you never see too much of. So I'd kind of like to do a renovation on that planet of his, entirely free you understand, gratis, it wouldn't cost him a cent. If he'd go for it, I could turn that planet into a showplace, a real paradise. I'm really a hell of a good engineer, let me tell you; it's quite unfair to judge me by the borax I have to turn out to earn a buck."

"I'll tell him," Carmody said. "But very frankly, I don't think he'll take you up on the offer."

"I don't think he will, either," Maudsley said morosely. "He's a stubborn old man and he doesn't want favors from anyone. Still, I do want to make the offer, and I mean it in all sincerity." Maudsley hesitated, then said, "You might also ask him if he'd care to drop around for a chat sometime."

"Why don't you go to see him?"

"I tried that a couple of times, but he wouldn't see me. He's got quite a vindictive streak, that old man of yours! Still, maybe he'll relent."

"Maybe," Carmody said doubtfully. "Anyhow, I'll tell him. But if you want to talk to a God, Mr. Maudsley, why don't you talk to Melichrone?"

Maudsley threw back his head and laughed. "Melichrone! That imbecile? He's a pompous, self-centered ass, and he has no character worth considering. I'd rather talk metaphysics with a dog! Technically speaking, Godhead is a matter of power and control, you know; there's nothing magical about it, and it's not a cure-all for what ails you. No two Gods are alike. Did you know that?"

"No, I didn't."

"Bear it in mind. You can never tell when a piece of information like that will prove useful."

"Thank you," Carmody said. "You know, before this, I didn't believe in any God at all."

Maudsley looked thoughtful and said, "To my way of thinking, the existence of a God or Gods is obvious and inevitable; and belief in God is as easy and natural as belief in an apple, and of no more or less significance. When you come right down to it, there's only one thing that stands in the way of this belief."

"What's that?" Carmody asked.

"It is the Principle of Business, which is more fundamental than the law of gravity. Wherever you go in the galaxy, you can find a food business, a house-building business, a war business, a peace business, a governing business, and so forth. And, of course, a God business, which is called 'religion,' and which is a particularly reprehensible line of endeavor. I could talk for a year on the perverse and nasty notions that the religions sell, but I'm sure you've heard it all before. But I'll just mention one matter, which seems to underlie everything the religions preach, and which seems to me almost exquisitely perverse."

"What's that?" Carmody asked.

"It's the deep, fundamental bedrock of hypocrisy upon which religion is founded. Consider: no creature can be said to worship if it does not possess free will. Free will, however, is *free*. And just by virtue of being free, is intractable and incalculable, a truly Godlike gift, the faculty that makes a state of freedom possible. To exist in a state of freedom is a wild, strange thing, and was clearly intended as such. But what do the religions do with this? They say, 'Very well, you possess free will; but now you must use your free will to enslave yourself to God and to us.' The effrontery of it! God, who would not coerce a fly, is painted as a supreme slavemaster! In the face of this, any creature with spirit must rebel, must serve God entirely of his own will and volition, or must not serve him at all, thus remaining true to himself and to the faculties God has given him."

"I think I see what you mean," Carmody said.

"I've made it too complicated," Maudsley said. There's a much simpler reason for avoiding religion."

"What's that?"

"Just consider its style—bombastic, hortatory, sickly-sweet, patronizing, artificial, inapropos, boring, filled with dreary images or peppy slogans—fit subject matter for senile old women and unweaned babies, but for no one else. I cannot believe that the God I met here would ever enter a church; he had too much taste and ferocity, too much anger and pride. I can't believe it, and for me that ends the matter. Why should I go to a place that a God would not enter?"

Chapter 14

Carmody was left to his own devices while Maudsley began construction of a machine to take him back to Earth. He became very bored. Maudsley could only work in utter solitude, and the Prize had apparently gone back into hibernation. Orin and Brookside, the junior engineers, were dull fellows, preoccupied with their work and uninterested in anything else. So Carmody had no one to talk to.

He filled in his time as well as he could. He toured an atom-building factory and listened dutifully while a red-faced foreman explained how it was done.

"This used to be all handwork," the foreman told him. "Now machines do it, but the process is really the same. First, we select a proton and attach a neutron to it, using Mr. Maudsley's patented energy-binding. Then, we spin the electrons into position with a standard microcosmic centrifuge. After that, we put in anything else that's called for—mu mesons, positrons, that sort of gingerbread. And that's all there is to it."

"Do you get much call for gold or uranium atoms?" Carmody asked.

"Not much. Too expensive. Mostly, we turn out hydrogen atoms."

"What about antimatter atoms?"

"I've never seen much sense in it, myself," the foreman said. "But Mr. Maudsley carries it as a sideline. Antimatter is made in a separate factory, of course."

"Of course," Carmody said.

"That stuff explodes when it comes into contact with normal atoms."

"Yes, I know. It must be tricky stuff to package."

"No, not really," the foreman assured him. "We put it up in neutral cartons."

They continued to walk among the huge machines, and Carmody tried to think of something else to say. Finally he asked, "Do you make your own protons and electrons?"

"Nope, Mr. Maudsley never wanted to fool around with that really small stuff. We get our subatomic particles from subcontractors."

Carmody laughed and the foreman looked at him suspiciously. They continued to walk until Carmody's feet began to hurt him.

He felt tired and dull, and this annoyed him. He ought to be fascinated, he told himself. Here he was, in a place that actually manufactured atoms, and had separate facilities for creating antimatter! Over there as a gigantic machine that extracted cosmic rays from raw space, and purified them, and bottled them in heavy green containers. Beyond that was a thermal probe, used for doctoring up old stars; and just to the left of it...

It was no use. Walking through Maudsley's factory elicited in Carmody the same sensations of boredom he had experienced during a guided tour through a Gary, Indiana, steel foundry. And that wave of sullen fatigue, that sense of mute rebellion—he had felt just the same after walking for reverent hours through the hushed corridors of the Louvre, the Prado, the British Museum. One's sense of wonder, he realized, is only capable of a small amount of appreciation. Men remain inexorably true to themselves and their interests. They stay in character, even if that character is suddenly transported to Timbuktu or Alpha Centauri. And, being ruthlessly honest about it, Carmody realized that he would rather ski the Nosedive at Stowe or sail a Tahiti ketch beneath Hell Gate Bridge than see most of the marvels of the Universe. He was ashamed of this, but there wasn't much he could do about it.

"I guess I'm just not particularly Faustian," he said to himself. "Here are the secrets of the Universe spread around me like old newspapers, and I'm dreaming about a nice February morning in Vermont before the snow has gotten carved up."

He felt bad for a while, but then he began to feel rebellious: "After all, not even Faust had to walk through this stuff like it was an exhibition of Old Masters. He had to work his ass off, if I remember correctly. If the devil had made it too easy for him. Faust would have probably given up knowledge and taken up mountain-climbing or something."

He thought for a while. Then he said, "Anyhow. What's such a big deal about the secrets of the Universe? They've been overrated, just like everything else. When you come right down to it, nothing's as good as you think it's going to be."

All of that, even if it were not true, at least served to make Carmody feel better. But he was still bored. And Maudsley still did not come out of his seclusion.

Time passed with apparent slowness. It was impossible to judge its true rate; but Carmody had the impression that it dragged on and on, and could have been subdivided into days and weeks, perhaps even a month. He also had the feeling—or the premonition—that Maudsley was not finding it easy to do what he had promised so lightly. Perhaps it was simpler to build a new planet than to find an old one. Becoming aware of the complexity of the task and its many unexpected dimensions, Carmody grew disheartened.

One day (to speak conventionally) he watched Orin and Brookside construct a forest. It had been ordered by the primates of Coeth II, to replace their old forest, which had been struck by a meteor. This new one had been paid for entirely out of schoolchildren's donations; a sufficient sum had been raised to purchase a first-class job.

When the engineers and workmen had left, Carmody wandered alone through the trees. He marveled at how good a job Maudsley and his team could do when they put their minds to it, for this forest was a marvel of creative and considerate planning.

There were natural glades for walking, with a leafy arbor above and a springy, dappled loam below—enticing to the foot and restful to the eye. The trees were not Earth species, but they were similar. So Carmody chose to ignore the differences and name them after the trees he had known.

That forest was all prime first-growth timberland, with just enough underbrush to keep it interesting. It was landscaped here and there with bright, rushing streams, none deeper than three feet. There was a shallow, intensely blue little lake, flanked by ponderosa pine or its equivalent. And there was a miniature swamp, dense with mangrove and cypress, studded with blackgums, magnolias and willows, and liberally sprinkled coconut palms. Farther back from the water's edge, on drier land, was a grove in which could be found wild plum and cherry trees, and chestnuts, pecans, oranges, persimmons, dates and figs. It was a perfect place for a picnic.

Nor had the arboreal potentialities of the forest been overlooked. The young primates could race up and down the straight-backed elms and sycamores, play follow-the-leader in the many-branched oaks and laurels, or teeter precariously across the tangled network of vines and creepers that interconnected the treetops. Nor had the needs of their elders been ignored; there were giant redwoods for them, where they could doze or play cards, high above the screaming children.

But there was much more than this; even an untrained person like Carmody could see that the little forest had been given a simple, pleasant and purposeful ecology. There were birds, animals, and other creatures. There were flowers, and stingless bees to cross-fertilize them and gather the pollen, and jolly fat little bears to steal the bees' honey. There were grubs to feast on the flowers, and bright-winged birds to feast off the grubs, and quick red foxes to eat the birds, and bears to eat the foxes, and primates to eat the bears.

But the primates of Coeth also die, and are buried in the forest in shallow, coffinless graves, reverently but without undue fuss, and are fed upon by grubs, birds, foxes, bears and even one or two species of flowers. In this way the Coethians have an integral place in the forest cycle of life and death; and this pleases them very much since they are born participants.

Carmody observed all of this, walking alone with the Prize (still a cauldron) under his arm, and thinking tremulous thoughts about his lost homeland. Then he heard a branch rustle behind him.

There was no wind, and the bears were all bathing in the pond. Carmody turned around slowly, knowing something was there but wishing it weren't.

There was indeed something there. There was a creature wearing a bulky, gray plastic space suit, Frankenstein-type shoes, a transparent bubble helmet and a belt from which dangled a dozen or more tools, weapons and instruments.

Carmody immediately recognized this apparition as an Earthman; no other creature could dress that way.

Behind and to the right of the Earthman was a slighter, similarly clad figure. Carmody saw at once that this was an Earthwoman, and a very attractive one.

"Good lord!" Carmody said. "How did you people happen to come here, of all places?"

"Not so loud," the Earthman said. "I just thank God we arrived in time. But now, I'm afraid, the most dangerous part is ahead of us."

"Do we have any chance at all, Father?" the girl asked.

"There is always a chance," the man said, with a grim smile. "But I wouldn't bet any money on it. Still, maybe Dr. Maddox can figure something out."

"He's very good at that, isn't he, Dad?" the girl asked.

"Sure he is, Mary," the man replied in a gentle voice. "Doc Maddox is the finest there ever was. But he—all of us—may have overreached ourselves this time."

"I'm sure we'll find a way," the girl said, with heart-breaking serenity.

"Maybe," the man said. "Anyhow, we'll show 'em there's still a few pounds of thrust in the old brain-jets." He turned to Carmody, and his expression hardened. "I just hope you're worth it, Mac," he said. "Three lives are going on the line for you."

It was a difficult proposition to respond to, and Carmody didn't even try.

"Single file quick-step back to the ship," the man said. "We'll get Doc Maddox's assessment of the situation."

Drawing a bulb-nosed gun from his belt, the man turned into the woods. The girl followed, giving Carmody an encouraging look over her shoulder. Carmody fell into line behind her.

Chapter 15

"Hey, wait a minute, what is all this?" Carmody asked as he followed the space-suited people through he forest. "Who are you people? What are you doing here?"

"Criminy!" the girl said, flushing with embarrassment. "We've been rushing around so, we haven't even introduced ourselves! A fine lot of fools you must take us for, Mr. Carmody!"

"Not at all," Carmody said courteously. "But I would like to know—well, to *know*, if you know what I mean."

"Of course, I know what you mean," the girl said. "I am Aviva Christiansen, and this is my father, Professor Lars Christiansen."

"You can knock off that 'Professor' stuff," Christiansen said gruffly. "Just call me Lars, or Chris, or anything else that comes to mind."

"All right, Dad," Aviva said, with a mock show of fond petulance. "Anyhow, Mr. Carmody—"

"The name's Tom."

"Tom, then," Aviva said, coloring prettily. "Where was I? Oh yes, Dad and I are connected with the Terran Interstellar Rescue Association (TIRA), which has its offices in Stockholm, Geneva, and Washington, D.C."

"I'm afraid I've never heard of your organization," Carmody said.

"There's nothing surprising about that," Aviva said. "Earth has just entered upon the threshold of interstellar exploration. Even now, in laboratories all over the earth, new sources of power far exceeding the crude atomic devices with which you have been accustomed are now in the experimental stage. And very soon indeed, spacecraft piloted by men of Earth will probe to the farthest corners of the galaxy. And this will, of course, usher in a new period of international peace and cooperation upon our tired old planet."

"It will?" Carmody asked. "Why?"

"Because there will no longer be anything significant to fight about," Aviva said, somewhat breathlessly since all three were trotting through low underbrush. "There are countless worlds out there, as you may have noticed," she continued, "and there is room for all kinds of social experiments, and adventures, and everything you could possibly imagine. So man's energies will be directed outward instead of dissipated inward in the form of disastrous internecine warfare."

"The kid's giving you the straight dope," said Lars Christiansen, in his deep, gruff, friendly, no-nonsense voice. "She may sound like a scatter-brain, but she's got about eleventy-seven Ph.D.'s and Doctorates to back up her line of gab."

"And my pop may sound like a roughneck," Aviva flashed back, "but he's got three Nobel prizes in his footlocker!"

Father and daughter exchanged looks which were somehow threatening and affectionate at the same time;

"So anyhow," Aviva said, "that's how it is, or I should say, how it's *going to be* in a couple of years. But we got a headstart on it all due to Dr. Maddox, whom you will meet shortly." Aviva hesitated a moment, then said in a lower voice, "I don't think I'll be betraying a confidence if I tell you that Dr. Maddox is a—a—mutant."

"Rats, there's no need to be nervous about the word," Lars Christiansen growled. "A mutant can be every bit as good as we are. And in the case of Dr. Maddox, he can be about a thousand times better!"

"It was Dr. Maddox who really put this project into orbit," Aviva went on. "You see, he made a projection of the future (how he does it I don't know!) and he realized that soon, with the imminent discovery of cheap, unlimited power in a safe, portable form, there were going to be space-ships all over the place! And a lot of people would just rush into space without proper equipment or navigational instruments or stuff—"

"A lot of half-baked fools," Christiansen commented dryly.

"Dad! Anyhow, these people were going to need help. But there would be no organized Galactic Rescue Patrol (he computed this figure very carefully) for 87.238874 years. Do you see?"

"I think so," Carmody said. "You three saw the problem and—and you stepped in."

"Yes," she said simply. "We stepped in. Dad's very keen on serving oth-ers, though you could never tell it from the grouchy way he talks. And what's good enough for my dad is good enough for me. And as for Dr. Maddox—well, he's just the utter maximum top realized-potential of any human being of my acquaintance."

"Yeah, he's that all right, in spades, doubled," Lars Christiansen said quietly. "The man has had quite a history. Mutations are usually of nega-tive value, you know. Just one or two out of a thousand pan out gold instead of pyrites. But in Dr. Maddox's case, there is a family history of massive mutation, most of it favorable, all of it inexplicable."

"We suspect benevolent alien intervention," Aviva said, almost in a whisper. "The Maddox family can only be traced back for two hundred years. It's a strange story. Aelill Madoxxe, Maddox's great-grandfather, was a Welsh coal miner. He worked for nearly twenty years in the notorious Auld Gringie Mine, and was one of the few laborers to retain his health.

That was in 1739. Recently, when Auld Gringie was re-opened, the fabulous Scatterwail uranium deposits were found adjacent to it."

"It must have begun there," Christiansen said. "We pick up the family next in 1801, in Oaxaca, Mexico. Thomas Madoxxe (as he styled himself) had married the beautiful and imperious Teresita de Valdez, Contessa de Aragon, owner of the finest hacienda in southern Mexico. Thomas was out riding herd on the morning of April 6th, 1801, when La Estrella Roja de Muerto—Red Star of Death (subsequently identified as a large, highly radioactive meteorite)—fell within two miles of the ranch. Thomas and Teresita were among the few survivors."

"Next we come to the 1930s," Aviva said, picking up the tale. "The next Maddox generation, much reduced in wealth, moved to Los Angeles. Ernest Maddox, the doctor's grandfather, was selling a newfangled contraption to doctors and dentists. It was called an 'X-ray machine.' Maddox demonstrated the machine twice weekly for at least ten years. He used himself as subject. Despite the massive overdose of hard radiation, *or perhaps because of it,* he lived to a very respectable age."

"His son," Lars said, "moved by we know not what compulsion, traveled to Japan in 1935 and became a Zen monk. He lived in a *tsuktsuri,* or corner of an abandoned basement, throughout the war years, never once uttering a word. The local people left him alone, thinking he was an eccentric Pakistani. Maddox's basement was in Hiroshima, just 7.9 miles from the epicenter of the atomic explosion of 1945. *Immediately after the explosion,* Maddox left Japan and went to the Hui-Shen monastery, situated on the most inaccessible peak in northern Tibet. According to the story of an English tourist who was there at the time, *the lamas had been expecting him!* He settled there, devoting himself to the study of certain Tantras. He married a woman of royal Kashmiri blood, by whom he had one son: that was Owen, our doctor. The family left Tibet for the United States one week before the Red Chinese launched their invasion. Owen was educated at Harvard, Yale, UCLA, Oxford, Cambridge, the Sorbonne, and Heidelberg. How he found us is quite a strange story in itself, which you shall hear upon a more propitious occasion. For now we have reached the ship, and I think we dare not waste any more time in palaver."

Carmody saw it in a little clearing, a majestic spaceship which rose upwards like a skyscraper. It possessed vanes, jets, hatches, and many other protuberances. In front of it, seated in a folding chair, was a man somewhat above middle age, with a benevolent, deeply creased face. It was immediately apparent that this man was Maddox the Mutant, for he had seven fingers on each hand, and his forehead bulged hugely to make room for the extra brain behind it.

Maddox rose in a leisurely manner (on five legs!) and nodded in welcome. "You have come only just in time," he said. "Lines of inimical force have very nearly reached the intersection point. Come into the ship quickly, all of you! We must erect the force-shield without delay."

Lars Christiansen marched forward, too proud to run. Aviva took Carmody's arm, and Carmody perceived that she was trembling, and that the shapeless gray cloth of her suit could not conceal the lissome lines of the beautiful girl, though she seemed unaware of it.

"It's a nasty situation," Maddox muttered, folding his canvas chair and putting it within the ship. "My calculations allow for this sort of nodal point, of course, but by the very nature of interminable combination one cannot predict their configuration. Still, we do our best."

At the wide entrance hatch, Carmody hesitated. "I really think I should say goodbye to Mr. Maudsley," he told Maddox. "Perhaps I should even ask his advice. He's been very helpful, and he's working on a way to get me back to Earth."

"Maudsley!" Maddox cried, exchanging significant glances with Christiansen. "I suspected he was behind this!"

"It looked like his damned handiwork," Christiansen grated.

"What do you mean?" Carmody asked.

"I mean," Maddox said, "that you have been victim and pawn in a vast conspiracy involving no less than seventeen star-systems. I cannot explain it all now; but believe me, not only your life and ours is at stake, but also the life of several dozen billion humanoids, most of them blue-eyed and fair-skinned!"

"Oh Tom, hurry, hurry!" Aviva cried, pulling at his arm.

"Well, all right," Carmody said. "But I shall want complete and satisfactory explanation."

"And you shall have it," Maddox said as Carmody stepped through the hatch. "You shall have it right now."

Carmody turned quickly, detecting the note of menace in Maddox's voice. He looked at the mutant intently and experienced a wave of shock. He looked again, at his three rescuers, and really saw them for the first time.

The human mind is adept at constructing gestalts. A few curves suffice for a mountain, and half a dozen broken lines can produce a passable wave. The gestalt was breaking down now under Carmody's particularizing gaze. He saw that Aviva's lovely eyes were stylized and suggestive rather than functional—like the design of eyes on the wings of a moth. Lars had a dark red oval in the lower third of his face, divided by a darker line; this was supposed to be a mouth. Maddox's fingers, all seven of them, were painted on his body at thigh level.

The gestalt broke down completely. Carmody saw the thin black line, like a crack in the floor, that connected each of them to the ship. He stood, frozen, and watched them move toward him. They had no hands to raise, no feet to move, no eyes to see with, no mouth to explain with. They were in fact round-topped and featureless cylinders, artfully but superficially disguised as human. They had no parts with which to function; they were themselves parts, and they were now performing their sole function. They were the exact and terrible counterpart of three fingers on a giant's hand. They advanced with supple bonelessness; they evidently wanted to drive him deeper into the black maw of the ship.

The ship? Carmody darted around the three and raced back the way he had come in. But the hatch extruded pointed teeth from top and bottom, opened a little wider, and then began to close. How could he have thought it was metal? The dark shiny sides of the ship rippled now and began to contract. His feet were caught in the spongey, sticky deck, and the three fingers were moving around him, blocking him off from the diminishing square of daylight.

Carmody struggled with the desperation of a fly caught in a spider's web (the simile was exact, but the insight had come too late). He fought with a frenzy and with no effect. The square of daylight had become round and wet, and shrunk to the size of a baseball. The three cylinders were holding him now, and Carmody could not tell one from the other.

That was the final horror; that, and the fact that the walls and ceiling of the spaceship (or whatever it was) had turned a moist and livid red, and were closing in and engulfing him.

There was no escape. Carmody was helpless, unable to move or shout, unable to do anything but lose consciousness.

Chapter 16

As from a vast distance, Carmody heard a voice say: "What do you think, Doctor? Can you do anything for him?"

He recognized that voice; it was the Prize.

"I'll pay for it," another voice said. He recognized this as Maudsley. "Do you think you can do anything for him?"

"He can be saved," said a third voice, presumably that of the doctor. "Medical science admits no limits to the feasible, only to the tolerable, which is the patient's limitation, not ours."

Carmody struggled to open his eyes or his mouth, but found that he was completely immobilized.

"So it's serious, huh?" asked the Prize.

"That is a difficult question to answer with precision," the doctor said. "To begin with, we must assign categories. Medical science is easier than medical ethics, for example. We of the Galactic Medical Association are supposed to preserve life; we are also supposed to act in the best interests of the particular form we treat. But what should we do when these two imperatives are in contradiction? The Uiichi of Devin V, for example, seek a physician's aid to cure them of life and help them achieve their desired goal of death. It a damnably difficult task, let me say, and only possible when an Uiichi has grown old and enfeebled. But what does ethics have to say about this strange reversal of normal desire? Are we to do as the Uiichi desire, and perform acts which are reprehensible in nearly every corner of the galaxy? Or are we to act upon the basis of our own standards, and thus doom the Uiichi to a fate quite literally worse than death?"

"What has this got to do with Carmody?" Maudsley asked.

"Not very much," the doctor admitted. "But I thought you might find it interesting, and it will help you see why we must charge the high fees we do."

"Is he in a serious condition?" the Prize demanded.

"Only the dead can be said to be in a really serious condition," the doctor stated. "And even then, there are exceptions. Pentathanaluna, for example, which laymen refer to as Five-Day Reversible Death, is really no worse than a common cold, despite vulgar rumors to the contrary."

"But what about Carmody?" Maudsley asked.

"He is definitely not dead," the doctor said soothingly. "He is merely in a state of—or tantamount to—deep shock. To put it more simply, he has, in a manner of speaking, fainted."

"Can you pull him out of it?" the Prize asked.

"Your terms are unclear," the Doctor said. "My work is difficult enough without—"

"I mean, can you restore him to his original state of function?" the Prize asked.

"Well! That is rather a large order, as I think you will admit if you give it a moment's thought. What *was* his original state of function? Does either of you know? Would he know himself if, miraculously, he could be consulted in his own cure? Of the million subtle alterations of personality, some of which take place at the mere instigation of a heartbeat, how can we know which was most characteristically *his?* Is not a lost personality like a lost second—something we can approximate but never truly reproduce? These, gentlemen, are questions of some weight."

"Damnably heavy," Maudsley said. "Suppose you just get him as near to what he was as you can. Will that be very tough?"

"Not on me," the doctor said. "I have worked for a considerable time in my profession. I have become inured to the most ghastly sights, accustomed to the most hideous procedures. That is not to say that I have grown *callous,* of course; I have merely learned through sad necessity to direct my attention away from the soul-searing procedures which my profession demands of me."

"Cripes, Doc!" the Prize said. "What do you gotta do to my buddy?"

"I must operate," the doctor said. "It is the only reliable way. I shall dissect Carmody (speaking in layman's terms) and put his limbs and organs into a preserving solution. Then, I shall soften him in a dilute solution of

432   ROBERT SHECKLEY

K-5. I will draw his brain and nervous system out through various orifices. The procedure then is to hook up the nervous system and brain to a Life-Simulator, and fire the synapses in carefully timed series. Thus we see if there are any breaks, bad valves, stoppages, and the like. Assuming the absence of these, we disassemble the brain, coming at last to the interaction point between mind and body. Removing this very carefully, we check all internal and external connections. If everything is all right up to this point, we open the interaction-point reservoir, looking for leaks, of course, and then checking the level of consciousness within. If it is low or depleted (and in cases like these, it almost always is) we analyze the residue and create a new batch. This new batch of consciousness is tested exhaustively, then injected into the interaction-point reservoir. All parts of the corpus are then reassembled, and the patient can be reanimated with the Life-Simulator. That's pretty much the whole process."

"Hooee," said the Prize. "I wouldn't treat a dog that way!"

"Nor would I," the doctor said. "Not until the canine race has evolved further. Do you wish me to perform this operation?"

"Well..." The Prize mused. "I guess we can't just leave him lying around unconscious, can we?"

"Of course we can't," Maudsley said. "The poor fellow has been counting on us and we must not fail him. Doctor, do your duty!"

Carmody had been struggling with his malfunctioning functions through this entire conversation. He had listened with steadily mounting terror and with the growing conviction that his friends could do him more harm than his enemies could even imagine. Now, with a titanic effort, he burst open his eyes and wrenched his tongue away from the roof of his mouth.

"No operation!" he croaked. "I'll cut your goddamned heart out if you try any goddamned operation!"

"He has recovered his faculties," the doctor said, sounding quite pleased. "Often, you know, a verbalization of our operating procedure in the patient's presence serves as a better anodyne than the operation itself. It is a placebo effect, of course, but certainly not to be sneered at."

Carmody struggled to stand up, and Maudsley helped him to his feet. He looked at the doctor for the first time, and saw a tall, thin, mournful man in black clothes, who looked exactly like Abraham Lincoln. The Prize was no longer a cauldron. Evidently under the stress, he had changed into a dwarf.

"Send for me if you need me," the doctor said, and departed.

"What happened?" Carmody asked. "That spaceship, those people—"

"We pulled you out just in time," the Prize said. "But that was no spaceship, keed."

"I know. What was it?"

"That," Maudsley said, "was your predator. You walked right into his mouth."

"I guess I did at that," Carmody said.

"And by doing that, you may have lost your only chance of getting back to Earth," Maudsley said. "I think you'd better sit down, Carmody. You have only a few choices now, and none of them is particularly enticing."

Carmody sat down.

Chapter 17

First and foremost, Maudsley talked about predators, their folkways and mores, habits and reactions, ways and means. It was important for Carmody to know just what had happened to him, and why, even if that knowledge came subsequent to the event.

"*Especially* if it comes after the event," the Prize put in.

Maudsley went on to say that, just as for every man there's a woman, so for every living organism there's a predator. The Great Chain of Eating (a poetic image for the totality of life in a state of dynamism in the universe) must go on, for reasons of inner necessity if for nothing else. Life as we know it involves creation; and creation is inconceivable without death. Thus—

"Why is creation inconceivable without death?" Carmody asked.

"Don't ask stupid questions. Where was I? Oh, yes. Thus murder is justified, though some of its concomitants are less readily appreciated. A creature in its natural habitat lives off certain other creatures and is lived off by still other creatures. This process is usually so natural and simple, and in so fine a state of balance, that preyers and preyed-upon alike tend to ignore it for great stretches of time, putting their attention instead upon the creation of art objects, the gathering of groundnuts, the contemplation of the Absolute, or whatever else the species finds of interest. And that is as it should be, because Nature (whom we may personify as an old lady dressed in russet and black) does not like to find her rules and regulations the subject of every cocktail party, swarming nest, Konklave, or what you will. But you, Carmody, by inadvertently escaping the checks and balances of your native planet, still have not escaped the inexorable Law of Process. Thus, if there were no existing predator for you in the farflung reaches of space, then one would have to be found. If one could not be found, then it would have to be created."

"Well, yeah," Carmody said. "But that spaceship, those people—"

"—were not what they seemed," Maudsley told him. "That must be evident to you."

"It is now."

"*They* were actually *it*, a single entity, a creature created especially for you, Carmody. *It* was your predator, and it followed almost classically the simple, standard Laws of Predation."

"Which are?" Carmody asked.

"Yes, which are," the Prize sighed. "How nicely you put it! We may rant against fortune and the world, but we are left at the end with the stark proposition: *These are the things which are.*"

"I wasn't commenting," Carmody said, "I was asking. What are these Laws of Predation?"

"Oh, sorry, I misunderstood you," the Prize said.

"That's quite all right," Carmody said.

"Thank you," the Prize said.

"It's nothing," Carmody said. "I didn't mean… No, I did mean! What are these simple, standard Laws of Predation?"

"Must you ask?" Maudsley said.

"Yes, I'm afraid I must."

"When you put it in the form of a question," Maudsley said severely, "predation ceases to be simple and standard, and even its status as a law becomes dubious. Knowledge of predation is inherent in all organisms, just like arms and legs and heads, but even more certain. It is much more basic than a law of science, you see, and therefore not subject to simplistic reductionism. The mere asking of that sort of question imposes a severe restriction upon the answer."

"Still, I think I should know everything possible about predation," Carmody said. "Particularly mine."

"Yes, definitely you should know," Maudsley said. "Or rather, you *should have known*, which is by no means the same thing. Still, I'll try."

Maudsley rubbed his forehead vigorously and stated: "You eat, therefore you are eaten. That much you know. But *how*, precisely, are you to be eaten? How are you to be trapped, seized, immobilized, and prepared? Will you be served up piping hot or nicely chilled or at room temperature? Obviously, that depends on the tastes of that which feasts upon you. Shall your predator leap at your undefended back from a convenient height? Shall it dig a pit for you, or spin a web, or challenge you to single combat, or dive upon you with outstretched talons? That depends upon your predator's nature, which determines his form and function. That nature is limited by and respondent to the exigencies of your own nature, which, like his, is informed by free will and thus ultimately unfathomable.

"Now to particulars. Diving, digging or spinning are straightforward, but they lose effectiveness against a creature with the faculty of memory. A creature like yourself, Carmody, could you avoid the simplistic deadly attack once, might never be deceived again.

"Straightforwardness is not Nature's way, however. It has been said that Nature has a vested interest in illusions, which are highways to death and birth. I for one will not argue the proposition. If we accept the concept, we see that your predator must engage in complex maneuvers in order to snare a complex creature such as yourself.

"There is another side to the problem also. Your predator was not conceived solely in order to eat you. You are the single most important single thing in his life, granted; but he does possess free will, just as you do, and therefore is not limited to the strict logic of his eating function. Barn mice may think that the owl in the rafters was conceived and delineated for the sole purpose of hunting mice. But we know that the owl has several other things on his mind. This is how it is with all predators, including yours. From this, we draw an important conclusion: that all predators are functionally imperfect by virtue of their free will."

"I never thought of it that way before," Carmody said. "Does that help me?"

"Well, not really. But I thought you should know it anyhow. You see, practically speaking, you may never be able to exploit your predator's imperfections. Indeed, you may never even learn what they are. In this situation you are just like the barn mice. You may find a hole to scamper in when you hear the whirr of wings, but you will never be able to analyze the nature, talents, and limitations of the owl."

"Well, that's just great," Carmody said, with heavy sarcasm. "I'm licked before I start. Or, to use your terminology, I'm as good as eaten even though nobody's stuck a fork in me yet."

"Temper, temper," the Prize cautioned. "It isn't quite as bad as that."

"So how bad is it? Can either of you tell me anything useful?"

"That's what we're trying to do," Maudsley said.

"Then tell me what this predator looks like."

Maudsley shook his head. "That is quite impossible. Do you think any victim can learn what his predator looks like? If he could, the victim would become immortal!"

"And that's against the rules," the Prize put in.

"At least give me an idea," Carmody said. "Does he always go around disguised as a spaceship?"

"Of course not," Maudsley said. "From your point view, he is a shape-changer. Have you ever heard of a mouse walking into the jaws of a snake, or a fly lighting on a frog's tongue, or a fawn stepping between the fore-paws of a tiger? *That* is the essence of predation! And you must ask yourself: where did those deluded victims think they were going, and what did they think was in front of them? Similarly, you must ask yourself what was really in front of your eyes when you talked to three of the predator's fingers and followed them straight into his mouth!"

"They looked like people," Carmody said. "But I still don't know what the predator looked like."

"There is no way I can enlighten you," Maudsley said. "Information about predators is not easily gained. They are too complementary to one-self. Its traps and concealments are based upon your own memories, your dreams and fantasies, your hopes and desires. The predator takes your own treasured dramas and plays them for you, as you just saw. To know your predator, you must know yourself. And it is easier to know the entire Universe than to know oneself."

"What can I do?" Carmody asked.

"Learn!" Maudsley said. "Be eternally vigilant, move at top speed, trust nothing and no one. Don't think of relaxing until you have reached your home."

"Home!" Carmody said.

"Yes. You will be safe on your own planet. Your predator cannot enter your lair. You will still be subject to all commonplace disasters, but at least you will be spared this."

"Can you send me home?" Carmody asked. "You said you were working on a machine."

"I have completed it," Maudsley said. "But you must understand its limitations, which are concomitant with my own. My machine can take you to Where Earth is now, but that is all it can do."

"But that's all I need!" Carmody said.

"No, it is not. 'Where' gives you only the first W of location. You will still have to solve for When and Which. Take them in order, is my advice. Temporality before particularity, to use a common expression. You will have to leave here at once; your predator, whose appetite you foolishly aroused, may be back at any instant. I may not be so lucky this time in my rescue attempts."

"How did you get me out of his mouth?" Carmody asked.

"I hastily fabricated a lure," Maudsley told him. "It looked just like you, but I built it a little larger than life-size and gave it a bit more vitality. The predator dropped you and bounded after it, dribbling saliva. But we can't try that again."

Carmody preferred not to ask if the lure had felt any pain. "I'm ready," he said. "But where am I going, and what is going to happen?"

"You are going to an Earth, almost undoubtedly the wrong one. But I will send a letter to a person I know who is very clever at solving temporal problems. He'll look you up, if he decides to take your case, and after that…well, who can say? Take it as it comes, Carmody, and be grateful if anything comes at all."

"I am grateful," Carmody said. "No matter what the outcome, I want to thank you very much."

"That's quite all right," Maudsley said. "Don't forget my message to the old fellow if you ever do get back home. All set to go? The machine is right here beside me. I didn't have time to make it visible, but it looks almost exactly like a Zenith battery-operated shortwave radio. Where the hell did it go? Here it is. Got your Prize?"

"I've got him," the Prize said, holding onto Carmody's left arm with both hands.

"Then we're ready. I set this dial here and then this one, and then these two over here… You'll find it pleasant to be out of the macrocosm, Carmody, and back on a planet, even if it isn't yours. There's no qualitative difference, of course, among atom, planet, galaxy or universe. It's all a question of what scale you live on most comfortably. And now I push *this*—"

Bam! Pow! Crrrrunch! Slow dissolve, quick dissolve, lap dissolve, electronic music denoting outer space, outer space denoting electronic music. Pages of a calendar flip, Carmody tumbles head over heels in simulated free fall. Kettledrums sound ominous note, ominous note sounds kettledrums, bright flash of colors, woman's voice keening in echo chamber, laughter of children, montage of Jaffa oranges lighted to look like planets, collage of a solar system lighted to look like ripples in a brook. Slow the tape, speed the tape, fade out, fade in.

It was one hell of a trip, but nothing Carmody hadn't expected.

PART III
WHEN IS EARTH?

Chapter 18

With the transition completed, Carmody took stock of himself. A brief inventory convinced him that he still had all four limbs, one body, one head, and one mind. Final returns were not in, of course, but he did seem to be all there. He also noted that he still had the Prize, which was somehow recognizable even though it had undergone its usual metamorphosis. This time it had changed from a dwarf into a badly constructed flute.

"So far, so good," Carmody said to nobody in particular. He now surveyed his surroundings.

"Not so good," he said at once. He had been prepared to arrive at the wrong Earth, but he hadn't expected it would be quite so wrong as this.

He was standing on marshy ground at the edge of a swamp. Miasmic vapors rose from the stagnant brown waters. There were broad-leaved ferns, and low, thin-leaved shrubs, and bushy-headed palms, and a single dogwood tree. The air was blood-warm and heavily laden with odors of fertility and decay.

"Maybe I'm in Florida," Carmody said hopefully.

"Afraid not," said the Prize, or the flute, speaking in a low melodious voice but with an excess of vibrato.

Carmody glared at the Prize. "How come you can speak?" he demanded.

"How come you didn't ask me that when I was a cauldron?" the Prize replied. "But I'll tell you, if you really want to know. Affixed up here, just inside my mouthpiece, is a CO_2 cartridge. That serves me in place of lungs, though for a limited time only. The rest is obvious."

It wasn't obvious to Carmody. But he had more important matters on his mind. He asked, "Where am I?"

"*We,*" said the Prize, "are on the planet Earth. This moist bit of ground upon which we are standing will become, in your day, the township of Scarsdale, New York." He snickered. "I suggest you buy property now, while the real-estate values are depressed."

"It sure as hell doesn't look like Scarsdale," Carmody said.

"Of course not. Leaving aside for a moment the question of *Whichness,* we can see that the *Whenness* is all wrong."

"Well... *When* are we?"

"A good question," the Prize replied, "but one to which I can only make an approximate and highly qualified reply. Obviously enough, we are in the Phanerozoic Eon, which in itself covers one sixth of Earth's geological time. Easy enough; but what *part* of the Phanerozoic are we in, the Paleozoic or the Mesozoic Era? Here I must hazard a guess. Just on the basis of climate, I rule out all of the Paleozoic except, just possibly, the end of the Permian Period. But wait, now I can rule that out, too! Look, overhead and to your right!"

Carmody looked and saw an oddly shaped bird flapping awkwardly into the distance.

"Definitely an Archeopteryx," the Prize said. "You could tell at once from the way its feathers diverged pinnately from its axis. Most scientists consider it a creature of the upper Jurassic and the Cretaceous Periods, but certainly not older than the Triassic. So we can rule out the entire Paleozoic; we are definitely in the Mesozoic Era."

"That's pretty far back, huh?" Carmody said.

"Quite far," the Prize agreed. "But we can do better than that. I think we can pinpoint what part of the Mesozoic we are in. Let me think for a bit." He thought for a bit. "Yes, I think I have it. *Not* the Triassic! That swamp is a false clue, I fear. However, the angiospermous flowering plant near your left foot points an unmistakable direction, periodwise. Nor does it constitute our sole evidence. You noticed the dogwood tree in front of you? Well, turn around and you will see two poplars and a fig tree in the midst of a small group of conifers. Significant, eh? But did you notice the most important detail of all, so commonplace in your time that you would be apt to overlook it? I refer to grass, which we see here in abundance. There was no grass as late as Jurassic times! Just ferns and cycadeoids! And that decides it, Carmody! I'd wager my life savings on it! We are in the Cretaceous Period, and probably not far from its upper limit!"

Carmody had only the vaguest remembrance of the geological periods of the Earth. "Cretaceous," he said. "How far is that from my time?"

"Oh, about a hundred million years, give or take a few million," the Prize said. "The Cretaceous age lasted for seventy million years."

Carmody had no difficulty in adjusting to this concept; he never even tried. He said to the Prize, "How did you learn all of this geology stuff?"

"How do you think?" the Prize replied spiritedly. "I studied. I figured, since we were going to Earth, I'd better find out something about the place. And it's a damned good thing I did. If it weren't for me, you'd be stumbling around here looking for Miami Beach, and you'd have probably ended up being eaten by an allosaurus."

"Eaten by a who?"

"I refer," the Prize said, "to one of the uglier members of the order Saurischia, an offshoot of which—the sauropoda—culminated in the renowned brontosaurus."

"You mean to tell me there are dinosaurs here?" Carmody asked.

"I mean to tell you," the Prize said in obbligato, "that this is the one and original Dinosaursville, and I would also like to take this opportunity to welcome you to the Age of the Giant Reptiles."

Carmody made an incoherent noise. He noticed a movement to his left and turned. He saw a dinosaur. It looked about 20 feet high, and might have stretched 50 feet from nose to tail. It stood erect on its hind legs. It was colored slate-blue, and it was striding rapidly toward Carmody.

"Is that a tyrannosaurus?" Carmody asked.

"Yes, it is," the Prize said. "*Tyrannosaurus rex*, most highly respected of the saurischians. A true deinodon, you will note, its upper incisors running half a foot in length. This young chap coming toward us must weigh upwards of nine tons."

"And he eats meat," Carmody said.

"Yes, of course. I personally think that tyrannosaurus and the other carnosaurs of this period feasted mainly on the inoffensive and widely distributed hadrosaurs. But that is only my own pet theory."

The giant creature was less than 50 feet away. There was no refuge on the flat, marshy land, no place to climb, no cave to scuttle into. Carmody said, "What should I do?"

"You must change into a plant at once!" the Prize said urgently.

"But I can't!"

"You can't? Then your situation is serious indeed. Let me see, you can't fly or burrow, and I'd wager ten to one you'd never outrun him. Hmm, this becomes difficult."

"So what do I do?"

"Well, under the circumstances, I think you should be stoical about the whole thing. I could quote Epictetus to you. And we could sing a hymn together if that would help."

"Damn your hymns! I want to get out of this!"

The flute had already begun to play "Nearer My God to Thee." Carmody clenched his fists. The tyrannosaurus was now directly in front of him, towering overhead like a fleshed-out and animate derrick. It opened its awesome mouth.

Chapter 19

"Hello," said the tyrannosaurus. "My name is Emie and I am six years old. What's your name?"

"Carmody," said Carmody.

"And I'm his Prize," said the Prize.

"Well, you both look very strange," said Emie. "You don't look like anybody I've ever met before, and I've met a dimetrodon, and a struthiomimus, and a scolosaurus, and lots of others. Do you come from around here?"

"Well, sort of," Carmody said. Then, reflecting on the dimensionality of time, he said, "But not really, actually."

"Oh," said Emie. Childlike, he stared at them and fell into a silence. Carmody stared back, fascinated by that huge, grim head, larger than a slot machine or a beer keg, the narrow mouth studded with teeth like rows of stilettos. Fearsome indeed! Only the eyes—which were round, mild, blue and trusting—refuted the rest of the dinosaur's ominous appearance.

"Well, so," Emie said at last, "what are you doing here in the park?"

"Is this a park?" Carmody asked.

"Sure, it's a park!" Emie said. "It's a park for *kids,* and I don't think you're a kid, even though you are very small."

"You're right, I'm not a kid," Carmody said. "I stumbled into your park by mistake. I think perhaps I should speak to your father."

"Hokay," Emie said. "Climb on my back and I'll take you to him. And don't forget, I discovered you. And bring along your friend. He's *really* strange!"

Carmody slipped the Prize into his pocket and mounted the tyrannosaurus, finding hand and foot holds on the folds of Emie's iron-tough skin. As soon as he was securely in place on the dinosaur's neck, Emie wheeled and began to lope toward the southwest.

"Where are we going?" Carmody asked.

"To see my father."

"Yes, but where *is* your father?"

"He's in the city, working at his job. Where else would he be?"

"Of course, where else indeed?" Carmody said, taking a firmer grip as Emie broke into a gallop.

From Carmody's pocket, the Prize said, in a muffled voice, "This is all exceedingly strange."

"You're the strange one around here," Carmody reminded him. Then he settled back to enjoy the ride.

They didn't call it Dinosaursville, but Carmody could think of it in no other way. It lay about two miles from the park. First they came to a road, a wide trail, actually, stamped to the firmness of concrete by countless dinosaur feet. They followed it and passed many hadrosaurs sleeping beneath willow trees by the side of the road and occasionally harmonizing in low, sweet voices. Carmody asked about them, but Emie would only say that his father considered them a real problem.

The road went past groves of birch, maple, laurel and holly. Each grove had its dozen or so dinosaurs, moving purposefully beneath the branches, digging at the ground or pushing away refuse. Carmody asked what they were doing.

"They're tidying up," Emie said scornfully. "That's all that housewives ever do."

They had come to an upland plateau. They left the last individual grove behind and plunged abruptly into a forest.

Evidently it was not a natural growth; it showed many signs of having been planted purposefully and with considerable foresight. Its outer trees consisted of a broad belt of fig, breadfruit, hazelnut and walnut. Past that there were several nicely spaced rows of tall, slim-trunked gingkos. Then, there was nothing but pine trees and an occasional spruce.

As they moved deeper into the forest, it became more and more crowded with dinosaurs. Most of these vere theropods—carnivorous tyrannosaurs like Emie. But the Prize also pointed out several ornithopods, and literally hundreds of the ceratopsia offshoot represented by the massively horned triceratops. Nearly all of them moved through the trees at a canter. The ground shook beneath their feet, the trees trembled, and clouds of dust were flung into the air. Flank scraped against armored flank, collisions were avoided only by quick turns, abrupt halts and sudden accelerations. There was much bellowing for right-of-way. The sight of several thousand hurrying dinosaurs was almost as fearsome as their smell, which was overpowering.

"Here we are," said Emie, stopping so quickly that Carmody was nearly thrown off his neck. "This is my dad's place!"

Carmody looked around and saw that Emie had brought him to a small grove of sequoias. The big trees formed an oasis within the forest. Two or three dinosaurs moved among the redwoods with a slow, almost languid pace, ignoring the turmoil 50 yards away. Carmody decided that he could get down without being trampled upon. Warily he slid off Emie's neck.

"Dad!" Emie shouted. "Hey, Dad, just look what I found, look, Dad!"

One of the dinosaurs looked up. He was a tyrannosaur, somewhat larger than Emie, with white striations across his blue hide. His eyes were gray and bloodshot. He turned around with great deliberation.

"How often," he asked, "have I asked you not to gallop here?"

"I'm sorry, Dad, but look, I found—"

"You are always 'sorry,' " the tyrannosaur said, "but you never see fit to modify your behavior. I have spoken with your mother about this, Emie, and we are in substantial agreement. Neither of us wishes to raise a graceless, loud-mouthed hot-rodder who doesn't possess the manners of a brontosaurus. I love you, my son, but you must learn—"

"Dad! Will you please save the lecture for later and look, just *look,* at what I've found!"

The elderly tyrannosaur's mouth tightened and his tail flicked ominously. But he lowered his head, following the direction of his son's outstretched forepaw, and saw Carmody.

"Well, bless my soul!" he cried.

"Good day, sir," Carmody said. "My name is Thomas Carmody. I am a human being. I don't think there are any other humans on Earth just now, or even any primates. How I got here is a little difficult to explain, but I come in peace, and—and that sort of thing," he finished lamely.

"Fantastic!" Emie's father said. He turned his head. "Baxley! Do you see what I see? Do you hear what I hear?"

Baxley was a tyrannosaur of about the same age as Emie's father. He said, "I see it, Borg, but I don't believe it."

"A talking mammal!" Borg exclaimed.

"1 still don't believe it," said Baxley.

Chapter 20

It took Borg longer to accept the idea of a talking mammal than it took Carmody to accept the idea of a talking reptile. Still, Borg finally did accept it. As the Prize remarked later, there is nothing like the actual presence of a fact to make one believe in the existence of that fact.

They retired to Borg's office, which was under the lofty green foliage of a weeping-willow tree. There, they sat and cleared their throats, trying to think of something to say. At last Borg said, "So you're an alien mammal from the future, eh?"

"I guess I am," Carmody said. "And you are an indigenous reptile from the past."

"I never thought about it that way," Borg said. "But yes, I suppose that's true. How far ahead in the future did you say you came from?"

"About a hundred million years or so."

"Hah. Quite a long time away. Yes, a long time indeed."

"It *is* quite a long time away," Carmody agreed.

Borg nodded and hummed tunelessly. It was evident to Carmody that he didn't know what to say next. Borg seemed a very decent sort of person; hospitable, but set in his ways, very much a family man, no conversationalist, just a decent, dull, middle-class tyrannosaur.

"Well, well," Borg said, after the silence had become uncomfortable, "and how *is* the future?"

"Beg pardon?"

"I mean, what sort of a place is the future?"

"Very busy," Carmody replied. "Bustling. Many new inventions, a great deal of confusion."

"Well, well, well," Borg said. "That's very much as some of our more imaginative chaps had pictured it. Some of them have even predicted an evolutionary change in the mammals, making them the dominant species on Earth. But I consider that farfetched and grotesque."

"I suppose it must sound that way," Carmody said.

"Then you *are* the dominant species?"

"Well...*one* of the dominant species."

"But what about the reptiles? Or more specifically, how are the tyrannosaurs doing in the future?"

Carmody had neither the heart nor the nerve to tell him that dinosaurs were extinct in his day, and had been extinct for sixty million years or so, and that reptiles in general had come to occupy an insignificant part in the scheme of things.

"Your race is doing every bit as well as could be expected," Carmody replied, feeling positively Pythian and rather sneaky.

"Good! I thought it would be like that!" Borg said. "We're a tough race, you know, and most of us have will power and common sense. Do men and reptiles have much trouble coexisting?"

"No, not much trouble," Carmody said.

"Glad to hear it. I was afraid the dinosaurs might have become highhanded on account of their size."

"No, no," Carmody said. "Speaking for the mammals of the future, I think I can safely say that everybody likes a dinosaur."

"It's very decent of you to say that," Borg said.

Carmody mumbled something. He suddenly felt very ashamed of himself.

"The future holds no great anxiety for a dinosaur," Borg said, falling into the rotund tones of an after-dinner speaker. "But it was not always that way. Our extinct ancestor, the allosaurus, seems to have been a badtempered brute and a gluttonous feeder. His ancestor, the ceratosaurus, was a dwarf carnosaur. To judge from the size of his braincase, he must have been incredibly stupid. There were other dawn-age carnosaurs, of course; and before them there must have been a missing link—a remote ancestor from which both the quadruped and the bipedal dinosaurs sprang."

"The bipedal dinosaurs are dominant, of course?" Carmody asked.

"Of course. The triceratops is a dull-witted creature with a savage disposition. We keep small herds of them. Their flesh rounds out a meal of brontosaurus steak quite nicely. There are various other species, of course. You might have noticed some hadrosaurs as you came into the city."

"Yes, I did," Carmody said. "They were singing."

"Those fellows are always singing," Borg said sternly.

"Do you eat them?"

"Good heavens, no! Hadrosaurs are *intelligent!* They are the only other intelligent species on the planet, aside from tyrannosaurs."

"Your son said they were a real problem."

"Well, they are," Borg said, a little too defiantly.

"In what way?"

"They're lazy. Also sullen and surly. I know what I'm talking about; I've employed hadrosaurs as servants. They have no ambition, no drive, no stick-to-it-iveness. Half the time they don't know who hatched them, and they don't seem to care. They don't look you forthrightly in the eye when they speak to you."

"They sing well, though," Carmody said.

"Oh, yes, they sing well. Some of our best entertainers are hadrosaurs. They also do well at heavy construction, if given supervision. Their appearance works against them, of course, that duckbilled look… But they can't help that. Has the hadrosaur problem been solved in the future?"

"It has," Carmody said. "The race is extinct."

"Perhaps it's best that way," Borg said. "Yes, I really think it's best."

Carmody and Borg conversed for several hours. Carmody learned about the problems of urban reptilian life. The forest-cities were becoming increasingly crowded as more and more tyrannosaurs and hadrosaurs left the countryside for the pleasures of civilization. A traffic problem of some severity had sprung up in the last fifty years. Giant saurischians like to travel fast and are proud of their quick reflexes. But when several thousand of them are rushing through a forest at the same time, accidents are bound to happen. The accidents were often severe: when two reptiles, each weighing forty tons, meet head-on at thirty miles an hour, broken necks are the most likely result.

These were not the only problems, of course. The overcrowded cities were a symptom of an exploding birthrate. Saurischians in various parts of the world lived on the edge of starvation. Disease and warfare tended to thin their numbers, but not enough.

"We have these and many other problems," Borg said. "Some of our finest minds have given way to despair. But I am more sanguine. We reptiles have seen difficult times before and have won through. We shall solve these problems just as we have solved all others. To my way of thinking, there is an innate nobility about our race, a spark of conscious, unquenchable life. I cannot believe that this will be extinguished."

Carmody nodded and said, "Your people will endure." There really was nothing for him to do but lie like a gentleman.

"I know it," Borg said. "It is always good, however, to receive confirmation. Thank you for that. And now I suppose you would like to speak with your friends."

"What friends?" Carmody asked.

"I refer to the mammal standing directly behind you," Borg said.

Carmody turned quickly and saw a short, fat, bespectacled man in a dark business suit, with a briefcase and an umbrella under his left arm. "Mr. Carmody?" he asked.

"Yes, I'm Carmody," Carmody said.

"I am Mr. Surtees from the Bureau of Internal Revenue. You have given us quite a chase, Mr. Carmody, but the IRS always gets its man."

Borg said, "This is none of my concern." He exited, making very little noise for so large a tyrannosaurus.

"You have some unusual friends," Mr. Surtees said, gazing at the departing Borg. "But that is no concern of mine, though it may be of some interest to the FBI. I am here solely in regard to your 1965 and 1966 tax returns. I have in my briefcase an extradition order, which I think you will find in order. My time machine is parked just outside of this tree. I suggest that you come along quietly."

"No," said Carmody.

"I beg you to reconsider," said Surtees. "The case against you can be settled to the mutual satisfaction of all concerned. But it must be settled at once. The government of the United States does not like to be kept waiting. Refusal to obey an order of the Supreme Court—"

"I told you, no!" Carmody said. "You might as well go away. I know who you are."

For this was the predator beyond any doubt. Its mimicry of an Internal Revenue man had been unbelievably clumsy. Both the briefcase and the umbrella were jointed to the left hand. The features were fair, but an ear had been forgotten. And, worst of all, the knees were hinged backwards.

Carmody turned and walked away. The predator stood there, not following, presumably unable to follow. It gave a single cry of hunger and rage. Then it disappeared.

Carmody had little time for self-congratulation, however, for a moment later, he disappeared.

Chapter 21

"Well, come in, come in."

Carmody blinked. He was no longer exchanging views with a dinosaur in the Cretaceous age. Now he was somewhere else. He was in a small, dingy room. The floor was of stone, chilly to his feet. The windows were covered with soot. Tall candles trembled uneasily in the draft.

A man was seated behind a high rolltop desk. The man had a long nose jutting out of a long, bony face. His eyes were cavernous. There was a brown mole in the middle of his left cheek. His lips were thin and bloodless.

The man said, "I am the Honorable Clyde Beedle Seethwright. And you are Mr. Carmody, of course, whom Mr. Maudsley so kindly referred to us. Do take that chair, sir. I trust that your trip from Mr. Maudsley's planet was a pleasant one?"

"It was fine," Carmody said, sitting down. He knew he was being ungracious, but the abrupt transitions were beginning to get him down.

"And Mr. Maudsley is well?" Seethwright said, beaming.

"He's fine," Carmody said. "Where am I?"

"Didn't the clerk tell you on your way in?"

"I didn't see any clerk. I didn't even see myself come in."

"My, my," Seethwright said, and clucked mildly. "The reception room must have gone out of phase gain. I've had it fixed a dozen times, but it keeps on desynchronizing. It is vexing for my clients, and even worse for my poor clerk, who goes out of phase with it and sometimes can't get back to his family for a week or more."

"That is a real tough break," Carmody said, and found himself near hysteria. "If you don't mind," he said, keeping a tight control on his voice, "just tell me what this place is and how I'm supposed to get home from here."

"Calm yourself," Mr. Seethwright said. "Perhaps a cup of tea? No? This 'place,' as you refer to it, is The Galactic Placement Bureau. Our articles of incorporation are on the wall, if you would care to read them."

"How did I get here?" Carmody asked.

Mr. Seethwright smiled and pressed his fingertips together. "Very simply, sir. When I received Mr. Maudsley's letter, I had a search made. The clerk found you on Earth B3444123C22. This was obviously the wrong place for you. I mean to say, Mr. Maudsley had done his best, but he is *not* in the placement service. Therefore, I took the liberty of transporting you here. But if you wish to return to that aforementioned Earth—"

"No, no," Carmody said. "I was just wondering how... I mean, you said that this is a Galactic Placement Service, right?"

"*The* Galactic Placement Service," Seethwright corrected gently.

"OK. So I'm not on Earth."

"No indeed. Or, to put it more rigorously, you are not on any of the possible, probable, potential or temporal worlds of the Earth configuration."

"OK, fine," Carmody said. He was breathing heavily. "Now, Mr. Seethwright, have *you* ever been to any of those Earths?"

"I'm afraid I have never had the pleasure. My work keeps me pretty well tied to the office, you see, and I spend holidays at my family's cottage at—"

"Right!" Carmody thundered abruptly. "You've never been to Earth, or so you claim! In that case, why in God's name are you sitting in a goddamned room like out of *Dickens* with *candles* yet and wearing a stove-pipe hat? Hey? Just let's hear you answer that one, because I already *know* the damned answer, which is that some son of a bitch must have *drugged* me and I dreamed this whole damned cockomamie thing including *you,* you grinning hatchet-faced bastard!"

Carmody collapsed in the chair, breathing like a steam engine and glaring triumphantly at Seethwright. He waited for everything to dissolve, for funny shapes to come and go, and for himself to wake up in his own bed in his own apartment, or maybe in a friend's bed or even in a hospital bed.

Nothing happened. Carmody's sense of triumph trickled away. He felt utterly confused, but he was suddenly too tired to care.

"Are you *quite* over your outburst?" Mr. Seethwright asked frigidly.

"Yes, I'm over it," Carmody said. "I'm sorry."

"Don't fret," Seethwright said quietly. "You have been under a strain; one appreciates that. But I can do nothing for you unless you keep control of yourself. Intelligence may lead you home; wild emotional outbursts will get you nowhere."

"I really am sorry," Carmody said.

"As for this room, which seems to have startled you so, I had it decorated especially for you. The period is only approximate—the best I could do on short notice. It was done to make you feel at home."

"That was thoughtful of you," Carmody said. "I suppose that your appearance—"

"Yes, precisely," Mr. Seethwright said, smiling. "I had myself decorated as well as the room. It was no trouble, really. It is the sort of little touch which so many of our clients appreciate."

"I do appreciate it, as a matter of fact," Carmody said. "Now that I'm getting used to it, it's sort of restful."

"I hoped you would find it soothing," Seethwright said. "As for your proposition that all of this is happening to you in a dream—well, it has some merit."

"It has?"

Mr. Seethwright nodded vigorously. "It has definite merit as a proposition, but it has no validity as a statement of your circumstances."

"Oh," Carmody said, and sat back in the chair.

"Strictly speaking," Seethwright went on, "there is no important difference between imaginary and real events. The opposition you create between them is entirely verbal. You are not dreaming any of this, Mr. Carmody; but I mention that only as a point of incidental information. Even if you were dreaming it all, you would have to pursue the same course of action."

"I don't understand all that," Carmody said. "But I'll take your word that this is real." He hesitated, then said, "But the thing I *really* don't understand—why is all of this *like* this? I mean, the Galactic Center looked a little like Radio City, and Borg the dinosaur didn't talk like any dinosaur, even a *talking* dinosaur, ought to talk, and—"

"Please, don't excite yourself," Mr. Seethwright said.

"Sorry," Carmody said.

"You want me to tell you why reality is the way it is," Seethwright said. "But there is no explanation for that. You must simply learn to fit your preconceptions to what you find. You must not expect reality to adapt itself to you, except very infrequently. It can't be helped if things are strange; and it also can't be helped if things are familiar. Am I getting through?"

"I think so," Carmody said.

"Splendid! You're sure you won't have some tea?"

"No, thank you."

"Then we must see about getting you home," Seethwright said. "Nothing like the dear old place to pick up one's spirits, eh?"

"Nothing at all!" Carmody said. "Will it be very difficult, Mr. Seethwright?"

"No, I don't think I would characterize it as *difficult,*" Seethwright said. "It will be complicated, of course, and rigorous, and even somewhat risky. But I do not consider any of those things to be *difficult.*"

"What *do* you consider truly difficult?" Carmody asked.

"Solving quadratic equations," Seethwright answered at once. "I simply cannot do them, even though I've tried a million or more times. That, sir, is a difficulty! Now let us proceed to your case."

"Do you know where Earth is?" Carmody asked.

" 'Where' poses no problem," Seethwright said. "You have already been to Where, though it didn't do you much good, since When was so far off the mark. But now I think we can pin down your particular When without undue travail. It's the Which which gets tricky."

"Is that likely to stop us?"

"Not at all," Seethwright said. "We must simply sort through and find which Which you belong in. The process is perfectly straightforward; like shooting fish in a barrel, as your people would say."

"I've never tried that," Carmody said. "Is it really easy?"

"That depends upon the size of the fish and the size of the barrel," Seethwright told him. "It is, for example, nearly effortless to pot a shark in a bathtub; whereas it is a considerable undertaking to bring down a minnow in a hogshead. Scale is everything. But whichever project is before you, I think you can appreciate its essential straightforwardness and simplicity."

"I suppose so," Carmody said. "But it occurs to me that my search for *Which* Earth may be straightforward and simple, but may also be impossible to complete due to the interminability of the series of selections."

"That's not quite true but it's very nicely said," Seethwright said, beaming. "Complication is often very useful, you know. It helps to specify and identify the problem."

"Well… What happens now?"

"Now we go to work," Seethwright said, rubbing his hands together briskly. "My staff and I have put together a selection of Which-worlds. We confidently expect that your world will be one of them. But of course, only you can determine the right one."

"So I look them over and decide?" Carmody asked.

"Something like that," Seethwright said. "Actually, you must *live* them over. Then, as soon as you are sure, signify to us whether we've hit your probability-world or a variant. If it's your world, that's the end of it. If it's a variant, then we move you on to the next Which-world."

"That sounds reasonable enough," Carmody said. "Are there a lot of these probability-worlds?"

"An interminable number, as you suspected earlier. But we have every hope of early success. Unless—"

"Unless what?"

"Unless your predator gets to you first."

"My predator!"

"He is still on your trail," Mr. Seethwright said. "And as you know by now, he is reasonably adept at setting snares. These snares take the form of scenes culled from your own memories. 'Terraform scenes,' I suppose we could call them, designed to lull and deceive you, to convince you to walk unsuspecting into his mouth."

"Will he interfere with your worlds?" Carmody asked.

"Of course he will," Seethwright said. "There's no sanctuary in the searching process. On the contrary—the better and more informed the search, the more fraught it is with dangers. You had asked me earlier about dreams and reality. Well, here is your answer. Everything that helps you does so openly. Everything that seeks to harm you does so covertly, by the use of delusions, disguises, and dreams."

"Isn't there anything you can do about the predator?" Carmody asked.

"Nothing. Nor would I if I could. Predation is a necessary circumstance. Even the Gods are eventually eaten by Fate. You will not be an exception to the universal rule."

"I thought you'd say something like that," Carmody said. "But can you give me any help at all? Any hints on how the worlds you send me to will differ from the worlds of the predator?"

"To me the differences are obvious," Seethwright said. "But you and I do not share the same perceptions. You could not make use of my insights, Carmody; nor I, of yours. Still, you have managed to elude the predator so far."

"I've been lucky."

"There you are! I have a great deal of skill, but no luck whatsoever. Who can tell which quality will be most needed in the trials ahead? Not I, sir, and certainly not you! Therefore be of stout heart, Mr. Carmody. Faint heart ne'er won fair planet, eh? Look over the worlds I send you to, be extremely cautious of the predator's scenes of delusion, get out while the getting's good; but do not be unmanned by fear into passing up your true and rightful world."

"What happens if I do pass it by inadvertently?" Carmody asked.

"Then your search can never end," Seethwright told him. "Only you can tell us where you belong. If, for one reason or another, you do not locate your world among the most likely, then we must continue our search among the merely likely, and then the less likely, and finally the least likely. The number of probability-worlds of Earth is not infinite, of course; but from your viewpoint, it might as well be; you simply do not have enough inherent duration to search through them all and then begin again."

"All right," Carmody said doubtfully. "I don't suppose there's any other way."

"There's no other way I can help you," Seethwright said. "And I doubt if there is any way at all that would not involve your active participation. But if you wish, I can make inquiries into alternate galactic location techniques. It would take a while—"

"I don't think I have a while," Carmody said. "I think my predator is not far behind me. Mr. Seethwright, please send me to the probability-Earths, and also accept my gratitude for your patience and interest."

"Thank you," Seethwright said, obviously pleased. "Let us hope that the very first world will be the one you are seeking."

Seethwright pressed a button on his desk. Nothing happened until Carmody blinked. Then things happened very quickly indeed, for Carmody unblinked and saw that he was smack dab on Earth. Or on a reasonable facsimile thereof.

PART IV
WHICH IS EARTH?

Chapter 22

Carmody was standing on a neatly trimmed plain, beneath a blue sky, with a golden-yellow sun overhead. He looked around slowly. Half a mile ahead of him he saw a small city. This city was not constructed in the common manner of an American city—with outliers of gas stations, tentacles of hotdog stands, fringe of motels, and a protective shell of junkyards; but rather, as some Italian hill towns are fashioned, and some Swiss villages as well, suddenly rising and brusquely ending, without physical preamble or explanation, the main body of the town presenting itself all at once and without amelioration.

Despite its foreign look, Carmody felt sure that he was looking at an American city. So he advanced upon it, slowly and with heightened senses, prepared to flee if anything was amiss.

All seemed in order, however. The city had a warm and open look; its streets were laid out generously, and there was a frankness about the wide bay windows of its store fronts. As he penetrated deeper, Carmody found other delights, for just within the city he entered a piazza, just like a Roman piazza, although much smaller; and in the middle of the piazza there was a fountain, and standing in the fountain was the marble representation of a boy with a dolphin, and from the dolphin's mouth a stream of clear water issued.

"I do hope you like it," a voice said from behind Carmody's left shoulder.

Carmody did not jump with alarm. He did not even whirl around. He had become accustomed to voices speaking from behind his back. Sometimes it seemed to him that a great many things in the galaxy liked to approach him that way.

"It's very nice," Carmody said.

"I constructed it and put it there myself," the voice said. "It seemed to me that a fountain, despite the antiquity of the concept, is esthetically functional. And this piazza, with its benches and shady chestnut trees, is copied from a Bolognese model. Again, I did not inhibit myself with the fear of being old-fashioned. The true artist, it seems to me, uses what he finds necessary, be it a thousand years old or one second new."

"I applaud your sentiment," Carmody said. "Permit me to introduce myself. I am Thomas Carmody." He turned, smiling, his hand outstretched. But there was no one behind his left shoulder, or behind his right shoulder, either. There was no one in the piazza, nobody at all in sight.

"Forgive me," the voice said. "I didn't mean to startle you. I thought you knew."

"Knew what?" Carmody asked.

"Knew about me."

"Well, I don't," Carmody said. "Who are you and where are you speaking from?"

"I am the voice of the city," the voice said. "Or to put it another way, I am the city itself, the veritable city, speaking to you."

"Is that a fact?" Carmody said sardonically. "Yes," he answered himself, "I suppose it is a fact. So all right, you're a city. Big deal!"

The fact was, Carmody was annoyed. He had encountered too many entities of great magnitude and miraculous power. He had been one-upped from one end of the galaxy to the other. Forces, creations and personifications had jumped out at him without cessation, causing him time and time again to lose his cool. Carmody was a reasonable man; he knew there was an interstellar pecking order, and that humans did not rate very high on it. But he was also a proud man. He believed that a man stood for something, if only for himself. A man couldn't very well go around all the time saying "Oh!" and "Ah!" and "Bless my soul!" to the various inhuman entities that surrounded him; he couldn't do that and keep any self-respect. Carmody cared more than a little for his self-respect. It was, at this point, one of the few things he still possessed.

Therefore, Carmody turned away from the fountain and strolled across the piazza like a man who conversed with cities every day of his life, and who was slightly bored with the whole thing. He walked down various streets and up certain avenues. He glanced into store windows and noted the size of houses. He paused in front of statuary, but only briefly.

"Well?" the city said after a while.

"Well what?" Carmody answered instantly.

"What do you think of me?"

"You're OK," Carmody said.

"Only OK?"

"Look," Carmody said, "a city is a city. When you've seen one, you've pretty much seen them all."

"That's untrue!" the city said, with some show of pique. "I am distinctly different from other cities. I m unique."

"Are you indeed?" Carmody said scornfully. "To me you look like a conglomeration of badly assembled parts. You've got an Italian piazza, a couple Greek-type statues, a row of Tudor houses, an old-style New York tenement, a California hot-dog stand shaped like a tugboat, and God knows what else. What's so unique about that?"

"The combination of those forms into a meaningful entity is unique," the city said. "I present variety within a framework of inner consistency.

These older forms are not anachronisms, you understand; they are representative styles of living and as such are appropriate in a well-wrought machine for living."

"That's *your* opinion," Carmody said. "Do you have a name, by the way?"

"Of course," the city said. "My name is Bellwether. I am an incorporated township in the State of New Jersey. Would you care to have some coffee and perhaps a sandwich or some fresh fruit?"

"The coffee sounds good," Carmody said. He allowed the voice of Bellwether to guide him around the corner to an open-air cafe. The cafe was called "O You Kid" and was a replica of a Gay Nineties saloon, right down to the Tiffany lamps and the cut-glass chandelier and the player piano. Like everything else that Carmody had seen in the city, it was spotlessly clean, but without people.

"Nice atmosphere, don't you think?" Bellwether asked.

"Campy," Carmody pronounced. "OK if you like that sort of thing." A foaming mug of cappuccino was lowered to his table on a stainless-steel tray. "But at least the service is good," Carmody added. He sipped the coffee.

"Good?" Bellwether asked.

"Yes, very good."

"I rather pride myself on my coffee," Bellwether said quietly. "And on my cooking. Wouldn't you like a little something? An omelette, perhaps, or a soufflé?"

"Nothing," Carmody said firmly. He leaned back in his chair and said, "So you're a model city, huh?"

"Yes, that is what I have the honor to be," Bellwether said. "I am the most recent of all model cities and, I believe, the most satisfactory. I was conceived by a joint study group from Yale and the University of Chicago, who were working on a Rockefeller fellowship. Most of my practical details were devised by M.I.T., although some special sections of me came from Princeton and from the RAND Corporation. My actual construction was a General Electric project, and the money was procured by grants from the Ford Foundation, as well as several other institutions I am not at liberty to mention."

"Interesting sort of history," Carmody said, with unbearable nonchalance. "That's a Gothic cathedral across the street, isn't it?"

"Yes, completely Gothic," said Bellwether. "Also, interdenominational and open to all faiths, with a designed seating capacity for three hundred people."

"That doesn't seem like much for a building that size."

"It's not, of course. But my idea was to combine awesomeness with coziness. Many people liked it."

"Where are the people, by the way?" Carmody asked. "I haven't seen any."

"They have left," Bellwether said mournfully. "They have all departed."

"Why?" Carmody asked.

Bellwether was silent for a while, then said, "There was a breakdown in city-community relations. A misunderstanding, really; or perhaps I should say, an unfortunate series of misunderstandings. I suspect that rabble-rousers played a part in the exodus."

"But what *happened,* precisely?"

"I don't know," Bellwether said. "I really don't know. One day they simply all left. Just like that! But I'm sure they'll be back."

"I wonder," Carmody said.

"I am convinced of it," Bellwether said. "But for the nonce, why don't you stay here, Mr. Carmody?"

"Me? I really don't think—"

"You appear to be travel-weary," Bellwether said. "I'm sure the rest would do you good."

"I have been on the move a lot recently," Carmody admitted.

"Who knows, you might find that you liked it here," Bellwether said. "And in any event, you would have the unique experience of having the most modern, up-to-date city in the world at your service."

"That does sound interesting," Carmody said. "I'll have to think about it."

He was intrigued by the city of Bellwether. But he was also apprehensive. He wished he knew exactly what had happened to the city's occupants.

Chapter 23

At Bellwether's insistence, Carmody went to sleep that night in the sumptuous bridal suite of the King George V Hotel. He awoke in the morning refreshed and grateful. He had been in great need of a cessation of consciousness.

Bellwether served him breakfast on the terrace and played a brisk Haydn quartet while Carmody ate. The air was delicious; if Bellwether hadn't told him, Carmody would never have guessed it was filtered. The temperature and humidity were also exquisitely satisfactory. In front of the terrace was a splendid view of Bellwether's western quarter—a pleasing jumble of Chinese pagodas, Venetian footbridges, Japanese canals, a green hill, a Corinthian temple, a parking lot, a Norman tower, and much else besides.

"You have a splendid view," he told the city.

"I'm so glad you appreciate it," Bellwether replied. "Style was a problem that was argued from various positions from the day of my inception. One group held for consistency: a harmonious group of shapes blending into a harmonious whole. But that had been tried before. Quite a few model cities are like that. They are uniformly dull, artificial entities created by one man or one committee, unlike real cities."

"You're sort of artificial yourself, aren't you?" Carmody asked.

"Of course! But I do not pretend to be anything else. I am not a fake 'city of the future' or a mock-Florentine bastard. I am a conglomerate entity. I am supposed to be interesting and stimulating, as well as being functional and practical."

"Bellwether, to me you look OK," Carmody said. "Do all model cities talk like you?"

"No," Bellwether said. "Most cities up to now, model or otherwise, have never said a word. But their occupants didn't like it. They didn't like a city that did things without saying a word. The city seemed too huge, too masterful, too soulless. That is why I was created with an artificial consciousness."

"I see," Carmody said.

"I wonder if you do. The artificial consciousness personalizes me, which is very important in an age of depersonalization. It enables me to be truly responsive. It permits me to be creative in my reactions to the demands of my occupants. We can reason with each other, my occupants and I. By carrying on an incessant and meaningful dialogue, we can help each other in the creation of a truly viable urban environment. We can modify each other without any significant loss of individuality."

"It sounds fine," Carmody said. "Except, of course, that you don't have anyone here to carry on a dialogue with."

"That is the only flaw in the scheme," Bellwether admitted. "But for the present, I have you."

"Yes, you have me," Carmody said, and wondered why the words rang unpleasantly on his ear.

"And, naturally, you have me," Bellwether said. "It's a reciprocal relationship, which is the only kind worth having. But now, my dear Carmody, suppose I show you around myself. Then we can get you settled in and regularized."

"And what?"

"I didn't mean it the way it sounded," Bellwether said. "It simply is an unfortunate scientific expression. But you understand, I'm sure, that a reciprocal relationship necessitates obligations on the part of both involved parties. It couldn't very well be otherwise, could it?"

"Not unless it was a laissez-faire relationship."

"We're trying to get away from all that," Bellwether said. "Laissez-faire becomes a doctrine of the emotions, you know, and leads nonstop to anomie. If you will just come this way…"

Carmody went where he was told and beheld the excellencies of Bellwether. He toured the power plant, the water-filtration system, the industrial park, and the light-industries section. He saw the children's park and the Odd Fellows Hall. He walked through a museum and an art gallery, a concert hall and a theater, and a bowling alley, a billiards parlor, a

Go-Kart track, and a movie theater. He became tired and footsore and wanted to stop. But Bellwether insisted upon showing itself off, and Carmody had to look at the five-story American Express building, the Portuguese synagogue, the statue of Buckminster Fuller, the Greyhound Bus Station, and several other attractions.

At last it was over. Carmody concluded that the wonders of the model city were no better and no worse than the wonders of the galaxy. Beauty was really in the eye of the beholder, except for a small part that was in his feet.

"A little lunch now?" Bellwether asked.

"Fine," Carmody said.

He was guided to the fashionable Rochambeau Café, where he began with *potage aux petits pois* and ended with petits fours.

"What about a nice gruyère to finish it off?" Bellwether asked.

"No, thanks," Carmody said. "I'm full. I'm too full, as a matter of fact."

"But cheese isn't filling. A nice Camembert?"

"I couldn't possibly."

"Perhaps a few assorted fruits. *Very* refreshing to the palate."

"It's not my palate that needs refreshing," Carmody said.

"At least an apple, a pear, and a couple of grapes?"

"Thanks, no."

"A couple of cherries?"

"No, no, no!"

"A meal isn't complete without a little fruit," Bellwether said.

"My meal is," Carmody said.

"There are important vitamins which only fresh fruit can give you."

"I'll just have to struggle along without them."

"Perhaps half an orange, which I will peel for you? Citrus fruits have no bulk at all."

"I couldn't possibly."

"Not even one quarter of an orange? If I take out all the pits?"

"Most decidedly not."

"It would make me feel better," Bellwether said. "I have a completion compulsion, you know, and no meal is complete without a piece of fruit."

"No! No! No!"

"All right, don't get so excited," Bellwether said. "If you don't like the sort of food I serve, that's up to you."

"But I do like it!"

"Then if you like it so much, why won't you eat some fruit?"

"Enough," Carmody said. "Give me a couple grapes."

"I wouldn't want to force anything on you."

"You're not forcing. Give me, please."

"You're quite sure?"

"Gimme!" Carmody shouted.

"So take," Bellwether said, and produced a magnificent bunch of muscatel grapes. Carmody ate them all. They were very good.

"Excuse me," Bellwether said. "What are you doing?"

Carmody sat upright and opened his eyes. "I was taking a little nap," he said. "Is there anything wrong with that?"

"What should be wrong with a perfectly natural thing like that?" Bellwether said.

"Thank you," Carmody said, and closed his eyes again.

"But why nap in a chair?" Bellwether asked.

"Because I'm *in* a chair, and I'm already half asleep."

"You'll get a crick in your back," Bellwether warned him.

"Don't care," Carmody mumbled, his eyes still closed.

"Why not take a proper nap? Over here, on the couch?"

"I'm already napping comfortably where I am."

"You're not really comfortable," Bellwether pointed out. "The human anatomy is not constructed for sleeping sitting up."

"At the moment, mine is," Carmody said.

"It's not. Why not try the couch?"

"The chair is fine."

"But the couch is finer. Just try it, please, Carmody. Carmody?"

"Eh? What's that?" Carmody said, waking up.

"The couch. I really think you should rest on the couch."

"All right!" Carmody said, struggling to his feet. "Where is this couch?"

He was guided out of the restaurant, down the street, around the corner, and into a building marked "The Snoozerie." There were a dozen couches. Carmody went to the nearest.

"Not that one," Bellwether said. "It's got a bad spring."

"It doesn't matter," Carmody said. "I'll sleep around it."

"That will result in a cramped posture."

"Christ!" Carmody said, getting to his feet. "Which would you recommend?"

"This one back here," Bellwether said. "It's king-size, the best in the place. The yield-point of the mattress has been scientifically determined. The pillows—"

"Right, fine, good," Carmody said, lying down on the indicated couch.

"Shall I play you some soothing music?"

"Don't bother."

"Just as you wish. I'll put out the lights, then."

"Fine."

"Would you like a blanket? I control the temperature here, of course, but sleepers often get a subjective impression of chilliness."

"It doesn't matter! Leave me alone!"

"All right!" Bellwether said. "I'm not doing this for myself, you know. Personally, I never sleep."

"OK, sorry," Carmody said.

"That's perfectly all right," Bellwether said.

There was a long silence. Then Carmody sat up.

"What's the matter?" Bellwether asked.

"Now I can't sleep," Carmody said.

"Try closing your eyes and consciously relaxing every muscle in your body, starting with the big toe and working upward to—"

"I can't sleep!" Carmody shouted.

"Maybe you weren't very sleepy to begin with," Bellwether suggested. "But at least you could close your eyes and try to get a little rest. Won't you do that for me?"

"No!" Carmody said. "I'm not sleepy and I don't need a rest."

"Stubborn!" Bellwether said. "Do what you like. I've tried my best."

"Yeah," Carmody said, getting to his feet and walking out of The Snoozerie.

Carmody stood on a little curved bridge and looked over a blue lagoon.

"This is a copy of the Rialto bridge in Venice," Bellwether said. "Scaled down, of course."

"I know," Carmody said. "I read the sign."

"It's rather enchanting, isn't it?"

"Sure, it's fine," Carmody said, lighting a cigarette.

"You're doing a lot of smoking," Bellwether pointed out.

"I know. I feel like smoking."

"As your medical advisor, I must point out that the link between smoking and lung cancer is conclusive."

"I know."

"If you switched to a pipe, your chances would be improved."

"I don't like pipes."

"What about a cigar, then?"

"I don't like cigars." He lit another cigarette.

"That's your third cigarette in five minutes," Bellwether said.

"Goddamn it, I'll smoke as much and as often as I please!" Carmody shouted.

"Well, of course you will!" Bellwether said. "I was merely trying to advise you for your own good. Would you want me to simply stand by and not say a word while you destroyed yourself?"

"Yes," Carmody said.

"I can't believe you mean that. There is an ethical imperative involved here. Man can act against his best interests, but a machine is not allowed that degree of perversity."

"Get off my back," Carmody said sullenly. "Quit pushing me around."

"Pushing you around? My dear Carmody, have I coerced you in any way? Have I done any more than advise you?"

"Maybe not. But you talk too much."

"Perhaps I don't talk enough," Bellwether said. "To judge from the response I get."

"You talk too much," Carmody repeated, and lit a cigarette.

"That is your fourth cigarette in five minutes."

Carmody opened his mouth to bellow an insult. Then he changed his mind and walked away.

"What's this?" Carmody asked.

"It's a candy machine," Bellwether told him.

"It doesn't look like one."

"Still, it is one. This design is a modification of a design by Saarinomen for a silo. I have miniaturized it, of course, and—"

"It still doesn't look like a candy machine. How do you work it?"

"It's very simple. Push the red button. Now wait. Press down one of those levers on Row A; now press the green button. There!"

A Baby Ruth bar slid into Carmody's hand.

"Huh," Carmody said. He stripped off the paper and bit into the bar. "Is this a real Baby Ruth bar or a copy of one?" he asked.

"It's a real one. I had to subcontract the candy concession because of the pressure of work."

"Huh," Carmody said, letting the candy wrapper slip out of his fingers.

"That," Bellwether said, "is an example of the kind of thoughtlessness I always encounter."

"It's just a piece of paper," Carmody said, turning and looking at the candy wrapper lying on the spotless street.

"Of course it's just a piece of paper," Bellwether said. "But multiply it by a hundred thousand inhabitants and what do you have?"

"A hundred thousand pieces of paper," Carmody answered at once.

"I don't consider that funny," Bellwether said. "You wouldn't want to live in the midst of all that paper, I can assure you. You'd be the first to complain if this street were strewn with garbage. But do you do your share? Do you even clean up after yourself? Of course not! You leave it to me, even though I have to run all of the other functions of the city, night and day, without even Sundays off."

"Must you go on so?" Carmody asked. "I'll pick it up."

He bent down to pick up the candy wrapper. But just before his fingers could close on it, a pincer arm shot out of the nearest sewer, snatched the paper away and vanished from sight.

"It's all right," Bellwether said. "I'm used to cleaning up after people. I do it all the time."

"Yuh," said Carmody.

"Nor do I expect any gratitude."

"I'm grateful, I'm grateful!" Carmody said.

"No, you're not," Bellwether said.

"So OK, maybe I'm not. What do you want me to say?"

"I don't want you to say anything," Bellwether said. "Let us consider the incident closed."

"Had enough?" Bellwether said, after dinner.

"Plenty," Carmody said.

"You didn't eat much."

"I ate all I wanted. It was very good."

"If it was so good, why didn't you eat more?"

"Because I couldn't hold any more."

"If you hadn't spoiled your appetite with that candy bar…"

"Goddamn it, the candy bar didn't spoil my appetite! I just—"

"You're lighting a cigarette," Bellwether said.

"Yeah," Carmody said.

"Couldn't you wait a little longer?"

"Now look," Carmody said. "Just what in hell do you—"

"But we have something more important to talk about," Bellwether said quickly. "Have you thought about what you're going to do for a living?"

"I haven't really had much time to think about it."

"Well, I *have* been thinking about it. It would be nice if you became a doctor."

"Me? I'd have to take special college courses, then get into medical school, and so forth."

"I can arrange all that," Bellwether said.

"Not interested."

"Well…what about law?"

"Never."

"Engineering is an excellent line."

"Not for me."

"What about accounting?"

"Not on your life."

"What do you want to be, then?"

"A jet pilot," Carmody said impulsively.

"Oh, come now!"

"I'm quite serious."

"I don't even have an airfield here."

"Then I'll pilot somewhere else."

"You're only saying that to spite me!"

"Not at all," Carmody said. "I want to be a pilot, I really do. I've *always* wanted to be a pilot! Honest I have!"

There was a long silence. Then Bellwether said, "The choice is entirely up to you." This was said in a voice like death.

"Where are you going?"

"Out for a walk," Carmody said.

"At 9:30 in the evening?"

"Sure. Why not?"

"I thought you were tired."

"That was quite some time ago."

"I see. And I also thought that perhaps you could sit here and we could maybe have a nice chat."

"How about if we talk when I get back?" Carmody asked.

"No, it doesn't matter," Bellwether said.

"The walk doesn't matter," Carmody said, sitting down. "Come on, we'll talk."

"I no longer care to talk," Bellwether said. "Please go for your walk."

"Well, good night," Carmody said.

"I beg your pardon?"

"I said, 'good night.' "

"You're going to sleep?"

"Sure. It's late, I'm tired."

"You're going to sleep now, just like that?"

"Well, why not?"

"No reason at all," Bellwether said, "except that you have forgotten to wash."

"Oh… I guess I did forget. I'll wash in the morning."

"How long is it since you've had a bath?"

"Too long. I'll take one in the morning."

"Wouldn't you feel better if you took one right now?"

"No."

"Even if I drew the bath for you?"

"No! Goddamn it, no! I'm going to sleep!"

"Do exactly as you please," Bellwether said. "Don't wash, don't study, don't eat a balanced diet. But also, don't blame me."

"Blame you? For what?"

"For anything," Bellwether said.

"Yes. But what did you have in mind, specifically?"

"It isn't important."

"Then why did you bring it up in the first place?"

"I was only thinking of you," Bellwether said.

"I realize that."

"You must know that it can't benefit *me* if you wash or not."

"I'm aware of that."

"When one cares," Bellwether went on, "when one feels one's responsibilities, it is not nice to hear oneself sworn at."

"I didn't swear at you."

"Not this time. But earlier today you did."

"Well... I was nervous."

"That's because of the smoking."

"Don't start that again!"

"I won't," Bellwether said. "Smoke like a furnace. What does it matter to me? They're your lungs, aren't they?"

"Damned right," Carmody said, lighting a cigarette.

"But my failure," Bellwether said.

"No, no," Carmody said. "Don't say it, please don't!"

"Forget I said it," Bellwether said.

"All right."

"Sometimes I get overzealous."

"Sure."

"And it's especially difficult because I'm right. I *am* right, you know."

"I know," Carmody said. "You're right, you're right, you're always right. Right right right right right—"

"Don't overexcite yourself before bedtime," Bellwether said. "Would you care for a glass of milk?"

"No."

"You're sure?"

Carmody put his hands over his eyes. He felt very strange. He also felt extremely guilty, fragile, dirty, unhealthy, and sloppy. He felt generally and irrevocably bad, and he knew that it would always be this way.

From somewhere within him he found strength. He shouted, "Seethwright!"

"Who are you shouting to?" Bellwether asked.

"Seethwright! Where are you?"

"How have I failed you?" Bellwether asked. "Just tell me how!"

"Seethwright!" Carmody wailed. "Come and get me! This is the wrong Earth!"

There was a snap, crackle and pop, and Carmody was somewhere else.

Chapter 24

Whoosh! Krrrunch! Kerpow! Here we are somewhere, but who knows where and when and which? Surely not Carmody, who found himself in a persuasive city much like New York. *Much* like; but was it?

"*Is* this New York?" Carmody asked himself.

"How the hell should I know?" a voice answered promptly.

"It was a rhetorical question," Carmody said.

"I am quite aware of that; but, since I have my rhetorician's papers, I answered it."

Carmody looked around and saw that the voice had come from a large black umbrella in his left hand. He asked, "Are you my Prize?"

"Well, of course I am," the Prize said. "I don't suppose I look like a Shetland pony, do I?"

"Where were you earlier, when I was in that model city?"

"I was taking a short, well-earned vacation," the Prize said. "And there's no use your complaining about it. Vacation time is stipulated in the contract between the Amalgamated Prizes of the Galaxy and the Recipient's League."

"I wasn't complaining," Carmody said. "I just…Forget it. This place certainly looks like my Earth. It looks like New York, in fact."

He was in a city. There was heavy traffic, both human and vehicular. There were many theaters, many frankfurter stands, many people. There were many stores which proclaimed that they were going out of business and selling their entire stock regardless of cost. Neon signs flashed everywhere. There were many restaurants, most prominent of which were The Westerner, The Southerner, The Easterner, and The Northerner; all of these had specials on steak and shoestring potatoes. But there was also The Nor'easterner, The Sou'wester, The East-by-Northeast, and the West-by-Northwest. A movie theater across the street was featuring *The Apocrypha* (Bigger and Stranger than The Bible), with a cast of thousands. Near it was the Omphalos Discothèque wherein a folk-rock group calling itself The Shits played raucous music, which was danced to by immature virgins in middleless dresses.

"Lots of action," Carmody said, wetting his lips.

"I hear only the jangle of cash registers," the Prize said, in a heavily moralistic voice.

"Don't be stuffy," Carmody said. "I think I'm home."

"I hope not," the Prize said. "This place gets on my nerves. Please look around you and make sure. Remember, similitude need not imply exactitude."

There was an IRT subway entrance in front of him. He saw that he was at Fiftieth Street and Broadway. Yes, he was home. He walked briskly to the subway and went down the stairs. It was familiar, exciting and saddening all at the same time. The marble walls were damp with ichor, and the gleaming monorail came out of one tunnel and disappeared into another…

"Oh," Carmody muttered.

"How's that?" the Prize asked.

"Never mind," Carmody said. "On second thought, I think I'll take a little stroll in the streets." He began to retrace his footsteps, moving quietly toward the rectangle of sky framed in the entrance. A crowd had formed, blocking his way. Carmody pushed through them, and the crowd pushed him back. The wet walls of the subway began to tremble, then to convulse rhythmically. The gleaming monorail pulled free of its stanchions, curled back on itself like a brazen tongue, and flicked out toward him. Carmody ran, bowling over the people who stood in his way. He was dimly aware that they rolled immediately to their feet, as though they had weighted bases. The marble pavement beneath him grew soft, syrupy. His feet were sticking, the figures were close around him, and the monorail was poised over his head.

Carmody shouted, "Seethwright! Get me out of this!"

"Me, too!" the Prize shouted.

"Me, too!" screamed the cunning predator; for it was he and none other, cleverly disguised as a subway, into whose mouth Carmody had strayed.

Nothing happened. Carmody had the terrible feeling that Seethwright was perhaps out to lunch, or on the toilet, or answering a telephone. The blue rectangle of sky became smaller as the exit sealed itself. The figures around him lost their resemblance to humans. The walls turned a purplish-red, began to heave and tremble, then to contract. The slender monorail curled hungrily around Carmody's feet. Within the predator's body, vast ululations were followed by protracted slaverings. (Carmody-eaters are notoriously piggish and lacking in any table manners.)

"Help!" Carmody screamed, as digestive juices ate away the soles of his shoes. "Seethwright, help me!"

"Help him, help him!" the Prize sobbed. "Or, if that seems too difficult, help me! Get me out of here and I will take advertisements in the leading newspapers, convene committees, form action groups, carry posters on the streets, all to the purpose of insuring that Carmody does not go unavenged. And I further pledge myself to—"

"Stop babbling," a voice said, which Carmody recognized as belonging to Seethwright. "It's disgraceful. As for you, Mr. Carmody, you must, in future, make up your mind *before* stepping into the mouth of your predator. My office is not set up for hairbreadth rescues."

"But you will save me this time, won't you?" Carmody begged. "Won't you? Won't you?"

"It is already done," Seethwright said. And when Carmody looked around, he saw that it was indeed already done.

Chapter 25

Seethwright must have mishandled the transition, for, after a brief blank spell, Carmody found himself in the back seat of a taxi. He was in a city very much like New York, and he seemed to be in the middle of a conversation.

"What didja say?" the driver asked.

"I didn't say anything," Carmody replied.

"Oh. I thought you were saying something. Well, what *I* was saying is, I was saying that's the new Flammarion building over there."

"I know," Carmody heard himself say. "I helped build it."

"Is that a fact? Some job! But now you're finished, huh?"

"Yes," Carmody said. He took the cigarette out of his mouth and frowned at it. "I'm finished with these cigarettes, too." He shook his head and threw the cigarette out the window. These words and actions seemed perfectly natural to one part of him (the active consciousness). But another part of him (the reflective consciousness) was watching with considerable amusement.

"Well, why didn't you say so?" the cabby said. "Here, try one of mine."

Carmody looked at the open pack in the driver's hand. "You smoke Kools, eh?"

"It's my regular smoke," the cabby said. "Kools have that light touch of menthol and the taste that's right!"

Carmody raised both eyebrows to show disbelief. Nevertheless, he accepted the pack, extracted a coffin nail and lit up. The smiling cabby was watching him in the rearview mirror. Carmody inhaled, looked surprised and pleased, exhaled slowly and luxuriously.

"Hey!" Carmody said. "You got something there!"

The driver nodded sagely. "A lot of us Kool smokers think so… Here we are, sir. The Waldorf-Astoria."

Carmody paid and began to step out. The cabby leaned back, still smiling. "Hey, mister," he said. "How about my Kools?"

"Oh!" Carmody said. He gave back the pack. He and the cabby smiled at each other. Then the cabby drove off and Carmody stood in front of the Waldorf-Astoria.

He was wearing a sturdy Burberry topcoat. He could tell this by reading the label, which, instead of being inside the collar, was sewn securely to the outside of his right sleeve. Now that he looked, he saw that all his labels were outside: anyone could tell that he had on a Van Heusen shirt, a Countess Mara necktie, a Hart, Schaffner & Marx suit, Van Camp socks, and Lloyd & Haig cordovans. Upon his head was a Borsolino made by Raimu of Milan. His hands were encased in deerskin gloves from L. L. Bean. His wrist was covered by a self-winding chronometer (Audemars Piccard) which had a slide rule, a timer, an elapsed-time indicator, a calendar, and an alarm;

all this in addition to keeping time within a guaranteed accuracy of plus or minus six seconds a year.

Finally, he smelled faintly of Oak Moss men's cologne from Abercrombie & Fitch.

He considered it a *fairly good* outfit, though by no means first-rate. It would pass muster, but he expected more of himself. He was ambitious, he planned to move up, he expected to become the sort of man who serves Chivas Regal on days other than Christmas, wears Brooks Brothers shirts, blazers from F. R. Tripler, uses Onyx after-shave lotion by Lentheric, slips into Country Warmer jackets by Paul Stuart...

But he would need a class A-AA-AAA Consumer Rating for goods like those, instead of his commonplace B-BB-AAAA which a mishap of birth had stuck him with. He *needed* that rating! Wasn't he good enough? Why, damn it, at Stanford he'd been first in his class in Consumer Techniques! His Use-Index for three years now had been in the ninetieth percentile! His car, a Dodge Ferret, was immaculate! He could cite other examples.

Why hadn't they moved him up?

Was it possible that they did not have their eye on him?

Carmody quickly put such heretical thoughts out of his mind. He had more immediate concerns. Today he had a thankless task before him. What he had to do in the next hour might well cost him his job, in which case he would be relegated to the empty-faced ranks of the proletarian users of Irregular Oriental Merchandise Seconds (IOMS).

It was still early, but he needed fortification for the ordeal ahead. He walked into the Men's Bar of the Waldorf.

He caught the bartender's eye. Quickly, before the man could speak, Carmody said, "Hey, friend, do it again." The fact that the man had not done it for him previously, and therefore, technically, could not do it again, was of no significance.

"Here you go, Mac," the bartender said, smiling. "Ballantine's got the deep-brewed flavor and the taste that's right."

Carmody knew that he should have said that himself. He had been caught napping. He sipped his beer thoughtfully.

"Hey, Tom?"

Carmody turned around. There was Nate Steen from Leonia, New Jersey, an old friend and neighbor, drinking a Coke. "It's funny," Steen said, "but did you ever notice? Things go better with Coke."

Carmody was caught without a line. He drained off his beer at a gulp and called to the bartender, "Hey, friend, do it again!" It was a poor expedient, but better than nothing at all. "What's new?" he asked Steen.

"Wife's gone on vacation. She decided to come on down to Miami and sneak a week via American Airways, number one to the sun."

"That's great," Carmody said. "I just sent Helen to Nassau; and if you think the Bahamas are lovely from the air, wait until you land. And do you know, I was asking her just the other night why, in this fast-moving world of ours, would anyone want to take the time for an ocean voyage to Europe? And she said—"

"Nice idea," Steen interrupted. He had a perfect right, of course; the Holland-American bit was entirely too long for verisimilitude. "Now me, I thought I'd pack us all off to Marlboro Country."

"Fine thought," Carmody said. "After all—"

"—you really *do* get a lot to like in a Marlboro," Steen finished (his privilege: he had begun the plug).

"Sure," Carmody said. Hastily he slopped down his beer and called out, "Hey, friend, do it again! Ballantine beer!" But he knew that he wasn't holding up his end. What on earth was wrong with him? For this very moment, this particular situation, there was an obligatory dialogue. But he couldn't remember, he couldn't seem to find it...

Steen, calm and collected with new improved ice-blue Secret clinging to his hairy armpits, came to it first. "With our wives away," he chuckled, "we get to do the wash."

Beaten to the punch! Carmody could do no more than to string along. "Yeh," he said. He gave a hollow laugh. "Remember that stuff about 'my wash is whiter than yours'?"

Both men indulged in scornful laughter. Then Steen looked at his shirt, looked at Carmody's shirt, frowned, raised his eyebrows, opened his mouth, portrayed disbelief, incredulity, amazement.

"Hey!" Steen said. "My shirt *is* whiter than yours!"

"Gee, so it is!" Carmody said, not bothering to look. "That's funny. We used the same model of washing machine set for the same cycle. And we also used the same bleach... Didn't we?"

"I used that Clorox stuff," Steen said carelessly.

"Clorox," Carmody said thoughtfully. "Yeah, that's gotta be it! *My bleach was too weak!*"

He portrayed mock exasperation while Steen feigned triumph. Carmody thought of ordering another beer, but he hadn't enjoyed the last two. He decided that Steen was too quick for him.

Carmody paid for the beers with his American Express credit card and then continued to his office, which was on the fifty-first floor of 666 Fifth Avenue. He greeted his fellow workers with democratic camaraderie. Several people tried to involve him in their gambits, but he ignored them. Carmody knew that his situation, life-positionwise, was desperate. He had thought about his alternatives all last night. Worry had brought on an acute migraine and an upset stomach, and he had almost missed the Charleston contest. But his wife, Helen (who hadn't really gone on vacation), had given him an Alka-Seltzer, which had fixed him up in a jiffy, and they had gone as planned and had taken first prize thanks to Alka-Seltzer. But the problem had remained. And when Helen told him, at three in the morning, that Tommy and little Tinker had had 32 percent fewer cavities this year over last, he had replied, "Do you know... I'll bet it's the Crest!" But his heart hadn't been in it, although it had been sweet of Helen to feed him the line.

He knew that no wife could feed her husband enough lines to make any real difference. If you wanted to advance in the Consumer Ratings, if you wanted to show yourself worthy of the things that counted in life—a Tech-built Swiss-type chalet deep in the Untrammeled Wilderness of Maine, for example, and a Porsche 911S, which people who considered themselves a breed apart purchased, and an Ampex for people who couldn't be bothered with anything less than the best...well, if you wanted that sort of thing, you had to deserve it. Money wasn't enough, social position wasn't enough, simpleminded perseverance wasn't enough. You had to prove that you really *were* of that Breed Apart for whom those goods were intended. You had to risk everything in order to gain everything.

"By jingo!" Carmody said to himself, striking his right fist into the palm of his left hand, "I said I'd do it and I will do it!" And he boldly advanced to the door of Mr. Übermann, his boss, and boldly threw open the door.

The room was empty. Mr. Übermann had not arrived yet.

Carmody entered the office. He would wait. His jaw was tight, his lips were compressed, and three vertical lines had appeared between his eyes. He fought to keep himself under control. Übermann would be here any moment. And when he came, Tom Carmody would say to him, "Mr. Übermann, you could have me fired for this but you've got bad breath." He would pause. *"Bad breath."*

How simple it seemed in contemplation, how difficult in execution! Yet still, a man must stand up, must fight for cleanliness and its extensions, must scramble for advancement. At this very moment, Carmody knew, the eyes of those half-legendary figures, the Manufacturers, were on him. If he were found worthy...

"Morning, Carmody!" said Übermann, striding long-legged into the room. He was hawk-faced and handsome; his temples were streaked with gray, a mark of privilege. His horn-rimmed glasses were a full three centimeters wider than Carmody's.

"Mr. Übermann," Carmody began in a quavering voice, "you could have me fired for this—"

"Carmody," the boss said, his diaphragmatic voice cutting through Carmody's weak chest tones as a Personna surgical-steel blade cuts through flab, "today I have discovered the most amazing mouthwash. Scope, it is called. I believe my breath will be sweet for hours and hours."

Carmody gave an ironic smile. What a fantastic coincidence! The boss had lucked into *the very mouthwash* that Carmody had been about to recommend. And it had worked! No longer did Mr. Übermann's breath smell like a garbage pit after a heavy rain. Now it was kissing-sweet (for girls, of course; Carmody himself was not interested in that sort of thing).

"Ever hear of it?" Übermann asked, and then left the office without waiting for an answer.

Carmody smiled even more ironically. He had failed again. And yet, he could feel an unmistakable sense of relief at the failure. Executive consumption was terribly trying, fantastically wearing. It was proper for a certain kind of man; but perhaps he was not that kind. Suppose he had made it? He could sense even now the regrets with which he would have given up his fifty-eighth-percentile consumption artifacts—his Raleigh coupons, his pigskin suede cap, his light-up Christmas tie, his Executive "Quick-Trip" Business Case made of Skai, his KLH Model 24 stereo music system, and particularly his Lakeland top-of-the-line coat of imported, soft, supple New Zealand Sueded shearling with the framed collar and lapels. And he would have had to dispose of all the rest of his dear, familiar objects as well.

"Sometimes things just work out right even when you think they're going wrong," Carmody said to himself.

"They do? Just what in hell are you talking about?" Carmody replied to himself.

"Oh my God," Carmody said to himself.

"Yeah," Carmody's self answered Carmody. "Acclimatized a little too quickly, didn't you?"

The two Carmodys looked at each other, compared notes and reached a conclusion. They coalesced.

"Seethwright!" Carmody shouted. "Get me out of here!"

And Seethwright, that faithful man, did just that.

Chapter 26

With his usual punctuality, Seethwright sent him into another of Earth's probability-worlds. The transition was somewhat faster than instantaneous. It was so rapid, in fact, that time became ever so slightly retrograde, and Carmody had the eerie experience of giving a response before receiving the requisite stimulus. That was a contradiction, of course, a very small one, but still illegal. Seethwright took care of it by a standard obliteration procedure, and no one bothered to report it to the proper authorities. Its effect was nil except for the wear and tear on the space-time continuum, which Carmody didn't even notice.

Carmody found himself in a small town. Superficially, there was no problem of identification; this town was, or purported to be, Maplewood, New Jersey. Carmody had lived here between the ages of three and eighteen. This was his home, insofar as he had a home anywhere.

Or, more precisely, this was his home if it was what it seemed to be. But that remained to be proven.

He was standing on the corner of Durand Road and Maplewood Avenue, at the upper end of the town. Straight ahead was the shopping center. Behind him were suburban streets rich in maple, oak, chestnut, elm, dogwood, and others. On his right was the Christian Science reading room. On his left was the railroad station.

"How now, voyager?" said a voice near his right thigh.

Carmody looked down and saw that he was carrying a fair-sized transistor radio. This, he knew at once, was the Prize.

"So you've come back," Carmody said.

"Back? I never left."

"I didn't see you in the last probability-world."

"That's because you weren't looking very hard," the Prize said. "I was in your pocket in the form of a badly forged denarius."

"How am I supposed to know that?" Carmody inquired.

"All you have to do is ask," the Prize said. "I am metamorphic by nature, and unpredictable even to myself. But you know that. Must I announce my presence each and every time we go somewhere?"

"It would help," Carmody said.

"My pride would not allow such anxiety-ridden behavior," the Prize said firmly. "I answer when called; when not called, I do not assume that my presence is required. It was quite obvious that you didn't need me in the last probability-world. Therefore I took the opportunity to go to Sloklol's Restaurant for a decent feed, and then to the Haganicht Proparium to have my hide dry-cleaned, and then to Varinell's Solar Beacon Pub for a few drinks and a chat with a friend who happened to be in the neighborhood, and then to—"

"How could you have done all that?" Carmody asked. "I wasn't in that world for over half an hour."

"I told you that our duration-flows are quite dissimilar," the Prize said.

"Yes, so you did... But whereabouts are those places?"

"That would take quite a little while to explain," the Prize said. "As a matter of fact, it's easier to go there than to explain how to go there. Anyhow, they're the wrong kind of places for you."

"Why?"

"Well... there are many reasons. But to cite only one, you would dis-approve of the food eaten at the Solar Beacon Pub."

"I've already seen you eat *orithi*," Carmody reminded the Prize.

"Yes, of course. But *orithi* are an infrequent delicacy, morsels to be eaten once or twice in a lifetime. Whereas at the Solar Beacon Pub we Prizes and related species eat our staple subsistence diet."

"And what is that?"

"You wouldn't want to know," the Prize warned him.

"I do want to know."

"I know that you *do* want to know; but after you hear, you will wish that you *didn't* know."

"Out with it," Carmody said. "What is your staple diet?"

"All right, Mr. Nosey," the Prize said. "But remember, you insisted upon knowing. My staple diet is myself."

"Is what?"

"Myself. I said you wouldn't like it."

"Your diet is yourself? You mean that you feast off your own body?"

"Precisely."

"Damn it all," Carmody said, "aside from being repulsive, that's im-possible. You can't live off yourself!"

"I can and I do," the Prize said. "And I'm quite proud of the fact. Morally, it is an outstanding example of personal freedom."

"But it just isn't possible," Carmody said. "It violates the law of con-servation of energy, or mass, or something like that. It sure as hell violates *some* natural law."

"That's true, but only in a specialized sense," the Prize said. "When you come to examine the matter more closely, you can, I think, see that the impossibility is more apparent than real."

"What in hell does *that* mean?"

"I don't know," the Prize confessed. "It's the answer in all our text-books. Nobody ever questioned it before."

"I want to get this straight," Carmody said. "Do you mean that you actually and literally *eat* portions of your own flesh?"

"Yes," the Prize said. "That's what I mean. Though you shouldn't con-fine it solely to my flesh. My liver is a tasty morsel, especially when chopped up with a hard-boiled egg and a little chicken fat. And my short ribs have served me well for a quick, casual sort of dinner; whereas my hams ought to be mild-cured for several weeks before—"

"Enough," Carmody said.

"I'm sorry," the Prize said.

"But just tell me this: how can your body provide enough food for your body (this sounds ridiculous) throughout a lifetime?"

"Well," the Prize said thoughtfully, "for one thing, I'm not a particularly heavy eater."

"Perhaps I haven't made myself clear," Carmody said. "I mean, how can you provide bulk for your body if you are simultaneously *using* that bulk to feed your body with?"

"I'm afraid I don't quite understand that," the Prize said.

"Let me try again. I mean this: if you consume your flesh—"

"And in fact I do," the Prize put in.

"If you consume your flesh, and utilize the product of that consumption for the nutrition of that same flesh… Just a minute. If you weighed fifty pounds—"

"In point of fact, on my home planet I weigh precisely fifty pounds."

"Excellent! Well, then. If you weigh fifty pounds, and, over the course of, let us say a year, consume forty pounds of yourself in order to support yourself, then what are you left with?"

"Ten pounds?" the Prize asked.

"Goddamn it, can't you see what I'm driving at? You simply cannot nourish yourself on yourself for any length of time."

"Why can't I?" the Prize asked.

"The Law of Diminishing Returns," Carmody said, feeling lightheaded. "Eventually there will be no more of you left for you to feed upon, and you will die."

"I am quite aware of that," the Prize said. "But death is an inexorable fact, as true and unavoidable for the self-eaters as for the other-eaters. Everything and everybody dies, Carmody, no matter who or what it feeds upon."

"You're putting me on!" Carmody howled. "If you really did feed like that, you'd be dead in a week."

"There are insects whose lifespan is but a single day," the Prize said. "Actually, we Prizes do rather well, longevity-wise. Remember, the more we consume, the less of us there is to be nourished, and the longer the remaining food lasts. And time is a great factor in autopredation. Most Prizes consume their future while in their infancy, thus leaving the actual corpus untouched until they have come into their maturity."

"How do they consume their future?" Carmody asked.

"I can't explain how," the Prize said. "We simply do it, that's all. I, for example, gobbled up my substance for the ages eighty through ninety-two— senile years, by the way, which I wouldn't have enjoyed anyway. Now, by rationing my intake of myself, I think I can make it to my late seventies."

"You're giving me a headache," Carmody said. "And you're also making me somewhat nauseous."

"Indeed?" said the Prize indignantly. "You've got a hell of a nerve to feel nauseous! You bloody butcher, how many animal sections have you consumed in your lifetime? How many defenseless apples have you gobbled, how many heads of lettuce have you callously ripped from their beds? I have eaten an occasional *orithi,* to be sure; but at Judgment Day you will have to face the herds you have devoured. They will stand before you, Carmody, hundreds of brown-eyed cows, thousands of defenseless hens, endless rows of gentle little lambs; to say nothing of the forests of raped fruit trees and the acres of savaged gardens. I will pay for the *orithi* I have eaten; but how will you ever atone for the shrieking mounds of animal and vegetable life that you have feasted upon? How, Carmody, how?"

"Shut up," Carmody said.

"Oh, very well," the Prize said sulkily.

"I eat because I must. It's part of my nature. That's all there is to it."

"If you say so."

"I damned well do say so! Now will you shut up and let me concentrate?"

"I won't say another word," the Prize said, "except to ask you what you are trying to concentrate on."

"This place looks like my home town," Carmody explained. "I'm trying to decide if it really is or not."

"Surely that can't be so difficult," the Prize said. "I mean to say, one knows one's own home town, doesn't one?"

"No. I never looked at it closely while I lived here, and I didn't think about it much after I left."

"If you can't figure out what is your home and what is not," the Prize said, "then no one can. I hope you realize that."

"I realize it," Carmody said. He began to walk slowly down Maplewood Avenue. He had the sudden terrible feeling that any decision he made would be wrong.

Chapter 27

Carmody looked as he walked, and observed as he looked. It seemed like the place he thought it should seem like. The Maplewood Theater was on his right; today's feature was *The Saga of Elephantine,* an Italian-French adventure film directed by Jacques Marat, the brilliant young director who had given the world the deeply moving *Song of My Wounds* and the swiftly paced comedy *Paris Times Fourteen.* On the stage, for a limited engagement only, was the new vocal group, Iakonnen and the Fungi.

"Sounds like a fun film," Carmody remarked.

"Not my sort of thing," the Prize said.

Carmody stopped at Marvin's Haberdashery and looked in the window. He saw loafers and saddle shoes, hound's-tooth check jackets, wide, boldly patterned neckties, white shirts with spread collars. Next to it, at the stationery store, he glanced at the current *Colliers*, leafed through *Liberty*, noticed *Munsey's*, *Black Cat*, and *The Spy*. The morning edition of *The Sun* had just come out.

"Well?" the Prize asked. "Is this the place?"

"I'm still checking," Carmody said. "But it looks pretty favorable so far."

He crossed the street and looked into Edgar's Luncheonette. It hadn't changed. There was a pretty girl sitting at the counter, sipping a soda. Carmody recognized her at once.

"Lana Turner! Hey, how are you, Lana?"

"I'm fine, Tom," Lana said. "Long time no see."

"I used to date her in high school," he explained to the Prize as they walked on. "It's funny how it all comes back to you."

"I suppose so," the Prize said doubtfully.

At the next corner, the intersection of Maplewood Avenue and South Mountain Road, there was a policeman. He was directing traffic, but he took time to grin to Carmody.

"That's Burt Lancaster," Carmody said. "He was all-state fullback on the best team Columbia High School ever had. And look, over there! That man going into the hardware store, the one who waved at me! That's Clifton Webb, our high-school principal. And down the block, do you see that blonde woman? That's Jean Harlow. She used to be the waitress at the Maplewood Restaurant." He lowered his voice. "Everybody said she was *fast*."

"You seem to know a lot of people," the Prize said.

"Well, of course I do! I was raised here! Miss Harlow is going into Pierre's Beauty Parlor."

"Do you know Pierre, also?"

"Sure. He's a hairdresser now, but during the war he was in the French Resistance. What was his name again? Jean-Pierre Aumont, that's it! He married one of our local girls, Carole Lombard."

"Interesting," the Prize said in a bored voice.

"Well, it's interesting for me. Here comes a man I know... Good day, Mr. Mayor."

"Good day, Tom," the man said, and tipped his hat and walked on.

"That's Fredric March, our mayor," Carmody said. "He's a tremendous person! I can still remember the debate between him and our local radical, Paul Muni. Boy, you never heard anything like it!"

"Hmm," said the Prize. "There is something strange about all this, Carmody. Something uncanny, something not right. Don't you feel it?"

"No, I don't," Carmody said. "I'm telling you, I grew up with these people, I know them better than I know myself. Hey, there's Paulette Goddard over there. She's the assistant librarian. Hi, Paulette!"

"Hi, Tom," the woman said.

"I don't like this," the Prize said.

"I never knew her very well," Carmody said. "She used to go with a boy from Millburn named Humphrey Bogart. He always wore bow ties, can you imagine that? He had a fight once with Lon Chaney, the school janitor. Licked him, too. I remember that because I was dating June Havoc at the time, and her best friend was Myrna Loy, and Myrna knew Bogart, and—"

"Carmody!" the Prize said urgently. "Watch yourself! Have you ever heard of pseudo-acclimatization?"

"Don't be ridiculous," Carmody said. "I tell you, I know these people! I grew up here, and it was a damned good place to grow up in! People weren't just blobs like they are now; people really stood for something. People were *individuals* then, not crowds!"

"Are you quite sure of this? Your predator—"

"Rats, I don't want to hear any more about it," Carmody said. "Look! There's David Niven! His parents are English."

"These people are coming toward you," the Prize said.

"Well, sure they are," Carmody said. "They haven't seen me for a long time."

He stood on the corner and his friends came down the sidewalk and the street, out of stores and shops. There were literally hundreds of them, all smiling, all old friends. He spotted Alan Ladd, Dorothy Lamour and Larry Buster Crabbe. And over there he saw Spencer Tracy, Lionel Barrymore, Freddy Bartholomew, John Wayne, Frances Farmer—

"There's something wrong with this," the Prize said.

"Nothing's wrong," Carmody insisted. His friends were all present, they were moving closer to him, holding out their hands, and he was happier than he had ever been since leaving his home. He was amazed that he could have forgotten how it had been. But he remembered now.

"Carmody!" the Prize shouted.

"What is it?"

"Is there always this music in your world?"

"What are you talking about?"

"I'm talking about the music," the Prize said. "Don't you hear it?"

Carmody noticed it for the first time. A symphony orchestra was playing, but he couldn't tell where it was coming from.

"How long has that been going on?"

"Ever since we got here," the Prize told him. "When you started down the street there was a soft thunder of drums. Then, when you passed the theater, a lively air was played on a trumpet. This changed, when you looked into the luncheonette, to a rather saccharine melody played by several hundred violins. Then—"

"That was background music," Carmody said dully. "This whole damned thing was scored, and I didn't even notice it."

Franchot Tone reached out and touched his sleeve. Gary Cooper dropped a big hand on his shoulder. Laird Cregar gave him an affectionate bear hug. Shirley Temple seized his right foot. The others pressed closer, all still smiling.

"Seethwright!" Carmody shouted. "For God's sake, Seethwright!"

After that, things happened a little too fast for his comprehension.

PART V
THE RETURN TO EARTH

Chapter 28

Carmody was in New York City, on Riverside Drive and Ninety-ninth Street. To the west, above the Jersey shore, the sun was dropping down behind Horizon House, and, to the right, the Spry sign had come on in all its glory. The trees of Riverside Park, clad in green and soot, rustled faintly in the exhaust fumes from the West Side Drive. Around him he could hear the screams of frustrated, high-strung children, punctuated by an occasional bellow from their equally frustrated and high-strung parents.

"Is this your home?" asked the Prize.

Carmody looked down and saw that the Prize had metamorphosed again, appearing now as a Dick Tracy watch with hidden stereo speaker.

"It looks like it," Carmody said.

"Seems like rather an interesting spot," the Prize said. "Lively. I like that."

"Yeah," Carmody said reluctantly, not at all sure how he felt about his home.

He began to walk uptown. The lights had come on in Riverside Park. Mothers with baby carriages were leaving, and soon the park would be left alone to police cars and muggers. All around him the smog rolled in on little cat feet. Buildings could be glimpsed through it like giants who had lost their way. To either side, the sewers ran merrily into the Hudson, while at the same time the Hudson ran merrily into the sewers.

"Hey, Carmody!"

Carmody stopped and turned. A man was walking briskly toward him. The man wore a business suit, sneakers, a bowler, and a white canvas ascot. Carmody recognized him as George Marundi, an indigent artist of his acquaintance.

"Hey, man," said Marundi, coming up and shaking hands.

"Hey, hey," said Carmody, smiling like an accomplice.

"Well, man, how you *been?*" Marundi asked.

"Oh, you know," Carmody said.

"Indeed, do I *not* know!" Marundi said. "Helen's been asking about you."

"That a fact?" Carmody said.

"Most assuredly. Dicky Tait's throwing a party next Saturday. You wanna come?"

"Sure," Carmody said. "How is Tait?"

"Well, man, you know."

"Sure, I know," Carmody said, in a tone of deep compassion. "Still, eh?"

"What would you expect?" Marundi asked.

Carmody shrugged.

"Isn't anyone going to introduce me?" the Prize asked.

"Shut up!" Carmody said.

"Hey, man, what's that you got there?" Marundi bent down and peered at Carmody's wrist. "Little tape recorder, huh? That's the greatest, baby, the greatest. You got it programmed?"

"I am not programmed," the Prize said. "I am autonomous."

"Hey, that's beautiful!" Marundi said. "I mean, it really is. Hey there, Mickey Mouse, what else you got to say?"

"Go screw yourself," the Prize said.

"Stop it!" Carmody whispered urgently.

"Well now," Marundi said, grinning, "little fellow's got a lot of spunk, eh Carmie?"

"That he has," Carmody said.

"Where'd you get it?"

"I got it—well, I got it while I was away."

"You've been away? I guess that's why I haven't seen you around for these last several months."

"That must be it," Carmody said.

"Where away have you been?" Marundi asked.

It was on the tip of Carmody's tongue to say that he had been in Miami. But instead he was inspired to say, "I have been out in the Universe, the Cosmos itself, wherein I have passed through certain selected short subjects which shall henceforward be known as reality."

Marundi nodded with understanding. "You been on a Trip, yes, man?"

"Indeed I have."

"And on that Trip you have perceived the molecular all-in-oneness of all things and have listened to the energies of your body, *nicht wahr?*"

"Not exactly," Carmody said. "Upon my particular Trip, I observed most particularly the discretionary energies of other creations and went beyond the personal-molecular into the external-atomic. That is to say, my Trip convinced me of the reality, to say nothing of the existence, of creatures other than myself."

"That sounds like powerful acid," Marundi said. "Where might it be obtained?"

"The Acid of Experience is distilled from the dull weed of Practice," Carmody said. "Objective existence is desired by many but obtained by few."

"You won't talk, huh?" Marundi said. "Never mind, baby, any Trip you can make I can make better."

"I doubt that."

"I doubt not that you doubt that. But never mind. Are you coming to the Opening?"

"What Opening?"

Marundi looked at him with amazement. "Man, you have not only been away, you have been out of touch besides. Today is the opening of what is past a doubt the most important art exhibit of our times and perhaps of any times."

"What is this paragon of esthetics?" Carmody asked.

"I am going there," Marundi said. "Accompany me."

Despite the mumblings of the Prize, Carmody fell into step beside his friend. They walked uptown, and Marundi told the latest gossip: how the House Un-American Activities Committee had been found guilty of Un-Americanism but had gotten off with a suspended sentence; the success of Pepperidge Farm's new Freez-a-Man Plan; how five U.S. Air Cavalry divisions had yesterday succeeded in killing five Vietcong guerillas; how NBC-TV had begun a wildly successful new series entitled *Adventures in Laissez-Faire Capitalism*. And he also learned that General Motors, in a gesture of unprecedented patriotism, had sent a regiment of clerical volunteers led by a vice-president to Xien Ka near the Cambodian border.

Thus they conversed, and at length they came to 106th Street, where several buildings had been razed and a new structure erected to stand in their stead. This structure appeared to be a castle, but such a one as Carmody had never before seen. And he addressed his companion, the high-spirited Marundi, asking for an explanation.

"This massy building that you see before you," Marundi said, "was designed by the architect Delvanuey, who also planned Death Trap 66, the famous New York toll road which no one has succeeded in driving from start to finish without accident. This same Delvanuey, you may recall, drew up the plans for Flash-Point Towers, Chicago's newest slum, the only slum in the world in which form follows function; that is to say, the first slum which is proudly and avowedly designed *as* a slum, and which has been certified 'unrenewable' by The President's Commission on the Perpetration of Fine Arts in Urbanamerica."

"That is a singular accomplishment," Carmody said. "What does he call this particular structure?"

"This is his opus magnus," Marundi said. "This, my friend, is The Castle of Garbage."

The roadway to the Castle, Carmody perceived, was cunningly constructed of egg shells, orange peels, avocado stones and clam shells. It led to a great doorway whose two sides were made of rusty bedsprings. Above the gate, in letters formed by varnished fishheads, was the motto: "Wastefulness in the defense of luxury is no vice; moderation in the dissemination of excess is no virtue."

They entered and walked through hallways of pressed cardboard, coming at last to an open courtyard in which a fountain of napalm blazed merrily away. They went past it into a room made of aluminum, steel, polyethylene, formica, styrene, bakelite, concrete, simulated walnut, acrilan and vinyl. Beyond that, other corridors branched out.

"Do you like it?" Marundi asked.

"I don't know yet," Carmody said. "What on earth is it?"

"It is a museum," Marundi told him. "It is the first museum of human waste."

"I see," Carmody said. "How has it been received?"

"With great enthusiasm, to my amazement. I mean, we artists and intellectuals knew it was good, but we didn't think the public at large would catch on so fast. But they have. In this regard they have displayed innate good taste and have recognized this is the only true art of our times."

"Do they? I, personally, find all of this a little hard to take."

Marundi looked at him with sorrow. "I had not thought that you of all people would be an esthetic reactionary. What would you like? Greek statuary or Byzantine icons, perhaps?"

"Certainly not. But why this?"

"Because this, Carmody, is the real present, upon which true art must be constructed. We consume, therefore we are! But men have been unwilling to face this vital fact. They have turned away from Garbage, that irreducible residue of our pleasures. Yet consider—what is waste? Is it not a memorial to our needs? Waste not, want not: this was the ancient counsel of anal anxiety. But now the false axiom has been changed. Why talk about waste? Indeed! Why talk about sex, or virtue, or any other important thing?"

"It sounds reasonable when you put it that way," Carmody said. "But still…"

"Come with me, observe, learn," Marundi said. "The concept grows on you, very much like waste itself."

They walked into the Extraneous Noises Room. Here Carmody listened to the sound of a continually flushing toilet, the musical pageant of traffic noises, the thrilling screech of an accident, the deep-throated roar of a mob. Mingled with this were Retrospective Sounds: the burr of a piston aircraft, the chatter of a riveting gun, the strong thud of a jackhammer. Past that was the Sonic Boom Room, which Carmody hastily backed out of.

"Quite right," Marundi said. "It *is* dangerous. But a lot of people come here, and some stay in this room for five or six hours."

"Huh," said Carmody.

"Perhaps," Marundi said. "Now, right over here is the keynote sound of our exhibit: the beloved bellow of a garbage truck chewing up garbage. Nice, eh? And right through here is an exhibit of empty pint wine bottles. Over there is a replica of a subway. It is built to convey every lurch, and its aerial environment is smoke-conditioned by Westinghouse."

"What's that shouting?" Carmody asked.

"A tape of heroic voices," Marundi said. "That first one is Ed Brun, all-pro quarterback for the Green Bay Packers. The next, a high-pitched whine, is a sound-portrait of New York's most recent mayor. And after that—"

"Let's go on," Carmody said.

"Certainly. To the right is the Graffiti wing. To the left is an exact replica of an old-law tenement (a spurious bit of romanticism, to my way of thinking). Straight ahead you can see our collection of television antennas. This one is a British model, circa 1960. Note the severity, the restraint. Compare it to that 1959 Cambodian job. Do you see the luxuriant flowing of lines on the Oriental model? That is popular art expressing itself in a viable form."

Marundi turned to Carmody and said earnestly, "See and believe, my friend. This is the wave of the future. Once upon a time men resisted the implications of actuality. That day is gone. We know now that art is the thing itself together with its extensions to superfluity. Not pop art, I hasten to say, which sneers and exaggerates. This is *popular* art, which simply exists. This is the age in which we unconditionally accept the unacceptable, and thus proclaim the naturalness of our artificiality."

"I don't like it!" Carmody said. "Seethwright!"

"What are you shouting for?" Marundi asked him.

"Seethwright! Seethwright! Get me the hell out of here!"

"He's flipped," Marundi said. "Is there a doctor in the house?"

Immediately a short swarthy man in a one-piece jumpsuit appeared. The man was carrying a little black bag with a silver plaque on it, upon which was written, "Little Black Bag."

"I am a physician," the physician said. "Let me see him."

"Seethwright! Where in hell are you?"

"Hmmmmmm, I see," the doctor said. "This man shows every sign of acute hallucinatory deprivation. Hmm. Yes, I palpate the head and find a hard massy growth. That much is normal. But going beyond that…hmm, amazing. The poor man is literally starved for illusion."

"Doc, can you help him?" Marundi asked.

"You called me just in time," the doctor said. "The condition is re-versible. I have here the divine panacea."

"Seethwright!"

The doctor drew a case out of his Little Black Bag and fitted together a glittering hypodermic. "This is the standard booster," he said to Carmody. "Nothing to worry about, it wouldn't hurt a child. It contains a highly pleasing mixture of LSD, barbiturates, amphetamines, tranquillizers, psychic elevators, mood stimulators, and various other good things. And just a touch of arsenic to make your hair glossy. Hold still now..."

"Damn you, Seethwright! Get me out of this!"

"It only hurts while the pain is present," the doctor assured him, poised the hypodermic and thrust home.

At the same moment, or nearly the same moment, Carmody disappeared.

There was consternation and confusion in the Castle, which was not resolved until everyone had fixed. Then it was passed over with olympian calm. As for Carmody, a priest intoned the words: "Superfluous man, goest thou now to that great realm of the Extraneous in the sky, where there is place for all unnecessary things."

But Carmody himself, propelled by the faithful Seethwright, plunged onward through the endless worlds. He moved in a direction best charac-terized as "down," through the myriad potentialities of Earth, and into the clustered improbabilities, and finally into the serried ranges of the constructed impossibilities.

The Prize chided him, saying, "That was your own world that you abandoned, Carmody! Are you aware of that?"

"Yes, I am aware of it," Carmody said.

"And now there can be no return."

"I am aware of that, too."

"I suppose you thought you'd find some gaudy utopia in the worlds ahead?" the Prize said, with a marked sneer.

"No, not exactly."

"What then?"

Carmody shook his head and refused to answer.

"Whatever it was, you can forget about it," the Prize said bitterly. "Your Predator is close behind you and will infallibly be your death."

"I don't doubt it," Carmody said, in a moment of strange calm. "But in terms of long-range planning, I never did expect to get out of this Universe alive."

"That is meaningless," the Prize said. "The fact is, you have lost every-thing."

"I don't agree," Carmody said. "Permit me to point out that I am presently still alive."

"Agreed. But only for the moment."

"I have always been alive only for the moment," Carmody said. "I could never count on more. It was my error to expect more. That holds true, I believe, for all of my possible and potential circumstances."

"Then what do you hope to achieve with your moment?"

"Nothing," Carmody said. "Everything."

"I don't understand you any longer," the Prize said. "Something about you has changed, Carmody. What is it?"

"A minor thing," Carmody told him. "I have simply given up a longevity which I never possessed anyhow. I have turned away from the con game which the Gods run in their heavenly sideshow. I no longer care under which shell the pea of immortality might be found. I don't need it. I have my moment, which is quite enough."

"Saint Carmody!" the Prize said, in tones of deepest sarcasm. "No more than a shadow's breadth separates you and death! What will you do now with your pitiable moment?"

"I shall continue to live it," Carmody said. "That's what moments are for."

Minotaur Maze

1. How Theseus got his first Minotauring job.

It is said that Theseus was passing through Delphi, a little town west of the Corinthian Pecos, and went into a saloon for a glass of beer and a hamburger. He noticed a newspaper which someone had left behind on the mahogany counter. He began leafing idly through it.

He was broke, as usual, an out-of-work hero, and totally unqualified to do anything but kill monsters and have trouble with women. He had been drifting through the high country on the old Dorian trail, eating small and sleeping lumpy. He was a long way from home and not planning to go back there anyway, heroes doing their best work on the road, it's in the nature of the calling. But nothing had turned up so far and, without much hope, Theseus turned to the classified ads. There he read:

"Hero wanted for dangerous job of a mythic nature. Must be fully qualified. Undying fame for right man."

"Well, now," Theseus said, rubbing a finger gently along the unshaven left side of his jaw.

Theseus went to the address given in the newspaper. It was a large, gloomy red brick office building on the edge of town. Theseus was directed to an office on the second floor. There Theseus saw filing cabinets, a goose-neck lamp, a coffee maker, a bald man, and a redheaded woman, all arranged in a standard way.

"Take a seat," said the man. "You've come in answer to the ad? Very good, we're in need of qualified sales personnel on Rigna II and Fortis Minor. Our line of hydrostatically stabilized comfort-controlled woolen outerwear sells itself, though we do need someone to accompany the goods and collect the money. Have you ever had a selling job before, Mister—?"

"My name is Theseus," Theseus said, "and I think there's some misunderstanding. The ad I'm answering called for a hero, not a salesman."

"Oh, of course, the hero ad," said the man. "Have you any credentials, Mr. Theseus?"

Theseus showed his graduate certificate from the Famous Hero School of Maplewood, New Jersey, his letter of recommendation from Achilles, with whom he had apprenticed for six months, and his other papers, commendations, proclivities, engagements, statements of exhortio and the like.

"Yes, we do have an opening in the hero line," the man told him. "It concerns one of our customers, Mr. Rhadamanthys, a very important man in these parts, a Justice on the Supreme Court of Hell and a brother of King Minos. Rhada, as we call him, had a good-sized ranch nearby where he raised filet mignons. They came completely encased in a living animal, of course, and there was quite a lot of work involved in extracting them. But Rhada had invented a process which he called *slaughtering* and it handled that nicely. Anyhow, Rhada's business was going along just fine when all of a sudden this Minotaur appeared in the vicinity and started raising merry hell with the filets in their primary stage, when they are known as *cows.*"

"I see," Theseus said. "And what is a Minotaur?"

The man explained that the Minotaur was one of those beast-men or men-beasts who used to inhabit the earth together with real men, until Solon passed the Freedom of Suppression Act which allowed the humans to get rid of them.

Theseus later learned that all this had begun in The Age of the Hybrid Monsters, a socially relaxed time when you wouldn't be afraid of being seen in public with a chap half goat and half bear, even if he had a pair of eagle's wings thrown in for good measure. That was back in the Golden Age, when people had no standards at all and thought everything was wonderful because they didn't know any better. It was a pleasant enough time in its undiscriminating way, but then the spirit of æsthetics was born out of the cauldron of undifferentiated good times, and people became ashamed of having conversations with creatures who grew fur and turned to eating or wearing them instead.

And so began the Last Vast Roundup, when the beast-men were captured and taken to Animal Corrective Hotels, where they were transformed into atoms and molecules and sent out to try again. But the Minotaur and a few other monsters escaped and took to the woods and mountains and lonely places. There the Minotaur lived and planned his revenge upon mankind, a sort of prefiguring of the Caliban figure, sinister, animalistic, cunning, savage, treacherous, disloyal, a mirror reversal of a Boy Scout. And now this creature had come down to the habitations of men and was playing hell with the filet mignons, giving them ideas above their station and even mounting raids against the *meat packing plants,* as the places where the filet mignons were put into cardboard boxes were called.

"So that's the situation," the man said. "Think you can handle it?"

Theseus knew that at this point he was supposed to express his detestation of the Minotaur, and his hatred of the rule-breaking bestiality that he stood for, and to further express his great pleasure at the high honor bestowed on him, a simple hero, for this chance to rid the earth of an embodiment of a detestable principle that rendered human life incomplete, flat, stale, tasteless, the Albanian in the woodpile, as the Hellenes say, the evil principle that keeps us from achieving our oneness.

But in fact, Theseus had a soft spot in his heart for monsters. It was inevitable, heroes and monsters share a special understanding since they are in the same line of work. Heroes and monsters also have this in common, that they are constitutionally unable to live on their income.

"Oh, yeah," Theseus said. "Minotaurs, nasty customers them critters; I've never tackled one before; chimæras are more in my line, but what the hell, a monster's a monster and I reckon I can cut it. I recollect this chimæra I was tracking out in Apache country near the Pæonian Gulf—"

"We'd love to hear about that some other time," the woman said. "But right now we need an answer."

"Oh, I'll do it all right," Theseus said.

"How soon can you start?"

"Well, now," Theseus said, sitting back in the batwing chair and putting one of his high-heeled Josiah Starke handtooled cordovan boots on the barrail nearby. "I reckon we ought to have a drink on it before I go out and start reading sign."

"Reading sign?" the man inquired. He turned to the redheaded woman. "My dear, do you have any idea what he's talking about?"

"Why shucks," Theseus said, "it ain't no special thing, reading sign, but when you deal with Indians, especially them Minotoor Indians, you got to have some savvy or import some right quick."

"Theseus," the woman said, "I think you're slipping out of context."

"Them Minotoor Indians," Theseus said, blowing the head off his mug of beer, "can move across bare rock without making a sound except a scuffle from their moccasins. When they're on the warpath they can equip their moccasins with silencers."

"Hey, snap out of it," the man said.

Theseus looked up, dazed. Heroes frequently dream of being allowed to change some of the basic rules of the hero and monster game, like changing the context, sending the spectators away, combining forces and assaulting the castle of love, heroes and monsters together, we'd be unbeatable. But it could never happen, the hard wiring of the universe wouldn't allow it, so if you can't love a monster, the next best thing is to kill a monster.

"Sorry," Theseus said, "just a momentary lapse."

"You're not by any chance mentally disaffected, are you?" the redheaded woman asked.

"I'm normal for a hero," Theseus said. "You have to be a little weird to do this job."

Theseus signed a provisional contract, to be read, approved, and finalized by his agent, and received the customary monster-hunt advance check. With the preliminaries completed, everyone was hungry and it was time to go to lunch. Lunch with the impresario after signing the contract is usually the best part of the monster hunt.

2. Mann. T. goes forth after the Minotaur.

After lunch they went straight to the command post. The redheaded woman did not go with them. Between chapters, she received a telegram telling her that she had won the Miss Abilene beauty contest and that oil had been discovered on the family estate in Sulk City, Florida. So departs a sulky and uncooperative character. Let it stand as a warning to others.

The Command Post was filled with that air of tension and imminent disaster that accompanies so many best-sellers. Updates on the location and predilections of the Minotaur were flashed on television screens. Technicians hurried back and forth with equation-laden clipboards, making science fiction possible. There was a low hum of electricity, and the odd stuttering sound of the Phase Two Synthesizer, sending forth its mood forecasts. In spite of all this, Theseus did not fail to notice the dark-haired girl carrying a small stack of computer printouts, which were created for the sole purpose of giving her something to do with her hands. She was adorable, the short skirt, the high heels, the pertness, and a look passed between them, not even an entire look, more of a looklet, or even a glancelet, and yet what future spells of sexual discombobulation were revealed in that stomach-twisting glance that tells you that she has noticed you and is considering thinking about you.

Theseus didn't know that now. He had just noticed that the green and red indicators on the Minotaur sweep search indicator had crossed and locked. The Minotaur had been located!

The high priest of the Technical Scribes, in his green and orange uniform, with the flared gloves and pleated cape, wrote the numbers on a piece of paper and gave it to him.

"Coordinates these the," he said, his odd construction and sibilant delivery marking him as an Asper Futile from Gnagi Prime.

Theseus studied the numbers, committing them to memory. Theseus didn't really have a very good memory. Things never stayed in it for long. Theseus shouldered his knapsack, filled with Minotaur finding and killing equipment, and headed for the outskirts of town where the trail of the Minotaur began, stopping only at a grocery store on his way out of town to cash his Monster Advance. It was a Greek grocery store, as you might imagine.

3. I hate to blame Dædalus for everything,

but a lot of the present complication was his fault. Before he introduced uncertainty and gave us a maze contemporaneous with all space and time, we'd been doing all right, we Hellenes. Our history was a little complicated, but straightforward, even though people have made a lot of work over it. After Dædalus broadened our horizons there was high confusion. Before Dædalus there was just the normal confusion.

Nowadays I'm anyone who happens to pick up the Theseus archetype. I've been universalized, and I don't much like it. But in the old days, before Dædalus decided that Hume was right, Sequence did not imply Causality.

Theseus' history, which is also mine: My father was named Ægeus, and he was a son of Pandion, whose father was Erectheus, King of Athens. Erectheus was killed by Poseidon and his sons fell out over the succession. Cecrops was chosen, but was forced to flee to Megara, and then to Euboea, where he was joined by Pandarus, another brother. Grandfather Pandion came to the throne, but could not hold it against his brother Metion, and, after Metion's death, against his sons.

Grandpa had to flee from Athens, and he went to Megara, where he married Pyla, daughter of Pylus, the king. He eventually took on the kingship when Pylus had to go away for some years.

After Grandpa Pandion's death, his four sons marched against Athens and drove out the sons of Grandpa's other son Metion. These four cast lots for the country and my father won the main portion, Athens itself. The others inherited outlying regions.

Of course, I didn't know this as a child. I was raised without knowledge of who my father was.

Dramatists usually portray my childhood and the famous incident of the sword and the stone. But for the purposes of brevity I'm going to tell the other part of the tale, the part you usually don't hear, why and how my father, Ægeus, was put into a position in which he could not acknowledge me.

Dad had tried marriage twice, but had been unsuccessful in having a son. His first wife, Melite, was cute, but barren, and his second, Chalciope, despite her husky voice and winning manner, proved no more fertile.

This was worrisome, and Dad consulted the oracle at Delphi. He learned that he was not to untie the mouth of his wineskin until he had reached the highest point in Athens, lest he die one day of grief. Ægeus couldn't figure out what this meant.

He stopped at Corinth on his way back from Delphi. There ensued the famous scenes with Medea.

But to go on, next he stopped at Troezen, where his old friend Pitheus was king. His brother Troezen was there, too. They were both sons of Pelops and had recently come from Pisa to share a kingdom with King Ætius.

There was a problem with Pitheus, and that was his daughter, Æthra. My mother. If Æthra had married Bellerophon, as had originally been planned, mine would have been a very different story. But Bellerophon got into trouble and had to be sent away. And that left Mother in a spot. She had to have a child in order to fulfill her destiny, which was a divine one, but there was no suitable consort in sight. My father's coming was a godsend. Not that my father could be expected to look at it that way.

Pitheus succeeded in getting Dad drunk, and got him into Æthra's bed. After that, according to the story, the god Poseidon had intercourse with my mother. Which raises the interesting point that if I really were Poseidon's son, I would be semi-divine, which, in ancient Hellas, was a very good thing to be.

In any event, Poseidon waived any claim on me, or on my mother. I mention the incident only because it's part of the record.

Dad told Mom that if she were to have a child, she was to keep quiet about whose it was. He was trying to protect her from the fifty children of Pallas. Pallas himself was a brother of Dad's old enemy Metion. He would try to kill Mom if he suspected her of carrying Ægeus' child, with his inherent claim to the kingship of Athens.

And so it was that I grew up in Troezen, and did not know my parentage, but suspected that I was one for whom a great future was expected. And this is how I began in the days before Dædalus constructed his maze and introduced Indeterminacy and made it possible for me to undertake my life in many different ways.

4. Dædalus.

Many complications came to pass when Dædalus built his great maze for King Minos of Atlantean Crete.

For a long time, there had been the classical period. Golden Age of Athens. Gods, Homer, Plato, all that stuff.

Only one man, in the short sweep of antiquity, knew that his way of life was passing. Dædalus was able to do something about it. He can well claim to be the first modern man.

Dædalus had learned through computer studies that Knossos, Crete, the entire Atlantean civilization, was due to go down the tubes shortly due to unavoidable natural catastrophe. Knowledge of this leaked out and there was unrest throughout the kingdom. People felt that this state of affairs could not be allowed to continue.

Minos agreed and set up a think tank with the Seven Wise Men of Hellas. They came up with the idea of the maze and recommended Dædalus for the job.

5. Theseus. About the Maze.

So here is Theseus searching for the Minotaur in the labyrinth which Dædalus constructed for King Minos back in the great days of Atlantean civilization.

It is a day, a featureless day, a day like so many others in the labyrinth.

The labyrinth, or maze, is a magical creation, a testing ground for heroes, a place of simultaneous realities and repetitions. The maze is the highest achievement of Atlantean scientific alchemy, the supreme monument to a civilization already in decline and soon to be destroyed by natural cataclysm, but destined to live forever through Dædalus' art.

The basic situation is simple enough: Theseus has to find the Minotaur, a monstrous creature part human, part beast. Theseus must kill the Minotaur and then find his way back to the everyday world.

The situation has been played out many times, with many different outcomes, and with different people in the leading roles. I'm not the only Theseus there's been or the only one there'll be. I'm just the current one; the one in the narrator position, though not, actually, the narrator of the entire story. I'll explain that a little later. Just now I'm Theseus, a professional Minotaur-killer, or rather, one of a long line of Theseuses, who have been recurring with almost sickening regularity ever since Dædalus introduced Recurrence into his scheme for the maze more complicated than the world it was modeled upon.

6. The Maze: Dædalus' Achievement.

Theseus wasn't at all sure he could bring off this minotauricide. The old legends made it seem quite simple and straightforward, but they were just popular tales for public consumption. The reality was something else again. Even leaving aside the nature and attributes of the Minotaur for the moment, and ignoring his considerable record of victories, and considering only the vastness of the maze and its endless interconnections and ramifications, one might think that Theseus' task was hopeless. How could he find the Minotaur within the maze?

It was Dædalus' achievement to build a maze more complex than the world upon which it was modeled. Past and present were simultaneously present in Dædalus' maze, and all times and places could be found within its twists and turns. You can find anything within the maze, but it's best not to expect anything specific; you can never tell who or what will turn up, because there are so many people and things in the maze. In fact, in the maze you encounter a greater variety of creatures than is found in nature itself, chimæras and harpies, Titans, Lapiths and Centaurs, Nemean lions, Stymphagian birds, and so forth. The fabulous was always just around the corner, but the chance of encountering something you were actually looking for was very slight indeed. A man might wander forever through the interlocking complications of Dædalus' maze without finding anyone who has even seen a Minotaur, let alone finding the monster himself.

Right now Theseus was hungry. He had a knapsack filled with items that might prove useful in the quest, but none of them was edible, at least not at the moment. Nor was there any food in sight. There was nothing in sight. Theseus was standing in the middle of a gray character-less limbo. This part of the maze is incomplete, although Dædalus planned to finish it as soon as he found the time.

Rummaging through his knapsack Theseus found a roadmap, a miraculous roadmap with the property of generating whatever it represents. The map shows a sector of Knossos, Minos' city, itself a part of the maze.

Here it is, the magical moment, the transformation, and no one can tell you how it happened. He opened the roadmap, and when he looked up, he found that the limbo had disappeared, perhaps into some other limbo, and he was standing on a narrow cobblestoned street. On either side of him were tall narrow houses with steep roofs and bay windows. He was in front of a hotel with a restaurant downstairs, marked in red on the map with two stars. The cheerful owner was standing outside in his shirt sleeves in the mild spring weather, smiling, obviously a man who knows how to take care of hungry heroes.

That's how it goes. That's how life or Dædalus or whatever it is puts us, the Theseuses and Minotaurs, into play. There's no way of finding exactly what you're looking for, nothing can be planned, but sometimes things just work out, and so Theseus was not surprised to find himself here. In the maze the description can become the described and the map is sometimes the territory. Theseus entered the restaurant.

The owner guided him to a sunny table near a window. Theseus folded the map and put it back in his knapsack, leaned the knapsack against the wall, unbuttoned his denim jacket, lighted a cigarette, made himself at ease.

The menu was written in an incomprehensible local dialect, but Theseus was an intuitive menu reader, like all heroes who journey to distant places, and he made a selection and asked for a beer right away. It was brought by a pretty blonde waitress in an embroidered white blouse and black skirt. He took a sip of beer and watched with appreciation as she moved away. She brought his food soon after, and he ate his fill, loosened his belt, settled back in comfort with coffee and a cigarette.

The maze afforded some pleasant moments like this, when danger seemed far away, when the Minotaur was forgotten, when the troubles of the past with Ariadne were forgotten, when the troubles of the future with Phædra were forgotten, when he could even forget that he was in the maze for professional reasons, on a dubious adventure which he performed for the amusement of others, the people of Minos' court, who watched his movements and the movements of other heroes in their spherical television sets, and whose interest provided the real motivation for his efforts.

Not for the first time he considered kicking back, giving up the quest for the Minotaur which had led him so far from Athens, so far from the repetitive comforts of the Maze, so far from Ariadne and the children. He wouldn't mind staying right here in this pleasant hotel, living in one of the rooms upstairs, getting to know the blonde waitress, visiting the local museums, the art galleries, the rock clubs, and other places of interest in the vicinity.

It is true that he didn't speak the local language, but that was not a serious obstacle. Theseus has found in his travels that he got along nicely with just a few words of the local lingo, plus his menu-reading ability, which is essential for survival in any world. He found advantages in his ignorance of the local tongue; it saved him from having to engage in political discussions with foreigners, or cultural disputes, which are worse. And lack of a common language had never prevented him from having charming little foreign girlfriends who indicated their pleasure by smiles and gestures rather than words, endless words.

Theseus loved foreign women, their look, their smell, their exotic clothing and unfamiliar mannerisms. But he also loved the pert and lively women of his native Hellas. In fact he had a hero's appetite for women, and a poet's appreciation of them. But his relationships never seemed to last, something always went wrong, and unpleasant guilt and unbearable complication followed. He knew this, knew he'd be wise to stay out of trouble, get on with the job, fulfill his contract, find and kill the Minotaur. But wisdom has never been the virtue of a hero and there was something about this blonde waitress...

He watched her. How demurely she moved between the tables with her trays of food and drink, in her little waitress's costume with the black stockings, eyes downcast, a vision of sweet innocence and childlike sexuality! And she was aware of him as something more than a mere customer, something to be used "in the context of equipment," in Heidegger's immortal phrase, a phrase which he shouldn't know but through Dædalus' machinations has come to know all too well, along with a lot of other knowledge more appropriate to a time-traveler than to the hero of an ancient quest. Anyhow, she seemed interested in him. He was sure of it, a hero could tell these things.

She came over to his table and addressed him in broken Hellenic. He loved the way her light clear voice mangled his native language. She was only asking if he wanted more coffee, but he was half in love with her already.

How nice it would be to settle down with this charming feminine person who conveyed her meanings in smiles and nods, how nice to live in an apartment with tall windows on an upper story of a cobblestoned street like this one. How nice to wake up with this warm, fragrant and delightful person beside him. Already he was sure she would get right out of bed, because, true to her waitress heritage, she'd be getting him his coffee. And she'd be smiling, even early in the morning…

Yes, of course he'd like more coffee! She went off to get it and he leaned back in his chair, wily Theseus wondering yet again if another adventure more pleasurable than this old matter of the Minotaur might not be beginning for him.

7. Ariadne Telephones.

Theseus hailed originally from Troezen, up near Scythian territory. Naturally, that's where Ariadne tried to telephone him first when she found that the hero had abandoned her on Naxos.

Not that it should come as any surprise to her. She knew the old legends as well as anybody, but she just never believed that Theseus would abandon her in a place like Naxos. And now he'd gone and done just that.

But she couldn't get through to Theseus; the only person she could reach was Max, Theseus' agent.

"He's on a quest," Max told her. "The new Minotaur gig finally came through."

Poor Ariadne. Tears streaked her cheeks. She said, "Will you give him a message? Tell him it's morning in Naxos and it rains all the time. Tell him he has no right to do this but don't tell him that he'll just get angry. Tell him I've forwarded his blue hero coat which he'll need if he follows the Minotaur into the northern regions of the maze. Tell him there's one version of the old legend which says that Theseus and Ariadne settled down in Naxos and lived there for the rest of their lives. Tell him that's the one we decided was true, in case he's forgotten.

"Tell him Dionysus arrived last week on his sailboat and told me in no uncertain terms that he's not responsible for me despite the legend that says he will fall in love with me and marry me and live happily with me on Naxos ever after. Dionysus says it may well turn out that way and he does consider me cute, but he's got a few things to do before getting to that. He has to find his motorcycle which someone borrowed, and he has to evict some Titans squatting in his apartment in downtown Naxos, and until he settles these things I'm on my own.

"Tell Theseus I've had to sell his orange suit of armor, his pin-striped shield, his matched set of swords, and a few other things just to make ends meet.

"Tell him I can't think of anything I've done to warrant this sort of behavior on his part; I'll admit it was hectic in the last weeks before our departure from Crete when we were searching all over the island for someone to clean the head of the Medusa he'd caught, and build an olivewood presentation case for it with a viewing mirror so they wouldn't be turned to stone. But it's not my fault it was raining all the time; do I make the

weather? Dionysus asked me to tell Theseus that he's got the Soma he asked
for, and he'll meet up with him somehow somewhere and get it to him.

"Tell him I think Dionysus is starting to get extremely interested in
me despite his gruff manner. I don't know what to tell Dionysus; which
version of which old legend am I supposed to follow? Tell Theseus to please
let me know something; I really need some answers, and that I am his
loving Ariadne."

"Don't worry about a thing," Max said. "I'll tell him."

8. The Minotaur.

The Minotaur, despite his enormous stature, his knife-edged hooves,
his lashing black-ox tail, his dagger-shaped teeth of a carnivorous bull
birthed from a nightmare, despite his needle-pointed horns and dazzling
speed, despite his unimpeachable victories over the Nemean lion and the
winged oryx of the Sabateans, despite all that, but in keeping with the
inner bovinity of his nature, was a fearful and trepidatious creature diseased with compunctions and covered all over with pinpoint doubts.

The Minotaur didn't spend much time in his lair. It left him too vulnerable to surprise attack; he knew that a moving defense is the best defense, and so he roamed everywhere, up and down and in and out of the
convolutions of Dædalus' maze.

He regretted the loss of the old labyrinth, the one they had built for
him under the palace at Knossos, where they sent him the pretty little
bull dancers to feast upon each year. He had sneered at it then, a dinner
once a year, where's that at? Now he'd give anything to have it back again—
the comforting stone walls, that he once thought were gallingly familiar,
the passageways of a thousand turns and complications, which he once
knew better than the inside of his own mind. Yes, and considered boring,
simple monster that he was back then.

Now it was different. The old labyrinth was gone, or rather, the labyrinth was everywhere, the old world was falling apart, and only Dædalus
was holding it together by sheer force of will and magical schemes. This
was to be applauded, no doubt, but where had it gotten the Minotaur?
Here he is out in the wilderness, and when he sleeps in the forest he is
guarded by flocks of tiny birds who feast off the parasites that live in his
hairy ears, paying for their dinners by taking turns staying awake and
watching out for trouble: "Look, over there, a leaf moved, a branch stirred,
a shadow cut across the moon."

Most of these are false alarms. The Minotaur has asked the birds on several occasions, please, as a personal favor to me, apply to your perceptions of
danger a degree of discrimination so that I can get a little sleep without having to jump to my feet twenty times a night in response to your premature

reports of suspicious shadows that turn out to be owls, strange noises that turn out to be mice. The tiny birds argue back in their twittering language, with much indignant fluttering of iridescent wings: "Isn't it enough that we spend our nights in your service listening and watching for danger? We are your early warning system, O Minotaur, indiscriminate but acute, but that's not enough for you; you want us, poor brainless feathered things though we are, to attempt the logical computations of analysis, not only to detect but to interpret, to decide not only what noise or sight should alert you, but which should not. You are unreasonable, O Minotaur, and unkind, and perhaps you'd like it better if we went away to visit our relatives the humming birds, leaving you to figure out what every little sound means in the darkness of the night by yourself since you re so smart."

The Minotaur apologizes, even a poor warning system is better than none, excuse me, I was asking too much, the Minotaur's got enough trouble without making new enemies or losing old friends, "I'm sorry, stay with me, please." Although he knows the tiny birds wouldn't leave him anyhow, these humming birds they speak of, who has ever seen them? But he goes through the formalities of asking them to stay, just carry on as before, and in the end they agree, grudgingly at first, then forgivingly, flying around his head like a circle of dusky motes.

Since he can't have his old stone labyrinth back, the Minotaur feels safest in the woods, in deep forest where the trees are crowded together shoulder to shoulder and connected by dense and stringy shrubs with hooked and rattly leaves, the sort of mazelike terrain that a monster can slip through without much difficulty, but that a man, even a hero like Theseus, finds difficult and noisy going.

And the forest is filled with good things to eat. The Minotaur's senses operate by human equivalents. Where a man might see acorns, decayed logs and rotting muskrats, the Minotaur sees olives, pizza, jugged hare. A good place, the forest, with its dappled greens and grays, the primeval colors of camouflage.

The Minotaur would cheerfully spend the rest of his life here. But that's not to be, the forest seems infinite when you're in it, but all too soon you come to cleared land, you see human habitations, you see thin streamers of smoke from the cooking fires and hear the sounds of children playing, and you know you're back in it again, civilization. You even think of retracing your steps, going back into the dear sweet woods, but no, from afar comes the sound of the hunter's horn, and the yap and squeal of the dogs, and there's nothing for it but to go on, keep moving on, moving on.

The Minotaur was by no means without resources when he came into human-occupied territory. You might think that a bull-headed man standing seven feet tall and colored jet black with gouts of foam around his muzzle would be more than noticeable. But this is not the case. People are unobservant. And the Minotaur has several disguises which have proven effective in the past. One of his ruses is to dress himself up as a Renault police van, painted dark blue, with policemen appliquéd on the windows. Deep in his throat the Minotaur makes the sound of a motor ticking over, the van just crawling through the streets, its tires whispering of atrocious pain and meaningless retribution. People tend to avoid him when he wears his van disguise, and even those who see through it move away and mind their own business, because the police have been known to disguise their vans as Minotaurs disguised as vans; there's no end to their twisted subtlety, a wise man keeps his nose out of such matters.

That damned elusive Minotaur! With his predilection for flight and his talent for dissimulation you might wonder how anyone, even a hero, even a god, for that matter, could hope to overwhelm him, could dream of finding him, for example, eating a quiet dinner in an Indian restaurant. But they do, and they say, "That's him, let's git him, ha, ha, take that, and that, look boys, we got ourselves a Minotaur or whatever they call them critters. Otis, you and Charlie hold his knackers while Blue cuts off his head with the chain saw, and then we're off to Ma Tatum's for a little well earned diversion." Unlikely, but it happens.

Not this time, though. This place looks all right, it feels safe, and the Minotaur, a beleaguered monster, knows about these things. Up ahead, in the middle of a cobblestoned street, is a nice restaurant. It would be nice to go in and have a civilized meal for a change, yes, and a glass of wine. The monster has money, or rather, traveler's checks, good anywhere in the universe. Monsters with traveler's checks are always welcome. In fact, the Minotaur has discovered that money is the best disguise of all. If you have enough of it, no one suspects you of being a monster; they just think you're an eccentric foreigner.

Yes, a nice meal would pick up his spirits considerably. The Minotaur starts toward the restaurant, his hooves clicking on the cobblestones.

9. The Maze Larger than the World.

For a long time it was impossible to be sure of anything. That was because indeterminacy ruled the maze world, and nobody liked it but Dædalus. The inhabitants detested it. Dædalus, they said, you have gone too far. No good will come of this, you're letting yourself be seduced by a mere proposition. Come, be reasonable, lay down a few hard facts, promulgate some operating instructions; at least give us some defaults. We need a little order around here. A little order is all we ask for, Dædalus; it keeps things nice, please, just for us, okay?

Dædalus wouldn't listen. He considers his critics negligible, old-world sentimentalists in love with obsolete ideas. The old order that they dream of never was, and will not be again.

The people in the maze, despite Dædalus, despite the rule of uncertainty, have set up some rules for themselves, just to avoid the chaos, and in order that a few things could be planned.

This matter of the Minotaur, for example. Many Theseuses came through these parts looking for the fabulous beast. A regular industry had sprung up to supply all of them. You could stop at any newsstand and buy a Standard Guide to Minotauronics, with thumb index and handy chart. You could try Hermes' adaptation of Pythagoras' Negative Inference System. There were many other methods and all of them worked to some extent, not through their intrinsic merit but because, for reasons not yet fully understood, the maze shaped its interminable topology to the intentions of the players within it, so that, although you cannot plan to find what you are looking for, you also cannot hope to escape it.

10. The Spool of Thread.

It is not often that a spool of thread becomes a central character in a drama. But so it is. The main components of our story are Theseus, the maze, the Minotaur, Dædalus, Ariadne, and the thread, the all-important link with the outer world that Dædalus gave to Ariadne, who gave it to Theseus.

By following the twists and turns of a magical spool of thread, Theseus was able to find his way to the depths of the maze where the Minotaur slept, kill him, and find his way out again. Or so the received version of the legend has it.

Actually, this was a simplified explanation which was given out to the barbaric Dorians of the post-Atlantean civilization after Dædalus' sophisticated technologies were lost in the holocaust that engulfed the ancient world.

The spool of thread was actually a homing device, a mechanical "hound" programmed to pursue the Minotaur through visual, audio, and olfactory modalities.

A quasi-living entity, the thread was susceptible to transformation, just like everything else in Dædalus' maze. In its thread form it was a kind of fly-by-wire missile, whose speed could be adjusted by the thought impulses of its operator. But it was also liable to change form without warning, in response to the rigorous but little-understood laws of Magical Engineering.

So it was that as Theseus sat there, relaxing in his chair at the restaurant, and with a comfortable flirtation going on with the waitress, he heard a squeaking sound from his knapsack. Theseus opened a flap and out crept a mouse, a rather pretty mouse, on the small side but daintily proportioned, and colored chartreuse.

"Why, hello, little mouse," Theseus said. "Have you been riding long in my knapsack?"

"Spare me the baby talk," said the mouse. "You knew me last as a spool of thread."

"Why have you changed into a mouse?" Theseus inquired.

"It was required by the exigencies of the situation," the mouse replied.

"I see," Theseus said, and asked no more, for he could tell by the reply that the mouse, like so many magical creations, was a master, or mistress, of the dialectics of evasion. But Theseus thought to himself that the mouse might be a symbolic solidification of the mouse that does the questing across the screens of computers.

"It's time for us to go," the mouse said.

"Right now?" Theseus asked. "It's really quite comfortable in this restaurant, and there's no real urgency about this quest, is there? I mean, we have forever, or at least quite a long time, in which to find each other, the Minotaur and I. How about I get you a bowl of milk and a nice bit of cheese and we plan to get started in about a week?"

"That won't do at all," the mouse said. "It's not that I'm in any rush, personally. When I finish this quest, I'll just be sent out on another. Finding a Minotaur or finding a hypotenuse is all the same to me. That's life for a homing device. But things tend to happen rather suddenly around here, when they happen at all. The Minotaur is on the move, and unless we make a simultaneous move, I'm apt to lose his location-trace. Then you really would have forever in which to search, and perhaps a bit longer."

"Oh, very well," Theseus said, getting to his feet. "Landlord, my bill! You take Visa card, I suppose?"

"Oh, yes," the landlord said. "All major credit cards are honored in the maze."

Theseus signed and looked around for the waitress to say goodbye, but the mouse told him, "Never mind that, you'll meet her again."

"How can you know that?" Theseus asked.

"Because you have no luck at all," the mouse said, snickering. "And now, my fine hero, let us be off."

The mouse climbed into his knapsack, then popped her head out again. "My name, by the way, is Miss Mouse. But you may call me Missy." She crept into the knapsack and made herself comfortable in a pair of his hiking socks.

Theseus left the restaurant and set off down the main road. It was a fine day. The sun—not the real sun but a substitute that Dædalus had found that looked just like the real thing, only with nicer colors—was climbing toward the zenith. Midday already! Theseus felt the first pangs of a familiar sensation. Theseus was able to identify it without difficulty: yes, Theseus was getting hungry again already. That's the trouble with meals in imaginary restaurants: they never satisfy for long.

11. Theobombus, leading cybernetician

at the Mount Parnassus computer works, looked up, an expression of disquiet passing over his handsome, aquiline, middle-aged features like the wings of a bat trembling just above the surface of a newly discovered painting by Manet, or like the way certain sounds seem to rebound in the caverns of the ear with an appeal so insidious, and so overwhelming, that we may be glad that music does not bear a moral imperative. Yes, there could be no doubting it. He had the biggest and best array of computing equipment the world had ever seen. He had to hand it to Dædalus; he was a man who got his men what they needed. What made it all the more neat was the way Dædalus had bypassed technology, letting intuition bear the point it so often seems to tend to, despite the cryptic tergiversations from our so-called reason. Dædalus' machines were damned good, his programs were brilliant, and the result of it all, the fruits of so much intellectual toil, the crowning achievement of what science can bring you, was the knowledge that the world had approximately ten and a half years of normaltime left to continue in, after which it would be annihilated.

A bummer, right? Nobody wants to hear they're going to be wiped out in about a decade. Four and a half years left and still counting. Dædalus could see he was going to have a crazed electorate on his hands unless he did something.

Dædalus swung into action. He created the self-enclosed Maze of the Minotaur, the Maze larger than that which contains it, the Maze that contains the rest of the universe that observes the Maze.

It was a neat solution. As any advanced mathematician could see, Atlantean civilization couldn't be saved in realtime, but in *mazetime®*, Dædalus' own invention. Minos, the nobles of his court, his civilization, could go on forever.

The maze which Dædalus had proposed was more complicated than the civilization it was based upon. It was a universe with its own space-time, with built-in spectators and a high degree of self-consistency. It had been expensive, but well worth it.

The maze had no objective existence, of course. Not even Dædalus could arrange that. But it didn't matter. What Minos and his court got was just as good as the real thing.

Within Dædalus' maze, all of the legends and myths of the Hellenes could be played out. There were creation myths, the stories of the Olympian gods, the *Odyssey* and the *Iliad*, Agamemnon and Clytemnestra, Orestes and Electra, Iphigenia, just about everyone of any importance.

The people of Atlantis could sit around and watch the action on their small spherical television sets.

For people of importance, Minos' inner circle of cronies, there were very large spherical television sets in which they could sit and watch the action from the inside.

From the inside of the very large spherical television sets, a member of the audience could even participate in the drama. This was useful when one of the main players needed a vacation.

There was no lack of dramatic material. The stories of the Greeks are interconnected and overlapped. Connections existed between all of the myth cycles. Each myth was a world of possibilities, and was connected at many points to other mythic worlds. Major myths could be rerun many times, and each time with a different outcome.

This made betting possible, which was taxed, and became one of the major sources of revenue for the upkeep of the maze.

The capital city of Knossos, known throughout Hellas as The Big Olive, was incorporated into the maze. Due to the maze's enhancement features, Knossos became contemporaneous with all space and time, and Minos found himself the ruler of the universe's largest city.

Minos and his friends also got immortality out of it, an important plus.

Since the labyrinth was a plenum, entirely filled with its contents, there was no room in it for anything new.

All that could be found in the maze, theoretically at least, were variations on the formal possibilities already contained within it.

This wasn't a very restricting condition, since the maze was so large, so complicated, so interconnected, that originality was never missed. It was replaced nicely by the seemingly fortuitous.

The only thing that irked Dædalus about the maze was that he could never meet anyone new in it. But old friends are the best friends, and this was a small price to pay, considering what he got.

12. King Minos.

King Minos lived in the new palace that Dædalus built for him within the maze. So magnificent was the result that it used up all the descriptive materials for millions of miles and thousands of years on all sides.

Unfortunately, Minos didn't have the place all to himself as he had originally planned. When Zeus came for a visit, he decided that Minos' place was where he'd like to stay when he was away from Olympus. He asked Minos if he could have an apartment somewhere in it, and even offered to pay rent. Minos couldn't very well refuse.

"I may bring in a few friends from time to time," Zeus said.

"Oh, certainly," Minos replied. "Feel free."

"I will," Zeus said.

Zeus took over a suite of rooms right above the apartments where Minos lived, overlooking the Fountain of Innocents, the Forum, the Beauborg, and the sex shops of the Rue St. Denis. Zeus did his own decorating. He put in a cocktail lounge and a bowling alley. Topless nymphs served Coors beer and Slim Jim sausages to the sounds of country rock. In Minos' estimation Zeus' suite had no class at all.

There was even a moldy deer's head mounted on one of the walls, overlooking the pool table. It had been a gift from Hades, who had searched through all the gift shops of hell until he found just the right thing.

Hades was Zeus' brother. Minos didn't like him, either. Hades was a gloomy fellow, always filled with moralistic ideas and cruel, very cruel, which is proper for a ruler of hell but not much fun in a brother.

Minos sat in his throne room. There was a low rumble of thunder overhead. Zeus had just bowled a spare. The deed was accompanied by gusts of homeric laughter. Minos sighed, gritted his teeth and walked to the window. Far below, crowds moved along the wide paved areas. There were fire eaters, mimes, clowns, magicians, orators and musicians. Minos had thought they would be amusing. Now he wished they'd all go away.

They couldn't go away, of course. They lived in the vicinity, both the entertainers and the crowds who came to be entertained. Minos was stuck with them. And it was his own fault.

13. How Knossos was Peopled.

Soon after his palace was built, Minos had asked Dædalus to find him a population. His own had perished in the destruction of Atlantis and Minos felt that it was important to have people around, since they gave a place a certain liveliness and color. Dædalus, in a hurry as always, and with a lot of other things on his mind, had simply taken the first population that came to hand, that of 20th century Paris. Minos actually had had quite a different population in mind. He'd thought that it might be nice to have Andean Indians, or Balinese, or possibly Eskimos. But he'd never gotten around to mentioning it, and he didn't want to ask Dædalus to take the Parisians back since the Master Builder had gone to quite a lot of trouble to get them.

The loss of the population of Paris did not pass unnoticed on 20th century Earth, and was especially remarked upon in France. The new French government had to act quickly. A statement was issued declaring that the Parisians had been carried off by an anomaly, and the event could confidently be expected never to happen again, such being the nature of anomalies. This satisfied everyone except for the lunatic fringe addicted to conspiracy theories. Paris was quickly repopulated. People were imported from other parts of France, and from Africa, the Caribbean and southeast Asia. Soon it was business again as usual.

As for the kidnapped Parisians in Knossos, they adjusted to their new situation without undue hardship. For one thing, Knossos looked just like Paris, except for the Assyrian tourists whom most people mistook for Americans. For another, Minos granted all the inhabitants free vacations in luxury hotels in the nearby Hanging Gardens of Babylon, thus proving the superiority of enlightened monarchy to any form of socialism.

14. In the Maze of Juxtapositions.

Life is crazy in Dædalus' maze. Theseus found himself standing on a dusty white country road under the shade of a solitary olive tree. To his left there was a range of low mountains. He studied them for a while, aware that there was something unusual about them.

Then he realized what it was: the mountains were moving slowly toward him. Or he was moving slowly toward them. Or both the mountains and he were moving toward each other.

The olive tree started edging away from both him and the avalanching hill.

Then a nearby hill went into motion and began bearing down on him. He studied it and considered taking evasive action. But where can you go when a hill is chasing you? It's like a landslide of elephants and there's nowhere to run. So Theseus stood his ground. Heroics are cheap when you're dead anyway. Still, what can you do?

He was more than a little surprised when the hill collected itself like a great ocean wave and flowed beneath him instead of pouring over him and grinding his flesh and bones to gravel. He was able to surfboard over it on his sneakered feet, wearing the soles of those sneakers down to an eighth of an inch by friction due to the abrading they took from rocks, gravels, sand, sea shells, fossils, old cigarette butts, and all the other matters of which a hill is composed. He was grateful to be shod at all when he stepped off the now-spent hill.

Theseus realized at once that he was in one of Dædalus' experimental areas. The maze, at this point in space and time, could be likened to a series of mobile walkways, as at an airport. Mountains, trees, lakes, and Theseus himself, were all mounted on movable surfaces, which approached, retreated and circled around each other, flowed into and around each other, approached and retreated in accordance with laws which Dædalus had invented but not elucidated, following the ancient dictum that mysteries give an air of pleasurable profundity, whereas explanations always smack of the banal.

Nothing in this collage of moving surfaces ever collided. Interaction was suspended; only passing juxtapositions were possible. It was magical and delicious, this section of the maze of juxtapositions. Theseus loved the way things suddenly appeared, moved toward him for a while, then went away. A whole castle passed in this manner, and the people on the battlements waved, like tourists anywhere. Then, without warning, he was in a bog.

It was dark in the bog, in a twilight sort of way, and twisting shadows interlaced the long diagonal lines of the tree trunks. There was a hush broken only by the whirring of distant wings. The waters seemed to rise as color bleached out of the evening sky, and it was for a while a white world with a few smudged lines here and there like one of those artful Japanese sketches that some feel are too clever by half. And then the long desolate call of a seabird—distant wings against the sky, and the whirr of mosquitoes.

The bog was old, very old. Lying in it now, in mud-blocked sea-caves far below the surface, congeries of blind skeletons sat in long aisle seats, their delicate tendrils that once were hands applauding soundlessly the sight they could see. Above all, the bog was a motivator of elevated language, bog talk, as it was called, a sort of heightened form of discourse that well set the mood for the next thing that was about to happen.

With a pull like suction gone berserk, Theseus broke his way through the clinging clay fingers of the mud bank and scrambled up to safe ground. He breathed a sigh of relief. Just then the construct began to collapse due to shoddy constructionmanship. And Theseus found himself walking on a road rather than riding on it, and that the mountains had stopped moving.

The road ended. Theseus walked through a thicket of thorny plants, not paying too much attention to his surroundings. But he was alert enough to spring back when something long and thin and bluish-gray reached out to grasp him.

15. Sorrows of the Minotaur.

Like so many of us, the Minotaur has a greater reputation for monstrousness than he deserves.

The Minotaur doesn't feel particularly monstrous. It's no fault of his that he has an unusual physical appearance. He's no killer, except in self-defense, as in the case of this crazy person Theseus who keeps on coming after him with intent to do grievous bodily harm.

The Minotaur would be perfectly willing to shake hands and forget the whole thing, if that could be arranged.

He's made his offers, his overtures, but they have been ignored. Apparently there's nothing he can do but keep on running around Dædalus' silly maze until he can arrange an ambush, catch Theseus unawares, do for him once and for all, or make him listen to reason.

None of the variations of his legend favor this outcome.

The Minotaur finds this discouraging. But, as a creature with Buddhistic leanings, he knows that no situation is entirely unworkable.

The Minotaur finds it all the more ridiculous having to go on with this monster thing, having to work through his Minotaurish situation, since, in his heart of hearts, he doesn't really consider himself a Minotaur at all. The Minotaur is convinced that, despite outward appearances, he is actually a unicorn.

The reason he thinks this is because, from as far back as he can remember, the Minotaur has had this desire to lay his head in the lap of a virgin.

The Minotaur has the body of a minotaur and the soul of a unicorn.

So far he has kept the secret of his true nature to himself. He hasn't even told Theseus, who is his closest friend, circumstances being what they are. He hasn't told anyone, not that people would think badly of him if they did know. People who work in the maze are show business people, after all, modern and tolerant, well known for their liberal views. It's the Minotaur himself who is old-fashioned. Well, not exactly old-fashioned, but very much a private person, or monster. He doesn't want everyone knowing his sexual preferences, discussing them at the parties the Minotaur knows they have, from which they exclude him.

He's finicky, and this is very typical of unicorns, who are shy, proud creatures, not at all like Minotaurs, who tend to be hairy-chested monsters who go about their work of sex and violence and don't give a damn who knows about it.

To lay his head in the lap of a virgin—that would be very heaven! But the Minotaur never seems to meet any live virgins, only dead ones, through no fault of his own, and anyhow, even if he could meet live virgins, he wouldn't be interested because he's in love with Ariadne; she's the only one he wants, unicorns are not promiscuous and he's certain he's a unicorn.

It is true that Ariadne is probably not a virgin. Or so the Minotaur assumes. Not that he's ever asked. But after all, she *did* marry Theseus, a move that carries strong sexual implications.

But despite her marriage to Theseus, despite the fact that she lives now with Dionysus, Ariadne has a definite virginal air about her, something unicorns have a very strong sense about. Unicorns know the truth about these matters in their infallible virgin-detecting hearts.

It's entirely possible that Theseus and Ariadne never consummated their union. For whatever reason. And that could be the real reason why Theseus has abandoned her on Naxos. Because Theseus, a Hellenic jock, a Greek macho, would never stand for his lady not putting out. Heroes don't stand for that sort of thing. Failure to *come across* would give Theseus ample grounds for abandoning the lady. And Theseus would be unlikely to talk about it afterwards, because it would reflect badly on his all-important manhood.

The Minotaur knows how unlikely all of this is. Still, so what? Maybe she's not virgin enough for other people, but she's plenty virgin for him. What he wants more than anything else in the world is to get together with her under intimate circumstances and lay his head in her lap.

He has pictured this to himself many times. He even plans, when he has time, to have one horn cut off to facilitate matters, and to prevent gouging her soft thigh. He hasn't entirely decided which horn to sacrifice, but he'll decide that when he finds a good surgeon, Asclepius by preference, the king of the sawbones, and charging fees in accordance with his reputation, wandering around somewhere in the maze with his little black bag.

The Minotaur will find Asclepius and arrange for the operation, a monohornectomy, a straightforward procedure, one of the simplest of the sex-change operations.

Then the Minotaur plans to do something about his passion. He will kidnap Ariadne, tuck her under one foreleg and gallop away snorting; it's the only way of bringing it off, no time for persuasion, not until later. After he has taken her to a safe place, he'll set her free, or almost free, as free as he dares, for he can't have her running away from him before they have a chance to talk. He won't hold her against her will no matter what she decides. But at least he will have had a chance to state his case and to tell Ariadne what he really wants—to provide for her every need and sleep with his head in her lap every night. You can never tell, she might go for it.

16. Although Minos is king, Dædalus

is the greatest man in Atlantean Crete, the wealthiest in the ancient world after Midas, the most respected, the one on terms of mutual respect with the gods themselves.

This is very gratifying, of course, but Dædalus is not entirely satisfied with his situation.

Granted, his maze is the greatest creation known to men or gods. But he did build it quite a while ago. What has he done recently? This question bothers him.

And Dædalus has to spend a great deal of his time doing upkeep and general repair work on the maze, and filling in the blank sections. And something is always breaking down. This irritates him because the thing ought to work perfectly. It is apparent that the maze lacks something, and Dædalus knows what it is.

His maze lacks a unified field theory.

Dædalus didn't bother to formulate one at the beginning, because he was busy with other matters. Now the maze is working more or less as it was supposed to, but parts of it keep on breaking down for no discernable reason, and there's always the danger of a really fatal Anomaly, and all for lack of a unified field theory.

Dædalus hasn't told Minos about this. The king wouldn't understand, because laymen never really grasp these matters. Minos would just get nervous and ask if the whole thing was going to go smash. And Dædalus couldn't even answer that apparently simple question without the damned missing unified field theory.

He works on it in the time he can spare from upkeep and maintenance. He's got a team of scientists working on it, too, the best men available, selected from everywhere and everywhen. Some of them don't believe he'll ever find what he's looking for. They cite Gödel and smile knowingly.

Dædalus has dedicated his life to the proposition that everything is quantifiable. He's been able to build a maze more complicated than the world upon which it is based, an achievement that will go down in universal history. He's doing all right by any standard, but he's not really happy.

It bothers Dædalus that there's no novelty possible in his maze. Unexpected things do occur rather frequently, but they're unexpected only because he lacks a unified field theory by which to predict them.

Sometimes Dædalus would just like to chuck the whole thing, go somewhere else, do something else.

The trouble is, he can't figure out where to go and what else to do.

That's the situation you get into when you're master of a maze which incorporates everything except a unified field theory by which it can explain itself.

Dædalus is working on it.

17. The Hornectomy.

The Minotaur has decided to take the big step and get the hornectomy that will transform him from a Minotaur into a unicorn. He will go to Asclepius, the master surgeon of the maze, and have one horn surgically removed. The remaining horn will be off center, but he will still be able to pass himself off as an Asymmetrical or Lopsided Unicorn.

But there's a difficulty. The Minotaur doesn't have the sizable fee that Asclepius charges for cosmetic surgery. Where will he get the money? None of his friends have any. And there are no jobs in the maze, only roles, which pay only in non-negotiable units of fame or in the small change of notoriety.

18. The Midas Touch.

Most of the money that exists in the maze tends to accumulate around a few individuals who need it for archetypal reasons. King Midas, for example, is extremely wealthy, since he can produce his own gold objects. But there's nothing frivolous about Midas; he is aware of his importance as a symbol of eternally unsatisfied greed and he takes his work seriously.

It is well known that Midas possessed the ability to turn anything into gold by his touch alone. But this was not an instantaneous process as the old legends would have you believe. Small pebbles, twigs, acorns, could be held in the hand or under the armpit and transformed overnight. They provided Midas with plenty of small change and an endless supply of knickknacks useful for birthday presents and bar mitzvahs. Larger objects took months, sometimes years, of Midas' unique and unremitting tactility, his chrysomatic touch. It was a great gift, but Midas had to spend almost all his time holding onto or leaning against the objects he wanted to aurefy, and this was boring, even though he could read or watch television at the same time.

Midas did make loans from time to time. Although he hated to decrease his treasure trove, even temporarily, he was unable, by virtue of his archetypal drive, to forgo any opportunity to increase it. That is how he came to be known as the Loan Shark of the Gods, and was recognized, even in his own lifetime, as the embodiment of the profit motive.

One small bonus that Midas gets from his knack: he is able to have all the fillings in his teeth made of wax. Within a day or so they turn into gold of their own accord. It is not a really large economy, but every bit helps when you're trying to compile a really impressive treasure hoard.

Some people ask why money is needed in the maze at all, since the necessities of life and adventure are supplied free. This is a naive question. You might as well ask why love is needed in the maze, or fame. Money, love, and fame are alike in their ability to provide pleasure on a low level, and motivation for great deeds on a high level.

Midas was a son of the Great Goddess of Ida by one of those anonymous satyrs who spring up all over the ancient world. A lot of stories have sprung up around Midas. The fact is, he managed the gold thing very nicely.

19. The Profit Motive.

Dædalus had never considered the profit motive when he set up the maze as the world's first welfare state. He thought it wasn't important. He provided everyone with food, shelter, clothing, weapons, everything you'd need to conduct your life and kill your enemies. He thought that would be enough. More than enough, in fact. He saw no need for commerce. Shopping bored him. The pleasures of consumption were beyond his understanding. He had built his maze back in the old days before commerce first became respectable, then habitual, and finally, indispensable.

Back when Dædalus was a boy, if someone wanted a fur coat they went out into the woods and shot one, rather than the more humane modern method of going to a store and buying one.

But times change, and since the maze is contemporaneous with all space and time, it is susceptible to new ideas. *Buying things* began as a novelty, but soon replaced *making things* as the standard way of getting a hold of things.

There's no stopping an idea whose time has come.

Dædalus passed a law forbidding most categories of buying and selling, but this was about as effective as a proclamation against measles.

People acquired money by selling to Midas and other middlemen who were legally entitled, demanded of, in fact, by archetypal force, to acquire the statues, golden cups, ivory combs, amber amulets, embroidered tapestries, and so forth, with which the maze was furnished. Midas paid for them in gold and silver coins and resold them at a great profit to museums and private collectors in the 20th century.

It wasn't perfect but at least it provided everyone with a source of income.

Soon everyone had money. But for a long time there was nothing to buy with it. Back then there were no bookstores, no movies, no boutiques or supermarkets. Of more concern, there was no entertainment.

Dædalus had tried to do something about the entertainment gap. He provided classical dramas in open-air theaters. They were free for everyone and about as interesting as government sponsored art usually is.

The people of Dædalus' maze weren't content with classical stuff. It was Dædalus' fault. He had provided everyone with spherical television sets so that they could communicate with each other electronically, instantaneously and at no cost, since, Dædalus proclaimed, it was the duty of the state to provide freedom of communication. Fine, said the Maze dwellers, how soon can we get cable? How soon can we tune in on the past and the future, which you say is all around us?

In vain Dædalus preached the old-fashioned pleasures, everyone gathering around the lyre on a Friday night singing the old songs. No use, pirate cable stations sprang up and set themselves to recording and presenting segments of the future which Dædalus had tried to forbid to his people, arguing that such knowledge was Anomalous and sure to bring on Catastrophe. And he decreed stern penalties for those caught sullying the philosophical purity of the maze with commercialism.

And of course it did no good at all. Dædalus was active in policing his maze, but he couldn't be everywhere at the same time. Clandestine enterprises sprang up here and there, usually run by furtive men with black mustaches selling from the backs of station wagons which of course shouldn't be in ancient Greece at all, brought there god knows how by the quick-witted exploiters of official government secrets, like Prometheus stealing fire from heaven. These unlicensed and illegal enterprises could be moved quickly if Dædalus was reported in the vicinity.

Prediction of where Dædalus would turn up next became an important industry in itself, a meta-industry, since the survival of all other commercial pursuits was ultimately based upon it. Predicting the times and locations of Dædalus became a career in itself, Dædalology, the science of knowing at all times where Dædalus was. There were quite a few systems of prognostication, most of them based upon data bases of the Master Builder's previous visits and, of course, Dædalus' psychological profile. But no heuristic could be established, it was all haphazard, unscientific, unreliable, and the resultant anxiety had potentially serious social consequences, especially since, given the unsettled conditions and the uncertainty of land tenure due to Dædalus' wiping out of industry wherever he found it, mankind could not take the next great step forward and build shopping malls.

The great breakthrough came when Pythagoras published his Locative Proposition, stating that, whereas it was impossible to predict where Dædalus was likely to show up next, due to the general condition of commercial indeterminacy, one *could* predict with a high degree of correlation where he was *least likely* to appear, and for how long.

The equations of Pythagoras' method of Negative Inference are very elegant, but we cannot go into them now. Suffice it to say that this powerful reasoning tool enabled men to build shopping malls at last, thus ending the Age of Commercial Furtiveness.

20. The Attack of the Self Pity Plant.

"Ah, no you don't!" Theseus cried, for he had recognized just in time the telltale trefoil leaves marked with dark spatulate blotches that characterized the Flowering Mood Dump, popularly known as the Self Pity Plant, a small, squat ambulatory shrub with a talent for indiscernability.

The self pity plant grasps passersby with its hooked leaf-ends, implanting tendrils of self-deprecating irony into the victim. This preliminary stage frequently goes unnoticed. The poison goes to work at once in the bloodstream, where it creeps along the artery walls holding as it were a cloak in front of its face and trying to pass as a member of the family. In this way it deceives the antibodies, who go on playing cards as if nothing had happened.

Reaching the central nervous system, the poison begins propagating dolons, tiny herring-shaped creatures that generate the enzyme of metaphysical doubt. Once it has reached this stage, you've got a pounding headache and you can consider your day is shot.

Although not usually fatal, the poison of the self pity bush has been known, in some cases, to infect people with the belief that they are Søren Kierkegaard.

Theseus had avoided the bush's first mad rush, but he was by no means safe. The plant had him backed up against a sheer granite cliff which seemed to ascend endlessly into the azure of the uncaring sky. There were shallow steps cut into the granite, and Theseus hastily began to climb, the plant in pursuit.

He managed to gain a few steps on the plant, but was brought to a stop when he encountered a three car garage blocking his path. The Flowering Mood Dump moved toward him with its strange cry, "Look, did I choose this situation?" It was a cry that has been known to unnerve even strong men, sending into fibrillation the delicate organ whereby humans monitor whining.

It looked like the end for Theseus' good mood. But then suddenly there appeared, just to his right, a small vehicle which rested upon a monorail which plunged downward through a steepening catenary of fear into a mysterious place that lay beneath impenetrable cloud cover. He wondered, was it a good bet to take this way? But it was too late to think about all that, even had there been time.

Theseus got into the vehicle and released the brake, which was the old-fashioned kind with a geared toe-in device to prevent accidental overruns. As it plunged into the previously described landscape, Theseus wondered, characteristically, if he had really made the right decision.

The Flowering Mood Dump was momentarily baffled. But then, with a resolution quite unexpected in so sketchy a creation, it leaped onto the back of a passing skateboarder, wrapped its short nuzzling limbs around his neck, hypnotized him, and sent him off in pursuit of Theseus.

Looking back, Theseus saw that the paths of the skateboarder and the monorail would converge at a point well short of infinity. It was coming right up, in fact. He would have to do something quickly, for the enraged plant was now capable of inflicting him with the most annoying and virulent form of critical self-analysis.

Theseus reached into his knapsack hoping to find something useful. He discarded a shoehorn as inapropos, set aside a pass to Dreamland for two as premature, and pulled out the homing device.

"Do something, please," Theseus said.

The homing device looked at him with irritation. It had its own problems.

It had crept into Theseus' pack because it had thought that was a cute thing to do, and it had its scholarly interests as well. But it found that Theseus had failed to provide it with mouse food, or any food at all, since heroes are well known as poor providers; for others, that is, since they usually do all right for themselves.

So the mouse was in a delicate situation. It had to eat immediately, or turn into an upright piano. It was ridiculous, but those were the rules.

One last desperate resource remained. The mouse took out the single Speedo capsule he always kept taped to his left armpit, and ingested it in the usual way. The drug, potent albeit proscribed, came on at once. Waves of power broke over the mouse. He rode the psychic shock wave to its peak, then changed himself into a cat.

Artificially boosted by the Speedo, the cat he was was able to catch the mouse he had been and devour it and thus save himself from upright pianoization before anyone had a chance to make a rule that it couldn't be done.

"Your problem is clear enough," the cat said. "But it has nothing to do with me. I'm along to help you find the Minotaur, nobody said anything about self pity plants. Theseus, I suggest that you apply to the gamemaster or whoever's in charge around here."

"No time for that," Theseus said, as the roller coaster car approached the end of the track where the self pity plant waited, having previously infected the hapless skateboarder with a rare form of Manichæism, then discarded him like the useless hulk he had become.

There was no gainsaying the inherent nastiness of the spot. But Theseus' cool did not desert him. Even in this extremity he was able to notice the small deviant aperture that had opened to one side of the track. Unhesitatingly he threw himself over the side of the car and plunged into the aperture.

There was an indescribable moment of transition. Then Theseus found himself in the center of a large sticky net made of some tarry black substance. It was a spider's web, but a very large one, the sort you used to encounter in old movies, and Theseus was stuck fast. Now he noticed the self pity plant nearby, wearing its spider's hat, and creeping rapidly across the integuments of the web toward the hapless hero.

"How come he gets to run along the web and I can't move a finger?" Theseus asked the homing device cat.

"I think it has something to do with Ohm's Law," the homing device said. "Try not to get any of that sticky stuff on me." Catlike, it had climbed onto Theseus' chest.

The self pity plant, smiling in an unpleasant manner, spider hat cocked rakishly over one eye, continued to advance.

"What do I do now?" Theseus asked—a rhetorical question for which Dædalus, in his wisdom, had provided an answer; or at least the possibility of an answer. For there appeared in the air above Theseus, in the midst of a rosy glow of magical shimmerings, the figure of a beautiful young woman clad in the finest descriptive materials.

"Ariadne!" Theseus cried.

"You have been very careless," Ariadne said, "and I ought to leave you to your fate, especially after the way you're going to leave me on Naxos without even a valid credit card."

Theseus was momentarily taken aback, then remembered that in the Maze, chronology was merely a suggestion, like a stoplight to a Roman, certainly not a directive, and so you were liable to encounter the results of your future misdeeds before you had the pleasure of performing them.

"But if I don't rescue you," Ariadne said, "I stand to lose a torrid love scene with Dionysus later. So here is what you need, Theseus."

She put into his fingers a small flask of a glassine substance, which Theseus immediately recognized as of Olympian manufacture, the veritable Soma, colored green and with runes inscribed on its sides.

"It is the Soma!" Theseus cried, recognizing the runic label, "the blessed Soma of the gods, without which a man, even a hero, can't expect to do much except fall prey to a self pity plant while his homing device sits on his chest trying to keep its paws clean."

Prying out the wax stopper with a small tool he always kept handy for this purpose, and which was the ancient world's equivalent of the Swiss Army knife, Theseus drained the flask to the dregs, and then chewed and swallowed them, too.

And there it was, the power! A harsh laugh of exultation rose in his throat, but he choked it back as the homing device cat said to him in a testy voice, "Oh get on with it, do please get on with it!"

By the power conferred on him by the Soma of the gods, Theseus made an effort of will more intense than any recorded since the beginning of the universe. Through sheer crazed stubbornness of the human kind he forced a Chinese restaurant into existence.

It wavered uncertainly for a moment, its red and orange pagoda superimposed ghostily upon the spider web and the advancing self pity plant in its black spider hat. Then the catastrophe occurred, the new thing happened, and the self pity plant, the spider web, the discarded skateboarder, and the spider hat all vanished back into the misty realm of the unrealized, the unrationalized, the unactualized.

Theseus approached the restaurant cautiously, because creations of this kind are apt to vanish suddenly, leaving you with a sore throat and a feeling of having slept in the wrong bed.

This Chinese restaurant passed the test of banality, however, by being there when he walked through the door and was shown a table by an impassive Chinese waiter.

Theseus ordered an assortment of dim sum. "Oh, and a bowl of soup for my homing device," he added, in response to a small sharp claw digging into his shoulder.

21. Minotaur & Midas.

The Minotaur came to see Midas, hoping to get a loan to finance his hornectomy. Midas' palace was splendid. The Minotaur passed through landscaped lawns and artificial lakes, past heroic sculptures, belvederes, ruined abbeys, and arrived at the main building. A uniformed major domo led him inside, down endless corridors, dimly lit and hung with indifferent oil paintings of classical subjects, through leaf-choked interior courtyards, to an audience chamber deep in the building's interior.

Midas, the richest man in antiquity, was a small plump monarch with a gray goatee. He was seated at a long table covered with parchment scrolls and wax tablets. He had a typewriter capable of cutting cuneiform strokes into clay tablets. A ticker tape machine chattered in one corner. Beside it was a computer terminal. Despite his love of tradition, Midas found it impossible to get along without these things.

King Midas was a good host. He offered the Minotaur a plate of straw ice cream, and then, a thoughtful specialty, a bowl of lightly poached maiden's hearts with bread sauce on the side.

He listens to the Minotaur's request and begins shaking his head almost at once. The Minotaur has come at a bad time, the money market is down, interest rates are up, or perhaps it's the other way around, in any case, money is tight and loans to individuals are out of the question at the moment. Midas regrets this, he would like to accommodate the Minotaur. The king is a great respecter of mythology and is aware of the Minotaur's contributions to the Hellenic scheme of things, his secure place in the history of the fabulous. Midas' very deep respect for the Minotaur and what he stands for made it all the more painful for him to have to refuse him, for he would really have liked to grant this loan, and would do so at once if it were only up to him—he is notorious for his soft heart—but he was accountable to his board of directors, who kept him on a tight rein; he has no discretion in these matters, alas.

Midas went on at such length about the galling restrictions that hemmed him in and restricted his ability to grant loans that he passionately desires to make that the Minotaur began to feel quite sorry for him, poor wretched king with all his fabulous treasures, with his golden touch and his triple A credit rating, unable to assist the causes closest to his heart.

The Minotaur said that he understood, and began to make a respectful exit. At the door Midas called him back, asking, Oh, by the way, what did he want the loan for?

The Minotaur explained about the hornectomy that will change him into a unicorn. Midas was thoughtful for a moment, then he made a telephone call, whispering in a Phrygian dialect which the Minotaur could not understand even if he could make out the words. Midas put down the telephone and beckoned the Minotaur to take a seat again.

"My dear fellow, you should have told me about this operation in the first place. I had no idea. I assumed you wanted the money for something frivolous, like so many of our heroes and monsters do. But this hornectomy, that's business of a mythical nature, and that's just what we're trying to encourage. I mean, after all, mythology, it's what Dædalus' maze is all about, isn't it? What did you plan to do, by the way, with the excised horn?"

"I hadn't really thought about it," the Minotaur said. "Keep it on the mantel as a souvenir, I suppose."

"Then you wouldn't mind parting with it, once it has parted with you, so to speak?"

"I don't suppose so," the Minotaur said. "But I don't see—"

"I can arrange the loan," Midas said.

"But what about the money market? What about the interest rate? What about your board of directors?"

"Leave all that to me," Midas said. "All I need is for you to sign over that horn to me as collateral."

"My horn?" the Minotaur asked, raising a hoof protectively to his forehead.

"Not that it's worth much," Midas assured him, "but it does give me something to show to the Banking Triumvirate."

The Minotaur had no plans for the horn after its removal. Nevertheless, he felt a bit strange about giving it to someone else.

"No objections, then?" Midas asked. The Minotaur nodded reluctantly. "Good, I have a standard loan application form right here. I'll just fill in the details for you."

Midas takes a parchment, selects a stylus, scribbles.

"I don't suppose you know yet which horn you're going to have removed? Well, no matter, we'll just write in, 'one Minotaur horn, either dexter or sinister, to be delivered no later than—' " He glances at his calendar watch. "Let's say, three days after the operation."

"I suppose that will be all right," the Minotaur says. "But you know how it is in the maze, it's impossible to say how long it will take to get from one place to another."

This was, in fact, one of the complaints the inhabitants of the maze expressed most often. Even a simple journey across town could take forever. If you had to go on a trip, it was a good idea to take your passport, all your money, a paperback book and a change of socks and underwear.

"I don't even know where to find Asclepius," the Minotaur said.

"I've already checked that out," Midas said. "Asclepius is presently in Jackson Memorial Hospital in Miami, performing a nose job and face lift on Hera."

"Miami? Where's that? Somewhere near Mallorca?"

"Only spiritually," Midas said with a snicker. "Never mind where it is. I can arrange for you to get there. As for getting back, that's a little more tricky, but we'll manage."

He looked through one of his desk drawers, found a card, gave it to the Minotaur.

"This is an Instantaneous Transfer Card, quite valuable in its own right. Play it after the operation and it will bring you back here by the quickest possible means. And here is a voucher to give to Asclepius, guaranteeing his fee for the operation."

He gave the card and the voucher to the Minotaur. The Minotaur signed his name at the bottom of the parchment.

"That's it," Midas said. "Good luck to you, my dear fellow. Oh, I almost forgot. One last formality."

He searched through his desk drawer again, found a plain gold ring, and, before the Minotaur knew what was happening, clipped it into the Minotaur's nose.

"What are you doing?" the Minotaur asked, startled.

"Nothing to get upset about," Midas said. "It's just a standard insurance device required by the underwriters. We remove it as soon as you deliver the horn. Don't try to remove it yourself—it's fitted with an explosive device to prevent unauthorized tampering. It looks quite nice on you, actually. Goodbye, Minotaur, and good luck. See you very soon."

"But when do I get the operation?"

"Oh, I think the Alien Observer can tell you that better than a novice in temporal travel like myself."

"What Alien Observer? What are you talking about?"

But Midas would say no more. He had spent enough time with the Minotaur; now there were other things to be done, profits to be made, objects to be turned into gold. Midas hated to be away from work long, his real work, turning objects into gold. Already his armpits had that itch they get when they've gone too long without some object clutched under them, like a small ink bottle or paperweight, to aurefy by their contiguity.

They shook hands. The Minotaur left. He was annoyed; he felt that Midas had acted in a high-handed manner. But never mind, now he could have his operation, that was the important thing. And it was nice, too, that he would finally have a chance to visit that part of the maze called Miami.

22. Dædalus Dispenses with Causality.

There was consternation when it was learned that Dædalus had decided to dispense with causality in his maze. People usually let the Master Builder have his own way in these matters, but this seemed to call for some explanation. A special meeting of the Mayor's Maze Committee was convened, and Dædalus was called upon to explain why he had taken this unprecedented step.

"Gentlemen, let us face facts," Dædalus said. "As you know, we have designed our maze as a pure entertainment object, untainted by the faintest tinge of moral uplift and incorporating no socially redeeming material whatsoever."

"And quite properly, too," muttered the Committeemen, doctrinaire æsthetes of an unbending nature, like most of the Mayor's appointees.

"Nevertheless, despite all our efforts, it has come to our attention that the taint of *significance* has infected some parts of our maze, clouding the crystal-

line meaninglessness of our structure like a fungus growth of elucidation. It
is because of that, gentlemen, that I have canceled the causality in the maze."

"I fail to see the connection," said a member of the committee.

"I had thought it obvious. Moral purpose attaches itself to objects by
way of causality. By dispensing with causality I defeat the purposes of
morality, which are to set standards by which men follow predetermined
rules, or fail to follow them, and so judge themselves harshly. It is this
circumstance which we are trying to avoid at all costs. Our project, gentlemen, is no less than the conquest of guilt itself."

This bold statement of purpose was greeted by cheers from the committee, all except for one old gentleman with forked white whiskers, who
said, "But it's all a lot of fuss over nothing, is it not? Canceling causality
just to avoid guilt seems to me an unnecessarily heroic measure. Why
don't people just constumpterize away their guilt like I do?"

Dædalus said, "I must remind you that most people lack the constumpter
gland which is given only to creatures of fiction."

"True, true," said the old gentleman.

"Remember that we are trying to provide the human race with happiness, something which has been in short supply during its short and miserable history."

"If I am not mistaken," another committeeman said, "you hold the
view, Dædalus, that mankind does not have to be goaded into upward
evolution by the continual pain of war, famine, social inequity, and every
sort of cruelty including the final result of self-judgment and self-doubt.
That's quite a radical view. Aren't you afraid their natural laziness will
prevail and they'll grow tails again and take to the trees?"

"It wouldn't matter," Dædalus said. "Who are we to judge the goal or
even the direction of evolution? From the standpoint we're considering
there's no difference between eating a banana and inventing Gödel's Proof."

"That's somewhat distressing," said Gödel's representative, who was
present as an observer.

Dædalus shrugged. "That's the way the cosmic cookie crumbles. We
can no longer permit a discredited morality to penalize all self-defined
deviations of the moral maze with *karma,* the internalized consequences
of action, the automatic payoff of causality."

"Hmm, yes, go on," said a tall, handsome man, the author's representative, hastily scribbling notes.

"By canceling the cause and effect mechanism," Dædalus went on,
"we remove the payoff factor from decision-making, and thus render karma
bankrupt, permitting the maze-runners of the future to pursue their
courses free of interior moral consequence."

"Letting people get away with murder, you mean," said the forkbearded
committeeman.

"Then as now," Dædalus said. "Murder, to take your example, will have no necessary karmic consequence. By dispensing with karma, we merely put things onto their true basis. The actual consequence of murder may be something quite different from what we imagine: the flowering of a bed of violets, for example. There will be no hard connections in our maze, no necessary consequences, only juxtapositions, arrived at by hazard or by plan, it makes no difference. All of them will be invested with a purely situational meaning, and will carry no greater burden than that. In our maze, gentlemen, any anything can be any other anything any time it pleases, and this, I submit, is the only freedom worthy of the name."

There was a hearty round of applause at the conclusion of these words, and several cries of "Onward with the non-karmic universe!" The committeemen gathered around Dædalus, eager to grant him sexual favors of an exquisite nature, or their equivalent in whatever value-system Dædalus favored. But the Master Builder declined all offers with thanks. "Just doing my job, ma'am."

23. The Chinese Waiter—Theseus & Minotaur.

"I'm looking for the Minotaur," Theseus said.

"Ah," said the smiling Chinese waiter, setting in front of him a plate of gingered crab with spring onions and black bean sauce, a dish usually available only at the Parthenon Palace Chinese restaurant on Green Goddess Street in downtown Knossos. "You rook for Nimotoor?"

"Minotaur," Theseus said, taking care with his enunciation.

"Enunciation," the Chinese waiter said.

"You're supposed to read my lips," Theseus said, "not my mind. Minotaur. Short horns, cowhide coloring, a sort of wonky expression around the muzzle, typical Minotaur look."

The Chinese waiter's face took on that look of intense expressionlessness that so often betrays inner perturbation. "Maybe you come back room talk with wise man, okay?"

Theseus followed the waiter through the glass-beaded curtains that separated the front of the restaurant from the back, down a corrugated yellow corridor where a toothless oriental man sat carving shrimps into gargoyles to decorate the lobster castle of some local dignitary. He went past the kitchen area where skylarking scullery boys dropped sizzling slices into potbellied tureens, past the provisions room where three Chinese chefs played fan tan with sow belly futures, and came at last to a small apartment upholstered in red velvet and hung with tiffany lamps.

"I keep you crab warm," the Chinese waiter said softly, and exited.

Theseus could not help but notice that there was another person in the room, a young man who looked strangely familiar.

"Hi, Dad," the young man said.

"Jason!" Theseus cried. For it was no other than the famous Jason of the Golden Fleece, Theseus' son, a relationship mentioned in no other Greek myth and revealed here for the first time.

"What are you doing in this part of the maze?" Theseus asked. "I thought you were supposed to be getting the Golden Fleece."

"I just haven't gotten around to it yet," Jason said. "And anyhow, there's plenty of fleecing to be done right here."

"You live here?" Theseus asked.

"I have a suite of rooms. Mr. Subtlety, the owner, gave them to me when he employed me."

"Not as a cook, I hope."

Jason looked pained. His father's criticism of his cooking, and especially of his sweet-sour sauces, had been one of the recurring traumas of his childhood.

"As a matter of fact," he said, "Mr. Subtlety hired me as resident hero."

"What does he need a hero for?"

"Protection. He's been serving hoisin sauce without a permit. He's afraid Zeus will learn about it and send Ares here to close him down."

"Would Ares do that?"

"Of course not. Ares is the god of war, not foreclosures. But try to tell Mr. Subtlety that. Meanwhile I do my job, it's a living, and it leaves me with plenty of time to take on special roles, like now, when a wise man is needed to advise you and none is available."

"You?" Theseus asked. "A wise man?"

"Those are my instructions."

"Well, go ahead, give me some wisdom, I'm listening."

Jason's words of wisdom were lost in the earthquake that destroyed the great library of Atlantis, where they had been stored in a bronze briefcase for the edification of posterity and others.

Just at that moment the Minotaur appeared at the window. A wisp of a woman hung from his mouth, giving him a goofy look.

"Excuse me," the Minotaur said, "is there a drugstore around here? I stuffed myself on sacrificial maidens last night and am now in need of Alka-Seltzer or its ancient equivalent."

"I've got just what you need," Theseus said, drawing his sword.

The Minotaur jumped back wildly, tried to turn and run, tripped over his own fetlocks and fell heavily. Theseus sprang through the window brandishing his sword and crying, "Tallyho!"

Since there was no other way out, the Minotaur had to play the whoosh card he had kept hidden away for just such an emergency as this. He played it. At once a large, gray, semi-liquid whoosh formed around him, quivered for a moment, then shot off at incredible speed. Theseus ran after it and tried to catch its tail gate, but the whoosh pulled away and soon had accelerated off the infrared end of the visual scale, not to become visible again until it slowed for its next station stop.

"Damnation!" Theseus cried. "When is the next whoosh due?"

Jason consulted his timetable. "That was the last for today. The milktrain whoosh is due tomorrow morning."

Theseus thanked Jason for his hospitality and his words of wisdom and set out on foot, his homing device chattering as it registered the trail of whoosh residue.

24. Minotaur Meets Minerva.

At least, the Minotaur thought, I'm sympathetic and likable, not like that Greek son of a bitch with the sword.

At least I *suppose* I'm sympathetic. Even attractive, in my way.

Though maybe a bull's head isn't to everyone's liking.

Still, it turns some people on.

The Minotaur looked at his wristwatch. He was half an hour early for his appointment. He had meant to be half an hour late. He figured that would show class, and the Minotaur was always concerned about showing class because he was convinced that he had class but that it just didn't show. It was the fault of his bull head, which gave people a bucolic sort of impression, vague and sweet, utterly without class.

The Minotaur was too nervous to ever actually be late for an appointment. He wanted to be, though. He dreamed of showing up for an appointment three-quarters of an hour late, breathless, arriving just as his appointee was leaving in a huff, extremely annoyed and needing a drink. It would be at that moment that the Minotaur would arrive, breathless, apologetic, and, putting a hoof around his appointee's shoulders, say, "I'm really sorry, the traffic this morning was unbelievable, let's get a drink…"

The Minotaur dreamed of delivering a speech like that, a speech with class. But on the morning of his appointment he was up early, he shaved and dressed and he still had hours to kill. He sat down and tried to read a magazine but it was no use, he couldn't concentrate; he kept on checking his wristwatch, and he ended up pacing up and down, hooves clicking on the polished wood floor of his apartment, adjusting his tie, tugging at his jacket, wiping his shoes, until finally he couldn't stand it any longer and out the door he went.

He had definitely decided not to be early for his appointment, however, so he went there the long way, by the route across the Alps. Even if he couldn't manage to be half an hour late he was sure he could manage a respectable fifteen minutes late. But of course he arrived half an hour early and of course his appointee was not there.

This wouldn't be too serious a situation in the real world. But in Dædalus' maze, if you arrive too early for your appointment you're apt to miss it entirely.

In the maze, being early can put you into a special time slot that other people can't get into. You move along encased in your special bubble of earliness, and other people are either late or on time so you never get to meet them. You have to get rid of some of that excess time you're encased in. Sometimes you can rub it off against a time-absorbent rock, sometimes you can sell it, but sometimes it's difficult even to give it away. People are suspicious about being offered your excess time, they think there must be something wrong with it, why else would you be trying to give it away? And it's hard to find a time-absorbent rock in a town or city.

The Minotaur had met his appointee yesterday. He had been passing through town in his usual furtive way when he heard a woman's voice call out, "Minotaur! Could I have a word with you?"

The Minotaur overreacted as usual, whirling around so fast he lost his balance and fell flat on his rump, the sort of pratfall that the Minotaur feared above anything, feared even more than death at the hands of the Greek butcher, Theseus.

"Let me help you up," the woman said. Through tears of chagrin, the Minotaur couldn't help but notice that she was a young woman, dressed in severe clothing that accentuated her angularity, with her hair pulled back in a scholarly bun and hornrimmed glasses perched on her sharp nose. She was definitely a virgin. Minotaurs have a sense for these matters. The Minotaur felt the first anticipatory tremors of love, and allowed himself to be helped to his feet and brushed off.

The young woman explained that she had noticed him while he was passing through town, and had observed that he was a Minotaur, by which she was just stating a fact, not passing a moral judgment. She hoped her observation would not be taken amiss. She had decided to speak to him because he was a victim and she and some of her friends were dedicated to reforming the various sexist, racist, and other discriminatory laws that presently prevailed throughout so much of the maze.

The Minotaur nodded politely, though he had very little idea what she was talking about.

"Minotaurs," she told him, "are members of an untouchable class called Monsters. They are designated as victims from birth, giving no thought to their individual aspirations. Denied an education in anything but the rudiments of Escaping and Avoiding, they are thus prevented from competing in the job market. Their inalienable rights as sentient beings possessing a reflexive consciousness are thus violated as they are feudally bound to a single occupation without respect to their own wishes."

"At least we have job security," the Minotaur quipped, for he was a little miffed. He had always considered his predicament unique and it annoyed him to learn that he was merely representative of the general situation for all monsters. But of course, monsters have little aptitude for politics, and it occurred to the Minotaur that she was right, of course, nobody had ever given him a break; it's monster this and monster that and monster 'ow's you soul, but it's thin red line of monsters when the drums begin to roll. The Minotaur wasn't sure how that fit in, he had failed Metaphor in school and so was careful not to make comparisons in public lest he be thought a fool.

"Well, it's nice of you to care," the Monster said cautiously. "What happens next? Do we talk about it some more?"

She shook her head decisively. "I'm part of the action arm of the Resistance. Minerva's the name, action's the game. A hero is in pursuit of you, I suppose?"

"That's for sure," said the Minotaur.

"Then what you need is a Safe House," Minerva said. "A place where you can rest and regain your orientation, or acquire a new one, while we consider what to do with you, sorry, *for* you, next."

"Minerva," the Minotaur said. "Nice name. You wouldn't happen to be also known as Athene, by any chance?" Because he was sure he had seen her picture on the political page of the *Labyrinth Times*.

She nodded. "Athene was my slave name back when I was a goddess to the Hellenes. Then I learned about Scientific Futurism. My mind was opened to the possibilities of human development, by Shekovsky and other 20th century thinkers. I took the Latin name Minerva as a sign of faith in the civilization destined to supplant the rule of the Hellenes. Does that answer your question?"

"More than amply," the Minotaur said.

And so she had told the Minotaur to meet her at this street corner, tomorrow, at noon. And here he was, regrettably early. But where was she?

"Here I am," Minerva said. "Let's go."

25. The Alien Observer.

The Minotaur followed Minerva to a street corner where a large black car had pulled up. The car had tinted windows so the Minotaur couldn't see in. He did notice that the car had diplomatic license plates, Alien Observer, for Alien Observer, something you saw more and more these days, since Dædalus' maze had excited considerable comment throughout the civilized portions of the galaxy.

As he got in, the Minotaur thought what a perfect setup this would be for Theseus to try to get at him. He wouldn't put it past Theseus to hire a couple of stooges and a woman, lure the Minotaur into the car, and then, wham, bam, it's another monster dead and general rejoicing throughout greater Hellas.

It's just the sort of sneaky stunt that Theseus *would* pull, but the Minotaur was a fatalist, what the hell, he got into the car. It sped away.

Sitting beside him was the Alien Observer, immediately noticeable as such because he had no hair and wore blue lipstick.

"Don't worry, old man," the Alien Observer said, "we will get you out of this." He talked in a funny way, like most aliens, with a pronounced weakness in the fricatives.

"It's very good of you," the Minotaur said, relieved to find that he was not in a trap after all. "I hate to put you to the trouble."

"Oh, do not lambaste yourself over it, old man," the Alien Observer said. "It is incumbent upon us to assist fellow sentient creatures in distress."

"I'm a monster, however," the Minotaur pointed out, thinking that an alien, with his inscrutable modalities of perception, might not have noticed.

"I am well aware of this," the Alien Observer said. "On my planet, we do not recognize such distinctions. That is why we have been given the Good Sentient Being Award of the Galactic Planets three years running. Do you say running?"

"Oh, yes," the Minotaur said, "that's quite correct."

"On my planet," the Alien Observer said, "we would say, 'three years of passing in the usual way.' We do not go in for action metaphors. Nor do we recognize the category of 'monster.' On my planet, ou-'Fang, or just 'Fang for short, we recognize only the category of intelligent being."

"That's good," the Minotaur said.

"Oh, yes. It is what we would call a preemptory fact."

"Local usage," the Minotaur said.

"Yes, precisely. And all of us belong to a single occupational group."

"I see," said the Minotaur.

They rode along in silence for a while. Then the Minotaur asked, "What category?"

"I beg your pardon?"

"What is the single category of occupational group that all you people on 'Fang belong to?"

"We are all railroad engineers," the Alien Observer said.

"How does that work?" the Minotaur said.

"We all get the same wage and the same fringe benefits: three weeks' vacation a year, and maternity leave for those of us who elect to become child-bearing females. We are all employed by the Planetwide Railroad Corporation of 'Fang, and we are all stockholders in it. We take turns being chairman of the board and other high offices."

"You can't get much more democratic than that," the Minotaur said.

"I can't imagine why other planets haven't tried it," the Alien Observer said. "They wouldn't have to be railroad engineers, of course. It just happens that we are all interested in trains. But they could be vegetable farmers or automobile manufacturers or whatever they pleased. The important point is that everyone should do the same thing. That way there's no dissension."

The Minotaur thought carefully about how to phrase his next question. Then he asked, "I can't help wondering what happens when you have produced all the railroads you could possibly need. I don't mean to pry, but I *am* curious."

The Alien Observer laughed good-naturedly. "We're asked that all the time. It's really a matter of definition, isn't it, deciding when you have all the railroads you could possibly need. What might satisfy some races who do not possess the Transportational Æsthetic might not suit us. In our view there's no such thing as too much railroad."

"You must have a lot of track," the Minotaur suggested.

"Most parts of the planet are triple-tiered," the Alien Observer said, in the careless tone of someone who doesn't want to let on how terribly pleased he is with local arrangements. "And I can assure you of one thing."

"What's that?" the Minotaur asked.

"Nobody's ever late for work."

"I should think not."

"That's a joke, actually," the Alien Observer said.

"Oh, I see," the Minotaur said, chuckling hollowly.

"I must admit, though," the Alien Observer said, "that we are reaching a point of virtual capacity, beyond which the tracks are liable to collapse into one solid mass. The railroad phase of our civilization is about at an end."

"Ah," said the Minotaur. "What will you do?"

"A civilization," the Alien Observer observed, "must either evolve or perish."

"Yes, I believe that's true," said the Minotaur.

"My mission here," the Alien Observer said, "is to see if Dædalus can use some first-rate track in his maze, which we can let him have at unbeatable prices. Meanwhile, we of 'Fang are already moving into the next phase of our evolution."

"What's that?" the Minotaur asked.

"Fashion design," the Alien Observer said.

"Really?" said the Minotaur.

"Yes. We have voted to throw away our old wardrobes at the end of each year and buy new ones, thus ensuring a permanent market for our industries. There may be a limit to how much railroad track you can lay, but there's no end to the home market for fashions. The social necessity of doing it keeps us alive, and its frivolity keeps us happy. It's really a good system. But of course I don't suppose that what makes blue-lipped aliens happy would be of interest to Earth people."

"There might be a market for your fashions here in the maze," the Minotaur said. "Among my people."

"Your people?"

"The monsters. Most of us wear no clothes at all. But it may be time for a change. I could speak to some of my friends about it."

"That would be very good of you," the Alien Observer said. "I have samples of our new line back in the hotel."

"I'd be happy to do it," the Minotaur said. "Ah, but I forgot for a moment, I'm a hunted monster."

"Ah, yes," the Alien Observer said. "I had forgotten."

"I can assure you," the Minotaur said, "that Theseus hasn't forgotten."

"Hmm," said the Alien Observer.

"Beg pardon?" said the Minotaur.

"'Hmm' is a term in 'Fang that means that an interesting thought has occurred to me. I have a plan, good monster, that might enhance our mutual positions in this convoluted world that Dædalus has wrought."

The car came to a stop.

26. The Telephone Booth.

Theseus entered the telephone booth.

Inside, on one of the walls, he found a telephone number scrawled in black crayon, and under it the initials M.R. Theseus realized, with quickening excitement, that these were the Minotaur's initials, Minotaurus Rex.

But how had this lucky circumstance come about? Theseus, on a hunch, stuck his head outside the telephone booth and looked skywards. Yes, sure enough, there was a fading purple glow near the horizon, sure sign that a synchronicity-rich sun had just gone nova.

Theseus fumbled in his pockets and found a universal telephone token, put it into the telephone, dialed.

In another part of the maze the Minotaur sat on a giant toadstool, holding a blue flower in his hand and feeling hung over and stuffed from last night's dinner of maidens, not live ones, concentrated maidens in the form of large blonde candy bars with nuts, standard emergency rations for Minotaurs on the run. The Minotaur was trying to abstain from eating live maidens; he was no barbarian, but canned, frozen, freeze-dried or concentrated maidens were something else again; they didn't even look like maidens. He still didn't feel completely right about eating them, but he consoled himself with the thought that the Cannibal Island Canneries would go on producing them whether he ate them or not.

There's a telephone beside the Minotaur on a small toadstool of its own. The telephone rings. The Minotaur answers it.

"Minotaur speaking."

"Hello, Minotaur, this is an old friend, three guesses."

"It's Theseus, isn't it?"

"You win the prize, my friend: immolation, followed by hard words. I'm coming after you, Minotaur, I'm going to get you."

The Minotaur shuddered—that horrible redneck voice! He pulled himself together. "Listen," the Minotaur said, "can't we make a deal, come to an arrangement, find an accommodation? This is crazy, why should you go running around after people threatening to kill them, what did I ever do to you?"

"I'm just following the legend," Theseus said, "no hard feelings."

"Give me a little more time," the Minotaur said, "I'm getting out of this Minotaur gig; they have plastic surgery these days. I'm going to move to another country and take up soil banking."

"You can't get out of it," Theseus said. "I'm coming for you."

The Minotaur wondered if Theseus could be having his telephone traced. Theseus was an ingratiating fellow. The Minotaur wouldn't put it past him to come on to a telephone girl, seduce her, dazzle her with promises, ingratiate himself with promises, get her to trace the call late at night when the supervisors have gone home to their tents and their swimming pools and leave the world to darkness and to me. He knew he should hang up, get moving, but he goes on listening.

"What's it like where you are?" Theseus asked the Minotaur. "Is it sunny? Raining? Night or day? Is there enough air? Are you in a place which is entirely water? What's the first thing you see when you wake up? Who do you hang out with? Are there any decent restaurants out your way?"

The Minotaur knew that as long as he had Theseus on the telephone he wouldn't have him sneaking up on him.

"Oh, it's pretty nice around here," the Minotaur said. He looked around. He was sitting on a giant toadstool at the edge of a bog, with dark oak trees growing nearby. The sky was overcast, and some fellow was walking on the ridge above him, smoking a clay pipe and rubbing his hands together and whistling to himself.

"Yes, I'm in quite a nice village," the Minotaur said. "It's perched on top of the only mountain for miles around; you can't miss it."

"Give me another clue," said Theseus.

"The only other thing I can tell you," the Minotaur said, "is that the sky hereabouts is an unusual shade of green."

There's a pause. Then Theseus said, "You're putting me on, aren't you?"

"I'm not clever enough for that," the Minotaur said. "Now tell me something about where you are."

"I'm in the lounge of a cruise ship," Theseus said. "The waitress is just coming with my drink."

"What does she look like?" the Minotaur asked.

"She's blonde and sexy," Theseus said. "I think she puts out. Eat your heart out, monster."

The Minotaur felt a sudden despair. Not only was his life in danger, his dialogue was dragging, too! It occurred to him that death might be a considerable improvement over the current situation.

"I have it on good authority," said Theseus, reading the Minotaur's mind, "that death is not nearly as bad as people say. Why don't you just let me kill you so we can get on to something else?"

"Well, I'll think about it," the Minotaur said.

"I really think you ought to," Theseus said. "I'm speaking as your friend now. When will you know for sure?"

"I'll call you in a couple of days," the Minotaur said, "and let you know for sure one way or the other."

"You won't forget?"

"Minotaurs never forget," the Minotaur said, and hung up.

Theseus planned to go home immediately and await the Minoraur's telephone call. But then he remembered he didn't have a home just now, that would come later and earlier. He needed a home quick, one with a telephone.

27. Girl Named Phædra.

Theseus is sharing an apartment with a girl named Phædra.

Several months have passed. He is still waiting for the Minotaur's phone call.

He knows it's not too likely that the Minotaur will simply give up. But it has been known to happen; Minotaurs get into these moods sometimes, it's not entirely unprecedented, other monsters in the past and in the future have been known to throw it in, say, "kill me, baby," or whatever words they please, and bare their necks to the blade, their shoulders to the axe, their ankles to the noose, their lungs to the fire. And then it's all over except for the royalties and the movie options.

Theseus would really like to get this over. Then he can marry this girl he lives with, Phædra.

Theseus knows that marrying Phædra may not be such a good idea. According to all the old legends, he will have a very bad time with her.

The Phædra legend as it is generally known: After marrying Theseus, Phædra, a daughter of King Alcæous of Crete, falls in love with Theseus' son by a previous marriage, Hippolytos. She tries to seduce him, but Hippolytos is a jock, only interested in athletics, and a very self-righteous guy. He gives her lectures instead of love, and this gets her so angry that she accuses him of raping her, then commits suicide by hanging herself from a doorpost.

Heavy, hysterical stuff, the sort of thing that happens in Grand Operas, but not in Dædalus' maze.

Theseus thinks the Phædra matter has been much exaggerated by the mythographers.

People simply don't act that way, especially Phædra, who seems a level-headed girl, rather pretty, not too tall, with large gray eyes and a kissable mouth.

Theseus thinks that the Phædra legend is one of Dædalus' tricks, presenting an alternative that you don't take because it looks bad, whereas actually it could work out very well. That's the sort of thing Dædalus does to complicate his maze.

Of course, Dædalus could be presenting a situation that looks bad figuring you'll try to outsmart him by choosing it anyhow, and then it turns out to be worse than bad.

Maze makers are devious people.

Maybe Phædra *is* a little unstable. Maybe marrying her *is* a little extreme, not to say heroic. It's been pretty good living with her, why get married? Because Phædra wants to be married; she's a conventional girl; she thinks a lot about what people will think, and Theseus always marries them, Ariadne, Phædra, Antiope, probably a few others he's forgotten.

Well it's something he doesn't have to think about just yet. He's still waiting for the Minotaur's call. Nothing can happen before that.

And the telephone *does* ring; sometimes it's for Phædra, sometimes it's for Theseus, but it's never the call Theseus wants.

There's some man who calls Phædra all the time. He has a heavy foreign accent. He never leaves his name when Theseus answers.

Theseus suspects it might be his son, Hippolytos, calling from a future part of the maze, trying to horn in on his father's act before Theseus has even properly consummated his relationship.

The fact is, Theseus hasn't slept with Phædra yet.

He has tried to get Phædra to sleep with him, because Theseus is something of a traditionalist in these matters and he figures that if he's going to be stuck with a messy situation in the future he might as well get a little fun out of it in the present. And Phædra is quite attractive, a toothsome little morsel, and young. Theseus likes them young, but she refuses: it's not that I don't love you, it's just that it doesn't feel right. I could never face my parents, oh, if only we could be married! But Theseus is still married to Ariadne, the divorce from Delphi hasn't come through yet; everybody is going to have to wait.

Theseus doesn't take Phædra's calls anymore. Theseus has his own special signal; he knows the call is for him if, between each ring, there is a lightly aspirated S sound. He has asked all his friends to produce this sound when they call him so he can differentiate his phone calls from Phædra's. This will make it harder for the Minotaur to get through, but Theseus is sure the resourceful beast will find a way. Theseus has tried to explain all of this to Phædra, but it's no use; they have no language in common. This was appealing when Phædra was a blonde waitress with a come-hither look in her eyes. Now she wears horn-rimmed glasses and has lost what little she had known of the Hellenic language. The only phrase they have in common is "will you have a drink," and, "will you have another drink?" She's always on the telephone with someone. Could it be the Minotaur? What in hell is going on around here?

It's raining outside, so Theseus smokes a couple of baguettes to calm his nerves. He goes out for a walk. When he comes back the telephone is ringing, and the aspirated S is clear, yes, it's for him, his call, and he races upstairs, five flights, fumbles with the locks, gets in at last, heart pounding, "Hello, yes, who is it?"

"It's me," says the Minotaur.

"Gasp."

"Beg pardon?" says the Minotaur.

"Just trying to catch my breath," Theseus says, his lungs laboring for air, light metaphor.

"I hope," the Minotaur says, "that you didn't run up those five flights."

"How did you know about that?"

"And how is Phædra?"

"How did you know about her?"

"We have our ways," says the Minotaur.

"No doubt," says Theseus. "What have you decided?"

"I'm going to wear the blue organdy," the Minotaur replies. "The choice was not as easy as you might think. I look good in jeans, and it's not really a formal occasion, eating moules in the Tarzan Trajectory, but I think it's the right decision."

"What about giving up, letting me kill you?"

"Had I said something about that? Oh, I remember now. But I was depressed then. And now there's a party. You can't expect me to give up before the party."

"I suppose not," said Theseus. "Is it going to be a good party?"

"It looks like it'll be a lovely party," says the Minotaur.

"Could I come?" Theseus asks.

"Really!" the Minotaur says.

"We could declare a night's truce. I haven't been to a party in a long time."

"Theseus, you're a cunning Hellenic bastard, but I could almost feel sorry for you. Almost but not quite. It is against the law of conflict for me to invite you to the party."

"For the love of God, Montressor!" Theseus cries.

"Yes," the Minotaur says quietly. "The cask of Amontillado." He hangs up.

Phædra comes home, makes a phone call, gets out again.

Theseus goes to bed.

28. Modalities of the Reclinational.

Theseus is asleep now, or, if not actually sleeping, at least lying down on his bed, smoking a baguette, reading a book, listening to his cassettes.

It is strange how little time authors give to describing the life of a man as it is lived when he is *lying down.* Yet what a topic there is in the modalities of the reclinational!

Perhaps a third of our life is spent sleeping, an activity essential to the propagation of dreams and fantasies. Another large percentage of our time is given to such activities as reading, getting a suntan, and talking on the telephone. Then there are the hours we devote to the amateur theatricals of sex. These are not limited strictly to the reclinational, since they take man, or couples, through a bewildering repertoire of postural possibilities for conjoined bodies, yet return ever again to that fundamental proneness which is our subject.

Even eating, an activity which just escapes our list of sedentary pursuits, since an upright or semi-slouched posture is generally considered desirable for its pursuit, may be viewed as nature's way of getting you to lie down, a full stomach being a powerful inducement to this end.

The ancient Greeks and Romans needed no such inducement. They took all their meals lying down, or, to be precise, in a reclinational position as close to lying down as was possible given the necessity of keeping the mouth elevated in order to enlist the assistance of gravity in moving the food from mouth through throat to stomach. They were clear-sighted and active, those clean-shaven men in their togas and chlamys. The Orient was amazed at how much bustling around these fellows did, usually in phalanxes and carrying spears. They were practical hedonists, and when they had fulfilled the necessities of the upright they turned to the arts of the reclinational with a will.

Petronius is to the point here, the author of the first novel which considers *lying down* in some depth. The central portion of the fragment of Petronius' *Satyricon* that has come down to us describes the feast of a fellow named Trimalchio. At this feast, which was, of course, a lying-down feast, everything was brought to you, food, girls, drink, entertainment, you didn't have to move at all. Instead of considering this a good thing, Petronius affects to find the spectacle coarse and laughable and to be avoided at all costs. Perhaps Petronius and his small circle of effete friends didn't like parties. A modern reading of the situation, however, puts the matter in a different light. There aren't many of us who would turn down a party where there were a lot of good things to eat, pretty girls dancing on the table, an abundance of wine and plenty of laughs. What in heaven's name is vulgar about this? It is precisely the party we all wish to be asked to.

Compare it to Plato's *Symposium,* where a bunch of gay men sit around talking about the meaning of love, which, since Socrates has ruled out sex, they find very complicated. In fact, the high point of the evening is when a guest announces how remarkable it is, the way Socrates is able to keep his hands off the delectable Alcibiades.

Trimalchio's feast comes out looking a lot more fun than Plato's, but different feasts for different folks; the essential thing is that both were important occasions in the cultural history of the world, and both were performed in their entirety in the reclinational mode, i.e., *lying down.*

The reader of the future will put down our facile action-oriented novels of today and ask, "Why doesn't the author ever say anything about the characters' thoughts while *lying down?* Why doesn't he tell us about the sensation of a scratchy blanket spread over a lumpy couch? What is it like to lie on your back on a dusty rug on the floor gazing up at a white sky with dead trees black against it? What about lying on a narrow wooden bench at a friend's house, sharing a bottle of wine while the radio plays and the baby chases the cat?" Our upright-oriented books will give him no reply, unless, of course, he happens to look into this one.

So here is Theseus, lying on the bed, half asleep, listening to the muffled and barely discernable conversation between Phædra and Hera in the other room. It was Hera's mother's apartment they were staying in, but the old lady was in the hospital with a broken hip and Hera had come over to get a few of her things. It was a rainy Sunday afternoon. Hera and Phædra were looking through Hera's old family album. On this page is Aphrodite at her first communion; here is Poseidon on his Sailfish; here is the infant Zeus teething on his pink baby thunderbolt. The women talked softly in the other room in their gentle foreign voices, car tires slushed on wet tar roads, the lights of Olympus glowed in the distance.

There was a loud buzzing sound. It came from Theseus' knapsack, which he had thrown into a corner. It was the thread, of course, no other piece of equipment had so annoying a sound.

"What time is it?" Theseus asked.

"Time to go Minotauring," the thread said.

Theseus sighed heavily, stubbed out his baguette, got out of bed. He strapped on his sword and armor, put on his knapsack, left a note for Phædra, went quietly out the door.

Delicious though *lying down* is, it always gives way, at last, to the demands of the upright and the motile. All our upright movements are but a dance of postural rotation as we hurtle through the unbelievable on our way to the unknowable.

29. *Phone Call to Naxos.*

Theseus looked around, but there was nothing to see for miles on all sides. There was just a telephone booth, painted red, and a copy of the Universal Maze Directory which connects everybody to everybody else and automatically updates itself whenever someone moves.

This was one of the less built-up parts of the maze, and although it was convenient to everything, it lacked amenities. Theseus took out his address book and leafed through it. It was one of the new models. The names of people well-disposed to you glowed in the dark. It was difficult to read the names of your enemies: they faded out, along with the memories of their better points.

After making a few calls, Theseus went to stay with his ex-wife, Ariadne, and her new boyfriend, Dionysus.

They were happy to see him. Things had been a little quiet on Naxos, an island never known for shows of unseemly mirth. Dionysus had a big farmhouse on the northwestern corner of the island. It occupied a pretty headland looking out to the sea. Below the property was a narrow beach and a little cove where shallow-draught boats could shelter.

Dionysus loved boats. And boats brought in the bootleg Soma, the divine intoxicants of the gods, which he sold to heroes at a modest markup.

Dionysus was also writing a novel, and Ariadne was studying to become a real estate broker.

The original problems between the three of them have been forgotten. Now the memory of the old days has become the special bond that keeps them together.

In the evenings, when the archaic red sun goes down into the sea, they sit at the kitchen table and play bridge. The spool of thread makes a fourth for the game. The thread is capable of splitting itself into seven different personalities, though this talent is rarely called for.

Ariadne seems to have quite a lot of children.

Some of them may be the neighbor's children, but some of them are surely hers. Hers and Theseus'. Theseus is almost certain that he and Ariadne had at least one child together, maybe two, just possibly three. He can't quite remember, though; his memory's not what it used to be, all those past and future wives, all those past and future children, all those changes.

Theseus doesn't like to ask which, if any, of the children are his. It seems disrespectful, somehow. It's the sort of thing you just don't ask. It looks rotten, not remembering which, if any, are your children, not remembering which wife you had which children, if any, by. And anyhow, he doesn't have to ask, Theseus is sure he wrote all this information down somewhere. He's a dedicated diarist; he keeps notes, about who he met, what he ate for lunch, how he feels. He's Theseus; his memoirs are sure to be in demand, the true account, what really happened. It's all there; he's recorded the whole thing, but he can't carry all those bales of paper around with him; he has stored portions of his diary here and there, but it's all somewhere, if only he could find time to put it together, publish the Memoirs of Theseus, and know which are his children.

Meanwhile the pleasant life on Naxos goes on. The peasants plow their fields, feed their animals, hold their famous shouting contests and their ancient Breadfruit Dances. They are a short, stocky, broad-faced people, always dressed in black, except on special holidays, when they wear white.

The Breadfruit Dances are danced to the accompaniment of indigenous musical instruments, the tamerland, the snap drum, the bug and the accordance. Theseus likes the plaintive sound, although he is more accustomed to the Hellenic electric syrinx and pedal pan pipes.

It is a simple life. At night the yelodians come up from the sea. Dark and sinuous, they slither along the beach and climb the nearby stupa trees in search of oysters. Further up the hillside the broad-leafed snappers are found, characteristic trees of the island. They are not true trees, but belong to a more ancient species, the arboleums, gray plants with characteristic crosshatching under their armpits. Sometimes a yellow-throated harbinger is sighted, flapping heavily through the arboleums. The harbinger is not a true bird. It is a member of the flappian family, an antique species that populated the skies of Naxos back when the earth was young and foolish.

Theseus has a good life on Naxos, but it has to end at last. Nothing can go on forever, specially if it is fun. The inexorable law of nature is that things shall pass from the all right to the unbearable, and that all the days of a man's life shall be as dead leaves on the tree of metaphor.

The end of his stay came about in an almost inconsequential way, as these things do. Theseus came back to the house one day and asked if there had been any calls for him. Ariadne said there hadn't been, and added that it was unlikely that he would receive any. "Why is that?" Theseus asked.

"Because the phone isn't connected," Ariadne said. "I thought you knew."

Theseus left the next day.

30. Falling Through the Story.

Theseus got back to the mainland, landing at a little harbor on the rocky coast of Attica. There was a town nearby, low white beehive shaped buildings gleaming under the midday sun. Entering, he saw that there was a celebration underway. But what festival could this be?

Walking into the town, he saw a great banner stretched between two buildings. It read, SAVE OUR MINOTAUR!

By a strange coincidence, he had come here on Minotaur Preservation Day.

Other banners pointed out that Minotaurs are an endangered species. It was evident that the people were determined to stop the unauthorized slaughtering of the fabulous beasts, to stamp out that little group of selfish men whose work was sure to obliterate one of the oldest species of the classical world.

One man, standing on a little pedestal, was making a speech. "You have seen other fabulous species disappear! Where nowadays are the Stymphagian birds? Where is the golden-headed walrus, the curly-tailed narwhal; where are the pixilated harpies? They are vanishing. And what is Dædalus doing about it? Nothing, that's what he's doing! Dædalus doesn't care for preservation; it's only new creation he wants!"

Theseus walked through the town and noted the carnival atmosphere. There were booths selling Souvlaki and stuffed grape leaves. Some of the troglodytes of Libya, themselves threatened with extinction, were present and handing out finely inscribed shards of pottery, the ancient world's equivalent of leaflets.

Theseus realized that this could work to his advantage. From overheard conversations he learned that the Minotaur himself was making an appearance here.

Theseus considered the situation. He will have an opportunity if he positions himself at a strategic location where he can get a clear shot. He was armed with a lightning bolt which Hermes had borrowed from Zeus. It was the ancient world equivalent of a guided missile, a Minotaur-homing device, and it was certain to reach its mark.

He looked around and planned his strategy. The procession, with the Minotaur riding in one of the chariots, would go right up the main street of this town. Quickly he found a vantage point, the old scroll repository on the corner of Classikos Street and Cornucopeia Way.

He entered. The building was deserted. On the second floor there was a place where he could prop up the lightning-bolt barrel, fasten the retaining pins to the clay floor, take a careful and leisurely aim. Who would ever dream of an assassin lurking in a scroll repository? This was going to work out just fine.

He still had half an hour before the procession was due to begin. Hiding the thunderbolt in a pile of rubble in a corner, he went out. Nearby there was a luncheonette where he bought a Souvlaki sandwich with grape leaf sauce. He always fired best on a full stomach.

He returned to the repository, and found a man standing at the doorway through which he had entered. Theseus didn't like that, but decided to carry off the matter boldly. Whistling, he nodded to the man and began to pass him.

"What are you doing up in that scroll repository?" the man asked.

"I just want a good place to watch the action."

"What's wrong with the grandstand?"

"I get dizzy from being high up and being crowded by people. Anyway, is there a law against it?"

"Not at all," the man said. "But you'd better watch yourself up there. The flooring is none too secure. Hasn't been permanently bonded yet with reality cement. You could say it's held together by spit and prayer."

"Don't worry, I'll be careful."

Theseus went upstairs. He waited a few moments, but no one followed him. He set up the thunderbolt on the window ledge, carefully zeroing in the crosshairs. Now he was ready! His pulse started to quicken. He was going to get the Minotaur at last!

Within a few minutes crowds had begun to gather on the street. Most of them took seats in the hastily erected grandstands on either side. There was a distant sound of a brass band. The Minotaur was coming! Little children ran up and down the street, blowing penny whistles. Theseus watched carefully, bent low over his thunderbolt launcher. He didn't want to blow this one! Then the procession came into sight. He could see the leading chariot, filled with classical secret operatives. They were armed with small bows and arrows.

The procession drew near. Theseus let the secret service chariot pass, the one with the press corps. The third chariot drew near. It was filled with cheerleaders from Classical High School. He let that one go by, too. Now, coming up quickly, he could see another chariot approaching. The Minotaur was in it, huge, blue-purple in color, foam-specked as usual, smiling like he owned the world, waving to the crowd. How happy he looked! Theseus watched, feeling almost regretful over what he had to do. Almost but not quite. He sighted through the crosshairs, took aim as the chariot drew near, then found that his position wasn't quite as perfect as he'd like.

He could see that the further window would give him a better shot. He picked up his thunderbolt and started across the creaking floor.

He was almost in position, when suddenly, with a heavy tearing sound, the whole construct gave way. Theseus realized too late that he had stumbled onto an unjustified spot. He tried to backpedal, but it was too late. Suddenly he was falling.

Theseus fell through the gauzy descriptive materials that the maze was constructed of. He passed quickly through a region of colossals, cylindrical in shape and gray in color, stacked with their cognates against a lurid background of horrifics. Then he passed through a region of nanoseconds and standard hesitations, and then through some oddly shaped slights, and, after them, a warehouse full of grandioses and etioses.

None of these materials looked like much close up. But it was amazing what Dædalus had done with such uncompromising materials.

Then the maze machinery kicked in and Theseus found himself standing on a standard classical city street. The premise could be seen wavering, there were repercussions of a rhetorical nature, and the author could be glimpsed, a ghostly figure of unbelievable beauty and intelligence, trying desperately, despite his many personal problems, to put things together again.

AFTERWORD

BY TOM GERENCER

So, now you've done it. You've read through all five of the Sheckley books bound together in this volume, and we've met here at the end. Or, if you're like me, you finished reading Resnick's foreword and you flipped to the back to see what somebody else has to say about Sheckley and/or to get all the damn forewords and afterwords out of the way so you can get to the actual WORDS for God's sake and also (and possibly finally but I wouldn't bet on it) to see if somebody can offer some kind of coherent picture of what this book is supposed to be and why it's here at all.

Well, Mike's probably done an excellent job of saying why the book is here (I haven't seen his introduction yet), and I'm willing to bet my eyeteeth that he's given you some insight into the length and breadth of Sheckley's career, and I might throw in my molars on the probability that Mike also introduced each of the included books in turn, so the best I can do is to tell you what I know about Robert Sheckley.

First, of course (and most important), there is his work. I came across the wonderful stuff after reading a Douglas Adams interview some eight years ago. In the interview, Adams was politely challenged that he might owe more than a trifling debt to a science fiction writer by the name of Robert Sheckley. Adams, while admitting that the coincidences were startling (neurotic robots, spaceborne hippies, the man who made the Earth), claimed he hadn't heard of Sheckley before he was accused of cribbing from him. (On later reflection, I find this hard to believe, especially since Adams' original idea for *The Hitchhiker's Guide to the Galaxy* was to have a lost Earthling searching for home through alternate dimensions and various versions of the planet. Sound familiar? If not, I was right about you and you *haven't* read this book yet! Get going, keed!)

I hardly cared back then, though, about who was cribbing whom (to crib the great Todd Thromberry) but being a fan of Adams' stuff, I decided to check out Sheckley.

I was, and I forever will remain, ecstatic that I did.

It seems now, to me, that Douglas Adams is not the only one who might be said to owe a debt to Robert Sheckley. Take, for instance, the Sci-Fi

Channel's series *Sliders*, also about a cross-dimensional search for the real Earth, or the vilified and popular adolescent game known as Killer, which was, in the eighties, blamed on Sheckley's *The Tenth Victim*. And how about Sheckley's 1958 story "The Prize of Peril" which bears a striking resemblance to Stephen King's *The Running Man?* (Sheckley's came first, of course.)

You could argue that such ideas as this are too old, too clichéd to attribute to any one man, but then I could argue back that *somebody* came up with this stuff, and that a guy like Sheckley (who came on the scene in the fifties, after all) might well have been the first to the summit of a lot of these speculative Everests. Whether he was or he wasn't is academic. But what he did do was to put a spin on these concepts that nobody put there before. Maybe another writer dreamed up legalized murder, but I doubt they saw it being made sport of by men whose falsely suicidal wives faked casual Cheyne-Stokes breathing at them while they watched TV. And it's almost certain that Sheckley wasn't the first one to think of time warps, but you can bet your moonboots that nobody else sent a long-lost uncle through one, from a golf course, by accident, to complain later (on a distant planet) that the greens committee ought to build a small fence or other enclosing structure.

Still, as Mike Resnick would no doubt say, if we got rid of every speculative story that was similar to another in some way, we'd have ten books left at most, and a handful of short stories. What counts, he'd say (and I believe), is how the stuff is written.

And how are Sheckley's stories written?

I won't say the man's not capable of a blunder, or a bit of wooden prose, because let's face it, who ain't? (I tend to think his equitable acceptance of his depths is what allows him to reach such heights, but let that go.) However, when he's good (and he so often is—you know this if you've done your reading) he's the crème de la crème.

Like most aspiring writers, I've tried to analyze why my favorite author's best stuff works so well. How does he manage to grip me into his stories with such a hold that I honestly can't find a place to put the things down? How does he achieve that oft-claimed (on book jackets) but seldom realized (in the armchair at home) effect of making his readers laugh out loud? As for the latter, I still don't know. But I love the results. And in answer to the question of Sheckley's page-turner power, what I've found is this: his stuff is *present*. Fluid. Or as Resnick says, it flows.

It puts you at the still point of the turning world, the average Joe (or Tom, or Marvin Flynn) in the center of the maelstrom. It seems to manifest the advice of Taoists when they say not to become attached to anything. When you read Sheckley, you're definitely not attached, and if you read him much you know the bottom can and will drop out at any second and you'll find yourself, well, absolutely anywhere. Like for instance in a Melden forest, hunting argumentative alien eggs; at the galactic center, preparing to be executed for crimes you're statistically likely to commit; or on a future Earth, where an idealistic youth asks, "Is love very difficult to find?" and the answer comes, "Walk up two blocks. Tell 'em Joe sent you." Sheckley's stuff *moves*. It jumps with invention and grandiloquence, and you get the feeling that, while he writes, he's thinking (as one character of his says), "What did I say? Never mind, the construction is right, even if the words are wrong." And as you read, you sometimes think (as another of his creations once observed), "That's not strictly true, but it's very nicely said."

And he's been saying it so well and for so very long. Sheckley was writing cynically slanted science fiction before Douglas Adams even *heard* of space. He was suspicious of technology before William Gibson saw his first old *Star Trek* episode. He has written loads of short stories and books, as well as television scripts and a few episodes of the old radio SF thriller *X Minus One*. He came on the scene when he was sorely needed—in the early 1950's—when so many of our sf heroes (and especially the ones on television) were whitebread, tight-lipped North Americans in space who could accomplish anything provided they were polite about it, approached the situation logically, and paid proper attention to their personal hygiene. Sheckley took those whitebread, by-the-book, crisply-jumpsuited (God love 'em) Americans in space and put them into situations for which they had no frame of reference. He made food giggle at them, stuffed bombs up their noses, and had planet-builders order them to be stuck back in the protoplasm vat with the cows.

Traditional writers said: The future is coming and here's how it's going to be. Sheckley's hopeful cynicism said: No, wait, this is the unknown. There is no form, no recipe to follow. Things are going to happen (and they do, and do they ever) that we won't be prepared for. Honest people might struggle to break into prison. We might find out dinosaurs were not only intelligent, but bigots to boot. A spaceship might be cleverly disguised to look like Fairlawn, New Jersey, while the real Fairlawn is lifted out and put down in India's Rajasthan province, *and no one might notice*. And sometimes, yes, the gods are going to speak, but when they do it's not going to be about life or death or the other well-turned eternal verities, but chronic boredom, or stew, or they might simply ask us, "How did you like my entrance?"

Peopled with idealistic youths, eager shysters, and girls with hair the color of rocket exhaust, Sheckley's dimensions presented and continue to present a much-needed argument to the speculative constructs of the era. And if he was needed in the past to "lay down the word, deacon, and let the people know the divine formula," then he is needed even more today. And is he here?

He is, thank God, he is.

I got to wondering about this question myself when, after reading as many of his books and stories as I could hunt down in used book shops, I looked him up on the Internet. To my surprise, he was not only easy to find, but glad to talk—about writing, or life in general, or any old thing. I guess my first contact with him was out of a sort of fan worship that anybody who has a hero feels, but that has (more or less) dropped away as I've realized there's a person behind the words, and a really kind and helpful one at that.

I've asked him for lots of advice over the years since then, and he's always given the same: Just keep trying. Write a sentence. Write another. Then another after that. Or if that doesn't work, try something else. Have a bad day? Keep working. Have a good day? Again, keep putting down the words. But above all, write. Frustrating advice, that, but advice that rings true. What fledgling success I have had, I owe to those words.

And the giver of that advice? He's out West, deeply in love, and enjoying a sort of *Spinal Tap*-type renaissance of his work, both in Europe and at home. And at an age when many past masters would be sitting around and waiting to give Martin H. Greenberg the opportunity to release yet another tribute anthology, Sheckley's still at it; writing stories about sentient, conversational viruses, mental visitors who get delivered to the wrong minds by incompetent mail carriers, and plate-specific, scallop-shaped aliens who appear on the dinner table during suppertime and then say, "Oh, hey, it's the Earth guy."

In this way, Sheckley still embodies that much-touted sense of wonder, and (as when I first read his stuff) I'm still drooling on the pages. He changed my way of looking at the world and at fiction, and made me see that life is an infinity of possibilities and anything—literally anything, right down to the existence of human beings—can happen.

And yet just you ask him how he did it (and believe me, I have) and he replies, exactly as one of his own bewildered characters might, "I don't know. I've written some nice things and people have said some nice things about me for it." And like one of his characters he seems, to me, to drift through life, accepting good and bad together, with the same bemused attitude. Almost Taoist, almost Buddhist, dyed-in-the-tie-dye, drug culture/counter-counterculture Sheckley. Wise and foolish all at once, and dangerous and kind. You get the idea that if you could meet the God of Sheckley's near-infinite dimensions (and if you were in one of them, such a meeting would be, at some point, almost inevitable), he or she would shrug at you and, not unkindly, say, "Gosh, keed. I really don't know, either."

ACKNOWLEDGMENTS

Thanks to:

Bill Shawcross of Rotten Apple Press, Rick Katze and John Lorentz for scanning and OCR.

Bonnie Atwood, Seth Breidbart, Ann Broomhead, Ann Crimmons, Pam Fremon, Deb Geisler, Chip Hitchcock, Rick Katze, John Lorentz, Gary McGath, Ruth Sachter and Tim Szczesuil for proofing and other help.

Priscilla Olson, who did all the typesetting (and gave me encouragement throughout the entire process).

Alice Lewis for designing a wonderful cover.

George Flynn for final proofing.

Mark Olson, Suford Lewis, Rick Katze, Seth Breidbart and especially Priscilla Olson for advice and assistance.

And Mike Resnick, who proposed this project for NESFA and was there with suggestions when needed.

Sharon Sbarsky
December 2001